THE LAST REGRET

A NOVEL

by

ANTHONY SIDERIS

ISBN: 978-0-9600009-9-9

Library of Congress Control Number: 2018913660

Published 2019 by H&B Radiance Inc

Printed in the United States of America

ISBN: 978-0-9600009-4-4 EPUB Edition

For permission requests, please address: H&B Radiance Inc
PO Box 23
Manchester, WA 98353

www.anthonysideris.com

To all the men and women who selflessly serve their country, protecting it from those wishing to do it harm. At great sacrifice to themselves and their families, they serve in the silence of their profession, mostly without ever receiving recognition or thanks from their fellow citizens.

Chapter 1

It was 11:00 p.m. on a cool and damp Friday night in March. Michael Blackstone ran down the empty streets of Queen Anne, one of Seattle's oldest residential neighborhoods. From the top of the hill just north of downtown, he watched a ferryboat pull away from the terminal down on the waterfront. The lights of the high-rise buildings glimmered in the background as he took in the view. He could smell the freshness in the air of spring approaching as he ran under the glow of each successive streetlight. For fifty-four years old, Michael was in pretty good shape despite his back injury. He tried to maintain a healthy lifestyle, watching what he ate and exercising regularly. His only weaknesses were pizza and soft chocolate chip cookies, which he managed to avoid except for special occasions. He was obsessed with staying fit. He worked out six days a week, maintaining a strict exercise regimen to compensate for the three damaged discs in his lower back.

He was amazed at the pace he was keeping. He hadn't run this hard for over twenty years, the way he used to before his injury and the steady decline of stamina that came with age. His legs burned and his heart pounded, but his kick was strong and he was actually picking up his pace. Perhaps it was the thought of it being his last run that pushed him beyond what he normally could endure. He knew that, despite the oxycodone he had taken to dull the pain, he would pay dearly the next day for the beating he was giving his back, but he was no longer concerned about that.

Michael always ran when he faced a big decision and needed to clear his head. This one was the biggest decision of his life, one that would change things forever. It had finally reached the point where he felt he had no other options left. He wasn't even sure how he'd gotten to this point, only that he couldn't bear to let the situation continue any longer. He had thought it through a hundred times, and each time, he'd arrived at the same decision. It was a drastic thing he was about to do, but he had made up his mind and was determined to go through with it. Shortly, it would be over and done with. He felt no apprehension. If anything, he felt a sense of calm.

The fifteen minutes Michael had been running felt more like five. Time seemed to have slowed. It was as if the memory center in his brain had been stimulated with an electronic probe; he recalled scenes from his past as if they were being displayed on a screen in front of him. Some of those memories, he had not thought about for decades. Those from his earliest childhood, recalled often only as scattered images of people and places, he now remembered in vivid detail. The summers he spent as a child with his grandfather and grandmother at their home in New Jersey came back to him. He remembered riding bikes with his best friend Gary behind the mosquito fumigating truck that drove through the neighborhood in the evenings, billowing out thick white smoke into the street. He laughed at the thought of how horrified mothers today would be at the idea of their kids riding their bikes behind a giant can of bug spray. How much life had changed during the past fifty years. Today it was unusual to even see a kid outside riding a bike. He remembered the sound of the mesmerizing tune coming from loudspeaker of the Italian Ice truck as it drove through the neighborhood each afternoon during the summers. He would run to his grandmother and beg for a quarter so he could buy one of those delicious frozen treats. Those were the days before cell phones and video games. In later summers, he and his friends would head out on their bikes in the morning and not return until dark. When he would finally get home, his mother would chastise him about being gone all day without her knowing where he was and what he had been up to. Unlike the fear parents had today about all the possible harm that could come to their children, back then, there was never any real worry of something bad happening. It was the last age of innocence.

Michael revered his grandfather George. He remembered hearing his grandfather's stories about growing up in Greece amidst all the poverty and hardships during World War I, then immigrating to the United States and fighting against the Germans in World War II. Michael could sit for hours listening to his grandfather tell those stories over and over, as if they were enchanting fairy tales from a faraway mystical place. How in 1929, at the age of nineteen, he had illegally immigrated to the United States by jumping ship off a Greek freighter that had docked in New York Harbor. He had been working in the Merchant Marine since the age of fifteen, supporting his widowed mother and brothers and sisters back in Greece. After arriving in New York, he found work as a laborer with Starrett Brothers, the company that was building the Empire State Building.

Michael remembered being transfixed as his grandfather told him about walking untethered along eight-inch-wide steel I-beams a thousand feet above Fifth Avenue. Those who worked on New York's skyscrapers were called roughnecks. It was dangerous work, but if one had nerves of steel, they could make a good living compared to most of the other low-paying jobs that were available to newly arrived immigrants. George had only completed the sixth grade, but he was a fast learner and not afraid of hard work. He quickly gained the respect of his coworkers and foreman, rapidly moving up to positions of greater responsibility. By the time construction was completed two years later, he was supervising a crew of fifty riveters. He had even come to the attention of Paul Starrett, the president of Starrett Brothers, as their youngest foreman.

George rose through the ranks of the company and by the age of twenty-six had become a project supervisor. Throughout those years, he'd regularly wired money back to his family in Greece. He had even saved enough for a trip back to visit them, but there was one small problem: he was in the US illegally and had no passport. Even if he could get into Greece, he would not have any way to get back into the United States legally. It was a growing concern that made him feel more uneasy with each passing year. He knew he needed to figure out a way to get his citizenship or it would catch up with him someday.

That day came on February 8, 1942. George had just entered the lobby of his apartment building in the evening following a long day at work. He noticed old Mr. Costello, the building manager, sitting behind his counter with a nervous look on his face. As he walked past Costello on the way to the stairs, George saw him give a nod to the two men sitting on the tattered sofa in the lobby. Before George could get to the stairs, the two men walked up to him and flashed their badges, identifying themselves as US Immigration officers. Mr. Costello shrugged at George with a guilty look on his face that said sorry, he had no choice.

With the entry of the United States into World War II, the country was scurrying to draft a military to fight on two fronts. As part of that effort, the Immigration Service was ordered to round up all illegal aliens and offer them a choice. They could either fight for the United States and obtain their citizenship after the war, or be deported back to their country of origin. Because Greece was occupied by the Germans, he couldn't be deported to Greece. Instead, he would be sent to Egypt to be used as manual labor by the British, who had been fighting the Germans in North Africa. It didn't take long for George to decide. Rather than work as slave labor for the British, he chose to take his chances with the US military and obtain his citizenship if he somehow managed to survive the war.

George, along with fifty-nine other illegals, was taken by bus to the military induction center at Fort Dix, New Jersey, where he lined up with several thousand other inductees in a large hangar waiting to enlist. George thought that since he had served in the Merchant Marine and was familiar with life at sea, the US Navy would be the logical choice for him. As he moved to the head of the line, he realized the line he was standing in was for the Army since it had a soldier at the front processing the inductees. He looked around for a line with a sailor. As he heard "next," he stepped forward and stood in front of a burly Army master sergeant sitting behind a table. The master sergeant looked up at him and asked him his name. Rather than giving his name, George told the master sergeant he wanted to enlist in the Navy and asked where he could find that line.

The master sergeant, looking George up and down, sneered. In a Southern drawl, he said, "All youse illegals is going into the Army. We gonna use yas as cannon fodder against the Natzees and Japs, before we start going through aw boys."

Realizing what his chances were of surviving the war in the infantry, George asked, "Do I have any other choices than the infantry?"

The master sergeant looked at him impatiently. "The Army is a-startin' a new unit called Aebone. It pays an extra thirty dollars a month if you'se interested."

Thinking he may as well get a little extra money if he was going to be risking his life either way, George said he would take it. He then asked, "Uh, what does Aebone do?"

The master sergeant looked back at George in annoyance. "What part of Aebone don't ya understand, boy? They call it Aebone because y'awll be gettin' to your destination in an aeplane, and once you get there, then y'awll gonna jump out with a pareeshoot."

George felt the first wave of nausea hit him as what he had just heard began to sink in. The master sergeant asked him his name again. George, in a mild state of shock, answered, "George Mavropetrakis."

"Gioj Maevo what? Shiiit, I can't even say that. What the hell kind of name is that?"

George, not quite sure what the master sergeant was asking, answered, "Actually, it means a black stone in Greek."

"Well, now that's somethin' I can pronounce." He wrote Blackstone down on George's induction form, and from that day, Michael's grandfather became Private George Blackstone, 82nd Airborne, US Army.

After seeing significant action in North Africa, Sicily, and Italy, George was recruited into a special commando unit under the control of the US Army's Office of Strategic Services. The OSS was the predecessor of the Central Intelligence Agency, which was established after the end of World War II. The unit was comprised of Greek-American GIs who could understand and speak Greek. They were sent into German-occupied northern Greece with the mission of sabotaging German communications and supply lines, along with causing general mayhem behind enemy lines. Awarded a Silver Star and two Purple Hearts for his role in capturing a critical railhead held by the Germans, to Michael, his grandfather was a hero, larger than life.

After the war, George obtained his citizenship and went to Greece to marry Grandma Stella, the girl from his village that he'd had a crush on as long as he could remember. Returning to the United States, George and Stella went on to have four children: Pete in 1946, Anna in 1949, Nick in 1952 and Michael in 1955. Tragically, Michael had died three years later after contracting pneumonia. It was devastating to the family; however, with the passing of each year, the rawness of their loss slowly dissipated, and life went on for the Blackstone family. George started his own construction company. He grew it into a successful business with over thirty employees by the time he retired in 1975 and turned the reins over to Pete, Michael's father.

Pete graduated high school in 1963 and married his high school sweetheart, Mary Ann Ortello. He immediately went to work in the family construction business, but with the escalation of the Vietnam War, he was drafted into the Army in 1964. Before he shipped off to Vietnam in early 1965, Mary Ann became pregnant. Pete was trained to be a medic in the 1st Cavalry Division. In November of 1965, he fought in the Battle of the Ia Drang Valley, which was the US military's first major battle of Vietnam. During that battle, Pete risked his life repeatedly while under enemy fire, saving the lives of seven men before getting shot in the chest. That same day, halfway around the world back in New Jersey, Mary Ann gave birth to a baby boy. Pete, barely hanging on to life, was medivacked to an army hospital in Pleiku. After four hours of surgery, he finally pulled through. He was awarded a Purple Heart and the Bronze Star for valor in action. After being discharged from the Army because of his injury, Pete returned home to see his two-month-old son for the first time. Pete and Mary Anne named him Michael, in memory of Pete's youngest brother who had died ten years earlier.

Michael stopped on a corner, running in place as he waited for a car to pass. He remembered working during summer vacations for his father, who had taken over the business after Grandpa George retired. His father had always encouraged him to consider other opportunities and challenges in life beyond the construction business. He would tell Michael from an early age that there was nothing a man couldn't accomplish if he used his head, had determination and worked hard. He encouraged Michael to become involved in athletics and was unyielding when it came to Michael's education, not cutting him any slack for anything less than his best effort. Pete wanted Michael to have every opportunity possible. He realized a good education didn't guarantee success in life, but it went a long way towards opening doors. Going all the way back to grade school, when Michael brought home anything lower than an A, Pete, rather than chastise him, would look him in the eye and ask if it was truly the best he could do. That question alone motivated Michael to try harder. He realized it was the stories about his father and grandfather that had caught his imagination from a young age and fed his hunger for action and adventure.

They instilled in him his sense of identity and a desire to accomplish something meaningful with his life. That desire was what drove Michael to succeed in everything he attempted.

At six foot tall, Michael was a handsome and athletic teenager. He grew up excelling in sports and academics. He was the quarterback of his high school football team and graduated with a 3.8 grade point average. He was recruited by many top universities his senior year, but of all the schools, Columbia University in New York City appealed to him the most. Columbia offered him only a partial scholarship to play football, but more importantly, it provided him the opportunity to pursue a degree in finance at one of the country's most prestigious universities. A finance degree from Columbia would open many doors for him, with the possibility of getting hired by one of the big Wall Street investment firms. What better way to achieve success in life and control his own destiny? Or so he thought at the time.

Michael went off to Columbia during the fall of 1983. There, he met Karen Sumner, a journalism major who wanted a career in television news. She was intelligent and attractive, with an easygoing personality and a smile that would put both men and women at ease. That concealed a hidden drive and determination for success in whatever challenges she faced, a trait that made her even more appealing to Michael. As it happened, Michael only played backup quarterback at Columbia, but he studied hard and graduated magna cum laude with a degree in finance. Following graduation in 1988, Michael was hired by Bear Sterns, one of the heavy hitters of investment banking on Wall Street, as an assistant portfolio manager. Karen got a job with WNBC, the local network affiliate in New York, as a reporter covering city hall and other New York City politics. Michael and Karen married the following year. Michael felt he was on top of the world. What more could he have wanted out of life? He was living in Manhattan, with a beautiful and intelligent wife and a career that would lead to financial security at a young age and possibly even make him rich if he played his cards right.

Michael recollected those years. He had done well at Bear Stearns, earning large commissions from managing several multimillion-dollar investment accounts. Between their two salaries, they had lived very comfortably in an upscale condo on the Upper East Side and still had managed to put money away into savings. After four years at Bear Sterns, however, he had become bored. Although he was making tons of money, he had felt something was missing in his life. He had a desire for something more than wealth. He wanted challenge and excitement. It wasn't that his job was not challenging, but it hadn't provided him the type of challenge he desired, and certainly not much excitement. His grandfather's stories had left him with a longing for something other than sitting in an office behind a desk staring at numbers all day, regardless of how much money he was making.

Despite trying his hardest to maintain a brave face, Karen had sensed a restlessness brewing inside Michael. He remembered the evening that brought the first big change to their lives. They had been relaxing on their couch, finishing off a bottle of red wine after dinner, when Karen asked Michael if he was happy. Michael sat there silently for several moments, searching for the right words to explain how he felt.

He finally blurted out, "I hope you know how much I love you and how thankful I am for all the blessings we have in our lives. But I hate my job. I can't stand it. I can't stand sitting in an office for ten hours a day. I can't stand the greedy and superficial people I work with. But what bothers me the most is that I feel like such a fool for having invested so much time and effort in pursuing a career I thought would bring me a sense of fulfillment and accomplishment, only to realize that there's more to life than just making money. I need something more than that."

"Well, what would you do if you could start over?" Karen asked.

Michael hesitated before answering, knowing that she would think he was crazy when she heard what he was about to tell her. "I want to join the Army and go into Special Forces."

"Oh," Karen reacted, surprised, "I didn't know you had an interest in the military. You never said anything about that in all the time I've known you."

"Yeah, I know. I always figured I had to do what everyone else thought was important in life. Making lots of money, a big house in the suburbs, having kids, Little League, vacations in Florida—you know, the American Dream."

"You don't want to have kids?" Karen asked.

"Of course I do, sweetheart, eventually. I just don't want to be stuck with a conventional boring life, waking up every morning and hating what lies ahead for that day. Doing it over and over again for the next thirty years. That's just not me. I guess I tried to convince myself it was, but it's not. I know you probably think I'm nuts, but the thought of that just terrifies me."

After a long silence, Karen spoke up. "Well, if you're sure that's what you really want to do, then do it."

Michael looked into her eyes, not expecting that kind of reaction from her. "But what about your career? You love your job. I couldn't take that away from you."

"Yeah, I love what I do, but I can do that even if you're in the military. And besides, I wasn't planning on working when the kids were born. I want to be home with them until they're in school. My family is the most important thing to me."

"You know, I won't be making the kind of money I am now, not even close. We'll probably be moving around a lot. I'll be going on deployments, leaving you alone with the kids, sometimes for weeks or months at a time. That's going to be a big change from what we have now."

"Of course it will be a big change, but money's not everything. We've managed to put a good amount away in savings. As long as we have a roof over our heads and can live fairly comfortably, I'm okay with that. It'll be a big adventure. And besides, I thought you knew me better than that. I'm not the kind of girl that cares about driving around in a new Mercedes and living in a huge house in the suburbs just to impress everyone with how much we have. I grew up with that, and I can't stand being around people like that. They're so shallow and superficial, like most of the people you work with. I got enough of that growing up in Seattle with my mom and all the other Boeing executives' families. They bore me to death," Karen reassured Michael.

"I love you!" he told her and gave her a big hug, not believing how lucky he was to have such a wonderful wife.

A few weeks later, Michael gave notice to his boss at Bear Stearns. His boss thought Michael had suffered a nervous breakdown and tried to convince him to see a therapist. That didn't bother him as much as his father's reaction. Pete was incredulous. He blasted into Michael. "Are you crazy? Enlisting in the Army!"

"I'm not enlisting, Dad, I'm going in as an officer," Michael corrected him.

"I don't care if you go in as a general, you have too much talent and ability to waste in the military. You're throwing away your future. What does Karen think of this harebrained idea of yours?"

"She supports me. And besides, I don't understand why you're so against it. You and Grandpa both served."

"That was different. Neither of us had a choice," his father replied testily.

"What about all the times you told me to consider other opportunities in life beyond construction?" Michael persisted.

"I didn't mean the military!"

There was a long uncomfortable silence between them until Pete finally said, "Son, it's your life and your decision. I just think you haven't thought things through very well and you're going to eventually come to regret this decision."

"You're right, Dad, it is my life and my decision. I already made one decision I regret because I didn't think it through and just did it because everyone else thought it was the right thing to do. You always told me to think for myself, and that's what I'm doing now."

Grandfather George, on the other hand, now eighty years old, told Michael not to pay too much attention to what his father said. "Michael, life passes by quicker than you realize. Sometimes it seems just like yesterday I was a young man with my whole life in front of me. Every morning when I look in the mirror, I'm reminded just how fast the years have rolled by. You only have a short amount of time to pursue your dreams in life. You don't get a second chance. Don't end up with regrets later, when it's too late to change things."

Michael always felt better after talking to his grandfather. It wasn't that he didn't respect his father's opinion, but Michael was a different type of person than his father. His father lived life conservatively. Michael was more like his grandfather, with a thirst for challenge and adventure. Karen stayed at her job in New York while Michael went off to Army Basic Combat Training and then to Officer Candidate School at Fort Benning, Georgia. After graduating first in his class, Michael had a choice of follow-on assignments. Knowing that the route to Special Forces was through Ranger school, Michael continued his training. Ranger school was one of the toughest courses, both physically and mentally, in the Army. Lasting over two months, the course started out at Fort Benning, then moved on to a mountain phase located in the rugged mountainous terrain out in the middle of nowhere in the Chattahoochee National Forest north of Atlanta. Following the mountain phase, training continued in the coastal swamp environment near Eglin Air Force Base in Florida, where students received training in waterborne and small-boat operations. The course concluded with desert training at Fort Bliss in Texas.

The grueling physical fatigue, sleep deprivation, dehydration, cold, and psychological stress made this the most difficult challenge Michael had faced in his life up to that point. There were times during the course when Michael questioned whether he would be able to complete it. Of the 357 students who started the course, only 153 graduated. Michael was one of them. Despite his concerns, Michael excelled at everything that was thrown at him. At graduation, he received the Ralph Puckett Award as the officer honor graduate for passing all graded leadership positions and the LTC Keith Antonia Officer Leadership Award, which was awarded to the commissioned officer chosen by his peers for demonstrating initiative, motivation and outstanding leadership. Receiving one award was an honor; receiving two made Michael stand out above his entire class. It boosted his confidence that he had made the right choice with the new direction his life was taking him.

Michael was again given a choice of assignments. It wasn't the norm for a second lieutenant to go directly into Special Forces without first having a command position, but the Army was engaged in an effort to expand its Special Operations and needed officers to fill those positions. Because of Michael's stellar performance in Ranger school, he was offered the opportunity to advance directly to the Special Forces Qualification training, known as the Q course. The Q course lasted for another fifty-six weeks, and although not as physically demanding as Ranger school, it was mentally challenging training in unconventional warfare and small-unit tactics. Michael thrived in that environment. It was everything he had imagined it would be going back to his earliest memories of the stories of Grandpa George's exploits with the OSS during World War II.

Michael and Karen had been separated for close to nineteen months by the time he graduated from the Q course. They would see each other between courses and anytime Michael could take any leave, which was pretty much limited to long weekends on federal holidays. Karen tried to make the best of it, but the time spent apart was tough on them. Michael missed her dearly, but he was preoccupied with the excitement and challenge of his training, making his awareness of their time apart much less noticeable. She tried to keep herself distracted by delving into her career back in New York, but she felt a distance forming between them. They both became aware of small cracks that were developing in their relationship. For the first time, there were awkward silences when they were together. Although it seemed as if their lives were starting to diverge, both of them believed things would return to normal when they were reunited.

After Michael completed the Q course, he was assigned as the executive officer of 1st Platoon, Charlie Company, 2nd Battalion, 10th Special Forces Group at Fort Devens, Massachusetts. Karen quit her job in New York and joined him. She intended to look for another news job in Boston, about an hour away, but became pregnant shortly after joining Michael. Their time at Fort Devens was very brief. Michael picked up his promotion to first lieutenant along with orders to 1st Battalion, 10th Special Forces Group at Panzer Kaserne in Stuttgart, Germany. They arrived there in August 1995. He was excited about picking up command of a platoon, as was customary for new first lieutenants. Because of his experience on Wall Street, however, it became apparent to the battalion's commanding officer, Lieutenant Colonel Danforth, that Michael possessed exemplary administrative skills. Thus, he was assigned as the battalion's planning officer, or S5 as it was called in the Army. Michael was disappointed at not having been given a command, but he soon fell into the rhythm of his new assignment and began enjoying the challenge it offered. He had a natural ability for evaluating complex tactical situations and coming up with innovative operational plans. He quickly established his reputation as a highly competent officer with insight and the ability to think outside the conventional box that went beyond what was already a hallmark of Special Forces.

After all the time spent apart, life for Michael and Karen in Germany transitioned into a wonderful period in their lives. Karen gave birth to Samantha, three months after they arrived in Germany. The three of them spent weekends exploring Germany and neighboring Austria. Michael had a fascination with World War II history going all the way back to the stories he'd heard from his grandfather, so they visited many of the historical sites of the war. Michael's other passion was skydiving. From the first time he'd stepped out of an airplane at jump school and experienced the exhilaration of free-falling through the sky, he had been hooked. Michael became good friends with Lieutenant Bill Pickett, the battalion's training officer or S7, whose office was next to his. This allowed Michael the opportunity to finagle training jumps from Bill and tag along with the different platoons of their battalion every time he could come up with an excuse to get out from behind his desk.

Michael's attention was drawn back to the car in the intersection in front of him. He paused on the corner, running in place as he waited for the car to make a turn. He sucked in as much air as his lungs would hold, trying to catch his breath, yet felt as if he could continue running all night. The surreal vividness of his memories, along with the thought of what lay ahead, had put him into a trance-like state that caused him to lose all concept of distance and time. The car made its turn, and he resumed running as his thoughts returned back to last training jump in Germany.

He was tagging along with 2nd Platoon, Alpha Company on a C-130 transport for a jump from fourteen thousand feet. It was late afternoon on a clear and crisp autumn day during late October 1993. As the rear cargo door of the C-130 opened, Michael could see the German countryside below, a dazzling collage of red, orange and yellow. The soldiers of 2nd Platoon stood and lined up to prepare for the jump. Michael was second from the rear. Not being a member of 2nd Platoon, he would be the second-to-last man to exit the aircraft. The last jumper was the platoon staff sergeant, whose responsibility it was to verify every jumper had left the aircraft. They stood one behind the other with their eyes on the jumpmaster as the cold air whipped through the fuselage. At the thirty-second mark, the jumpmaster gave the hand signal for one final check. Each jumper responded with a thumbs-up. When the green jump light came on and the jumpmaster yelled, "Go, go, go," the soldiers quickly shuffled down the ramp and stepped out of the aircraft. When it was his turn, Michael paused momentarily and then stepped out into the frigid air. Adjusting his body position to stabilize his descent, he closed the distance with the rest of the platoon. The training jump called for the platoon to keep a tight formation and land within the designated drop zone. As the air rushed by him, he glanced at the sun, which looked like a huge orange ball low on the horizon. He looked down at the approaching ground and marveled at the array of brilliant colors. Although he had done close to one hundred jumps, the thrill he experienced each time was just as intense as his first.

Michael glanced at the altimeter strapped to his wrist; it indicated he was falling through three thousand feet. The designated altitude to deploy chutes for this jump was two thousand feet. As he saw the first canopies deploying below him, he prepared to deploy his chute, waiting to see the jumper in front of him deploy his own first. He watched as the chute below him came out and then collapsed, twisting itself into a propeller and sending its jumper into a spin. Michael waited for the jumper to detach his main chute and deploy his reserve, standard procedure for a main chute malfunction. Seconds ticked by as Michael fell through two thousand feet, and the jumper below was still attached to his main chute, spinning even more wildly now. Michael realized he had only seconds to act before he would pass him by. Glancing at his altimeter again, he saw that he was passing through fifteen hundred feet. Adjusting his body position, Michael dove towards the jumper in the hopes of intercepting him. He knew if he timed it perfectly, he would detach the jumper's main chute and deploy the reserve, leaving him barely enough altitude to then deploy his own chute, assuming both of them weren't knocked unconscious by the midair collision. As Michael closed on the jumper, he spread out his arms and legs just before colliding with him. After recovering momentarily from the impact, Michael reached for and detached the jumper's main chute, then pulled the reserve rip cord. As the reserve chute deployed and yanked the jumper away from him, Michael pulled his ripcord. His canopy deployed and slowed his descent for the remaining five hundred feet. He prepared for a hard landing as he saw the ground coming at him fast. He hit hard and felt a sharp pain in his lower back as he tucked and rolled.

Michael lay on the ground motionless, trying to catch his breath after having the wind knocked out of him. Second Platoon's medic came running over to Michael and told him to lie still while he assessed his condition. Able to move his fingers and toes, Michael knew he was not paralyzed but could tell from the severe pain that he was seriously injured. As he lay there, Sergeant Thompson, the jumper with the parachute malfunction, came running over and knelt beside him. With tears streaming from his eyes, he looked at Michael and thanked him repeatedly.

"You saved my life, Lieutenant, I don't know how I'll ever repay you."

"Don't mention it, Sarge. Anything to get me out of the office for a few hours," Michael replied, trying to make light of what he realized was his serious condition. He closed his eyes and lay on his back, thinking that he wouldn't be jumping again anytime soon, perhaps never.

Michael was transported to Landstuhl Army Hospital. After having a CAT scan and MRI of his spine, the orthopedic surgeon came to Michael's room and broke him the news. He had sustained spinal compression fractures in two vertebrae and had ruptured three discs in his lower back. The doctor told him he would eventually recover after several months in a back brace and restricted activity, but his days in Special Forces were over. His spine would never be able to withstand the punishment imposed by the physical demands of Special Forces, let alone jumping out of aircraft. Michael tried to come to terms with what the doctor had just told him. It didn't seem real. Michael recalled all the hours spent in his hospital bed, somehow hoping it was all just a bad dream, and he would eventually wake up in his bed and find Karen lying next to him. Reality slowly set in over the course of the next month as Karen made the daily drive with Samantha, or Sam as they'd started calling her, to visit him, until he was finally released to return to limited duty.

On Michael's first day back at the battalion, he was told to report to LTC Danforth's office. He wondered what his commanding officer was going to say to him as he hobbled down the hallway towards Danforth's office. Stopping outside his door, he knocked and waited for a response.

"Enter," Danforth barked from inside the office.

"Sir, Lieutenant Blackstone reporting for duty." Michael saluted as he entered his CO's office.

"Have a seat, Lieutenant," Danforth instructed him.

"I'd prefer to stand, sir. A lot more comfortable."

"Oh yeah, I suppose it is after what you did to yourself. How ya feeling?"

"I'm doing okay, sir. Just feels like I got blindsided by a two-hundred-and-fifty-pound linebacker coming at me with a full head of steam," replied Michael.

LTC Danforth looked at him silently from behind his desk for a moment before he continued, "I read the accident report and spoke to Sergeant Thompson about what happened. You have some pretty big balls, Lieutenant, doing what you did. You saved that man's life, while risking yours. Your selfless actions are a shining example of the type of bravery that has made Special Forces worthy of the honors earned by them throughout their history of fighting for this country. I know from your file that both your father and grandfather served their country bravely and were recognized for their heroic actions. Let me just say that you've done them both proud. I'll be putting you in for a Soldier's Medal. It would have been a Bronze Star if this had happened during combat, but nonetheless, I just want you to know how damn proud and honored I am to have men like you under my command."

"Thank you, sir, but I really didn't have time to even think about what I did. I just reacted. Any one of those other men who jumped with me would have done the same thing if they were in my position."

"Hey, Lieutenant, just learn how to accept a little recognition and say thanks. I'm sure many other men would have displayed the same type of courage, but the fact that you were able to keep your wits about you and act quickly and decisively under such stressful circumstances is an ability not all men possess. It's that type of trait that can make the difference between life or death, victory or defeat on the battlefield. You would have made an outstanding officer."

Michael realized Danforth said, "would have made" rather than "are going to make" and was about to respond to him, but Danforth continued. "Lieutenant, I've read the medical report and spoken to your doctor. The extent of your injuries precludes you from remaining in Special Forces and qualify you for a medical discharge. You could probably stay in the Army behind a desk somewhere, but knowing the type of soldier you are, I don't think you could live with that. I know these are hard words for you to swallow, but I would suggest taking the medical discharge and getting on with your life. It pains me to say it, but as your commanding officer and more importantly a fellow Green Beret, the most decent thing I can do is to be brutally honest with you."

Michael stood there in stunned silence, his head spinning. After recovering, Michael addressed his commanding officer: "Sir, I know I messed myself up pretty bad. But I also know that I can fully recover physically, at least get myself back to ninety-five percent, which will make me fit enough for anything that's expected of me in Special Forces. I just need a little time."

LTC Danforth looked at Michael compassionately, as a father would a son. "Lieutenant, I'm sure if anyone could do it, you could. But even if you were able to get yourself back to that level of conditioning, there's no way you would be cleared medically to stay in SF, or any other combat unit for that matter, with your injury. That's the type of injury most people don't bounce back from, and the medical regs aren't flexible about those things. That's just the way it is. You can't fight Army bureaucracy any more than you can pull an elephant with a dog leash. Hell, it wouldn't matter if your father was the Army chief of staff."

Michael felt as if his whole world had come undone. "I don't know what I'd do. I can't stay in the Army behind a desk. I'd rather not have survived that fall." The words slowly drifted out of his mouth.

"Listen, Lieutenant, there's someone I want you to talk to at the US embassy in Bonn. I think he would be very interested in you, especially your analytical skills. There's still a way you can serve your country," Danforth told him. "I'll let you know after I talk to him in the next few days. In the meantime, you may want to start with admin on the paperwork for your medical discharge. If you decide to consider this other opportunity, you'll probably want to get moving with the next phase of your life as quickly as possible."

"Okay, sir, thanks," Michael answered with a slightly renewed sense of hope.

"All right, then. You'll be fine, Lieutenant, in whatever your future holds for you. You have that rare quality I've seen in only a handful of men who can excel in whatever challenge life throws at them. Don't get discouraged. Anyway, we're going to have one hell of a drunk before you escape from here. Dismissed."

Michael saluted and walked out of LTC Danforth's office, a million thoughts flying through his head. He felt like his world had come crashing down around him, but at the same time, he was intrigued by what Danforth had said about the man at the embassy. After a week, LTC Danforth instructed Michael to report to the embassy to meet with Mr. Bob Johnson.

Two days later at 7:00 in the morning, Michael pulled out of his driveway on base housing and drove up the A61 to the US embassy in Bonn. After passing through security screening and obtaining his visitor's badge, Michael waited in the security office for his escort. A few minutes later, an attractive brunette in her mid-thirties, dressed in high heels, a snug charcoal-gray skirt and a white silk blouse, which showed off her tall, slender figure, walked into the security office.

"Lieutenant Blackstone?"

"Hi, uh, yes, that's me."

"Would you please follow me? I'll show you to Mr. Johnson's office."

"Yes, ma'am—I mean miss. Sorry, it's an occupational habit," he fumbled, a bit embarrassed.

"Don't worry," she replied with a slight giggle and a smile. "My father was a Marine and demanded my brothers be respectful to ladies."

As Michael followed her, he wondered whom she worked for and if all female embassy employees looked like her. She was dressed professionally, yet she certainly knew how to accentuate her feminine qualities. She led him up the stairs to the fourth floor and punched the code into the keypad, unlocking the heavy security door. They walked down the hallway and turned left into a room that was the first of an executive office suite. A woman sat behind a desk.

"Hi, Sue. Bob asked me to bring Lieutenant Blackstone to see him," his escort said to the lady behind the desk.

"He's inside." Sue nodded her head towards the other door leading past her desk.

The brunette peeked her head into the adjoining office, saying, "Bob, Mr.—I mean Lieutenant. Blackstone is here." She glanced back at Michael and smiled.

"Bring him in," a gruff voice barked from the other side of the door.

They walked into the office, where Michael saw a man with salt-and-pepper hair, wearing an oxford shirt with the sleeves rolled up, sitting behind a large mahogany desk. He had striking looks. Michael tried to guess his age but couldn't tell if he was in his late forties, fifties or early sixties. He looked like he kept himself in shape and had a youthful face, although it was weathered, as if he had spent a good part of his life outdoors. It was his eyes, however, that drew Michael's attention. There was an intensity in those dark blue eyes that made Michael feel as if Johnson was able to peer into his soul and see his deepest secrets. Even without knowing anything about him, Michael could tell this man had seen and done things that the average person couldn't imagine. He remembered seeing that same look in his grandfather's eyes when he would tell Michael about his missions behind enemy lines.

"Michael, thanks for coming. I know your CO, LTC Danforth. He filled me in on what happened to you. That was a damn brave thing you did, son. Not only brave, but also pretty impressive the way you kept your cool in a tense situation like that. You're a credit to SF." He stood and shook Michael's hand.

"Thank you, sir, nothing any other SF soldier wouldn't have done."

"No doubt. You guys know how to look after each other's back when you're out there operating all on your own. Not like big Army that goes in with overwhelming firepower and air support. I was with the 75th Infantry Regiment in 'Nam. If we didn't take care of business on our own, there was nobody else we could call on to come get us out of a jam."

Michael had heard of the exploits of 75th Infantry Regiment, or LRRPs as they were called, for Long Range Reconnaissance Patrol. They worked in small units of six to eight men, deep behind enemy lines, for thirty to forty days at a time. They were completely self-sufficient, living off the land while beating the Vietcong at their own game of stealth in the jungle. They had a kill ratio of 400 to 1, the highest of any unit in US military history. Michael realized this man was pretty bad-ass, even if he was now sitting behind a desk, dressed in gabardine wool slacks and an oxford shirt.

"You guys definitely knew how to look after yourselves. I read about your outfit's missions. During interrogations, the Vietcong would refer to you guys as the ghosts of death. Even they were scared of running into you guys," Michael told him, trying not to appear too awed by Johnson's background.

"Yeah, we dispatched our share of Gooks. Still didn't make up for what all they did to our boys. Too many of them got killed for nothing, and in the end, we just turned tail and handed the commie North everything they wanted. What a damn waste of good men. It was one of the sadder moments in our country's history. A hard lesson learned, but I hope it finally woke us up not to get involved in wars unless there's a clear objective and the politicians let the war fighters get the job done right."

"I hope so, sir."

"So, Michael, sorry to hear about your injury. Tough break. I'm guessing you've decided not to stay in the Army and push a desk the rest of your career."

"No, that's not for me. I'd feel like a caged animal stuck in an office all day."

"Don't blame you, I'd feel the same way. As a matter of fact, sometimes I do now. I don't get out into the field as much as I used to. Got any plans for when you get out?"

"No, sir. I worked on Wall Street before joining the Army. I guess I could always go back. If I have no other choice other than being stuck behind a desk, I might as well make some decent money," Michael said, dejected at the possibility.

"Well, Michael, how would you like to still be able to serve your country, working for the CIA?"

Michael stood in silence, studying Johnson's face. Here was a man who, after having experienced the things he had in Vietnam, had chosen to go work for his country's clandestine spy agency. Michael wondered how he would like that kind of work.

Michael asked him, "You got any regrets so far?"

"Nope, not a one. But then again, I was never the conventional type who wanted a house in the suburbs and a wife nagging me all the time about when I was going to cut the grass."

Michael thought about his answer. He wondered how Karen would react if he said yes. Would she understand his decision and be supportive, or would she be upset at the idea of Michael going from being a soldier to a spy? Would it be too much to ask of her? After all, she had given up enough of her life already, following him with his career in the Army. This job would probably be similar to the Army, he thought. They would be moved around every few years, and he would have to travel some. But she'd probably like it better than Army life, he tried to convince himself. He was pretty sure embassy dependents were treated better than most military dependents. The housing accommodations must surely be better. He tried to picture himself trading in his uniform for a trench coat.

"I'll have to run it by my wife. Well, not run it by her, but at least be able to tell her what I'll be doing once I leave the Army. Otherwise, it's not going to work. We have an honest relationship, and there's no way I can go through the rest of my life looking her in the eye every day and lying about half of my life."

"Michael, if you accept this job, it's a commitment that you're devoting the rest of your working life to serving your country. Of course, it's in a different capacity than what you've been used to as an officer in the Army, but no less important. In many ways, the individual impact you'll have in the CIA protecting your country will probably surpass anything you would do in the Army. I suppose if there was a war, you could have done some heroic deed or taken some decisive action to win a battle, but on a day-to-day basis, you will be in the midst of a battle that's been going on for almost fifty years between the CIA and the rest of the world, less of course the Brits, Canucks and Aussies. Everybody thinks that it's a big kumbaya party now that the Soviet Union is no longer and that drunken buffoon Yeltsin is giving Russian bear hugs to Clinton. But let me tell you, between what China's world ambitions are going to be in another ten years, along with that Russian psyche of hurt pride and a paranoia of the West trying to subjugate Mother Russia, not to mention all the trouble those fanatics in the Middle East are going to be causing, things in this world are going to get much worse despite what most people think. The CIA will need to double its size just to keep up. Think of all the possibilities for someone with your ability. Getting in at the beginning of a drastically changing world, you'll be able to write your own ticket for what targets and types of operations you want to pursue. There'll be more work than there are soldiers for the foreseeable future. So, getting back to your question, if you tell me the CIA is where you want to dedicate your life, then, yes, you can tell your wife about what type of work you'll be doing. Of course, she will have to learn your cover story and sign confidentiality disclosures about not revealing your true employer to anyone, including parents and your children, but that's about it."

"Well, that's good. That was a pretty long answer to a fairly simple question. You're not trying to pitch me, are you?" Michael asked half-jokingly.

"What do you think we do here at the CIA?" Johnson stared back at Michael with those piercing blue eyes and a big barracuda smile on his face.

Michael started nodding before the words even came out of his mouth. "I'll do it. What have I got to lose?"

Michael remembered that question as he reached the end of his run. Standing in front of his condo, sucking in as much of the cool night air as his lungs could hold as he tried to catch his breath, he now knew what the answer to that question had been. It was more than he could have imagined when he'd originally asked it. In a few hours, it would not matter what the answer to that question had been. He entered his security code on the keypad next to the front door of his building and entered, walking through the lobby. As he stood there waiting for the elevator, he thought about how much his life had changed since then. The elevator door opened, bringing Michael's attention back to his surroundings. From inside the elevator, he heard his name. As he stepped in, he saw his eighty-year-old neighbor, Dolores Diamond, eyeing him up and down as she smiled at him. She was wearing an orange-and-black oriental silk robe over what Michael could clearly see was black lingerie with fuzzy cheetah slippers on her feet. In her right arm was Chloe, her thirteen-year-old Yorkshire terrier. A gold-tipped cigarette holder with an unlit cigarette stuck out between her bright red lips. She never seemed to be able to get her lipstick and eyeliner quite right in her older years, but she never left her condo without her makeup and her hair done.

"Hello, handsome," she greeted Michael with her usual seductive, raspy voice from years of smoking Virginia Slims.

Between the length of the cigarette holder and the extra-long cigarette, Dolores looked like something out of a Humphrey Bogart movie. She claimed that the cigarette holder had been a gift from Sean Connery during the filming of the 1965 James Bond movie *Thunderball*, in which she had been a supporting actress. Michael had never bothered renting the movie to see if Dolores had actually acted in it or was simply a lonely old lady craving a little attention. Despite often being trapped by her in the hallway while coming or going, Michael was always kind to her, spending more time than he really wanted listening to stories about her days in "entertainment," as she called it. Several times over the past five years since Michael and Eva had moved into the building, Dolores had shown them old photographs of her as a Las Vegas showgirl. Michael had to admit she was pretty hot back in her day, especially in some of those showgirl costumes, which didn't leave much to the imagination. Michael always found it amusing looking at photos of a beautiful half-naked twenty-something-year-old woman as she sat between him and his wife fifty years later. Michael and Eva considered her a sweet old lady, treating her more like their eccentric old aunt than just a neighbor. Always trying to help her out as much as possible, they would regularly pick up groceries for her and fix things that needed repair in her condo.

"Hi, Dolores, what are you doing out this late?" Michael asked, thinking it was a bit odd she was in the elevator with Chloe at this hour.

"I'm just so upset about Johnny Carson passing away. He was such a sweet guy, a real ladies' man, but always a gentleman," she said as if she knew him personally.

"Uh, Dolores, Johnny died about ten or so years ago," Michael responded, trying to sound neutral while determining whether Dolores was mentally all there.

"Oh, I know that, tiger. I may have a vivid imagination, but I'm not senile yet. I was just watching a documentary about him on the History Channel. It made me sad, thinking about him and all my other friends that aren't around anymore."

"Did you ever meet Johnny Carson?" Michael asked, somewhat intrigued.

"Did I meet him? Honey, I knew Johnny from when he was just starting out on the *Tonight Show* back in the early sixties. Where do you think he used to spend all his vacations? I knew the inside of his suite at the Sands just like it was my own place," she answered as if stating the obvious.

"Is that where you worked as a showgirl?"

"Of course that's where I worked. How else would I have met Johnny?"

"I see. Did you and Johnny have a thing going on?" Michael asked delicately, not wanting to embarrass her?

"Johnny and I? Heavens, no!" She burst out laughing. Her face lit up with a big smile as she recalled happy memories from long ago.

"Sorry, Dolores, I just thought from what you said about knowing his room, you and he might have had a relationship or something," he said sheepishly.

"Young man, your mind is in the gutter," she teased. "Johnny would come to Vegas several times a year to hang out with his pals, Frank, Dean, Sammy and Joey. They would have some wild parties. They were the type of fellas that needed women around them all the time, like a sheik needs a harem. Those parties sometimes went for three days and nights straight, with a never-ending supply of booze and broads. When we girls would finish up with our shows, we'd hang out in the party suite. If you managed to catch a few hours of sleep before your next performance, you were lucky. Those were the days when getting those little black beauties to perk you up before the show wasn't a problem, honey."

It suddenly hit Michael as he asked, "Dolores, do you mean the Rat Pack?"

"Of course that's who I mean. And by the way, they didn't call themselves the Rat Pack. That was Bogey's gang back in the fifties. Frank, Dean, Sammy and Joey called themselves the Clan. It was the press that called them the Rat Pack and that's what stuck," she corrected him as if he was in school and she was his teacher.

"Wow, I never any idea that you knew them. Did you ever have a fling with any of those guys?" he asked her teasingly.

"How do you think a showgirl was ever able to afford a condo like this?" she replied with a devilish smile and a raised eyebrow just as the elevator doors opened. They stepped out onto the fifth floor and headed down the hallway.

"Dolores, you must have been more than a handful for any guy. Sounds like you have a lot of good memories," he said as they walked side by side.

"Yeah, honey, I do. You go through life meeting lots of different people. Some you know for a long time, some only for a short while. It's not how long you've known them that's important, it's the intensity of the relationship that counts. That's what you end up carrying around with you the rest of your life. Who you are as a person is shaped a little bit by each one of those people that has passed through your life."

They reached Dolores's door and stopped. She opened her door and put down Chloe, who ran into the living room and jumped up onto the white leather couch. Dolores turned in her doorway and looked into Michael's eyes as she said, "I'm really sorry about what happened between you and Eva. You two made a good couple."

"Yeah, I'm sorry too." He looked back at her, wondering if she had ever found lasting happiness with anyone at some point in her life. As far as he knew, Dolores had never married. Michael placed his hands on her shoulders as if he were saying goodbye to an old friend. "Dolores, you're a wonderful gal. If I was born thirty years earlier and had run into you someplace, I'd probably have butterflies in my stomach trying to come up with some smooth line just as an excuse to talk to you. I'm lucky to have met you and have you as a friend, even if I am thirty years too late."

She looked back at him with a sweet smile, as if she were a young woman again, waiting for him to give her a good night kiss at the end of a date. He didn't know what made him do it, but he slowly moved his face towards hers and kissed her gently on the lips, pausing briefly before their lips parted without it feeling uncomfortable for either of them. Michael smiled warmly at her as he studied her face. For a second, it seemed as if he could see beyond the wrinkles and age spots on her face, past the smudged lipstick and crooked eyebrows, as if he were looking at the beautiful young woman he saw in the photographs. He felt a warm tenderness towards her, sensing that although she was old and in the final chapter of her life, she still longed for the closeness of having someone by her side.

"You take care," he whispered softly into her ear before he turned, leaving her standing there as she savored that brief moment of intimacy.

That was a strange encounter, he thought as he walked down the hallway to his door, especially while experiencing the mix of emotions over what was about to take place. He unlocked the door and entered his condo. He walked into the kitchen and pulled a glass out of the cupboard and stuck it under the ice dispenser of the refrigerator, filling it with ice. He pulled open the freezer door and reached for the bottle of Finlandia vodka, his favorite. He always kept his vodka in the freezer, which caused it to thicken into a syrupy liquid. Michael wasn't a big drinker but occasionally enjoyed a vodka straight, preferring it to any other type of liquor. He filled the glass and walked into the living room, carrying the bottle with him. He set it down on the glass coffee table in front of the couch, then continued into the master bath, sipping his vodka as he took off his sweaty clothes and tossed them onto the floor. He turned on the shower, letting the hot water run until he saw the steam billow out, before stepping in with his glass of vodka. He didn't know why he was taking a shower considering what lay ahead, but for some reason, it did not sit right with him to go ahead with what he was planning without cleaning himself up first. It wasn't as if it would make it any less distasteful, but as always, Michael was very methodical and conscientious in everything he did, something that had stayed with him from his time in Special Forces and at the Agency.

He let the hot water hit his back as he sipped his vodka, going over the mental checklist of everything that had needed to be taken care of before going ahead with what he was about to do. After his father had retired fifteen years ago and sold the construction business, he and Michael's mother had moved to St. Augustine, Florida, trading in the cold New Jersey winters for balmy Christmases and scorching Fourth of Julys. They were now well into their seventies, but both still in good health. They didn't have an inkling about what

Michael was about to do. He knew how devastated they would be when they heard the news but hoped that they would be able to forgive him.

Sam, his daughter, now in her second year at UCLA medical school, would be taken care of financially with the life insurance money. That would pay off all of her school loans and leave her with enough to get her life started. Some of the money would also go to Eva, his soon-to-be ex-wife. He didn't have the heart to remove her as a beneficiary. Although she had left him, part of him knew that he hadn't tried very much to keep her from going. She had put up with his slow spiral into depression over the past few years. She had given him ultimatum after ultimatum to get counseling, telling him over and over again that she couldn't live with a man who didn't show her any emotion. The more she desperately tried to find the man she had first met, the man she remembered being full of passion and a hunger for life, the more he withdrew from her. He hadn't seen or talked to her in over four months, other than the occasional texts back and forth regarding the divorce. Any emotional connection between them had dissipated long ago. The divorce would be final next week. He felt a slight sense of guilt about not waiting until then. Not that he thought it would make the slightest difference to her emotionally, but he disliked the thought of leaving her with the label of widow to carry around for the rest of her life, with the connotation of having suffered loss. It didn't make him feel good that this would be the last thing she would remember him by. He knew his promises about what their lives would be like after they married and moved back to the United States hadn't turned out as he had envisioned. He had ruined his first marriage and had hoped the second time around would be different. It hadn't turned out that way.

As he let the hot water hit his head and run down his face, he remembered the day he had come home from his meeting with Bob Johnson, and how Karen had reacted to his announcement that he was joining the CIA. Unlike how she had supported him in his decision to join the Army, that time she was visibly shaken, almost to the point of tears. He didn't understand the severity of her reaction. He remembered trying to convince her that his new job wouldn't affect their family life. Other than the first year at the CIA's training course, he would probably be away from home far less, rarely for more than a few weeks at a time. At least, that was what he'd told her then. He had also said that it was much less dangerous than the Army. As a spy, he wouldn't be trying to kill anyone or have anyone trying to kill him. That wasn't part of the job description.

Michael remembered Karen's response, that at least in the Army, he could tell her about his day when he came home from work. In the CIA, things would be different. There, half of his life she would never have any idea about. It would be like living with a stranger, and would cause them to drift apart. She didn't know if their marriage could survive that. After a few days had passed and Karen had gotten over the initial shock of Michael's announcement, they'd talked about it again. He had been able to reassure her that they would never drift apart, but he also remembered the little voice inside him that told him what Karen feared wasn't something that should be taken lightly. It was a voice he obviously hadn't paid enough attention to.

Michael grabbed the shampoo and squeezed a shot into his hand. As he lathered his hair, he remembered how, after he'd returned home from the Farm, the CIA's training academy near Williamsburg, VA, he had sensed a slight shift in their relationship. It wasn't as if they weren't happy to see each other again. They spent as much time as they could in bed the first month, trying to make up for lost time, but he could feel an almost unperceivable distance had developed between them. It seemed like a conscious effort to make conversation with each other. At first, neither of them gave it much thought. Sam had recently turned three and was getting more and more of Karen's attention. Karen had quickly come to the realization that Michael's career would have them moving regularly to various places throughout the world. She thought most of his postings would have decent schools for the dependent children of US embassy employees, but it would up to her to ensure that Sam received enough attention so she would have as normal a childhood as possible.

Michael's first assignment was to CIA Headquarters in Langley, as an assistant staff operations officer, more commonly referred to as a desk officer, responsible for supporting intelligence operations of CIA stations throughout the world. It was a customary assignment for new recruits to be paired up with a more senior desk officer, during which time they would learn the ins and outs of how the CIA functioned, while getting an introduction to how real-world operations worked before they were dispatched out into the field. After twelve months at Langley, Michael received his first posting to Istanbul, Turkey. The US embassy was located in Ankara, Turkey's capital. The primary CIA station was stationed at the embassy, but a secondary CIA station was located at the US consulate general in Istanbul. Istanbul was not only Turkey's largest city and trading hub but also the crossroads between the West and the rest of the Muslim world. As a member of NATO, Turkey was a military ally of the United States and Western Europe, while at the same time being the descendant of the Ottoman Empire, which had controlled most of the Muslim world up until its defeat during World War I. Although it had since become a secularized democracy, many Muslims still considered Turkey part of the Muslim Caliphate that would rise again one day and rival the West for dominance of the world. Whether it was other foreign intelligence services, terrorism or organized crime, Istanbul was the center of it all. It was a city of terrorists, criminals and spies.

Michael was assigned to the station's counterterrorism unit as a specialized skills officer, or SSO. While case officers were primarily responsible for recruiting foreign assets to spy for the CIA, SSOs were primarily responsible for supporting CIA operations. They commonly had unique attributes such as fluency in foreign languages, paramilitary operations and other specialized skill sets. Michael's new assignment was as the liaison with Milli İstihbarat Teşkilatı, known as MIT, Turkey's National Intelligence Service. Whereas some new CIA officers might have considered a liaison assignment undesirable because it was out of the mainstream of CIA intelligence operations, Michael saw it from an entirely different perspective. He took advantage of the independence his new position offered him, working outside the direct scrutiny and oversight of his boss, the chief of station, and CIA headquarters. It gave him the opportunity to develop a close working relationship with MIT and earn their trust, thus facilitating his involvement in several joint CIA-MIT counterterrorism operations. Unlike the CIA's foreign collection operations, which were worked unilaterally without the host country's knowledge, counterterrorism operations needed to be worked with the host country's intelligence service, since it was they who were familiar with the terrorist groups in their country, along with how and where they were operating. He was assigned to work with a young, intelligent MIT liaison officer who spoke fluent English. With her help, he quickly integrated into MIT's counterterrorism operations.

Michael loved the excitement that his new job brought him, but his family life suffered. Often after returning home during the early-morning hours after a surveillance operation, he would get a few hours of sleep, then leave the house before Karen and Sam woke, for a day of writing cables back to Langley before going back out again the following night. The routine began to take its toll on his relationship with Karen. They managed to get away occasionally for short vacations to nearby Greece or Italy, but he spent more and more time away from home, leaving Karen and Sam to fend for themselves. The resentment Karen felt towards Michael's obsession with his job built steadily over time. After three years in Istanbul, Karen threatened to return to the US with Sam if things didn't change. Michael pleaded with her to have patience and promised he would be transferring back to Washington the following year, where their lives would return back to normal. Karen and Sam were the most important part of Michael's life. He couldn't imagine life without them. He realized he needed to focus more attention on them and not take them for granted. It wasn't that he purposely neglected them; it was just that his job had a way of consuming him. The gratification he got from the challenge of his work, along with the occasional adrenaline rush, was like a drug. It had a way of taking him over and blinding him to what was going on with his family life.

After spending four years in Istanbul, Michael's transfer back to Langley came just in time during the summer of 2002. He realized his relationship with Karen had been stretched to its breaking point. His new position at headquarters was as the assistant to the deputy director for operations, the DDO. It was a choice assignment because it put Michael in the midst of the CIA's operational nerve center, providing him a rare view into all of the CIA's worldwide operations. His family situation also got better as his relationship with Karen slowly improved. He still spent ten to twelve hours a day at work, but it was typically Monday through Friday. Sam was in third grade, and Karen had resumed her journalism career, working as a part-time research assistant at the *Washington Post*. It wasn't television, but it allowed Karen more flexibility to have a career in the news and still maintain a family life. Michael and Karen slowly developed a network of friends, mostly other couples with children, enjoying birthday parties, barbeques and dinner parties typical of middle-class suburban couples in northern Virginia. Michael's passion, however, was working out in the field, and he soon developed an itch for a new assignment. He wanted another overseas posting so he could go back to running operations. He had hoped it would be as a counterintelligence case officer. Rather than chasing down terrorists, this time he wanted to recruit assets to target other foreign intelligence services that were spying against the United States. In other words, he would be running spies against other spies. That opportunity came quicker than he expected during the summer of 2004.

Michael remembered the day he announced to Karen that he had received orders to Athens, Greece. It was the beginning of the end for their marriage. Karen had told Michael she and Sam wouldn't be going with him. She couldn't take having their lives turned upside down again after finally reaching some semblance of normalcy following all the years of putting up with Michael's self-centeredness with work. Michael left for Athens without Karen and Sam. Although they hadn't discussed divorce, Michael knew their marriage was on thin ice. He flew back to visit every three or four months, whenever he could break away for a week, but each time, the distance between him and Karen grew. Sex had become merely a physical act, devoid of any emotional connection. Michael remembered his last visit after being in Athens for a year and a half. They hadn't even had sex. They were cordial to each other, but it was obvious to both of them something had permanently changed in their relationship. The day before Michael was to return to Athens, Karen told him she wanted a divorce. Realizing it was no use trying to pretend their marriage was salvageable at that point, he had told her that it was probably the best for both of them.

As Michael stood under the shower with the hot water beating down on his head, he recalled Sam's reaction later that evening when they'd told her about their decision. Michael could still remember the hurt he saw in her face. It had been etched into his memory ever since. She'd burst out sobbing, "No, no, no!" Even though he had been gone often with his work, he had never failed to make Sam the center of his attention when he was home. She had been daddy's girl, and Sam had placed him on a pedestal. It was that day that he had been knocked off his pedestal. Ever since, he had tried to restore their relationship, but as Sam had entered her adolescent years, she'd wanted less and less to do with him. Other than the occasional phone call on Christmas or her birthday, he had become a virtual stranger to her.

After toweling himself off, he paused for a moment, trying to decide what to wear. He slid open the closet door and looked inside. For some reason, jeans seemed too casual for such an occasion. He decided on a pair of khaki pants. Should he put on socks? he wondered. *The hell with socks. You're making this way too complicated*, he answered himself. What difference would it make if he wore socks? He pulled on his pants and grabbed a blue-and-yellow striped polo shirt, pulling it over his head. He glanced at himself in the full-length mirror of the closet door. He looked all right for what he was about to do, he thought. He walked over to the nightstand and opened the top drawer, reaching in and grabbing the Glock 21. He kept the .45 auto next to his bed out of habit. He wasn't a gun nut, nor did he get any particular enjoyment from shooting guns. He had certainly had more than enough experience handling them in the past. To him, firearms were just tools that served a specific purpose, just like a hammer or screwdriver. In the case of guns, their purpose was to kill, whether it was animals or human beings. Michael had used them for both. He hadn't hunted in years, but as a teenager, he'd accompanied his father and grandfather on hunting trips every fall in the western forests of Pennsylvania. In Special Forces, he had become proficient with a multitude of weapons, both small and large, from handguns, assault rifles and machine guns to hand-held antitank and antiaircraft weapons, not to mention a wide range of explosives. Until that fateful day in Athens twelve years ago, however, he had never had to use one to kill another human being. As a CIA officer operating in a foreign country, having to shoot two people dead meant something had gone terribly wrong.

He grabbed his empty glass and walked into his office. Opening the middle drawer of his desk, he pulled out a prescription bottle of oxycodone and the perfectly rolled joint he had bought from the recreational marijuana store earlier that day. Michael hadn't smoked marijuana since his days at Columbia. Not because of any legal or moral reason; he just didn't care for the effect it had on him. He had never bought into the government's ridiculous reasons for classifying marijuana as a highly dangerous drug. It seemed hypocritical to consider alcohol a socially acceptable drug when it was responsible for so much devastation in people's lives, destroying families and leaving death in its wake. He'd never heard of anyone smoking marijuana and then beating his wife or child in a fit of rage. He walked back into the living room and sat down on the couch, placing the Glock on the coffee table. He refilled his glass from the bottle of vodka he had left there and looked out through the floor-to-ceiling windows to the waterfront and lit buildings of downtown Seattle.

Michael and Eva had timed it well with the purchase of their top-floor condo in 2010, when the bottom of the real estate market had dropped out, buying it at half the price the previous owner had paid four years earlier. Following Michael's divorce from Karen, they had first met sitting next to each on the beach in Glyfada, a suburb just outside of Athens. Originally from the Czech Republic, Eva Slovensky had been a swimsuit and lingerie model in Europe, spending time modeling in France and Italy. She had moved to Greece in 2004 as her career began the inevitable decline that all models face as they reach their late twenties and are replaced by younger women just beginning their modeling careers. Michael had become enamored with her beauty. They began seeing each other on a regular basis, spending the night at each other's apartments several times a week. Michael had told her he was an economics attaché at the US embassy, dealing with economic development issues between the United States and its European Union trading partners.

With Eva being a foreign national, Michael realized his relationship with her put him in a precarious situation as an intelligence officer, but he couldn't keep her out of his life. He was very careful about separating his work life and his personal life with her. He had told his boss, Harry Barso, the chief of station, about her and had introduced her to him when they'd run into him at a local Athens taverna. Barso had warned Michael to be extremely careful in his relationship with her. It was inevitable that CIA officers who spent most of their careers overseas would come into contact with foreign nationals and in some cases establish friendships. There was always the added risk, however, with members of the opposite sex, and in some cases, the same, being honey traps, a term used to describe efforts by intelligence services to compromise their target through the use of sex, with an additional option of blackmail. They had known each other for two years when, following Michael's unexpected and sudden transfer back to Washington and his subsequent departure from the CIA, he asked her to marry him and move to the United States. Michael had never leveled with Eva about his employment with the CIA, instead telling her that he had decided to call it quits with the State Department and the federal government in general. It was a secret that had brought about one of many fissures in their relationship, widening as time passed.

They had initially rented a small apartment in the Capitol Hill neighborhood of Seattle. Following their divorce, Karen had moved to Seattle with Sam, where she had been hired by one of the local television stations as a reporter, and Michael wanted to be close to Sam. Having left the CIA under less than optimal circumstances, Michael didn't have many job prospects and had decided to go into real estate. He had been away from Wall Street for too long to go back at the age of forty-three and try to compete with twenty-two-year-olds coming straight out of college into entry-level positions. Seattle was to be a fresh start for Michael and Eva.

Eva had tried to be Sam's friend, but all her efforts were in vain. In Sam's mind, Eva had stolen her father away from her mother, and Sam made it very clear she didn't care to have any type of relationship with Eva. While trying to restart her modeling career in the United States, Eva enrolled in Seattle Central Community College to brush up on her English and meet new friends.

At thirty-one, Eva still had a youthful face and sexy figure. The fine lines just beginning to make their appearance under her eyes were easily disguised with a bit of makeup. She figured she still had a good five to ten years left for a career in modeling. Perhaps not as a swimsuit model, but with any luck, she could get a job modeling women's clothing or makeup. Her high cheekbones and striking Slavic looks could certainly catch some modeling agency's attention. It wasn't long before she had landed her first job at Nordstrom's, modeling women's fashions with the style and sophistication she had developed during the years modeling in Europe.

Michael gulped the last bit of vodka in his glass and filled it once more. He opened the bottle of oxycodone and took out six pills, popping them into his mouth and chasing them down with another swig of vodka. He had already taken one pill prior to his run for his back pain. The combination of alcohol and oxycodone had put him in a comfortably numb state in which he felt no pain. He sat there thinking about how he had gotten into his current situation. It seemed that despite the fair amount of success he'd had in real estate, he couldn't find any meaning or sense of contentment in his life. What had happened in Athens twelve years ago hung on him like the weight of an anchor. The passing of time didn't lessen his anguish. Despite trying to forget the past and get on with his life, he was still haunted by those nagging memories. They had dragged him into a downward spiral of depression, causing him to slowly withdraw from everyone around him, including Eva. Although he had plenty of personal and professional acquaintances, he kept them at a distance, never allowing anyone to get too close to him.

As his relationship with Eva continued to decline, he withdrew even further, barricading himself emotionally from her. Even his parents noticed the difference in him, but he had shut them out also, rarely speaking to them. He was aware of the change in himself, but couldn't understand why it was happening or how to stop it. It was especially striking to all who knew him, since he had been such a social person. He had loved the company of friends and meeting new people from all walks of life. He could still turn on the charm and engage people, as was evident with his success in real estate, but he had just been making use of one of the many skills he had developed that had made him so effective in recruiting spies.

Now, he just felt emptiness, a void that he was unable to fill despite how hard he tried. He had reached the point where he couldn't stand it any longer. It wasn't that he was psychologically or emotionally weak. He had faced many challenging situations in life. He had gone through the Level C SERE training, the toughest of all Survival, Evasion, Resistance and Escape courses, when he was in Special Forces. The course was designed to train one how to resist torture after being captured by the enemy. Even though participants are aware that everything is simulated and the course will eventually end, after a few days of being subjected to extremes of both physical and mental stress, combined with continuous sleep deprivation, almost all break and disclose their information to their captors. Michael was one of the few that had made it through without being broken. While he had found the strength back then to withstand the stress of physical and psychological torture, he didn't know how to fight the emotional emptiness that had brought him to this point.

Michael lit the joint and took a slow, deep drag. He instantly coughed violently as the smoke tore out of his lungs. Grabbing his glass, he gulped a swig of vodka to coat his raw, burning throat. *Shit*, he thought, *that wasn't too smart*. His next inhale was a bit more conservative, but he still struggled to hold back his lungs' natural reaction to cough. He felt the sensation of the marijuana start to seep through his head. The combination of vodka and oxycodone caused him to feel lightheaded as the relaxing numbness began drifting over him.

He sat back on the couch and stared out the window. He wondered what, if anything, he would find when he departed this life. He wasn't particularly religious. Although he had grown up going to church every Sunday and even served as an altar boy, he hadn't stepped inside a church in over thirty years. It wasn't that he didn't believe in the existence of God or some type of supreme being, but he was an analytical and objective person who only believed in things he could understand. He had never found anything in religion that offered rational answers to the many questions he had about what he observed in the world around him. He had studied history and had experienced enough during his travels throughout the world to realize that religion, whether it was Christianity, Judaism, Islam, or any other, rather than offering answers, instead was used to manipulate people into believing in the self-serving interests of its leaders. He saw the hypocrisy of so many who preached about how God wanted everyone to live in peace and show love and compassion to their fellow man, yet turned a blind eye to all the injustice that was happening right in front of them. If there was a God, it certainly didn't appear he cared about what happened in this world, despite what religion claimed.

Michael turned his gaze to the coffee table and tried to focus on the Glock lying on top of it. He was beginning to feel disoriented, as though he was standing outside his body. He reached for the Glock and picked it up. The feel of its weight in his hand reoriented him back to his surroundings. He stared at the gun, transfixed by its appearance in his hand, almost as if it was an illusion. His mind started to wander. It was a strange sensation, as if he was recalling everything that happened during his lifetime all at once. He was a child sitting on the floor next to the Christmas tree with his parents and grandparents on Christmas morning. He was sitting next to Karen with Sam in his arms in their living room on another Christmas morning twenty-five years later. He was making love to Eva on their living room floor in front of the Christmas tree, with the two men he had shot and killed in Athens sitting on the couch staring at them as blood oozed out of the bullet holes in their bodies.

Michael squeezed his eyes shut and shook his head back and forth. When he opened them again, he was alone back in his condo. He saw the Glock was still in his right hand. Raising it, he placed the end of the barrel against his temple and felt the cold steel against his perspiring skin. Leaning his head against the barrel, he remained motionless, with his eyes closed. He had no awareness of how long he remained in that position. It was as if time had stood still. He slowly opened his eyes and saw the two dead men standing in front of him, their white shirts stained with blood. Michael stared at them, transfixed by the look on their faces.

"Why are you here?" Michael asked.

They didn't respond, just stood in front of him, just staring at him in silence.

"Why are you here?" Michael repeated, louder this time. "What do you want from me?" he shouted.

They continued standing there silently, staring at him.

"Leave me! Please, just leave me alone!" Michael pleaded with them.

"Why did you have to kill us? I had a daughter who loved me," Michael heard one of them say.

"I'm sorry, I'm so sorry," Michael sobbed. He placed the pad of his index finger against the trigger, pausing momentarily as he glanced at them once last time. His finger slowly began pulling the trigger. He felt the resistance of the trigger spring build as it approached its breaking point. The last thing he heard was the sound of his cell phone ringing, followed by the distinct ping of the Glock's firing pin as it traveled to its mark, striking the primer of the round in the chamber. He didn't hear anything else, he didn't see anything else, he didn't feel anything else. There was only darkness.

Chapter 2

It was early Friday evening as the meeting between Iranian and the United States delegations concluded for the day. President Martin Steele had promised to take a tough stance against Iran and scrap the nuclear deal negotiated under his predecessor, President Andrew Walker. With the support of Russian President Dimitri Markov, President Steele was pressuring Iran to return back to the negotiating table following Israel's allegations that Iran had violated the original agreement by developing an intercontinental ballistic missile capability whose only purpose was to deliver nuclear weapons whenever the country chose to restart their uranium enrichment. Shortly after he'd taken office, President Steele's first official invitation to a head of state was extended to President Markov, much to the surprise of the United States' NATO allies. Following the three-day official state visit, with President Markov standing next to him in the Oval Office, President Steele announced Russia's agreement to pull all military assistance out of eastern Ukraine; in exchange, the United States wouldn't pursue Ukraine's admittance into NATO. Despite the criticism he faced, even from members of his own party in Congress, President Steele was able to spin it as a foreign policy success, stating that there were many common interests the US and Russia shared in which they could work together to bring stability to an increasingly unstable world. The governments of the UK and the European Union voiced their alarm, saying that President Steele was recklessly endangering the stability of Europe and the rest of the world. In his customary belittling manner, President Steele responded by chastising their leaders in the media as shortsighted and weak in their leadership, blaming them for the dire political and economic situation in which the EU currently found itself. The international community was caught on its heels, trying to recalibrate where it stood in its relations with the United States.

The negotiations were being held at the renowned Four Seasons Hotel in Istanbul, Turkey. The hotel was a converted Ottoman palace situated on the Bosphorus, the strait that separated the European part of Turkey from the Asian side. It was the world's narrowest strait used for navigation, connecting the Black Sea with the Mediterranean Sea. Istanbul had been selected as the venue for the talks because of its symbolic location as the crossroads between East and West. Turkey was also a Muslim country as well as a member of NATO. The delegations, which included US Secretary of State William Payton and Iranian Foreign Minister Farid Mohammedi, were meeting in the Atik Pacha Grand Ballroom. It had been set up in a huge rectangular configuration of tables to accommodate both delegations. The US delegation sat opposite the Iranian. Secretary Payton, a retired four-star Army general and former SACEUR,

Supreme Allied Commander of NATO forces in Europe, had been President Steele's first cabinet post nominee following his surprise election victory over Vice President Sam Russell, whom Steele had ridiculed as being the weak "yes man" of President Walker. Also known as "Wild Bill Payton" in the military community, he had been relieved as SACEUR and forced to retire because of comments he made to a German magazine critical of President Walker's efforts in negotiating the Iranian nuclear deal. Payton, with his no-nonsense, tell-it-like-it-is style, was what President Steele wanted in his Secretary of State to reflect the administration's tough new foreign policy stance.

As the delegates rose from the table, Secretary Payton walked over to Foreign Minister Mohammedi with his interpreter, Ali Shiravi. "Mr. Foreign Minister, may I have a word with you?"

Ali began repeating the Secretary's request in Farsi, but Mohammedi raising his hand and said in perfect English, "I understand English very well, thank you."

Payton continued, "Foreign Minister, I think we've made our concerns very clear regarding your country's efforts to circumvent the restrictions it had agreed to concerning its nuclear weapons program. In addition, your country's continued efforts in trying to destabilize the Middle East are something that will no longer be tolerated. It would be a monumental mistake for your government to underestimate President Steele's resolve when it comes to the national security of the United States. As difficult as the sanctions from the last administration were on your economy, I can assure you they will be nothing compared to what your country will face if it continues down the same path. I understand the difficult position President Rostami finds himself in trying to keep the hardliners in check, but he needs to understand the new reality your country is facing when it comes to its relationship with the United States. It would be a real tragedy for the people of Iran if their leaders continued pursuing a policy of hostility and antagonism towards their neighbors and the United States, especially when economic conditions in Iran have been steadily improving. I hope I've made myself clear."

"Mr. Secretary, it is not the intention of Iran to threaten or destabilize any country. Iran wishes only to protect its national security and develop its economy for the benefit of its people. Iran has the sovereign right to defend itself and develop its military capabilities in furtherance of that goal. We acknowledge that the United States has interests in the stability of the Middle East. Iran also has such interests, which is the reason we have played an integral role in the fight against ISIS. Iran, however, cannot accept being treated as a child and being told with whom and in what manner it can exercise its sovereignty. We have abided by all the terms imposed upon us by the nuclear agreement in order to convince the world that our nuclear program is for peaceful purposes, but it is our right, just as any other nation's, to be able to control our means of energy production. Iranian sovereignty will not be threatened, nor will Iran be intimidated, by the United States or any other country."

"I am not questioning Iran's right to pursue nuclear energy, Foreign Minister, but what reason would there be, then, for your country's development of an ICBM capability if it has ceased its nuclear weapons program?" Payton asked accusingly.

"Mr. Secretary, Iran's adversaries have the military capability to inflict heavy damage on our country. It is only reasonable that Iran keep its options open to defend itself should it be threatened at some future time. That is exactly what Iran is doing, without violating the terms of the nuclear agreement forced upon us by the United States five years ago. Now it is the United States that is attempting to violate the terms of the agreement by threatening Iran. It is the actions of the United States that have destabilized the Middle East. How ironic it is for the United States to accuse Iran of meddling in the affairs of other nations, when your country has intervened repeatedly in the Middle East and elsewhere. It was your CIA that deposed the rightfully elected government of Iran in 1953 and reinstated the Shah, the puppet of the United States who tortured his own people for decades while doing the bidding of your government," Mohammedi replied testily.

"The United States may have been shortsighted in some of its past foreign policy decisions, but it was always part of the broader goal of defending the ideals of human rights and democracy against the aggressive efforts of the Soviet Union to instill its control over peace-loving peoples. It was the Soviet Union that, for close to half a century, kept half of Europe subjugated behind an iron curtain of fear and repression. The United States may not have always lived up to the ideals that it was founded upon, but that was as a result of human frailty and not reflective of what we aspire to as a nation," Payton fired back.

"Let us not attempt to justify each of our country's shortcomings and failures. Yes, in Iran we do face certain challenges from powerful elements within the regime that attempt to exert undue influence in our society. However, the Persian people have a long history that spans over two thousand five hundred years. Do not expect to see changes in Iranian society according to the timeframe of United States, when your country is still struggling to overcome the racial prejudice and inequalities that remain pervasive in your society going back to your civil war one hundred and fifty years ago. Let us focus on resolving our current issues, and as trust is slowly reestablished between our two countries, perhaps then we can debate these other matters. As far as Iran's missile program goes, President Rostami is willing to consider any reasonable suggestions your government may offer that would reassure the international community of Iran's peaceful intentions," Mohammedi offered.

"I'll confer with President Steele regarding our discussions. I look forward to our return to these talks tomorrow, when we can hopefully arrive at an acceptable solution for all parties involved. Have an enjoyable evening, Foreign Minister," Payton concluded.

"You also,

Mr. Secretary," Mohammedi reciprocated.

Bill Payton turned and headed for the exit of the ballroom. Ali and the Secretary's personal security officer (PSO) followed him. As they passed through the lobby, Ali's attention was drawn to a man sitting in a leather chair drinking coffee. As Ali walked by, their eyes met, and Ali instantly recognized the face. It was Jonathan Canton from the embassy in Athens twelve years ago. Ali wondered what he was doing here.

Ali continued to look at him while following Secretary Payton to the elevators. The PSO radioed his colleague on the third floor to release the elevator reserved for the Secretary and his staff, who were staying at the hotel. As a show of good faith, the US and Iranian delegations had agreed to stay at the Four Seasons for the duration of the talks. The Iranian delegation occupied the second floor, with the US delegation above them on the third. Overall security was the responsibility of the Turkish Army, while each delegation's security detail maintained control of their respective floors. The technical countermeasures team of the Secretary's security detail had swept the entire floor for bugs and set up secure communications for the Secretary to talk with Washington. With the hotel bordered by Çirağan Street, the major thoroughfare paralleling the Bosphorus, in the front and back, and the grounds of Bahcesehir University and Besiktas Anadolu Lisesi High School on each side, the Four Seasons was a highly secure venue.

***

As they rode up in the elevator, Secretary Payton asked Ali, "What did you think about Mohammedi's performance?"

"Are you asking me my opinion about his reaction or his sincerity, Secretary Payton?"

"Both."

"I think he had reasonable demands from their point of view. They already feel that they've had everything shoved down their throat. The Persian people have a long and great history, but they've also experienced conquest and suffered humiliation at the hands of many other nations, especially in the last hundred years. So, for them, it's a matter of maintaining their last bit of dignity and self-respect. I think if President Rostami can't deliver a face-saving agreement from this conference, it's the end for him, and the hardliners will be back in charge, Secretary Payton."

"Ali, stop repeating my name every time you say something to me. You're probably right about Rostami. The question is what can we offer them that will help give Rostami the upper hand when it comes to dealing with the hardliners," Payton muttered as the elevator doors opened to the third floor.

"We can offer them the same dignity and respect we expect from them, Secretary Payton."

"I didn't ask for your opinion on how I should negotiate with them," Payton snapped at Ali.

"Yes, Secretary Payton."

Payton scowled at Ali as he walked down the hallway to the door of the suite adjacent to his personal suite. The adjacent suite had been configured as a working office, set up with a meeting table in the living room and secure communications equipment in the bedroom. The primary communications center was monitored twenty-four hours a day by the Secretary's staff in another room down the hallway, but this allowed Payton to have a secure workspace next to his bedroom. The PSO opened the door for Payton and Ali, following them in.

"Will you be going out, Mr. Secretary?" asked the PSO.

"No, I'm just going to order room service and catch up with work. I'll let you know if anything changes," Payton answered.

"Yes, sir." The PSO turned and exited the suite.

"That will be all, Ali. I won't be needing you until tomorrow morning, but make sure you're available. I expect I'll be able to find you in the hotel if I need you before then. You can go now." Payton walked through the connecting doorway to his suite.

***

Ali turned to leave, opening the door to the hallway but stopping short and letting it swing shut. Wanting to quickly check his SIPRNET account for any emails from Foggy Bottom, as the State Department was referred to by its employees because of the neighborhood it was located in back in D.C., Ali walked into the communications bedroom. The SIPRNET, which stood for

Secret Internet Protocol Router Network, was a secure network of computers used by the Department of Defense and the State Department to transmit classified information. Ali sat down behind the laptop and logged in with his user name and password. He saw that he had received twelve emails. He opened the first and began reading through it.

***

Bill Payton threw his file folder on the mahogany desk and walked over to the mini-bar. He took out two small bottles of Jack Daniels and a Coca-Cola, along with the ice tray. He was twisting the small plastic tray, trying to land a few ice cubes into his glass, when all sixteen of the small ice cubes dropped out onto the counter and floor. "Damn it! Why can't the Secretary of State get a decent ice machine in a ten-thousand-dollar-a-night room?" he muttered as he swept the remaining ice cubes off the counter into his glass. He poured both Jack Daniels and a third of the can of Coca-Cola into his glass, swirling it with his finger. He heard a knock on his door and walked over to answer it. Opening the door, he found Jonathan Canton standing in front of him with a smug grin on his face.

"What are you smiling at?" he asked sarcastically before turning and walking back into the living room.

Canton followed Payton in and walked over to the mini-bar. He pulled out a small bottle of Johnnie Walker Blue Label and poured it into a glass, then opened the ice compartment. "No ice?"

Payton turned to Canton with a hint of annoyance. "Make yourself at home on the US taxpayer's dime. That little bottle there probably costs fifty bucks."

"Not being charged to my room," he replied sarcastically.

"You just better watch how you address the Secretary of State."

"A bit edgy, aren't you? Mohammedi rub you the wrong way?"

"Oh, he's one arrogant camel jockey, lecturing me on the foreign policy of the United States. He'll get what's coming to him," he hissed.

"Actually, Iranians are Aryans, not Arabs," Canton corrected him.

"Don't get smart with me. Remember how you got to where you are in the Agency. If it wasn't for me suggesting to the DCI that you would be a valuable asset to me as the deputy director of the Counterproliferation Division for these negotiations, you'd still be just another desk officer. I can just as easily suggest to him that you were completely useless and you'll be sent to some shithole in the third world, sending cables back to Langley about which twelve-year-old girl has been with their president this week," Payton warned him.

"That's right, you can, but just remember how deep in this you are. You have a lot more to lose than I do if any of this were somehow to get out. You think Steele would come to your rescue and give you cover? He would let you hang out to dry before he takes a hit for a Secretary of State who's gone rogue on him. You might even find yourself in a nice cozy ten-by-ten room in Leavenworth," Canton replied with an amused expression on his face.

"Is that a threat?"

"No, it's not. You just need to come to the realization that both of us are in this together. You take care of your end and I'll take care of the operational side. Without me, where would you be?"

"You know, if you weren't the only CIA officer without any principles or conscience, I wouldn't put up with your bullshit," Payton snapped back.

"Well, lucky for you, I'm your man," Canton replied smugly.

Ali, who had been going through his email, paused as he heard a discussion going on in Payton's room. He recognized the other voice from somewhere but couldn't place it. It wasn't Ali's intention to eavesdrop on the Secretary's conversation, but he couldn't avoid overhearing what was being said through the open doorway leading to his private quarters. There was something about the other man's voice that pulled Ali's attention away from his email to the conversation going on next door.

"Well, is everything on track?" asked Payton.

"Nothing to worry about. Everything is good."

"That doesn't tell me anything. What does 'everything is good' mean?"

"It means their team is in place and standing by to execute the operation," answered Canton.

"I hope for all our sakes the Russians don't screw this up. The Iranians have to believe it was the Israelis who killed their foreign minister. Everything has to point to them. They better not leave a shred of evidence that could raise suspicion otherwise," Payton warned him.

"Don't worry, I've been assured that they've gone over every detail. The Spetsnaz team that's executing the operation is their best, their Delta Force. They're even using Israeli ammo so the Iranians find the spent shell casings," Canton assured him, referring to Rostov, the SVR operative in charge of the operation in Istanbul. The SVR was Russia's foreign intelligence service that had replaced the KGB after the breakup of the Soviet Union.

"Doesn't that seem a bit too obvious? I mean, come on, if the Israelis were going to carry out a hit on the Iranian foreign minister, don't you think they would use ammo that wouldn't point directly back to them?" Payton replied sarcastically.

"It doesn't matter what the obvious would be. The effect this is going to have on the hardliners back in Tehran—it will get them so spun up, it won't matter what any Iranian security official might think about the casings. The fact that spent Israeli ammunition was found where their foreign minister was assassinated will set things into motion so fast that no security officer's suspicions are going to stop their leadership from pulling out of the nuclear agreement. And once the Israelis believe the Iranians are going to resume their nuclear program, they won't hesitate to launch an attack against Iranian nuclear facilities. The Iranians will of course retaliate with every medium-range missile they have, and with any luck the Israelis will retaliate with a nuke back to Iran. Before you know it, the whole Middle East will be in complete chaos, leaving Russia and the United States controlling most of the world's oil supply," Canton said, attempting to sound impressive.

"Oh, I'm glad you're so confident about how everything is going to play out," Payton shot back.

"You need to have a little bit of confidence that the professionals know what they're doing. That's why you're going to suggest to the President to appoint me as the new DCI when all this is over and done with, right?"

"Don't get ahead of yourself. Let's see how all this turns out before you start popping the cork off the champagne," Payton said, trying to curb Canton's sense of self-importance.

Ali was in a state of shock. He couldn't believe what he had just heard. The US Secretary of State was conspiring with the Russians to assassinate the Iranian foreign minister, and throw the entire Middle East into complete turmoil in order to control the world's oil supply? What was even more shocking to Ali was the identity of the other man. It suddenly hit him; it was Jonathan Canton. As Ali sat there trying to gather his thoughts, the secure fax machine next to him let out a loud tone that startled him. Turning his head toward the doorway leading through to the living room and the Secretary's adjoining suite, he heard the conversation abruptly cease. Ali tried not to panic. He couldn't be discovered. There would be no plausible way for him to deny overhearing their conversation. He stood up and thought desperately about what he could do. He wanted to run out of the suite but realized there would be no way of doing so without being discovered. He looked around the room frantically, focusing his attention on the closet with the louvered doors. He quickly tiptoed over and slowly slid the door open. He ducked into the closet and quietly slid the door shut.

Payton and Canton looked at each other in silence. Canton put his glass down and walked into the living room of the adjoining suite. He paused in the middle of the room and looked around, listening for any movement. His gaze turned towards the communications room. He walked to the bedroom door, stepped in and looked around. The bed had been removed to make space for the tables that had been set up for the array of communications equipment. He walked over to the notebook computer on the table and glanced at the screen. He saw an open email from the State Department to multiple recipients. Canton scanned the list of approximately thirty addressees. One caught his eye: shiravi_ali@state.secure.gov.

Ali's heart raced as he held his breath. He could see Canton through the slats in the closet door. He tried to stay calm, but he could feel himself beginning to shake. What would he say if Canton discovered him? Canton slowly turned around and walked towards the bedroom door, pausing momentarily at the threshold, then continuing through to the living room and returning to Secretary Payton's suite.

"What's up?" Payton asked.

"Nothing, just the comm gear in the other room," replied Canton.

"Do I have anything to worry about when this thing goes off? The Russians know I'm on the floor right above Mohammedi, right?"

"Just relax, you're in no danger. It'll be a surgical operation. They'll be in and out so quickly, you won't even be woken up until after the fact."

"And you actually think I'm going to be able to fall asleep tonight?"

"You're a general. You should be used to these types of operations."

"Not when I'm on the floor above the X and it's the Russians doing the operation. You remember how things went with their botched rescue attempt in 2003, when a hundred and thirty hostages were killed in the theater in Moscow. That doesn't inspire a great degree of confidence in their special operations capabilities. Where are you going to be when all this is going down?" Payton asked Canton.

"I'll be with Rostov, monitoring how things are going."

"Who's Rostov?"

"He's the SVR guy in charge of the operation. Don't worry, he knows what he's doing," Canton reassured him.

"He'd better, for all our sakes," Payton stated with concern, not liking the fact that their success or failure was in the hands of the Russians.

Ali slowly slid open the closet door and stepped out, carefully closing it behind him. He walked over to the computer and logged out of his email. Being as quiet as possible, he moved to the bedroom door and slowly looked out into the living room. He could hear Payton and Canton talking again. He knew he had to get out of the suite before his luck ran out and he was discovered. He quietly tiptoed across the living room to the hallway door, trying to keep his steps as silent as possible across the marble floor. He slowly turned the doorknob and pulled the door open ever so carefully, trying not to make a sound, stepping into the hallway and gently closing the door behind him. He nodded at the security officer standing at the end of the hallway and then turned and walked around the corner to his room down the hallway.

Canton picked up on the almost imperceptible sound of the door in the next room latching shut. His attention was diverted from what Payton was saying as he walked to the doorway of the adjoining suite and looked in.

"What?" asked Payton with a perplexed look on his face.

"Nothing, I must be hearing things," replied Canton.

"Who's getting paranoid now?"

"Yeah, I guess it's getting on all our nerves some. Well, I'm out of here. I'll get back up with you afterwards. Thanks for the scotch, by the way," he said jokingly.

"Oh, don't mention it. I'll send you the bill," Payton grumbled as Canton left the room.

Canton looked up and down the hallway. He turned and walked toward the security officer. "How's it going?" he asked.

"Everything is just fine, sir."

"That's good. Did you happen to see anyone come out of the suite next to the Secretary's?"

"Just his interpreter, Mr. Shiravi."

"When was that?" Canton asked.

"Just a few minutes ago."

"I see. I need to talk to him. What room is he in?"

"I believe he's in 322, just around the corner," replied the security officer.

"Thanks," Canton told him and walked towards the elevator. "Oh shit," he murmured to himself, suspecting Ali had heard their conversation. He took the elevator down to the hotel lobby and walked into the Yali lounge. He took a seat in one of the plush burnt-orange chairs in the corner and ordered a Johnnie Walker Blue Label on the rocks. The waiter brought him his drink. He took the bill and charged it to room 302, Secretary Payton's suite. He sipped his scotch as he thought about how to deal with Ali. He had to find out exactly what Ali knew before deciding what course of action to take. Looking around, he spotted a house phone.

***

Ali returned to his room and sat down on the edge of his bed. He looked at his hands and saw that they were shaking. He clasped them together and rested his forehead in them. What should he do? Who could he call? The FBI, the CIA, the President? Was the CIA even involved in this? Was the President? He knew he had to do something. His mind raced as he struggled to think. He was starting to hyperventilate. He tried to calm himself and slow his breathing. Who would believe his story that the Secretary of State was involved in a conspiracy with the Russians to assassinate the Iranian foreign minister? It sounded so ludicrous, he was beginning to question his own sanity and whether he'd actually heard what he thought he'd heard. As he sat there trying to make sense of it all, he almost flew off the edge of his bed when his room phone rang. He stared at the phone as it continued to ring, until he finally walked over and picked it up. "Hello," he answered.

"Hello, Ali."

Ali's heart pounded so hard he thought it was going to rip out of his chest. "Is this Jonathan Canton?" he asked, trying to sound as normal as possible.

"Yeah, it is, Ali. I thought I recognized you earlier in the lobby with Secretary Payton. How long's it been? Close to twelve years now?"

"Uh, yes, it must be," Ali managed to spit out.

"Well, I'd sure like to talk with you and catch up some. I'm down in the lounge having a drink. Why don't you come down and join me?"

"Well, I was just about to hop in the shower. Maybe some other time," Ali stammered.

"No, Ali, I think we really need to talk now. There are some important issues that can't wait. So, why don't you throw on some clothes and come down?" Canton replied, making it clear that he expected to see Ali shortly.

There was a short period of silence until finally Ali answered, "Okay, give me a few minutes and I'll be down."

"I'll be waiting for you," Canton finished and hung up the phone.

Ali put the phone down. A wave of nausea came over him. His whole body shook as he was overcome with fear. There was something about Canton that had always made Ali uncomfortable around him. It wasn't anything Canton had done in particular; just a sense Ali had of something dark and untrustworthy about him. Ali wondered what would happen if he just did not go downstairs to meet him. He could stay in his room. Canton wouldn't try to do anything to him with so many security personnel around. But then he thought about Secretary Payton finding out that he had overheard their conversation. What would he do then? Finally, he realized he had no other choice but to go down and face Canton, if for no other reason than to try to find out what Canton knew or suspected. He was fairly certain he would be safe as long as he stayed in the hotel with all the security personnel. He could order room service and not leave his room unless he was with the Secretary. He would wait it out in the safety of the hotel until it was time to fly back to the United States. Once back there, he could figure out who he needed to talk to about what he knew. But what about the assassination plan? It sounded like it was going to happen soon, possibly even tonight. Should he warn the Iranians? Would they even believe him? It sounded so crazy.

He walked into the bathroom and splashed cold water on his face. He toweled off and looked in the mirror. Despite his naturally dark complexion, his face looked pale, as if all the blood had drained out. He took several deep breaths and walked back into the bedroom. He looked out his balcony towards the Bosphorus Bridge just north of the hotel. It was illuminated with purple lighting along its entire length and was one of two suspension bridges spanning across the Bosphorus, connecting Europe and Asia. He had faced risk and danger in Athens years earlier, but nothing close to what he was facing now. He left his room and walked around the corner, past Secretary Payton's room toward the security officer and the elevators. He stopped and spoke to the security officer.

"I'm going down to the lounge for just a little bit. I should be back shortly in case anybody's looking for me."

"Okay, Mr. Shiravi. You don't have to check in with me," the security officer answered. "Did that guy ever get a hold of you?"

"What guy?" asked Ali.

"You know, the guy that was with the Secretary just a short while ago. Weren't you in there with them?"

"Oh, you mean Mr. Canton? Yeah, he did."

"All right, I thought it was kind of odd he was looking for you just after you left the room."

"Oh, he just needed to ask me something," Ali explained. "I should be back shortly," Ali said for a second time.

"Okay," answered the security officer, looking slightly puzzled.

"See you soon."

Ali took a deep breath and headed over to the elevators. The elevator reserved for the US delegation stood ready with its doors open. Ali stepped in and hit the button for the ground floor. As the doors closed, he told himself to stay calm when he met Canton. He would be safe in the hotel lobby within public view. He would try to learn what Canton suspected and deny anything Canton might accuse him of knowing. The elevator doors opened and Ali stepped out into the lobby and headed towards the lounge. He passed a Turkish soldier with an MP5 submachine gun slung around his neck, standing guard duty in the hotel lobby. Ali entered the lounge and looked around. He spotted Canton sitting at a corner table in a section of the lounge that had no other customers. Canton looked up and made eye contact, signaling him over with a nod of the head. Ali swallowed and walked over to him.

"Hello, Ali," Canton greeted him.

"Hello, Jonathan," Ali replied.

"Have a seat." Canton gestured to Ali.

Ali pulled out a chair across from Canton and sat down. He tried to look calm and act as normal as possible. His mouth was dry, and he felt as if his whole body was shaking. He looked Canton straight in the eye, trying to force a polite smile.

"What a coincidence running into you here after so many years. When did you get out of the Air Force and start working for the State Department?"

"In 2012."

"I lost track of what happened to you after we shut down the operation and you were transferred. Real shame how everything turned out. I know it must have been tough on the family to uproot them like that all of a sudden. Where'd they transfer you to? Fort Mead, wasn't it?" asked Canton.

"Yes, it was," Ali answered, knowing full well Canton knew where he had been transferred after Athens.

The waiter walked over to their table. "Anything for you, sir?"

"No, thank you," Ali replied, shaking his head. The waiter turned and headed back to the bar.

"So how do you like working for State?" Canton asked.

"I like it," said Ali, keeping his answer short.

"Good. What's it like working for Secretary Payton?"

"He's an okay boss."

"Yeah, I bet he is. You must hear some pretty interesting conversations when you're around him. Things not many others know about," Canton probed.

"Well, that's part of my job," replied Ali.

"Did you ever hear him say anything that surprised you?" Canton asked.

"I'm not sure what you mean."

"You know, something that you never expected to hear from him."

Ali's heart raced. He was doing everything in his power to keep his breathing under control. It felt as if his facial muscles had become numb and he couldn't control the expression on his face.

"No, nothing I can think of," Ali stammered.

"So, you never overheard him say anything that you thought was unusual?"

"No, not really."

"Weren't you just with Secretary Payton a short while ago?" Canton asked.

"Well, yes, in the negotiations, just before I saw you in the lobby."

"Didn't you accompany the Secretary to his room?"

"No, I went to my room," Ali blurted, then instantly regretted his false answer.

"Oh, I see. The security officer must have been confused, then. I went up there earlier and asked if the Secretary was with anyone, and he said you were with him." Canton looked accusingly at Ali.

Ali momentarily averted Canton's gaze as he replied, "He must have been thinking of earlier today."

"Yeah, must have," Canton echoed. "Well, got any plans for this weekend? Going to see any of the sights?"

"I'm not sure. I've been to Istanbul before. I have a good book I'd like to finish," Ali managed to get out as he stood to leave.

"Where you going?"

"I need to get back to my room. I have some calls I need to make," was the only thing Ali could come up with.

"Who you going to call?" Canton asked suspiciously.

"Oh, um, my daughter. I have to see how she's doing. I haven't talked to her in a while." Ali regretted the words as soon as they came out of his mouth. Why had he even brought up his daughter to Canton? He had panicked.

"Oh, that's right. You have a daughter. How's your wife?"

"She died," Ali answered, feeling very uncomfortable talking about his family with Canton.

"Ah, too bad. So how old is your daughter now?" Canton asked with a menacing smile.

"She's in her twenties. Well, I have to go. Nice seeing you again. Goodbye." Ali turned away from Canton, forcing himself to walk as normally as possible, which at the moment was a challenge in itself.

"I'm sure we'll be seeing each other again," Ali heard as he made his way towards the lobby. He walked past the Turkish soldier with the MP5, straight to the elevators, pushing the up button for the reserved elevator. As he stood waiting for the elevator, he glanced up into the camera above the elevator doors. He silently chastised himself for lying about not being with the Secretary earlier. He knew why Canton had asked him that question, and his lie had just confirmed Canton's suspicions that he had overheard the conversation. He had panicked and committed a costly mistake. The elevator arrived and Ali stepped in. He pushed the third-floor button and waited for the doors to close while he considered his situation. When the elevator reached the third floor, he exited and hurried past the security officer, rounding the corner to his room. He entered his room and quickly shut the door, turning the dead bolt and flipping the security latch. He sat down on his bed and tried to focus on what he needed to do. For now, he would just stick with his original plan and stay confined to his room unless he had to be with Secretary Payton. Once he made it safely back to the United States, he would have more options available to him.

***

After five minutes, Canton stood and headed out of the lounge. He walked to the elevators and headed back up to the third floor. He stepped out and headed towards Secretary Payton's room. He knocked on the door and pushed his way in before Payton had fully opened it. Payton looked at him with a bewildered expression. Canton walked past him to the door connecting the adjoining suite and closed it.

"What the hell do you think you're doing, barging in like that?" he asked.

"He heard," Canton let out.

"Who heard? Heard what?"

"Ali, your interpreter, that's who. He was in the other room when we were talking earlier. He heard everything. He knows we're involved."

Payton's eyes widened in shock. He stood staring back at Canton in silence as he tried to embrace all the implications. Besides jeopardizing the success of the operation, Ali's knowledge implicated him in what was, for all practical purposes, treason. He realized everything he was, everything he had, his entire future, was threatened by Ali. "That little prying snoop. You're going to have to kill him," he finally told Canton.

"It's obvious someone's going to have to kill him, but it's certainly not going to be me. Not that I have any problem with doing it myself, but that's not possible here or now. I think it might be a little obvious walking past your security to his door and politely asking if he would let me in," Canton replied sarcastically.

"Well, any suggestions? You're the supposed expert on these types of things. This could become a disaster really quick."

He put his hands over his face as he stood there silently for several moments, thinking. "I have an idea, but we're going to need the Russians' help," Canton finally let out.

"Oh great, bring the Russians into the middle of this monumental screw-up. That will inspire a lot of confidence in us. Do whatever you have to do, just make sure it's done right."

"Okay, there's someone I have to get a hold of right away. I'll be back as soon as everything is arranged," he said as he turned towards the door.

"You better make sure this is taken care of. That's all I'm going to say," Payton addressed Canton's back as he walked out of the room.

As he made his way through the lobby to the front doors of the hotel, Canton pulled out the prepaid mobile phone he used for communicating with Rostov and dialed the number for Rostov's own prepaid mobile phone. After three rings, he heard a "*Da*" on the other end.

"We need to meet. Something has come up," Canton said.

"Now is not a good time," Rostov answered.

"This is something that can't wait. It may jeopardize everything."

There was a pause on the other end, then Rostov said, "You know where to meet. Be there in forty-five minutes."

Canton walked to his rental car, an Alfa Romeo Giulietta parked in the front lot of the hotel. The chill of the night air sent a shiver down his spine. Spring was just around the corner, but it had been unusually cool for this time of the year. He started the engine and pulled out of the hotel parking lot, turning right onto Çirağan Street and driving towards the Bosphorus Bridge. He crossed the bridge and turned right onto Paşa Limanı Avenue, which paralleled the Bosphorus Straight on the Asian side of Turkey. He headed south for several miles until he reached an industrial port area. He drove down the dimly lit streets amongst warehouses and rail yards, making a series of turns to ensure he wasn't being followed. Finally, he pulled into a lot on the side of a large warehouse. It was close to 8:00 p.m., and other than the occasional truck leaving the port area, most activity had ceased for the day. Canton turned off his car and waited. From his position he could see down the street and observe the prearranged meeting location with Rostov, while still remaining hidden in the shadows of the warehouse. After fifteen minutes, Canton saw a dark blue Opel pull into the lot a block down the street and back in between two warehouses. Canton waited another five minutes, looking for any signs of surveillance, before starting his car and driving down the street towards the Opel. Shutting off his lights, he turned into the parking lot and drove in between the two warehouses. He pulled up next to the driver's side of the Opel and rolled down his window to face Rostov, sitting across from him.

"What is so urgent that we had to meet five hours before the operation is going to begin?" Rostov asked with annoyance in his Russian accent.

"We've had a little security breach."

"What do you mean, security breach?"

"The Secretary's interpreter overheard him talking about the plan to kill Mohammedi."

"Overheard him talking with who?" asked Rostov with alarm.

"It was with me, actually. He didn't realize he was in the other room connected to his suite."

"With you? And is this what you consider using good tradecraft in the middle of a highly sensitive operation? It is a wonder how we lost the Cold War with that kind of incompetence in the CIA," Rostov replied with a disgusted tone.

"Hey, Rostov, I don't want to hear it. I'm sure if you were summoned by your foreign minister, you wouldn't ask him if it was safe to talk in his presence. Now's not the time for this, just because you still have issues you haven't worked through yet since we won the Cold War. I don't think President Markov or your boss Petrovich is going to look too favorably on you if this operation unravels because you couldn't handle the situation. If I have to call Petrovich and speak to him personally, I'll do it right now," Canton shot back at Rostov in a condescending tone, letting him know who was ultimately calling the shots between the two of them.

Rostov stared back at Canton with his cold steel-gray eyes in silence. There was no doubt from the expression on Rostov's face that under different circumstances, he wouldn't have allowed Canton to dictate the terms of their relationship. Realizing he had no choice for the time being, he asked, "Where is he?"

"He's in his hotel room at the Four Seasons. I don't think he's going to leave it unless it's with the Secretary. There's no possible way for me to get to him. I don't think he's figured out what to do yet. Who is he going to tell that the Secretary of State and the Russian President are involved in an assassination plot against the Iranian foreign minister? Your team is going to have to take him out when they do Mohammedi," Canton instructed him.

"That is insane. It is less than five hours before the mission starts. How do you expect them to do that when they have no intelligence or plan put together? The operation to kill Mohammedi is planned precisely down to the minute. Any attempt to alter it now could jeopardize the whole operation."

"Don't worry, I've thought of that. Your team is coming in from the water, I'm assuming?" asked Canton.

"Of course, where else would they come from? The lobby?" Rostov remarked sarcastically.

"I'll have the Secretary tell his interpreter to meet him outside under one of the gazebos by the seawall. He'll come out just in time for your team to take care of him before they go after Mohammedi. I'm assuming there will be other casualties outside before your team makes it inside to Mohammedi."

"There are too many variables that are unaccounted for, too many things that can go wrong," Rostov replied.

"Well, we don't have many options right now. He's a slender bald guy, about five feet eight inches—that's, what? About a hundred and seventy centimeters. In his mid-fifties. He's originally from Iran, so have them look for an Iranian-looking guy. It'll look like he was at the wrong place at the wrong time. Just one more dead Iranian. It's perfect. Tell me what time you want him out there and I'll make sure he's there," Canton told him.

Rostov thought in silence for a moment before he answered Canton, "Make sure he is out there at exactly one o'clock."

"I'll do my part, you make sure your team does theirs," Canton replied dismissively, then rolled up his window and drove off.

He drove back to the Four Seasons and headed back up to Payton's suite. The security officer acknowledged him with a nod as he walked past towards the Secretary's door. He knocked on the door and waited. Payton opened the door wearing a hotel robe and slippers. Canton walked in and went into the adjoining suite, checking each room to make sure no one was there before returning to Payton's room, where the Secretary was standing with a look of anticipation.

"Well, did you come up with a solution to our problem?" Payton asked.

"It's taken care of. I just need you to call Ali at twelve forty-five"—Canton looked at his watch—"that's in a little over three hours, and tell him you need him to meet you outside at the gazebo by the seawall at exactly one a.m."

"Why would I tell him to meet me outside at that hour of the night?"

"I don't know. Make something up. Tell him you just spoke with the President and you need to discuss something with Mohammedi right away. The Russians will take care of him right before they get to Mohammedi."

"Will they be able to do that?" Payton asked.

"They will if he's out there. So make sure that you make it clear to him you expect him out there promptly. Understand?"

"I don't like this. It seems like too many things could go wrong," he told Canton with concern.

"There's no other option right now. Just do what I told you and everything will be fine."

"That's not reassuring." He paused. "What are you going to do until then?"

"Well, I was planning on waiting here to make sure everything goes as planned," Canton told him.

"You are, are you? Just keep away from my mini-bar," Payton warned him.

***

The eight Spetsnaz commandos exited from the moon pool of the Russian bulk freighter *Yevgeni Alekseyev*, which was anchored in the commercial port on the Asian side of Istanbul approximately four miles south of the Four Seasons across the Bosphorus. The moon pool was an opening in the base of the ship's hull that gave access to the water below. Also known as wet porches, moon pools were normally found on research vessels and allowed divers to lower equipment into the sea. The *Yevgeni Alekseyev* was a relic of the Cold War, and like other Soviet cargo vessels designed with similar moon pools, it had allowed Soviet special forces and intelligence officers to infiltrate ports throughout the world without being detected. The commandos submerged ten feet below the hull of the ship and activated their Protei-5 propulsion units as they started to make their way across the channel. The Protei-5, developed during the time of the Soviet Union, was a small one-man diver propulsion vehicle that operated with an electric motor that used six lead-acid batteries. It attached under the diver with a clip over each shoulder and one up between the legs. Using these and their Soviet-era IDA71 military oxygen rebreather units, the commandos were virtually invisible as they made their way towards the Four Seasons.

***

It was 12:30 a.m. Canton opened the balcony door that looked out over the terrace and walked out into the chilly night air. He looked down onto the grounds of the hotel. The area between the hotel and seawall was a terraced courtyard of inlaid marble slabs, with an assortment of manicured shrubs and trees. There were benches scattered throughout and several gazebos over along the seawall. It was empty this time of the year. In another month, it would have tables set up for outdoor dining. Floodlights illuminated the exterior wall of the hotel; however, the subdued ambient lighting in the courtyard, along with the shrubs and trees, cast a multitude of shadows throughout the grounds. Canton could see a couple of Turkish soldiers standing guard duty by the seawall. Whatever the Russians had planned for the operation, Canton hoped they were good enough to be able to quickly adapt and take care of Ali without it affecting their ability to kill Mohammedi. Canton knew the Russian Spetsnaz were formidable special operations forces, but he didn't know their level of proficiency in carrying out highly complex operations compared to the US military's elite units such as Delta Force and the SEALs. He looked at his watch and saw it was 12:40 as he walked back inside. He found Payton sitting in an easy chair, smoking a cigarette.

"I didn't know you smoked," Canton remarked as he closed the door.

"I gave it up years ago," Payton answered nervously.

"It's almost twelve forty-five, you ready to make the call?" Canton asked.

"I'm ready," he said as he stamped out the cigarette.

"Remember, tell him you need him to meet you at the gazebos down by the seawall at one o'clock, that's in fifteen minutes. Got it?"

"I got it. I didn't get to where I am because I don't understand what needs to be done and when," Payton snapped. He picked up the phone that was next to him and dialed Ali's room.

***

Since returning to his room, Ali had paced, sat, stood and lain on his bed, trying to come to terms with his surreal situation. He would momentarily sink into the comforting illusion that it was all just a dream, but his brain would steer him back to reality, leaving him with no choice but to deal with his situation. He knew he had to tell someone about everything he had heard as soon as possible, but who would believe such a preposterous story of the Secretary of State being involved in an attempt to assassinate the Iranian foreign minister? The irony of his predicament was that, if he told someone before it actually happened, it would be his word against that of the Secretary of State and a CIA agent. He was fairly certain he would lose that credibility contest and probably be deemed mentally unstable. He needed some proof, but short of the assassination actually taking place, he had none. Ali paced his room, trying to think of who would believe him about the Secretary of State, when it occurred to him he should focus on Canton instead. Just as he finally realized who he needed to contact, he was startled by the ring of his room phone. He stopped and looked at the phone, wondering who could be calling him at this hour. His brain finally shifted into gear, and he walked over and picked up the receiver.

"Hello?"

"Hello, Ali. This is Secretary Payton. I hope I didn't wake you?"

"Oh, no, Secretary, I wasn't sleeping."

"That's good. Listen, I've been on a call for the past hour with the President regarding our discussion from earlier today. I'm going to be meeting the Iranian foreign minister very shortly to iron out some details. I know it's late here, but it's something the President wants to hear back on before he calls it a day back in D.C. I'll need you with me to make sure everything is clearly understood on both sides. We're going to be meeting outside at the gazebo by the water. I need you there at one, that's in fifteen minutes. Don't be late, understand?" Payton instructed him.

"Uh, yes, Secretary Payton," Ali answered automatically.

"Good, see you there."

Ali slowly put the receiver back in its cradle. He thought about what Secretary Payton had just said to him. Under any other circumstances, he wouldn't have been alarmed at the Secretary's instructions to meet him at this hour of the night. Ali knew that foreign diplomacy kept strange hours, especially considering diplomats' capitals were often many time zones away. He felt fairly certain that he would be safe in the presence of the Secretary, especially with his security officer present, but he had a strange feeling about this. He looked at his watch. It was 12:47 a.m. He had thirteen minutes. His mind turned back to who he had to contact. Although he hadn't spoken to him in years, he still had his number written down in his little black phone book back in his home in Alexandria, Virginia. Ali sat down on the side of his bed and thought. He glanced at his watch again. It was already 12:50. He felt the pounding of his heart clear up through the carotids in his neck. A drop of sweat trickled down his forehead. He grabbed his cell phone and scrolled through his contacts until he came to his daughter Roxanne's number. He touched her name and waited as it dialed. The few seconds it took to connect seemed like an eternity to Ali. He desperately hoped she would answer. Finally, he heard ringing on the other end. Ali nervously tapped his foot as he waited through three rings, then a fourth. He began to sink into despair as he heard his last chance passing away, when suddenly he heard, "Daddy? Hi. You're back early."

"Hi, sweetheart. No, I'm not back. Just listen to me very carefully, okay? Grab something to write down what I'm about to tell you," Ali said hurriedly.

"Why, what's going on?" Roxanne asked, confused.

"I don't have time to explain right now. This is a matter of life and death, sweetheart. Just do what I say, please," Ali instructed her.

"Okay, just give me a second," she said, putting her phone down to look for a pen and paper.

Ali looked at his watch. It was 12:52.

"Daddy—okay, what do you need me to do?" she asked nervously.

"Write this name down: Michael Blackstone. He's an old friend. Do you remember him from Athens? You met him once when he came to our home."

"I can't remember, Daddy. That was like over ten years ago."

"Okay, that's not important. I need you to get to my condo as soon as possible and find his number in my little black telephone book I keep in my desk. Call him and tell him the following. Listen very carefully and write it down. Secretary Payton, Jonathan Canton and the Russians are going to try to kill the Iranian foreign minister. Did you get that?"

"Oh my God! What's going on?" Roxanne asked with panic in her voice.

"Just call him and tell him exactly what I told you. Keep trying until you get a hold of him. Tell him who you are and where I am. Do you understand what I need you to do, sweetheart?" Ali asked her frantically.

"Yeah, okay, Daddy, I will. Are you okay?"

"I'm fine. I'll explain everything later. Please, just get to my place as soon as possible. How long will it take you to get there?"

"If I leave now, I can catch a train from Boston South Station and be there in seven or eight hours," Roxanne told him.

"Okay, that's good, sweetheart. I have to go now. I love you," he said to her as if it might be the last time he would ever have a chance to do so.

"I love you too, Daddy," Ali heard, then hung up.

He looked at his watch. It was 12:54 a.m. He closed his eyes as he realized the inevitable had finally arrived. He had to go downstairs to meet the Secretary. He took a deep breath and stood up. He left his room to go downstairs. He turned the corner and walked toward the security officer sitting in a chair by the elevators.

"Excuse me, did you see the Secretary come by here yet?" Ali asked him.

"Nope."

"Do you know if he's going downstairs soon?"

"I don't know, sir. I just man this post. You can ask his security officer, but it's pretty late," he told Ali without much enthusiasm for assisting him any further.

"Okay, thanks," Ali replied, knowing he wouldn't get any more information.

Ali pushed the down button and waited for the elevator doors to open. He stepped in and hit the L button to take him to the lobby. The doors closed as the elevator began its journey down.

***

The man dressed in the dingy hooded poncho stopped his donkey-drawn wagon across the boulevard approximately fifty yards down the street from the Four Seasons. The back of the wagon was full of cabbages. Earlier that day, he had approached its owner, a farmer who had brought his produce to the market, and asked if he would sell the entire wagon-full of cabbage along with donkey and wagon. The farmer had initially thought he hadn't heard the stranger correctly. The stranger spoke passable Turkish but with a heavy foreign accent. Although the stranger again explained what he wanted to buy, the farmer thought it was some kind of joke and told him he could have everything for ten thousand lira, approximately four thousand dollars, easily twice the actual worth of his animal, the wagon and the produce. The stranger agreed without even bothering to haggle over the price, pulling out a stack of two-hundred-lira banknotes. Counting out fifty of them, he handed them to the farmer. The farmer looked back and forth from the banknotes to the stranger in disbelief. He finally smiled and handed the stranger his donkey and walked off on his merry way, thinking of the good news he would tell his wife later that evening after he had made his way home.

The hooded stranger stepped down off the wagon and grabbed the donkey's bridle, attaching a rope to it. He tied the other end around a tree on the sidewalk and casually walked off away from the cart, disappearing into the night.

***

The Spetsnaz commandos easily evaded the Turkish Navy patrol boat that was patrolling up and down the waterway about three hundred yards off the hotel. As they approached the seawall along the hotel's waterfront, the Spetsnaz switched off their Protei-5s and secured them with small anchors connected to thin cables, keeping them from drifting away while submerged awaiting their return. They swam the last few yards to the concrete platform that allowed guests to arrive by boat to the hotel. The platform was eight feet below the level of hotel grounds and had two sets of concrete stairs going up opposite directions. They quietly climbed onto the platform, removing their rebreathers, fins and masks, staging them for their escape following the execution of the mission. They removed their night vision goggles and their Israeli CTAR-21 assault rifles from their watertight packs. Because of the special nature of their operation, rather than using the standard Spetsnaz AK-9 assault rifle, they were using the compact commando version of the Tavor, the Israeli military's standard-issue assault rifle. Other than the metal clink of the slide, the sound suppressor mounted at the ends of their barrels made them virtually silent when fired. The Spetsnaz team had trained with them in preparation for this operation. The commander looked at his watch. It was 12:55. He activated the microphone of his tactical comm unit and conducted a radio check with his team. Each team member acknowledged. He then gave them a hand signal, and they split into two groups of four and made their way up both sets of stairs. The two lead Spetsnaz slowly peeked their heads over the top of the concrete bulkhead and scanned in each direction searching for Turkish military sentries. Fortunately, they had been supplied with the layout of the hotel and Turkish security arrangements, which Rostov had obtained through Canton. They spotted the outline of a sentry on the roof of the hotel, as well as two sentries standing approximately forty yards away along the seawall, talking to each other. The commander gave a hand signal to his man at the top of the other stairs, indicating he had the sentry on the left, which was returned with a hand signal acknowledging the other commando had the sentry on the right. They switched on their infrared laser sights, which put a red dot on each sentry's torso that could only be seen with their night vision goggles, and waited.

***

The two stolen motorcycles headed north up Çirağan Street, one trailing fifty yards behind the other. As the first approached the Four Seasons, the rider, who was wearing a full-face helmet, a black leather jacket and leather riding pants, abruptly shifted his weight, laying the motorcycle down and sending it sliding across the road towards the donkey and wagon. The rider let go of his motorcycle and slid on his leathers across the asphalt as he watched the motorcycle hit the donkey's front legs, bringing it crashing down onto the street. The rider stood up as the second motorcycle pulled up next to him, pausing long enough for him to hop on the back before it accelerated down the street away from the raucous scene. The donkey lay on the street with its two deformed broken legs amidst heads of cabbage strewn all over the street. Its loud, painful cries could be heard permeating the night.

***

The rooftop sentry moved from the back of the hotel to the front, investigating the commotion. He had heard the screeching of the motorcycle sliding across the street and then the loud wailing of the donkey. The Spetsnaz commandos also heard the donkey's cries and initiated their operation. With one shot each, they took out the two sentries as they were distracted by the sound of the donkey's scream. The commandos advanced up the stairs and took cover behind the two-foot-tall concrete planter boxes along the edge of the seawall. The commander then called for an enemy threat count. One of the Spetsnaz reported two soldiers by the pool at their ten o'clock. Another reported two by the corner of the hotel at their one o'clock. All four had turned their backs to the water and faced the horrendous noise coming from the front of the hotel. The commander designated each of his team target assignments and waited until all replied they had acquired their target and were standing by. The commander gave his order: "On my count. Three, two, one—execute."

There was a brief flurry of eight metallic clinks from their silenced rifles as each of the team members fired a round at their assigned sentry. All four of the Turkish soldiers fell nearly simultaneously. The commander instructed his team to remain ready to execute the main objective of their operation as soon as he had taken care of the newly added target Rostov had dropped on them two hours prior. He looked at his watch and saw that it was 12:58.

***

The elevator doors opened, and Ali walked out into the lobby. He saw a few hotel lobby staff along with the Turkish Army sentry standing by the front doors, looking out across the hotel's grounds towards the direction of the street and the horrendous wailing of what sounded like a donkey. Ali walked to the front entry to see what was going on, but could see nothing beyond the confines of the hotel parking lot. He turned and started towards the Aqua Restaurant, which he knew led outside to the hotel grounds by the waterside. The restaurant was empty at this time of night. Ali walked through the subdued lighting of the restaurant towards the glass doors that led to the exterior. He paused and looked out through the doors to see if Secretary Payton was outside. The bright floodlights shining on the massive white stone walls of the hotel lit up the back of the hotel. Ali strained to see out towards the gazebo by the waterfront. The bright lighting shining on the hotel made that area of the grounds appear dark from Ali's vantage point. Ali pushed on the lever and opened the door, slowly stepping outside. He took a few steps as he scanned back and forth, looking for any signs of someone by the waterfront amidst the faint cries of the donkey off in the distance.

***

The Spetsnaz commander saw Ali come out of the hotel and stop after a few steps. He attempted to manually adjust the sensitivity of his night vision goggles to reduce the bright halo that was being caused by the lights reflecting off the back of the hotel's massive white walls. The commander activated his IR laser and aimed at Ali as he steadied his assault rifle on top of the planter box. He could clearly see Ali's outline, but his night vision goggles wouldn't pick up the little red dot that would normally have been easily seen in even partial darkness. He lifted his goggles off his eyes and switched to the optical sights of his rifle, trying to locate Ali. Although there was plenty of lighting against the backdrop of the hotel, Ali stood in a slightly recessed area in the shadows along the glass wall of the restaurant. Without his night vision goggles, the commander could only make out the subtle outline of Ali. He took aim and slowly squeezed the trigger, hearing the clink of the slide as he fired at Ali.

Ali heard a sharp pop behind him an instant before he felt the sharp sting of small glass fragments hitting the back of his neck. He ducked his head as he realized he had been shot at. He heard another pop behind him, and then another. Ali turned to run back into the restaurant but found the door had locked from the inside. He could hear additional pops against the stone walls as he turned and ran along the back of the hotel towards the pool deck. He made his way to the pool on the far side of the hotel, half jumping, half falling over the three-foot hedge that separated the pool deck from the rest of the hotel grounds. He searched for a place to hide. He looked to the far end of the pool and saw the eight-foot wrought-iron fence separating the grounds of the hotel from the grounds of Bahcesehir University next door. He ran towards the fence, looking for an escape route. Realizing he couldn't make it over the fence, Ali ran along the fence line towards the seawall along the edge of the hotel grounds. He would be dead in a few seconds if he didn't escape. With no other option, he lowered himself down over the seawall and let himself drop. He gasped as he entered the fifty-degree water. Despite the freezing water taking his breath away, the adrenaline that was by now pumping through him enabled him to swim the few yards to the university's dock. He pulled himself out of the water and found a dark area in the shadows along the boathouse located on the pier. He could see the Bosphorus Bridge lit up in the background as he looked back at the hotel through the wrought-iron fence. He could see some sign of movement amongst the ambient lighting on the grounds of the hotel but couldn't make out exactly what was happening. He stayed crouched in the shadows, shivering in the cold night air, as he tried to bring his breathing under control and keep from hyperventilating.

***

"*Govno!*" the Spetsnaz commander uttered under his breath. He looked at his watch. It was 1:02. They had eight minutes to complete the mission before the risk of discovery increased exponentially with each passing moment. He didn't have time to worry about the American now; otherwise, he would jeopardize their mission. He ordered his men to commence with the primary objective. Leaving two men at the seawall to provide cover, the commander and his five remaining men quickly ran across the hotel grounds to the left side of the hotel where the service ramp was located. There was another Turkish soldier posted at the top of the service ramp; his eyes widened in surprise as he saw six men dressed in black wet suits running towards him. Before he had a chance to react, the Spetsnaz commander stopped, brought his rifle up to his shoulder and double-tapped the soldier, putting one round in his torso and one in his head. One of the Spetsnaz took a post at the top of the delivery ramp as the remaining five moved down the ramp to the delivery area in the basement.

The commander peeked around the concrete wall and spotted the State

Department diplomatic security agent dressed in a suit and tie standing by the service elevator. He lowered his assault rifle to his side, letting it hang in its sling, and reached behind him, pulling the CO_2 tranquilizer rifle slung on his back to the ready-aim position. After acquiring the sight picture of the diplomatic security agent's neck, he slowly squeezed the trigger. There was a barely audible pop of compressed air as the dart exited the barrel of the rifle, finding its mark a second later. The security agent winced and reached for his neck when he felt what he thought was a bee sting, but before his hand made it to the source of his pain, his legs gave out from under him and he slumped to the concrete floor. The use of the dart gun to tranquilize any American security personnel rather than kill them was all part of the plan, which had been created far above the Spetsnaz commander's level. His responsibility was only to execute the plan he had been given. He knew not to be concerned with what political considerations had factored into the operation. The team moved quickly across the parking garage to the elevator. Four of them got into the elevator, leaving one man behind to cover the basement area while they continued on to their objective.

When the doors opened on the second floor, two Spetsnaz exited to the left, with the other two going right. The two going right immediately ran into an Iranian security guard, who froze momentarily at the sight of two men clad in black pointing submachine guns at him. As he reached for his pistol at his side, the Spetsnaz closest to him fired two shots, instantly dropping him to the floor. As they continued past him, the second Spetsnaz fired one more round into his head, ensuring he was dead. The four Spetsnaz continued down opposite ends of the hallway, circling around until they ran into each other again. The commander glanced at the number written on the underside of his wrist, verifying the correct room of the Iranian foreign minister. They moved down the hallway, covering their respective fields of fire until they came to room 207, the Atik Pasha Suite. One of the commandos got down on a knee in front of the door as the other three covered both ends of the hallway. He removed a small electronic unit that was connected to a card key by a bundle of wires. The commando stuck the key into the door's card receptor and watched the screen flash through a series of numbers, then heard the sound of click in the lock. He removed the key and quietly opened the door.

The commander entered first, dropping his night vision goggles over his eyes, followed by one of his men, with the remaining two moving to opposite corners to cover the hallway. As the two quietly made their way through the foyer, a dim light could be seen from one of the rooms down the hallway. The two Spetsnaz lifted their night vision goggles up and continued down the hallway, passing the living room and dining room, until they arrived at the partly closed door from which the light was emanating. With his assault rifle raised to his shoulder and his one eye peering through his optics, the Spetsnaz commander slowly made his way around the door. As he came within full view of the master bedroom, he saw the Iranian foreign minister dressed in light blue pajamas, sitting in a chair reading a book he had placed in his lap. The foreign minister slowly looked up to see the end of the sound suppressor as the Spetsnaz commander fired two rounds into his head. The foreign minister's head slumped forward as small drops of blood dripped from the two bullet holes in his forehead, staining the light blue fabric of his pajamas. The commander looked to make sure the shell casings were visible on the floor next to the dresser against the wall so that they would be easily spotted upon a cursory examination of the room. Leaving the dead foreign minister in his chair, they turned and quickly made their way back out to the hallway, where their other two team members were waiting.

The four of them hurriedly made their way down the hallway to the stairs, which led all the way down to the basement. The commander looked at his watch. It was 1:08. He radioed the rest of his men that they were headed back down to the basement. They exited the stairwell into the parking garage, meeting up with the teammate they had left there, and headed to the service ramp. The team member posted at the top of the ramp gave them the all-clear signal as they made their way up the ramp to the side of the hotel. The anguished cries of the crippled donkey could still be heard from the front of the hotel. As the six Spetsnaz made their way across the grounds, they saw one of their teammates by the seawall aim his rifle towards the hotel roof and fire. The Spetsnaz commander turned back towards the hotel just in time to see the form of a Turkish soldier fall from the roof and land on the pool deck with a dull thud. Meeting up with their other two team members by the seawall, they made their way down the stairs to the platform by the water, where they removed their night vision goggles placed them, along with their weapons and other gear, into their watertight packs. They quickly donned on their rebreathers, fins and masks and silently slid into the water, disappearing into the darkness.

***

The foreign minister's head of security could hear the wailing of the donkey through his window. Despite the well-insulated windows, the dull sound of horrendous screams coming from the injured animal was enough to keep him from falling asleep. Intending to go downstairs to investigate the disturbance, he dressed, grabbing his sidearm and placing it in his waistband under his sports jacket. Opening his door, he stepped out of his room. He paused in the middle of the hallway. Something didn't seem right. There was a peculiar smell. He took another whiff and immediately recognized it as the acrid odor of burnt cordite unique to the discharge of a firearm. His demeanor instantly changed from annoyance to concern. Why was he smelling that odor in the hallway? As he rounded the corner leading to the elevators, his attention was instantly drawn to his man lying in the hallway in a pool of blood. His eyes opened wide as he pulled out his pistol and pointed it in front of him as he ran to his fallen man. He checked the man for a pulse; there was none.

With his gun drawn, he made his way down the hallway, slowly turning the corner and heading to the foreign minister's suite. He checked the door and saw that it was locked. He pulled out his master key for the entire second floor and inserted it into the slot, unlocking the door. He stepped quietly through the foyer and looked around the corner down the hallway. He could see a faint light coming from the bedroom. He moved slowly down the hallway until he came to the bedroom. With his pistol raised in front of him, he turned the corner and came face-to-face with the foreign minister. It looked as if he had fallen asleep while reading in his chair, until he spotted the bloodstains on his pajamas. He ran over to him and lifted his head, seeing the two bullet holes in his forehead. Touching the foreign minister's neck and feeling that his skin was still warm, he realized he must have been shot very recently. He looked around the room. His eyes were drawn to the two spent brass shell casings on the floor. Reaching down, he picked them up and examined them. He recognized the 5.56mm rounds as the standard NATO round, but what caught his attention was the TZZ stamped on the back of the shell casing. He knew TZZ was Israeli-manufactured ammunition used exclusively by the Israeli military. That made no sense to him at the moment, but he had another immediate issue to be concerned about. Fear at the thought of the assassin still being nearby swept over him.

He moved methodically through the rest of the suite, clearing each room. He stepped back out into the hallway and did the same. After making sure he was out of immediate danger, he ran down to the room of another of his subordinates and pounded on the door. After several seconds, a sleepy-eyed Iranian security officer opened the door. The chief of security hurriedly stepped in and closed the door. His subordinate instantly came to a state of alertness when he saw the look on his boss's face and the gun in his hand.

"The foreign minister's been shot. He's dead. Heydar is dead also. He's in the hallway. Get dressed and grab your weapon. We need to secure the floor. I didn't see any sign of the assassin still here. Go around to every room and find out if there are any other casualties. I'm going downstairs to alert Turkish security, then I'll call Tehran. Nobody goes into the foreign minister's room. Understand?" Assad instructed his man.

"But who did this? How? When?"

"Don't ask questions, Naveed. Do you understand what I expect from you?" barked his boss.

"Yes, yes, I understand."

"Good, I'll be back," he told him as he left the room.

He took the stairs down. As he came out into the lobby, he saw the Turkish soldier standing just outside the front door facing the street and talking into his radio. The Iranian security chief ran up to him and asked him in broken English what was going on.

The soldier answered, "Accident with animal. *Esek*. How do you say, ee ah, ee ah?"

"That is not accident. It is diversion!" he yelled at him. "The foreign minister has been shot. Call your general. I need to speak now to him."

The soldier looked confused. "Sorry, not understand," he replied.

"My foreign minister is dead! *Olü!*" he repeated in Turkish.

The soldier keyed the mike of his radio and hurriedly spoke into it. The voice on the other end responded back with alarm. A frantic conversation ensued back and forth until finally the Iranian security officer heard the repeated blast of a whistle outside. He saw the platoon of Turkish soldiers standing by the street looking out towards the accident scene scramble as they formed a perimeter around the hotel. Previously, they had been sitting and smoking cigarettes or sleeping in their vehicles that were parked at the far corner of the parking lot. The Iranian head of security came to the realization that they were too late. The assassin or assassins were long gone. His head dropped in despair as he began thinking about what he would tell Tehran.

***

Secretary Payton's PSO jumped awake when he heard the blast of the whistle. He put on his pants and a sweater and grabbed his gun as he hurried out of his room to check on the Secretary. He glanced around the corner, throwing the security officer posted by the elevator an inquisitive look, to which he responded with shrugged shoulders. He walked to the Secretary's door and knocked. Secretary Payton came to the door and asked, "What is it?"

"Are you all right, Mr. Secretary?"

"Yes, I'm fine. What's all the commotion?"

"I don't know. I'm going downstairs to find out," he replied.

"Okay. Let me know what's going on," he said from behind the door. He turned and walked back into the living room, glancing at Canton.

"Sounds like things went as planned," declared Canton.

"Let's wait and see what Simpson finds out downstairs before we get too excited. If two of the dead bodies are Mohammedi and Ali, then we can start celebrating," Payton said cautiously.

***

Ali was stooped in the shadows next to the boathouse, shivering in his wet clothes. He had seen the man fall from the roof and several figures run to the seawall and disappear into the darkness. His mind didn't want to believe what was happening, but his cold, wet clothes reminded him he wasn't dreaming. Now that he knew Secretary Payton was involved in trying to have him killed, he knew he couldn't go back to the hotel. As he sat there thinking about what to do, he heard the blast of the whistle coming from the direction of the hotel. A large spotlight on the Turkish patrol boat turned on and began sweeping back and forth along the hotel. Off in the distance, Ali could hear the faint sound of an approaching helicopter. Looking south down the Bosphorus channel, he spotted the searchlight in the air. He realized he had to get out of there quickly. Shortly the whole area would be swarming with Turkish military and police, and he couldn't risk being discovered until he had time to figure out his next move. He got up and cautiously ran off the pier onto the grounds of the university. The headed towards the street, cutting in between various buildings. This time of night, he didn't see a soul on the university grounds. As he made his way across the campus, he could hear sirens off in the distance. He reached the front of the campus and nonchalantly stepped out onto the sidewalk, briskly walking down Çirağan Street towards the old part of the city. He was tempted to run, but he forced himself to walk, knowing that running would draw too much attention. As he made some distance from the hotel, the blaring "weee ooo weee ooo" of sirens and flashing blue lights passed him as police raced to the hotel.

Ali walked for close to half an hour until he came to Atatürk Bridge. The span crossed over into the old section of Istanbul that contained the ancient walled city of Constantinople, from the time of the Byzantine Empire until it was conquered by the Ottoman Turks in the fifteenth century. He was starting to feel lightheaded. Although it was almost spring and the temperature normally climbed into the sixties during the day, the nights had been chilly, dropping down into the forties. He knew he would start going into hypothermia soon if he didn't find a way to get warm. He wandered for another fifteen minutes before he started becoming disoriented with exactly where he was. He checked his watch. It was 2:05 a.m. Even at this hour, the old city had some pedestrian traffic. There were the restaurants and coffeehouses that remained open for the all-night crowd, whether they were the younger secular Turks out socializing on the weekend or workers from any of the many businesses that stayed open throughout the night. Ali kept to side streets, not wanting to attract attention to himself. He turned down an alleyway and was overwhelmed with the fresh smell of baked bread coming from somewhere. He walked a bit further down the alley and came across wooden pallets stacked along the back of a building. He walked around the pallets and found a space three feet wide along the wall of the building with a metal exhaust grate blowing out warm, delicious-smelling exhaust. Ali had stumbled upon a bakery that was busy baking the day's delivery orders. Although it was a cruel joke having the delicious aroma torment him, he knew the warm air would end up saving his life, at least for the time being. He sat down with his back against the grate. The warm air blowing against his back helped bring his shivering under control. He pulled off his shoes and socks and placed them against the grate. He reached over and dragged a couple of pallets towards him, placing them against his side. He laid his arms down on the pallets, resting his head and closing his eyes. He just needed a few hours of sleep and some time to recover. He would figure out what to do in the morning, he thought as he drifted off to sleep.

Chapter 3

It was 7:00 a.m. Saturday morning in Moscow. Victor Petrovich was at the Senate Building, which was the Russian President's official residence within the Kremlin complex. President Dimitri Markov was sitting at the dining room table, being served breakfast by his house staff. Although President Markov had several residences throughout Russia, some known to the Russian public and others not, he stayed at the official residence when he needed to be in direct contact with his ministers running the routine day-to-day affairs of Russia. In this case, he was there in order to be kept apprised of the most important event of his presidency since coming to power in 2010. Petrovich was briefing him on the results of the mission in Istanbul, which had taken place just a few hours ago.

"President Markov, I am happy to report that the mission was a success. Mohammedi is dead, and our team escaped without detection. They are all back on the *Yevgeni Alekseyev,* and as soon as the ship is finished loading its cargo later today, they will be heading back to Novorossiysk," Petrovich briefed his boss.

"Excellent, Victor. What has your man Rostov told you about the situation in Istanbul? How are the Turkish authorities reacting?" asked Markov.

"They have done the usual—increased security at the airports and border crossings, a more visible police presence out in the street—but it is still early, and they are still trying to get an understanding of the situation. Ambassador Antonov will be contacting the Turkish foreign ministry in a few hours to see what information he can obtain. Our man-and-wife team staying at the Çırağan Palace Kempinski Hotel, down the street from the Four Seasons, has reported that police vehicles have cordoned off the street in front of the Four Seasons since the time of the incident."

"What about the Americans? Have we heard anything from them? Payton's CIA man, Canton, have you spoken to him at all?" Markov inquired.

"Rostov spoke with him a few hours ago. We had—I should say *they* had—a problem that has now also become our problem. It appears one of Secretary Payton's interpreters overheard him speaking with Canton about the operation. Canton contacted Rostov a few hours before the operation to inform him of this and request that our team also eliminate the interpreter during the operation. According to Rostov, Canton was supposed to have the interpreter at a certain location outside the hotel when our team arrived, but he was not where he was supposed to be. Our team attempted to neutralize him nonetheless but were unable to do so without jeopardizing the mission, so he escaped," Petrovich advised as he prepared for the onslaught that he was about to receive from his boss.

President Markov stared at Petrovich in silence. There was no expression on his face. This was even more distressing to Petrovich than if Markov had screamed at him. Markov had served in the KGB years ago and was quite familiar with clandestine operations. Now he used the SVR as his personal secret police, suppressing all dissent to a degree not seen since the days of the Soviet Union. Yes, he had always managed to put some twist on it, justifying the imprisonment of his critics as men involved in corruption, and in the cases of those being killed as provocations the West was behind, but everyone knew what would happen if one crossed President Markov. Petrovich felt a shiver down the back of his neck as he looked back at Markov, waiting for a reaction.

"Why is it we had to get involved in taking care of the Americans' mess?" Markov asked with his steely eyes staring back at Petrovich.

"Mr. President, Rostov explained the situation to me. The Americans caused this mess, but they also dragged us into it whether we liked it or not. The risk that the interpreter posed to the operation was so critical that he had to be eliminated immediately. Canton had no way of taking care of it without risking being compromised, so our team was the only option available. As with any last-minute change to an operation with so many unknowns, there is always the possibility things will not go as expected. That is what happened," Petrovich explained.

"Do not tell me about what can happen during an operation, especially when you have incompetents involved. That careless fool Payton reveals the most sensitive operation to a lowly government employee and then cannot clean up his own mess. Where is this interpreter now?"

"We do not know. Rostov is working his connections with the Turkish authorities to see what he can come up with. I will speak with Canton later today to see what he knows. I do not think this interpreter will get very far, if they have not already found him. Once the Turkish authorities find him, they will hold him until he can be turned over to the Americans. I would not be surprised if Payton and Canton do not perhaps attempt to make it appear this interpreter may have been involved in the assassination. According to what Canton told Rostov, he is of Iranian descent, so all the more reason to make it appear this man may have had some type of vendetta against the Iranians," Petrovich tried to reassure Markov without invoking any more of his wrath.

"Make sure you stay on top of this personally. I do not care what needs to be done, this man must never make it back to the Americans alive. Do what you have to do to make sure this does not happen. Do you understand what I expect from you?" Markov said it more as a statement than a question to Petrovich.

"Yes, Mr. President. It will be taken care of. You can rely on me," Petrovich answered, trying to sound self-assured.

"That is what some of your predecessors had said also," Markov replied in the flat but menacing tone he used when he wanted to convey that he would not tolerate any failures. Markov did not bother saying anything more to Petrovich. He reached for some papers on his desk and began looking over them. Petrovich knew he had been dismissed. He turned and headed for the door. Petrovich understood what it meant for him if the interpreter wasn't found and eliminated. It might be he who would be eliminated if this became a liability for Markov. He cursed Canton under his breath for putting him in this situation.

***

Ali awoke to the sounds of the city coming to life. He had fallen asleep from exhaustion following the two plus hours of adrenaline-filled terror. His neck and back ached from being bent over the stack of pallets, but his clothes were dry and he was warm. He rubbed his eyes as he recalled what he had just been through. It would have been very easy to think that it was all just a wild dream, except for the fact he had awoken in an alleyway rather than his hotel room. He sat there trying to think through his situation. Going back to the hotel was out. The Turkish authorities were more than likely looking for him. He knew if he surrendered to them and told his story, he would probably not be believed and would be turned over to the US authorities anyway. Despite trying to avoid where his thoughts were leading him, he found it harder and harder to deny that his only chance of survival was to turn to the Iranians and tell them what he knew. It was the only way he could expose the conspiracy. He didn't know how it would eventually all unfold, but he couldn't think of any other options.

Ali winced from the soreness he felt running throughout his body as he slowly stood up. He was fairly certain there was an Iranian consulate in Istanbul because he had seen the myriad of Iranian diplomatic personnel coming and going from the hotel during the negotiations. He had to find out where it was located. He stuck his hand into his left pants pocket for his cell phone, hoping for a miracle. He was disappointed when he found a dark screen because of the phone being submerged in the water. He reached around to his back pocket for his wallet but found it missing. He felt his other pocket and found his room key. He tried to remember if he had left his wallet in his room or could have lost it in the water. Either way, it didn't matter, because he had no money or any identification.

Ali listened for any signs of movement. He peeked his head around the stack of pallets and found the alleyway clear. He was about to step out when the door at the rear of the building swung open and an old man with several days of white stubble dragged out a plastic garbage can. Peering between the gaps in the pallets, Ali could see it was full of bread scraps. The old man threw open the lid of the dumpster and with a grunt heaved the contents of the garbage can into the dumpster. He closed the lid and dragged his garbage can back inside, closing the door behind him.

A deep rumble came from Ali's stomach, reminding him he was hungry. He knew he had to eat to keep his strength up. He cautiously stepped out from behind the crates and hurried over to the dumpster. He lifted the lid and peered in. The mixture of the fresh bread remnants and rotting food made him put the lid back down in disgust. He reconsidered his options. He could either try to steal some from a vendor and risk drawing attention to himself, or he could swallow his pride and see what he could recover from the dumpster. Holding his breath, Ali opened the dumpster, reached in and scooped out two handfuls of bread scraps. He filled his pockets with as much as they would hold and reached in for another handful. He then headed off down the alley, stuffing a handful of crumbs into his mouth. Away from the rotting smell of the dumpster, the bread scraps tasted surprisingly delicious.

Ali glanced at his watch and saw that it was 7:40 a.m. He walked out to the main street and found a fair amount of pedestrian traffic already at this hour of the morning. He looked up at the sky, trying to get his bearings. It was an overcast day, but he spotted the brighter section of the horizon, indicating where the sun was rising in the east. He knew if he headed that direction, he would eventually run into the Bosphorus and would then be able to find the Grand Bazaar. He didn't speak Turkish but guessed he would be able to find some vendors who spoke a bit of English in what was one of Istanbul's main tourist attractions. As Ali walked amongst pedestrians on their way to work, he considered what he would say to the Iranians. He knew his story would sound just as unbelievable to them as it would to anyone else he tried to convince. He vacillated on his decision to go to them. Why did this have to happen to him? he asked himself with a hint of self-pity. He wished he could have remained naïvely ignorant of the truth that the Secretary of State was involved in the plot to kill a foreign diplomat. Now he was unwillingly cast into the position of being the only one who knew the truth about one of the biggest conspiracies in modern times, one that had the potential to destabilize the Middle East and disrupt the entire world. After walking for what seemed like an eternity, he finally reached the eastern wall of the old city. He had a distorted concept of time following the events of earlier. He walked through one of the gates that led out onto Kennedy Avenue, the waterside boulevard running along the outer wall of the old city. Orienting himself, he walked back inside the old city and headed southwest. After a short walk, he ran into the Hagia Sophia and the Blue Mosque, two more of Istanbul's tourist attractions. He recalled the Grand Bazaar being a short distance past them. He continued walking for another ten minutes until he finally reached one of the entrances.

The Grand Bazaar was one of the world's oldest indoor markets. It was constructed by the Ottoman Sultan Mehmet II during the fifteenth century following the capture of Constantinople and defeat of the Byzantine Empire. It was also the world's largest covered market, with over three thousand shops and sixty streets. He made his way through the narrow streets as merchants opened their shops and kiosks. There was a variety of goods sold there, everything from rugs, antiques, jewelry, leather goods and clothing, along with an assortment of souvenir shops and places to eat. The bazaar was already filling with people. Ali felt comfortable here. He could blend in with crowds of shoppers and hopefully get information on how to find the Iranian consulate without attracting attention. He casually walked around and browsed into the various shops.

Ali entered an antique shop and asked, "Hello, do you speak English?"

"English, yes, yes," replied the elderly shopkeeper.

"Can you tell me where is the Iranian consulate?" Ali asked very slowly.

"Yes, yes, please look." The shopkeeper smiled at Ali, motioning with his hand to the furniture in his shop.

"No, thank you. Do you know where the consulate for Iran is?" Ali asked again slowly.

"Yes, yes, thank you, please look," the shopkeeper said again, smiling and nodding his head.

"Okay, thank you." Ali headed back out to the street, realizing he had just heard the extent of the shopkeeper's English. He had similar results in the next shop he tried. Ali's luck improved on his third try when he wandered into a rug shop that had both Turkish and Persian rugs stacked in piles and hanging on its walls.

"Hello," Ali said to the shopkeeper, testing the waters.

"Hello, please come in and look around. I am Habib," the shopkeeper of about sixty replied to Ali with a big smile in his broken English.

"Oh, you speak English," Ali answered.

"Yes, yes, my friend, I speak English. You are American?" the shopkeeper asked.

"Yes," answered Ali.

"Where are you from originally?" the shopkeeper asked, observing Ali's Middle Eastern complexion.

"I am originally from Iran," replied Ali.

"*Salaam*, brother," the shopkeeper responded to Ali in Farsi, increasing the size of his smile. "I am also from Iran."

Switching the conversation to Farsi, Ali asked the shopkeeper, "How long have you lived in Istanbul?"

"I am here thirty-five years. My wife is Turkish and my four children only speak Turkish, and English they are learning in school. I have a brother still in Tabriz. He is my business partner. He runs the export end in Iran and sends me the rugs, where I sell them in my shop," Habib answered proudly. "When did you leave Iran?"

"My parents sent me to my uncle in the United States in 1979, shortly after the revolution." Ali answered.

"And your parents?" Habib asked.

"I don't know. I never saw them again after that. They were professors at Tehran University," Ali answered sadly.

"I am sorry to hear that, brother. There were many who disappeared during that time," Habib responded sympathetically. "Are you interested in a rug? What would you like me to show you?"

"Actually, I was wondering if you could tell me where the Iranian consulate is?" Ali asked.

"It is very close, on Ankara Street, just a five-minute walk from here back towards the water. You will recognize it by its big black iron gate and statues of lions on each side. Why is it you want to know where the consulate is?" Habib asked curiously.

"I've been thinking about trying to make a trip back to Iran to visit after all these years. I need to find out about getting a visa," Ali replied as nonchalantly as possible.

"Brother, I don't know what you expect to find, especially in Tehran. Things have changed very much since the days you remember. You have to be very careful where you go and watch what you say, especially as an American citizen. The authorities will be very suspicious of you, especially VEVAK." Habib referred to the Ministry of Intelligence and Security, or MOIS as Iran's intelligence service was called in the West.

"Thank you, Habib. I will be careful if I go. *Hodahafez*," Ali said, bidding the man goodbye before he turned and left the shop.

"*Hodahafez*, brother," Habib replied with a smile. Apart from noticing his wrinkled clothes and bulging pants pockets, Habib thought there was something unusual about Ali. He just couldn't pinpoint exactly what it was.

***

Israeli Prime Minister Ehud Akerman was sitting at the head of the conference table with his security cabinet, which included Defense Minister Moshe Rozen and Mossad director Benjamin Schimmel. They were discussing the current situation regarding the assassination of Foreign Minister Mohammedi and what it meant for the negotiations between Iran and the United States. They had received sketchy reports regarding the details of what happened from the Israeli consulate in Istanbul, but it was confirmed that Mohammedi had been killed.

"You all know why we are here. Mohammedi has been assassinated. I don't trust the Iranians. It would not surprise me if it were elements within their own government that were responsible for his assassination. Who else would have such easy access to him? More importantly, who else would have a motive to do this other than us or the hardliners within their Republican Guard? We know it wasn't us, so that leaves only them. Benjamin, what do you have for us?" Akerman looked to the Mossad director.

"Mr. Prime Minister, our station in Istanbul has nothing to tell us at this time. The Four Seasons Hotel where this happened has been cordoned off by the Turkish authorities. Secretary Payton with the US delegation was staying there, which has complicated matters. I am certain continuation of the negotiations will cease for the time being. This early, it is difficult to judge the reaction of the Iranians. Aside from the official rhetoric the government will be putting out for public consumption, this situation will more than likely lead to a power struggle between the hardliners and the more moderate elements within President Rostami's administration. This may weaken Rostami enough that he has to abandon the negotiations for now or risk losing control to the hardliners," Schimmel briefed those in the room.

"What is the latest status of their weapons program?" Akerman asked his intelligence chief.

"Our latest intelligence gives us estimates that Iran can reconstitute their nuclear program to where it was three years ago fairly quickly. We have reliable intelligence that their underground Fordow facility, near the city of Qom in northern Iran has the capability to get two thousand, seven hundred and eighty-four IR-1 centrifuges up and running within six months. The centrifuge equipment has been disassembled under the original agreement, but we suspect it has been kept in storage at Fordow. Our estimates are that after reassembly and calibration, they can be up and running within six months. They will then have the capability of enriching ninety percent U-235 weapons-grade uranium," Schimmel advised the prime minister.

"That is unacceptable! Right under their noses, Iran has been developing their missile program so that they can be ready with a delivery system whenever they decide they are done abiding by the nuclear agreement. In less than a year, they will have produced enough weapons-grade uranium and have a ready delivery system that will be able to threaten our nation." Akerman pounded his fist on the table in front of him.

"Prime Minister, we have confidence in our sources, but keep in mind that these are only estimates. As with any intelligence, there is always a margin of error. We could be off by a year or even two on their current capabilities. The real question is how they are going to proceed from here," the Israeli intelligence chief cautioned the prime minister.

"I suspect they will publicly accuse us of being behind the assassination. The question is, was such a bold measure done at the direction of the Supreme Leader or by rogue elements within the Republican Guard who believe the Supreme Leader will not be willing to challenge them and acquiesce, thereby giving them his tacit support? Either scenario is not good. The only reason they would do something this bold is to resume their nuclear weapons program. We cannot let that happen. Since the negotiations have for all practical purposes been permanently sabotaged by the Iranians, we have no other choice but to take matters into our own hands now," Akerman declared.

"Ehud, what you state about the Iranians being behind this may be correct, but we do not yet know what will happen. We do not know how the Americans and the others will react. We do not yet even know how the Iranians are reacting. Let us not rush into anything too hastily without first having a clearer picture of the situation as it develops over the next few days," Defense Minister Rozen counseled Akerman.

Only Moshe Rozen addressed the prime minister by his first name. Rozen was the last of the Israeli leadership who had served in the Arab-Israeli wars of the late '60s and early '70s. He had been a captain in the Israeli Army during the

Six-Day War in 1967, during which the Israeli Army had completely routed the combined forces of Egypt, Syria and Jordan. Rozen had been in command of an Israeli armored company of twelve M-51 Super Sherman tanks that single-handedly destroyed thirty-seven of the Egyptian Army's T-34 Soviet-made tanks during the Battle of Abu-Ageila in the Sinai Desert. As a decorated war hero, he had gone on to serve in the Israeli governments of various Likud prime ministers, to include Menachem Begin, Yitzhak Shamir, Benjamin Netanyahu, Ariel Sharon and now Ehud Akerman. At eighty-one, he was the oldest serving minister in the Israeli government and was respected as an elderly and wise statesman by the Israeli population.

"Moshe, it's obvious what's at play here with the Iranians. What are the Americans going to do? They're not going to do anything. President Steele talks tough and thinks he can take a hard line with the Iranians by forcing them to renegotiate. Steele thinks he has leverage over the Iranians, but he doesn't know his head from his ass. He really believes Rostami's government has control over their nuclear program, when it always has been and always will be the Republican Guard. We cannot wait any longer, especially considering how bold the hardliners have become in reaction to Steele's arrogance. If we do not put a permanent and final stop to their program now, they could have a nuclear weapon in less than a year, and then we will not be able to do anything about it without risking the destruction of Israel," Akerman responded, pushing his point about the urgency to act immediately.

"It may have to come to that, but we need to make sure that, however we decide to act, the consequences we suffer are not greater than whatever benefit we may gain. We will have to live with whatever the fallout will be with the Americans. President Steele will react very strongly to something like this," Rozen persisted, making sure Akerman thought through whatever decision he was going to make.

"Of course, Moshen, our esteemed old *Hakham*. What would we do without your wise counsel?" the prime minister replied half-jokingly, attempting to lighten the atmosphere and reassure his cabinet that he was in command of the situation. "What I am saying is that we need to prepare to be able to execute the plan all of us agreed upon when the time has come. We will know in the next few days if it is the right time, and if that is the case, our military must be ready to act swiftly and decisively. Moshe, I want you to put the Air Force on seventy-two-hour standby to launch Operation Yem Sevp," Akerman ordered his defense chief.

Operation Yem Sevp, meaning Red Sea in Hebrew, was the Israeli military's attack plan to destroy the Fordow nuclear facility in Iran. The General Staff of the Israeli Defense Force, or IDF as it was called in Israel, had been instructed by Defense Minister Rozen to devise a plan that would effectively cripple Iran's nuclear program. The Israeli Air Force had presented him with a plan that would require the use of almost a third of the Israeli Air Force's aircraft. If successful, it would destroy the Fordow facility and kill many of Iran's nuclear scientists and technicians. With the current sanctions in place, it would be very difficult if not virtually impossible for Iran to rebuild its nuclear program for years, perhaps even decades.

"Does anyone else have anything to add?" Akerman paused for a moment to see if there were any other concerns. "All right, gentlemen, we know what each of us has to do in order to prepare for what lies ahead. With God's help, we will defeat our enemies who want to destroy our nation," the prime minister said, concluding the meeting.

It was 3:00 p.m. on Saturday afternoon in Istanbul. Secretary Payton was sitting in the US consulate's sensitive compartmented information facility, or SCIF as it was called, about to join via secure video-conference a meeting President Walker was holding with his National Security Council in the White House Situation Room. Housed in the basement of the West Wing, it was the intelligence management center where the NSC met anytime there was a crisis. It had been created by President Kennedy in 1961 as a result of the Bay of Pigs debacle, at which time the President and his cabinet had no real-time intelligence of what was happening with the doomed operation. It was staffed twenty-four hours a day by senior personnel from the intelligence agencies and the military, who constantly monitored world events and kept the President and his staff informed of significant incidents. Present in today's meeting were the Vice President, the Secretaries of Defense, Energy and Homeland Security, the Chairman of the Joint Chiefs, the Director of National Intelligence (DNI), the Director of Central Intelligence, the National Security Advisor, the White House Chief of Staff and the Attorney General. As the female Air Force technical sergeant brought up the secure link with the consulate in Istanbul, Bill Payton's face appeared on the large flat-screen hanging on the wall at the end of the conference table.

"Bill, can you hear me?" asked President Steele.

"Yes, Mr. President, I hear you fine," replied Secretary Payton.

"Let's start off with you recapping for everyone what has happened since yesterday along with any new developments," the President instructed Payton.

"Gentlemen. As you all know, we were in discussions with Foreign Minister Mohammedi and his delegation regarding Iran's missile program as it relates to their being able to reconstitute their nuclear program to develop a nuclear weapons delivery system. Following the meeting, he approached me to speak in private. We had a frank discussion in which I made it very clear to him the United States would not stand for Iran developing that type of capability. I can't say we had come to any level of understanding, but we agreed to resume discussions the next day, that being today. I then retired to my room at the hotel. At some time around one thirty this morning local time, the foreign minister's security chief discovered one of his men shot and killed in the hallway on their floor and Foreign Minister Mohammedi shot dead in his room. Seven Turkish soldiers were also found dead on the grounds of the hotel on the water side. The foreign minister and his delegation occupied the entire second floor of the hotel, with us above them on the third. None of our delegation was injured or was even aware that anything had happened until I was woken by one of my security personnel after the Turkish military guarding the hotel went on alert following the discovery of the bodies. During the attack, one of my security detail standing a post in the hotel basement was shot with a tranquilizer dart but, other than a bruised neck, wasn't injured. He wasn't able to provide any information regarding the attack. My interpreter is MIA, but we're trying to track him down. At this time, I don't have any additional information as to who may have been responsible for the assassination. The Turkish authorities have cordoned off the hotel. It's a chaotic scene here. Between the Turkish military, the Turkish police conducting their investigation and Iranian personnel attempting to maintain control of the second floor, it's almost impossible to get in or out. We still have some staff there but are in the process of getting packed up and moving to another hotel until we can determine what the next move will be. Ambassador Reynolds and the chief of station are coordinating with the Turkish government and security services to obtain any additional information and determine what if any assistance they may need from us," the Secretary of State briefed the President and NSC.

"When you spoke with Mohammedi, did you notice anything unusual or observe any signs of concern on his part?" the President asked.

"No. He was his usual self, attempting to lay blame for all of the world's ills on the United States," answered Payton.

"What's your take on all this, Bill?"

"Hopefully we'll know more soon, but I think it's pretty obvious it was the hardliners within Iran who wanted to make sure there would be no possibility of giving in to any of our demands regarding their missile program, so they staged this attack to create a crisis within their country."

"You mean the IRGC," said the President, referring to the Iranian Republican Guard Corps. The IRCG was a special branch of Iran's national security establishment with approximately one hundred and twenty-five thousand personnel responsible for protecting Iran's Islamic system against foreign threats or domestic dissent. The IRGC was the Iranian hardliners' shock troops, independent of the Iranian military's chain of command, much the same way as the SS had been for the Nazi regime during World War II. It answered directly to the Supreme Leader and was outside the control of the president and his government. It was also very wealthy, having developed into a multi-billion-dollar empire by controlling many of Iran's heavy industries, which also gave it additional autonomy even though it was officially under the control of the Supreme Leader.

"Yes, Mr. President. The IRGC is the only element within Iran that would have the means and the boldness to assassinate their own foreign minister. It was no secret that the IRGC was at odds with President Rostami over reaching a nuclear settlement in order to have the sanctions lifted. The IRGC could care less how badly their economy is hurting or how much the Iranian people are suffering, as long as they maintain their hold on power. There is no way they would have stood for any more concessions on their part regarding their nuclear weapons program," he answered the President.

"Mahdavi has come out and publicly accused Israel of being responsible for the assassination. What's his angle?" President Steele asked, referring to Iran's Supreme Leader.

"That's to be expected. Even if the assassination took place without his orders or knowledge, he can't appear not to be in control. Either way, Iran will be forced to respond against Israel. How they respond is anyone's guess. There's definitely going to be a power struggle in Tehran. Mohammad Bardari, the commander of the IRGC, wields a lot of influence and power. If this was done without the Supreme Leader's consent, Mahdavi may realize that he's better off taking a hard stance and dropping his support of Rostami, rather than trying to cross or remove Bardari," Payton said, offering his assessment.

"Thanks, Bill, I think you may be right about the Iranians concocting this and trying to make it look like it was the Israelis. John, what do we have as far as intel goes?" the President asked the DNI.

"NRO has satellite imagery as of a few hours ago showing the Iranians mobilizing their missile forces. NRO is redirecting CRYSTAL satellites to make more frequent sweeps across the Middle East, and we have an older KEY HOLE bird in geosynchronous orbit above Iran that will provide us twenty-four-hour coverage, although not with quite the same capabilities as the CRYSTAL birds. NSA has picked up increased chatter from both their conventional and IRGC forces. From what we've been able to decrypt so far, it sounds like there's a lot of confusion going on right now. Everybody is mobilizing without really knowing why," the DNI said.

"Ed, what do you guys have at CIA?" Steele asked the DCI.

"Nothing definitive yet. The chief of station in Turkey has met with the director of MIT, that's their national intel service, and so far, they have nothing. Our satellite station at the consulate in Istanbul is working all their sources to see what they can find out. That goes for all our stations in the Middle East. We also have Jonathan Canton in Istanbul, our deputy director of the Counterproliferation Division, who was there advising SecState during the negotiations. I spoke to him this morning. As Secretary Payton mentioned, his interpreter has gone missing. Shiravi was born in Iran and is a former US Air Force linguist. We have no reason to suspect him of anything at this point, but the fact that he has disappeared and is Iranian makes him a person of significant interest. Canton knew him personally back in Athens, when Shiravi was assigned to the Defense Attaché's Office at the embassy. I'm going to let him coordinate our efforts in Istanbul. Canton will be working with the Turks trying to locate Shiravi—that will allow the chief of station to coordinate the overall effort and still maintain all the operations they have going on. I've made it clear that they have all the CIA's assets at their disposal to find out who's behind this. Whoever was responsible for this attack kept it pretty tight," the DCI answered President Steele.

"What makes you say whoever? You're not convinced it was the Iranians?" asked the President.

"It doesn't add up, Mr. President. Why would they risk something going wrong in an environment they don't have much control over, especially with our delegation staying at the same hotel? It was a pretty sophisticated operation to pull off. The Quds Force is the special operations unit of the IRGC, but this falls outside the scope of their capabilities and past operations."

"So, who are you saying was responsible? The Israelis?" Steele asked.

"Mossad has a history of attempting some pretty bold operations, but again it would be a pretty high-risk operation, and the blowback if something went wrong would be devastating. I know Benjamin Schimmel, the Mossad director. He's a pretty cautious guy, and that's not something he would try. I can't speak for Prime Minister Akerman. He has a tendency to be impulsive as you very well know, but he would have to get Defense Minister Rozen on board. From what we know about Rozen, he's not hesitant to act boldly when it's called for, but he's also very cautious and calculating. He thinks things through very carefully before acting. The risk versus gain just doesn't add up for them either," the DCI advised the President.

"Well, who's responsible, then?" the President asked, somewhat annoyed.

"I don't know, Mr. President. I don't want to offer any preconceived judgments because I have absolutely no evidence to support them, but it would definitely benefit the Russians if the negotiations fell apart. With the price of oil at almost half of what they need to keep a balanced budget while still being able to update their military and keep domestic spending up for Markov to retain a firm grip on power, instability in the Middle East will definitely cause the price of oil to skyrocket. And this has the potential to cause a whole lot of instability."

"Are you saying the Russians could be behind this? That's the most idiotic thing I've heard," Steele belittled the DCI.

"Mr. President, I'm saying they would benefit from this the most, and they have the capability to carry out this type of operation. Our assessment of Markov's personality leaves it entirely possible he would attempt a bold if not reckless move like this," the DCI defended his assessment.

"Interesting theory, Ed, but I've met with Markov, and I think I know him well enough to know that he wouldn't try something like this and risk the inroads he's made trying to rebuild his relationship with us. Bill, what do you think about Ed's crazy theory?" the President asked his Secretary of State.

"It's an interesting twist Ed has on the situation, Mr. President, but I'd advise not to start focusing our attention on any one direction just yet until we get some more definitive information on who was behind it. The bigger issue is what's going to happen internally back in Tehran and how they're going to respond. If they decide to do an about-face on the nuclear deal, that's going to make the Israelis feel they have no other choice than to respond militarily. If they do that, then Iran is going to launch every long-range missile they have back at Israel, and then who knows how the Israelis may respond? They might even retaliate with a nuke if they suffer significant loss of life," Payton advised the President.

"What do you think about your interpreter going missing?"

"I don't know what to think, Mr. President. I was told about it this morning. I was just with him yesterday afternoon during the negotiations, and everything seemed fine with him. He's always been very diligent in his duties. I've never noticed anything out of the ordinary with him," Payton replied matter-of-factly.

"Okay, keep me informed if anything develops with that." President Steele put his hands over his face and rubbed his eyes. He turned to Secretary of Defense John Russell and asked, "John, what's the situation militarily with everyone?"

John Russell was an imposing man. At six feet four inches tall, the Secretary of Defense had played on Harvard's basketball team while attending college there in the mid-sixties. He came from a prominent and wealthy Boston family who could trace their roots back to the Revolutionary War. Upon graduating, he had been scheduled to start Harvard Law School but had opted to join the Army as an officer instead, to the great consternation of his family. Following completion of Officer Candidate School, he had been sent to Vietnam as a new second lieutenant and served as an artillery officer. He'd left the Army when his service commitment ended four years later and returned to Harvard to obtain his law degree. He had gone on to serve as legal counsel for various Fortune 500 companies, and eventually on the boards of some of those same companies. As a Vietnam War veteran and a blue blood of American aristocracy, Russell was a very prominent man in the circles of wealth and power.

"I've been in contact with the Israeli defense minister, and no surprise, he told me they were putting their forces on high alert in light of Iran's accusations that Israel was responsible for the assassination. That's to be expected. He assured me that they won't do anything before advising us. As you heard from our imagery and intercepts, the Iranians are also going on high alert. They're mobilizing all their antiaircraft batteries and lighting up their airspace. Everybody else's military over there is also increasing their alert status. I'm going to talk with the Saudi, Jordanian, Egyptian and Iraqi defense ministers and try to keep everyone from getting too spun up. The earlier we try to get out in front of this, the less chance we have of things escalating out of control. I'll let General Donovan brief you on the status of US forces," the Secretary of Defense said as he turned to the Chairman of the Joint Chiefs.

"Mr. President, I've directed Central Command to put their forces on high alert. The Navy is moving another carrier task force into the Indian Ocean. The Air Force is increasing its surveillance capabilities by having the 38th Reconnaissance Squadron redeploy another RC-135 Rivet Joint from Offutt in Nebraska forward to Souda Bay on the island of Crete. We'll be able to monitor all of the Gulf's airspace as well as Iranian tactical military traffic. We're also putting the 1st and the 2nd Ranger Battalions on alert to be ready to deploy in twenty-four hours if necessary. Beyond that, Mr. President, we're standing by to implement whichever course of action you decide to take," the Chairman advised Steele.

"Thank you, General. Dave, how does this affect us domestically?"

"We've increased our security posture at airports and at the border, and the Coast Guard is deploying additional patrols in our major ports. Additionally, we're coordinating with state and local authorities to make sure everyone is kept in the loop should anything develop that may impact our domestic security,"

David Saunders, the Secretary of the Department of Homeland Security briefed the President.

"Okay, that's good, everybody. I want everyone to give Bob updates every twelve hours," said the President, referring to his National Security Advisor. "Let's stay on top of this. No statements to the press unless it's coordinated with Gene," he added, referring to the White House press secretary. "That will be all. Bill, don't go, I want to speak with you individually."

Everyone rose and departed the Situation Room, except the female Air Force technical sergeant who was monitoring the secure video link equipment. "You can leave also, miss," Steele instructed her. The President waited until everyone had left the room before he continued. "Bill, what the hell is going on over there? Who is this interpreter of yours that's missing, and what's he got to do with all of this? Is this going to be a problem for us?"

"Everything is under control. He was just at the wrong place at the wrong time. Canton is on top of things trying to track him down. The Turks are also looking for him. There is no way for him to get out of the country. We have his passport and wallet, and he has nowhere to go without them. He'll turn up eventually."

"What do you mean, he was at the wrong place at the wrong time?"

"He may have overheard something regarding the planning."

"Overheard! How the hell did he hear anything about the planning?"

"It was a slight oversight. Canton was briefing me on things, and he was in the adjoining room. He may not know anything. But we're not taking any chances. Canton is on top of it," Payton tried reassuring Steele.

"He better be. And the Turks! Why the hell do you have them involved in this?"

"Because it's their country and they're the only ones who can find him. How else did you think we could track him down in a foreign country?"

"So help me, Bill, if this starts to go sideways on us, we are screwed. Take whatever steps are necessary to get the situation under control over there. I don't care what needs to be done. Do you understand?"

"Don't worry."

"Don't tell me not to worry, Bill. You know what's at stake here," Steele shouted at the monitor on the wall.

"I know, I know. After I'm done meeting with Akerman in Jerusalem, I'm heading to Moscow to reassure Markov that we have everything under control," Payton told his boss.

"Markov? Why do you need to reassure him?" Steele asked suspiciously.

"Well, because considering the circumstances, I'm sure he'll want to know how we're handling things. They have as much at stake in this as we do. You and he want the same thing out of this, don't you? To bring back some semblance of order in the world, the way things used to be. Isn't that the purpose behind all this?" Payton tried to sound convincing.

"Yeah, you're right. Okay, size up how far the Israelis might escalate things if the Iranians take any retaliatory measures against them. For the record, tell them we expect them to exercise restraint, but let them know we will have their back even if we have to condemn them publicly for any measures the international community may declare were excessive. Brief me as soon as you're done meeting with Markov. I want to know what he's thinking. I'm sure he believes that he can play me, but he's going to figure it out eventually that he's the junior partner in this relationship," Steele instructed his Secretary of State.

"Yes, Mr. President. I'll convey your messages to Akerman and Markov," Payton assured the President.

"All right, Bill, we'll talk again after you meet with Markov," the President disconnected from the secure link with Istanbul.

***

After spending several hours wandering through the bazaar agonizing over his situation, Ali finally forced himself to make his way to the Iranian consulate. He headed east, back towards the Bosphorus. It was a short five-minute walk to Ankara Street, and Ali quickly located the consulate with its black iron gate and lion statues as Habib had described. It was an imposing three-story building with a large portico and a ten-foot black iron fence on top of a stone wall surrounding its grounds. Ali walked past the gate trying to peer into the grounds but couldn't see over the tall iron doors. He continued past the consulate down Ankara Street, towards the water. He had lost his nerve.

He kept walking until he reached Gülhane Park. Located within the ancient walls of the city, the expansive park was bordered by the Bosphorus on the east side and was part of the grounds of the Topkapi Palace, the royal residence of the Ottoman sultans. Ali wandered through the park until he came to a bench situated on the cliff side overlooking the Bosphorus. He sat down and looked out across the strait to the Asian side of Istanbul. He reached into his pocket and pulled a handful of bread crumbs, shoving them into his mouth. He had to find something else to eat, but he had no money. He thought about going back to the Grand Bazaar and stealing some food from a shop, but he quickly dismissed that idea, not wanting to risk getting caught. The sun had broken through the clouds and it was starting to warm up. He looked at his watch. It was already 2:30 p.m. He knew he couldn't avoid doing something. He guessed the US embassy had already contacted the Turkish authorities and requested assistance in locating him. The longer he waited, the greater the chance he would be discovered. He also realized the risk he would be taking by going to the Iranians. Who knew how they would react and what they might do to him? His story sounded so outrageous that they might think he was deranged and throw him out. On the other hand, they might believe him to be some kind of provocateur and do something far more unpleasant to him. He had no illusions about what might happen to him if he couldn't convince them he was telling the truth. He might end up spending the rest of his life in an Iranian prison or even worse.

He thought of turning himself in to the Turkish authorities and attempting to convince them of his story. That was a possibility, he tried to tell himself. He pulled himself back to reality, admonishing himself for thinking like a fool. Who was going to believe such an outlandish tale? At best, he might be judged mentally insane and be committed to a psychiatric facility for a while, until the Turks eventually turned him over to the American authorities. Something inside him told him he would never get a chance to tell his story to any American authorities. Canton would somehow ensure he was killed while in Turkish custody. Whether it was as brazen as a bullet in the head or made to look like a suicide, he knew there was no way he could be left alive to tell his story, no matter how unbelievable.

Ali agonized for another half hour. He could no longer put it off. He got up and headed through the park back towards the Iranian consulate. He walked back down Ankara Street to the large black iron gates of the consulate. Not seeing any intercom or other way of contacting anyone inside, he walked around the corner to look for another entrance. He came across the public entrance, which had a thick ballistic glass window on the side, through which he could see a small empty booth. He looked at the sign taped inside the window, which said business hours were 8:30 a.m. until 11:30 a.m. daily, other than Friday, when they were closed for the Muslim holy day of worship. He hung his head in frustration and was about to turn and walk away but saw the intercom on the wall next to the window, with a call button. He hit it once and waited. He hit it again, waiting a good thirty seconds, but no one came. He began frantically hitting the button over and over until the door behind the booth opened and in walked a strikingly beautiful Iranian woman of about thirty years old. She was wearing violet eye shadow, eyeliner and maroon lipstick with a brightly colored turquoise scarf covering her hair.

"We are closed," she said in Turkish through the intercom, pointing to the sign.

"Hello. I have information about what happened last night at the Four Seasons Hotel. May I please speak to someone? It is important," Ali answered in Farsi.

Ali observed the look of bewilderment on her face. She stared back at him in silence, trying to determine if he was serious or just some sort of crazy person. She finally responded in Farsi, "Are you Iranian?"

"I'm originally from Iran, but I'm a US citizen. Please, it is important I speak with someone," Ali pleaded with the woman.

Having recovered from her initial surprise, she asked Ali, "Your name, sir?"

"Ali, Ali Shiravi," he answered.

"Do you have your passport or any identification?"

"No, I lost my wallet and passport. But once I can talk with someone, I will be able to prove who I am. Please, this is very important," he replied.

The woman studied him for a few moments longer before she answered, "Please wait here." She turned and left her small cubicle through the door behind her.

Ali stood there waiting, his heart racing and his mouth dry. He knew this was his last opportunity to change his mind before he would pass beyond the point of no return. He looked around. He wanted to just turn and walk away, but where would he go? It took everything he had to overcome his urge to leave. He could see a waiting room inside the consulate through the open door of the booth that the stunned young Iranian woman forgot to close in her excitement. He glanced up above the window at a security camera. He stood there looking into the lens, wondering who was watching him on the other end.

After what seemed like an eternity, the woman returned and spoke to Ali through the intercom, "Mr. Shiravi, please come in. You can enter through the door to your left."

Ali heard the buzz and the clink of the electronic lock releasing the door. He pulled open the heavy security door and walked into the sally port. When the door behind him shut, he heard the interior door leading into the waiting room buzz and unlock. Ali pushed open the door and walked into the empty waiting room. A male consular employee behind a counter with a thick glass shield like those found in a large city bank greeted Ali in Farsi. "*Salaam*. Please sit, someone will be with you shortly."

"Thank you," replied Ali as he sat down in one of the black plastic chairs in the empty waiting room. Ali looked around, noticing the photographs of the Supreme Leader and President Rostami hanging on the wall. There was a flat-screen television on the wall that had on Al-Alam News, the officially sanctioned news station of the state-owned media corporation, Islamic Republic of Iran Broadcasting. He also noticed the large five-by-three-foot mirror built into one of the walls, obviously a two-way mirror. Ali wondered if anyone was watching him from the other side. He looked back over towards a consular employee sitting at his desk behind the counter, reading a Turkish variety magazine that had a photograph of Demet Akalin, one of Turkey's most famous female pop singers, in a low-cut sequined dress on its cover. Unlike in Iran, where popular music was heavily regulated through the Ministry of Culture and Islamic Guidance, which was responsible for restricting any media that the government didn't approve, Turkey had a flourishing music industry with female pop singers that rivaled their Western counterparts in their sexual suggestiveness. Along with its vibrant music industry, Turkey also was known for its steamy soap operas that were permitted in more liberal Muslim nations of the Middle East. Although Turkey was a Muslim country, a Western secularism had been fused into its society since its founder, Atatürk, had transformed the remains of the Ottoman Empire into modern-day Turkey following World War I. Diplomatic duty in Turkey was a choice assignment for embassy personnel of many other Muslim countries, which had strict codes that determined what was acceptable popular entertainment.

It seemed like half an hour had passed while Ali waited, until finally a door opened and a man of about forty with a neatly trimmed beard, wearing a gray suit without a tie, appeared.

"Mr. Shiravi?"

"Yes, that's me," replied Ali.

"Please, this way." The man gestured for Ali to come through the door.

Ali stood and walked over to the door. The man in the suit held it as Ali passed through into a wide hallway. Ali immediately noticed something unusual was going on. Personnel were busily hurrying around, phones were ringing and there was a buzz of activity. Ali wondered what the outcome of the attack had been. He had an uneasy feeling that the attack had been successful and that Foreign Minister Mohammedi had been killed. Ali's escort led him down the hallway to a large foyer, up a large marble staircase and down another hallway to a door with a cipher lock. The embassy employee depressed a series of buttons on the combination and twisted the knob, opening the door and gesturing Ali into the room. Ali entered the room and observed a small wooden table with three chairs around it. Apart from those furnishings, the room was bare, with only a duplicate set of photographs of the Supreme Leader and President Rostami hanging on the wall. There was also a two-way mirror on the wall.

The embassy employee told Ali to sit in one of the chairs and someone would be with him shortly. He closed the door and left Ali in the room. Ali saw that the door had a cipher combination on the inside also. He walked over to the door and tried turning the knob. The knob turned but didn't open the door. Ali realized he was locked in the room and now a prisoner. He felt the hairs of his neck stand as the realization set in that he no longer had the freedom to leave and was no longer in control of his own destiny. He looked around, then walked over to the two-way mirror. He stopped in front of it and looked at his reflection. It felt odd looking at himself in the mirror and not being able to acknowledge the person he was certain was on the other side looking back at him. He walked back over to the table and sat down in one of the chairs. He glanced at his watch. It was almost 5:00 p.m. As he sat there waiting, Ali's mind wandered from thought to thought on how everything would end for him. He struggled to stay focused on his present circumstances, trying to keep himself keep calm and levelheaded. He believed he would eventually be able to convince someone that he was saying was the truth, even if they initially suspected him of being sent by the CIA. How ironic it was that ten years ago, he actually had been such a provocateur, gaining the trust of an Iranian official. He hoped now that he was reaching out in earnest to them, they would believe him.

After almost an hour, Ali heard the buttons on the cipher lock being depressed right before the door opened and an imposing man dressed in a wrinkled light gray suit with a heavy five-o'clock shadow entered the room. He walked over and sat down in the chair next to Ali. Ali waited for the man to say something, but he just stared at Ali in silence. Ali tried to maintain eye contact with him as long as possible until his discomfort finally made Ali say, "*Dorood*," smiling politely as he greeted him in Farsi.

Without warning, Ali felt the man's open hand strike him on the left side of his face with such force that it knocked Ali off the chair. Using his hands to steady himself on the floor, Ali struggled to maintain his composure from the shock of the man's blow. He slowly stood up while seeing stars in front of him and sat back up in his chair. He gingerly rubbed the side of his face as he cautiously watched the man in case he would try to strike him again.

"Don't say anything unless I ask you. Do you understand?" the man said in Farsi.

"*Baleh*," Ali said, answering yes.

"You look familiar. What is your name?" the man asked him.

"Ali Shiravi. I am the Secretary of State's interpreter."

"Yes, that is where I have seen you. You are Iranian, then." It was more of a statement than a question.

"I was born in Iran, but I am an American citizen," Ali replied.

"Once an Iranian, always an Iranian," the man responded in a menacing tone.

Ali sat in silence, waiting for the man to speak. The last thing Ali wanted was to appear argumentative and risk being struck again.

"So why are you here, Mr. Shiravi?" the man asked.

"I came because I have some information about the attack against your foreign minister," Ali kept his response short.

"And what is this information?"

Ali hesitated as he thought about where to start. He finally decided to just come out with the simple facts and hope the man's reaction wasn't going to be another slap across the face.

"The Russians were responsible for the attack against Foreign Minister Mohammedi. The US Secretary of State and President Markov are involved. They did this to sabotage the nuclear deal and start a war in the Middle East." Ali postured himself to dodge any incoming blows from the man as he waited for a response.

The man looked at Ali in silence for a moment, then finally burst out laughing. He couldn't contain himself for several seconds as the intensity of his laughter increased. The man suddenly stopped laughing, and his right hand came up and struck Ali across his face again. This time Ali was on guard and pulled his face back, deflecting most of the man's blow. The man stood up and slowly walked around the back of Ali. Ali raised his arms above his head to protect himself from any other incoming blows. The man came around and leaned his hands on the table, placing his face directly in front of Ali's. Ali lowered his arms since the man's hands were now on the table and their faces were inches apart. Ali looked at him, maintaining eye contact, while trying not to appear defiant.

"That is the most preposterous story I have ever heard. Why did you come here and not report this to American security personnel?" the man shouted as his spittle hit Ali's face.

"Because an attempt was made on my life also," Ali answered him vehemently. "I could not tell the Americans because the Secretary of State knows that I know about the attack, and I will be killed."

"And how do you know this information?" the man lashed back at Ali.

"Because I overheard the Secretary discussing it with another individual involved."

The man stared at him in silence as the stink of the man's body odor and his foul cigarette breath permeated Ali's nostrils. The man finally shouted at Ali, "You are a CIA spy sent here to mislead us! Why would the US Secretary of State and the Russian President do such a thing? That is insanity. The Zionist Jews were behind the foreign minister's assassination!" the man ranted on.

"So, the foreign minister is dead?" Ali asked, hoping that the attack had somehow failed.

"Yes, he has gone to Allah now. Do not act as if you do not know this. This is a plot by the Great Satan to destroy the Islamic Republic!" he shouted at Ali with contempt.

"Please, sir, what I'm telling you is the truth. I can prove it. I just need a chance to explain everything," Ali pleaded. The man had reverted to the typical paranoid mindset of some Iranians that the United States was continually plotting the overthrow of Iran. Ali realized he needed to speak to someone above this man, someone in a position of authority. Ali guessed he was a low to mid-level security official, probably IRGC, that had a limited aptitude to comprehend the significance of what Ali was trying to explain to him.

The man began pacing back and forth, contemplating what to do. He finally turned to Ali and told him to stand up. "You will get a chance to explain everything." He walked over to the door and entered the combination on the cipher lock, opened the door and motioned Ali to get up.

Ali walked out into the hallway, and the man stepped behind, holding Ali from the shoulder as he led him back down the hallway to the marble staircase. They went down the staircase to the foyer. The man gave Ali a shove, directing to continue down the staircase to what was evidently the basement level of the consulate. They descended the stairway, which led to a dimly lit hallway with a concrete floor. A feeling of panic swept over Ali as he wondered where he was being taken. He thought about turning on the man and trying to make a break for it, but then thought about what he would do next. He was certain that he would never make it out of the consulate, trying to force his way past all the personnel that would try to stop him. Some might even have guns. He risked being shot and killed. They finally came to a solid green metal door with a heavy slide bolt. The man pulled the slide to the side and pulled the door open. He motioned Ali inside. Ali hesitated, indicating he wasn't going inside the room. The man reached inside his sports jacket, drawing out a black semi-auto and pointed it at Ali. Any thoughts of resistance immediately left Ali's mind. Ali walked through the door, accepting that he would just have to be patient and wait for the opportunity to speak to the right person. That was his last thought as something hard struck the back of his head and everything went black.

Chapter 4

Rays from the late-morning sun streamed in, filling the room with brightness, as Michael's eyes slowly opened to a sideways view of the world. He perceived that he was lying on his side on what he assumed was his couch. His view took him across the top of the coffee table and out the floor-to-ceiling windows, to the sun sparkling across the waters of the Puget Sound. He attempted to lift his head, but it seemed as if it was disconnected from his body. He wondered if he was actually awake or dreaming. With great effort, he tried to focus his mind and orient himself to his present situation. He moved his left eye around, exploring the limits of his peripheral vision. From what he could see, everything appeared to be normal in his living room. He could see his left arm hanging off the couch, and what looked like his left knee. He shifted his gaze and saw a half-empty bottle of Finlandia and a half-empty glass on the coffee table. It jolted his memory to the events of last night. He was overcome with a feeling of panic as he recalled putting the Glock to his head and pulling the trigger. Had he blown part of his head off but somehow managed to survive to be left paralyzed, lying on his living room couch along with fragments of his brain? He started hyperventilating and his heart began to race as that thought set in. He knew he would pass out if he didn't get his breathing under control. He slowed his breathing, struggling to remain calm and not panic. The fact that he could control his breathing brought a slight sense of relief. If part of his brains were spread out across the living room, he would probably not be able to exercise that kind of control. Why couldn't he move, then? Michael focused on his hands, trying to move his fingers. He had a sensation of the fingers on his left hand moving, but nothing on his right. He tried his toes next. He thought he could feel his feet moving. Out of his peripheral vision, he caught the sight of his left knee moving ever so slightly as he wiggled his toes. He breathed a sigh of relief knowing he wasn't paralyzed, but couldn't understand why he felt numb, as if his entire body had fallen asleep and left him without any sense of feeling.

"Oh man," he mumbled to himself. Michael's ears perked up as he heard the raspy sound of his voice. That was a relief. So, he could speak, move his toes, move the fingers of his left hand and control his breathing. It was something. He knew he had to see if he could get up from the couch; that would be the real test of how bad his situation really was. He tried to push himself up, but nothing happened. He tried to raise his head again. With a sustained effort, he slowly lifted his head off the couch and was able to see his right arm was pinned under his torso. *That arm isn't going anywhere*, Michael told himself, figuring out why he couldn't get up from the couch. Maybe he could roll off the couch. To his surprise, he was able to twist his midsection easier than expected, rolling off the couch and crashing with a thud onto the floor. He let out a groan from his new position between the coffee table and couch. Michael lay there motionless, staring at a lost Christmas ornament under the couch, wondering if he wouldn't have been better off dead. After resting there for several moments, he reached for the couch with his right arm while planting his left hand on the floor and gingerly lifted himself up onto his knees. That was as far as his strength would take him, and he momentarily rested his head and chest on the couch cushion. With another concerted effort, he lifted himself up onto his wobbling legs before half sitting, half falling back onto the couch. He was in a daze and disoriented. He didn't know how long he had sat there attempting to adjust to the sensation of dizziness and lightheadedness while trying to keep from passing out. He felt something hard against his back as the feeling slowly started returning to his body. Reaching behind him, he discovered the Glock on the couch. He carefully grabbed it and pulled it out from behind him, laying it on the coffee table. He stared at the handgun while he contemplated the events of last night. Despite his disorientation, the details of what had happened were slowly returning to him. He noticed the trigger of the Glock was in the depressed position, indicating that it had been pulled. That struck him as odd. After being fired, it would have normally cycled back to the ready position.

Michael raised both hands to his temple and cautiously walked his fingers across his head searching for any wounds. Everything felt normal but, still somewhat disoriented, he didn't fully trust his senses. He slowly pulled his hands away from his head and looked at them for any sign of blood. He took in a deep breath and let it out a sigh of relief at the sight of his clean hands. He sat there, looking out the window at the sparkling waters of the Puget Sound. He was bewildered. How he could still be alive, let alone unharmed? He picked up the Glock from the coffee table, depressing the magazine release, dropping it into his left hand. He turned it and looked through the small holes on the back of the magazine that showed the remaining rounds. He counted twelve, which meant the thirteenth round was still in the chamber and hadn't fired. That didn't make sense. He had obviously pulled the trigger when he had raised the gun to his head—or had he imagined it all? He grabbed the slide and slowly pulled it back, ejecting the .45-caliber Hydra-Shock round in the chamber onto the coffee table. He picked up the ejected round and examined it. He couldn't believe what he was looking at. There was a depression on the primer from being struck by the firing pin, yet the round hadn't discharged. Michael had fired thousands of rounds throughout his career, both in the military and afterwards in the CIA, but he had never experienced a misfire like this. Machine guns had jammed on occasion from the accumulation of powder debris and gunk after having fired several thousand rounds, but never a well-maintained handgun or rifle using good ammunition. Hydra-Shock was one of the most reliable and trusted ammunitions there was, used by police departments and various military special operations units. The odds of a misfire were astronomical, especially considering it was the round that should have killed him.

Michael placed the unspent round on the coffee table in front of him. He stared at it while trying to come to terms with what had happened. He was trying to figure out what he felt. His emotions were in turmoil. Everything that had happened to him since last night seemed surreal. He kept wanting to believe it was all a dream, but the .45-caliber round standing in the middle of the coffee table reminded him it was real. He looked around his living room. Everything looked normal, yet somehow felt different. Things seemed brighter and more vivid. It was as if all his senses had switched from a normal channel on the television to the same channel in HD. He studied the rays of sunlight streaming into the living room. He never remembered them looking so defined and concentrated, yet they were the same beams of light from the sun he had seen every day of his life. Something had changed, but he could not place his finger on what it was.

Michael looked at his watch. It was 11:30 a.m. He estimated it had been around twelve hours since he had taken the oxycodone with the alcohol and had smoked the marijuana. He knew all the toxins he had poisoned himself with would eventually clear out of his system and he would return to normal. It was going to take some time, and he just needed to take it easy and be patient.

His thoughts turned to what had gone so wrong in his life that it had led him to try something as drastic as ending it. He was never the type of person who would just give up when things got difficult. He could never have imagined himself reaching that point of desperation. What had changed him so much? He had mixed emotions. On one hand, he felt guilt and anger for failing to accomplish what he had set out to do a few hours ago. On the other hand, he felt a sense of relief that he was still alive. He searched for reasons for what had driven him to take his own life but couldn't come up with anything so significant that it had caused him to attempt such a desperate act. Yes, he was upset that his marriage with Eva had ended in divorce, but he also felt a sense of relief of finally being out of a dysfunctional relationship. Financially, he was doing well. His medical retirement from the Army and his investments were enough for him to live comfortably. His real estate income was just icing on the cake. His life hadn't been that bad. Why, then, had he tried to end it? Was it that his life lacked purpose? He knew real estate didn't challenge him or give him much satisfaction. He just couldn't get excited about driving couples from house to house, waiting for them to decide which they were interested in, vacillating for weeks and sometimes even months before ever making a decision. At times, he felt like a glorified used car salesman. Although his pride made it hard for him to admit, he guessed he was probably suffering from some depression.

Michael just didn't know what he could do to change the circumstances of his life. It wasn't as if all his specialized training and work experience in the military and the CIA could translate into something useful in the private sector. Going back to Wall Street at his age was out of the question. He had been away for too long and didn't feel like starting from the bottom again, competing with the twenty-something-year-olds trying to make a big name for themselves in the financial industry. He had considered corporate security but knew it wouldn't bring him the same challenges covert operations against foreign intelligence services and terrorist organizations had. It would have been a big disappointment compared to what he had been used to. It certainly wouldn't have given him the adrenaline rush he got in the CIA or Special Forces. Was he some sort of excitement junkie, addicted to the adrenaline rush just like any other addict? He wondered if there was an Adrenaline Anonymous for those who were hooked on thrill-seeking addictions like base jumping, untethered rock climbing and the like. Was that it, then? Was he simply an adrenaline junkie and life had become boring? He knew it had to be something more than that. There was an emptiness inside him, but he just couldn't figure out what had caused it.

Michael turned his attention back to the unspent .45 round. He thought he should keep it for good luck, or at least as a reminder of the yet unknown reason why his life had been spared. He picked it up off the coffee table and put it in his pocket. It suddenly came to him that the last thing he remembered from last night was hearing the ring of his cell phone. He looked for his iPhone, searching the couch and under it until he realized it was in his left pants pocket, where he always kept it. Pulling it out, he opened it and saw that he had one missed call. The call was from a number with 703 area code. He didn't recognize the number, but he remembered that 703 was the area for Alexandria, Virginia, a stone's throw away from Washington, D.C. He saw that there was also voicemail from that number. Michael touched the screen and listened to the message.

"Hi, this is Roxanne Shiravi. I'm Ali Shiravi's daughter. I'm calling for Michael Blackstone. You know my father. He said you're an old friend from Athens. He asked me to call you and pass a message to you. He said it was very important and you would understand. He told me to tell you that Secretary Payton, Jonathan Canton and the Russians are going to try to kill the Iranian foreign minister. I know it sounds pretty crazy, but those were his exact words. He sounded really stressed out when we talked. I don't know what's going. Does any of this make sense to you? I'm really worried. Please call me back. This is my cell phone I'm calling you from. Let me leave you my number just in case, it's 703-509-3578. I hope I hear from you soon. Bye."

Michael held the cell phone next to his ear while he sat motionless, trying to process what he had just heard. Was he still having auditory hallucinations from the effects of the drugs? He put his phone on speaker and set it down on the coffee table, listening to the message again. No, he wasn't having an auditory hallucination, unless hallucinations could repeat themselves word for word. Ali Shiravi, of all of the people to pop back into his life at this moment. Everything was getting stranger by the minute. What in the world was his daughter talking about—the Russians, Canton and the Secretary of State trying to kill the Iranian foreign minister? It sounded crazy. Was somebody from his past messing with him? Was it some kind of joke? Who in the world would even know about Ali and Canton? It was almost too much for Michael to handle at the moment. Just having come out of a drug-induced coma after unsuccessfully trying to kill himself, his brain was just barely clinging to reality.

Michael closed his eyes and lowered his face into his clasped hands. He tried to make sense of everything. He had tried to kill himself, but for whatever unexplained reason, his handgun had malfunctioned and he was still alive. At the same time, he had received a telephone call from a person claiming to be the daughter of Ali Shiravi with a crazy story about the Russians, one of his former colleagues and the Secretary of State wanting to kill the Iranian foreign minister. Was everything that happened to him within the past twelve hours simply coincidental, or was there something more to it? Michael wasn't one to believe in coincidences. The laws of probability were like the laws of physics to him; they weren't flexible. Michael had a thorough understanding of how those laws functioned. Every decision he had ever made in planning a covert mission while in Special Forces or a double-agent operation in the CIA depended on his ability to factor in the odds of every possibility. Michael knew what the odds were of receiving that phone call at the exact moment that the round that had been supposed to kill him had misfired. They were astronomical. Somehow, he had to find out how and why that happened and what that meant for how his life would progress from this moment forward. The first step was to call Roxanne back to find out if she could tell him anything more that would shed some light on the astonishing message she had left him.

He looked at his watch. It was 11:35 a.m. in Seattle, so 2:35 p.m. back in Virginia. He touched the call back button on Roxanne's voicemail and placed his phone next to his ear. The phone rang once before it was answered on the other end.

"Hello?" Michael heard the voice of a young woman answer.

"Hi. Is this Roxanne?" asked Michael.

"Yes, it is. Is this Mr. Blackstone?"

"Hi, Roxanne, yeah, this is Michael."

"Oh, I'm so glad you called back, Mr. Blackstone," Roxanne said with relief in her voice.

"Well, the message you left definitely caught my attention. And by the way, it's Michael. So, what's going on?"

"I don't know, Michael. My dad called me out of the blue and just told me it was very important I pass that message on to you. He said he didn't have time to explain, but that it was a matter of life and death. He sounded really anxious. I've never heard him sound that way before. He said you were an old friend and that I had met you once at our home when we lived in Athens. I can't remember you, but then again, I was only six or seven when we lived there. Do you know what my dad's talking about?"

"I don't have a clue, Roxanne. I haven't spoken to your dad for over ten years now. Where is he? What's he doing?" Michael asked her.

"He works for the State Department as an interpreter. He's in Istanbul right now with the Secretary of State. There's some kind of meeting going on with the Iranians, and he's the Secretary's interpreter. He's been there for a few days now. I think he's supposed to be there until next week sometime," Roxanne informed him.

Michael's gut reaction was one of concern. Learning that Ali was with the Secretary of State and had contacted his daughter with such a shocking story set off the alarm bells for Michael. He vaguely remembered reading in the news that the Secretary of State was involved in negotiations with the Iranians over their missile and nuclear program, but he hadn't followed things closely enough to know any of the details. It had been over a decade since Michael had seen Ali, but he knew him well enough to know that he would never have made such an outrageous allegation unless there was something behind it. From the time he had spent working with Ali, he knew him to be a dependable and levelheaded individual. He had come to Michael's attention shortly after arriving in Athens from Langley. From when Michael first met Ali, he'd realized what a valuable asset Ali had the potential to become. That was the reason Michael had recruited him and spent a year training him. Michael knew the kind of person Ali was, better than just about anyone else other than perhaps Ali's own family. He had more trust in Ali than he did in many of his fellow officers in the CIA.

The fact that Ali mentioned Canton made Michael feel very uneasy. That was a name that, even after ten years, still brought out a strong visceral reaction of mistrust in him. Michael had heard Canton was still with the Agency and had advanced up the ranks. How was he connected to this? Michael knew he had to look into this and find out what was going on. He also knew he had to be careful, especially if Canton was involved. Even after all these years, he considered Ali a friend and someone who he still felt a sense of responsibility to look after. He grabbed the remote control off the coffee table and turned on the TV. He tuned it to CNN International in the hopes of catching a report on what was going in the world of international affairs. What he saw on the screen in front of him made his eyes open wide. He increased the volume to hear what the reporter was saying.

"Michael, are you still there?" His attention was drawn back to Roxanne, who was still on the other end.

"Oh, sorry, Roxanne. My mind was off racing from one thought to another, trying to make sense of what your father said. Where are you at right now?" Michael asked her, shifting his attention back to the CNN correspondent.

"I'm at my dad's condo in Alexandria. I came here to find your number. I go to school in Boston. I took the train down."

Michael paused while he listened to the reporter. "The Turkish authorities are neither confirming nor denying that the Iranian foreign minister has been killed. But as you can see behind me in the distance, the Turkish police and military have completely cordoned off the area surrounding the Four Seasons Hotel here in Istanbul, where the negotiations between Iran and the United States were taking place. Back to you, New York…" Michael's eyes widened as he listened to the CNN correspondent finish his report.

"Hello?" Michael heard Roxanne again.

"Yeah, I'm still here, Roxanne, sorry. Does anyone else know where you are at right now?"

"No, I'd just finished with class Friday afternoon when I got the call from my dad. I went back to my dorm and grabbed a few things and headed for the train station."

"Listen, Roxanne, I'm not exactly sure how your dad is involved in all this, but he wouldn't have reached out to me unless he had no other choice. I'm going to try to help him, but I'm going to need you to stay put at his place until I can get out there. Don't go outside, don't answer the door and don't make or answer any calls except from me. If your father has a house phone and it rings, check if you can see the number that's calling and jot it down. I'm going to check on airline tickets and catch a flight out there as soon as possible. Okay?"

"Sure, Michael, whatever you want me to do," Roxanne answered.

"What's your dad's address?"

"Um, 702 Prince Street in Old Town."

"Is there any food there for you?" he asked, hoping she wouldn't be tempted to order takeout.

"I'll find something. Don't worry, I'm not going to order Domino's, if that's what you're thinking."

Her response reassured him. She at least sounded like she could exercise some good judgment considering how worried she must have felt about her father. "Okay, Roxanne, as soon as I make my travel arrangements, I'll call you and let you know when I'm going to be there. Are you going to be all right on your own until I get there?"

"Yeah, I'll be fine. I may have been in grade school the last time you saw me, but I'm twenty-two now and a senior in college. I'm sure I can manage on my own in my father's condo without getting myself into trouble. I'll just stay put on the couch and watch a few seasons of something on Netflix until you get here," Roxanne answered him mischievously.

"Okay, bye, see you soon."

She sounds like she has a bit of spunk in her, Michael thought. He tried to think back to what he remembered about Roxanne when he'd visited Ali at his home in Athens twelve years ago. He vaguely recalled a little girl asking him quite a few questions and talking a lot about herself. *She probably had that spunk in her from back then*, he thought.

Michael turned his attention back to the TV. There was another CNN correspondent reporting from the State Department in Washington, D.C. "The State Department has confirmed that Secretary Payton was at the Four Seasons at the time of the alleged attack on the Iranian foreign minister, but was unharmed. There have been some fatalities, but none were US personnel. A State Department security officer was injured during the attack, but it is not considered life-threatening and he is expected to make a full recovery. One State Department personnel is unaccounted for. However, the State Department cannot provide any additional details at this time. We will continue to bring you updates on this breaking story..." The reporter's voice drifted off as he lowered the TV volume on the remote.

Michael stood up quickly and started towards the hallway, almost losing his balance but catching himself by grabbing the end of the couch. He paused while adjusting to his sudden lightheadedness. The excitement from his conversation with Roxanne and the revelations on the news had jump-started his brain into high gear, but his body was still working off the effects of last night's smörgåsbord of drugs. He slowly walked back to his office and retrieved his laptop, bringing it back to the living room and setting it down on the coffee table. He opened up the browser and Googled "airline tickets, Washington D.C." Clicking on the travel website at the top of the list, he searched for all available flights from Seattle to any of the three D.C. area airports. He found a nonstop Alaska Airlines flight from Sea-Tac to Reagan National that departed at 11:05 p.m. that evening and arrived 7:40 a.m. the next morning East Coast time. That was perfect, he thought as he selected it. It would give him the rest of the day to get ready for his trip and recover from the effects of last night, and he'd get into D.C. first thing in the morning. The next screen asked him to select his return date. He paused to think. How long would he need? What was he going to do? The longer he spent thinking about it, the more he realized that he had no idea what he was expecting to accomplish by going out there. Roxanne had told him pretty much everything she knew, so what more was he expecting to learn by heading out there and meeting her in person? He thought he could search Ali's home to see if he could uncover any clues as to what Ali might have been involved in but doubted he would find anything. He knew only Ali had any answers. Michael hoped Ali was okay, but he remembered the CNN reporter's words about one State Department personnel being unaccounted for. He told himself not to jump to any conclusions without knowing the facts, but he had a bad feeling it was Ali who was missing. He selected a return date a week later. That should give him enough time to find out what was going on, he hoped as he completed his purchase.

Michael's attention was caught by the image of Secretary of State Payton on the TV. He turned up the volume and listened to what Payton was saying in front of a barrage of cameras from the international press. "It is with great sadness that I have to announce the death of Foreign Minister Mohammedi. The foreign minister, along with one of his security personnel and several Turkish military, was killed last night during an attack that took place at the Four Seasons Hotel here in Istanbul, the venue of the negotiations between the United States and Iran. I want to extend my condolences to the Iranian and the Turkish people, as well as the families of the deceased for their loss in this terrible tragedy. Fortunately, no US personnel were killed or seriously injured. One State Department employee is unaccounted for, and we are trying to determine his status and whether it is related to this attack. No group has claimed responsibility for the attack, but it is clearly evident that whoever was responsible carried it out with a high degree of precision and expertise.

The United States has pledged its assistance and cooperation to the Turkish government as well as the Iranian government in helping them uncover those behind this attack. Whatever the attackers thought to accomplish by disrupting these negotiations, they should know that they will not deter our efforts to reach an agreement that will ensure no countries in the Middle East should feel threatened by their neighbor. Over the next few days, I will be meeting with leaders from countries that are stakeholders in the peace process for the Middle East. The international community will not be shaken or intimidated by the barbaric actions of terrorists attempting to impose their distorted beliefs on the civilized world. Thank you, that is all I have for now." The CNN commentator in Istanbul added that Secretary Payton was conferring with President Steele regarding the direction the United States will pursue should Iran withdraw from negotiations. "With the apparent assassination of the Iranian foreign minister, it is unclear how the Iranian government will respond and how it will affect further negotiations and the current nuclear agreement. Although there are yet many unanswered questions, the one thing that is clear is that, just when you think one small step that will bring some semblance of stability to the Middle East is achieved, something else always seems to come out of nowhere and redirect everything," the commentator finished.

The CNN anchor switched to Iran's Supreme Leader Mahdavi on Iranian television. An interpreter translated to English as he spoke, "We will not allow such a cowardly act to go unpunished. The Zionist infidels with the support of the Great Satan continue to act aggressively and at will against all their neighbors. Only the Zionists would act so insolently, with such a barbaric act as assassinating a senior member of a sovereign government. They will suffer the consequences of their actions."

The coverage turned to Ehud Akerman, the prime minister of Israel, responding to Iran's accusations. Prime Minister Akerman was making his remarks in English, clearly intending his audience to be the international community more so than the Israeli populace. "Iran has leveled this preposterous accusation against Israel, claiming that it was somehow involved in the assassination of their foreign minister. First, let me unequivocally state that Israel does not assassinate leaders of sovereign nations, even if they are our enemies. Second, there would be no reason for Israel to jeopardize the nuclear agreement at this stage. We have stated all along that we believe this agreement will not prevent Iran from pursuing nuclear weapons, but we respect our allies' efforts to halt Iran's nuclear weapons program regardless how misguided they may be. We would not undermine them in such an underhanded way. The only ones who would clearly benefit if the nuclear agreement was derailed are the hardliners in the Iranian government. Rather than making unfounded allegations against Israel, the Iranian leadership should look internally to determine who has the most to gain by this outrageous act. Finally, I want to make it clear that Israel will not tolerate any attack or attempt to compromise its security without responding decisively and overwhelmingly," Akerman concluded with a clear warning to Iranian leadership.

The CNN anchor next introduced JalAl Rezi, PhD, from the Center of Middle East Policy of the Brookings Institution, one of America's oldest foreign policy think tanks. "Dr. Rezi, what are your thoughts on what has transpired over the past twenty-four hours with the apparent assassination of the Iranian foreign minister and how it will impact not only the nuclear agreement, but the entire Middle East?" asked the CNN anchor.

"This will have far-reaching implications beyond the nuclear agreement. Although it is still too early to conclude the full impact it will have, under the current circumstances, it seems unlikely that the Iranian government will agree to cease the development of its ballistic missile program. President Rostami had faced significant opposition from hardliners regarding the nuclear deal. With the assassination of his foreign minister, who was also one of his closest allies, it will be very difficult if not impossible for Rostami to continue wielding influence over the hardline elements within the Iranian leadership and convince them they should not respond rashly and scuttle the nuclear agreement. If anything, the hardliners will increase their influence, particularly with Supreme Leader Mahdavi, which could mean the end of Rostami's efforts in moving Iran towards normalizing relations with the West. Although he is the Supreme Leader, Mahdavi has to be cautious about the perception to hardliners such as Mohammad Bardari, the commander of the IRGC, that he has allowed too much compromise in dealing with the West. Even though the IRGC falls under the direct control of the Supreme Leader, it still is a powerful element within the Iranian society that enjoys a significant amount of autonomy from the control of any administration. The Supreme Leader's authority is to a great extent dependent upon support from the conservative power blocs within Iranian society, of which the IRGC is definitely one of the biggest players. As to the question of who may have been responsible for the assassination of Foreign Minister Mohammedi, I would have to agree with the comments of Prime Minister Akerman, that certain elements within the Iranian leadership would have the most to gain from such an act. If it was in fact the IRGC that was responsible for the assassination, the important question that needs to be answered is whether the Supreme Leader gave his tacit approval beforehand to go forward with it, or whether he learned about it after the fact and finds himself in the difficult position now of having to provide his de facto approval, or else risk the perception that he does not have firm control over the IRGC. Neither situation is good, but the second is the worse of the two. The only thing that has kept the IRGC in check is the effect of the economic sanctions against Iran.

They have had a crippling effect on the economy, which has to a certain extent limited the IRGC's influence. However, for as much difficulty and pain as the sanctions have brought on to the average Iranian, the IRGC's main concern is maintaining its power base. The success of the nuclear agreement is something the IRGC realized was going to shift the power balance to President Rostami and more progressive elements in Iran, at their expense. This is something they cannot allow. As far as the Middle East as a whole is concerned, this could have a catastrophic effect depending on how all the parties involved respond from here forward. Iran pulling out of the nuclear agreement may leave Israel in a position where it feels it has no other choice but to take military action against Iran's nuclear and missile program. As if it is not enough that Syria has become a proxy war between Iran, Saudi Arabia, Turkey, Russia and the United States, threatening the stability of the entire region, military action by Israel could be the spark that ignites the powder keg and brings the whole region into an all-out war," Professor Rezi finished.

"That sounds very worrying for not just the situation in the Middle East, but the entire globe. Let's hope cooler heads prevail. Thank you, Dr. Rezi, for that insightful analysis. And now let's turn to something closer to home. Our own Lisa Reynolds has been following up on the latest trend of facial tattooing. More and more Americans are expressing their identity by tattooing the animal they identify with onto their face. Lisa is with Charisma Chambers, the owner of Mystic Nymph Tattoo in Los Angeles..." Michael lowered the volume on the TV as he contemplated what he'd just learned.

He looked at the clock on the wall. It was 12:15 p.m. He had the remainder of the day left to get ready before his flight that evening. That left him enough time to recover and let the remaining effects of the drugs and alcohol clear out of his system. He sat on his couch, looking out across the Puget Sound on what was shaping up to be a mild spring day. His mind kept taking him back to Ali's message. Judging from the time Roxanne had called him from her father's house after having traveled from Boston, Ali must have called her sometime around when the attack had actually taken place. From what had been reported on the news, the attack took place during the early-morning hours, which would have been eighteen to twenty hours ago. The question was whether Ali had called prior to the attack, in an attempt to relay a warning, or afterwards, perhaps after having witnessed the attack.

Michael replayed Roxanne's message on his voicemail and verified what he thought she had said: "...are going to try to kill..." But were those Ali's exact words or what Roxanne thought she'd heard her father say? It really didn't matter. Whatever the case was, Ali had gotten himself into a dangerous situation, especially if he was the missing State Department employee.

Michael wondered if he was getting himself into something he had no business being involved in. After all, he no longer worked for the government, and it had been ten years since he had last seen Ali. He had no responsibility for what might have happened to Ali. Ali was a State Department employee now, and whatever he might have been involved in would be investigated by the State Department as well as the CIA and a host of other agencies within the US government's intelligence and national security community. What happened would eventually come to light. At least, that's what Michael tried to convince himself. The fact that Ali had mentioned Jonathan Canton being involved, however, was what kept forcing Michael back to the decision that he had no choice but to follow up on what happened, as far as was reasonably possible. It went against his better judgment, but he felt he had a sense of responsibility to try to help Ali, even after all this time.

Michael pondered what connection Canton still could have had with Ali after Athens. Was it just coincidental that the two were both involved in this situation? Michael knew the odds of that were slim. As far as he knew from occasional conversations with the few former CIA friends that he still kept in touch with, Canton had transferred back to D.C. after Athens and had been there ever since. He'd had a few liaison assignments to other agencies and had also served as the DCI's special assistant, which was essentially a high-profile errand boy position, but one which nonetheless put its occupant in close proximity to one of the most powerful persons in the US intelligence community. Even though Canton had never developed any significant operations or held a leadership position, he had somehow managed to get appointed to a deputy director position at Langley, something highly unusual for one who had never been a chief of station. A chief of station was the senior-most overseas CIA position located in US embassies throughout the world. The chief of station had his own independent fiefdom, independent of the US ambassador's oversight and control. Although the chief of station was required to keep the ambassador advised of any intelligence issues that might affect his duties as the President's representative in the host country, his chain of command was back to DCI at Langley. Michael's concern about Canton wasn't his competence. On the contrary, Michael considered Canton very cunning and calculating when it came to pursuing his objectives, which usually involved his self-interests. He wouldn't think twice about gaining someone's trust and then betraying them if it could benefit him. Michael knew Canton couldn't be trusted, especially after what he had done in Athens, even if Michael had no proof.

More than ten years later, it was still hard at times for Michael to think about Athens. He had tried to put it all behind him and get on with his life, attempting to compartmentalize it as a distant memory from a previous chapter in his life. Sometimes it seemed like none of it had actually taken place, as if he hadn't lived those events but rather seen them acted by a character in a movie. The rawness of emotions he occasionally still experienced, however, was a painful reminder of just how real and unfinished everything still felt after all these years.

Michael's thought took him back to when he had arrived in Athens without Karen and Sam during the summer of 2004. He'd immediately hit it off with his boss, Harry Barso, the chief of station. Barso was seventeen years older than Michael. He had an easygoing style but expected his case officers to aggressively recruit foreign intelligence assets and come up with operations that produced results. Working for an operationally minded boss was the type of environment Michael thrived in. In both the Army and the CIA, he had experienced the type of bosses whose entire focus was self-promotion. The easiest way to move up the ladder was to avoid doing anything that could go wrong and put one in the spotlight. It didn't matter if anything was ever accomplished; as long as nothing major went wrong during one's watch, one could usually count on moving up the ladder with just the passage of time. That was just the nature of bureaucracies, which both the CIA and the military were, however unique was their purpose. This often led many in leadership positions to be risk-averse. Michael couldn't understand that way of thinking. Everything the military and the CIA did involved a certain amount of risk. The challenge was knowing how to assess the risk accurately and mitigate as much of it as possible. Fortunately for Michael, Barso was the kind of boss who had climbed the ladder because of his professional accomplishments. Athens was his second chief of station posting. He was well respected, with a solid reputation, and was considered likely to eventually move up to senior leadership back at CIA headquarters. Single and divorced three times, Barso spent most of his time working, often seven days a week. He had high expectations of his people, but he was also very personable and would often share a beer with some of the other single or unaccompanied Athens Station personnel. Michael had spent many a Saturday night closing down a local neighborhood taverna with Barso.

After arriving in Athens and spending his first few months getting familiar with the city and the station's operational tempo, Michael started working towards putting together his own operation to pursue one of the intelligence collection requirements of Athens Station. As part of the CIA's mission to support decision makers in the US government, the CIA had a long list of specific intelligence requirements throughout the world. Some of the intelligence sought was what foreign leaders were thinking and planning. Other intelligence requirements involved the military capabilities of other countries. Yet other intelligence was focused on terrorist groups and threats against the United States and its allies. Then there was the intelligence concerning the activities of other foreign intelligence services against the United States. This was also known as counterintelligence. The collection requirement that caught Michael's attention was concerning Iranian intelligence activity in Greece and the rest of Europe. The MOIS, Iran's foreign intelligence service, was the successor to SAVAK, which under the Shah brutally suppressed any political dissent by torturing political prisoners at the infamous Evin Prison. Under the current Islamic government, the IRGC was responsible for taking care of political dissent and anything else that threatened the Islamic government, leaving the MOIS to the more traditional role of intelligence gathering. A new MOIS chief had recently come to Athens, and Michael saw this as a perfect opportunity to determine if it would be possible to target him, with the ultimate goal of someday turning him into a spy for the US. After all, that was the main purpose of the CIA.

A few months before Michael's arrival in Athens, Farzan Karbashi had shown up as the MOIS chief. Michael had looked through Karbashi's file in the intelligence database the CIA kept of all known foreign intelligence officers and discovered that Karbashi had attended Oxford University from 1976 through 1977, working on a postgraduate degree in international law—until his father, a well-respected cleric from the city of Tabriz, had run afoul of the Shah for criticizing some of his practices. As a result, Karbashi was forced to return to Iran and attend Tehran University. He was studying to become a lawyer when the Iranian Revolution took place in 1979. His father was involved in the revolution, supporting the Ayatollah Khomeini. His family's newfound status and connections with the Islamic leadership opened the door for Karbashi to become one of the early recruits to MOIS after he finished his studies. From early in his career, he was well respected for his intelligence and abilities and rapidly rose up through the ranks of the MOIS. His file mentioned that he was a devout Muslim but had several setbacks in his career due to clashes with conservative hardliners within the MOIS. He was considered to be more of a pragmatist. After the moderate Mohammad Khatami had been elected president of Iran in 1997 and had appointed a more pragmatic MOIS director, Karbashi's career surged ahead again.

What had really caught Michael's attention was that Karbashi had run a successful honey trap operation against the Israeli Defense Force Liaison Officer to NATO headquarters in Brussels in his previous overseas posting. Karbashi had co-opted a young and attractive Belgian national of Iranian descent on her mother's side, who worked at the Israeli embassy's consular section as a clerk. The married Israeli Air Force colonel, on an eighteen-month unaccompanied tour to NATO HQ, had made the tragic error of becoming involved in an extramarital affair with the attractive twenty-six-year-old clerk. After months of regularly spending nights at her apartment so as not to attract any unwanted attention at his residence, the Israeli colonel found himself receiving an envelope with dozens of compromising naked photos of the two of them in various lovemaking positions and a blackmail note with a relatively trivial demand of one thousand euro, warning that the photos would otherwise be sent to the Israeli ambassador. He had confronted his young mistress, who had burst into tears, claiming she had been coerced by her ex-boyfriend, a low-level drug dealer, to let her plant the hidden camera in her bedroom. Believing her story and desperate to protect his reputation and future career as a general officer in the Israeli Air Force, he had foolishly agreed to meet with the young Iranian MOIS officer posing as her ex-boyfriend to exchange the money for an envelope with the remaining photos and a memory card. The entire exchange of course photographed by Karbashi. In addition to the compromising images on the memory card, a hidden executable program had infected the colonel's personal laptop when he inserted it. It had given Karbashi access to the colonel's emails, schedules and other sensitive information concerning IDF matters that should not have been on the colonel's personal computer. A few months later, the colonel had received another envelope with copies of his emails and other sensitive data, along with photographs of him exchanging money and an envelope with a young MOIS officer. Ensnared in the web, the Israeli colonel had provided Karbashi with a steady supply of Israeli Air Force capabilities for a few months, until the colonel had decided to take his life—but not before leaving a note confessing his failures to his wife and country. Michael was surprised not only by Karbashi's ingenuity and professionalism but also that, as a Muslim, he would resort to an intelligence operation using a female, sex and blackmail, methods that were traditionally within the repertoire of the Russian SVR.

After that success, Karbashi had been transferred to Athens in 2003. Athens was considered a highly sought-after post for the MOIS because it was one of the main MOIS stations in eastern Europe. Greece's membership in the EU, along with its historical connections to the East going back thousands of years to the time of the Persian Empire and Alexander the Great, made it Iran's gateway to the rest of Europe. If Michael could somehow find a way to target Karbashi with the goal of co-opting him to either knowingly or unknowingly provide information about MOIS operations and other important intelligence, it would be a CIA officer's dream recruitment. A successful recruitment such as that, he would be able to write his own ticket for the direction of his career, perhaps even as a chief of station in one of the smaller embassies after he was done in Athens.

Before he started planning out the future of his career, he reminded himself that he needed some way to get to Karbashi. The Iranians were a hard target for Western intelligence agencies. Unlike the Soviets, which the CIA was able to recruit for ideological reasons during the Cold War, most Iranians who worked for the Islamic government had a deep mistrust for anything having to do with the United States as a result of its support of the Shah, who had oppressed his own people for decades. Many Iranians were also devout Shia Muslims with a disdain for what they considered corrupt Western ideals, making it all the more difficult for the CIA to recruit Iranians to spy, especially anyone working for their intelligence agency. It would be a real chess match going up against a seasoned professional like Karbashi.

Michael knew he had to find a way to get to him before he had any chance of being able to co-opt him. He would have to learn everything he could about Karbashi's routine. He had to find where he was most susceptible, where he shopped, where he socialized, where he did everything outside his workplace. In order to do that, Michael would need a surveillance operation to track Karbashi's movements to and from the Iranian embassy. That required manpower, which always came at a premium when it involved pulling personnel off other operations and duties. It would be a challenge selling a preoperational surveillance op to his new boss when he didn't even have any idea yet what kind of operation he was going to run against Karbashi. But Michael also knew that sometimes one had to go trolling in uncharted waters when it came to going after bigger fish. He hoped his boss wouldn't want to play it safe and stick to more a conventional approach.

Michael remembered pitching his surveillance request to Barso a few months after he had arrived in Athens. Leaning back in his chair with one shoe up on the edge of his desk, Barso looked over Michael's operational plan, uttering occasional grunts as he read through it. With his reading glasses slopped down to the edge of his nose, Barso looked over his desk at Michael on occasion to ask him a question about some detail. Finally, pulling off his reading glasses, Barso looked directly at Michael and said, "That's a significant amount of manpower for surveillance coverage when you don't even have a viable operation yet."

"I know, Harry. But if you consider the potential intelligence value of someone like Karbashi, isn't the investment in manpower worth it to at least find out if there's any opportunities of going after him?" Michael addressed his boss by his first name, as was customary in the CIA's culture of informality combined with secrecy.

"Even if you were able to find a vulnerability in his routine, you'd still have to come up with a way of making contact with him. Do you even have any assets to do that with?" Barso asked.

"No, I don't. But until I can determine what vulnerabilities he has, it's useless for me to try to speculate how to target him. I'm not too concerned about an asset just yet, as I am about figuring out if it's even feasible to go after this guy. It's one of those questions of which came first, the chicken or the egg?" Michael attempted to convince his boss.

Barso sat behind his desk with his hand on his chin, thinking as he stared past Michael. Michael looked at his boss, waiting for him to ask another question. Michael began to wonder if he should say something when Barso broke the silence and said, "I like your attitude. You're not afraid to push the envelope and go after the hard targets. They're not easy, but if you can recruit one, they can be a treasure trove of intelligence. Those don't happen often. Most intelligence officers go through their entire careers without running a major asset like that. You think you're up for the challenge?"

"If you're asking whether I'm confident I can manage an op like this, yeah, I am. I've always been at my best when I'm challenged. If there's a way to go after this guy, I'll figure it out and put together a good op. I guess it comes down to whether you have confidence in me that I can run something like this," Michael said, trying to reassure his boss without coming off sounding cocky.

"From what I've read in your file and heard from people who know you, you've never shied away from being in the middle of all the action. I've been around this agency long enough to know the difference between a good bullshitter and someone who actually walks the walk. You have a pretty good reputation. You've used your wits and kept pretty cool in some pretty sticky situations. I think you can handle something like this. But just remember, the bigger the prize, the bigger the fallout if something goes wrong. If you manage to make inroads with Karbashi, the deeper it goes and the more complicated things get. It's your operation, but I want regular updates on what's going on, especially if and when you get to the point that you're ready to pitch him. For now, you can rent an apartment for surveillance of the Iranian embassy for three months, not six, and you can have two personnel, not four. If you can't figure out Karbashi's routine and a way to him by then, then you're wasting your time. I'm going to give you Schmitty from tech and Canton. He's been here a year now and still hasn't gotten anything up and running. May as well make him useful. Set the surveillance schedule and use them as you see fit, but try to be considerate. Canton's single, but Schmitty's married and has a couple of young kids. You can budget two rentals rather than using our surveillance vehicles, just switch out the plates with cover plates. And one final thing, don't get caught by the Greeks. If we're going to do this, it's going to be a unilateral op without letting the Greeks in on it. It would be embarrassing enough getting rolled up by the Greek police, but I don't want to spoil my relationship with Papadopoulos over at EYP," Barso warned, referring to the director of Greece's national intelligence service.

That was what Michael wanted to hear. While he did his best to keep his composure in front of his boss, inside, he was silently doing his end zone celebration spike. "Thanks, Harry, you won't regret it. Are you going to let Schmitty and Canton know they're assigned to the surveillance?" Michael asked.

"Yeah, I will. Now get out of here, and let me get back to whatever I was wasting my time with before I change my mind," Barso dismissed Michael.

Michael didn't know Canton very well. In the three months since Michael had arrived in Athens, he hadn't spoken much to him. During social occasions, when Michael attempted to engage him in conversation, Canton came off somewhat snooty. Michael couldn't tell if it was insecurity on the part of Canton or he was just a jerk. The CIA had its share of them, just like any other organization. Canton was four years Michael's senior at the CIA. From what Michael knew about him, his first posting overseas had been at the US embassy in Israel. He had spent six years back at Langley, where he'd held a variety of desk officer jobs and staff positions. Michael and Canton had overlapped at Langley for one year before Canton transferred to Athens. Other than running into each other in the hallways at Langley, they had never spoken. Michael wondered why, as a junior CIA officer, Canton had spent such a long time at headquarters after his first overseas posting. As far as Michael was concerned, being assigned overseas was what being a CIA officer was all about. Operations were run out in the field in foreign countries, not back at headquarters in Virginia. Being stuck at Langley was something that was to be avoided as much as possible, at least early on in one's career.

Michael thought about Harry's comment about making Canton useful since he wasn't running any of his own operations. Michael hoped he could rely on Canton. He wasn't concerned about Schmitty. Techies, as technical services officers were referred to, were for operational support. Whether it was surreptitiously installing cameras and listening devices or hacking into computers, surveillance was just another one of the many things they did as part of their duties supporting the field. A case officer, on the other hand, being assigned to support someone else's operation usually meant they didn't have any of their own initiatives they were working on. Depending on the type of person Canton was, Michael knew that as his senior, being assigned to assist on his operation might rub him the wrong way. Michael hoped that wouldn't be the case, especially since Canton had already been frosty towards him.

Michael remembered how their first conversation went later that day. Canton strolled into Michael's office and remarked sarcastically, "Looks like I'm going to be stuck doing grunt work for you for the next three months."

Michael tried to sound considerate in his reply. "Hi, Jonathan. We'll all be doing some grunt work, you, me and Schmitty. I hope it's not going to interrupt what you've been working on too much."

"I've been working on a few things that have the potential to turn into something pretty heavy, but apparently Harry thinks your fishing expedition is more important. I told him I would be willing to help you out temporarily," Canton sneered as if he was being inconvenienced.

"Sorry your stuff got put on hold. I just asked Harry for some bodies. He made the call on who he was going to give me," Michael answered nonchalantly. It was obvious Canton wasn't happy about having to help him.

"I hope you'll be putting in the hours chasing this guy around also and weren't expecting Schmitty and me to do all your work for you," Canton came back abrasively.

"I'm going to be right there with you guys. It'll actually require all three of us. One on static and two mobile," Michael attempted to mollify him.

"Well, I think you're wasting your time with the Iranian. You really think you're going to find a way into this guy? And even if you do, how do you expect to pitch a senior MOIS guy? What could possibly motivate him to spy for us?" Canton said mockingly.

"Guess we'll just have to wait and see how things turn out. It's not going to happen if no one tries," Michael responded, trying not to let his annoyance at Canton's obvious insult show.

"Yeah, whatever, just make sure you give me plenty of notice on the schedule. I'm not going to be at your beck and call whenever you need me."

"Sure, I'll make sure you and Schmitty know a week ahead of time what the schedule will be. But it will pretty much be seven days a week at first until we can pick up on what Karbashi's routine is like. We'll get started as soon as I find an apartment for rent across the Iranian embassy to set up our static surveillance post. That's it for now," Michael told him, meeting his stare until Canton finally broke contact and walked out of Michael's office.

***

Michael glanced at the clock on his living room wall as his attention returned back to the trip he would be going on in a few hours. He had no idea if he was making the right decision or even if he could be of any help to Ali, but the more he thought about Canton, the more he was certain he had no other choice than to stick with his gut instinct. If nothing else, he would see if he could get together with Harry Barso while he was in the D.C. area. Michael hadn't seen him since

Athens but had kept in periodic contact with him over the years, calling during the holidays to wish him a merry Christmas. Harry had decided to retire from the Agency a few years after his tour as the Athens chief of station had ended. Although the findings of the internal CIA investigation had cleared Harry of any blame, the fallout from it having happened on his watch had pretty much ended any real chance of his career advancing. Harry had transferred back to Langley a year after the incident and was assigned to the National Security Agency as the CIA liaison. It was technically a senior management position, but it was no secret that it was also a position that didn't lead to the higher echelons of leadership within the Agency. Much like a commanding officer of a naval vessel getting a follow-on assignment as the commanding officer of a naval base, it pretty much ended any hopes of getting the highly sought-after star of a flag officer. In the seniority structure of the CIA, being a chief of station was similar to a medieval lord ruling over his own little fiefdom, but CIA headquarters was like the king's court, where the real power resided. After a couple of years, Harry had retired from the Agency and gone to work as a consultant for a defense contractor. Michael felt bad that Harry's future at the Agency had suffered because of what happened in Athens, especially after how much Harry had fought on his behalf when Langley wanted to crucify him. He had paid the price for staying in Michael's corner and supporting him. Not many bosses would have stuck up for one of their people under similar circumstances. Michael had a great deal of respect for him. He hoped they could get together. He was looking forward to seeing him after so many years, but he also wanted to get his take on the situation with Ali. There was no one else he could trust, especially with Canton being involved.

Chapter 5

Slivers of light shone through the small round holes on either side. The muffled sound of a car engine was the next thing that registered with him. Ali sensed the vibration and jostling of being in a vehicle, but he felt disoriented, the way one does when coming out of anesthesia following surgery. He tried to make sense of where he was. His face felt strange. He tried to open his mouth but couldn't. Something held it shut. He detected a hint of a slightly sweet and putrid odor as he took in air through his nostrils. Trying to focus his eyes, he could make out something blocking his vision a few inches from his face. It finally occurred to him that he was lying on his back in a tight space. He felt beads of sweat running down his face. Wherever he was, it was uncomfortably hot. He reached to wipe his forehead but realized his wrists were bound behind his back. He could feel his hands, but something seemed odd, as if his hands had partially fallen asleep. It was a strange sensation that added to Ali's confusion. Confusion turned to alarm as it hit him his hands weren't touching each other, but rather someone else's. He frantically began feeling around for whatever he could grasp. Alarm turned to panic when he realized he was lying on top of someone. He tried moving his legs but discovered they were bound at the ankles. He began thrashing about wildly, lurching forward and hitting his forehead against a solid surface. The back of his head came back down, smacking the face of the person beneath him. He tried to scream but couldn't get anything out of his mouth. He started breathing furiously through his nose. He began feeling faint. He knew he would pass out if he didn't get his breathing under control. With everything he could muster, he tried slowing his breathing, pausing in between each breath and trying to hold still and determine if the person under him was moving. He couldn't feel any movement or detect any sign of breathing. Ali tried suppressing the thought that began seeping into his mind, but his worst fear finally overcame him. That sweet putrid odor was the beginning stages of human decomposition. He was trapped inside a crate with a corpse.

Ali lay there, trying to make sense of how he had gotten into his present situation. The last thing he remembered was being in the Iranian consulate. He remembered being questioned. He remembered being taken down to the basement by the man and being forced at gunpoint into a room. From there on, everything was blank. Ali realized despite his dire situation, he had to try to keep his wits about him. Being trapped in a casket with a corpse would have been bad enough under any other circumstances, but the thought of what lay ahead for him was a more pressing concern. They obviously wanted to keep him alive—what other reason for the holes drilled in the wooden crate he was trapped in? Corpses didn't need to breathe. He turned his head, trying to see through the holes, but could not make out anything through the small openings. He wondered how long he had been unconscious. He had no concept of how much time had passed since he was at the consulate, but guessed it was the next day from the bright light coming in from the outside. The back of his head ached, and he had a splitting headache. The more he thought about it, the more he realized he had probably been knocked out by the man at the consulate. He guessed it was possible that he had also been drugged.

After what seemed like an unbearably long time, the vehicle finally came to a stop. Ali could barely make out voices talking in what sounded like Turkish. There was silence for several minutes other than the idling of the engine, then some more talking, and then the vehicle began moving again. Eventually a new sound came into range. It grew louder until it overwhelmed the sound of the vehicle's engine. Ali recognized it immediately as the unmistakable sound of jet engines. The vehicle jolted to a stop. A moment later, he felt the crate being lifted and jostled about. He was carried for a few feet, then set down on an inclined surface. The container began moving upwards. The crate was on a conveyor belt, being loaded onto the aircraft. A sick feeling came over Ali at the realization that he was leaving Turkey. There was only one place he could be going—Iran. He agonized over the thought of being taken to Iran, but what had he expected? That they would keep him at Iranian consulate? That they would just believe his story and release him? It made sense they would want to get him out of Turkey and take him to Iran. It wasn't so much that he was being taken to Iran but more the manner in which it was happening that made it difficult to come to terms with. Was this how they treated anyone who voluntarily came to them and provided very important information? It was a far different experience than his last dealings with them as the Secretary's interpreter.

Ali's container was lifted, carried a short distance, then put down. He heard another heavy object being set down beside him. A horrible thought entered his mind. If he had been loaded into the cargo bay of the aircraft, he would freeze to death once the aircraft had taken off and climbed to the subzero temperatures of its flight altitude. He had been sweating profusely. The discomfort of being soaked in his own perspiration along with the stench of the corpse brought on a wave of nausea. He felt he was going to vomit. That was the last thing he needed right now to add to his misery. His body ached from being confined in the tight space. The thought of freezing to death didn't seem that terrible in some ways, especially considering what might lie ahead for him instead. He felt like such a fool for naïvely believing the Iranians would listen to him. Despite realizing those involved in the assassination would never have allowed him to remain alive, he regretted his decision. He resigned himself to the fact that he had become a dead man the moment he had learned about the assassination plot. He thought about Roxanne. The idea of her never knowing what had happened to him tore at him. He wished he had said more to her when they had last spoken on the phone. He wished he had told her how much he loved her, how precious she was to him.

Ali heard the thud of the aircraft door being shut. There was silence other than the sound of the aircraft's engines idling in the background. He knew it would be just a matter of minutes now before the aircraft started taxiing for takeoff, and shortly afterwards the slow process of freezing to death would begin. He thought about what death by hypothermia would be like. He imagined that after he moved beyond the uncontrollable shivering, he would eventually just start feeling disoriented and slowly drift off to sleep, then after that, the inevitable would happen. In an odd sort of way, that peculiar thought comforted Ali somehow. Better than being tortured to death or beheaded or burned alive, as had happened to so many hapless souls for religious reasons during the Middle Ages. Strange, he thought, the peculiar ways one's mind starts rationalizing things, rating the least preferred ways of death when one knows theirs is imminent. Thinking how fortunate it would be to leave this world by freezing to death was a sign of losing grip on reality. He felt helpless not having any control over his destiny. He wanted to scream, but his lips were sealed shut. No one could hear the terror he was experiencing, but inside his mind, he was screaming his lungs out.

There was the faint sound of voices, just loud enough that Ali could hear them over the hum of the plane's engines. He couldn't make out what they were saying, but they were definitely speaking in Farsi. He felt an overwhelming sense of relief with the realization that he wasn't in the aircraft's cargo bay. He wanted to laugh. Of course, they wouldn't have loaded him into the cargo compartment to freeze to death. Why else had they drilled holes in the crate for him to be able to breathe? He realized he wasn't thinking rationally. He knew he needed to stay calm and keep his wits about him. It was the only way he was going to survive this ordeal. The engines began to spool up, and a few seconds later they began moving. Ali sensed the aircraft taxiing, rolling, then braking; a turn, a slight increase in power, then another turn and eventually they came to a full stop. They sat there a few minutes, then was the sound of the aircraft's engines coming to full power, followed by the release of the brakes, and the aircraft beginning its acceleration down the runway. He felt the nose pull up, followed by the aircraft lifting off the runway as they began their climb through Turkish airspace. He didn't know the exact distance between Istanbul and Tehran but guessed the flight would be two to three hours. It was going to be a miserable flight being crammed into such a confined space for that long. At least his traveling companion wouldn't have to suffer through any discomfort. How ironic was that, he thought. He knew by some of the bizarre thoughts he was having that everything he had been through in the past forty-eight hours was finally starting to catch up with him.

Ali felt the aircraft finally level off from its climb. As he lay there thinking about what awaited him when he reached Iran, he heard movement outside. He was startled by the sound of an object hitting the top of his casket, followed by the "tap" of metal hitting metal. He saw the end of a crowbar pry a small gap between the top and side of the crate, then again further down the lid and around the other side, until a pair of hands reached underneath and pulled it off entirely. Ali was momentarily blinded by the sudden brightness. As his eyes adjusted, he saw looking down at him the man who had interrogated him at the consulate. He reached down and grabbed Ali by the shoulders, lifting him up and over the crate and letting him come crashing down onto the hard aluminum deck of the aircraft.

Lying on his side with his wrists and ankles bound, Ali observed another casket next to the one he had just been pulled out of. The caskets were in a cargo area at the rear of the aircraft, an aging Boeing 727 from the mid-1970s. Ali wondered if he should still feel relieved his life was no longer in danger. Due to the embargo placed on Iran by the United States, the country was unable to purchase any new aircraft to replace its aging fleet of Boeings from before the Iranian Revolution. It had resorted to buying used aircraft and parts utilizing middlemen from countries willing to sell Iran their retired aircraft as they updated their own fleets. But more importantly, it wasn't able to obtain the technical support from aircraft manufacturers, which created significant reliability and safety issues. Iran had the third-largest oil reserves in the world, but its national airline trailed behind those of many third-world African nations.

The man positioned the lid back on top of the casket and tapped it shut again with a hammer. When he was finished, he turned to Ali and lifted him to a sitting position. He grabbed the end of the tape over Ali's mouth, and with a sudden jerk, ripped it off his face. Ali winced, then took a deep breath through his mouth now that he was finally able. He stared at the man, waiting to see what he would do next. Ali's eyes opened wide as he saw the man pull a knife out of his pocket, opening the blade as he made his way towards Ali. Ali instinctively tried to scoot away from the man as he approached him.

"Relax, I'm just going to cut you loose," the man said in Farsi as he grabbed Ali's legs and cut through the cord securing his ankles. He then walked around the back of Ali and did the same with the cord binding Ali's wrists. "Get up," he ordered Ali. "If you try anything foolish, I will kill you, do you understand?"

"Yes, I understand," Ali answered, shaking his head.

"Move," the man gestured to Ali, pointing forward.

"Please, sir, tell me your name," Ali asked as he stood up.

"Just call me Assad, and don't ask any more questions."

"*Mamnoon*," Ali thanked Assad, trying to establish a rapport with him.

"Get moving." Assad shoved him towards the front of the aircraft.

Ali walked towards the front of the aircraft, where there was a small seating area. Assad followed behind him. Ali was concerned about men like Assad. He guessed Assad was probably IRGC. Ali knew the kind of individuals who were in the security apparatus of the Iranian government. It attracted the most authoritarian elements within Iranian society, individuals who were staunchly opposed to any engagement with the West. They saw any attempts to loosen the strict morality and accepted standards of behavior imposed by Islamic Sharia law as attempts to undermine the Islamic Republic. They were usually not highly educated and were very suspicious of moderates within the Iranian government, particularly in the administration of President Rostami. For that matter, they were suspicious of any progressive elements within Iranian society, particularly the university-educated class who had become more and more vocal during the past two decades about their ideas of a more open society in Iran. Men like Assad wouldn't hesitate to employ cruelty to anyone they perceived possibly challenging their authority and power. As Ali approached the front of the aircraft, he saw another man sitting in one of the seats, looking back at him. Reaching the first row, Ali turned to Assad, awaiting his instructions.

"There." Assad pointed to the window seat across the aisle from the man who had been looking at him. "Naveed, if this traitor tries anything foolish, I want you to put a bullet in his head. Do you think you can do that without bringing the plane down?" Assad instructed his associate loud enough for Ali to hear.

"No, Assad, I will not discharge my weapon in the aircraft. But if he just looks at me the wrong way, I'll cut him open slowly so I can watch him bleed to death until we get to Tehran," Assad's partner responded with a menacing glare at Ali.

Ali slid across two seats and sat down next to the window. Assad sat in the aisle seat next to him, leaving the middle seat between them. Ali looked out the window at the ground below, thinking how two days ago, everything in his life was normal. He'd had a good job with the State Department, a comfortable life with a nice condominium in Alexandria, a daughter who adored him and was doing well in college, not a worry in the world. Then suddenly, his life had been yanked out from under him. He wondered if he would ever see Roxanne again.

He told himself to try to stay positive and not let negative thoughts overwhelm him. He was still alive, and that was a good sign. The Iranian consulate had to have briefed someone of importance back in Tehran about his story. Why else would they have gone to such trouble to smuggle him out of Istanbul? He would have a chance to convince someone with more intelligence than Assad that he was telling the truth. But then what? Even if they believed him, what would they do with him? Would they allow him to leave Iran? And go where? He couldn't just show up on a flight to the United States. He didn't even have his passport. Would they let him stay in Tehran and live like a normal citizen? That seemed completely implausible, particularly with the knowledge he had about what had happened to the foreign minister. Could they afford to let him live, especially after he was no longer of any value to them? He would just be a liability to the Iranian regime. He imagined himself being told to kneel down in some prison cell with someone standing behind him and putting a bullet into the back of his head. He knew there would be no public trial in which his existence would be acknowledged by the government. The acid churned in his stomach amidst waves of nausea as he sat contemplating his future.

Ali turned to Assad, trying to engage him in conversation. He was hoping he could get Assad to reveal some clues of what lay ahead for him. "Those two caskets back there, is one the foreign minister?"

"Yes, it is him!" Assad answered angrily.

"And the other, in the casket I was in?"

"That was Heydar. He was part of the foreign minister's security. He was also my friend. He is with Allah now, in paradise." Assad spoke in a more subdued tone.

"I am sorry for your loss."

"His death will be avenged!" Assad yelled.

"I also want the truth to be known about who did this, so they can be punished," Ali responded, hoping Assad would discern his sympathy for the injustice done to Heydar. "That is why I came to the consulate. I know you think I'm involved in this, but I'm not. The people who are responsible for the death of the foreign minister and your friend also want me killed. Even though I'm an American citizen, I was born in Iran. I'm Iranian by blood. It angers me that such a cowardly act was committed against my fellow Iranians."

"Do not call yourself an Iranian. You are a traitor. You betrayed your country when you left and gave your allegiance to the Great Satan! You will have a chance to tell your lies to others in Tehran. If it were up to me, you would be coming back in your own casket without air holes instead of your filthy presence desecrating Heydar's body. Now shut your mouth before I shut it for you!" Assad threatened him.

Ali turned away from Assad and looked back out the window. That hadn't gone as he had hoped. He realized he would have to wait until he could speak with someone who was hopefully more reasonable once he arrived in Tehran. He should have known better than to expect someone such as Assad to believe his story. Men like him were only motivated by hatred and violence. They had no tolerance for anyone or anything that didn't agree with their distorted ideas. Understanding and compromise were not a part of their narrow view of how to interact with the world around them.

* * *

Michael sat at gate N27 at Sea-Tac Airport, waiting to board a red-eye flight from Seattle to Reagan National Airport in Washington, D.C. He strained to hear the ceiling speaker while he watched the CNN news coverage flat-screen monitor. He got up and stood under the speaker, where he could here Iran's President Rostami giving a televised news conference to the people of Iran. Rostami, who normally had a reserved and amiable public demeanor, was shouting and slamming his fist on the podium in front of him as he addressed his nation. Michael listened to the voice of the interpreter as Rostami's words were translated into English.

"It is reprehensible that the Zionist regime would, with so much audacity, carry out such a cowardly act to assassinate a sovereign nation's foreign minister in front of the whole world to witness. The Zionists then have the impudence to make the outrageous claim that the Iranian government would kill one of its own senior leaders. The Zionists have shown there are no limits to how far beyond the norms of the civilized world they are willing to go. Iran came in good faith to negotiate, while the Great Satan again continues to threaten us with unjustified economic warfare, simply because we are exercising our sovereign right to defend our nation. In good faith, Iran disclosed the extent of its nuclear program amidst the threats and ultimatums of the West and has stood by its side of the agreement. This is the way we are repaid for our sincerity, by being stabbed in the back by the illegitimate Zionist regime that has been unlawfully occupying the rightful lands of the Prophet Muhammad's people. The Zionists deny their complicity in this despicable act, yet there is undeniable proof it was them. The cowardly murderers did not hesitate to kill Turkish and Iranian personnel yet spared the life of one of their American benefactors, tranquilizing him rather than killing him. We also have additional proof from their carelessness in leaving behind evidence that directly implicates them. This is an act of war against the nation of Iran, against the people of Iran. We will not allow this act to go unanswered. The Zionist regime will not escape punishment for their treachery. Iran will have to reconsider if it is in its best interest to remain in the nuclear agreement under such circumstances," Rostami finished his tirade.

"And that was the Iranian president, Nouri Rostami, addressing his nation, obviously convinced the Israelis were behind the assassination of their foreign minister yesterday in Istanbul. Prime Minister Ehud Akerman held a news conference earlier today, addressing the accusations leveled by Iran against his country, and this was his response." The CNN anchorman transitioned to the Israeli prime minister.

"The Iranian regime has leveled these preposterous accusations against Israel as a pretext for them to withdraw from the nuclear agreement in order to restart their nuclear weapons program. The barbarity of how far Iran is willing to go in killing their own foreign minister defies what any civilized nation would resort to. This should be no surprise to us. All along, we have been warning our allies in the United States and Europe that the Iranians would never actually give up their nuclear weapons program, and we have been proven correct. As we have always maintained, we will not allow Iran to develop nuclear weapons that could threaten the existence of Israel. We are within our rights to defend ourselves from such a threat and will do whatever is necessary to ensure that Iran will never have the capability to threaten our nation. Attempting to use this absurd subterfuge as a justification to take any hostile action against Israel will not succeed. Make no mistake, any aggression by Iran against Israel will be answered with a certain and overwhelming response," Akerman declared.

"That was the Israeli prime minister, Ehud Akerman, with an obvious warning to the Iranian government. The United Nations Security Council is slated to hold an emergency meeting tomorrow to discuss this developing crisis. Never a dull moment in the Middle East. And now here's Valerie Watson on the latest celebrity plastic surgery fad making news in Hollywood," Michael heard as he turned his attention away from the monitor.

That's not good, Michael thought. When a moderate like Rostami started sounding like the hardliners who had always opposed him, that was something to be concerned about. Things could spiral out of control pretty quickly if they didn't figure out a way to deescalate the situation. Michael hoped Israel wouldn't attempt anything rash, such as a military strike. That could destabilize the whole Middle East for years.

Michael's thoughts returned to Ali's message. It didn't make sense to him. What would be the purpose of killing the Iranian foreign minister and threatening the nuclear agreement? It wouldn't serve the interest of the United States or Russia. Was he missing something? Perhaps Ali had been mistaken?

But Michael knew what type of person Ali was. He was certain Ali wouldn't make such an audacious claim unless there was something behind it. Michael, however, kept coming back to the fact that Canton was somehow involved. He wondered if he was letting what happened in Athens cloud his judgment now.

With the announcement that boarding was about to begin, waiting passengers began queuing in their respective lines. Michael glanced at his watch and saw that it was 10:35 p.m. He hoped that he would be able to at least get a few hours of sleep on the five-hour flight to D.C. He hated flying coach. He was never able to get comfortable, especially after his back injury. He never understood how, in an age of smartphones and self-driving cars, they still hadn't figured out how to make a coach airline seat somewhat comfortable, considering how many millions of passengers sat in them every day. He was still feeling the effects from the previous night. His body ached, but the excitement from the uncertainty of what lay ahead made him less aware of his discomfort. It was a familiar feeling, but one that he hadn't experienced in a long time. This time, however, feelings of doubt invaded his thoughts. He was fifty-four, not an old man, but certainly nowhere near his prime for what he might be getting himself into. It had been ten years since he had operated in the intelligence and counterterrorism world. For the majority of the public, their exposure to this world amounted to a two-hour movie about some secret agent single-handedly going up against a terrorist organization to recover a nuclear device amidst a never-ending barrage of bullets and explosions, just after just having gotten out of bed with some beautiful supermodel. Michael had experienced firsthand how quickly things could go bad and people could get killed. He tried to reassure himself that he still had it in him to figure out what had actually happened to Ali and come up with a plan that would hopefully be able to help his friend.

Strange, he thought, thinking of Ali as his friend. Michael knew a fundamental rule of running intelligence assets was never to get personally attached to them. One had the responsibility of protecting them and ensuring their well-being, but never should one allow any feelings of friendship to develop towards them. At the same time, one of the techniques used to develop the asset's loyalty and trust in his handler was to make them believe you were their friend and really cared about them. There was a reason they were referred to as assets, because when their intelligence usefulness was finished, they were discarded and any further contact with them ceased. Michael reflected on the duplicity and insincerity that was such a central attribute of the intelligence world. He wondered how much his old world changed him as a person, how much it contributed to both his divorces. Perhaps since he had been away from that world for so long, he saw things from a different perspective, the way most normal people did. A world where people were supposed to have genuine friendships and relationships. But then again, he had just tried to end his life twenty-four hours ago. He knew he was messed up, despite his wishful thinking.

Michael got in the line for his boarding zone and waited. After ten minutes, he was inching down the aisle, hoping that there would still be room in the overhead for his carry-on. He had only packed the basics, enough for four days. He had no idea where his journey would lead or what to expect. He could always buy more clothes and supplies if he needed some later. As he neared his seat, he spotted an opening in one of the overheads and shoved his carry-on into it. He considered himself lucky to have found such a last-minute ticket, but he had to make do with the last open seat available, which was a middle seat. He was hoping he would be lucky enough to be squeezed in between two petite women so at least he wouldn't feel crowded. He looked at his seat number on his boarding pass while glancing at the overhead seat numbers until he reached aisle twenty-eight. He looked down at the high-school-aged Samoan kid squeezed into the aisle seat and the young mother with the six-month-old infant in the window seat, trying his hardest not to let the disbelief show on his face. He stopped in front of the Samoan teenager with the headphones over his ears and waited for him to disconnect from the gangster rap he was plugged into and notice Michael standing there. Already starting to feel irritated at what lay in store for him over the next several hours, Michael felt his patience wearing thin. Tapping the Samoan kid on the shoulder, he finally got his attention.

"Oh, sorry, dude, didn't see ya." He looked up at Michael and started to get out of his seat. Michael stepped back as the huge teenager grabbed the seat in front of him, trying to pull himself up and extract himself out of his tight space, while simultaneously almost taking out the grandma in the seat in front of him. Throwing the gray-haired elderly lady a sympathetic look, Michael shook his head back and forth ever so slightly, brooding over his misfortune. He dreaded the thought of how he was going to feel by the end of his flight. He slid into his middle seat, giving a slight smile to the young mother who returned an apologetic look as she tried to calm her crying baby.

Michael grabbed his seat belt and buckled it before the Samoan kid sat back down. He closed his eyes, trying to tune out the crying baby on one side of him and the huge teenager encroaching on his other side. He thought he should give Roxanne just one more call to let her know what time to expect him. His old instincts made him feel uneasy about calling her again. He tried to tell himself not to get paranoid. No one was likely to be tapping her phone because of Ali's contact with her. At least, he hoped that was the case. Not knowing what Ali was involved in, he told himself he couldn't afford to be careless, especially if he was going to be poking his nose into the world he'd left a decade ago. He pulled out his cell phone and hit the redial.

"Hello?" Michael heard the sleepy voice of Roxanne on the other end.

"Oh, sorry, Roxanne, this is Michael. I didn't even think that it's almost two a.m. there," he said, feeling bad that he had woken her up.

"That's okay," she said groggily. "I've just been on the couch most of the day napping anyway. What's up?"

"I just wanted to check in with you and make sure everything was okay."

"Yeah, just sleeping and waiting for you to get here."

"I'll be there sometime around seven thirty in the morning, by the time I get a rental car and drive from the airport. Listen, Roxanne, I don't want you making any calls or texting from your phone unless it's an emergency. I don't mean to sound paranoid, but without knowing what your dad's involved in, you need to be careful about using your phone. I don't know who may know about you, but your phone is the easiest way somebody can get information about you that may put your father in danger."

"Okay, Michael."

"Good girl. Just sit tight until I get there, and we'll figure things out. See you in a few hours," Michael tried to reassure her.

"Bye, see you soon." He could hear the worry in her voice. Michael ended the call, noticing the young mother glancing at him.

"Sorry, I didn't mean to eavesdrop. I hope everything is okay," she told Michael while breastfeeding her baby.

"It will be," he answered, wondering if there were any certainty to his statement. Michael felt the aircraft push back from the gate as the safety video came on the screens on the back of every seat. Michael put his head back and closed his eyes. It was a habit he had picked up years ago in the Agency, when he would travel on a routine basis to different parts of Europe, the Middle East and North Africa. During those often-frenzied times, sleep was a luxury Michael snatched in bits and pieces whenever the opportunity presented itself. Traveling by plane was always a chance to catch up on a few hours of sleep. But in those days, he reminded himself, he was almost always sitting in a business-class seat. With the Samoan kid's belly pushing Michael's left arm into his lap as he listened to the baby suckling his mother to his right, he realized that probably wasn't going to be the case on this flight. He just hoped his lower back would hold up, so he wouldn't end up having to hobble through the terminal to the rental car counter.

As the aircraft began to taxi towards the runway, Michael's thoughts returned to Canton again. He recalled the months he'd spent with him and Schmitty in the apartment across the street from the Iranian embassy, eating gyros from the fast-food restaurant around the corner while taking turns looking through the spotting scope at those coming and going from the embassy, hoping to spot Karbashi. Schmitty was the easygoing type, originally from Minneapolis, Minnesota. He could talk about the most mundane topics, from which pro sports team had the hottest cheerleaders to the latest in microchip technology of the CIA's collection of technical gizmos. Michael fondly referred to him as their Q, the fictional head of the R&D branch of the British Secret Service, or MI6, from the James Bond films. Michael would on occasion bring him a box of Greek pastries from the bakery a few blocks from the US embassy, a flagrant bribe, anytime he wanted to try out some new high-tech spy toy, which Schmitty guarded as if they were his precious children, always fussing about not bringing it back broken. With Canton, however, it was always a tiresome effort to engage in any type of enjoyable conversation. It wasn't that Canton didn't want to talk. On the contrary, he liked hearing himself talk more so than whoever else was in the conversation. The problem was, he always wanted to steer the conversation to him. Regardless of the topic, Canton would somehow inject himself into the center, either through his personal experience or level of expertise. Michael remembered Schmitty's frequent eye rolling when Canton would attempt to hijack the conversation. It wasn't only his narcissistic tendencies, but there was also some other spiteful predisposition about his character Michael had noticed, as if he was entitled to everyone's respect. In some instances, Michael and Schmitty would listen to Canton's statement about how he was in some way connected with the topic of conversation and continue on with their conversation as if Canton hadn't said anything. They never did it to be rude, but they also wanted to make it clear they weren't interested in talking about him, often needling him by calling him Mussolini. Despite Canton's continuous self-aggrandizement, the three of them managed to keep a good-humored atmosphere considering the many hours they initially spent together.

When almost one had month passed, they still hadn't spotted anyone matching Karbashi coming or going from the embassy. They knew from satellite imagery that there were no other entrances on the back or sides of the embassy, which abutted other properties. Everyone came and left from the front gate. Having burned through one-third of his surveillance allowance, Michael was beginning to feel a bit discouraged. Listening to Canton's continuous comments about it all being a waste of time didn't help his disposition either. He was beginning to second-guess himself. Had he missed something? Was the intel in their database about Karbashi being assigned to the embassy in

Athens wrong? He had double-checked with Langley and had been assured that NSA intercepts had confirmed Karbashi's transfer to Athens. Why, then, had they not spotted him in close to a month? Something was wrong. It was as if Karbashi wasn't even in Athens, which made Michael wonder if that was actually the case. Had he been transferred from Athens? Michael highly doubted it. The NSA had cracked the Iranian foreign ministry's encrypted diplomatic communications for many years and knew everyone who was assigned to each Iranian mission, as well as what each Iranian ambassador was discussing with the foreign ministry back in Tehran. What the NSA hadn't yet been able to decrypt was the separate MOIS communications from each of their embassies back to MOIS headquarters. Michael had put in an intercept request for any Iranian diplomatic message traffic that referenced Karbashi, but he could have also been recalled to Tehran by the MOIS temporarily for some reason without anything having been picked up by the NSA. Which got Michael wondering if Karbashi had left Greece at some point prior to the start of their surveillance without them knowing it. Maybe they had just had bad timing.

Michael had decided to check the airlines' computer reservation system, or CRS as it was called throughout the industry, to see if he could find a passenger name record for Karbashi. Depending on how long ago he had left Athens, his name might have still been in the database. Michael remembered the relief he'd felt after the CRS query revealed that Karbashi had left Athens two days before they had started their surveillance and, better yet, showed his return reservation on Turkish Airlines through Istanbul in two days, which was a Sunday. He knew that was their opportunity to pick him up at the international arrivals terminal at Eleftherios Venizelos International Airport just outside of Athens and hopefully tail him back to his home. It was going to require quite a bit of additional manpower beyond the three of them because of all the transportation options available for Karbashi to take into Athens, between the metro, a taxi, or even being picked up by someone. Michael remembered how he had to ask Harry on a Friday afternoon to make available almost every member of the station's surveillance team for Karbashi. Michael hated having to impose on so many of his colleagues' weekends at the last minute, but he also knew, just like everyone else who chose the CIA as their career, that weekends were whenever one was lucky enough to have two days off in a row. Despite Canton's grumbles about how much everyone was going to hate him for ruining their weekend, the surveillance team looked forward to every opportunity to practice their tradecraft.

They had prepositioned at the airport that Sunday afternoon, waiting for Karbashi to come off his flight. Michael was paired up with a female agent, the two of them posing as a traveling couple just outside the baggage claim of international arrivals. They were sipping coffees at a small table with their carry-on baggage on the floor beside them. There were two other surveillance team members in the arrivals area. One was an older gray-haired gentleman in a dark black suit, posing as a limo driver and holding a cardboard sign with a made-up name scribbled on it, faced the out-coming passengers. The other was a young female in torn blue jeans sitting on her backpack, who looked like the typical Euro hippie heading to the closest youth hostel that would be the first stop of wherever her journey was taking her. Three of them wore miniature and virtually invisible earpieces, and wireless encrypted Bluetooth microphones under their shirt cuffs, the latest in technology from Schmitty's storeroom of surveillance gadgets. The young girl instead had the communications gear built into her headphones, which were connected to the iPhone on which she was feigning listening to her favorite music, as was obvious from her head bobbing. Michael remembered the anticipation of sitting there with his surveillance partner, wondering if some unexpected last-minute occurrence would cause Karbashi to miss his flight. Having to call off the surveillance without netting any results was something he dreaded thinking about. Those types of things happened more often than not. That was just part of intelligence work.

His concerns were alleviated when the team member posing as the limo driver raised his hand to cover his cough and spoke into his microphone. "Coming out."

"Spotted him. Snapped his picture. Sending it to everyone," the Euro hippie advised the team, keeping her communications brief.

Karbashi walked around the end of the crowd standing there, waiting in anticipation for their expectant travelers. He pulled his suitcase behind him as he headed towards one of the escalators leading to the sky bridge.

"We got him," Michael announced to the rest of the team. He and his surveillance wife got up from their table and trailed Karbashi as he ascended the escalator. "Looks like he's taking the metro back to Athens. Mobile units, stand by to head back to Athens and stage along metro stops."

"Falling in behind you," the Euro hippie advised Michael and his partner.

They followed Karbashi across the sky bridge leading to the metro terminal. They walked to separate automated ticket machines and purchased their fares for the trip into Athens. Blending in with the crowd standing on the platform waiting for the next train to arrive, Michael sat holding hands with his surveillance wife as he kept sight of Karbashi, standing a few yards away. He glanced at the digital display overhead, which indicated four minutes until the next departure. He finally saw the train approaching the terminal. He stood up with his wife as it slowly pulled up the platform and the waiting passengers moved toward the edge of the platform. The doors on the opposite side of each car opened first, allowing arriving passengers to exit before the doors on their side opened to let them in. Michael and his wife got on board, using the other set of doors of the car Karbashi entered. They sat down on the far end of the car, holding hands and conversing like a normal couple arriving for a holiday in Greece, while keeping tabs on Karbashi, sitting down on the other end. Michael raised his hand to his partner's cheek and reached in, as if giving her a kiss, using the opportunity to activate his mic. "We both got eyes on. Mobile units, head to Athens. If for some reason we lose coms once we go under, I'll text locations," he said, referring to where the metro went from the surface rail section to underground once it entered Athens. Having recently been built by a German company for the 2004 Summer Olympics, it was a modern state-of-the-art metro system with mobile phone repeaters throughout. The comm units they were using piggybacked off the various mobile phone networks, using an encrypted signal that evaded detection by mobile carriers. This offered the CIA secure communications for surveillance anywhere in the world where there was a mobile phone network.

The Euro hippie had entered the next car, standing where she had a view of Karbashi through the windows of the adjoining cars. She activated the mic on her headphones and gave a reciprocal response: "I have eyes on." The team had planned for several contingencies, depending on which option Karbashi chose to leave the airport. In case he selected the metro, the plan was to keep eyes on him as he rode into Athens, with the three mobile units at the airport racing back to Athens to join the other two units standing by at the first two stops Karbashi might possibly get off at. Each of the five mobile units would rotate, advancing to each of the next stops on the metro line, until the team tailing him in the metro announced which stop he was getting off at. Each mobile unit would then drop off its passenger team member at a designated location, forming a box around Karbashi, to pick up the foot surveillance and diminish the likelihood of him noticing the couple on the metro and the hippie girl were following him. He was, of course, also an intelligence officer operating in a foreign country, who would likely be exercising a greater level of awareness than the average person going through the day-to-day slog of life, oblivious to their surroundings.

Michael remembered how they'd followed him all the way to the Syntagma Square stop, which was one of the central points in downtown Athens. The huge square had originally been the front lawn and gardens of the royal palace of King Otto in 1843. Today the palace was the Parliament Building, where the Greek government conducted business. Rather than a large sprawling lawn, Syntagma was an expansive public square of marble tiles interspaced with small sections of trees and grass. Surrounded on all sides by four lanes of traffic, there was a steady current of taxis driving around the square, dropping off and picking up passengers. It was also a hub for two metro lines and various public and charter buses as well as a major tourist stop for the Monument of the Unknown Soldier in front of the Parliament Building, which had an hourly rotating color guard. Tourist came there to have their picture taken in front of the two soldiers dressed in the traditional uniforms with the white leggings and wooden clogs that stood at attention, similar to the grenadier guards at Buckingham Palace in London. Located across the street from the Parliament Building, it was also the main venue for regular public demonstrations, which was how Greeks expressed their discontent with government policies they were unhappy about.

Karbashi rode up the escalator, exiting the metro station and cutting across Syntagma Square. Michael and his wife partner followed him, maintaining a comfortable distance but keeping him in their sight. Michael called out their location to the rest of the team. A mobile unit was already there, circling the square in the swirl of traffic. Although it was Sunday evening, the nearly constant flow of traffic, along with two traffic lights, meant that a rotation around the square took up to two minutes. The other mobile units were racing from previous metro stops to join the surveillance. Karbashi walked to the center of the square, then cut right and headed towards the corner across from the Hotel Grande Bretagne. The Euro hippie team member trailing behind Michael and his partner called out, "I have the eyeball," allowing them to break off Karbashi as she picked him up. When the crosswalk light changed, Karbashi crossed the boulevard with a crowd of pedestrians. Michael saw him as he walked up to the front of the hotel, entering through the large revolving door, then immediately exiting and walking up to the concierge attendant standing at the drop-off area.

Michael realized Karbashi was asking for a taxi. The Euro hippie member with the eyeball called it out to the rest of the team. Michael asked for the location of the other four mobile units. The Raven 5 replied it was stopped at a red light a block away. The Raven 3 and Raven 1, the other two closest units, advised they were still several minutes out. The Raven 2, the mobile unit circling Syntagma, called in that it was stopped at one of the traffic lights on the other side of the square. Michael began to worry. If Karbashi got into a taxi before some of the other mobile units arrived, they would lose him as his taxi took off and blended in with traffic. Michael and his partner standing on the opposite corner still in the square could only look helplessly across the boulevard as Karbashi waited for the concierge to flag a taxi. The Euro hippie had crossed with Karbashi onto that side of the street but continued on past him, since she would have attracted obvious attention standing in front of a five-star hotel. She walked another seventy yards and stopped by a sidewalk kiosk, blending in with other pedestrians while trying to keep Karbashi in her sight. A yellow taxi pulled up to the front of the hotel next to the concierge, who had his arm outstretched.

Michael watched as Karbashi walked up to the taxi and the concierge opened the rear door for him. "Raven 5, where are you?"

"Light just turned green, we're moving your way," Raven 5 answered.

"Raven 2, how about you?" Michael checked with the unit circling the square.

"Southeast corner, light's still red."

Karbashi handed the concierge a tip and stepped into the taxi, which pulled away from the hotel, merging with the traffic flow onto King George Boulevard.

"Taxi pulling out of the Grand Bretagne, looks like a late-model VW Passat," Michael advised the team. "Fox 2, do you have eyes on?" Michael asked his team member standing by the kiosk.

"I got him, but he's going to be out of my view shortly," the Euro hippie replied.

"This is Raven 5. We're just turning the corner onto King George. Where is he?"

Michael saw the blue Opel Corsa that was Raven 5 drive past them just as Karbashi's cab had turned the corner onto Syntagmatos Street, out of their sight.

"Raven 5, I see you. The Passat is in the outside lane just passing Ermou Street. He's behind a white Sprinter van," the Euro hippie vectored them in.

"Roger, Fox 2, we got eyes on," Raven 5 advised as they picked up the eyeball.

"This is Raven 2, we're finally moving. Just turned onto King George. We'll make our way in behind you, Raven 5."

"Roger, Raven 2," Raven 5 acknowledged.

"This is Raven 3. We're one minute out. Hang tight, Fox 1 and Fox 2, we'll swing by and pick you up," said Canton, who was in the silver Nissan van with Schmitty.

Karbashi's taxi headed north up Mesogeon Boulevard, one of Athens's main arterials, past all the metro stops they had passed coming from the airport. With all five mobile units joining the surveillance, they followed Karbashi's taxi to Neo Psychiko, a suburb just north of central Athens. The taxi stopped and dropped Karbashi off on a quiet residential street, where he walked down the sidewalk, pulling his suitcase behind him. The mobile units dispensed their passenger team members at various points in the neighborhood, boxing in Karbashi. They eventually followed him to a five-story apartment building, where they observed him pull out a key, open the front gate and walk up to the front door, opening it with his key and entering the building.

Michael remembered the sense of relief he had felt that day. He had finally found Karbashi and located where he lived, but now the real work began. He had to systematically track Karbashi when he wasn't at the Iranian embassy and find a vulnerability in his routine. Michael realized it wasn't going to be easy. Karbashi had obviously conducted a surveillance detection route on his way home from the airport. There was no other reason for him to have taken the metro all the way down to central Athens, past where he lived, and then double back, taking a taxi. He was obviously a professional intelligence officer who knew how to utilize good tradecraft. Michael would have to figure out a way to get to Karbashi without him realizing it. It was going to be Michael's abilities and expertise up against Karbashi's.

The Alaska Airlines Boeing 737 had come to a stop after several minutes of taxiing and waited at the end of the runway for takeoff clearance. Michael felt the engines come to full power as the aircraft picked up speed down the runway. Despite the Samoan teenager's mass encroaching into his space on one side of him and the crying baby on the other, Michael began drifting off as the plane lifted off the ground and climbed through the rainy night on its way to D.C. It seemed that Michael was going to get some sleep after all.

Chapter 6

Secretary Payton sipped his espresso while listening to Prime Minister Akerman drone on and on about Israel's right to defend itself against its enemies and Iran posing an existential threat to the security of Israel. From across the coffee table, he watched Akerman gesturing with his hands as he halfway shouted his words. Payton glanced at Defense Minister Moshe Rozen, sitting off to the right and slightly behind Akerman, catching his eye and detecting a hint of embarrassment for him having to sit and listen to Akerman rant. He was only catching half of what Akerman was saying, his mind split on the thought of their plot possibly being exposed if Ali wasn't found and silenced. After about five minutes, Akerman finished and looked at Payton, waiting to hear his response.

"Mr. Prime Minister, that was quite a speech. I'm sure that works wonders when you're addressing the Knesset, but it's not going to do much for allowing us to have a constructive conversation about ensuring Israel's security. Now you know that, despite some of our differences regarding settlements and the whole Palestinian issue, Israel is our staunchest ally in the Middle East, even more so than the Saudis. Yeah, they have their oil, but they're not a democracy like both our countries. As a matter of fact, Israel is the only stable government in the whole region. If they didn't have oil wealth or autocratic governments, none of these people would be able to govern themselves. The Arab Spring was proof of that. So, when it comes down to it, Israel is the only real ally the United States has in the Middle East, and we are not going to let anyone threaten your security. But, Mr. Prime Minister, if you continue to push President Steele on every issue and aren't willing to give a little to get a little, then we're not going to make any progress," Payton fired back at the Israeli prime minister.

"Secretary Payton, I'm not questioning the United States' commitment to Israel. I am just asserting that, as our ally, you must understand the position we find ourselves in. As I recall, it is the same position your country found yourselves in 1963 during the Cuban Missile Crisis. Back then, your country was willing to risk war with the Soviet Union when they placed nuclear missiles one hundred miles off your coast because it posed such an immediate threat to the United States. Now Israel finds itself in the exact same situation," Akerman said, backing off some.

"I understand your concerns, but that was the whole reason why we decided to stick by the nuclear agreement signed by the previous administration. Despite it making a good campaign slogan, we found it has actually been pretty effective in curbing Iran's nuclear weapons program. That's also why we set up the conference with Mohammedi, to discuss their ballistic missile program.

You see us constantly engaging to counter any military capability they have that would threaten Israel or any of its neighbors, yet you continuously criticize all our efforts, whether it's this administration or previous ones."

"It is not that we don't acknowledge and appreciate all the US's efforts. But, they have unfortunately not been effective. Your country is so naïvely trusting of the Iranian regime. They continue to mislead you, year after year, yet you can't see they are just stalling so they can develop all their other capabilities to complete their nuclear delivery system. When they have perfected their missile technology, it will only be a matter of months whenever they choose to reconstitute their nuclear weapons program and deliver a nuclear missile anywhere in the Middle East. And now, they have concocted this ludicrous story, blaming Israel for assassinating their foreign minister as a pretext to suspend the nuclear agreement. If those savages are willing to go that far, do you really believe the hardliners who control the IRGC and military are not preparing to take some action against Israel?"

"I don't know, Mr. Prime Minister; did they kill their foreign minister?" Payton finally asked, having been waiting for Akerman to bring it up.

"What do you mean? Do you actually believe we had anything to do with this?"

"The Iranians are claiming they have proof it was you, actual physical evidence," Payton baited him.

"That is ridiculous. If we had done such an operation, I can assure you there would never have been any evidence linking it to us. It is an obvious ploy by the IRGC to create chaos and weaken Rostami's government so they can obtain leverage and justify whatever action they take against us."

"I didn't say I believed them, I'm just telling you what they're claiming. I'm also inclined to believe it was them. After all, who else's interests would it serve to do something like this? The question now is, was it merely an internal power play, or do they have other reasons?"

"Mr. Secretary, we know the reasons. They intend to have a nuclear missile capability. That will never be acceptable to Israel. We will not allow that to happen," declared Akerman.

"So what do you mean by 'you will not allow that to happen'? Is there something you have planned that we should know about?" Payton asked, accusingly.

"At this time, we don't have anything definitively planned, but course, we always have contingency plans standing by. For now, we are waiting to see how the Iranians are going to respond." Akerman assured the Secretary of State.

"Ehud, that sounds like the same double talk I get from my Jewish jeweler when we're haggling over the price of a necklace for my wife. I keep asking him to give me a better price, and he just keeps telling me I won't find a better diamond from anyone else."

Payton's comment momentarily flustered the prime minister. Payton shot another glance at Defense Minister Rozen and caught the grin on his face from Akerman's reaction. After recomposing himself and forcing a smile, Akerman asked Payton, "Mr. Secretary, I just want your assurance that the United States will stand by Israel regardless of what transpires as a result of the situation that the Iranian's have instigated."

"Of course we will, Mr. Prime Minister, I would hope that is never in question. The United States will always stand with Israel. You have the assurance of President Steele."

"What are you planning on discussing with President Markov when you meet with him?" Akerman asked.

"I am going to ask him to use whatever influence he has with the Iranians to deescalate the level of rhetoric coming from their leadership. I'm also going to discuss the reports we've recently been made aware of regarding Iran's renewed interest in purchasing their S-400 air defense system. The capabilities of the S-400 are of concern to us, as I'm sure they are to you, should any future military action be necessary," Payton informed him.

"Yes, it is a concern of ours also, isn't it, Moshe?" Akerman deferred to his defense minister.

"Yes, it is, Mr. Secretary. The Iranians currently deploy the S-300, which they obtained from the Russians in 2007. Although it is a capable system, the Russians basically sold them their leftover junk from the Soviet era. The S-300 was developed in 1979, and although it can be a formidable air defense system against many of our fourth-generation F-15 and F-16 fighters, we have developed countermeasures against it. We also have our eight new F-35 Lightning IIs, which we recently took delivery of from you, and they are virtually invulnerable to it. But if the Iranians obtain the S-400, that would be a game changer, as you Americans like to put it," Defense Minister Rozen explained to Secretary Payton.

"I understand that, Moshe, and I will exert all my influence with Markov to make sure that doesn't happen," Payton told them both.

"Thank you, Mr. Secretary. We will see what transpires over the next few days with the Iranians. I have grave doubts, however, that they will come to their senses. The hardliners have made their move, and they know this is their only chance to seize power. If they seem weak now in front of the Iranian people, they will lose all credibility," Akerman concluded.

"We'll keep in close contact, Prime Minister," Payton told them as he shook hands on his way out.

***

Canton was in a meeting with Asya Tarhan, the chief of counterterrorism for MIT in Istanbul. He was in her office, sitting in a leather couch diagonally across a marble coffee table from Tarhan. She had just offered him coffee and was speaking to her assistant through the intercom on the table next to her, asking her to bring in two coffees. He discreetly stared at Tarhan's crossed legs while she was momentarily preoccupied with her assistant. Canton couldn't help but notice how fit she looked for a middle-aged woman. She was tall and slender, about five foot nine inches, but had an athletic look to her. With short black hair, high cheekbones and Persian eyes, she was sensually attractive but also a had subtle aura of assertiveness not commonly found in women. Although she looked like she was in her mid-thirties, Canton figured she had to have been at least in her mid-forties to be in charge of MIT counterterrorism operations for western Turkey. She must have been very competent to have such a central position in what was a normally a male-dominated organization, especially considering all the high-profile terrorist attacks that had hit Istanbul over the past several years. She wore a charcoal-gray women's business suit with a white silk blouse. The formfitting skirt hugged her hips down to her knees, with the rest of her exposed legs running down to the black pumps on her feet. He noticed her toned calves under the suntan nylons that covered her legs. She obviously must have been a secular Turk to be dressed in what was considered fairly provocative attire for women in many circles of the Islamic world.

Asya Tarhan was the only child of retired general Aslan Tarhan, a senior general in the Turkish Army. Her mother had died when she was nine years old. She was raised by her father, who showered all his love and attention on her after the death of his wife. He had taught her from a young age how to strive for excellence in whatever challenges she pursued in life. Unlike many Muslim men, he didn't treat the women close to him as possessions to remain silent and subservient. Not that he wasn't a devout Muslim. He said prayers five times a day, as was required by his faith, and lived a righteous life according to the teachings within the Quran. He was a dedicated soldier to his country and a dedicated father to his daughter, whom he treasured. Nowhere in the Quran or in any of the Prophet's teachings had he read that women must be treated as second-class citizens when it came to what they wanted to aspire in life. As a military man, he was also a pragmatist, realizing that the tenets of his faith had to be applied to the modern world they lived in without compromising their intended meaning by Allah. He did not hold his daughter back in any aspirations she had growing up as a child, encouraging her to excel in women's sports and academically. She attended the University of Istanbul, where she majored in classical studies while competing on the women's gymnastics team. She excelled in her studies and graduated with honors, but it was her success in gymnastics that led her to be noticed on the national stage. She had landed a spot on the Turkish Olympic Gymnastics Team, and while competing in the 1996 Olympics in Atlanta, her performance on the uneven bars earned her a gold medal. She had instantly become a celebrity, bringing home national honor to Turkey. Following her graduation, she chose what seemed an unconventional path to everyone except her father, who knew her best. She applied to MIT for an operational position. MIT was still a male-dominated organization, employing females primarily for secretarial positions, but her father's position, as well as her recent national celebrity, led her to be hired into one of few operations officer positions occupied by females within MIT at that time.

Canton looked up at her as she caught him staring at her legs. "Thank you for making the time to see me, Ms. Tarhan. I know you have a lot on your plate right now." Canton smiled.

"Things are a bit hectic right now, but I can always find the time to meet with our colleagues from the CIA," she replied cordially.

"The reason I wanted to speak with you, is because one of Ambassador Payton's staff is unaccounted for. It's his interpreter, Mr. Ali Shiravi. He hasn't been seen since Friday afternoon following the conclusion of talks at the Four Seasons. Apart from our concern over his disappearance, we believe he possibly may be connected to the foreign minister's assassination in some way. Mr. Shiravi is of Iranian descent, and although he wasn't in any security-related position, the fact that he's missing under these circumstances makes him a person of significant interest to the United States government," Canton explained.

"I see. What do you believe is his connection?" Tarhan asked inquisitively.

"Well, we're not sure if he's complicit in any way or a victim of foul play. Under any other circumstances, we would have treated his disappearance as a criminal matter for your national police to handle, but due to the sensitive nature, we're requesting the assistance of your service to use whatever means at your disposal to locate him. We have his passport and wallet, so unless he has fake travel documents, he can't get out of the country through normal means."

Canton pulled an eight-by-ten photograph out of an envelope and handed it to Tarhan. "This is a current photo of him. We would very much appreciate it if you could get this out to all airports, seaports and border crossings with instructions to be on the lookout for him. This request for assistance comes straight from the DCI," Canton told her, trying to emphasize the importance of his request.

"I can do that for you. It's been over twenty-four hours since the attack, so he may already have left the country, if that was his intent. I will also forward this to the national police for them to distribute throughout their precincts. If he still is in the country, there may be a chance of spotting him, or identifying his body if it turns up."

"Thank you, Ms. Tarhan. I'd like to offer any assistance that the CIA can provide your agency in this investigation. I'm sure our working together can greatly increase your effectiveness in resolving who was behind the assassination of the Iranian foreign minister. I know the DCI would greatly appreciate being updated on your progress. Would you mind if I came by your office for regular updates? Perhaps we could even have a working dinner together sometime," Canton said, nonchalantly slipping in the invitation.

"Yes, you are welcome to come back to my office for updates. My secretary can schedule you whenever I'm available," Tarhan answered, leaving out any mention of dinner. "Well, if there is nothing else," she said, standing up, "I'll see you out, Mr. Canton. As you can imagine, I need to be at three places at once lately. I will be in touch if there are any developments." She motioned him as she walked toward her door and opened it.

"Thank you." Canton stuck out his hand to her as he paused at her door. "By the way, you can call me Jonathan," he offered with a smile.

"Jonathan." She shook his hand briefly and showed him out the door. "My secretary will have someone escort you out."

What a creep, she thought, *trying to make a pass at me in my office during an official visit*. It was hard for her to believe that a senior officer in the CIA would so act with such a blatant lack of unprofessional. Fortunately, she knew how to handle misogynists such as him.

***

Canton exited the front of the MIT building and walked up to his waiting car. He got into the backseat and slammed the door shut. *What a cold bitch*, he thought, dwelling on how Tarhan had obviously snubbed his suggestion for dinner.

"Where to, sir?" his driver asked.

"Back to the consulate," he snapped.

"Everything okay, sir?"

"Just drive, and don't worry about things that don't concern you," Canton replied dismissively. He sat back in his seat as they drove through the busy morning streets, wondering what his next move would be if the Turks didn't locate Ali. Where could he be? He didn't have his wallet or his passport. He had no credit cards and most likely not much cash on him. But his damn phone. Just as he wondered what was taking Langley so long to get back with Ali's phone records, his encrypted cell phone rang.

"Canton."

"This is the technical collections division," said a female voice on the other end. "We have Ali Shiravi's cell phone records from the past seventy-two hours. Sorry it took so long. His carrier is AT&T, and he's been roaming on Turkcell while in Istanbul. It took us a little while to hack their network and obtain his call records. The only activity was one outgoing call from his phone Saturday morning at twelve fifty a.m. to another cell phone in the Boston area. We traced that number to a T-Mobile account belonging to Roxanne Shiravi. Various database checks along with Ali Shiravi's personnel records with the Office of Personnel Management disclose Roxanne Shiravi is his twenty-year-old daughter, who is currently attending Boston College. We checked her cell phone activity since receiving the call from her father. There was one outgoing call and two incoming calls from the same number in Seattle, Washington. That number is an AT&T account belonging to Michael Blackstone."

The woman continued regarding further checks disclosing that Michael Blackstone was a real estate agent in Seattle and a former CIA employee, but Canton wasn't paying attention. Hearing Blackstone's name mentioned shook him to his core. It was someone he hadn't thought about for over a decade. What did he have to do with any of this? Why would Ali's daughter call Blackstone?

"Where and when did the first call from Roxanne Shiravi to Blackstone take place?" Canton interrupted.

"Uh, let's see, that was Saturday morning at four twenty-three a.m. East Coast time, from a cell tower in Alexandria, Virginia."

"How about the first call from Blackstone to Shiravi?"

"That was Saturday morning at eleven thirty-five a.m. West Coast time, from a tower in north Seattle, Queen Ann Hill to be exact."

"And the second call from Blackstone to Shiravi?"

"Okay, that was on Saturday night, ten fifty-four p.m. West Coast time from a tower in SeaTac, Washington."

"Where the hell is SeaTac?"

"It's about fifteen miles south of Seattle. That's where Sea-Tac Airport is located."

"The airport? Tap into CRS right now and do a search for passenger Michael Blackstone departing from Seattle yesterday and today. I'll hold while you run that check," Canton directed.

"Yes, sir, stand by."

Shit, that's all I need, Blackstone poking his nose into this. What did Ali tell his daughter? What if he mentioned me? What if he mentioned Payton? Canton waited anxiously for the voice on the other end.

"Sir, it looks like he was booked on a Delta flight departing Seattle at eleven ten p.m., arriving Reagan National at six thirty a.m. local."

"Can you tell me the duration of Ali Shiravi's call to his daughter?"

"Hold on, let me see if I can pull that up. It was one minute, forty-seven seconds."

"Okay. Here's what I want. I need real-time monitoring on all three of those numbers. All incoming and outgoing calls. I want those conversations recorded and transcripts made. This is a level one national security request. I want to be contacted immediately. Do you understand me?" Canton stressed.

"Yes, sir. I'll submit the request to NSA right now. Is there anything else?"

"Yeah, what's Ali Shiravi's address?"

"Wait one…702 Prince Street, in Old Town, unit twelve, Alexandria, Vir—"

Canton hung up his phone before she had finished. He didn't know what Ali had told his daughter, but he had to assume the worst. There couldn't be any loose ends. "Change of plans, take me to the airport," he instructed his driver.

***

The plane began its descent into Tehran. Ali recognized various landmarks of the city he hadn't seen in a very long time. He'd never imagined going back to Iran after he'd left in 1979, in the midst of the Iranian Revolution. He was in his freshman year, studying architecture at Tehran University, when the Ayatollah Khomeini had returned to Iran and forever altered his future. Ali's parents, both law professors at Tehran University, were horrified by what they saw happening in their country. They had decided to send Ali to his aunt and uncle in Tysons Corner, Virginia, until they could make arrangements to permanently leave Iran for the safety of the United States. A month later, they had managed to make a call to Ali's uncle. They had told Ali that the new government had made it difficult to leave the country, but they were working on finding a way out. That was the last Ali had ever heard from them.

Ali's aunt and uncle had a very profitable Persian rug import business—that was, until the revolution, when all trade between the US and Iran came to a screeching halt. With their supply of rugs cut, they were forced to close down their store and open a small janitorial service, cleaning offices after hours. The best they could do for Ali was let him work with them as a means of getting back on his feet as he started his new life in the United States without his parents. After six years, he realized any hopes of getting ahead and making an independent life for himself were not going to be realized by cleaning offices until three a.m. six days a week. At the age of twenty-five, Ali went back to school at the local community college, studying computer programming. There he met his wife, Janet, an American girl who was seven years his junior. They eventually married and moved into the daylight basement of Janet's parents' home, which they converted into a separate apartment. Ali ended up working for Janet's father, who owned a small chain of tire stores, managing his inventory control system. Ali and Janet had wanted to have children. They had tried repeatedly, but Janet was unable to conceive. Another four years of working for Janet's father passed, and Ali found himself back in the same situation he had been in with his aunt and uncle. They were living in his in-laws' basement with Ali getting paid only ten dollars an hour, his father-in-law justifying it by the fact that they were living rent-free.

Ali had felt trapped. He wanted to get out from under his father-in-law's dominion and to be his own man. With whatever they had managed to put away, Ali and Janet moved to their own apartment and Ali opened his own computer shop in a local strip mall. This was in 1990, still the early days of home computing before the advent of the Internet, when computers were primarily used by businesses and enthusiasts building their own computers from individual components. Ali worked hard at making his business profitable, but there was just not enough public demand to generate steady sales. There were months when Ali barely made enough to pay the bills. The advent of large computer manufacturers such as Compaq and Gateway entering the market with their fully assembled home computers made it all the more difficult to compete and stay profitable. Finally, to both Ali and Janet's surprise, Janet became pregnant. With no health insurance and a child on the way, Ali realized he had to provide a stable income for his family and decided to enlist in the

US Air Force at the ripe old age of thirty-five. Roxanne was born the following year.

As the aircraft touched down at Mehrabad Airport, Ali remembered when he had departed from this same airport nearly forty years ago, with so much uncertainty. That same uncertainty returned, now that all control of his life had been cruelly snatched away from him. He knew that Mehrabad, located in central Tehran, had been replaced by Imam Khomeini International Airport located about ten miles southwest of the city. He looked outside as the aircraft taxied past the main terminal to a hangar at the far side of the airport complex. Ali read the large sign in Farsi above the hangar doors, which said Quds Force, meaning Jerusalem Force. The Quds Force was the special forces unit of the IRGC, responsible for all external operations. It reported directly to the Supreme Leader. A sick feeling came over Ali. He knew all too well it wasn't a good sign that he was going to be in the custody of the IRGC.

Assad looked at him, telling him with a threatening smile, "You are finally back home to face judgment for your betrayal of your country." When the aircraft had stopped and the doors were opened, Assad escorted Ali down the stairs and into the hangar, where two men wearing light gray jumpsuits were waiting outside an olive-green van.

"*Asalaam alaykum*," Assad said, using the traditional Muslim greeting meaning "peace be upon you."

The gave him the customary reply: "*Alaykum salaam*," meaning "and upon you peace."

"Here is your prisoner. I assume you have been informed of what his crimes are. God willing, this traitor will meet the fate he deserves," Assad sneered as he turned Ali over to their custody.

Walking on either side of him and holding his upper arms, they escorted Ali to the back of the van. Opening the rear doors and the interior steel cage door on the inside, they shoved him into the back of the van and locked the door from the outside. Ali sat on the wooden bench along one side of the prisoner transport van.

As they drove off, Ali asked, "Where are you taking me?"

"You'll learn soon enough," the guard sitting on the passenger seat told him through the cage that separated them. Ali looked through the windshield as the van drove past a guard post and out a gate on the opposite end of the terminal, turning onto one of the main arterials running through central Tehran. It was late in the afternoon, approaching evening, and all the commuters heading home from the workday slowed traffic as the van made its way down the busy thoroughfare. He didn't know exactly where they were, but was generally aware they were heading north. Everything looked different, yet strangely familiar in many ways. Ali recognized that they had finally made their way into the northern suburbs of Tehran when the realization hit him where they were taking him. A few minutes later, his worst fears were confirmed when the twenty-foot-high beige walls came into view. The van pulled off the road and stopped in front of the large steel gate with a blue sign above it that had written in both Farsi and English: "Evin House of Detention." Originally constructed by the Shah to house political prisoners, it was now used by the Islamic Republic of Iran to incarcerate enemies of the state. Just as under the Shah, Evin Prison's notoriety came from the fact that many who had the misfortune of being incarcerated there were never seen or heard from again. Stories of torture that took place within its walls were familiar to all Iranians.

After proceeding through the front gate, the van drove a bit further and stopped in front of a gray concrete block building. The two guards exited the van, walking to its rear. Ali heard the key go into the back door just before it was opened and his one of his captors motioned him out. As before, he was escorted by both arms to the two steel doors with wire-reinforced thick glass windows. The guard on his right pushed the red button on the panel next to the door and waited until he heard the buzz of the electric lock before pulling on the handle and opening the door. They walked into a room divided by a counter. One side of the counter contained a row of metal benches bolted to the floor and another security door that had a small window of reinforced glass at eye level. On the other side of the counter sat a fat prison guard in a gray corrections uniform, marked with food stains down its front and stretched to the point that one of the buttons had popped off, revealing a similarly stained undershirt. He looked up as they brought Ali in, taking a bite of the shawarma in his hand and dripping additional juice onto his uniform. "What kind of dog have you brought in tonight?" he hollered, spitting pieces of his half-chewed shawarma onto the counter.

"He's a special prisoner of the IRGC. He is to be put in isolation and have no contact with any of the other prisoners. He is also not to be harmed in any way. His safety is your responsibility. If anything happens to him, you will have to answer to the IRGC commander," one of the transport guards warned.

"Oh, a special prisoner," the fat guard blabbered with a mouth full of food. "Well, what's his name?"

"You don't need to know his name. Just make sure he's ready whenever the IRGC needs to interrogate him," one of them instructed the prison guard while the other handcuffed Ali to the pipe running along the back of steel bench. Having completed their responsibility of transporting the prisoner from the airport to the prison, they departed, leaving him in the custody of his new jailer.

"Well, well, Mr. Special. We'll make sure you get *special* treatment," he mocked Ali while stroking his hand back and forth along his wooden nightstick, until breaking out in laughter, spitting additional food particles into the air in front of him.

Ali stared in revulsion at the sight of the guard. For as bad of a reputation as prison guards had in certain parts of the United States, particularly in some Southern states, where low salaries attracted persons with minimal qualifications, Ali knew the situation here was far worse. Prison guards and sanitation workers were some of the worst-paid state employees in Iran. Sanitation workers at least were appreciated for the service they performed in keeping the densely populated city clean from refuse, especially during the sweltering summers. Prison guards, on the other hand, were reviled by many Iranians who either had family members or knew of someone else's family that had experienced their cruelty while incarcerated.

Despite the guard's vile threats, Ali remained handcuffed to the bench until the guard had finished processing his intake paperwork. When that was complete, he picked up the phone on the counter and told the person on the other end that the prisoner was ready to be taken to his cell. A few moments later, Ali heard the buzz of the electronic lock on the security door as another guard came into the room. He walked behind Ali, temporarily removing one of the cuffs to release him from the pipe then refastening it to his other wrist, and lifted him up from the bench. With one hand on Ali's shoulder and another holding the chain of the handcuffs, the guard walked Ali over to the security door, waiting for his colleague to buzz the door unlocked. Ali could smell the stink of the guard's body odor. Unlike the intake guard, this guard was tall and lanky, with several days' beard growth and oily hair that looked like it hadn't been washed in a week. Passing through the security door, the guard led Ali down a dingy gray corridor with no doors other than another security door at the far end. The guard pushed the red button on the wall and looked up at the camera above the door. Waiting to hear the buzz of the electronic lock, the guard pulled the door open and proceeded with Ali down another corridor. This hallway had a line of steel doors with metal slides that were obviously for passing food trays to inmates on the other side. They walked past several doors and stopped in front of the one marked with the number ten. The guard reached for the security key attached to his belt with a chain and unlocked the door of the cell. The guard removed Ali's handcuffs and motioned him inside with a nod of his head.

"When will I get to speak to someone?" Ali asked the guard, hesitating at the door.

"I don't know, that's none of my business," the guard answered him. "Now get in." He motioned again with another nod. Ali stepped into his cell. "Your belt." The guard stuck out his hand.

"Why do you need my belt?"

"I don't need it. That is the rules." The guard looked at him impatiently.

Ali realized it was a waste of time expecting the guard to answer any of his questions, so he pulled his belt off his pants and handed it to the guard. He stood there watching as the door slammed shut in front of him. He heard the key turn the bolt, locking him in. He knew eventually someone would come to question him. Until then, he would try to keep his wits about him and make the best of his situation. He walked over to the cot, which had a small pillow and gray blanket, and sat down on it. As he looked around the eight-by-ten-foot cell that was to be his new home for the time being, his confidence was shaken at the sight of the hole in the concrete floor and the short hose connected to the water faucet on the wall next to it. There was no window in the cell, the only light coming from the incandescent bulb hanging from the ceiling. It was a drastic change from where he had been a mere seventy-two hours ago. He wondered when he would ever see the outside again.

Chapter 7

Michael had picked up his rental car at Reagan National Airport and was heading south down the George Washington Memorial Parkway for the short drive to Old Town Alexandria. It had been nearly a decade since he had been to D.C. after being transferred back from Athens, but everything looked comfortably familiar to him. Part of him missed living here. He had spent most his CIA career overseas, but the two years he'd spent at Langley prior to Athens were exciting from the perspective of being close to the centers of power and witnessing how the levers of the US government operated. It also brought back sad memories. It was the last period of time he had spent together with Karen and Sam. Unfortunately, it was a time when his entire focus had been on his career, at the expense of his wife and daughter. Looking back, it was hard for him to imagine how he could have been so self-centered to put his ambitions before his family. It was the beginning of what had eventually become a downward spiral that had led him to attempt to take his own life just two days prior. For now, that downward spiral had been put on hold, as his focus was directed on trying to help an old friend that was in trouble. Michael reflected on considering Ali his friend. He had recruited Ali, trained him and tasked with his mission. He might have been responsible for Ali's safety then, but that was many years ago, and he certainly didn't owe him anything now, especially not knowing the extent of his involvement in what was quickly escalating into an international crisis. *I'm just going to make some inquiries and see what I can find out*, he told himself, *that's all I'm committing to.*

The drive down the parkway got Michael into Old Town in less than ten minutes, where it would normally have taken thirty minutes during the busy weekday commute. He followed the map display on his iPhone to Ali's address. He drove by what was once a large three-story colonial brick town-home, now painted teal green and converted into individual condominium units. It was 7:20 a.m. on a Sunday morning, and there wasn't much pedestrian traffic yet other than a middle-aged woman in black tights and a neon pink running jacket taking her manicured standard poodle out for its morning walk. The twenty-five miles per hour speed limit down the residential street gave Michael the opportunity to look for any signs of surveillance on Ali's condo. He knew it would only be a matter of time before surveillance would be put on his residence, either by the FBI or CIA, depending on whether or not Ali was wanted in connection with the Iranian foreign minister's assassination and whether Canton had anything to do with his disappearance.

Michael parked his rental car two blocks down and walked back up the street towards Ali's condo, scrutinizing the cars parked on either side of the street. Everything looked normal. There was a variety of newer high-end SUVs and luxury cars, what one would expect to find in that type of neighborhood near the Capitol, but Michael also noticed the new four-wheel-drive full-size van. It was black with tinted windows, with two side-by-side aerodynamic plastic cargo boxes on a roof rack and off-road tires on a raised suspension, the kind that many dual-income professional couples had to transport them to and from their extreme sport weekend excursions. It wasn't that the seventy-thousand-dollar expedition van looked out of place in the neighborhood; after all, it was a wealthy suburb of Washington, D.C. What caught Michael's attention was that, unlike the other parked cars, which had dew on them, the van was completely dry. Coming up to it from behind, Michael couldn't see anything through tinted windows of the rear doors. He continued past it, glancing with his peripheral vision, but was unable to see anything through the dark passenger-door window. He walked the remainder of the block, crossing the street at the intersection, to the corner where Ali's building was located. He hopped up the four steps through the arched portico onto the covered porch and looked at the directory on the security panel. He located the black button that had "A. Shiravi" next to it and pressed it. While waiting for an answer, he casually looked to his right down the street to where the black van was parked. It was too far away for him to see if there were any occupants sitting in the front.

A few seconds later, he heard the voice of Roxanne through the speaker on the panel. "Who is it?"

Michael turned and looked into the small camera lens on the panel. "Hi, Roxanne, it's me, Michael Blackstone." He gave her a reassuring smile.

"Okay, just give me a sec to figure this out," she told him.

The front door buzzed just as Roxanne's voice came over the speaker again, telling him it was unit G, up the stairs. Michael let himself into the foyer, which had a grand staircase going up to the second floor. As he climbed the staircase, the aged wood of each stair creaked under the weight of each of his steps. *No way anyone could make it silently up these stairs*, he thought, *pretty good security feature*. His awareness surprised him. He was already starting to revert to some of his old patterns of thinking from a previous life. He got to the top of the stairs and looked down the long carpeted hallway, where he spotted a door open partway and a young woman with dark hair peeking her head out and flashing a nervous smile. Michael walked down the hallway to the open door as Roxanne opened it fully, letting him into her father's home. She closed the door and turned the dead bolt.

Michael turned to face her. "Hi, Roxanne, I'm Michael. Nice to see you again after all these years. Do you remember me at all?"

"Hi, Michael. You look kind of familiar, but then again that was a long time ago. I was just a little kid."

"Yeah, and I was fourteen years younger."

"You sure don't look like you're anywhere close to my dad's age."

"Well, thanks, but sometimes rolling out of bed in the morning, I feel like an old car with a cheap paint job," he joked. "Besides, your dad's a few years older than me. So tell me, what's going on?"

"There's really not much more I can tell you than what I already said over the phone. I got this strange call from my dad late Friday afternoon. He sounded really anxious, and what he told me didn't make sense, but he wanted me to get a hold of you and tell you exactly what he told me."

"Did he say why he wanted you to call me and not the authorities?" Michael asked.

"No, he just said to call you, no one else."

"Hmm. I heard on the news that one State Department employee is missing. I'm assuming that's your dad?"

"I don't know. He was the Secretary of State's interpreter at the conference with the Iranians. He's been there since last Thursday. I tried calling him back after I got here, but I got a message saying 'the number you are trying to reach is not available,'" she informed him.

"How long has he been working for the State Department?"

"Almost four years now, since he retired from the Air Force. The State Department had a shortage of Farsi speakers, and my dad applied and got the job. This was the first time he was going to be the Secretary of State's interpreter. When I talked to him before he left for his trip, he was really excited about it."

"Did he say anything else to you before he left? Did he mention the name Canton or anything about Russians?"

"No, nothing else. The first time I ever heard the name Canton was when he called me with that strange message. Do you have any idea what he might be involved in?" Roxanne asked worriedly.

"I have no clue. I haven't spoken to your father since Athens. Last I heard, you guys were transferred from Athens to the D.C. area back in 2007."

"Yeah, that happened all of a sudden. I remember we moved without even packing up our household belongings. We lived in a hotel for a couple of months until all our stuff finally showed up. My dad spent the last eight years of his career at Fort Meade. He never said exactly what he did, but I'm pretty sure he was working at the NSA as a linguist. How else would he have gotten the interpreter job at the State Department?"

Michael was impressed with Roxanne's astuteness. While back at Langley following his abrupt transfer, he had heard that Ali had been reassigned to Fort Meade after he and his family had been hastily rushed out of Athens. "Huh," said Michael, feigning ignorance of Ali's assignment to the NSA.

He walked over and sat down on one of the barstools at Ali's kitchen counter. "Wow, I'm at a loss as to what your father may be involved in," he uttered, running his hand back along the side of his head. Michael sat there, looking at her while thinking about what to do. He observed that Roxanne had grown up to be an attractive young woman. Her medium-length black hair, high cheekbones and Persian eyes gave her an exotic look. She obviously hadn't gotten any of her mother's genes for light brown hair and a fair complexion.

"Have you talked to your mom at all? Does she know anything about what's going on?"

"My mom passed away two years ago. Lung cancer. It was pretty tough on both of us," she said with a melancholy tone.

"I'm really sorry to hear that."

"It's okay. When my dad found out my mom had cancer, he was by her side night and day until the day she finally left us. He would take her to her chemo treatments and stay with her, taking care of her through all the nausea and weakness. It actually brought them closer together than they had ever been before. It was bittersweet."

Michael didn't know what to say. He bit his lower lip, attempting to subvert the swell of emotion he felt at hearing the sadness his friend and daughter must have experienced with their loss. He turned his head and looked around the living room and dining room area. Strange again how Michael thought of Ali as his friend. He told himself there was no reason he should have felt that way. He didn't know why he was there or what he could even do.

"I'm going to look around your dad's place, if that's okay?"

"Sure, that's fine. Do you have any idea what you're looking for?"

"Not a clue. Just a shot in the dark to see if I can find anything that might point in some direction."

"Do you want me to help?"

"Might as well. You know your father better than I do."

Not wanting to overlook anything, Michael systematically went room to room, methodically searching all drawers and closets. He hadn't done something like this for more than a decade, but it came back to him naturally, without having to think much about what he was doing. They spent the next forty-five minutes going through the entire condo, looking for any hints that might shed some light on what Ali could have been involved in. Michael even turned on the PC that was in the spare bedroom being used as an office. Not surprised, he found that a password was needed to access it. By the time they were finished, they had found nothing that would tell them anything more than they already knew.

"That didn't turn out like I had hoped," Roxanne said, disappointed.

"I really wasn't expecting to find anything."

"So, what now?" Roxanne asked what appeared to be a simple question, but Michael could tell from her expression she was asking him much more. He stood silently, looking at her. He saw the worry in her face. She was scared. She was alone. She had no one else to turn to. He tried to think what else he could do to help her, to help Ali. But how could he help, if he had no information and absolutely nothing to go on? He needed some help. Someone who might be able to perceive something he was missing. There weren't many people he knew who could help him. The more he tried to think of who he could turn to, the more he realized he really didn't have anyone he could count on. He had several close acquaintances he had met through his real estate or at the gym that he occasionally had a coffee or drink with, but he didn't consider any of them truly friends, especially any who would be at all useful in a situation such as this. It was a depressing realization that, in the twelve years since he had left the CIA and moved to Seattle, he hadn't developed any close friendships. He knew that was messed up, more so, that he was messed up. It wasn't that he didn't enjoy interacting with people; that was a big part of what he did every day in real estate. It was just difficult meeting someone who had comparable life experiences to his. Someone who had a similar view of life. Someone he could share his personal thoughts with. Someone he could trust. That was the case for male friends as well as any female friend. After thinking in silence for a bit longer, he finally decided who his only real chance of getting help from might be, and just as importantly, whom he could trust.

"I'm going to go see an old friend, Roxanne. I don't know if he will be able to help at all, but he's the only one I know and trust who might," Michael said, finally broking the silence.

"That means you'll try and help my dad, then?" Roxanne asked anxiously.

"I'll do whatever I can. I can't make any promises, though. I have no idea what he's involved in and don't have a clue of where he might be."

"Oh, thank you, Michael!" she burst out. "There must have been a reason he asked specifically for you after all these years. He must have a lot of trust in you."

"Well, we went through a lot together some years ago. I just hope he doesn't have more faith in me than I deserve. In the meantime, you need to get back to your school while I look into things further. How did you get here?"

"I came down on Amtrak from Boston."

"Okay, well, I'll get you to the train station and you head back to...where do you go to school?" he asked her.

"Boston College, I'm a senior. Two more months and I'm finished!" she exclaimed.

"So, you go back to Boston College and get back to your normal routine. As soon as I find out something, I'll let you know. Okay?"

"How long do you think it will take before you find anything out?"

"Roxanne, like I told you, I'm not even sure if there is anything more I can find out. I promise I won't leave you hanging either way. Trust me on that."

"Well, if my father does, I guess I do too. I really don't have any other choice," she conceded.

"No, you don't. Okay, let's get out of here. There's nothing more for us to do here, and the longer we stick around, the greater the chance someone will see us," he told her and headed for the door. She grabbed her overnight bag and followed him out, shutting the door and turning the dead bolt.

"What do you mean, someone will see us?" she asked as they headed down the hallway. Michael was just about to answer her when he heard the front door below open as they neared the top of the staircase. Michael froze instantly and raised his hand to signal Roxanne, who was startled by his abrupt stop. He stood silently and listened, peering around the corner to look downstairs. He could only see the front door and part of the foyer, but he could hear movement. He waited to hear the creaking of someone walking up the stairs. Instead, he heard the turn of a key, a rustling of paper, then the sound of a small metal door slamming shut, and finally the sound of footsteps fading away down the hallway. Michael turned to Roxanne and saw her raised shoulders and upturned palms, along with the puzzled look on her face.

"Sorry, guess I'm a little paranoid. Listen, Roxanne, I don't know who else may be involved in this. If what your dad said in his message is true, this is serious enough that they're going to try to find out as much as they can about your father, which includes checking out where he lives. I don't think it would be a good idea for you to come back here. What are your plans after graduation?"

"If you're asking whether I was going to move back with my dad, no. I share an apartment with a friend, and I'm planning on staying there after graduation. And who is 'they'?" she asked as they descended the stairs.

"'They' is any number of government agencies, along with anyone who may wish your dad harm."

"How do you know all that?" she asked, baffled by his answer.

"Because I used to be 'they.'" He turned and looked her in the face.

"I get it now why my dad wanted me to call you."

They stepped out onto the porch. Michael didn't see any pedestrians other than a couple of joggers running down the sidewalk on the opposite side of the street. They walked in the direction of Michael's car, parked two blocks away. He could see the black van still parked where it had been. The reflection off the windshield made it difficult to see from a distance if anyone was in it. As they neared the van, Michael saw it was unoccupied, but his attention was drawn to the fact that he couldn't see anything past the front seats because of the charcoal-gray bulkhead behind them. Michael had seen vans configured like that before. He had sat in the back of them many times in his prior life. They continued past the van down the sidewalk to the intersection. Rather than continue straight down the next block, Michael turned left, heading perpendicular to his car.

"Where did you park?" Roxanne asked.

"Down that way." Michael nodded in the direction of his car.

"Then why are we going this way?"

"Just being cautious," he said, playing it down, not wanting to alarm her.

They walked to the next intersection and turned right onto a two-way street that had a bit of early Sunday morning traffic. They continued to the next intersection, making another right, and walked back to Prince Street, having made three sides of a rectangle instead of walking a straight line back to Michael's car. Michael pulled out the key fob, unlocking the doors and glancing around before getting into his parallel-parked Chevy Blazer. He started the engine and pulled out onto Prince Street. He stopped at the intersection before the black van and turned right rather than pass by the van. Another right turn, a few more blocks and a right turn again had them heading north towards the Capitol on Jefferson Davis Highway, which was US Route 1.

"Where we going? The train station's back there." She gestured towards the rear with her thumb.

"I'm not dropping you off at Alexandria Station. We're heading up to Union Station in D.C."

"Isn't that kind of out of the way, when there's a station just a few blocks that way?"

"It won't take that long this early on a Sunday morning. Besides, better safe than sorry."

"A little paranoid, are we?" she teased him.

"Maybe a little."

Although traffic was lighter than usual this early, there was always a steady flow inside the Beltway, even on weekends. As Michael drove, he kept glancing up at his rear-view mirror, looking for any signs of surveillance. They were approaching Reagan National Airport when he saw it. About a quarter mile back, over the tops of the other cars, Michael spotted the distinct roof rack on the top of the black van from Prince Street. He wasn't just paranoid. He felt a sense of satisfaction that his intuition was correct. He at least still possessed some of the instincts that made him good at his former vocation, if you could call it that. He also was upset with himself. He knew how they were following them. It was their phones.

I should have known better. They would have immediately checked Ali's cell phone records, found the call to Roxanne, checked her records and found the call to me. They have our cell phone numbers. They're doing real-time monitoring and tracking us through the GPS in these damn smartphones, he chastised himself. Smartphones had just made their debut when Michael had left the Agency. Back then, although they could zero in on the approximate location through triangulating the cell towers a phone was pinging, they still needed a tracking device on the vehicle to get an exact fix on the location. It wasn't as easy as today, when each cell phone had its own built-in tracking device for any law enforcement or intelligence agency with the proper equipment and legal authority. In this case, he had no idea if his followers were law enforcement—in other words, the FBI—or his former employer. He needed to be more careful, especially since he was going to continue trying to find out what happened to Ali. He would deal with the phones shortly, but for now, he had to buy them some time. Traffic was moving along at a nice clip of fifty-five miles per hour heading into D.C., when Michael spotted his opportunity. Coming up quickly was a service break in the median, a favorite of the state police to tuck into and run radar speed traps. He glanced in his rear-view mirror to see if he would have time to slow down, but a young woman driving a small SUV, talking on her cell phone while intermittently glancing up at her mirror trying to get her lipstick right, was right behind him. *Well, she's going to be in for a surprise,* Michael thought as he prepared to make his move.

"Hang on," he warned Roxanne a second before he braked hard as he came up on the gap in the median, dropping their speed instantly to thirty miles per hour, then spinning the steering wheel hard left. Glancing briefly in the rear-view mirror, he caught the expression of shock on the woman's face behind them, right before the back end of their car broke right, as Michael skidded the car into the break in the median. To his right, he heard, "Aaaaahhh!" as Roxanne clutched the front of the dash with both her hands. Looking past her out the passenger-side window, Michael saw his chance and stomped on the gas, reentering Highway 1 heading south in the opposite direction. He looked left across the divider just in time to see the black van, catching a glimpse of its driver looking back at him as they shot by each other.

"Sorry about that," Michael declared as Roxanne attempted to catch her breath.

"What was that!" she exclaimed.

"We picked up company."

"What are you talking about?"

"There was a black van parked down the street at your dad's place when I got there. It was there when we were leaving. It was just behind us," he explained the reason for giving her a scare.

"It could have been any black van. There's more than just one black van in Virginia," she declared, trying to stay calm.

"Not like that one."

"I almost peed my pants!"

"Yeah, that happens sometimes, when people get scared," he joked, trying to make light of the situation.

"What's going on? Why is someone following us?"

"Give me your phone."

"What?"

"I said give me your phone."

Roxanne pulled her phone out of her purse and handed it to Michael.

"Unlock it," he instructed her, handing it back to her. She pressed her index finger to the fingerprint reader and handed it back to Michael. Michael touched the settings icon, then the airplane mode button, disabling the phone's cellular, WI-FI, Bluetooth and GPS. He then did the same to his, before continuing.

"Like I told you earlier, there are people who are going to try to find out as much as they can about your dad. They apparently didn't waste any time. You can't go back to Boston."

"What do you mean, I can't go back to Boston? I'm graduating in two months. If I don't go back, that's not going to happen," she declared.

"It may not be safe for you there. I'm sorry, but you may have to put that off for the time being."

"Put it off? I can't put it off. I have plans."

"Listen, Rox, any plans you had changed the minute your dad got into whatever jam he's in. If he's still alive, they will be looking for him, and they will use whatever means necessary to get to him. His biggest vulnerability is you, and I can guarantee you they are looking for you right now. That's exactly what I would do if I were them. If you want me to help your dad, then you have to help me. If I am able to find him, it won't do him any good if they can use you as leverage over him. So, you have a choice: go back to Boston and wait for them to come for you, or do what I tell you and maybe see your dad again someday." Michael was brutally honest with her. He knew what he just told her would shake her up, but he had to make sure the gravity of the situation hit home. She had to understand that she was a liability to whoever was after her father, and therefore was a target herself.

"How would they know anything about me?"

"Because you're his daughter and it would be very easy for them to find that out."

"So? Just because I'm his daughter, why would they think I would know anything about my dad's work?"

"How do you think they found us?"

"I don't know."

"Our cell phones. They obviously know your dad's cell phone number. If they know that, then they know he called you. Then you called me. Do I need to go on? They have a record of every call either of us has made, all your friends' numbers, everyone in your life. That black van had two cargo containers on its roof rack. How much you want to bet they don't have camping gear in them? They were tracking our phones. You can't use that phone again. As a matter of fact, here—take this and start going through your contacts and writing them down." He handed her a small notepad and pen.

"I have hundreds of contacts in here. It'll take me forever to do that," she protested.

"Well, you better get started, then," he told her as he merged onto I-495 heading back towards Tysons Corner.

"So, what are we going to do now?"

"I'm working on that," he said, trying to reassure her, and himself for that matter.

They drove in silence around the Beltway while Michael contemplated what to do and Roxanne sat frantically scribbling the numbers from her contacts. His head spun as he tried to focus his thoughts on what his next move should be. Less than forty-eight hours ago, he had tried to kill himself, had failed as a result of some freakish ammunition malfunction, and was now with the daughter of a friend he hadn't seen in over ten years, with some spooks following them trying to find out what they knew and whether they were a liability to whatever plot Ali had uncovered. *How in the world did I end up in a situation like this?* he thought. As with everything he did, whether it was assessing investments when he worked on Wall Street or calculating risks when making plans in Special Forces and the CIA, Michael was a student of probability. He knew everything that occurred in the universe had to abide by certain principles that were governed by the laws of probability. Whether it was the weather or human behavior, each possible outcome could be statistically calculated to a certain degree. Michael didn't fail to appreciate what the odds were of everything that had happened leading him to his present situation. Probability-wise, they were astronomical. *Why did this happen to me? What am I supposed to do now?* He knew he had to get Roxanne somewhere safe before he could do anything. Somewhere completely unconnected to her. He had an idea, but first he needed to take care of their communications problem.

They continued up I-495. Michael searched his rear-view mirror for any other surveillance. When they got to Tysons Corner, he pulled off the expressway and drove towards where he remembered the retail area was located. Things had changed quite a bit since Michael had last been there, but he still remembered his way around. Finally finding what he was looking for, he pulled into the parking garage of the super-size Target.

"What are we doing here?" Roxanne asked, looking up and pausing from her scribbling.

"I'm going to get us some new phones," he informed her.

"Oh, okay. I'll just wait here and finish copying my contacts."

"I'll be right back. Don't go anywhere or talk to anyone."

"I wasn't planning on doing any shopping, but a cup of Starbucks would be nice," she answered him.

Michael shook his head in amusement at her sense of humor as he got out of the car. He walked into Target and headed to the electronics section. Finding the cheapest prepaid cell phones they had, he grabbed two along with a couple of fifty-dollar recharge cards, and headed to the self-checkout registers, paying cash for the phones and cards. He was back in the car in five minutes.

"That was fast," Roxanne commented.

"I wasn't planning on doing any shopping," he answered her with a witty comeback.

"Ha-ha, you're funny. So, have you figured out what our next move is?"

"Our next move is to get you somewhere safe. I have a plan, I just need to make a call first," he told her as he started the car and made his way out of the parking garage. "Are you done copying your contacts?"

"Yeah, just finished. My hand is numb," she told him as she shook it.

"Good. Give me your phone."

"How come? I'm not going to use. I won't even turn it on? I have all my photos and music on it."

"I'm going to need it," he told her.

"Will I get it back?"

"I'll get it back to you, eventually."

"You better," she said, reluctantly handing him her iPhone.

"Do me a favor, take the prepaid phones out of the bag and activate them. There's a couple of recharge cards also for each phone."

She reached in and pulled out the two LG flip phones, looking at them and commenting, "My, aren't these are cutting-edge technology? Can you even text with them?"

"Don't worry, you're not going to be texting anybody."

"Not texting anybody, what do you mean? I have to let someone know where I am. At least my roommate. Otherwise she's going to call the police."

"Roxanne, I don't think you fully understand. You can't tell anybody where you are or what has happened to you. They will be monitoring the numbers of anybody you've ever called. As soon as you contact anyone, they will know where you are," he schooled her.

"So, I'm just going to up and disappear is what you're telling me?"

"That's pretty much it. Don't worry, it's not like you're going to be stuck in some cabin without any electricity in the middle of the woods. You'll probably actually enjoy where you're going to be, even if you are a little bored."

"Where's that?"

"You'll know soon enough," he assured her as he merged onto I-66 east, heading back towards D.C. They drove across the Potomac and down Constitution Avenue, past the Vietnam Memorial and Smithsonian towards the Capitol Building, turning north onto First Street before pulling into Columbus Circle in front of Union Station. Michael drove into the entrance of the parking garage and found a spot on the third level overlooking First Street.

"Did you activate the phones?" he asked her.

"All ready to go."

"I'm going to call your phone, for us to have each other's numbers." Michael dialed the number from her phone's card and waited until it began ringing before hanging up.

"Got it," she told him, saving his number in her new contacts.

"Okay, hang tight for a little bit, I have to make a call," he told her as he got out of the car. He walked to the front of the car and stood by the wall, looking out over First Street. He unlocked his iPhone, which was still on airplane mode, and went to his contacts. Finding the number he was looking, he flipped open his new phone and dialed it. Funny how things had changed, he thought, as the number he dialed started ringing. *When I was Roxanne's age, I had every important number memorized in my head. Must have been at least twenty numbers. Nowadays, lose your phone and you're dead in the water.* Although he still embraced the latest technology out of habit from his days in the CIA, he was still old-school in many ways. He still kept a written schedule and notes in a planner, and he still kept a little black book with all his contacts, although his was actually dark blue.

"Hello?" he heard on the other end.

"Hi, Dad. How you doing?"

"Michael, hello, son. I didn't recognize the number. Where are you calling from?" Pete Blackstone asked. Michael could hear a sizzling sound in the background.

"I'm in D.C., Dad. How's Mom?"

"Your mother's fine. She's out in the yard with her garden. Any minute now, she's going to smell the bacon frying and march in here to give me an earful about my cholesterol. What are you doing in D.C.? You at some sort of real estate conference?"

"No, Dad, I'm not at a conference. Listen, I don't have time to explain everything right now, but I need your help with something. Actually, more like with someone."

"Why, what's going on? You in some sort of trouble."

"No, Dad, just an old friend that may be in a jam. I'm trying to find out what's going on, but he has a daughter that needs to be somewhere safe, where no one can find her. I was wondering if you and Mom could put her up for a while, until I can figure things out?"

"Michael, you're calling me from D.C., on a phone number I don't recognize, telling me an old friend is in trouble and you have to make his daughter disappear because she's in danger. I know what kind of people most of your old friends are. What in the world have you gotten yourself involved in?"

"I didn't say she's in danger, Dad, it's just a precaution. And, yeah, it is one of those old friends. He may be in some danger and he didn't have anyone else to turn to. I'm not involved in any of it, so don't worry. I'm just going to try and find out what happened and help him out if there's any way I can."

"Michael, you're fifty-four years old and you haven't done any of this kind of secret squirrel stuff in a long time. Aren't you getting involved in something that may be out of your league anymore, not to mention a bit more dangerous than getting one of your clients to make an offer on a home?"

"Yeah, Dad, I know I'm not young anymore, and you don't have to keep reminding me about having told me that I wouldn't like real estate. I already have enough regrets for a lifetime."

"Sorry, son, that's not what I meant. Of course we'll help you. How old is this friend's daughter?"

"She's around Sam's age. She's a senior in college. Her name is Roxanne. I'm going to put her on the train and send her down to you. What's the closest

Amtrak station to you?"

"That would be in Palatka, about forty minutes away."

"Can you pick her up when she arrives?"

"Sure, just give me the time."

"I'll have to get the ticket first, and then I'll call you, okay?"

"Sure. What would you like me to tell your mom?"

"I don't know, Dad. Just tell her it's a friend of mine's daughter who is going through a tough time and needs a place to take it easy for a short while. That way she won't be too nosy and ask her a lot of questions. I think you guys will both like her. She's a nice girl."

"Well, it might be nice to have her here for a while. We haven't seen Sam in close to three years now. Maybe we can take her out on the boat for some marlin or yellow tail."

"Yeah, I'm sure she'd love that. Okay, I'm going to get her a ticket and put her on the first train to you. I'll call you back with the info."

"Okay, gotta go. I'm about to be busted. I see your mom heading this way," Pete Blackstone told his son and hung up the cordless phone.

Michael shook his head and smiled. Ever since his father had retired to St. Augustine with his mother, he had surprisingly learned to relax and enjoy life. His mother had taken up gardening and whatever else she did with her social circle of similar transplants from the cold winters of the Northeast to the year-round warmth of Florida. His father had taken up golf at the age of sixty and bought a thirty-four-foot Bayliner Sport Fish, spending several days a week out on the water with his fishing buddies and occasionally Michael's mom. A wave of guilt came flooding over him as he thought how devastated they would have been at the news of his suicide. He stepped back into the car to face Roxanne's intense stare.

"Well?"

"Well, you're going to St. Augustine, Florida."

"What's in St. Augustine?"

"My mom and dad," he informed her.

"Your mom and dad? You're going to have them harbor a fugitive?" she asked him, astonished.

"You're not a fugitive. It's just a place to keep you safe and out of the way for a while."

"When you're running away from ninja guys following you around in a black van, what do you call that?"

"Trust me, they're not ninja guys. What I meant was, it's not like you're running away from law enforcement. You haven't done anything to break the law, so there's no reason to believe it's the police who are interested in you. If it were the police, I wouldn't be so worried. So, until I can find out exactly who all the players involved are, it's best if you just disappear for a while. I don't work for the government anymore, so it's not like I can put you in the witness protection program. My parents' place is the only option I have right now. You'll get along fine with them. They're very easygoing, and they live a block from the beach."

"The beach, huh? Well, I suppose there might have been a lot of worse places you could have hidden me away, like in some tenement building in Baltimore," she said, becoming more amenable at thought of lying on the beach every day.

"Let's get you a ticket, then," he told her, both of them opening their doors and getting out of the car. They walked down the stairs and entered the cavernous hall of Union Station, walking over to the ticket kiosk. They looked at the scheduled departures for Palatka, Florida and found the Amtrak Silver Star departing in a little over four and a half hours and arriving in Palatka the next day at 8:10 a.m., nearly seventeen hours later.

"Seventeen hours," Roxanne groaned.

"Sorry, you can't fly. They'd find you instantly through the airline reservation system. You don't have to give your real name for a train ticket. Tell you what, I'll get you a Viewliner cabin, so you can at least sleep and—look, even take a shower in your own private bathroom," he told her. *Ouch,* he thought when he saw the difference in price between a standard seat and a cabin. *Oh well, a plane ticket wouldn't have been much cheaper last minute like this.* He opened his wallet and pulled out four hundred-dollar bills.

"Oh wow, that's not cheap! I could have sat in a regular old seat."

"It's seventeen hours, you'll appreciate it later."

"I already appreciate it. Thanks."

"Well, we have over four hours to kill. There's a bunch of shops, and we can get a bite to eat. I think we'll be okay in here. The odds of anyone showing up here looking for us aren't that great. As far as they know, we're in a car heading somewhere."

They walked into the quaint Union Station Café and took a table in the corner.

"It's getting close to lunchtime. You hungry?" he asked her.

"Starved. Haven't eaten since last night."

"Yeah, me too."

After the waitress took their order, Roxanne asked, "So, Michael, are you going to tell me why of all the people in the world my dad could have turned to for help, it ended up being you?"

Michael sat there for a moment, thinking about what he should tell her. It wasn't so much about any of the specifics of what he and Ali and had been involved in Athens; he couldn't tell her anything about that. It was more about trying to come up with an actual reason Ali had decided to put all his trust in him at such a critical time.

"To be perfectly honest with you, I don't know why your dad turned to me. It's been a long time since we worked together. He was capable and reliable and picked up on things very quickly, but most of all, he was a good man, down to his core. I always trusted him. He never let me down. Unfortunately, others did."

"You mean my dad did secret agent kind of stuff with you?" she asked excitedly.

"Let's just say your dad was in a unique position to help his country, and he stepped up when he was asked," he told her, trying to deflect her question.

"Oh, I see. You can't tell me or you'd have to kill me," she giggled. "Well, whatever my dad did with you, he must have trusted you a lot also, for him to ask you for help now."

"I suppose he did. I just hope he's not overestimating what I'm capable of," Michael replied hesitantly.

"My dad's a pretty good judge of people. If he turned to you, there's a reason."

"We'll see. I'll do whatever is possible to try to help him, I just don't want you to get your hopes up too much. I don't know if you've watched the news lately, but the Iranian foreign minister was assassinated close to the time your dad contacted you. Whether he called before or after it happened really isn't that important. What is important is who he mentioned. This can have really serious international implications, and the parties involved will stop at nothing to make sure your dad never tells anyone. That's what I'm up against." He felt bad having to tell her that. She was obviously worried enough about her dad, even if she was making a good effort at maintaining her composure. Michael just thought it would be cruel to get her hopes up when he knew all too well the odds he was facing.

"I realize that, and I'm not expecting you to perform any miracles. I know who two of the people, I mean person and country, are, but who is Canton?"

Michael thought about what to tell her. He knew the significance of Canton's involvement, even if he didn't know any of the details yet. The mention of his name was what ultimately convinced Michael he had no other choice but to get involved. He finally answered her question. "He's someone I wouldn't trust further than I could throw him."

"Sounds like you know him pretty well."

"Yeah, I know him really well."

"Does my dad know him? I mean, other than from now?"

"Unfortunately, he does."

"Is he dangerous?"

"Only if you turn your back on him. But he may be the best lead I have at this point."

They finished eating and talked for another couple of hours. Their conversation shifted away from their current situation, and they talked about Roxanne's major in journalism and ambition to get into television news. It caught Michael by surprise when she mentioned it, but he enjoyed telling her his thoughts and observations based on Karen's career before they had Sam. At last, they heard boarding call announced over the PA system for her train.

"Looks like you're up. Listen, before you head down there, I want to give you something that you're going to need." He reached into his back pocket and pulled out his bulging wallet. Flipping it open, he pulled out the wad of cash and counted out ten hundred-dollar bills. Reaching across the table, he said, "Here, you're going to need a little spending money for clothes or whatever. Don't worry about food, my parents will have all that covered. I'm sure my dad will probably pester you the day you arrive for a list of whatever food you like so he can make a run to Costco. You can't use any of your plastic, not debit cards or credit cards, and that means no ordering on-line. If it's an electronic transaction, they'll know about it five minutes later. The same goes with your new cell phone. You can't ever use it to call anyone you know. The only ones you should ever call is me on my new phone, or my parents. Here's their home number and cell phones. Put them in your phone, Pete and Mary Ann." He recited the three numbers for her. "That's it. No one else. I mean it. Even though you don't know anyone down there, try to keep a low profile. I don't know how long you'll have to be there, but don't make any friends. Do you understand what I'm telling you?" he stressed.

"Yep, you want me to become a ghost. I got it. You see, I pick up this secret agent ninja stuff pretty quick," she said, making light of the circumstances.

"Yeah, you do. You'll probably make a good investigative journalist someday," he shot back.

"You really think so? I never really gave that much thought. Yeah, I can be like the Millennial generation's Christiane Amanpour," she bantered with him.

"Okay, we better start heading down to your train," he announced as he stood up and left cash on the table with their bill. They walked down to the platform and located Roxanne's car. They stood outside the door, looking at each other one last time. Michael held out his hand to her for a final goodbye, but instead he got her arms around his shoulders and her head on his chest. Michael felt her trying to hold back her sobbing.

"Hey, you're going to be okay. You need to stay strong and don't give up hope. I promise you, I'll do whatever is in my power to help your dad." He chose his words carefully, purposely not telling her everything was going to be okay. He didn't want to promise something he wasn't sure he could deliver.

"I'll be all right." She let go of him and wiped her tears. She looked at him one last time and forced a smile before turning and stepping into her train car and out of his sight.

He turned and walked back towards the doors to the main terminal, looking at faces to see if he spotted anything unnatural in anyone's demeanor. One thing that his surveillance detection training at the Farm had taught him was how to recognize anomalies in one's environment. Whether it was seeing the same vehicle over time and distance, or a person appearing out of place for their surroundings, Michael had mastered the tradecraft. It was one of the most important tools of an intelligence officer operating in foreign environments. The converse was true for surveillance tradecraft; being able to follow someone over a sustained period of time without being detected. It was the most tedious of the tradecraft disciplines, but it could also be the most challenging and exciting at times. It was one thing to remain hidden within a vehicle and follow from a distance; it was entirely different being on foot, having to maintain eyes on the target without being observed. One of the fundamentals was to avoid making eye contact, which drew attention to oneself. Michael knew this and directed his gaze at each face he encountered, looking for any reaction that could give an indication he was being surveilled.

It was a technique the instructors at the Farm had used to make trainees choke and give themselves away. The human psyche had an unconscious tendency to reveal things through the eyes. It was why it was also such an important tool in interrogations—focusing on the eyes of the subject—looking for any signs of deception. Of all the training Michael had undergone at the Farm, he had enjoyed the tradecraft segment the most. It had included a number of real-world simulations, staged in various locations up and down the East Coast. He had done very well, and it had paid dividends for him out in the field many times.

He walked to a convenience kiosk and purchased the Sunday edition of the *Washington Post*. He walked back out to the platform, where he found a bench that he could see down the full length of Roxanne's train. He sat down and looked at his watch. He had twenty minutes until her train was scheduled to depart. He opened up his paper and held it in front of him. Starting with the front page and making it to the second, he spent the remaining time glancing back and forth between his paper and the platform, until Roxanne's train finally started pulling out of the station. Other than a few loved ones of passengers, who were standing outside the train, waving their final goodbyes through the windows, Michael didn't spot anything unusual. He folded his paper and carried it with him into the terminal. He walked across to the doors leading to the stairs of the parking garage and double-timed it up to the third level, walking over to his car while trying to catch his breath. It surprised him he was winded, considering the fantastic run he'd had the day before yesterday. *Hmm. Knowing you're going to kill yourself as soon as you're done running must be a pretty good motivational factor. Could be a good mind trick for professional distance runners*, he thought. He unlocked his car door and got in. Opening his cell phone, he hit redial and waited for his father to answer.

"Hello," came his mother's voice.

"Hi, Mom."

"Well, hi, Michael. How are you, honey?"

"I'm good, Mom. How's everything with you?"

"Oh, you know me, I keep busy enough with my gardening and my friends. I also volunteer at the church whenever they need me. Your father told me we're going to have some company for a little while. Is your friend's daughter okay? He didn't tell me what's wrong with her, just that she needs some time away from her current situation. Is there anything I can do for her? Do you want me to set her up an appointment with Rhonda, to talk with her? You know

Rhonda, she's treated hundreds of artists, musicians and actors with all kinds of problems, depression, infidelity, alcohol, even pervert type things."

"Mom, who is Rhonda? And, no, there's nothing you need to do for her. She just needs a little time away. Just give her some space. She's a nice girl, you guys will like her."

"She was a therapist up in New York, for all those famous people. You know, those poor souls that have all those problems common with artists. Oh, I'm sure we'll like her. I wish Sam would come and visit us sometime. It's been so long since we've seen her. How is everything with you and Eva? We haven't seen you guys either. It's been over a year now."

"Yeah, I know, Mom. Listen, I can't talk very long now. I just wanted to let you guys know Roxanne's train will be arriving in Palatka tomorrow morning at eight ten. Tell Dad so he can go there and pick her up. Here's her cell phone number. Do you have something to write it down?" He waited before reading her the number twice to make sure she copied it correctly. "Okay, thanks, Mom, I really appreciate it. As soon as I'm done with a few things, I'll come and visit you guys. Talk to you soon. Love you."

"We love you too very much. Bye-bye, honey," he heard right before hanging up.

One issue taken care of, now time to make another call. He opened his little blue book and turned to the Bs, finding the number he was looking for. It had been several years since he had spoken to him, but he was the only person Michael thought might be able to help, at least give some counsel. He had no one else to turn to. He entered the number and hit call, listening to it ring.

"Hello," he heard on the other end.

"Harry, this is Mike Blackstone. How you doing?"

"Mikey! It's been a while. I'm doing great! Loving semi-retirement, even though I'm still collecting a full salary while working from home. How's everything with you? I think last time we talked, you were still doing the real estate thing back in Seattle."

"Yeah, that's me, Mr. Real Estate. Not much to get excited about, but I make my own hours and I'm not stuck behind a desk all day."

"I know what you mean. If I couldn't sit in my underwear and drink my morning coffee behind my desk at home, I'd have called it quits a while ago and moved back to the PI with Rose," Harry Barso bellowed in his familiar raucous tone, referring to the Philippine Islands. "Yep, heat, sun, water and lots of young pretty little things walking around in short shorts and tank tops year-round."

"That's right, you got married. As I recall, she's quite a bit younger than you."

"Thirty years. You should see the looks I get when I'm out with her. Wives look at me like I'm some dirty old man, while their husbands walking next to them are fantasizing what it must be like to have a hot little thing like her."

"So, what do you care about seeing pretty young things in shorts when you have one at home year-round now?" Michael said, giving him a hard time.

"Heck, it's not the same, buddy. They get to the US and everything changes. They become just like every other American gal. Shopping, television, Internet. I can't complain, though, she makes some mouthwatering lumpia. I think I've put on ten pounds since I married her. So, what made you call out of the blue after all this time? It's always great to hear from you, but I don't think you were just having fond memories of your old boss and decided to see how I was doing."

"Harry, you always knew how to get right to the point, even if you were halfway tanked on one of our Saturday nights. I'm in D.C. Something's come up from the past, and I need your help," Michael was short and straight to the point. He wasn't going to say much over an open line, even with his anonymous prepaid cell phone. Despite what the public already knew about NSA's meta data collection program, what was much less known was the PRISM program. PRISM intercepted virtually every mobile network call in the world and sifted the millions of calls every minute through NSA's supercomputers, analyzing them in seconds with algorithms for keywords and phrases, and triggering an immediate phone intercept if the conversation fell within specified parameters. He would wait to fill in Harry face-to-face.

"Well, why don't you plan on stopping by and staying for dinner? I'll have Rose whip us up something good to eat, and then we can sit out on the patio for a cigar and cognac."

"That sounds great, Harry."

"Come by around six. That's in a little over two hours. That work? I'll text you my address."

"Don't bother. I have a thirty-dollar dumb phone I'm calling you from. You can just give me the directions old-fashioned way."

"Hmm, must be serious if you're using a burner. Still remember all the old tricks of the trade, I see."

"Yeah. I'll fill you in over that cognac and cigar."

Harry gave Michael his address in Bethesda, Maryland, and step-by-step directions from downtown D.C. "That should take you about twenty, twenty-five minutes, depending on the traffic. Seems like there's always traffic here, even Sunday evenings."

"Sounds good. See you in a bit."

"See ya then, buddy."

It gave Michael a sense of reassurance that he would be able to confer with his old mentor and friend. Harry had been one of the sharpest bosses he had ever worked for in the CIA. Despite having a reputation for being the life of the party when it came to after-hours libations, Harry was one of the most adept and well-respected chiefs of station throughout the Agency. He had been on course to become part of the senior leadership back at CIA headquarters, if it hadn't been for the heat he'd taken for standing behind Michael, even when Langley demanded its sacrificial lamb. It was one of the things still hard to shoulder at times, the feeling of responsibility for sidelining Harry's career. All of a sudden, Michael's uncomfortable night sandwiched in between his two fellow travelers began catching up with him. Overcome with exhaustion, he figured he had time to recharge some before having to head out for Harry's. He reclined his seat back, set the timer on his watch for one and a half hours and closed his eyes. *I could definitely use a power nap if I'm going to be enjoying a cigar and sipping cognac with Harry. I may not get to bed before midnight*, he thought as he drifted off to sleep.

***

The unmarked white Gulfstream G550 landed at Joint Base Andrews just outside of Washington, D.C. In addition to being the home of Air Force One and the fleet of jets used by the various cabinet secretaries and senior Congressional leadership, it also had numerous other military and federal civilian tenants, including the large unmarked hangar at the far end of the field. The hangar housed the small fleet of executive jets that made up the CIA's own autonomous air force it used for transportation to all corners of the globe. As a deputy director, Canton was authorized to use an aircraft for the sensitive operation he was on. They had made it from Istanbul back to D.C. in just under eleven hours nonstop, thanks to the Gulfstream's max cruising speed and cruising altitude of Mach 0.87 and fifty-one thousand feet. The aircraft taxied over to the lone hangar and pulled in, concealing it from the rest of the airport activity. After coming to a stop, the CIA-employed flight attendant opened the Gulfstream's door and lowered the stairs, allowing Canton to exit and walk over to the black Chevy Suburban his assistant was standing next to, waiting for him.

"Steve. Bring me up to speed on the latest with Shiravi's daughter and

Blackstone. Where are they?"

"Sir, we don't have that information. The surveillance team lost them. We had both of them at Shiravi's home in Old Town earlier today. They left from there, heading towards D.C. on Highway 1, when Blackstone pulled a sudden U-turn. Both their cell phones went dark shortly afterwards," his assistant briefed him in the backseat as their driver pulled out of the hangar and headed for Langley.

"What do you mean, lost them? How the hell did that happen?" Canton asked, visibly cross.

"Like I told you, boss, he pulled a sudden U-ey in the middle of Highway 1 and then they lost tracking on their phones."

"That son of a bitch! He obviously made the surveillance team. Any transactions by either of them with any of their cards? Airline or hotel reservations?"

"Nope, not a thing since she purchased her train ticket from Boston, and for him, a hold on his card for a Hertz rental from Reagan National. It's a gray Chevy Blazer with Virginia plates. We're plugged into all D.C. metro area toll and traffic cams but haven't had any hits yet."

"Fuck! Fuck! Fuck!" Canton was livid. The last thing he needed was Michael Blackstone sticking his nose in the middle of this. It was bad enough Ali had overheard their conversation, but finding and eliminating him was a manageable undertaking, especially since he was trapped somewhere in Turkey. But to have their conspiracy compromised by Blackstone was an unacceptable risk. It was imperative he locate Blackstone and Roxanne Shiravi to find out exactly how much they knew, and permanently silence them if necessary. "I want to know the second we get a hit on his rental. I don't want that son of a bitch taking a shit without me knowing about it. Do you understand?"

"Yes sir. I'll make sure you're informed the second he passes gas."

"In case you haven't figured it out yet, Steve, I don't have a sense of humor, so don't try to kiss ass with me. It's not going to get you promoted any faster."

"Yes, sir. Do you want to go back to the office?"

"No, take me home. I'm not going to sit in my office on a Sunday afternoon waiting for Blackstone to show his face. I want you and—what's this guy's name?"

"Foster, sir," their driver volunteered.

"You and Foster to stand by with the Suburban in my driveway in case we get a hit on either of them. You can come in and use the bathroom, but otherwise make the best of it. It may be a while."

"We'll manage, sir," his assistant answered, all the while wondering how he had been so lucky getting an assignment as his assistant. *There's a good reason why everyone thinks you're a prick*, he thought, almost wishing Canton could read his mind.

Chapter 8

Michael heard the electronic beeping in the distance as he strained to maintain the vision of Eva lying face-down on her beach chair with the strings of her bikini top undone, exposing her tanned back and legs. They would often spend Sunday afternoons at Vouliagmeni Beach south of Athens, from the middle of April well into October when the weather cooperated. He lay back down on his chair next to Eva and closed his eyes, trying to ignore it, and focus instead on relaxing sound of the surf. The beeping grew louder until that was all he could hear. He sat up from his beach chair and opened his eyes, searching for the source of the annoying sound, but found himself staring at the steering wheel of his rental car, realizing he was dreaming of a distant memory that had somehow embedded itself into his subconscious. He took in a deep breath and blew it out slowly as he tried to reorient himself. He pushed the button on his watch and stopped the alarm he had set an hour and a half ago. It was 5:40 p.m. He brought up his reclined seat and started the engine. He pulled out of the Union Station parking garage and headed across town to Wisconsin Avenue, taking it north towards Bethesda. When he reached Chevy Chase just before Bethesda, he made a series of turns through some residential neighborhoods, conducting a hasty surveillance detection route to see if he had picked up a tail. He didn't observe anyone following him.

***

The officer sitting behind the console of monitors reached past his thirty-two-ounce insulated coffee jug for another Dunkin Donuts Old-Fashioned glazed. Sergeant Mahoney was almost a thirty-year veteran of the D.C. Metro Police Department. After suffering a minor heart attack chasing after two teenagers who had robbed a liquor store with only six months until retirement, he had been transferred the central traffic monitoring division at the Henry J. Daly Building, D.C. Metro's headquarters. He told himself he would start eating healthier after retirement as he brought the donut towards his mouth while looking up at one of his monitors. His elbow caught the top of his coffee jug, tipping it over onto the counter and popping its lid. Twenty ounces of still-steaming-hot coffee came flying towards him, hitting him square in his lap. He shot up, sending his chair flying backwards, shouting a series of obscenities as the scalding liquid soaked through his pants into his tighty-whities. He futilely looked around for something to soak up the coffee, but found nothing. Turning from his console, he headed out the door and down the hallway to the restroom just as all his monitors flickered and turned solid blue. Stripping out of his pants and underwear, he stood in front of one of the sinks, washing them with the soap from the hand dispenser. He figured he would use one of the hand dryers to dry them off. Hoping no one would walk in on him standing half-naked in his socks and shoes and top half of his uniform, he heard the creak of the door as it swung open and the deputy chief of the department walked in, stopping and staring at Sergeant Mahoney for a brief moment before turning and walking back out without saying a word. Unbeknownst to Michael, he had passed through thirteen intersections with traffic cameras during his drive to Harry's. All had failed to capture his license plate due to a temporary software glitch in the computer system of the D.C. Police Department's monitoring center, rendering the CIA's hack into their camera feeds blind for seventeen minutes.

***

Michael located Harry's home in a high-end neighborhood in north Bethesda. The smaller of the homes averaged three thousand square feet, with every home sitting on half an acre and backyards abutting a green zone. He pulled into the circular driveway of a two-story beige brick colonial with a columned portico over the front entrance. As a result of the recent change to daylight savings time, it was still light enough to get a good view of the neighborhood. Michael could see that Harry was obviously doing very well for himself ever since he'd left the Agency for the private sector. Michael pushed the doorbell and heard the chimes inside announcing his arrival. A few seconds later, the door opened and the tall presence of Harry Barso holding a glass of what Michael knew was scotch appeared before him.

"Mikey! My wayward son, come on in!" he shouted with exuberance.

"How ya doing, Harry?" Michael reached out his hand, instead getting a bear hug. Michael reciprocated the unexpected gesture of affection from his former boss. They had spent many close times shutting down a pub in Athens, but that was a long time ago and before the incident.

"I'm doing great! It's good to see you, Mike, after all these years. The few times we talked on the phone over the years just doesn't cut it. Come on in, buddy. We'll go sit outside in the enclosed patio until dinner's ready." They passed through the kitchen, where a young and attractive woman, wearing a red apron over a brightly flowered silk blouse and a clingy black skirt in tall cork platform heels, was busy cooking several dishes that were emitting mouthwatering aromas. "This is my sweet, beautiful Rose. Honey, this is Michael. He and I worked together a while back. He is a true gentleman," Harry said, making introductions.

"Nice to meet you, Rose. How did someone as pretty as you get stuck with an old fart like Harry here?" Michael poked a little fun at Harry's hair, which had turned completely white. He remembered Harry's salt-and-pepper hair from Athens, when Harry claimed it was a magnet for younger women after a sugar daddy.

"You know, that's what my father said also, that I should marry someone who at least was younger than him." She shot a smile of endearment towards Harry while having a little fun reminding him how lucky he was to have a wife so much younger than him.

"Oh! I look better than at least half the guys ten years older than me. Just remember, you married the best of the best." He let out a hearty laugh.

"Why don't you two go into the patio and catch up until dinner is ready?" she told them in her cute Filipino accent.

"Follow me, buddy, and let me make you a drink," he said, leading Michael into a large heated glassed-in patio that had dark green artificial turf and a collection of wicker furnishings. Harry walked over to a small bar with an impressive collection of liquors. "If I remember correctly, you were a vodka on the rocks guy. Stoli okay?"

"That's fine. You still remember after all this time?"

"Of course I do. We had our share of closing down the Galaxy Bar at the Hilton. I remember fondly some of those Saturday nights in the summer up on the rooftop. Great place to meet flight attendants. Remember that sweetheart that couldn't get enough of me? What was her name? Helene, from Swiss Air. Those were some good times. That's where you met Eva, if I remember correctly?" Harry asked as he handed Michael his drink and sat down in a wicker chair with his scotch.

"Yeah, it was."

"How is she? Last I remember you telling me, she was doing some modeling for some department store, Nordstrom, was it?"

"She did, still does, I think. I don't know, we haven't spoken much the past year."

"That doesn't sound good. You guys split up?"

"Actually, it'll be official tomorrow, but things have been pretty rocky for the past several years. Seems like both of us were way off with our expectations of how we thought things would turn out. Can't say it's her fault. I had a lot to do with it."

"Oh, Mike, I'm really sorry to hear that. Besides being a knockout, she was a nice gal, intelligent, good sense of humor, and not hung up on her looks.

Wow, did you hear that? I just described every man's dream. Did she know how to cook?"

"If you consider green smoothies cooking. That wasn't her forte, but she made up for it in other ways. Yeah, she is a great gal. Guess she wanted something different than what she got with me. Anyway, it's for the best, so both of us can move on with our lives," Michael told him, withholding the full extent of what that meant. "How long have you and Rose been married? I can't remember when's the last time we talked. Must have been a couple years now."

"We'll be married three years this May. I met her when I was on a business trip over there. She was singing in the bar at the Pan Pacific in Manila. The minute I saw her and heard that sweet voice of hers, I knew I had to do whatever was in my power to get her to have dinner with me. All I needed was fifteen minutes to work my charm, and she was mine."

"More like two days of asking me to go to dinner, and most of the night trying to convince me it was safe to go out on a second date with you," Rose interrupted them, bringing in a plate of hors d'oeuvres.

"Oh, you were just playing hard to get, trying to show me what an upright and proper woman you were. I could tell after your first glass of wine, you found me to be the most charming and witty man that ever swept you off your feet, not to mention handsome." Harry let out a hearty laugh, reaching around and hugging Rose as she gave him a peck on his cheek before walking back to the kitchen.

"She seems like a real sweetheart. I hope you're happy, Harry."

"I have no complaints. I got a great job that pays three times what I made working for Uncle Sam, a hot young wife who adores me and, knock on wood, my health is pretty good despite what my doctor says about my cholesterol and weight."

"I see you're getting a little soft in your old age. Now that you got Rose, the beer belly doesn't matter that much anymore," Michael needled Harry.

"I just don't have it in me anymore to be chasing tail around, acting like some forty-year-old. The years were rolling by and I would come home from some business trip to an empty house. I don't have any kids and not many people I can call real friends. I don't know what she may have seen in me other than a ticket to the United States, but Rose is a sweet girl and treats me like a king. I didn't want to spend my last years alone, without anyone. When I start drooling and can't feed myself anymore, I got it all planned for me to move to a care facility that she can come and visit me once a week. The house will be paid for, and there's enough left for her to live a comfortable life with whoever she chooses to afterwards."

"Yeah, that's what I was hoping I'd have with Eva. It's probably better I stay out of relationships. Makes things less complicated."

"That's not the Mike Blackstone I remember. What the hell happened to you, Mike? I never heard you sound down. Even after all that happened and you leaving the Agency, you always had this spirit of resilience and fortitude, like nothing could bring you down."

"I don't know, Harry. I guess I'm not that person. Life just didn't turn out the way I'd planned."

"Since when does life turn out the way anyone plans? Do you think I planned on being where I'm at now? I thought I'd be with the Agency until I was so old, the youngsters would be asking me to tell them stories about the Bay of Pigs. Life doesn't ask you what you want, nor does it care. You take what it gives you, and you make the best of it."

"I know that, Harry. It still bothers me that you ended up leaving early. You took a lot of heat for me, and it cost you. I know life's not fair, but you shouldn't have had to suffer the consequences for something that I was responsible for."

"That's not what I'm talking about. You weren't responsible for anything. You forget, I was your boss and knew everything you did was the way it should have been done. There's nothing you did or failed to do that caused what happened. Intelligence work isn't always neat and tidy. Things go wrong sometimes and people end up dead. That's just the way it is, and the way it will always be. What do you think happened the year after you left, when Mathews and the six others were killed in Afghanistan? Do you think they screwed up because they trusted their source and didn't search him? Do you think they were responsible for their deaths? Intelligence is a dark and ugly business with bad people that don't have your best interests in mind. I wouldn't have stuck my neck out for you if you'd screwed up. Langley just needed its pound of flesh and wasn't going to let things be without someone paying. That's the way federal bureaucracies work, and the Agency's no different," Harry admonished Michael as a teacher would his student.

"Yeah, Harry, I know that, and I know I'm not anyone special to think I deserve otherwise. It's just that I always felt I had a purpose. Whether it was in the Army or with the Agency, I believed I was doing something that had meaning, something that would make a difference. Ever since that got taken away, it seems like I've just been going through the motions. Hard to wake up every morning and get excited about driving around with a couple all day, showing them home after home. I went from being a secret agent to a real estate agent."

"Oh, so it's a matter of your ego being hurt. Your identity was taken away from you and now it's a big pity party. You know, Mike, it's easy to fall into the trap of thinking who you are as a person is all wrapped up in what you do, especially in the line of work we were in. Your idea of self-importance shapes the image you have of yourself, and when that's taken away, you feel inadequate, helpless, less of a man. You got to find purpose and meaning in life outside of your job. Otherwise, you'll either end up a bitter old drunk who's miserable, or even worse."

Harry's words stung Michael deeper than he realized, but they achieved their intended effect. Harry knew him better than he knew himself. He knew Michael wasn't one to roll over when the road got rough. In his case, it wasn't that the road was rough; it was just the opposite. There was no challenge, nothing to overcome, nothing to make Michael feel he was accomplishing something that made a difference in some way. He knew he had to strike at Michael's pride a bit to focus his attention away from the quagmire of self-pity he had gotten bogged down in. Michael sat silently for a few moments, contemplating Harry's words as they both sipped their drinks.

"You're right, Harry. For me, it was even worse. I was in a pretty dark place. I won't bother you with the details, but let's just say I wouldn't be here talking to you right now if something hadn't, or I should say had, happened that I can't quite wrap my head around just yet. Then I get this strange message out of the blue on my voicemail from the daughter of Ali Shiravi. Not someone I could have ever imagined crossing paths with again in this lifetime. That's the reason why I'm here," Michael confessed, feeling a sense of relief that he had been able to confide to his former boss and friend.

"Shiravi? I haven't heard that name in a long time. Why did his daughter contact you?"

"You're not going to believe what I'm about to tell you. Ali works for the State Department now as an interpreter. He was in Istanbul with Secretary of State Payton, who was meeting with the Iranian foreign minister to discuss Iran's missile program. He called his daughter from there and told her to contact me and pass on this message, that Payton, Jonathan Canton and the Russians are going to try to kill the Iranian foreign minister."

Michael paused a moment and allowed what he had just told Harry to sink in. After a couple of seconds elapsed, Harry came back with, "That sounds crazy, except for the fact that the Iranian foreign minister is dead. What else did he say?"

"That's it. His daughter said he was adamant about tracking me down and passing on that message. I just met with her at her dad's condo in Old Town. She took the train down here from Boston where she goes to school, to get my number from Ali's address book. His place was under surveillance when I got there. I can't say for sure who it was, but I made a black surveillance van parked down the block from his house. I'm guessing they got her mobile number from the call Ali made to her, and consequently mine, from the call she made to me. They may have tracked her there or just been sitting on his place, but from the looks of the van, I think they were tracking her. It looked like the same kind we used with the concealed arrays up on the roof rack. They followed us out of the neighborhood, but I lost them when I pulled a quick U-turn on US-1 going into D.C. That's the reason I picked up the prepaid cell phones. I don't know what Ali's involved in, but I told her I would try to help. She was desperate. She didn't have anyone else to turn to. Her mom died a few years back. I'm sure they know she contacted me, but I don't think they know what Ali told her. Otherwise, they would have already picked her up and probably me also. I don't know if she's in any danger, but I didn't want her going back to Boston under the circumstances. I bought her an Amtrak ticket under a fake name down to my parents' place in St. Augustine, with cash. She's going to stay with them for a while until I can find out something, anything about what happened to her father. I've told my folks she's the daughter of a friend that needs to get away from some things for a while. I've emphasized to her how important it is for her to keep a low profile and not attempt to contact anybody, even with her clean phone. I don't know if they've been able to get any info yet on my rental to track me through traffic cams, but I did an SDR on the way over here and I'm fairly confident I didn't pick up a tail. That's pretty much the gist of it. Is that crazy enough for you?"

"Holy shit, Mike, what the hell have you gotten yourself into? I didn't hear the specifics about Mohammedi's assassination, but Ali's message sounds beyond bizarre. The Secretary of State? The Russians? And what does that snake, Canton, have to do with all of this? It doesn't make any sense. Why would they do that? What would they have to gain? The entire Middle East is barely keeping it together. It will be total chaos if things spin out of control between the Iranians and the Israelis. It'll make Syria and ISIS seem like a birthday party," Harry exclaimed.

"Tell me about it. That's why I wanted to get your take on it. I don't know if there's anything I can do to find out what Ali's involved in, let alone help him, but I felt I had to give it a try."

"Mike, you don't owe Ali anything. You're going to risk your neck for someone you haven't seen in, what, ten years? Someone you don't even know that well? Who knows what he's gotten himself involved in? You may be getting yourself into something you can't get out of. It could even end up getting you killed. Do you understand what I'm telling you?"

There was a silence as Michael wrestled with the reality he was now facing. Once he took the next step, he was past the point of no return. For all he knew, he might already have passed it just by knowing what Ali had told them. The implications of that information itself alone would be enough to put some of the most powerful people in the world in a very vulnerable position, one they wouldn't hesitate a second to kill over. What did he really expect he could do? Go around asking far-fetched and absurd questions about the US Secretary of State and—who, President Markov, the man who didn't hesitate to use the blunt force of the Russian military against civilians and call it fighting terrorists? *I must be out of my mind. I don't know which is worse, giving Roxanne a glimmer of false hope, even if I told her not to count on anything, or actually thinking there was something I could do to help Ali. I must still be going through withdrawals from the drugs and alcohol.*

Michael looked up at Harry, not sure quite sure if he was just thinking it or had actually said it out loud. Harry just returned that kindhearted but penetrating look Michael remembered, the one that expected you to examine the truth of every situation, no matter how much you didn't like what the answer was going to be. Harry was particularly astute at using it during many of their well-oiled philosophical discussions at the Galaxy rooftop bar on warm Athens summer nights, with the lit-up Acropolis staring at them from a mile away. He had perfected it to the point of being able to convince the multitude of flight attendants overnighting at the Hilton that he was a well-known psychologist who had treated many famous celebrities. Harry had a personality that would fill the room when there was an audience of attractive women. The fact that he could play the piano half-decent and sang well enough to do a pretty good impersonation of a lounge singer meant there was never a dull moment hanging out with Harry. But along with the carefree side to him, there was another side that had the seriousness of a person who dealt with the matters of life and death and didn't have the patience for distorting facts and avoiding the truth.

"Harry, I know I've put myself in an impossible situation. I know I may get myself killed. But trust me when I tell you, that really doesn't faze me anymore. It's not that I don't care about it. I definitely have some issues I need to work through, but I've already been down that road before. You're right, I don't owe Ali anything. He was just an asset of mine, and it was a long time ago. But I do know him very well, more than just his basic motivators to control him. I don't know exactly what it was, but there was a friendship, a bond of trust, that was built between us. By the end, he was doing everything I was tasking him with out of some sense of loyalty or obligation, not wanting to let me down. In some ways, I could trust him more than many of the people I worked with. I at least owe him my earnest effort to try to help him somehow, even if it comes up way short." Michael disclosed the truth about what he was feeling, even if it didn't make rational sense to most people. It didn't even make rational sense to him.

Harry shook his head from side to side with a grin on his face. "Mike, you haven't changed a bit. The one thing you always had was a good internal compass pointing you in the right direction. Sometimes you just can't get all the facts and you got to go with your gut instinct. That's what made you such a good case officer. If you think this guy is worth putting your life at risk, then who am I to judge your decision? That's a pretty gallant thing you're doing. To tell you the truth, I don't know if I would be willing to do something like that if it was you in Shiravi's shoes."

"Harry, I know you. Of course you would."

"Well, maybe come bail you out of jail for urinating in public, but what you're doing is almost suicidal," Harry told him, admonishing him on one hand while admiring his courage on the other.

"Harry! Michael! Dinner is ready," Rose called from the other room.

"Let's pick this up again after we chow down on some mouthwatering Filipino food. I've been all over Asia, but there's nothing quite like what my Rose cooks up in the kitchen," Harry rubbed his stomach where it was stretching some of his shirt buttons. "Gotta get back to the gym someday. Otherwise I'm going to have to get myself some new clothes," he laughed, getting up from the wicker patio chair and leading Michael to the dining room table.

Rose had prepared a variety of Philippine dishes for their dinner guest. While Michael feasted on the abundance in front of him, he listened to Harry recount what it was like spending two weeks with Rose's family, something that was customary with many Filipinos whose daughter or sister was going to be bringing someone new into the family. After an hour of enjoyable conversation with Rose and eating until both of them were stuffed, they excused themselves and returned to the patio. It was dark outside by now. Harry switched on the cable lighting running around the perimeter of the ceiling, which, along with the numerous tropical plants filling the room, gave it an exotic ambiance of somewhere far removed from the Beltway.

"You up for a good cigar and another drink?" Harry asked.

"I'll never turn down one of your cigars," Michael answered, remembering Harry's passion for good cigars.

Harry walked over to the bar and made each of them another drink, stopping by a good-sized humidor and grabbing two cigars before returning to his chair next to Michael. "Here you go, buddy." He clipped the end of a cigar, handing it to Michael along with a cigar torch.

"Cohiba, you always liked a good cigar," Michael commented, examining the expensive Cuban he was handed.

"There are few pleasures in life you can enjoy in which the only cost is money, and this is one of them," Harry responded, placing the lighter at the end of his cigar while puffing on it to get it started.

"This room must be where you come to get away from everything. You live in a great neighborhood, Harry, but just driving here reminded me how much you can feel all the urgency and stress everywhere. How have you kept your sanity living here so long?"

"Yep, this is my little Shangri-La. You get used to it after a while, and with what Lockheed Martin's paying me, it makes it very tolerable. I get out of this place every month or so on business, and Rose and I have been going to the Philippines every winter to get out of the cold for a month. It's not a bad little gig. I'll keep doing it until they tell me it's time to leave because I'm starting to repeat myself, telling the same stories over and over again."

"Harry, you were doing that from when I knew you back in Athens. So, what is it exactly you're doing for Lockheed Martin?" "I am the VP of their foreign threat department. I'm the only VP I know that doesn't have a single person working under them, other than my secretary, who pretty much just manages my travel schedule and tells me when I've left my fly down. They had to give me the title of VP to justify the obscene salary they pay me. I advise them on what the terrorist and foreign intelligence threats are in places they're doing business overseas. All of it with foreign military sales. I fly into town and pay a visit to the chief of station, many of whom I've known since they were newbie case officers; some who've worked for me. I have a TS clearance because of all the classified defense contracts we have, so I can get an in-depth classified briefing about any threats to be concerned about in-country. I distill it down and give a briefing to company personnel that are going there and try to give them some common sense advice that will hopefully keep them from being kidnapped, killed or otherwise compromised. I have a weekly meeting with the vice president of security, a retired Air Force colonel who's a schmuck. He was with the Office of Special Investigations when he was active-duty, but he doesn't know his head from his ass when it comes to intel. He thinks he's my boss, and it drives him crazy that he has no oversight on when and where I travel and who I meet with. His name is Richard Payne. Can you imagine what it must have been like for him before he got promoted to lieutenant colonel? Major Dick Payne. Technically, I think he's probably my boss on some organizational chart, since my salary gets paid out of the security budget. I keep him updated on what I think he needs to be informed about. Anytime the company is getting involved in new business overseas, I meet directly with the COO to brief him on what the security concerns are and what needs to be done to mitigate them. It's a cake job. I almost feel guilty about how much they're paying me, but they probably charge it as overhead on one of their contracts. No wonder the F-35 is so over budget."

"And all this time I thought you were just scraping by working as a security guard at Walmart. I'm glad things worked out so well for you after leaving the Agency. I know it was a difficult decision. Do you miss it at all?"

"Was it a difficult decision? Yeah, at the time it was, but looking back now, I don't regret it in the least. Leaving the Agency was the best thing that could have happened to me. If I had stuck around until the very end, maybe I could have made it back into the pipeline and become an assistant director, but then where would I be? An extra eight hundred dollars a month for retirement and showing up once a year for the retirees' banquet recalling the old glory days with a bunch of other lonely pathetic drunks? I would probably never had landed this job and certainly never have met Rose and married her. I'm not a religious guy, but for whatever reason, the big guy upstairs must have been looking after my sorry ass and decided to give me a second chance. Believe it or not, Rose's even got me to show my face in church every once in a while. She's Catholic, you know, so I'm starting to get this guilt complex from all the dirty looks I get showing up Sunday morning with a hot little thing next to me. I know that dirty old priest is probably thinking he should have become a Protestant every time he lays eyes on her," Harry laughed.

"You're a lucky man, Harry. I envy you. You always knew how to keep the job from taking over and robbing you of your identity. That's something I wasn't very good at, and paid the price for it. Maybe that's part of the reason I feel I need to do this. Maybe it's just some unfinished business I need to take care of, before I can finally put whatever's been eating at me to rest."

"Mike, if this is something you have to do, then you're going to need all the help and support you can get. I still have enough contacts at Langley that I can poke around and see what I can find out about what happened with the Iranian foreign minister under the guise of how it's affecting the situation with Israel. They recently took delivery of eight F-35s from us, with another forty-two scheduled over the next few years. We got instructors, ground crews and a whole bunch of other support personnel over there, getting them operationally ready for their air force. If I can find out anything, it might be able to point us in the right direction."

"Us? Harry, I just came here to get some of your advice, not drag you into this. I already feel guilty enough about you taking the hit for me in Athens, justified or not, but no way am I going to let you risk losing everything again. And you know that is a real risk. If things go south, Lockheed Martin will terminate your ass in a second rather than risk any fallout if you're in any way implicated with helping me."

"I may also have some unfinished business. If Canton's involved in this, then he's finally going to have to account for his treachery. We both know he was the only other one who knew about the meet in Athens. Only he could have compromised it. He was the one responsible for what happened. And besides, everything I would be doing would be directly related to my responsibilities for the world's largest defense contractor. We just have to be very careful and make sure our communications are secure, and I have just the thing to make that happen. I'll be right back."

He stood up and left the patio, returning a few moments later with a briefcase-size Pelican case and setting it down on the glass patio table next to them. He unlatched the four clasps around the case and opened the lid. He reached in and pulled out one of the satellite phones from the dense foam securing it in place. He handed it to Michael.

"That's the latest encrypted Iridium sat phone. Even if the NSA knew which specific call to intercept, it would probably take them the better part of a week to crack the encryptions. So, what's your plan?"

"Plan? I have no plan, Harry. That's why I'm here. I don't even know where to begin."

"Well, what are we trying to find out?"

"That's the dilemma. The Iranian foreign minister was assassinated, just like Ali warned in his message. Did he know that ahead of time, or after it happened? We can't tell just based upon the time his daughter received his call and the exact time the foreign minister was killed, but his message said that Secretary Payton, Jonathan Canton and the Russians are going to try to kill the Iranian foreign minister, the key words being 'going to try,' which indicates it hadn't happened yet. So, if he knew ahead of time, the question is, how did he find out? Knowing the answer to that question would at least point us in the right direction in trying to find out what happened to him, but the only one who can provide us that answer is Ali. It's one of those predicaments—which came first, the chicken or the egg? Okay, bad analogy, but you know what I mean," Michael said.

"So, the Iranian foreign minister is dead, Ali has claimed the US Secretary of State, Canton and 'the Russians,' which obviously is referring to Markov since nothing happens without his express approval, are responsible for killing him, and Ali has disappeared. That's what you got to go on? Am I correct?"

"That's it, unless I'm missing something."

"Well, the way I see it, the only option you have of finding out what happened to Ali is to to go to the last place he was known to have been."

"You know, that thought has been resting in the back of my head since yesterday, before I even met with Roxanne. Part of me was hoping you might think of another option, something I was missing, but it looks like you've come to the same conclusion."

"I don't know how else you can possibly find out anything, unless you were planning on giving Canton a call to ask him if he's involved in the assassination of the Iranian foreign minister. I don't have any contacts in Turkey other than the chief of station, but for me to reach out to him for information about a missing State Department employee would seem out of place and possibly attract unwanted attention. I highly doubt the Agency would have been involved in something like this, but if Canton is, he'll be on high alert and have his tentacles in as many places as possible. He'll for sure be all over you, trying to figure out what you know, especially after meeting with Ali's daughter. And he can do it officially, using Agency assets under the pretext of investigating the assassination."

"Yeah, I know, and that's why I'm concerned about you being tracked to me. We're taking a chance just sitting here talking about it."

"Don't worry about that. See that little black box sitting on the bar back there?" Harry pointed behind them. "That's a Stealth jammer. It blocks wall mics and transmitters in outlets, along with laser and microwave reflections off windows. Comes in handy when traveling overseas on business. Even if anybody followed you here, we're just two old friends catching up on old times. Wasn't your first posting in Turkey? Do you have any contacts over there still?"

"Yeah, I was in Istanbul from '98 until 2002. I may still have a contact in MIT. It's been a long time since I've spoken with her, but she's my only possibility. I guess I'm heading to Istanbul to see what I can come up with. I'm going to need to get some cash out of my account for an airline ticket and operational funds when I'm over there. I used most of the cash I brought with me for Roxanne's train ticket and for some spending money so she doesn't use any of her plastic. Even if they track me through CRS purchasing a ticket, I'll pick it up last minute at the ticket counter—that way it'll give them the least amount of warning that I'm heading over there. If my old contact is still with MIT, I'm hoping she can help me get through the airport and avoid the tail Canton will have waiting to pick me on that end."

"I'll be right back." Harry stood up, leaving his cigar in the large crystal ashtray and walking out of the patio. Michael sat on his own, sipping his vodka and puffing on his cigar, wondering what Harry would come back with this time. After about five minutes, Harry walked back in with his drink in one hand and a stack of cash in another. "Here you go, Mike. It's ten grand. This should cover you for a ticket and operational expenses while you're over there." Harry handed him the wad of cash.

Michael looked at the bundle of bills. "Harry, you don't need to give me any money. I can cover whatever I need."

"That's all right. You can pay me back later. You need to maintain a low profile. You make any sizeable withdrawals out of your bank account, and Canton will know about it. You're going to have to operate the same way you would as if you were in Moscow during the good old days. Only now, instead of the KGB, it'll be your old employer monitoring your every move."

"Thanks, Harry, I really mean it. I hope I'm up to the task."

"Mike, if anyone can pull something like this off, it's you. You were one of the best case officers I ever had work for me. And besides, weren't you one of the snake-eating SF guys?"

"Yeah, that was me. But it's been a long time, half a lifetime ago, since I did any of that kind of stuff. I'm glad you have that much confidence in me, because I don't. Funny how age has a way of quelling one's sense of invincibility and making you realize just how vulnerable you are."

"I think that's just wisdom that comes with age. That's why us old farts know better than some of these younger kids that always want to leap before they look to see what's on the other side. I'll help you out whatever way I can from over here. I'll keep the sat phone on me so you can reach me whenever we need to talk. The phones are billed to a Lockheed Martin account, and we have hundreds of them worldwide, so don't worry about making calls. It's just a tiny drop in the bucket if you knew how much they spend on overhead like that. In the meantime, I'll see if I can get together for lunch with some of the old-timers at the Agency that I still keep in touch with. I'll try and steer the conversation to who's doing what these days and see what I can find out about Canton."

"You're a good man, Harry. You've always been there to back me up, even when it wasn't in your best interest. I can't tell you how much I appreciate it. I know the price you paid for doing that, regardless of how things may have turned out for you now. You knew what it was going to cost, but you didn't back down when a lot of others would have looked out for themselves and left me to the wolves."

"Hell, let's not get carried away here. I don't think I'm in the running for sainthood; too many venial sins in my past, but what's right is right when it comes to the truth about what really happened. I'll be damned if I was going to let some headquarters IG let you hang out to dry for something in which you had no choice. I would have done the exact same thing in your circumstances. Now that that's put to rest, how about one more drink before calling it a night? You're gonna stay here with us tonight in the guest room. No reason for you to be exposing yourself any more than necessary until you're ready to head over to Istanbul. We can check tomorrow on flights, and you can head out when you got everything lined up."

"Just like old times, Harry."

"Yeah, except no view of the Acropolis, and no pretty flight attendants to flirt with."

***

William Payton sat in the backseat of the US ambassador's armored limo, looking out the window as they passed by the State Kremlin Palace on his way to a meeting with Russian President Dimitri Markov. The only modern building within the vast Kremlin complex, it was formerly known as the Palace of Congresses in Soviet communist times. It was now Moscow's biggest and most prestigious concert hall, playing host to large official functions and entertainment events such as the ballet and symphony concerts. Payton wondered which Markov he would encounter—the cagey former KGB agent suspicious of the West's motives, or the inviting and charismatic leader of modern Russia he portrayed on the international stage. Whichever Markov was there, Payton was determined to make it clear the United States was the dominant partner in their joint venture to bring some stability back to the world, just like in the good old days of the Cold War. Despite their ideological differences back then, at least there had been stability in the world with each of the superpowers keeping their spheres of influence around the globe in check. This time, there were no ideological differences between the West and Russia. The Russians could care less about spreading any social ideology to any other parts of the globe. Their only interest was to maintain strict control over their internal politics and leverage their petroleum and natural gas reserves to magnify their position of importance in a world that was leaving them behind economically.

Not only was Russia's economy suffering with the drop of energy prices over the past several years, but its vulnerability in being able to project any significant influence beyond its immediate neighborhood had become apparent to the rest of the world. Other than attempting to interfere in other countries' domestic politics or being a spoiler in the UN Security Council, the ability for its military to be a decisive fighting force was limited to dropping non-precision-guided munitions over civilian areas in Syria undefended by antiaircraft weapons. Russia's military was a hollow force, with Soviet-era weapons still making up the majority of its arsenal and nukes. With oil prices being so low, it had to put much of its modernization plans for its military on hold. As a former SACEUR, the NATO Supreme Allied Commander Europe, Payton knew exactly the position Markov found himself in, despite all his posturing and bravado for public consumption.

The limousine pulled up to the front of the Senate Building, which housed President Markov's official working residence within the Kremlin. Sergey Dobrynin, the Russian foreign minister, was standing outside the entrance, waiting to greet Secretary Payton. Payton's security officer stepped out of the front passenger seat of the limo and opened the secretary's door. Payton stepped out and was greeted with a handshake by Dobrynin.

"William, how nice to see you again."

"Hello, Sergey, good to see you also."

"I hope you had a pleasant flight from Tel Aviv. How did things go with Prime Minister Akerman?"

"Oh, you know him. A lot of pounding his fist on the table with the same bombastic theatrics he puts out to the Israeli public about Iran so he can stay in power. For some reason, he seems to think that's how to conduct diplomacy. He really needs to get a foreign minister rather than doing it himself, but I don't think there's a politician in all of Israel that would be able to put together a reasonable foreign policy Akerman could live with."

"How very true. President Markov is looking forward to meeting with you. You have much to discuss. Come, Mr. Secretary." Dobrynin motioned him inside.

They walked down the columned hallway of the Russian White House. Passing several sets of thick solid wooden double doors, Payton admired the splendor of the arched ceiling with its ornate gold leaf that lined much of the hand-carved trim work and the intricate mosaic design of light and dark woods of the Parquet flooring. After walking what seemed the length of a football field, they arrived at President Markov's office. It was the first time Payton was meeting with Markov in his office rather than in the presidential library, where they normally met along with their staffs. Markov rose from behind his desk and walked over extending his hand. "*Zdrastvyte*," he said, greeting Payton in Russian.

"*Zdrastvyte*, Mr. President. It's good to see you again."

"Please, sit. We have much to speak about." He motioned Payton over to the table and chairs on the other side of his desk. Payton sat down on the oversized chair across from Markov, while Dobrynin pulled up a chair and sat at the end of the table. Markov motioned with his hand to his assistant standing by the door, at which he stepped outside, closing the door, leaving the three men alone in the office.

"Sergey, correct me if I misspeak. I do not want there to be any miscommunications in this meeting. I understand English perfectly. It is my speaking which sometimes falls short. It has been a good while since I have needed to speak rather than using an interpreter. No unnecessary personnel need to be present for what we are to discuss. There have been enough breaches already," Markov said, making it clear he was going to dispense with diplomatic formalities.

"Yes, Mr. President," the foreign minister acknowledged.

"Mr. Secretary, may I be permitted to call you William?"

"You may, if that is what you wish."

"Very good. I would like you to call me Dimitri. There is no reason why we should maintain formalities under the present circumstances. William, I would like you to tell me where things stand with the Israelis. Do you believe there is enough provocation that they will launch an attack against the Iranians?"

"That depends. Although Akerman didn't come out and say so, he intimated they have a contingency plan standing by should they need to take action against the Iranians. One thing he did make clear was that they had significant concerns about you selling them the S-400 air defense system."

"Interesting, considering they have your new F-35 fighters. I was under the impression that they had the latest military hardware from the United States," Markov baited Payton.

"Dimitri, I don't think discussing the capabilities of US military hardware has any bearing on what the Israelis decide to do. Rest assured, the equipment we have provided them over the years is more than adequate for them to take on whatever the Iranians have. I doubt the Iranians will take any direct military action against them, because they know they can't win going tit for tat with them. I'm certain there's a good amount of confusion in Tehran right now, while different political factions try to consolidate their power. The hardliners and IRGC may be itching to launch some sort of unconventional attack, but the Iranian military also has to buy into it. Ultimately Mahdavi is going to have to approve any military action, and he may not have the support of all the factions, even if he is the Supreme Leader. After speaking with Akerman, I'm convinced the Israelis have prepared to take some kind of military action against them. They just need a little push to get them there."

"Perhaps we can provide the push they need by announcing the sale of our S-400 air defense system to the Iranians."

"That could do it. One of the things I told Akerman I would try to dissuade you from doing was exactly that. He will be enraged when he hears the news. You're not planning on actually going through with it, are you?" Payton asked, somewhat concerned.

"I do not believe it will get that far. Besides, what we provide to them may look like the S-400, but things are not always how they appear."

"Good. Things need to get moving along sooner rather than later, if our enterprise is going to succeed. Can I tell President Steele you have everything under control, then?"

"We have everything quite under control. It seems it is you who are not capable of the same. What is being done about the interpreter who overheard the careless discussion with your CIA man?" Markov asked Payton, making obvious his displeasure.

Payton had anticipated Markov would eventually bring that up. He hated the fact he had to acknowledge his carelessness to Markov. After all, he was a former four-star general in the United States Army, a Supreme Allied Commander of NATO, while Markov had been a mere colonel in the KGB. Who was Markov to question his competence?

"That was an unfortunate incident. It was also unfortunate that your elite Spetsnaz team was unable to take care of such a routine task as eliminating an unguarded interpreter. My CIA operative is working on locating and silencing him. He won't pose any risk to us. Who would believe him anyway? Come on, Russia and the United States plotting together to throw the Middle East into turmoil, after all we've done to try to bring stability to it? That would sound ridiculous."

"Ridiculous or not, we cannot allow such accusations to surface, especially before our plan is executed. Once the Middle East is in flames, then no one will have time for any wild conspiracy theories. The world will only be thinking about where it will get its oil from. Between your shale oil and our petroleum deposits, we will control most of the world's oil supply and bring some order back, as things were before, when we were the only two superpowers and the rest of the world fell into place."

"Yeah, just like in the good old days, when there was a clear understanding of the rules. Now any camel jockey with a cell phone and a computer can cause endless headaches for us over there. Once the Middle East is out of the oil business, they can have whatever's left of their useless wasteland and do what they want with it. They want to build a caliphate in the middle of the desert, they can do it the same way they did centuries ago, living in their tents with their camels and goats. The best thing about all this is we'll have a rope tied around China's neck. They get out of line, then we can shut down the oil spigot on their economy. They'll be back riding bicycles through the streets of Beijing," Payton said zealously.

"It is good we finally can agree that working to both our countries' mutual benefit makes more sense than being adversaries. President Steele and I are practical men and see the world in much the same way. Both our countries share the same values based on our ethnic and Christian backgrounds, the same ones that undesirable elements in your country are trying to corrupt. He understands the need to preserve our way of life and not allow those lesser others to shape the world."

"Well, Dimitri, since we are on a first-name basis now, let me tell you this. Whatever you may think about our lesser others, they are American citizens and entitled to their beliefs even if they are completely screwed up. The difference between your country and mine is that your people have never had the chance to think for themselves, and anytime they've tried, the few of you who are in charge get so scared you shit your pants because you know they're going to see through all your hollow rhetoric about how you're looking after their welfare. Your country didn't do that during the time of the czars, under communism, and certainly not now. Don't bullshit me with your values. The only values you have is to stay in power. Now that's perfectly fine by us, as long as you understand one thing. Your economy is ranked twelfth in the world, and that's only because of your oil and gas. If it wasn't for that, you'd be neck and neck with Poland as far as what you actually produce. You can go ahead and build up your military when oil reaches a hundred and fifty dollars a barrel, but if you become a thorn in our side, we will outspend you just like we did in the eighties, which bankrupted the great Soviet Union. You are nothing close to the Soviet Union. We won't expand NATO as long as you stop with all your little incursions into your neighbors' sovereign territory. You don't see us invading Canada to annex Nova Scotia."

"Mr. Secretary, when your president and I spoke, we reached a mutual understanding that we would maintain our spheres of influence without each of us attempting to subvert the other. We do not want to start another arms race. We realize we cannot compete with the United States. But we also expect the United States to respect the sovereignty of Russia. We will not tolerate criticism and interference with our domestic politics as we have endured from the previous US administration. Russia is not the United States. The Russian people do not think the same as Americans. As long as they have their bread and their national pride, they don't care who leads them. Gorbachev foolishly thought he could give them a little freedom to decide for themselves what they wanted, and look what happened. Complete chaos all those years under that fool Yeltsin. By the time he left office, his approval rating was under five percent. My approval rating is over eighty percent. It is hard to criticize those kinds of numbers as to whether the Russian people are satisfied with their leadership. I don't believe your president has nearly that kind of approval rating. I expect President Steele will stay true to his word and drop the sanctions the previous administration imposed on us and will get the EU to do the same."

"Dimitri, I thought you said we were on a first-name basis. When we have control of the world's oil supply, the EU will do whatever we want of them. We will also deny NATO membership to Ukraine, while giving them assurances much the same way we do with Taiwan. It would go a long way in resolving many of these outstanding disputes if there was a gesture on your part to recognize the territorial integrity of Ukraine before the sanctions and NATO issues are addressed."

"What type of gesture are you suggesting?" Dobrynin asked, inviting a stare from his boss for interjecting.

"How about you withdraw all military support for separatists in eastern Ukraine and announce a referendum for the people of Crimea to determine if they want to stay with Russia or go back to Ukraine. Now before you get all up in arms, hear me out. In the big picture, what are you really getting out of eastern Ukraine other than a trickle of dead Russian soldiers coming back from there? We can certainly provide the Ukrainians with military hardware that will turn that trickle into a steady stream. Eventually even the Russian public will notice their sons coming back from Ukraine in body bags. Another Afghanistan is something you don't need politically to sully your popularity. As far as Crimea goes, you're not getting anything out of that other than your naval base at Sevastopol. Since you've annexed Crimea, it's costing you a hundred times as much to maintain your base now that you're responsible for taking care of two million of its inhabitants. You can present it to the Ukrainian government in terms of a similar arrangement as we have in Cuba with Guantanamo Bay, for all practical purposes being sovereign Russian territory. Either way the referendum goes, you keep Sevastopol and come out looking to the rest of the world like you respect the true democratic wishes of its people. It's a win-win situation, unless you continue to let your foolish Russian pride distort your ability to recognize what is in your best interest. Hasn't this indignation at the West over not getting the deserved respect since the breakup of the Soviet Union gone on long enough? You really have to get beyond this zero-sum game mentality. It didn't do much for the Soviet Union."

Markov sat in silence, his expressionless face and beady stare concealing his desire to cave in Payton's skull with the trophy-sized green granite paperweight on his desk. Payton returned Markov's stare with a feeling of satisfaction at finally being able to tell him his true standing when it came to his relationship with the United States. It was something he had wanted to do since his days as SACEUR. As a military officer, however, he'd had to bite his tongue when it came to making any type of comments about political leaders; otherwise he'd have been overstepping his bounds and would have been relieved of command with the certainty of forced retirement from active duty. Unlike some of his fellow flag-level officers, who didn't know when to keep their mouths shut and had made controversial public statements that led to their demise, Payton took pride in his skill at navigating those types of minefields, something that would serve him well in his future political ambitions. Upon his retirement from the Army following his tenure as SACEUR, Payton was finally able to speak out publicly as a staunch supporter of presidential candidate Martin Steele, for which he was subsequently rewarded by being nominated as Steele's Secretary of State. Just as, during the campaign his boss had played up the idea its soft foreign policy had diminished the United States' standing in the world, Payton called for a much more aggressive approach when it came to dealing with countries such as Iran, China, North Korea and Russia. Despite his confrontational public statements towards these adversaries, Payton realized the US needed Russia's cooperation if his and President Steele's vision for the future had any chance of succeeding. One thing he was determined however not to allow to happen, however, was for Russia to reassert itself as a global power. They could stabilize their economy and update their military with their oil revenues, but the US would no longer tolerate any further incursions or meddling in the domestic politics of other countries. In exchange, the United States wouldn't criticize Markov's efforts to clamp down on political opposition groups within Russia. That was the deal President Steele had privately put forth to President Markov during their first meeting following Steele's election victory. It was a deal that Markov had willingly accepted. Payton wanted to ensure Markov understood the conditions of their arrangement, while at the same time taking pleasure in asserting himself as the one who had the actual power in their relationship.

Saving his boss from having to immediately respond to Payton's proposal, Foreign Minister Dobrynin stepped in. "That is a very interesting proposal. We will have to study it and give it serious consideration. I am certain we can arrive at some course of action that will be mutually acceptable to both sides. Let us reconvene again shortly to finalize an agreement."

"That would be good, Sergey, but we need to have an agreement on this soon. If you're going to announce the sale of the S-400 to Iran, wouldn't it be prudent to have the referendum on Crimea and the withdrawal of support for the separatists standing by in the wings?. We all know the effect the S-400 sale is going to have in Israel and the rest of the Middle East, but the Europeans are going to be just as concerned. You can bet Israel will raise a stink to both us and the Europeans, expecting us to stand by them in denouncing the sale. Announcing the referendum and withdrawal from eastern Ukraine a few days after that will make you guys look magnanimous in the eyes of the Europeans. You have to be willing to work with us to get the sanctions lifted if you're going to be selling oil to Europe," Payton said, reminding them there were still some levers the United States had with its European allies. With that, he stood up, knowing their meeting had concluded."But how do we know the Ukrainians will accept such an agreement?" Dobrynin asked.

"Don't worry about that. I won't have any problem convincing President Ryabenko that it's in his best interest to accept such a deal. I think he'll be very amenable to what I have to tell him."

"Thank you, Mr. Secretary. We will talk again soon." The foreign minister gestured to Payton that he was ready to escort him to the door.

"Mr. President." Payton offered his hand to Markov.

"Secretary Payton, do not assume Russia will take a subservient position to the United States in this arrangement. We are equal partners, and I expect mutual respect for each other's interests. Otherwise, we will find ourselves back where we were with the previous administration." Markov took Payton's hand as he made clear his demands.

"Well, we wouldn't want that, Mr. President. That wouldn't be good for anyone," Payton answered before turning and heading towards Dobrynin waiting for him at the door.

"Goodbye, William, until we speak again. Yuri will escort you to your vehicle." The foreign minister handed him off to President Markov's assistant, waiting in the hallway.

"*Dosvedania*, Sergey, until next time," Payton told his Russian counterpart, then turned and followed Yuri down the hallway.

***

"That insolent son of a whore. Who does he think he is, speaking to me like that? He acts as if he is speaking to his equal, when he is merely Steele's messenger boy. I would crush his throat under different circumstances," Markov bristled to his foreign minister.

"It seems the secretary does not know his proper place. I would not allow him to irritate you, Mr. President. I remember something my father used to tell me about someone from his village who would brag about how he was going to get an important job because of all the influential friends he had in the Party. He was made the head dog catcher for the entire province. Since then, anytime he would be seen in the village square, he would be greeted by a hail of barking howls from all his fellow villagers. That is why my father used to say, 'A fool's tongue runs before his feet.'" "Yes, Sergey, it seems your father taught you well in the matter of discretion, something this American knows nothing about."

***

Payton sat in the back of his limo as it pulled out of the Kremlin and headed back to the US embassy. He had a smug smile of satisfaction on his face as he thought about his meeting with Markov. He had made it clear to Markov who was in the driver's seat. Russia would have to play the hand they were dealt. Markov might be a shrewd opponent, but in the end, the house always won, and the United States was holding all the cards.

Chapter 9

After spending an uneventful night catching a couple hours of restless sleep amid the relentless anxiety of what awaited him, Ali was wakened by the sound of a man crying and pleading in the hallway outside his cell. "Please, I beg you, I am not a traitor. I have never betrayed my country. They are all lies. Please, please, do not do this. I have a family. My wife, my children, they will have no one." His cries continued, fading as he was led away. Ali sat up in his cot and rubbed his neck, trying to get out the knots from sleeping on what was probably the original mattress from when Evin Prison was first built by the Shah in 1972. He glanced at his watch to see what time it was but only saw his bare wrist. He wondered what had happened to his watch, trying to remember the last time he'd looked at it. He was almost positive he had been wearing it the night everything had happened. Yes, he remembered looking at it the next day, prior to finally going to the Iranian consulate, but that was it. He let out an angry sigh at the realization it had been taken from him, probably when he was unconscious back at the consulate. *Assad! I can't believe he stole my watch. That vile man. And he probably considers himself a devout Muslim,* Ali thought. He had always wanted a nice watch but had never been in the financial position to spend that kind of money on an enlisted man's pay while being married with a family. His wife had gotten the Omega watch for him nine years ago, for his fiftieth birthday. She had put away a little bit of money over the years from various jobs she had at different duty stations Ali was assigned to while in the Air Force. Apart from the cost of the watch, which he guessed was at least a couple thousand, the true loss he felt was from the special meaning it held, connecting him to his wife, whom he still missed dearly.

He stood and walked over to the heavy steel door that confined him in his cinder block box. He examined the two metal slides, one at eye level, for the guards to look inside, and the other at floor level for passing meals through. He tried pushing each from side to side, but neither budged. *Probably latched from the outside,* he thought. He sat there silently with his ear next to the door, trying to hear on the other side. Other than a faint mechanical hum from somewhere beyond his walls, there was silence. He walked back over to his cot and sat down. He felt a dull ache in his stomach as he realized that he hadn't eaten since the day before yesterday, when he had retrieved the bread scraps from the dumpster behind the bakery. He wondered when he would be given any food. He thought about his decision to go to the Iranian consulate. With where he was now, it was hard to convince himself he had made the right decision. But what other option did he have? The logical side of him told him he would have been killed one way or another if he had turned to the Turkish authorities, who would have eventually handed him back over to the US government. Canton would have made sure of that. Considering his current situation, he wasn't too sure the eventual outcome would be any different. That was the uncertain side of him talking. He kept telling himself to be patient and not lose hope. Someone within the Iranian government would eventually be convinced he was telling them the truth, but then what? Would the Iranians just release him? Where would he go? What would he do? How could he ever return to the United States? Would he ever see Roxanne again? His thoughts brought on a feeling of despair. *What did I do to deserve this?* He started sobbing at the thought of never seeing his daughter again.

Ali heard the sound of a key being inserted into his door, then the lock turning. He quickly composed himself as he stood up, looking towards the door. As the door opened, he saw a different guard from the previous night gesture him to the door.

"Come."

Ali walked to the door. "Where are you taking me?"

"You will find out soon enough," the guard answered him curtly.

He was led down the hallway around a corner to a barred door with a guard sitting at a desk on the other side. Looking up as they approached, the guard stood up and inserted a key in the door, opening it and allowing them to pass through.

"Who is our new guest, Gazi?" the guard asked Ali's minder.

"I don't know, somebody they brought in last night."

"Where are you taking him?"

"To get his first taste of what life will be like in his new home."

"Oh, is that why he has the look of a frightened rabbit about to be skinned?" The guard laughed at Ali.

"If it were only that quick and easy," Ali's minder answered, continuing down the hallway and around the corner with Ali out in front of him. Ali did his best not to let the guards' comments get to him. He realized they were just trying to torment him. He would just have to wait and see what lay ahead for him and not allow them to get the better of him.

They came to a stairwell, and Ali's guard motioned him up the stairs. They climbed to the second level, coming across two guards who were half holding, half dragging a prisoner who was whimpering something unintelligible. As they passed, Ali caught the prisoner's eyes. The man returned a disturbing gaze, the look of a traumatized man, a man that had something broken inside him, never to be the same. Even his two guards had an unsettled look on their faces, in acknowledgment of what the man had obviously suffered. Ali struggled to maintain his composure as he fought off the queasiness that came over him at the thought of what the man had undergone to get to his current state. They turned a corner and came to a short hallway with six doors. Ali's minder escorted him to the second to last, unlocking the thick wooden door with one of the keys on the ring attached to his belt and motioning him inside.

Ali stepped into the room, hearing the door shut behind him and the key turn, locking him in. The dimly lit room had a wooden table with three chairs around it. On one wall were two sets of shackles attached to steel rings bolted into the cinder blocks, one set at shoulder level six feet apart and the other at ankle level three feet apart. The floor below was stained dark brown, what was obviously the discoloration of dried blood that had been absorbed into the concrete. The opposite side had a three-foot-by-four-foot mirror built into the wall, which Ali assumed was a two-way mirror. He resisted the temptation to walk over and look into the mirror, knowing someone was likely on the other side observing him. He took a seat at the table and waited for whoever was going to come in and question him. He hoped they would be more reasonable than Assad had been with him back at the consulate. As he sat there waiting, he studied the shackles on the wall. He pondered how many poor souls had been brutalized in this room. He wondered if his father had met his fate in a room similar to this, perhaps even this room itself. He looked at the dried blood on the floor. Could any of it be his father's? He tried not to think those thoughts, knowing they would only lead him to despair.

His fate was in Allah's hands now. That thought surprised him. How was it he looked to Allah now as being in control if his destiny? Although he was a Muslim, he had never practiced his religion. When Janet had been diagnosed with cancer, he had turned to Allah in prayer, asking that his wife be spared. His prayers had obviously fallen on deaf ears, as he watched her health rapidly deteriorate until she was taken away from Roxanne and him. If Allah did exist, he wondered what the Almighty thought about a religion that was used to justify the persecution and killing of thousands of innocent victims, just because their beliefs didn't line up with the those of so-called religious leaders. Ali knew this type of hatred wasn't limited solely to Islam. Christianity had its share of atrocities throughout history, all in the name of God. That animosity existed even today in both Europe and the United States, where so many so-called Christians looked at Muslims as if they were all hate-inspired terrorists, bent on the death of every Christian and Jew. Where was Allah or God in the midst of all this hatred amongst his children? Nowhere that Ali could see. Yet something inside him made him believe in his existence. *If you're there, I could sure use your help now. Give me the courage and strength to get through this. I know I haven't practiced my faith according to what the Qur'an says, but please let me see my daughter again,* he offered silently as he sat there waiting for what was in store for him.

Five minutes later, he heard a key being inserted into the lock. He stood up from his chair as the door opened and watched a guard carry in a car battery with a set of jumper cables and place it on the floor by the wall with the shackles. A man wearing a charcoal suit with a white shirt buttoned up to the top and no tie walked in and sat down across from Ali, motioning him to sit down. Ali watched as the guard left the room and shut the door. The man sitting across from Ali sat in silence, studying Ali for several moments before finally speaking in Farsi.

"Welcome back to Iran, Ali. How does it feel to be back in your country after so many years?"

"I am being treated like a prisoner. How do you expect me to feel?"

"Ah, so I take it you are not happy to be back in Iran?"

"I am not happy about how I have been treated."

"Perhaps you expected to be welcomed home like some type of hero after betraying your country and serving its enemy for so many years."

"I have never done anything to betray Iran. I voluntarily came to the Iranian consulate to provide important information about a plot to assassinate Foreign Minister Mohammedi."

"So, that is your story. What is this important information you are hoping I'll believe?"

"I will tell you everything I know, but please, I ask that you tell me who you are."

"My name is Hamed," the man told Ali.

"Who do you work for? Will you be able to verify what I am telling you is the truth?" Ali asked, wanting some reassurance he was speaking to someone in a position of authority.

"I am a colonel of the Ansar-ul-Mahdi. I am quite confident I will be able to determine if you are telling me the truth," Hamed answered him, looking over to the car battery. The Ansar-ul-Mahdi Corps was an elite section within the IRGC responsible for protecting top officials in the Iranian government, counterintelligence and covert operations, the equivalent of the Secret Service, the FBI and Special Forces all wrapped up in one. "I am the one who will determine if you will ever see the light of day again, or if you will spend the rest of your days rotting away in here. Do we understand each other?"

"Yes, I understand perfectly," Ali answered him.

"Very well, then. I will not ask you again. Tell me what information you have about who killed the foreign minister."

"I know it may sound unbelievable, but Secretary of State William Payton and a man named Jonathan Canton, who works for the CIA, are involved in a plot with the Russian government in the assassination of the foreign minister."

"How is it you came by this information?"

"I am Secretary Payton's interpreter. I overheard the Secretary and Canton talking about this just prior to the assassination taking place. They found out I learned about the plot and tried to have me killed also."

"How did they do that?"

"Secretary Payton called me and told me to meet him outside in the back of the hotel at one a.m. He said he was meeting with the foreign minister to discuss something. When I went outside, I was shot at, but they missed. I ran and hid in the darkness. It must have been right before they killed the foreign minister."

"And who was it that shot at you?"

"It was Russian special forces."

"Russian Spetsnaz? And how is it you are still alive?"

"I don't know. Allah must have been protecting me."

"Allah, you say. So, you are a believer?"

Ali paused while he considered how to answer that question. He didn't want to answer such a question untruthfully regardless of what Hamed's reaction might be. "If you are asking me if I have been a faithful Muslim, praying five times a day and living my life in the tradition of the Hadith, no, I have not. But I do believe in Allah, and that I will have to account to the Almighty someday for my actions in this life."

"At least you are honest about that. Your story, on the other hand, I do not believe. It is some sort of deception by the Americans to mislead us into believing the Russians were responsible for killing the foreign minister. We know it was the Zionist regime who did this. We have proof!"

"That is exactly what they want you to believe. They were even going to use Israeli ammunition."

"That is ridiculous. What reason would the Americans and Russians have to do something such as this? It would benefit neither of them."

"Yes, it would, if they created chaos and destruction in the Middle East. Then, between the two of them, they would control most of the world's oil supply."

"And how do you know all of this?" Hamed asked.

"As I told you, I heard Secretary Payton and Canton talking about it when they thought they were all alone. I was in the adjoining room. They did not know."

Hamed considered what he had just been told. How could Ali have known Israeli shell casings were found in the foreign minister's hotel room? Was it just a lucky guess or had the Americans somehow found out about the shell casings? As far as he knew, no one outside a small circle within the IRGC, along with the President Rostami and the Supreme Leader, knew about the shell casings. The Turkish authorities hadn't been allowed into the crime scene until after the casings and the foreign minister's body were removed. Perhaps other shell casings were found on the hotel grounds and the Turks had not shared that information with them but had told the Americans. If it was some sort of American ploy, they would certainly know the risk in sending someone to the Iranian consulate with such a story. Perhaps they did not care what happened to Ali, falsely telling him that he could tell this outlandish story and then just be able to walk back out of the consulate. Who would believe something like that? Ali did not strike him as being such a fool. None of it made sense.

"You are lying! Look over there." Hamed turned towards the shackles on the wall. "Do you know how many others have also tried to lie at first but eventually ended up telling the truth? There are many unpleasant ways we can arrive at the truth. I am not a sadistic man, but I will do whatever is necessary to make you tell me the truth. The choice is yours."

Ali was momentarily speechless at Hamed's reaction as he tried to come up with a way of convincing him. *How can he not see I'm telling him the truth? What more proof does he want? No one in his right mind would come to them with a story like this if it wasn't true.* He finally found his voice. "Colonel Hamed, please believe me, I am telling you the truth. I have no reason to lie. I know what you can do to me, but it would not change what the truth is. I am not some kind of spy. I just happened to be at the wrong place at the wrong time. I did not want any of this!"

Hamed studied him. Ali drew on every ounce of strength not to break eye contact with him, while at the same time trying not to appear to be challenging him. Finally, Hamed broke the silence and declared, "I will allow you to return to your cell to think carefully about what you are going to tell me the truth is next time we speak. You have not been subjected to any mistreatment this time. But, I can assure you, the next time it will not be the same if I am not convinced you are telling me the truth. Do you understand what I am saying?"

"Yes, I do," Ali answered, making every effort to look Hamed in the face. It was a struggle doing so. Unlike in Western culture, maintaining eye contact with someone in Persian culture, especially a superior, was a gesture of defiance. That was the last thing Ali wanted to convey.

Hamed stood up and walked to the door, opening it. The guard who had brought Ali, now standing in the hallway, came to attention. "Return him to his cell and get him some food."

Ali rose from his chair as the guard came in to escort him back to his cell. Hamed sat back down and evaluated what Ali had told him. *The Americans and Russians, conspiring against Iran? That sounds too unbelievable. They are back to being Cold War adversaries. They have not even been able to reach any level of cooperation in Syria or resolve their differences over Ukraine. Russia supports us, even selling our military advanced weapon systems. That does not make sense. Yet what would the Americans be hoping to accomplish by sending him to us with such a ludicrous story? The infidels are not idiots.* He didn't know what to believe. He certainly couldn't report such an outrageous story back to General Bardari without somehow being able to verify it. Bardari would consider him a fool. Yet again, what if, by some unlikely possibility, what Shiravi was saying was the truth? What were the implications for Iran? They could be catastrophic if his country misstepped and allowed the infidels to manipulate them towards their own destruction at the hands of the Zionists with their nuclear arsenal. He had to apply as much pressure on Shiravi as possible without inflicting excessive pain. Hamed knew there was a fine line in torture that, once crossed, would make a man say whatever was necessary to stop the suffering. Yet when properly applied with psychological distress, it was possible to break any man's resistance to disclosing the truth. He was not a cruel man, nor did he enjoy unnecessarily tormenting his subjects. But he would not hesitate to sacrifice Shiravi, a man who had deserted his country, to fulfill his duty. He could not afford to get this wrong. Too much was at stake for his country and his family.

***

It was 10:00 a.m. as Michael pulled out of Harry's driveway. Rose had cooked them a hearty breakfast, and after a couple cups of coffee while waiting for the morning D.C. rush hour to get over with, Michael was on his way to find a travel agency. His father had called him an hour earlier and told him Roxanne had safely arrived and they were driving back to St. Augustine, which took one concern off his mind. He left Bethesda, heading down I-495 to Tysons Corner.

Today, however, the CIA's feed of the D.C. area traffic cameras picked up the license plate of Michael's rental car and the system alerted the technician sitting in Langley's operations center. He immediately placed a call to Canton's office.

"Sir, we got a hit on Blackstone's rental. We picked it up heading south on Old Georgetown Road in Bethesda about thirty seconds ago, and now it's on southbound on I-495. We have a seventy percent positive ID based upon on a partial plate and vehicle type."

"Give me the info on the vehicle."

"Gray 2017 Chevy Blazer, Virginia plates Victor Bravo Kilo One Three One Three."

"Keep tracking it. I'm heading out. I want continuous updates. Call me back on my secure cell and keep the line open. Do you understand?" Canton directed him.

"Yes, sir. Calling you back on your cell now."

Canton heard his cell ring and answered it, "I'm here," as he called his assistant on his office phone. "Steve, I want three surveillance units ready to go in two minutes at the service entrance at L2. Tell them I'm on my way!"

"Roger that, sir," he answered his boss.

Canton grabbed his Sig Sauer 9mm from his desk, then stood up and ran out of his office down the hallway to the elevators. He entered the first elevator and pushed the button for the lower level of the underground service garage. *Finally, got him! Who does Blackstone think he is, poking his nose into something that's way out of his league? I'm going to jack that son of a bitch up!* Canton relished the chance of putting him in his place. The elevator door opened, and Canton stepped out just as two Suburbans, one charcoal and one navy blue, pulled up along with a black electronic surveillance van. He stepped into the passenger side of the lead charcoal Suburban and shut the door just as the driver floored it, screeching the tires as they headed out of the underground garage.

"What's the surveillance van's call sign?" Canton asked his driver.

"Eagle Seven," the driver answered.

"Patch the traffic camera feed to Eagle Seven," Canton instructed the technician back in the operations center. "What's the delay on the feed from the actual camera location?"

"About ten seconds," the technician answered Canton.

Canton grabbed the encrypted wireless surveillance kit, placing it in his ear and keying the microphone. "Eagle Seven, this is Canton. Ops center is patching the traffic camera feed to you. There's about a ten-second delay. I want you to track the subject vehicle, a gray Chevy Blazer, Virginia plate Victor Bravo Kilo One Three One Three. I want an intercept on this guy."

"Roger, Raptor One," the technician in the back of the surveillance van acknowledged.

"I take it the other Suburban is Raptor Two?" Canton asked his driver.

"That's affirmative, sir."

"Raptor Two, did you copy?" Canton asked the team in the other Suburban.

"Raptor Two copies."

The three vehicles sped out of CIA headquarters onto Georgetown Pike towards I-495.

"Subject vehicle just passed traffic cam right after GW Parkway off-ramp, looks like he's still heading south on the Beltway," Eagle Seven advised everyone.

"Raptor One copies."

"Raptor Two copies."

The three vehicles sped past Langley High School at twice the legal speed limit, trying to intercept Michael before he passed the Georgetown Pike exit. Thirty seconds later, they were at the I-495 overpass, waiting for the next traffic cam update before getting on the highway.

"Vehicle just passed traffic cam right after Georgetown Pike off-ramp, still on the Beltway."

"He just passed us ten seconds ago," Canton declared as the driver momentarily flicked on the red-and-blue strobe lights concealed in the front grill and top of the windshield. Disregarding the red turn signal and oncoming traffic, he floored it and turned onto the interstate entrance. Raptor Two and Eagle Seven fell in behind, as all three vehicles sped down the on-ramp onto I-495. Even past rush hour, the Beltway had substantial flow, making it difficult for the surveillance vehicles to pass traffic. Canton strained to see over the sea of cars in front of him, trying to spot the gray Chevy Blazer. He cursed as he looked at one gray SUV after another with the same nondescript body style of most late models.

"Just passed cam at Old Dominion Drive," Eagle Seven updated everyone.

"We're passing Old Dominion! He must be no more than a quarter mile ahead of us," Canton responded, viewing the speedometer, which showed fifty-two miles per hour. "We're coming up on Dulles Access Road, did he pass it or take it?"

"Don't know. No traffic cam there," Eagle Seven replied.

"Shit! What do you mean no traffic cam there? Raptor Two, take the exit just in case he got off!" Canton shouted into his microphone.

"Raptor Two taking Dulles exit," the second Suburban acknowledged as it peeled off onto the off-ramp.

"Just passed Tysons Corner Metro cam on Chain Bridge Road," Eagle Seven shouted. "He took the Tysons Corner exit!"

The driver of Raptor One yanked his steering wheel hard right just as they were about to pass by the exit, skidding the rear wheels of the Suburban and bringing the front swerving across the soft dirt of the off-ramp towards the guardrail. To avoid impaling the front of their vehicle on the end the of guardrail, the driver kept to the left of the guardrail, driving over the grass while trying to avoid sliding down into the marshy weeds, until finally clearing the other end and bringing the Suburban back onto the asphalt. Canton shot him an irritated look, the driver returning a quick glance that said he had no other choice.

"Whoa! That was a close one, Raptor One. Eagle Seven still behind you."

"Raptor Two copies. Turning as soon as we can to link back up with you."

The driver of Raptor One punched the accelerator on the ramp taking them off the Beltway onto Chain Bridge Road. Five seconds later, they were passing by the Tysons Corner Metro station.

"There he is!" Canton shouted into his mic. "Turning left onto International."

***

Michael slowed as he approached the stopped traffic at the red-light intersection. He moved to the left-turn lanes that would take him to Tysons Corner Mall. He remembered a travel agency being located inside the mall. He could check there to see what flights were available to Istanbul before deciding what time to head for the airport and buy a ticket there. He had purposefully not done so from Harry's home—not that he didn't think Harry had his computer set up to access the Internet through a VPN, but he wasn't willing to take any chances Harry could in any way be connected to him if things went sideways. He knew the NSA had all sorts of capabilities, probably even more so than when he had left the CIA over a decade ago. He glanced in his rear-view mirror, noticing the charcoal Suburban coming up quickly across five lanes of traffic to the left-turn lanes a few cars behind him. The light turned green, and the traffic in the turn lanes turned onto International Drive. Michael stayed to the left in order to turn into the mall entrance. He noticed the charcoal Suburban pull into the left-turn lane several cars behind him as he turned onto Tyson One Place. He drove a few hundred yards and turned into the parking lot in front of Macy's. Michael looked into his rear-view mirror. He saw the charcoal Suburban also into the parking lot. *Let's not get paranoid. Lot of people go to the mall,* he told himself. It was still fairly early, and there were plenty of open parking spaces. Michael turned into a space and pulled forward to the other open spot in front of him. In his peripheral vision, he saw the charcoal Suburban turn down his row and head towards him. As it came into his view, he could make out two men through the windshield. The Suburban drove up to the front of his vehicle and stopped, blocking him from pulling forward. *What the...?* Michael went to high alert and threw his car into reverse. As he was just about to floor it to get out of the kill zone, a black van pulled in behind him, blocking him in.

Michael quickly opened his door and jumped out, not wanting to be trapped inside his vehicle for whatever this was going to turn into. He did a quick scan of his surroundings, assessing his options. The spot next to him was empty, so he had some room to maneuver in case he needed to escape quickly on foot. He looked at the Suburban blocking the front of his car, then heard the door of the van behind him open. He looked behind him and saw two men step out, both holding pistols down low in front of them, trying not to draw attention to themselves. Michael looked back at the Suburban, assessing the threat coming from there. Finally, the passenger-side window came down and a man Michael hadn't seen for years looked at him with a contemptuous glare behind dark sunglasses. Michael returned the stare, having known all along that it would come down to confronting Canton at some point. He just didn't want it to be on Canton's terms.

"Jonathan, why am I not surprised to see you?" Michael didn't want to waste words trying to feign ignorance about their encounter.

"Well, well, Michael. Long time. Whatever brings you back to D.C.? Last I heard, you were some kind of salesman back in Seattle," Canton smirked as he opened his door and stepped out of the Suburban.

"Funny you asked, Jonathan. An old friend called and said he needed help with some asshole from his past. I flew out here to give him a hand. So, what brings you here with a bunch of youngsters from the Agency tagging along?" Michael smiled, glancing back at the two twenty-something-year-old

CIA officers trying to look intimidating for him in their leather jackets and sunglasses.

"Now that's real coincidental, because an old friend of both of ours, Ali Shiravi—you remember Ali, don't you?—has gotten himself into a real jam, and nobody can seem to find him in order help him out either. You wouldn't happen to have heard from him after all these years, would you?"

Michael studied Canton. He had aged quite a bit. He was two years younger than Michael but looked like he was pushing sixty with his receding hairline and all the gray that had overtaken the sandy blond hair Michael remembered. He knew he had to try and get some kind of reaction from Canton that might unwittingly reveal the extent of what he suspected. He needed to control the dynamics of the situation and keep Canton off balance.

"You know, I had heard Ali was working for the State Department now as an interpreter. I've been watching the news and what's been going on in Istanbul. That's really wild, what happened to the Iranian foreign minister. I wonder who could have been responsible for that? I'm sure you have some insight into that, but I guess I don't have a clearance any more for you to share that with me. I also caught something about a State Department employee that's missing. I'm guessing that must be Ali. You just happening to be here asking me about him must mean you're in the thick of it, one way or another. Was there anything you wanted to tell me about all this, or have you missed me so much after all these years that you just wanted to say hi?"

Michael watched as Canton's face turned red with anger as he restrained himself from saying something rash in front of the subordinate CIA officers. He stepped forward and stopped two feet from Michael's face, taking a deep breath before responding.

"Listen, Blackstone, don't go sticking your nose into something that's no longer your business. This is an official US government investigation at the highest level. Don't interfere, or I'll make sure your ass gets jacked up so bad, you won't even know what hit you. It will make the last time seem like it was a walk in the park," he threatened Michael, alluding to what had happened in Athens.

"You go and do whatever you need to do to catch the bad guys. Don't worry about me interfering in your investigation. I already have a pretty good idea of who they are. After all, that's what I used to do. And you're right, I certainly learned my lesson in Athens, and I won't ever let that happen again. So, did you want to join me for a cup of coffee in the mall? Maybe we can do a little bit of underwear shopping for you afterwards. I'm pretty sure there's a Victoria's Secret inside," Michael said, trying to push Canton's buttons in front of his subordinates.

"Fuck you, Blackstone! I don't want to see you again, or you're going to regret it beyond your wildest dreams. Do you understand me?" Canton could barely restrain his anger.

Michael blew him a mocking kiss as he locked his door, then turned and walked towards the entrance to Macy's. Canton got back into the Suburban, slamming the door, as it pulled away heading towards the exit. The other two CIA officers hurriedly got back into the black van and circled around the lot, pulling in behind the Suburban. In his peripheral vision, Michael saw the Suburban and van pull out of the parking lot. He turned and quickly jogged back to his car, opening the door and jumping in. He stuck the key into the ignition, starting the car and throwing it into drive, quickly making his way out of the parking lot towards the mall exit. He could see the Suburban and black van turn onto International Drive.

It was against his better judgment, but something made him follow Canton just to see if he could get under his skin a little bit more. He knew Canton would be all over him, trying to watch his every move, so he had to level the playing field some. Rather than allowing Canton to stay on his game, if Michael could unnerve him some so that his emotions clouded his judgment, it might cause Canton to slip up and do something foolish, opening up an opportunity.

He made the turn onto International before the light turned red. He saw the two vehicles turn right onto Chain Bridge Road, heading back towards I-495. So, what was he going to do now? he wondered as he followed them. Michael turned onto Chain Bridge and spotted them four cars in front of him. *Just enough cover to keep me out of their sight*, he thought as he followed some distance behind them. Then an idea struck him that put a smile on his face. If he could pull it off...***

Canton was silently fuming as he sat in the passenger seat of the Suburban. It hadn't gone as he'd wanted. He had made his point but felt like he had not been given the respect he deserved, especially in front of the other men. "Raptor 2, Eagle 7, you guys can split, don't need you anymore," he told the other two units. "Back to Langley," he instructed the driver.

***

Michael saw the black van pull out from behind the Suburban and take off down the road. He stayed with the Suburban as it veered right, getting onto the cloverleaf that put them back on the Beltway heading north. He followed behind, blending in with the late-morning traffic. As they approached the Georgetown Pike exit, Michael saw the Suburban's right turn signal go on.

Perfect, he thought, *they're headed back to Langley*. Maybe his idea would work. He stayed back from the Suburban, driving at a leisurely pace down the residential area surrounding CIA headquarters. The Suburban turned left onto Dolley Madison Boulevard drove a quarter mile, then turned left onto the drive leading to the main gate of Langley. Michael lagged behind, allowing several other cars to turn down the drive before making the left and committing himself. It had been many years since the last time he'd driven down this road. He hoped things hadn't changed much at the front gate. He would need to get the timing right if his plan was going to work. He pulled his iPhone out from his coat pocket and pressed his thumb to the fingerprint scanner, unlocking it. He touched the settings button, then the airplane mode button, linking his phone to the cellular network. Now, it was just a matter of timing. He could see the Suburban up ahead slow down as it approached the front gate of Langley. There was a small line of vehicles lined up, waiting to be checked through the gate. Michael pulled in behind the Suburban, with two cars separating them, as they queued in the line to get in. There were four vehicles in front of the Suburban. No one behind him yet. *Perfect*, he thought. He couldn't have asked for a better setup. He waited.

***

Canton heard his cell phone ring as they waited in line to get through the front gate. He looked at the number. It was the ops center. "Canton," he answered briskly.

"Sir, this is the ops center. Blackstone's cell phone just came on."

"Is he making a call?"

"No, sir, just pinged the system."

"Where is he?"

"Um, it looks like he's at the front gate."

"What front gate?" Canton asked, annoyed.

"That would be our front gate, sir."

"What the—?" Canton twisted back and forth in his seat, looking all around him. He opened his door and got out of the Suburban, looking behind him with a bewildered look on his face. That's when he spotted Michael through the front windshield. Michael opened his door and stepped outside, where Canton could get a good look at him. The expression on Canton's face went through a series of changes, from confusion, to surprise, to disbelief and finally to anger. Michael gave him a smile, raising his right hand and flipping him the middle finger. He watched Canton become incensed. He had never seen that shade of red come over a person's face. Having savored the moment, Michael sat back down in his car, put it in reverse and backed out, keeping his eyes in the rearview mirror until he came to a break in the median, where he crossed over to the opposite lanes. He glanced in his rear-view mirror and saw Canton still standing outside the Suburban. Part of him knew it was a childish thing to do, but it had given him a brief moment of pure satisfaction seeing Canton become unhinged. On a more practical level, he had been able to push Canton's buttons so that his attention would be diverted and focused on seeking revenge, which always made one think emotionally rather than rationally. Michael hoped he hadn't caused himself more trouble than good. He switched his iPhone back to airplane mode, disconnecting it from the network once again. He looked at the clock on the dash. It was 11:30. He would head back to the mall at Tysons Corner and check on flights. With any luck, he would find something leaving for Istanbul this evening. Until then, he would do some shopping to augment the clothing he had packed and pick up a few more supplies he thought he might need. He didn't know how long he would be in Istanbul. He would wait until two hours prior to the flight's departure time before heading to the airport and buying his ticket. He would also need to take care of the traffic cameras spotting his vehicle. With any luck, he would have several hours' head start and already be in the air before Canton was made aware that he was headed to Istanbul. Better to have him reacting and playing catch-up. Before then, however, he needed to make a call to an old friend he hadn't seen in almost seventeen years. A friend whose help he needed if he was to have any chance of helping Ali and keeping Canton off him. He hoped she would be able to come through for him, if she was still in a position to do so.

***

Farzan Karbashi, head of the MOIS, was sitting across from across the table from Major General Mohammad Bardari, the commander of the IRGC. Next to him was Major General Rezi Ashtari, the Iranian Armed Forces chief of staff, along with the chiefs of the Army, Air Force, Navy and Air Defense Force. Sitting next to Karbashi was Hossein Ali Shahidi, the Iranian vice president, Mohammad Amiri, the head of the Iranian nuclear program, and Major General Saeed Zidabadi, the Iranian defense minister. They sat in the conference room of the White Palace, the official residence of the president of Iran, which was located within the vast 750-acre Sa'dabad Complex on the western outskirts of Tehran. They conversed amongst themselves as they waited for President.

The door by the head of the long conference table opened and President Nouri Rostami walked in. The occupants of the table stood up as Rostami took his place at the head of the table, motioning everyone to sit back down. Karbashi listened as the president opened the meeting.

"*Asalaam Alaykum,*" Rostami greeted everyone.

"*Alaykum Salaam,*" came the chorus of replies.

"My brothers, our country has not faced such a despicable attack against our sovereignty since that infidel Saddam invaded our country shortly after the founding of our Islamic Republic. Our foreign minister was murdered in utter disregard of any principles of civilized conduct. The Zionist regime naturally denies any culpability, but who else would be so brazen to commit such a shameless act against our nation? Yet they have the insolence to claim it was elements within our own government that were responsible. Elements who have been against the nuclear agreement our government signed with the infidels in order to unburden our people from the unjust sanctions they imposed on our country. They are obviously referring to the Revolutionary Guard Corps. What would be their reasons for wanting us to believe such an astonishing story, General?" The president turned to the commander of the IRGC.

General Bardari was taken by surprise. For a moment, he didn't know whether Rostami was accusing him of the Zionists' ridiculous claim or was asking for his opinion on what they were up to. "Your Excellency, no doubt they are trying to misdirect us and cause confusion amongst us while they make plans to strike at our country. They have stated all along that was their intention. They are looking for a justification to take military action against us. The Army of the Guardians of the Islamic Revolution has never been fooled by any of their ploys. We are ready to unleash the fire of Allah on them if they should be so foolish to try and attack us," Bardari boasted.

"Yes, it would seem foolish for them to attempt something so brazen when they know what will result. That is why I am having difficulty understanding their reasons for doing so. Would they have reason to believe there is any instability within our own government? That we are all not in agreement regarding the direction of our country?" Rostami looked at Bardari before shifting his glance to the others sitting at the table. "The Islamic Republic faces threats from our enemies, who all around us. Let us not give them any reason to believe we are not completely united."

Everyone around the table nodded in agreement, even Bardari. He wasn't in favor of the government signing the nuclear agreement with the West. He believed President Rostami was too willing to appease the infidels, but the Supreme Leader had ultimately approved of the agreement, despite the IRGC's opposition. Whatever Israel was up to, they would bear the full force of his country's military if they were foolish enough to threaten its integrity. Wanting to impress upon all the others that the Guard Corps was on top of things, he informed them, "We have a prisoner we are interrogating who claims he has information about the foreign minister's assassination."

"Who is this prisoner?" Karbashi asked.

"He is a traitor who works for the Americans."

"What do you mean by traitor?"

"He is an Iranian who fled our country during the revolution. He betrayed his people and went to live with the infidels in the United States. He even went so far as to work for the regime of the Great Satan!"

"Are you saying your prisoner works for the American government?" asked Karbashi in surprise.

Everyone else's gaze was fixed on Bardari. The general sat quietly, thinking about what more to say. He hadn't wanted to divulge the fact that the IRGC was holding the US Secretary of State's interpreter prisoner. He knew the alarm it would cause amongst the others in the government. They were all so weak and frightened about how the infidels would react. He knew they were all bluster. They had foolishly thought they could march into Iraq and transform it into a perverted Western democracy that would serve their interests the way the sycophant Saudis did. In the end, they had withdrawn with their tails between their legs. The same thing happened to them in Afghanistan. Iran was no Iraq or Afghanistan. His country had the military capability to severely bloody the Great Satan's nose. The Americans wouldn't have the stomach to get involved in another aggression in this part of the world again. He would show them there was no need to fear the hollow bellicosity of the United States.

"He is no one of consequence. A low-level employee sent to us with false information as a ploy to mislead us," Bardari finally announced to the others, stretching his neck and raising his head high in a show of self-assurance.

"General, are you saying you have kidnapped an American government personnel and are holding him prisoner?" President Rostami asked incredulously.

"We did not kidnap him. He came to us," Bardari responded defiantly, defending himself from what he perceived was the questioning of his judgment.

"What do you mean he came to you?" Rostami returned.

"He came to the consulate in Istanbul after the foreign minister was killed and said he wanted to talk to someone about the assassination."

"And what did he have to say?"

"We have not finished questioning him yet."

"Not finished? And where is this prisoner now?"

"We are holding him in Evin Prison."

"Evin Prison? Have you lost your mind, General? You said you did not kidnap him. How did he get from our consulate in Istanbul to Evin Prison? You have unnecessarily created another major international crisis for us. As if the assassination of our foreign minister was not enough! You have imperiled us even further with this foolish act!" President Rostami was livid.

Not wanting it to appear in front of the others that the president had chastised him, Bardari defended himself. "I have not created anything. The Americans have no idea we are holding him. The only ones who know are those sitting at this table, along with a few of my men. There is no additional risk posed to us. We will question him and determine what he knows."

"Question him! And then what? I know what it means when you question someone. What do you intend to do with him then?" Rostami meant it more as a statement, implying that Bardari hadn't thought through all the implications.

The general remained silent for a moment, knowing he didn't have an answer. Finally, he acknowledged, "It is not my concern what happens to him. My responsibility is to defend our Islamic Republic. When he is no longer of any use to me in doing so, I do not care what happens to him."

"Is the Supreme Leader aware of your reckless actions, General?"

"I do not trouble the Supreme Leader with such mundane issues. If something important is disclosed by the prisoner, I will of course inform him of it."

"You will also inform me, immediately. I am the one responsible for the actions this government takes. We are in the midst of the greatest international crisis our country has faced. We cannot afford to have one segment of the government off on its own, acting independently of the rest. I am certain the Supreme Leader agrees with me on that issue. Do we understand each other, General?"

Bardari hated being scolded like some school-aged child. President Rostami was a cleric who obviously didn't grasp how Iran should respond to its enemies. He, on the other hand, was the commander of the Army of the Guardians of the Islamic Revolution. As a young man, he had fought against Saddam's forces in the Iran-Iraq War and repelled the invaders from his country. He knew the only way to defend the Islamic Republic was to show no mercy to its foes. Although Bardari ultimately reported to the Supreme Leader, he knew that as long as Rostami had the Supreme Leader's support, he would have to acknowledge Rostami's leadership in directing the government's response to the current crisis.

"Of course, your Excellency," Bardari said, yielding for the time being.

"Good, I am glad we are in agreement. There is too much at stake for us not to be united and pursuing a unified strategy. Whoever is responsible for this attack against us will not go unpunished. Let us not act rashly, however, without first ascertaining what their agenda is in committing this belligerent act against our nation. The Zionists are looking for any opportunity to take military action against us. We must be careful not to give them a justification for such action in the eyes of the international community. When we do retaliate against them, it must be clearly seen as defending our sovereignty against their aggression. Farzan, what do know about any military action the Zionists may be preparing for?" the president asked of his MOIS chief.

"We have no specific information of any immediate threat. As always, the main threat we face from any Israeli military action is an attack by their air force against any of our nuclear and missile facilities. We know their primary target is our Fordow facility. Although they have the capability to launch such an attack, the casualties they would face in lost aircraft would be substantial. But that is something General Fadavi would have more expertise on," Karbashi said, deferring to the chief of Iran's Air Defense Force.

"General, are we prepared to defend against any attack by the Israeli Air Force?" Rostami asked Fadavi.

"Your Excellency, we have air defense batteries at all of our strategic military and research facilities. At Fordow, we have deployed the two S-300 air defense batteries which we obtained from the Russians two years ago. We are fairly certain it will defend against any attack by the Israeli Air Force against that facility."

"What do you mean by fairly certain, General?" asked Rostami.

"The S-300 is capable of defending against most anything the Israelis have in their air force, except perhaps the F-35 stealth attack fighters they recently obtained from the Americans. We believe they have at least eight that are operational. The Russians have assured us the S-300 can detect them, but we are not completely convinced this is accurate. If they can penetrate our defenses and launch an attack, they could cause some damage to the facility."

"Is Fordow not deep underground? How could they damage the facility, even if they were to penetrate our defenses?"

"The facility is ninety meters deep. We believe the Americans have also supplied them with the GBU-28, which is a five-thousand-pound laser-guided bunker buster bomb they used against the Iraqis to penetrate their hardened facilities. It is capable of penetrating thirty meters of earth or six meters of solid concrete. If they targeted the facility with several of these bombs, they could theoretically penetrate it. If that were to happen, it would devastate the entire facility since it is confined underground," the general explained.

"Nonsense! The Zionists would never be able to penetrate that deep into our territory. Even if they do have the F-35 fighters, they would require other aircraft to penetrate all our other air defenses all the way to Fordow. It would be impossible for them to do that without most of their aircraft being destroyed!" Bardari interjected.

"General Bardari, I believe this is not your area of expertise. It would be wise for us to consider General Fadavi's concerns when it comes to defending our air space, since he is the one who is knowledgeable in this subject and is his responsibility." Turning back to Fadavi, Rostami asked, "General, were we not in talks with the Russians to purchase a more advanced air defense system?"

"Yes, we were. It is the S-400 system, their most advanced system, which they claim can defend against any stealth aircraft the Americans have. But Defense Minister Zidabadi felt we did not need it."

"Is this correct?" Rostami asked, turning to his defense chief.

"Yes, it is. The Russians wanted to sell us the S-400 at four times the cost of the S-300. I felt it would not be wise to spend so much of our military budget on the S-400 when we were suffering from the financial effects of the Western sanctions. The Russians were trying to pressure us into purchasing their most expensive military hardware at the same time they were supporting the sanctions against us. They claim to be our allies, yet when it comes to standing behind us against the Americans and Europeans, they always look after their own interests at our expense. We purchased the S-300 instead and have since engineered our own version of the system."

"Yes, the Russians seem to be our friends when it is convenient for them. We must always exercise great caution when dealing with them. Let us not forget, they are infidels also. The only principles which guide President Markov are those that he finds expedient for him to maintain power. He has allegiance to no one but himself. Let us all be vigilant over the coming days and prepare to defend our nation against anyone who may attempt to do us harm. Thank you all for coming," President Rostami said, dismissing everyone.

All those at the table stood and began filing out of the conference room.

As Karbashi was about to exit the room, President Rostami grabbed his arm. "Farzan, stay one moment. I would like to speak to you privately."

Karbashi paused, allowing the rest of the attendees to leave. Shutting the door, he returned to the table and sat down next to the president. "Yes, my President?"

"Farzan, we have known each other for quite some time. Your father was my spiritual mentor. It was he that inspired me to forsake a career as a legal scholar and pursue serving Allah. I imagine I could have had a very successful legal career, perhaps even becoming a judge, but it would not have led me to the position in which I currently find myself. In many ways, you are like a younger brother to me. You are one of the few in our government that I have the utmost trust in. You know how much I value your opinion. It is my obligation under Allah and my responsibility to the Iranian people to protect our country from those who would want to seek our destruction. I will not hesitate to take whatever means are necessary to do that. However, I am aware of what an all-out war with Israel or the United States would mean. Our military would certainly inflict stinging casualties on them, but in the end, our nation would be devastated. I will not allow that to happen as a result of our enemies manipulating us into inflicting such an outcome upon ourselves. Whoever was responsible for killing our foreign minister did not do it as an act of terrorism against us. They have a specific result they are trying to achieve. This act was merely the catalyst for some plot, whose intended outcome we do not know. It is of paramount importance we do not do anything rash that would play into the hands of our enemies. Cool heads need to prevail. General Bardari is undoubtedly a brave man whose courage is placed in Allah the Almighty, but even the Prophet was cautious in dealing with his enemies, saying that 'all war is cunning.' Bardari's zealousness blinds him and may lead him to attempt something foolish. I am confident I have the trust and support of our Supreme Leader, but Bardari may try to circumvent me and place us in a situation which will limit our options, such as with his foolhardiness in kidnapping the American. What do you know about this man that Bardari is holding prisoner?"

"Thank you, Nouri, for your confidence in me. Even from when I was in high school and my father would invite you to our home to dine with us, I knew you were destined for great things. Your devotion to Allah's word through the Prophet never hindered you from seeking the truth about all matters, regardless of where it led. As to the prisoner, this was the first I have heard about it. My officer at the consulate in Istanbul had been called back to our embassy in Ankara by his superior following the assassination, in order to brief him on what happened. He was obviously absent and not aware of this American. He should have been allowed to remain in Istanbul, where he could have been of some use. I will address this issue later. For now, I will make inquiries with Ankara and instruct them to find out whatever they can from consulate personnel regarding the circumstances surrounding the American. Bardari said he came to the consulate and wanted to speak with someone regarding the assassination. I hope whatever information he had was important enough to justify kidnapping him and not done as some form of retribution for the foreign minister's death. Even if he still is an Iranian citizen, kidnapping American government personnel is a brazen act that could provoke a significant response from them, putting us into a position we cannot maneuver out of," Karbashi advised the president.

"Very good, Farzan. Let us ask Allah for guidance so that we may proceed wisely. The fate of our country depends on it. Now I must go and apprise the Supreme Leader of where things stand. I will learn what General Bardari has been saying to him, which will be obvious from some of the questions he will be asking me. The Supreme Leader realizes Bardari can be overzealous at times but likes having him as his check on me to make sure I am not liberalizing our country more than what he is comfortable with. It can be quite trying at times having to counter Bardari's claims that I am too conciliatory to our enemies. If it were up to him, we would be in continuous strife with all our neighbors, along with the Zionists and the Americans. He would rather bring our country to utter destruction than acknowledge the fact we cannot take on all our adversaries single-handedly. *Asalaam Alaykum*, my brother."

"*Alaykum Salaam*, brother. May Allah guide you wisely." Karbashi wished his friend well as he stood up to leave.

Chapter 10

Michael made his way back to Tysons Corner Mall. He figured that after belittling Canton in front of the other younger CIA officers, Canton would be seething with anger towards him. But there wasn't much more Canton could do to him other than track his every movement until he got out of the United States. Then the playing field would be evened, especially if Michael could get the help of his old friend. The mall was as good a place as any for Canton to be able to track him back to, since that was the last place of their confrontation. It was a large, crowded place that diminished any advantage Canton would have if for some reason he decided to come after Michael again. He doubted that would happen, but better safe than sorry. It would also give Michael a place to hang out until he was ready to make his break for the airport fifteen minutes away. Keeping an eye on his rear-view mirror on the drive back, he thought about the last few days. Less than seventy-two hours ago, he had tried to kill himself because something was so wrong in his life that he couldn't think of a reason for allowing it to continue. He had failed because a bullet had misfired in some unexplainable miraculous way that defied all probability. Then the daughter of one of his assets from the CIA years ago left him a message about her father needing help because he had knowledge of a conspiracy that could turn the world upside down. And now, he was preparing to fly to Istanbul to try and help Ali, all the while being tracked by his old employer. *How in the heck did I get myself into this situation?*

He drove back into the shopping mall's parking, selecting the cover of the parking garage to leave his vehicle. He got out and locked the door, then glanced at the license plate in the front of his car before walking into the mall. He found the mall directory guide and searched it for the travel office. He found what he was looking for and headed towards the escalator, taking it down to level one. He walked up to the attractive thirty-something woman sitting at the travel agency kiosk and was greeted with a pleasant smile. "Hi there. May I help you?"

"Hi. You sure can. I need to check on flights to Istanbul, Turkey."

"What dates were you thinking of?"

"Today, actually."

"Wow, that's pretty short notice."

"Yeah, something came up unexpectedly and I need to get there fairly quickly."

"Okay, what return date would you like?"

"How about a week? But I'd like it to be a changeable ticket."

"All right, let's see what's available," she told him, turning to her computer and searching for flights. "Well, there's not much left to choose from. I take it you want nonstop?"

"Yep, want to make it as quick and painless as possible."

"The only nonstop still available for today is on Turkish Airlines out of Dulles at eleven fifty-five tonight. There's business class for six thousand, one hundred and ninety-seven dollars, and economy for one thousand and twenty-seven. Does that work for you?"

"Six grand for business? Well, I guess this late, that's to be expected. How booked is it?"

"Let's see," she said, typing on her keyboard. "Oh, there's plenty left in economy, over twenty seats, and five in business."

"Oh, that's good. I'll have to check on a few things before deciding," he told her, having obtained the information he needed.

"My name is Jennifer and I'll be here until three, but someone else will be here until nine."

"Thank you, Jennifer, you've been very helpful."

"You're very welcome. I didn't get your name."

"It's Tom," he told her, giving her a smile before turning and making his way down the mall. He realized he hadn't consciously thought about giving her a false name; it had just come as a natural reaction. Giving out a fictitious name to conceal his identity was something he hadn't done in a very long time. Somehow, old habits were starting to kick in without him even realizing it until after the fact. He hoped that he could still call on some of the skills he had used when running clandestine intelligence operations, even if he would be clumsily rusty over a decade later. He would need them if he stood any chance of accomplishing what seemed like an impossible endeavor from where he stood now.

He would need to get some additional clothing for his trip, attire that would blend-in in that part of the world and not make him stand out like an American. *What the heck are they wearing in Turkey today? Guess I should find out what I need to look for before I buy anything.* Even though he didn't care if Canton knew where he was, he didn't want to unnecessarily advertise his location by using his iPhone, so he would do the next best thing. There had to be an Apple store in a mall this size. He found his way back to the directory and saw that he was in luck. He climbed the escalator back up to level two and located the Apple store. He walked in, made his way to an open desktop and clicked on the browser. He typed in "Turkish public protests" and hit search. He scanned through the images of everyday Turks out on the street. It gave him a good idea of what the average Turk was wearing these days—pretty similar to what the average American male was wearing, less the baseball cap. The shoes were what usually gave away one's country of origin. He looked down at the topsiders on his feet. He decided he would need to start with his shoes. He looked at his watch. It was 2:30 p.m. He had nine and a half hours until his flight departed. To play it safe, he wouldn't cut it closer than 10:15 p.m. to make it to the airport, purchase a ticket and get through security for an international flight. There wouldn't be many flights that late at night, but with the current international tensions, security would undoubtedly be increased. He would find a place to grab a bite to eat and make the call that could end up making a significant difference to what lay ahead for him. With the remaining time, he would shop for shoes and clothes to augment his wardrobe, then catch a movie or two at the theaters located in the mall.

Michael decided on the Mexican Grill. The lunchtime rush was over, so he was able to find a quiet corner to himself, where he would have some privacy to make his call. The waitress came by and gave him his menu. He looked through it, trying to decide what he was in the mood for. There was enough time before his flight that he thought it safe to indulge himself with a spicy burrito. He reconsidered his choices and thought it wiser to go with the tostada salad instead. After all, he was already getting AARP junk mail, which reminded him he didn't have the cast-iron stomach he'd always liked to brag about during his younger days. Despite the effort he made to keep in shape, he was keenly aware of the changes his body was undergoing. It was tough coming to terms with the fact he wasn't the same physically as just ten years ago. He didn't remember such a drastic change in his forties. He hoped any wisdom he'd gained during that time would make up the difference, especially considering what he might be facing in the new reality he had just stepped into. The thought of was somewhat intimidating. It gave Michael an uneasy feeling he wasn't familiar with.

The waitress came back by and took his order. He looked at his watch once again. It was close to 11:00 p.m. in Istanbul. The time had finally arrived. He knew he would be calling late. He hoped he wouldn't be waking her up, but it was too important a call to worry about that. He knew she would understand. They had been through a lot together. He pulled out his small address book and flipped through the pages until he found her number. It was her home number. What if she didn't live in the same place any longer? He remembered her apartment. It was in one of the nicer residential areas of Istanbul. Her father had given it to her on her twenty-fifth birthday. His position had given him the connections to be able to afford such a gift for his only child. It wasn't huge, but spacious enough, with three bedrooms and a large open living room–dining room area. It was on the top floor of a six-story building, with balconies and retractable awnings running down the length of both sides of her half of the building. It was a very nice home, especially for a single woman in Istanbul. He paused at that thought. Why did he assume she was still single? That had been seventeen years ago. She might very well have met someone and be married. For that matter, she might even have children. That was presumptuous of him, thinking she was still single without any commitments, just waiting to help him. He might even be waking up her husband sleeping next to her. Suddenly he felt like he had butterflies in his stomach. Was he nervous about calling her? It surprised him. Even if she were married, it wouldn't make a difference as to whether she would help him. Of course she would. But then, if she was married and had children, then perhaps she was no longer working and not in a position to help him. His uncertainty began to annoy him. There was only one way to find out. He just needed to make the call. He flipped open his new phone and dialed the 011 for international, then the 90 country code for Turkey, followed by her number. He listened, waiting for the call to go through, then heard the distinct ring of a European call on the other end. On the fourth ring, he heard the phone pick up and a familiar female voice say in accented English, "Hello?"

"Hi, Asya."

There was momentary silence on the other end, then, "Michael, is that you?"

"Yeah. It's me. You recognized my voice after all these years," he answered, a bit surprised but pleased.

"Of course I recognize your voice. How many American men do you think I'm close enough with to recognize their voice with just two words," she ribbed him in the old familiar way he remembered. "Where are you? I see it is a US number."

"I'm in Washington, D.C. I hope I didn't wake you. I know it's late there."

"No, I was still up. You remember me, I'm a night owl. I'm still going over some things and planning for tomorrow. It seems that I can never just leave things at work."

Well, that didn't sound like someone who was married with children, although he told himself not to make assumptions. "I know you must be surprised to hear from me after all this time. Hard to believe it's been seventeen years already. Sometimes, it seems like just yesterday, while at others it feels like a lifetime ago."

"I know what you mean. The years pass by with or without your agreement. It's good to hear your voice again. What is it that makes you call after all these years?"

"I'm calling because I need your help. Do you still work for the same employer?"

"Yes. Do you?"

"No, I don't. That's why I need your help. I can't get into details over the phone, but I'm flying to Istanbul in a few hours and I can tell you in person when I arrive. I know this may sound like a strange request, but I'm likely going to have some former associates waiting for me when I arrive, which I would rather avoid. I was hoping you could arrange that for me."

"That is a strange request."

"I know. You'll understand after you hear what I have to tell you. I hope you know me well enough to trust that I would not do anything that would jeopardize your position."

"Of course I trust you Michael. I haven't forgotten what you did for me. Your word is enough."

"I'm glad to hear that. Here's my flight info. I'm arriving on Turkish Airlines flight number eight out of Dulles. It's expected in at five oh five p.m. tomorrow."

"Okay, I have it written down. I will take care of everything."

"Thanks, Asya. I really appreciate it."

"You're welcome, Michael. I will see you tomorrow."

"See you then. *Güle Güle*," he said, telling her goodbye.

"You remember," she laughed. "*Güle Güle*."

Michael ended the call and put his phone in his pocket, just as the waitress arrived and placed his tostada on his table. "Here you go. Can I get you anything else?"

"No, thanks."

"Enjoy," she told him as she walked off, leaving him to his meal.

The call couldn't have been any better. It was a short conversation, but he felt good about how it had gone. It wasn't so much what was said as the feeling he got from it. Yes, Asya would help him, which would make things much easier. He wouldn't have to worry about losing the surveillance Canton would have waiting for him at the airport. More importantly, the conversation with her felt as comfortable and natural as it had all those years ago, when they used to spend hours at a time together. Prior to making the call, he had feared that the awkwardness of talking again after so long would leave them both feeling uncomfortable, but he hadn't sensed it on her end and certainly didn't feel it himself. He was excited to see her again after all these years. He wondered how much she had changed. He had last seen her when she was thirty years old. He remembered her striking looks, but more so her boundless personality and impressive intellect that could mesmerize anyone she encountered. She was a remarkable person and had become a trusted friend, but it was also a challenge being around her so often. The amount of time he spent with her often exceeded the time he spent with Karen and Sam at home. He had never acted inappropriately towards Asya, despite how close they had become. He had been married and would never have betrayed Karen in that way, but he'd also valued the professional relationship and friendship he had developed with Asya too much to risk spoiling it all over some physical impulse, although there had been many of those. She was too appealing a person not to be attracted to her. She would draw the attention of every man when she walked into a room. At five foot, nine inches tall, with the body of a former Olympic gymnast, she looked incredible in anything she wore. But her face was what was her most striking feature. Her high cheekbones, pouty lips and bright-green eyes with a hint of Persian could enchant any man when she smiled. She wore her jet-black hair cut short, almost masculine, which in some ways heightened her femininity, especially when she accented her ears with the gold hoop earrings she wore dressed up for an evening occasion. Despite the sensuality she exuded, there was a fierceness that also emanated from her, which would make most men think twice before making a lewd comment about her looks within earshot. He wondered what she was thinking about him.

Despite the feelings of attraction she evoked, Michael had the utmost respect for her. Neither of them had ever acknowledged it, but the unstated sexual tension between them had been unmistakable. In certain instances, it was so strong, it almost felt as if there was some sort of gravitational attraction between them. Yet Asya never gave any indication or flirted in such a way as to suggest the possibility of something happening between them. If anything, she enjoyed busting Michael's chops as much as his buddies in Special Forces had. She could have gone toe-to-toe, tit for tat with any first sergeant when it came to the one-upping banter in the enlisted ranks of the Army. It was probably something she had become accustomed to from her father, who had made his career in the Turkish military. She could carry herself regardless of the company. She had never met Karen but had known he was married and had a daughter. Michael knew her; jeopardizing his marriage was something she would never do. Yet Michael never mentioned her to Karen. He never mentioned any of his colleagues or persons he associated with at work; after all, everything he did was classified. But it always made him feel he was consciously concealing something from Karen in not mentioning that his Turkish counterpart, with whom he spent an inordinate amount of time, was an intelligent and witty knockout with a great personality. Yes, he might never have betrayed Karen's trust with Asya, but he wasn't sure he could say that about the choices he'd made with his other mistress, his career.

Michael glanced at his watch and turned his attention to the tostada. He would have plenty of time to think more about things on the flight. He told himself not to let his expectations get the better of him. For all he knew, Asya might assist him in getting through the airport unnoticed and then leave him to go off and do whatever he came there to accomplish. He shouldn't expect anything more from her. She had her job and her own busy life.

When he finished his meal and paid the bill, he headed out into the mall on his first objective, to find a new pair of shoes. If he could wrap things up quickly with the clothes after that, he would have plenty of time to catch a movie or two until he needed to head out to the airport. Things were going better than he had initially expected at the time he was leaving on his first flight back in Seattle. Then, he'd had no idea what he would do or where things would lead. Now, at least, he had a direction he was moving in. Where it would eventually lead him and what it would entail was yet to be determined.

**

Hamed turned off Fereshteh Street, the main arterial going into the Elahieh district in northern Tehran, and drove down the residential street with apartment buildings on one side and a small park on the other. Elahieh was an upper-class residential and commercial area where many politicians, diplomats and artists lived. Being a colonel in the IRGC came with some privileges, such as his official Renault Mégane, which also served nicely for weekend family outings to escape the noisy congestion of Tehran. Another one of those privileges was the three-bedroom apartment he lived in with his wife and two children. Modest in comparison to some of the other residences in Elahieh, it nonetheless signified he was part of the upper hierarchy of the Islamic State's bureaucracy and a respected member in society. Apart from the luxuries of a personal vehicle and housing in an affluent neighborhood, he was a modest man. He thanked Allah for the blessings of being able to provide a nice home for his family and being able to take them on excursions throughout his beautiful country, and show his young sons some of the glorious history of the Persian Empire. Although Hamed was a pious man, faithfully praying five times a day along with keeping the other nine practices of his Shia faith, he also had great pride in the greatness of his country's history. He had taken his family to marvel at the ancient remains of Persepolis dating back to 500 BC, the capital of the Achaemenid kings, Cyrus the Great, Darius and Xerxes, who had rivaled the ancient Greeks for dominance of the civilized world. He had instilled in his sons a sense of pride in the history of their country but also explained to them the importance of submitting to Allah and obeying his word as given through the Prophet Muhammad.

He had taught them how to live a virtuous life by obeying the laws of Allah in the Holy Quran and expressing love towards righteous people while disassociating from evildoers and the enemies of Allah and His Prophet. He taught them how evil had corrupted other parts of the world. Places where the Great Satan had taken control over entire nations that sought the destruction of their people. Countries such as the United States, where the infidels lived like animals, fornicating amongst themselves, corrupting their bodies with drugs and alcohol and striving only to obtain physical pleasures and comforts in the absence of Allah in their lives. The Great Satan was attempting to spread his evil to other parts of the world, including their country, so that they might become corrupted also. Life was a continuous jihad, a struggle to please God by fighting against those who would do evil to his righteous people. That was what had inspired Hamed when, at the age of six, he had witnessed the Shah's secret police arrest his father, a young cleric in Tehran, for speaking out with others against the Shah for corrupting their country by introducing perverted Western customs into their society. His father, one of the young leaders and supporters of the exiled Ayatollah Khomeini, had accused the Shah of being a stooge of the Americans, who did their bidding by allowing them to exploit Iran's oil wealth, only so that he could remain in power. Hamed's father had returned home six months later a different man. Apart from the physical scars and burn marks he bore throughout his entire body, there were other scars that could only be seen through the blank stare in his eyes. He hadn't been able to preach after that. His mind was never the same. He remembered the morning not long after that when he found his mother crying in their kitchen, with two policemen who had just told her his father had stepped in front of a bus on one of the main boulevards. He had lain in the street for half an hour before the ambulance had arrived, but it had been too late.

His mother had been forced to take a job as a maid for one of the Shah's generals to keep him and his younger sister fed. They lived in the small shack in the back of the general's palatial home. He remembered the general coming down to the shack in the evenings and taking their mother into the large storage closet and shutting the door. He remembered the sounds of his mother whimpering amidst the repetitive sound of the general's grunts. He remembered the shame he felt at the sight of the general coming out of the closet zipping up his trousers, and the sorrow in his mother's eyes each time for those two years. He also remembered the day when they announced the return of the Ayatollah Khomeini to Iran after the Shah had fled the country. The general and his family had been packing frantically, preparing to leave the country along with other ranking members in the Shah's regime. Hamed remembered the general coming one last time to their shack that evening. He remembered how he had grabbed his mother and dragged her into the storage closet. He remembered the rage that had erupted inside him at the thought of his mother being violated one last time before the general fled the country like a thief in the night. The next thing he remembered was the sight of the large kitchen knife sticking out of the general's stomach as he lurched forward, trying to grab Hamed by the throat. He remembered his mother grabbing the large iron skillet from the table and smashing it repeatedly against the back of the general's head until he lay motionless on the floor, blood seeping out of him. His mother had grabbed his sister and him and fled the house.

She had sought help from the Khomeini revolutionaries and was taken under the protection of one of them, who would eventually become one of the founding members of the Islamic Revolutionary Guard Corps. Uncle Rahim, as he had become known to Hamed and his sister, had taken care of them through the time of Hamed's graduation from Tehran University and acceptance into the IRGC as a young officer. He owed his and his family's life to the Islamic revolution that had preserved the virtues he was now protecting against the Great Satan. His faith in Allah was unshakable, but he wasn't some naïve and ignorant Iranian who believed all the government propaganda about the United States. He knew both the freedoms and opportunities the West provided, as well as the temptations. Before meeting his wife and becoming married at the age of thirty-seven, he had spent his younger years as a single IRGC officer, being assigned to Iranian embassies in both England and Holland. He had experienced the sexual delights of the red-light district in Amsterdam, drinking Johnnie Walker while whores in their working attire pleasured him according to his every sexual fantasy. He would always ask Allah for forgiveness afterwards, but knew he would return again at his first opportunity. He had met his wife, Laleh, when he had returned to Tehran. She was a modest and pious woman from a good family. Her father was a well-respected cleric. They had decided a marriage to each other would be appropriate for both their stations in life. She bore him his two sons, Tahmin, who was nine years old, and Reza, seven, both of whom he loved more than life itself. The thought of his two little angels being contaminated by the immoral ways of the West terrified him. That was why he considered it his sacred duty to defend the Islamic Republic against the Great Satan.

He pulled his car into the basement parking garage of his building. He climbed the stairs to the fifth floor rather than taking the elevator. Reaching his mid-forties, along with his senior rank, kept him behind a desk more often now, making it harder and harder to stay fit with the passing of each year. The run up the stairs to his apartment each night gave him an intense if short workout. He hoped it wouldn't cause a heart attack someday. He reached his floor and walked down the hallway, taking deep breaths trying to catch his breath as he pulled out his keys and searched for the one to his apartment. He inserted the key and opened the door to the sound of his two children running to greet him. He had worked late the last few nights since the foreign minister's assassination. The entire IRGC had been put on high alert, along with the rest of the Iranian military. He saw their joyful smiles as they ran up to him, shouting, "Baba! Baba!" He let go of his briefcase and stooped down, opening his arms as they both jumped onto his shoulders, giving him a hug. He stood up, letting out a grunt as he hugged them close to him.

"You two are growing so big. Pretty soon, I won't be able to lift you both." He kissed them on their foreheads.

His wife came out of the kitchen and smiled at the sight of her children in her husband's arms. They had grown up so quickly. It seemed like just a few years ago she was changing their diapers. In a few more years, they would be grown-up men, leaving their parents' nest to begin the jihad of their adult lives. She had hoped they would choose a life as clerics in the service of Allah, rather than the soldier's life of their father. She knew they both adored their father, thinking he was the hero of their Islamic republic, wanting to be just like him. She had seen the kind and loving side of him, giving alms to the poor, helping the old widow on the ground floor with her grocery shopping, and teaching their children to show kindness to those in need. But she also knew the dark secrets he kept to himself, the cruel things he sometimes had to do to men who were the enemies of their country. He was a complicated man, but he always treated her with the utmost adoration and respect.

"Pretty soon they will be lifting their baba up and holding him in their arms," she said as he let them back down.

"They will! They will be bigger and stronger than me!" he shouted to them. "Have you both been good boys today, listening to Maman and finishing your homework?"

"*Bale, bale, Baba.*"

"They did after I had to tell them how upset their baba would be if they didn't get all twenties on their grades."

"Twenties? Your maman must think I'm some kind of strict monster."

"You are, Baba!" Reza shouted.

"I am? Well, then, I guess I will have to eat you!" he shouted as he picked up his youngest, burying his face into his stomach and tickling him until he was kicking his legs and screaming in laughter. He set him down and told them, "Go and get ready for bed, and I will be in shortly to say prayers with you."

They both ran down the hallway into the bedroom they shared. He turned to his wife and gave her a hug. She returned his hug. She could sense he'd had a strenuous day. His shoulders were tense and he had that look on his face that he got when something serious had happened. She knew not to ask him about his work. He wouldn't tell her anything anyway; it wasn't something he ever brought home with him. There were times when he had been called suddenly and was away for days, but when he was at home, his attention was focused entirely on his family.

"How are you, my *joon*?" she asked, referring to him as her life.

"I'm well. Just a long day."

"I can tell from the bags under your eyes that you are tired and have not eaten. There are some kababs and baghali polo for you in the kitchen."

"That is very thoughtful of you, my *delbar*," he thanked her, letting her know she had his heart. "I will pray with the children first and then eat."

He walked down the hallway to the boys' bedroom and found them wrestling around on Reza's bed. Tahmin had his younger brother pinned under his arms and knees and was dangling a string of spit above Reza's face as Reza screamed. It was an effort for Hamed to suppress his smile before he could utter in a stern voice, "Tahmin, get off your brother or I will pin you down and you will feel my belt across your backside. I told you to get ready for bed."

"We are, Baba! We were waiting for you to come," he answered as he quickly dismounted from on top of his brother.

"All right, the both of you come here and kneel next to me," he told them as he kneeled down on the rug in their room, facing southwest towards Mecca. His sons joined him, one on each side of him. They lowered their heads to the carpet, and Hamed began to recite the prayer, pausing intermittently, waiting for his sons to repeat the words.

"Allah! There is no God but you, the Ever Living, the One Who sustains and protects all that exists. Neither slumber nor sleep overtakes You. To You belongs whatever is in the heavens and whatever is on the earth. Who is he that can act except with Your permission? You know what happens to all in this world, and what will happen to all in the hereafter. No one may comprehend anything of Your knowledge except that which You will. Your throne extends over the heavens and the earth, and You feel no fatigue in guarding and preserving them. With Your name, I lay myself down, and with Your name I rise. O Allah, You have created my soul and You take it back. Unto You is its death and its life. If You give it life, then protect it, and if You cause it to die, then forgive it. O Allah, I submit myself to You, entrust my life to You, turn my face to You, and lay myself down depending upon You. I believe in Your Holy Book, the Quran, and the Prophet through whom You revealed it. O Allah, I ask You for strength. All glory is to You, Allah, all praise is to You, Allah, Allah the Most High and the Most Great."

They rose from their prayers, and Hamed tucked his children into bed. He gave them each a kiss on their foreheads and silently asked Allah to protect them against all the evil in the world. He closed their door and walked back to the kitchen, where he sat down at the small table. Laleh had warmed two lamb kebabs and the rice with dill and fava beans. He bit into his late supper and realized how famished he was. It helped that Laleh's culinary skills turned any food she laid her hands on into a mouthwatering delight. It was a miracle he hadn't gained more weight since marrying her.

As he sat there chewing his food, he thought about his initial interrogation of Ali earlier that day. He had been straightforward with him, treating him humanely but letting him know Ali know that he would not hesitate to inflict severe discomfort if he wasn't going to be completely truthful with him. He did not know what to think about Ali's story. He knew the Americans were constantly plotting ways to inflict damage upon his country, but the enormity of the conspiracy was almost too much for even him to believe. Could the government of the United States be so wicked that they were willing to bring about death and destruction upon his country, along with the rest of the Middle East, that would make the attacks on Hiroshima and Nagasaki seem insignificant?

Ali hadn't told him what their objective might be in killing the foreign minister, but Hamed saw the forces it had set in motion. He knew his country wouldn't sit by quietly without responding in some way when all appearances pointed to the Zionists. He just did not know the type and magnitude of the response. That was above his level of importance within the hierarchy of the Islamic Republic's leadership. Perhaps when he made general, he would be privy to those decisions, but for now, it was his responsibility to determine if there was any truth to the wild claims Ali was professing, or if it was some elaborate ploy to bring a wedge between Iran and its nominal ally, Russia. The Russians had been cooperating with Iran in supporting the Assad regime in Syria. In addition to Assad being both countries' only ally in the rest of the Middle

East, they, along with North Korea, were at odds with the United States. This led to an allegiance of convenience against the attempted dominance of their countries by the United States and its European allies. But he had no illusions about the Russians. They themselves were infidels. Their president professed to be a devout Christian, yet Hamed knew he was a godless man whose only motivation was to maintain power by allowing his corrupt underlings to rob the state in exchange for their loyalty while arresting and eliminating his opponents. He wouldn't put it past Markov to sell out his country if it benefited the immediate interests of his thugocracy. But it was still hard to imagine that the Americans and Russians could secretly conspire with each other to attempt such a bold outrage. He had to determine what the truth was. The future and well-being of not only his country but also his family depended on it. He would use whatever means were necessary to be certain he was getting the truth from Ali, no matter how unpleasant they might be. He finished the last kebab and washed it down with the last bit of tea in his cup. He looked at his watch. It was 10:30 p.m. He knew Laleh would be waiting in bed for him. There would be more late nights until this current ordeal that had befallen his country had run its course, one way or another. The fact that the outcome depended so much on his success or failure weighed heavily on him. He stood up and walked into the dark living room and kneeled down, facing southwest in the middle of the Persian rug adorning the marble floor. He lowered his forehead to the ground for one additional prayer before he retired for the night.

"Oh Allah, Your faithful servant asks for Your guidance and wisdom as he attempts to find the truth about what the enemies of Your faithful people are plotting against them. Reveal to me if it is the Great Satan who is manipulating this man to deceive me from the truth. Your servant knows the evil one's powers to lie and deceive Your faithful people. Give me the strength to employ whatever means are necessary to discern the truth, even if it requires bringing great harm or death to this man in order to save the lives of Your people against the plans of the evil one. You are the Most High, the most powerful, the knower of all truth, who peers into the hearts of men and sees their deepest, darkest lies. I ask for the truth to be revealed to me. All glory and praise is to You, Allah." He finished his prayers and rose, making his way towards the bedroom. The light was still on. Laleh was up waiting for him. She was a good wife, better than he deserved.

***

Secretary Payton had just landed at Andrews Air Force Base on his way back from Moscow. His motorcade with its D.C. Police motorcycle escorts was moving him through the evening rush-hour traffic up the Suitland Parkway on his way to the White House, where President Steele was waiting for him. He sat in the back of his armored limousine, looking out the window as they crossed the Anacostia River into D.C., wondering what would happen if something in their complex scheme failed to move in the direction they had planned. The dynamics they had set in motion seemed to be taking on a life of their own. Right now, they appeared to be leading towards the desired outcomes, but history was littered with examples of well-thought-out plans that had failed to turn out as anticipated. He thought of the German Army's invasion of the Soviet Union during World War II. The German High Command had put together perhaps one of the most brilliantly strategized invasion plans in military history, yet unanticipated factors beyond their control had turned it into one of history's greatest military disasters. Now the risk that their own plot could be compromised through inadvertent carelessness made his stomach churn. Common sense told him the odds of Shiravi disclosing what he knew were remote, but the uncertainty of not knowing where he was didn't sit well with him. He hoped his faith in Canton's ability to take care of that problem wasn't misplaced. He knew Canton was a capable operator, but there was something untrustworthy about him. Payton certainly didn't care for his air of arrogance. He was the US Secretary of State and a former four-star general; Canton was merely a CIA hack who had risen beyond his abilities just because he had managed to brown-nose the First Lady.

Prior to becoming First Lady, Alexandra Kinkaid-Steele was a Republican congresswoman from North Dakota, and the chairwoman of the House Intelligence Committee, until her husband had unexpectedly won the presidential race in 2016. Canton had been assigned to her staff as the CIA liaison, a go-nowhere position reserved for seasoned mid-level officers that didn't have what it took to make it as a chief of station in one of the Agency's overseas posts. Congresswoman Kinkaid-Steele had obviously trusted and thought enough of him to recommend him to her husband for his usefulness in their endeavor. Since they clearly couldn't task the CIA to carry out such an unsanctioned act, Canton, with his CIA access, along with the Russians taking care of the wet work, was what they needed to carry out their plan. President Steele had made it clear to his nominee for Director of Central Intelligence that he wanted his wife's former staffer promoted to a senior management position within the CIA, preferably as the deputy director for the Counterproliferation Division. It was a position that would warrant having him assist the Secretary of State in his negotiations with the Iranians over their nuclear and weapons programs. Canton's meteoric rise within the CIA hadn't gone unnoticed by many of his peers, who were familiar with his unimpressive record. Most, however, took it as just another example of how the administration was attempting to put its own people into the previously nonpartisan positions within governmental agencies. It didn't help matters that Canton made no bones about rubbing the noses of all his contemporaries in the fact that he now outranked most of them. He was not well liked at Langley, but it didn't bother him. There were very few people within the Agency that could tell him what he could and couldn't do. Specifically, there were only three: the DCI, the deputy DCI, and his boss, the deputy director of the National Clandestine Service, formerly known as the Directorate of Operations.

Payton hadn't been keen on the idea of having to work with Canton, but he hadn't had any say in the matter. President Steele had made that decision. Payton would be responsible for coordinating with Markov and Dobrynin, along with steering the Israelis in the right direction, while Canton would handle things at the operational level with the SVR. He would also be in a position to access and pass whatever sensitive intelligence was needed. So now his future and the success of the entire operation was in jeopardy unless Canton could ensure that Shiravi was eliminated. It wasn't a position he liked to be in. He dreaded having to explain the situation to the President in the next few minutes.

His motorcade cleared the security checkpoint on Pennsylvania Avenue and made its way down the drive to the West Wing of the White House. The US Marine Corps White House sentry standing post in his dress uniform outside the entrance stepped forward, offering the Secretary of State a salute as he stepped out of the rear of the limo. Still maintaining his four-star rank in retirement, Payton returned a sharp salute as he walked past. Inside, he made his way to the Oval Office, where he would meet with the President. The staff member standing outside the door greeted him, opening the door to the Oval Office.

"Please have a seat, Mr. Secretary. The President will be with you momentarily. Can I get you anything?"

"No, I'm good. Thank you." Payton nodded, taking a seat on one of the gold couches facing each other. The aide exited the room, closing the door. Payton looked at the portrait of George Washington hanging above the fireplace and wondered what he would have thought of their plan to secure the future their country's prosperity and well-being in the face of a world so hostile to their values of democracy. The idea of having to compromise those values and work with a thug like Markov was distasteful to him, but sometimes one had to deal with the devil to obtain noble goals. Roosevelt and Churchill had certainly had to with Stalin. That was just the reality of the world. Payton at least found solace in the fact that in the end, the United States would secure its place as the world's preeminent superpower, both militarily and economically. The Russians, of course, would prosper economically with their newfound oil revenues, but they were a hollow nation that didn't produce anything other than dictators. From the tsars, through the oppressive decades of communism, and now with

Markov controlling every facet of society, the Russian people had never had the opportunity to govern themselves by letting their voices be heard. They were content to have someone tell them what to do and what to think, as long as they had their bread and vodka. In a way, Payton felt sorry for them. Russians were essentially Westerners and Christians, yet they lacked the capacity to advance beyond the serfdom mentality that had held them captive for their entire history. Well, there were winners and losers in the world. As long as America was winning, he really didn't care about the plight of the losers.

The door in front of him opened and President Martin Steele walked in from the study next door, which was the actual working office of the President. Contrary to popular belief, the Oval Office was primarily used by the President for briefings and staff meetings, and for ceremonial events such as foreign dignitary visits or the signing of an important new bill into law.

"Bill, how are you?" President Steele asked, walking over and shaking Payton's hand before taking a seat on the couch across from him.

"I'm doing well, Mr. President."

"How was the flight back from Moscow? Did you get any rest?"

"It was fine. I managed a short nap."

"Good, good. So, a lot going on. How did things go with Markov? Did you manage to grab the tiger by the tail?" Steele let out a sarcastic laugh.

"More like trying to charm a cobra. He was his usual self, trying to intimidate with implied threats behind that impersonal smile and those steely blue eyes. It may work with all his lackeys over there, but I know what he's all about and what he can bring to the table to back up those threats. He forgets I was SACEUR and know exactly how far he can push his agenda on the world stage. Their military's been stretched to its operational limit between sustaining their undeclared insurgency in eastern Ukraine and keeping Assad afloat over in Syria. The *Kuznetsov*, that pile of scrap they call an aircraft carrier, barely limped back to its base in Severomorsk, billowing out thick black smoke you could see miles away. They're a paper tiger."

"Bill, you still think like a general. It's not just which kid on the block can kick everybody else's ass in a fight. Of course, next to our military, they're a third-world country. Markov doesn't hold a lot of cards, but the ones he does, he knows how to play pretty well. He hasn't stayed in power this long because he's a fool."

"Oh, I know that, Mr. President. He's as cunning as a fox. But he's got to learn just how far he can play his hand before the hammer comes down on the back of his neck. The only thing he understands is brute force. So he's got to understand, in the end, we're the ones who have final say on things."

"Okay, Bill. Why is it you have such a hard-on for the guy? At least he's got things under control in his country. Would you rather have a country with all that oil wealth and that many nukes with the type of chaos they've got going over in Pakistan? We and our European allies have stuck it to the Russians pretty good since the breakup of the Soviet Union, pushing ourselves all the way up to their western border. They feel threatened. That whole Ukraine and Crimea thing is just Markov posturing that he isn't going to let us walk all over him. In the big picture, they're just a hollow shell of what they used to be. Kind of like what happened to Sears. He just wants to hold on to what little they have remaining and knows he has to maintain complete control or he'll lose even that. Look what happened to them under that clown Yeltsin. They almost went completely bankrupt. I got to hand it to Markov, he turned his country around when they were on the brink. He's a winner. That's what the Russian people want. They could care less if their voices are heard. Look at their entire history. They've always been told what to do, and they do it. Better than a lot of the corporations in this country with their management taking them in the wrong direction. That's why I left Merrill Lynch and set out on my own. Didn't want anyone else dictating to me what I could or couldn't do. Worked pretty well for me."

"Whatever you say, Mr. President. We just need to keep the Russians in check and on a short leash."

"Bill, I thought we were both on the same page that it was the Chinese who were our greatest adversaries. In the end, isn't that what this is all about? Once we get control of the world's oil supply, they won't be able to compete with us economically. Our energy costs will be half of theirs. They'll still have their cheap labor costs, but we'll leave them behind when you factor in our energy savings. Our tax revenues will go up and we'll be able to continue outspending them militarily five to one, while they'll be struggling trying to meet the demands of an increasing middle class, let alone a generation of half a billion aging Chinese who will have to be supported by a workforce the same size as a result of the One-Child policy they had for twenty-some years. Same thing that happened to Detroit when things started going south for them in the nineties. They were bleeding tax revenue as factories shut down left and right, while drowning in red because of their pension obligations. The Chinese have been able to sustain their spending with seven percent economic growth, but that won't last forever, and when it does fall to three percent growth, which most industrialized countries would be ecstatic about, the shit is going to hit the fan over there. You think we had a lot of disgruntled voters last election that got me elected, just wait and see what happens when a hundred million pissed-off Chinese descend on Beijing."

"We're on the same page, Mr. President. Once we can choke off their oil supply, it'll all be over for them, just like what happened to the Germans in World War II."

"Well, then, I'm glad we're in agreement. So, how do things stand? Are we heading in the right direction?"

"We are. Akerman is so worked up with all the rhetoric, it's just going to take a little shove to push him over the line to launch some sort of strike against the Iranians. The Russians announcing the sale of their S-400 missile defense system to them will be that little shove. More than likely, it will be their Fordow underground nuclear facility. That's what the Iranians were talking about three years ago, when they wanted to purchase that system to defend Fordow. Over the past two years, the Israelis have purchased over two hundred GBU-28 laser-guided bunker buster bombs from us. There're very few facilities you need that many bunker busters for, and Fordow is one of them. I told Akerman that I would stress to Markov how much we were against the sale. He's going to come unglued when he hears they're going through with the sale. He'll feel he's got no other choice but to go through with an attack before it's too late. If that happens, you can bet to high heaven that the Iranians will retaliate significantly with a barrage of intermediate-range missiles."

"Do the Iranians have the capability to significantly hurt Israel?"

"They have somewhere in the neighborhood of a hundred medium-range missiles that can reach them. Even if it's a limited retaliation, Israel won't let a missile attack from Iran go unanswered. It'll only take a few dozen falling on Tel Aviv or Haifa before the Israelis respond with their own Jericho II intermediate-range missiles. Things will go tit for tat until they escalate to the point that each side starts sustaining significant civilian casualties. At some point, the Israelis are going to hit them with a nuke. It may not be Tehran; it might be one of their smaller cities. But when that happens, you can bet the rest of the Middle East will erupt into complete chaos. The Arabs may not care for the Iranians, but when the Jews nuke their fellow Muslims, it's going to be Armageddon over there. Who knows? With the way those rag heads think, you might even have the Iranians lashing out at the Saudis. It could turn into a real bloodbath over there."

"You almost sound enthusiastic about that," President Steele remarked.

"I'm just a realist. People have had to die throughout history for the sake of civilization. I don't think Alexander or Caesar flinched at the tens of thousands they killed in order to bring order to the world. The harsher things are in the beginning, the faster we accomplish what needs to be done to have peace and order in the long run. That's been the problem with this pinprick approach we've been stuck on over the last thirty years in dealing with these jihadi fanatics."

"Is there anyone you don't dislike, Bill?"

"I don't dislike anyone, Mr. President, as long as they don't threaten the United States. Once they start making hostile moves against us, then I got a serious problem with them."

"Once a soldier, always soldier, is that how it is?"

"I may be wearing a suit these days, but it doesn't diminish the sense of duty I feel to my country."

"It's good to know I can count on your loyalty. Which brings me to our other issue with the interpreter. Has that situation been rectified?"

"Not yet."

"What do you mean not yet?"

"He hasn't been found. For all we know, he could be lying dead somewhere. He may have been wounded by the Russians and wandered off somewhere or even drowned in the Bosphorus. I wouldn't worry too much about it," Payton said.

"The Russians? What the hell is going on, Bill? Why would he have been wounded by the Russians?"

"Canton arranged for their Spetsnaz team to take out my interpreter before they went after Mohammedi, just to be safe. Apparently, they weren't successful," Payton explained and waited for the onslaught from the President.

"The Russians! Why are the Russians involved? You told me Canton was handling it! It doesn't sound like he's handled anything." Steele was livid.

"It was the only option available under the circumstances. It was just a few hours before they were supposed to go after Mohammedi. We didn't want to take any chances."

"Why didn't Canton just take care of it himself? He's CIA."

"That would have left us with an even bigger mess than we already have now. Could you imagine how it would have complicated matters if he was found murdered in his room on my floor? This way, at least it was supposed to look like he was just an unfortunate additional victim connected to the assassination of Mohammedi. Collateral damage. Unfortunately, the Russians screwed things up."

"No, Bill, you and Canton screwed things up. If you'd been more careful with what you said and where you said it, we wouldn't be in this mess. For Christ's sake, you were a four-star general. You should have known better."

Payton sat there in silence. He wanted to tell Steele that he was still a four-star general, just retired, but he thought it would be wiser under the circumstances if he kept his mouth shut. What did he expect a Wall Street banker to know about the military anyway? He hated being put in this situation. Just a simple careless oversight, saying something at the wrong time, and now some GS-13 interpreter had put his whole future in jeopardy. He had never been so careless in his thirty-six years in the military, and now he had to stand in front of Steele and be berated by a man who had never served in the military.

"Yes sir, I should have been more careful," Payton offered contritely.

"I just hope you're right about him lying dead somewhere. I'll tell you, Bill, if you hadn't come up with such a brilliant plan when I asked you how we could take the whole Middle East out of the petroleum business, I would fire your ass for something so stupid. All right, for now, let's just keep moving forward with the plan. After the Russians announce the sale of the S-400 to the Iranians and Akerman blows his top, I'll hold a press conference. Everyone is waiting to hear a statement from the President of the United States on this situation. In addition to expressing my condolences to the Iranian people, I'll warn the Iran regime not to make any rash decisions about retaliating against Israel when there's a question as to who's actually responsible for the attack. I'll also warn them against any attempts to circumvent the nuclear agreement. That should get the Supreme Leader and all the hardliners riled up over there, and they'll respond with some inflammatory rhetoric, like pouring gasoline on the fire, hopefully enough to force the Israelis into launching their attack. Unless there's anything more, I have a meeting with the Secretary of Energy and a bunch of oil company CEOs, including my father-in-law. I hope that old coot behaves himself in front of the others and doesn't try to dictate the direction of the conversation just because he thinks his money got me elected. Keep me updated on the situation with the interpreter. I want that taken care of. Is that understood?"

"Yes, sir, Mr. President, it is." Secretary Payton stood up following the cue from the President.

"All right, then, let's make it happen and get this country back on top. We owe it to the American people and American stockholders. It's corporate America that makes this country what it is," Steele said as he led Payton to the door. "We'll talk again soon, Bill." He opened the door to find the Secretary of

Energy and fourteen oil company CEOs waiting out in the hallway. "Bob, come on in and bring all our guests," the President said enthusiastically, giving his practiced smile.

***

Michael walked out of the theater and looked at his watch. It was 9:30 p.m. Perfect, he thought. He would be at the airport by 10:15, drop off his rental car, hurry to the Turkish Airlines ticket counter, purchase his ticket and clear security to make it to the gate just in time for boarding. He was cutting it close for an international flight, but he didn't want to give Canton any more warning than was necessary. No reason to make anything easy for him. Canton would undoubtedly have enough time after he had been informed about Michael's reservation for Istanbul to contact the chief of station at Ankara and have him dispatch a surveillance team to the airport to pick him up after he cleared customs, but whatever Asya had planned would spoil their efforts. Michael smiled at the thought of Canton's reaction when he learned that the team had never spotted him at the airport. He would be able to confirm Michael had boarded the flight in Dulles but would become unglued trying to figure out how he hadn't come off it in Istanbul. He tried to think of what Canton's next move would be after that. He would most likely head back to Istanbul. That was Ali's last known location and that's obviously where he was, even if Canton wasn't able to figure out how he'd pulled off his disappearing act from the airport.

He walked briskly back to the parking garage and found his car. He pulled the Phillips screwdriver out of the black backpack stuffed with his new shoes and clothes he had purchased in the mall, walked around to the front of his car and squatted in front of the license plate. He quickly unscrewed the Virginia license plate from the front of the bumper, tossing it in the car and placing the screws in the cup holder. With the front license plate off, any traffic cameras between the mall and the airport wouldn't be able to track his movements, since most of them faced in the direction of oncoming traffic. It lessened the odds that Canton could get a jump on him before his flight left Dulles. The last thing he wanted to risk was giving Canton enough time to put someone on the same flight to Turkey and pick Michael up leaving the US. That would not be a good thing, although it wouldn't make much of a difference in the end. That person would have had to clear customs just like every other passenger, while Michael would somehow vanish into thin air. The only additional piece of information it would have given Canton was that someone actually witnessed him land in Istanbul, something he would conclude anyway. Either way, he would realize that Michael had some local assistance in leaving the airport undetected.

He pulled out of the mall and headed back to the Beltway. It would be a short drive to the airport from there, up to the next exit and then fifteen miles down the Dulles Access Road to the airport. Traffic should be very light this time in the evening, he thought. He would make it in good time.

As soon as he exited the cloverleaf from I-495 onto the access road, he knew he had a problem. Traffic was backed up and crawling at a snail's pace on all four lanes. *Oh crap. I don't need this now.* It was 9:50. *How can there be this much traffic going to the airport this time at night?* There had to be some sort of accident. He wanted to turn on his iPhone and check his WAZE app to find out the cause and extent of the traffic, but it would alert the technician back at Langley, giving away his location. He was stuck crawling twenty-five miles per hour in a sea of other frantic drivers also heading to the airport and worrying about making their flight. Well, things didn't always go as planned. Murphy's law was part of reality, even in intelligence operations. One could try and plan for every conceivable contingency, but the unexpected could always throw a monkey wrench into the most well-thought-out plan. He was upset at himself for cutting it so close. He could always wait at the airport and take the next available flight. The thought of finding some corner in the airport to spend the night didn't appeal, but once there, he didn't want to leave again to find a hotel to spend the night. The longer he remained in the US, the greater the chances of Canton tracking his movements. He would have to call Asya back and tell her he had missed his flight. He dreaded having to do so. What would she think? No use getting frazzled, he told himself; things were what they were. He just had to roll with the punches. He knew some things wouldn't go smoothly in his quest to help Ali, but he didn't want to start off by missing his flight.

He turned on the radio and searched for some calming music to get his mind off the traffic. His rental came with Sirius satellite radio, so he searched the channels until he came across the jazz stations, flipping through them until he heard something he liked. He loosened his grip on the steering wheel and relaxed his shoulders to the smooth voice of Sade coming over the speakers. His taste in music was wide-ranging. He listened to classical when the mood struck him, and other times blasted the driving beat of INXS on his car stereo driving down the highway with the sunroof open. Sade? INXS? It seemed such a short time ago their hits were being played over the airwaves. When he thought about it, that was three decades ago. He doubted anyone from his daughter's generation would even recognize the names. The deaths over the recent years of singers he had grown up listening to—David Bowie, Glenn Frey, George Michael, Prince, and others—had hit home with him. He was getting to be an old fart. How could so much of his lifetime have passed by so quickly? It seemed just like yesterday that he was young and had fallen in love with Karen and they had married. He felt a sense of melancholy at being without anyone close to him at this point in his life. Perhaps that was what had led him to try and take his life. Was it that bad, being alone? If he was being honest with himself, he actually liked the freedom of not having to be accountable to anyone other than himself. Despite being married twice, he had grown accustomed to doing things on his own. Whether it was a result of his occupations or something about his character, there was a big part of him that liked to keep some distance between himself and others. Maybe that distance was what had led Karen, and now Eva, not to be able to sustain such a relationship. He didn't blame them. He knew he had come up short by not making them feel included in his life. He was the one to blame.

In the distance up ahead, Michael could see the blue and red flashes of emergency vehicles. He glanced at his watch again. It was 10:00. Traffic was still rolling along at twenty-five miles per hour. At this rate, he didn't know if he had a chance of making his flight. He remembered how many times he had been in similar situations in some foreign country in the distant past, racing to catch a train or plane. The pace of daily life while he was in Special Forces and the CIA was constantly in overdrive, sixteen years of nonstop challenges with intermittent bouts of excitement-filled adrenaline rushes. At the time, he never really gave it much thought that his life was flying by in a nonstop blur. It was his world, and he had no other point of reference to go by. Looking back, he wished he had slowed things down some and made some different choices when it came to his personal life—choices that might have led him to a different place in life. The flashing lights slowly drew nearer as the traffic in the left two lanes merged to the right. He saw fire trucks up ahead and a Virginia State police trooper directing traffic to the right. It was 10:20 by the time Michael inched by the scene of a three-car accident along the median. The vehicles weren't severely damaged, but with all the emergency vehicles, it was enough to cause traffic to pile up for several miles.

As soon as he had cleared the scene, Michael stomped the gas pedal and accelerated down the wide-open lanes in front of him. He still had another ten miles until the airport, but with any luck, he might able to make his flight. He finally came across the first set of signs for the airport, directing him to the lanes for the rental car returns. He pulled into the Hertz area and got out of the car, looking for the attendant. He spotted her and waved, trying to draw her attention. After what seemed like an eternity, the heavyset older African-American gal finally made her way over to him. He handed her his rental agreement, waiting as she scanned it, got in and checked the mileage and gasoline level and finally walk around the car to inspect it.

"What happened to the license plate?" she asked.

The license plate? Crap! Michael realized he forgot about it in his rush. "It's on the passenger floor. It was loose and rattling. I tried tightening it, but the holes were stripped. I didn't want it to fall off, so I took it off." That was the only excuse he could come up with that quickly.

"Mm-hmm." She gave him an up-and-down once-over and entered something into her portable check-in unit. "And you know you didn't fill up your gas tank. Gonna have to charge you three ninety-nine a gallon to fill it back up to full, where it was when you got it."

"That's fine, miss. I'm a bit of a rush. If you could just finish checking me in and give me the receipt, I'm cutting it close on my flight," he told her, trying not to sound impatient with her.

"You know how many times I've heard that? The answer I give them is maybe they should have planned a little bit better before leaving for the airport. You know you should give yourself at least two hours for international flights. Mm, mm, honey, you need to really get your act together. Haven't you ever flown before?" she asked him as she printed his receipt and handed it to him.

"Yes, thank you. I'll have to remember that." He grabbed the receipt from her and hurriedly made his way towards the terminal. Just what he needed to hear, the parking attendant telling him how he couldn't plan the first leg of his operation without risking it unraveling before it even began. He made his way up to the departures level and located the Turkish Airlines counter. He walked up to the empty ticket counter and was greeted by the Turkish Airlines agent.

"May I help you?"

"I'd like to purchase a ticket for Istanbul, if any are still available on the flight leaving tonight," he told her.

"My, you're cutting it very close," she commented as she began checking her terminal. "Business or economy?"

"Economy is fine, a window or aisle seat if any are still available." He knew there should be plenty.

"I'm sorry, we're sold out of economy. We only have business left."

"Sold out? How can that be? I checked earlier this afternoon and it showed you had over twenty seats open," he asked with a hint of frustration.

"That can happen sometimes. Another airline was late with a connecting flight to Istanbul, so it booked the remaining seats on this flight to accommodate its passengers. We do have three business seats open, however."

"And how much are those?"

"Eight thousand, two hundred."

"That's two thousand more than what I could have purchased it for just a few hours ago," he exclaimed, exasperated.

"Tickets are always more expensive at the ticket counter," she informed him sadly, "but tell you what I can do. If you purchase an open unrestricted economy fare for tomorrow night's flight, I can switch you to this flight and put you in business since there are no other seats available. The fare costs twenty-one hundred dollars, but it will save you over six thousand dollars."

"I will take that offer!" he told her, his disappointment turning to thankfulness. *There is a God*, he thought.

"I am."

"I'm sorry, you're what?" he asked her.

She looked up at him with a smile, "I'm what?"

"You said, 'I am.'"

She giggled at him, "No, I didn't say anything. Maybe you're just so happy you're hearing things. May I see your passport?"

"Passport, oh yeah. Hold on a sec." He reached into the zippered inside pocket of his jacket and pulled out his passport. The last time he had used it was four years ago, when he and Eva had taken a trip down to Cancun. He looked at the nearly pristine passport and remembered what some of his older passports had looked like. He had used several, with various identities, including a Canadian passport obtained through a reciprocity agreement between the CIA and its Canadian counterpart, the Canadian Security Intelligence Service. The old ones were well worn, most of the pages filled with various countries' immigration stamps. It seemed like he was on a plane every other month during those years. He handed her his passport. She opened it to the first page and entered his passport number into her computer terminal, then handed it back to him and continued typing.

When she finished, she looked back up at him. "That will be two thousand, one hundred and seventy-seven, including the airport tax."

He pulled out the stack of cash Harry had given him and counted out twenty-two hundred-dollar bills, handing them to the ticket agent. She counted them and pulled out twenty-three dollars in change from her cash box, handing it to Michael. She typed some more and waited for the printer next to her to spit out Michael's ticket and boarding pass. She handed them to him and told him his gate would be B-51, concourse B. If he had any baggage to check, he would have to go to the other counter to check his baggage. Otherwise, he could proceed straight to the gate.

"Thanks for all your help, especially cutting me the break with the business-class ticket. That's going to make a world of difference on how I feel when I get there. You're a kind person."

"Well, thank you. I'm glad I could make things more pleasant for you. Have a wonderful flight," she said with a big smile. He turned and slung his backpack over his left shoulder. Grabbing the handle of his carry-on, he started moving towards the security screening checkpoint. He looked at his watch. It was 11:15. He hoped things weren't backed up. He was cutting it close, and boarding would be starting shortly. He got to the checkpoint and saw there weren't many people waiting in line. Despite it being close to midnight, TSA still had four lines open. Dulles was the main international airport for Washington, D.C. He figured TSA didn't want to draw any more unnecessary attention to itself by invoking the ire of angry members of Congress and the rest of the three hundred thousand federal employees who worked in D.C. and used Dulles on a regular basis. Dulles was also the main hub for US military members flying commercial in and out of the D.C. area. It was a night-and-day difference from the three New York–area airports, where security lines often stretched down the length of the terminal at peak hours.

He pulled his shoes and belt off and laid them in the bin. He pulled everything out of his pockets, and along with his watch, threw it into his backpack and placed it and his carry-on on the conveyor. He waited for the TSA screener to motion him into the body scanner and stepped in, placing his feet onto the yellow shoe outlines and raising his arms above his head while the scanner made its sweep. He stepped out of the machine and grabbed his belt and shoes from the bin, along with his backpack and carry-on. He headed towards his gate, trying to kick his heels into his shoes, while at the same time attempting to slip his belt through each pant loop as he pulled his carry-on behind him. Gate B-51 was a good distance down concourse B, and he didn't have much time to spare. He finally arrived at his gate and saw that boarding had already begun. Business class had already boarded, and now economy passengers were boarding the Airbus A340-300. He stepped into the empty business-class line, pulling his boarding pass from his pocket and handing it to the Turkish Airlines gate agent. She scanned it and handed it back to him, and he continued through the door and down the jet way. He reached the back of the line of passengers waiting to board the aircraft, shuffling along behind the mother trying to manage her three young children who looked like their sugar rush had just kicked in. He took satisfaction in knowing it was unlikely they would be sitting next to him. He finally boarded the aircraft and cut across his seat at 8D. He placed his carry-on in the overhead bin and took his seat.

He took in a deep breath and finally relaxed. He looked at his watch. It was

11:40 p.m. Things had worked out perfect despite the traffic, and he was flying business class. He couldn't have asked for anything more. A flight attendant came to his seat, welcoming him on board while holding a tray with orange juice and champagne glasses in front of him. He grabbed an orange juice and took a long swig, refreshing his dry mouth. It had been a chaotic few days. He knew things would likely get more chaotic, but for now, he had ten hours to relax and hopefully get some sleep on the flight over. He pulled the menu out of the holder on the side of his seat and looked at the choices for dinner. The rib-eye steak caught his attention. He would order that along with a glass of red wine and finish it off with cheesecake, then put his chair back for a good night's sleep and wake up with a few hours left until arrival at Istanbul. He heard the aircraft door shut, and then the captain come over the PA system, welcoming the passengers onto Turkish Airlines flight eight to Istanbul. After the announcement finished, the cabin crew began their pre-takeoff safety demonstration as the aircraft began its pullback away from the jet way.

Michael put his head back and closed his eyes at the thought that in a few hours, he would be facing Asya after all these years. He wondered how much she had changed. The conversation they'd just had made it feel like no time had passed at all, but he knew their lives had diverged, and after so many years, things wouldn't be the same. Each of them had changed from how the other remembered them. He wondered what she would think of him. Would she recognize the person he had become? Sometimes he didn't recognize himself. It seemed surreal that he was being catapulted back to an environment that felt as if it were from a different lifetime. People he hadn't seen for years, for decades, had come hurtling back into his life. Of all the people, however, Asya was the curveball. The sound of her voice had brought on all kinds of confusing emotions. On one hand, he was excited and looking forward to seeing her; on the other hand, he felt a good amount of anxiety. He had just tried to kill himself, and now he was going to have to be around her and act as if everything in his life was great. Maybe not great, but okay. He wasn't sure if he could pull it off and act natural around her. He wondered if she would sense something different about him. They had never been lovers, but during the time they had spent working together, a certain intimacy had developed between them. In some ways, what he had experienced with Asya was far more intense than anything he had with Karen, and then afterwards with Eva.

The four engines of the A340 came to full power, then he felt the large aircraft began its takeoff roll down the runway. As the plane accelerated and then lifted off, Michael dozed off to the thought of how he imagined Asya would look after all these years. He would have to wait for that ribeye steak until after all this was over and he had returned to the United States.

Chapter 11

Ali awoke to the sound of the call to prayer from somewhere off in the distance. He sat up in his cot and looked around, wondering where it was coming from, since his cell had no windows. He sat quietly listening, but he no longer heard anything. That was strange, he thought; it sounded just like he remembered as a child growing up in Tehran, when the muezzin would call out the time for prayers from the minarets of the neighborhood mosque. Had he just dreamt it? It was a strange dream to have. Although he was born and raised in Tehran, he hadn't spent much time in mosques. His parents, secular Iranians and university professors, had taught him the fundamentals of his religion and the formalities of worship but hadn't attended prayer services regularly, other than on special holidays and of course during Ramadan. As part of his attempts to Westernize Iran, the Shah had made great efforts to minimize the role of religion in society. With its nightclubs, fancy restaurants and recreational venues, Tehran during the early 1970s gave off a feeling closer to Los Angeles than to the crowded theocratic metropolis of today. It was easy to live one's life with religion being shoved into some corner as an antiquated relic of Iran's past, until Khomeini's Islamic revolution turned Iranian society upside down in a matter of just a few months after the Shah had fled. Although Ali's uncle was a kind man and treated him well, he never spoke to Ali about religion, nor did he ever attend a mosque. Ali was about as secular as they came in northern Virginia. He had even married in a civil ceremony at the courthouse in Richmond. Religion was something he was as unfamiliar with as quantum physics, so how was he ever going to convince Hamed that he was a God-fearing, truthful man?

The thought of what inhumane torture he would be subjected to overwhelmed him with dread. It wasn't so much the physical pain as the thought of not leaving this place the same man he had come in, if he ever did leave. He knew what happened to those who survived imprisonment by the IRGC. Something always snapped inside. The lucky ones may have come out with merely a facial twitch that stayed with them the rest of their lives. The less fortunate had difficulty functioning as normal members of society. He wondered if his parents had met such a fate. Perhaps one or even both had survived the revolution and managed to somehow scrape by in their new, unforgiving world. The more he considered that possibility, the more he felt it would have been better had they not lived after experiencing a place like this. He wondered what he would have found if he had managed to see them again after all these years. Two hunched and gray elderly people. Would he have even recognized them after almost four decades? Would they have recognized him?

He thought about seeing his daughter again. Would Roxanne be ready to handle what she would see standing in front of her—some broken man, vaguely resembling the father she remembered? Ali knew she would make a valiant effort to hide her shock behind a brave smile, but her eyes always gave her away. He remembered her that way from a little girl. He almost felt as if he should consciously make an effort to erase Roxanne from his mind, think of her as dead, no longer in his life. That way he would only have to endure the physical pain and be spared the mental anguish. The thought of her never knowing what had happened to him, however, was too much for him to bear. He didn't want to put her through the same grief he experienced, never having found out the fate of his parents. He identified with the suffering so many survivors of the Nazi death camps had gone through, never having seen their loved ones again or knowing their fate. If there was a God, it was cruel how he allowed the brutality of man to go unchecked. It was as if he wasn't even tuned in to what was going on around the world. How could he allow such unspeakable acts of evil to continue century after century and not do anything about it? He obviously disregarded the cries for help from all the victims who were suffering the consequences of such brutality.

It made him angry that he had learned about one of those evil acts, and now his life would never be the same because of it. The uncertainty about his future aroused so many raw emotions inside him. He didn't even think about what he was doing when he pulled the blanket off his cot and threw it down on the floor in front of him. He knelt down on the blanket, placed his forehead down in front of him, and burst out sobbing. He lost track of how long he had lain there when he heard the man's voice. He had missed the sound of the keys unlocking the door and the man entering. He attempted to stand up but found that he couldn't lift his head up off the floor. At first, he thought whoever had come into his cell was holding his head down, but he didn't feel any hands. Despite how hard he struggled, he remained in the same position.

He finally relented and called out to whoever was restraining him, "Please stop. Why are you doing this to me?"

"What is it I am doing to you?"

"You're not letting me get up."

"I did not put you there."

"Put me where?"

"Where you find yourself."

"I'm on the floor."

"Yes, you are. Why do you find yourself there?"

"What do you mean, why do I find myself there? I put myself there," Ali exclaimed.

"Why did you put yourself on the floor?"

"Why? I don't know why. I guess I wanted to ask God something."

"What did you want to ask?"

"I wanted to ask him why he put me in this situation. I wanted to ask him what I did to deserve this," Ali told his questioner.

"You believe you did something to deserve your current situation?" his questioner inquired of Ali.

"No, I didn't do anything. I just happened to have the bad luck of being at the wrong place at the wrong time."

"You believe it was bad luck?"

"Of course it was bad luck. I don't deserve this. I've never done anything to hurt anyone. I've just tried to live my life as best as I could. I've always done my best at my job, when I was in the military and now. I've tried to be a good father to my daughter after her mother died. I had to watch my wife slowly die in front of me. She was in so much pain. She was a good person and the best wife anyone could have asked for. She didn't deserve to suffer like that. We didn't deserve to lose her. My parents were good people and wonderful parents. They loved their country. They didn't deserve what happened to them," Ali cried out with a sob.

"Why do you believe any of these things have to do with what one deserves?"

"I don't understand."

"You said none of you deserved the things that happened. Why do you believe these things have anything to do with what you deserve?"

"Because—because we're not bad people."

"So, you are saying you are good people?"

"Yes, I am a good person, and so was my wife, and so were my parents, and so is my daughter. I've been around enough bad people to know the difference."

"I see. So, since you are good people, you believe you do not deserve what has happened to you?"

"Well, yes. I mean, no, we don't deserve it."

"And what is it you do not deserve that has happened?"

"What do you mean, what is it? We don't deserve all the bad things that have happened to us."

"You believe bad things do not happen to good people?"

"No, I didn't say that. I meant, we didn't do anything to deserve to suffer like this, to go through the pain and loss. We were punished for things we didn't do," Ali told him.

"And who is it that is punishing you?"

Ali remained silent for a moment. He didn't know what this person was trying to get at. He knew it wasn't Hamed, but there was something strange about his questioner's voice. Was he speaking to him in Farsi or English? Ali tried to think what language he was hearing and speaking himself, but had trouble making sense of the conversation. Was it some ploy on the part of his captors to get him to confess to something? He was confused. Had they spiked his food or water with some drug? He felt normal, yet something strange was happening. He thought of the question he had been asked. Who was it that was punishing him? What had made him say that? The current Iranian regime had punished his parents. Wasn't that obvious? His wife suffering through the cancer, who had punished her? Roxanne and him, losing their beloved mother and wife, who had punished them? Ali being here in this prison, who was punishing him? He didn't know what to answer. To whom was he attributing the responsibility for all these things that had happened to him?

"You have not answered me. Who is it that is punishing you?" Ali's questioner asked again.

"I don't know."

"You must know. You seem very certain you do not deserve to be punished. Who is punishing you?"

"You're trying to confuse me. I don't know what you want me to say," Ali answered agonizingly.

"I want you to tell me who is punishing you."

He struggled to maintain his composure. He didn't want to break down in front of his questioner and reveal anything more than he needed to, yet he felt compelled to tell his innermost feelings. Not being able to hold back any longer, Ali finally blurted out, "God! He's the one punishing me!" He broke out in uncontrollable sobbing. He didn't know how long he lay on his cell floor, languishing in turmoil, but at some point, he realized he was no longer being held down. He lifted his head and looked around his cell for his questioner, but he was alone. How had he not heard him leave? He hadn't even heard the cell door open or close.

Ali stood up and walked over to the door. He grabbed the handle and attempted to open the door but it was locked. He walked back over to his cot and sat down. What had just happened? Had he hallucinated everything? It didn't feel like a hallucination. He had never hallucinated before, that he knew of. But, then again, how would one know? It felt as real as when Hamed had questioned him just the day before. It was the strangest thing he had ever experienced, considering he had almost been killed by assassins in a foreign country, then kidnapped by the IRGC and taken back to Iran to be imprisoned. Perhaps he had just snapped. He would find out soon enough, he thought. He wasn't naïve enough to believe his captors would let him off without pursuing more severe measures to get him to say what they wanted to hear. That, he would not confuse with a hallucination.

***

Canton was awakened by the sound of his cell phone vibrating on his nightstand next to his bed. He was disoriented at first, but then he looked at the familiar blue numbers on his alarm clock telling him it was 1:12 a.m. and realized he was in his condo in Crystal City. He answered in a hoarse voice, "Canton."

"Sir, this is the operations center."

"What is it?"

"Sir, your phone is unsecure. Can you please go secure?"

"What? Oh yeah, wait. Hold on a minute." He pressed the secure button and entered his personal identification number, then waited for the sequence of tones that indicated his connection was now secure. "What is it?"

"Our last pass through the CRS picked up a Michael Blackstone having booked a ticket on Turkish Airlines flight eight from Dulles to Istanbul. You had submitted yesterday for any hits on airline travel."

"Yeah, I did. So when does the flight leave?"

"Unless it was delayed, it departed about an hour and ten minutes ago. It was scheduled for eleven fifty-five p.m."

"It already departed! Why am I just now being told?" he screamed.

"Sir, he purchased the ticket at eleven fifteen. Our last sweep through CRS was at one a.m., before that at eleven p.m. It's every two hours," the operations officer informed him.

"I don't need you to tell me how often the sweep is done. It doesn't do me any good, now does it? When is it scheduled to arrive in Istanbul?"

"At five oh five p.m. today."

"Connect me through to the chief of station in Istanbul. What time is it there?"

"Eight fifteen a.m. Hold on, I'll connect you."

Payton waited while the desk officer tracked down the Istanbul COS. He was going to teach Blackstone a lesson once and for all. Even if he needed to use every single resource the station in Turkey had available, he was going to track Blackstone's movements and let him lead them to Shiravi. Obviously, Blackstone had obtained some important information from Shiravi's daughter. Once Blackstone led him to Shiravi, he could take care of both of them at once and eliminate any chance that their plot would be compromised. He knew this was a presidential priority and he could pull upon as many resources of the CIA as he needed. Blackstone was his.

"Sir, COS Istanbul is on the line. I'm dropping out."

"Hello, Jonathan. Isn't it pretty late, or early back there in D.C., depending on how you look at it?"

"I don't know what's late or early anymore. Listen, we got a lead on someone who may know something about Shiravi's whereabouts. His name is Michael Blackstone, and he's in the air right now heading to Istanbul. I'm going to need a surveillance team at the airport ready to pick him up. Blackstone is a high-value target and pretty slippery, so don't scrimp on the surveillance team. We can't afford to lose this guy." He recited Blackstone's flight information. "I'll have Langley forward you a photo as soon as we hang up."

"Michael Blackstone? Didn't we have a Michael Blackstone who worked for us a few years back?" the COS asked.

"Yeah, we did, and it's the same guy. He got terminated for killing a couple of innocent victims in one of his operations that went bad. He's a loose cannon, so tell your people to use extreme caution when dealing with him. We'll eventually have to snatch him. He hasn't hesitated to kill before, so it may come down to getting this guy dead or alive. He doesn't get away. Do you understand how important this guy is?"

"I got it, Jonathan. I'll have the airport flooded. We have a few assets that work there, so we'll have the whole place covered. He won't get away."

"Good. I'll be out heading back out there sometime tomorrow—I mean later today. There're a few things I need to take care of on this end first. Let me know as soon as you guys pick up Blackstone. I'm going to try and get a few hours of sleep while I can."

"Got it. Talk to you in a few hours."

He looked at the clock. It was 1:34 a.m. He could squeeze in another three and a half hours of sleep before he headed back to Langley to figure out a way of snatching Shiravi's daughter, just in case he needed any leverage later. It was always good to have an insurance policy, he thought as he closed his eyes, hoping he could fall back asleep quickly. He was starting to feel a little run-down from the pace of everything since last Friday. He would get as much sleep as he could. He lay in bed with his eyes closed, but he couldn't get the vision of Blackstone humiliating him in front of his men earlier that day out of his head. One way or another, Blackstone would be a dead man.

***

Michael woke up to the aroma of fresh-baked croissants and coffee. His business-class seat was fully reclined and a blanket covered him. The cabin was brightly lit in addition to the sunlight coming in through several open window shades. That was strange, he thought. The last thing he remembered was waiting for his dinner to be served. He must have fallen asleep. He looked around and saw his fellow passengers eating their meals. The flight attendant with the pretty smile that had welcomed him on board saw that he was up and came to his seat.

"Well, good morning. I hope you had a restful sleep. Would you like anything from our brunch menu?"

Still a bit disoriented from waking up, Michael finally found the button to raise his seat.

"I put that down for you after we took off. You looked so exhausted and your head was hanging forward. I didn't want you to wake up with a stiff neck," she told him with a kind smile.

"Oh, thanks, that was really nice of you. I actually feel pretty good," he told her, stretching his arms above him. "How much longer until we land?"

"Two and a half hours."

"Oh wow, I got a good amount of sleep."

"You did. Eight hours. So, would you like something to eat?"

"Actually, that sounds good," Michael told her, noticing the dull ache in his stomach. He pulled the menu card out and flipped through it to the brunch section. "Um, how's the poached salmon with the white wine sauce?"

"It's very good. I've had it before. The asparagus that comes with it is also yummy. Just makes your pee smell," she giggled.

"Okay, I'll take that, with some orange juice and coffee."

"Great, I'll have that out to you in just a minute," she told him and headed back to the galley.

Michael looked at his watch and saw it was 8:12 a.m., still on Eastern Standard Time. He took off his Omega Seamaster Professional and moved it forward seven hours to Istanbul time. He studied his watch. He remembered when he had received it as a gift from Karen on his thirtieth birthday in 1995, when they had been living in Germany. Sam had been a year old. His SF buddies had given him a hard time because it wasn't a Rolex, the traditional watch of the Green Berets. Michael didn't know how the tradition with Rolex watches and Special Forces had started, but he didn't care. He loved his Omega. Karen had always had class and a knack for spotting quality. He wished he hadn't taken her for granted all those years and had shown her more affection, wished he had let her know she and Sam were the most important things in his life, instead of blindly pursuing his ambitions. He wished he had done a lot of things differently.

The flight attendant returned with his meal. "Here you go, enjoy."

"Thank you."

Michael took a bite of the poached salmon. *She was right, it is good*, he thought. As he worked on his brunch, he told himself to stop thinking about Karen, Asya and all the other things from his past, and focus on Ali. It troubled him that Canton was so deeply involved in the situation. He didn't know exactly what it was, but it was obvious from all the attention and threats he had gotten that Canton was worried about what he might find out. Michael knew he had to be careful when dealing with him. Canton was a manipulative individual without any principles and completely lacking any scruples. He was the type who wouldn't hesitate to stab someone in the back to get what he was after. He wasn't the most skillful operator, but he was ruthless, which made him dangerous. Michael remembered the last time he had experienced Canton's treachery.

After they'd finally tracked down where Karbashi lived in Athens, the real work had begun. Michael convinced Harry to authorize the rental of another apartment across the street from Karbashi's building. Harry also assigned two more young case officers to assist Michael with the surveillance operations.

Karbashi's routines, habits, places he frequented and people he associated with had to be established before Michael could determine the right approach to target him. It was manpower-intensive and involved many hours. Canton made it readily apparent he felt being assigned to support Michael's operation was beneath him, especially with junior case officers. He had gone to Harry in protest, but Harry would hear none of it. He had told Canton to get some of his own operations going, and then he would consider reassigning someone else in his place. There was a never-ending abundance of negative comments from Canton to the others on the surveillance about how it was a waste of time and would never lead to anything. It was all Michael could do not to ask Harry to remove him from the operation. He would rather be a man short than have to deal with Canton's discontent and resentment. He placed him on day shift, Monday through Friday, when Karbashi was mostly at the Iranian embassy. When it came to intelligence matters, a true professional operated outside the scope of regular business hours. Any real chance of uncovering Karbashi's vulnerabilities would be after hours. It also allowed Michael to avoid having to listen to Canton's grumblings. Michael spent most of his days at station in the embassy and worked with the other two young case officers starting at 4:00 p.m. until Karbashi would retire to his apartment for the evening. He didn't even bother with Canton on weekends, instead working both Saturdays and Sundays with one or the other of the young single officers, or Schmitty on occasion, giving him as much time as possible with his family.

Michael quickly discovered Karbashi was careful in how he conducted himself. He left his apartment at different times each day and never took the same routes to or from the Iranian embassy. He used a combination of taxis and the metro to get around Athens, always practicing good tradecraft and not taking shortcuts on his countersurveillance measures. It was what Michael expected from any professional intelligence officer. It took them several weeks to learn some of Karbashi's habits in moving around Athens. Even skilled intelligence officers fell into routines that would mostly go unnoticed to the average individual. With enough time, however, Michael and his team started picking up some of the subtle patterns Karbashi used in his surveillance detection routes. After about a month, they had been able to determine that Karbashi frequented various Persian restaurants throughout Athens and the neighboring port city of Piraeus for late dinners. There was a sizeable Iranian ex-pat community in the Athens area, perfect cover for Karbashi to meet whatever contacts and sources he was developing in Greece. One of the primary concerns of the Iranian regime was external efforts to subvert the Islamic Republic. Many of them came from the extensive community of some five million Iranians living outside Iran. It was one of MOIS's main intelligence requirements to collect as much information as possible about threats to the regime within that ex-pat community. Persian restaurants were an ideal place to gather with ex-pats, under whatever cover Karbashi was using, to infiltrate that community. If he was good, he might also be attempting to recruit some mid- or high-level Greek government officials in an attempt to obtain confidential information on some of the EU's positions on trade, defense and foreign policy towards Iran. Because it was easy to notice when unfamiliar faces started frequenting the restaurants, they were safe locations for Karbashi to avoid any possible surveillance by EYP, the Greek Intelligence Service.

After eight weeks, Michael's team had identified the six different restaurants Karbashi was using as his meet sites. Several times, Michael had been tempted to send in a team for dinner while he was in one of the restaurants, but he didn't want to risk blowing the surveillance in the off chance they would arouse suspicion. It would have been nice to see who Karbashi was meeting with, but that wasn't their objective. Their objective was to discover any potential vulnerabilities Karbashi might have, and after two months of following him, their efforts seemed to have paid off. Despite Karbashi's caution, one predictable aspect of his life was when he attended the unofficial mosque located near Omonia Square every Friday for the sunset prayer service. The Omonia neighborhood of Athens, once a vibrant area with many nice shops and places to eat up until the late 1990s, was now characterized by the number of vagrants, illegal immigrants, prostitutes and pickpockets who inhabited its streets, especially at night. Greece, being ninety-eight percent Greek Orthodox, hadn't permitted the existence of an official mosque since Greece had gained its independence from the Ottoman Empire in 1832. There was a network of unofficial mosques, however, ranging from people's homes to empty warehouses, which served as places of worship for Greece's one hundred thousand Muslims.

Michael determined that the mosque served the Shia Muslim population in Athens, which was made up mostly of Iranians, some Lebanese and a few Syrians. Its entrance was located down a narrow street next to a Persian rug store that occupied a section of the ground floor of a small warehouse, squeezed in between a run-down apartment building and a motorcycle and scooter repair shop. Michael quickly realized this would be his only opportunity to target Karbashi. The question was, how would he gain access to the mosque? He would need to recruit someone who was a Shia Muslim that would have a reason to attend the mosque—an asset that could make contact with Karbashi in a way that didn't arouse suspicion. It was a concern Michael had thought about from the very beginning. It made him question whether it had been wise to move forward with the operation without first having developed an asset to run up against Karbashi. Then again, why go through all that trouble, when it wasn't even certain if Karbashi was a realistic possibility? And besides, Farsi-speaking Shia Muslims weren't something Michael had a big supply of in Athens. It was a classic case of which came first, the chicken or the egg? Something that was all too common with intelligence operations. He struggled with his predicament. After all the time and manpower they had expended, how would he explain to his boss that he was dead in the water?

Michael remembered the Monday a little over a week after they had established that Karbashi attended the mosque every week. He had been in his office in the station. It was around lunchtime. He had been sitting at his desk in his small but private office, bouncing a red rubber ball onto the floor, then off the wall while racking his brain, trying to come up with a solution to his dilemma. He had thought of various possibilities. He would go to all the Persian rug shops in Athens and start eating in all the Persian restaurants to see if he could develop an asset from someone there. In the end, he'd shot that one down as a bad idea. The Iranian ex-pat community in Athens was tightly knit and not that large. His repeated presence at many of those places could arouse suspicion and even trickle down to Karbashi somehow. It wasn't worth the risk. He had thought of recruiting a Greek national and sending him into the mosque under the cover that he wanted to convert to Islam. That was an even worse idea than his first. Assuming he could have recruited a young Greek that fit the profile, the training it would take to prepare him for the off chance that he would eventually be accepted into the mosque made it a long shot at best. Even if he was able to attend the Friday evening worship service there on a regular basis, there would be no reason for him to approach Karbashi, or the other way around. Trying to force an introduction would have aroused too much suspicion. He was stuck.

He looked at his watch. It was 1:45 p.m. He hadn't eaten lunch yet, and the embassy cafeteria closed in fifteen minutes. He thought he'd run down and grab a bite to eat before leaving in an hour and a half to relieve Canton and Schmitty. He walked down to the end of the hallway, through the security door into the stairwell and down to the basement level. The cafeteria was in the center of the building, ringed on four sides by the administrative offices that kept the embassy running. He ran in and purchased a club sandwich to go. It was a pleasant early spring day in Athens, so he would sit outside in the center courtyard and enjoy his lunch. Michael sat down on one of the marble benches looking out over the green space in the center of the open-air square that characterized the distinctive architecture of the American embassy in Athens. It was unusually warm even for Greece that early in March, seventy-six degrees and a clear blue sky. That's one thing Michael loved about this country. The abundant sunshine, moderate winters and hot summers, along with the deep clear blue waters of the Aegean Sea, made it a country hard not to love, despite its chaotic politics and dysfunctional governments. Having just hosted the summer Olympics, Greece was riding high on a wave of enthusiasm, especially with the massive infusion of funding they had recently obtained from European Union loans. Some of it went for major infrastructure improvements, such as the newly constructed metro, which had opened just in time for the Olympics. Much of it, however, went to hiring additional government employees and extending salaries and the traditional thirteenth-month pay bonus to its bulging civil servant sector, politicians trying to curry favor with their constituents when it came time for elections again. Yeah, life was good in Greece in 2005.

As Michael sat in the warm sunshine taking bites of his sandwich, he overheard the conversation someone sitting on the next bench was having over his mobile phone. It was a little beyond Michael's range of hearing to pick up what was being said, but the conversation was not in English and certainly not Greek. He felt guilty attempting to listen in on somebody else's conversation when it wasn't work-related, but there was something about the language that drew his attention. Occasionally, a few words sounded familiar. He listened intently, taking a bite of his sandwich and trying not to be obvious. There it was again! Michael caught the word *man* being spoken by the fellow next to him. Michael nonchalantly moved his head from left to right, taking in the view, until his eyes fell on the man in the khaki trousers and light blue oxford shirt sitting next to him. He was of slender build and medium height, balding with black hair, and he had a darker complexion than your average Greek. He looked like he was in his mid- to late forties. Michael noticed the embassy security badge hanging around his neck, which showed he was cleared to enter the classified areas inside the embassy. He did not look familiar, but then again, Michael didn't spend much time congregating with many of the other embassy employees who didn't work in his little world inside Athens Station. *He's gotta be speaking Farsi*, Michael thought. Although he hardly had even rudimentary fluency, he knew enough to realize the man was saying the word *man* repeatedly, which was the Persian word for *I*. He caught other words that also sounded familiar. To make the time pass by quicker when they had first started surveillance on the Iranian embassy, Michael had purchased the Rosetta Stone language course for Farsi. He had become familiar with enough words that he was fairly certain the man next to him was speaking Farsi.

Michael sat there and slowly ate his sandwich, waiting for the man to finish his conversation. After another five minutes of talking, the conversation ended and he stuck his phone back in his pocket. As he sat there looking out over the bright sunshine shining down over the center courtyard, Michael turned toward him until he caught his eye, giving him a nod and greeting him with a "How ya doing?"

"Hello," the man answered with an ever-so-slight accent.

"Man, it's nice to have some warm sun again after that cold winter we had."

"Yes, it feels good. You had a cold winter here?"

"I wouldn't call it cold by D.C. standards, but it got down into the low forties for a pretty long stretch, which is unusual for here. You just visiting?"

"No, I recently PCS'd here," he told Michael, using the term for Permanent Change of Station, when active-duty military are transferred to a new duty station.

"Oh, military. I'm former Army myself."

"Air Force, here with the DAO," he said, referring to the Defense Attaché's Office.

"Oh, no kidding? I know Colonel Richards. He seems like a pretty nice guy," Michael said of the Air Force attaché.

"Yeah, he seems like he's going to be a good boss to work for."

"Well, welcome to Athens. My name's Michael," he said as he got up and moved towards him, offering his hand.

"Thank you, I'm Ali."

"Strange time to be PCS'ing."

"Yeah, the master sergeant I replaced had an emergency transfer back to CONUS. Found out his child had leukemia." Ali was referring to the continental United States.

"Oh, poor kid. At least they'll be able to get some better treatment back home. I wouldn't take the gamble trying to fight that here. You got family that came with you?"

"My wife and daughter will come out this summer, as soon as school is out. You?"

"I'm unaccompanied. My wife wanted to stay stateside. Didn't want to uproot our daughter again. Don't blame her. I've put them through a lot," Michael said solemnly. He hadn't spoken to Karen in over a month. He knew things weren't good. She had recently packed and moved with Sam from D.C. back to Seattle. They were slowly becoming strangers to him. He should have taken leave and flown out to see them during Christmas, but he couldn't afford to be away from the operation just when they'd determined Karbashi was still in Athens.

"Sorry to hear you guys are separated. It's tough being away from your family. It's only been two weeks for me, and I already miss them."

"Yeah, it's become an occupational hazard for me."

"Who do you work for?" Ali asked.

"RSS," Michael told him, using the cryptonym for referring to the CIA within the embassy staff.

"Oh, so you're a spook?"

"Well, my official cover is political attaché, but I tell my Greek friends I work in the consular section, reissuing lost or damaged passports. It's a boring enough job that I don't get many follow-on questions."

"Yeah, I'm sure you need to keep a low profile."

"That's right. I only wear my navy-blue T-shirt with big yellow CIA letters across the front when I want to pick up Greek girls out on the town," Michael laughed.

"I heard Athens has a pretty wild nightlife."

"I don't know what you call wild, but there are plenty of clubs with live entertainment and all-night partying, especially once the warm weather comes around, which is pretty soon."

"I'm not one for big crowds and loud music," Ali commented.

"Yeah, I prefer a smaller taverna with some good food and local wine. There's hidden treasures all around, some not too far from the embassy."

"I haven't ventured out much yet. They've got me at the Hilton down the street until they come up with permanent housing for me, so I hit the breakfast buffet in the morning before coming here, and a few times a week I walk down to Syntagma and grab some fast food."

"Ah, you're missing so much. Tell you what, why don't you come out with me one night this week after work? I'll show you a really good place not too far from where you're staying. It serves some great Greek food and has some of the best red wine I've ever tasted. You like red wine?"

"I like to have some every once in a while."

"Great! Once you get a taste of some real Greek food, you'll be hooked. Just let me know whatever day works out for you."

"Okay. Maybe tomorrow or Wednesday night?"

"Sure, how about tomorrow night around eight?"

"Eight? Isn't that kind of late for dinner?" Ali asked.

"Are you kidding? Not around here. That's early. Most places don't even open up before then. Greeks, they eat dinner pretty late. What's your ancestry?

Lebanese? Syrian? They eat pretty late, don't they?" Michael asked, trying to draw him into revealing his ethnicity.

"I'm actually Iranian. I was born there but immigrated to the US in 1979, right after the Iranian Revolution. I can't remember how late we ate. It's been so long, almost forty years."

"Wow, that must have been pretty wild witnessing all that happen. How old were you?"

"I was nineteen. I had just finished my first year at Tehran University."

"No kidding? I take it your parents didn't care for the changes that were happening in your country?"

"They were very concerned about the direction things were heading. They sent me to my uncle in the US and were planning on following, but they never made it."

"Never made it? Why? What happened?"

"I don't know. We never heard from them again."

"Ah man, I'm sorry. That must have been really rough on you, especially coming to a strange new country."

"Yes, it was challenging the first few years, but I made it through. You adapt to things eventually. Fortunately, I had my uncle, who took very good care of me. I was just talking to him. He's in a nursing home back in Virginia. I just wish my parents would've had the same chance I did to make a new life for themselves. I think they would have really prospered in the US."

"What did they do?"

"They were both university professors."

"Yeah, they would have had a lot of opportunities to teach in the US. I'm glad we bumped into each other. It was good meeting you, Ali. I'm looking forward to talking to you some more over some killer Greek food and good wine tomorrow night. I'll swing by the Hilton around eight. I gotta get back to work. You know, always some terrorist or spy to nab," he told Ali.

"Yes, I am also. Let me give you my number just in case something comes up."

"Good idea. Let me enter it into my phone." Michael repeated back Ali's number.

"That's it."

"I'll call it so you got up my number also. See ya tomorrow, Ali."

"See you tomorrow, Michael."

Michael headed back to his office. He felt giddy with excitement over his good fortune. Of all the places he could have imagined to find an asset to run against Karbashi, having one drop in his lap like this inside the embassy, defied all belief. *Okay, let's not get too excited about this yet,* he reminded himself. He still needed to determine if Ali had what it took to be a double agent, let alone if he would even be interested in doing what would be asked of him. But on the face of it, Michael couldn't have asked for a better candidate. He walked into his office and plopped down in his chair, swinging it around in a celebration spin.

Michael thought about his conversation with Ali. He had managed to obtain a good amount of information about Ali's background and his current situation; he hadn't wanted to press Ali further and seem too forceful. He would have plenty of opportunity to learn more about him tomorrow evening over some good food and wine. Michael had a natural ability to put people at ease with his easygoing style. It had served him well in developing friendships and intelligence sources. Alcohol was just another tool he used to lower his subject's inhibitions and get them to open up more than they would normally do. He didn't consider it unethical; after all, he had never attempted to manipulate anyone into something they didn't feel comfortable with. He had always felt a certain bond with his assets and a responsibility to look after their welfare. It was a unique type of relationship that was established. It was one in which a level of trust steadily developed over time, until there was no doubt that Michael was always straightforward and genuine in his dealings with them. His strategy was pretty simple: respect them, never lie to them, earn their trust, and they will want to be your friend. The fact that Ali was alone in Athens until gave Michael a great opportunity to establish a friendship with him and hopefully develop him as his asset to target Karbashi.

He was already considering all the different options Ali's situation offered. If he played things right, he could dangle him in a natural and unsuspecting way by having him attend the Omonia mosque for prayers. That would hopefully draw Karbashi's attention to him. If they could establish a relationship, and Karbashi learned he was working for a defense attaché in the American embassy, that would hopefully set the hook. It would be too tempting a prize for an intelligence officer to pass up. Of course, he would have to be careful in how he went about things with Ali. If Karbashi was a competent intelligence officer, he would be cautious to ensure Ali was not in fact a dangle of US intelligence. It was always a concern for intelligence organizations when an individual with access to foreign intelligence suddenly materialized out of nowhere, offering to spy for them. The ploy was as old as intelligence operations themselves. The

Soviets had used it against the West during the Cold War, and vice versa. In this case, however, Ali wouldn't be approaching Karbashi to offer him anything. If everything went according to plan, Karbashi would be the one making the first move.

The flight attendant came by holding a pot of fresh coffee. "Care for some more coffee?"

"Sure." Michael extended his cup.

"Are you going to Istanbul for business or pleasure?"

"Pleasure. Visiting an old friend that I haven't seen in a long time."

"You must be excited to see them again."

"Yeah, I am."

"Well, I hope it will be a nice reunion," she told him as she refilled his cup.

"Thanks, I hope so too," he said with anticipation at the thought of seeing Asya in just a few hours.

Michael sipped his coffee as his thoughts went back to that first dinner with Ali. He had left the other two case officers to handle the surveillance of Karbashi for the remainder of the evening and headed down to the Hilton to pick up Ali. He had taken him to the Skalakia Taverna, a small restaurant close to the Hilton that was known for its good cuisine and reasonable prices. He learned more about Ali's background, what his life was like when he'd first immigrated to the United States, how he had met his wife, had made a go at running his own computer business, and had eventually enlisted in the Air Force. Michael told Ali a little bit about himself, how he had worked on Wall Street and decided he wanted something different in life and joined the Army; the parachuting injury that brought another major change in his life, along with his daughter, Sam, who was close to the same age as Ali's daughter, Roxanne. Michael believed disclosing some personal information about himself laid the foundation for a relationship of trust to develop with whomever he was trying to pitch as a source—in this case, a fellow American and member of the military that he would be asking to do something potentially dangerous. After having spent a couple of hours conversing while enjoying the delicious assortment of lamb chops, grilled sausage and other Greek dishes, along with an abundance of red wine, Michael had a good feeling about Ali. On the walk back to the Hilton, Michael decided he would ask Ali if he would be interested in working for the CIA. It was noisy enough with all the traffic that he didn't worry about being overheard. The odds that EYP was monitoring his clean mobile phone were almost nonexistent. You could still purchase a mobile phone in Greece without having to provide any identification. It was a great convenience in conducting intelligence operations. Michael made his pitch.

"Ali, in addition to serving your country in the Air Force, how would you feel about being involved in helping the CIA? You have a unique background that has the potential to be very useful in operations we're running against our country's adversaries."

Ali looked at Michael as they walked up the busy street, trying to figure out exactly what he was being asked. "What do you mean about my background? And useful in what way?"

"I mean that you are of Iranian descent and you speak Farsi. I can't disclose any details about how you would be able to help until I get a commitment from you that you're interested. What I can tell you is that it would be challenging and exciting and may even involve a certain amount of risk, but most of all, you would be helping your country in a way not many others could."

Ali walked silently, contemplating what he had just been asked. Michael could tell he was uncertain. Finally, he turned to Michael and said, "I'm guessing by adversaries, you mean Iran. Why else would you be asking me?"

"That's right."

"What about my duties with the DAO?"

"It won't interfere. You'll still be doing your nine-to-five job here in the embassy. As a matter of fact, it will be important that you maintain your regular routine. We'll do your initial training on weekends. By the time your family gets here in a few months, you'll be done with that, and then it will just be a couple of hours once a week at first. A little bit more down the road if things hopefully go well. It shouldn't interfere with your family life that much."

"Will Colonel Richards know what I'm doing?"

"I'll have to ask my boss about that. That'll be his call. He may just tell him that you're assisting us with something because of your language abilities."

"I see," Ali said with a bit of hesitation.

"You seem unsure."

"No, it's not that. It's just it has stirred up a lot of emotions that I've kept buried for a long time."

"I know it's a lot to drop on you all at once."

They continued walking in silence until they reached the Hilton. Michael was just about to tell him to think about it for a few days before giving him an answer when Ali said, "Yes, I'll help you."

"That was a quick decision. Are you sure? Do you need some time to think about it?"

"No, I'm sure. I've had twenty-five years to think about it."

"Okay, great. I'll talk to my boss tomorrow about it and then get back in touch with you. We'll start training this weekend if that works for you."

"That's fine. I didn't have any plans."

"I'll see you tomorrow, then. Have a good night," Michael said.

"Goodnight, and thank you for the dinner. I had an enjoyable time. See you tomorrow."

Michael walked back to his apartment, which was a few blocks away on one of the streets behind the embassy. He had been fortunate enough to have had one of the apartments the embassy housing office had under contract come open. It was within close walking distance to work, convenient since he didn't have to drive in the chaotic Athens traffic every morning and evening. It was a good location, close to Kolonaki, which was one of Athens's oldest affluent neighborhoods, with upscale shops and cafes, and a short walk to the metro station by the Megaron concert hall.

He conducted his routine surveillance detection route, a circuitous course down side streets to ensure he wasn't being followed. He arrived back at his apartment at 11:50 p.m., which was a relatively early night for him, but he was tired. The weeks of ceaseless surveillance on Karbashi were starting to take a toll on him. He hoped to get a good night's sleep, but he knew it would take a while for him to unwind. He was ecstatic. He had finally found his asset.

He went to his refrigerator—small by American standards—and took an ice tray and bottle of Finlandia vodka out of the freezer. He twisted some ice cubes into a tumbler and filled it with vodka. He sat down on his couch, sipping his vodka while his mind raced, thinking about the operation. Things were looking very good.

The captain's voice came over the intercom, announcing that they would begin their descent into Istanbul in another ten minutes and be landing in forty, thanking them for choosing to fly with Turkish Airlines. The pretty flight attendant came to his seat and asked, "Is there anything you would like before landing, sir?"

"No, I'm good, thanks."

"Well, enjoy your stay in Istanbul. I hope you have a wonderful time with your friend," she told him, then moved on to the next passenger.

An overwhelming feeling of anticipation came over him as it finally kicked in that within the hour, he would be facing Asya. He had experienced a variety of intense situations and encountered many unique individuals in his past life but had never really been fazed by any of it. There were situations in which he had been at risk of getting injured or even killed, when the fear mechanism inside him had kicked in loud and clear. Though most people didn't want to admit it, fear was a primal and very useful emotion that had helped human beings survive for millennia. Fear was good, as long as you didn't let it overwhelm you and prevent you from thinking rationally. What he was feeling now was something he hadn't experienced before—it wasn't anxiety or nervousness. On the contrary, he was especially looking forward to seeing Asya again. He wondered why, after all these years, she was suddenly causing such havoc with his emotions. He would find out shortly, he told himself as he got up to use the restroom one last time before landing, realizing he probably wouldn't have the opportunity to do it at the airport.

***

Harry sat at the small kitchen table, drinking his coffee and eating his buttered toast while watching CNN International on the small television mounted on the wall. He was listening to the morning anchor interview some intelligence expert about the various possibilities of who was really behind the assassination of the Iranian foreign minister. He listened to the expert drone on about the possibility that the PKK or other terrorist organizations were trying to bring instability to Turkey. *Where do they get these so-called experts from?* Harry thought. *He probably also thinks 9-11 was staged by the CIA.* He flipped his remote through various news channels, pausing to hear what they were reporting before moving to the next. He stopped at BBC World and turned up the volume. File video footage of the Russian S-400 anti-aircraft missile system, with its four-missile mobile launcher and separate large rectangular mobile radar array, aired before the coverage turned to the Russian foreign minister, who was announcing the sale of the S-400 missile system to Iran, stating that it had nothing to do with recent events surrounding the foreign minister's assassination, but had been in the works for quite some time. He went on about Russia standing behind Iran in its right to defend itself against the hostile and aggressive threats of some nations, obviously referring to the United States and Israel.

"Those bastards," Harry said to himself. He was familiar with the S-400. After all, he worked for Lockheed Martin, the world's largest defense contractor and manufacturer of the F-22 Raptor and F-35 Lightning II stealth fighter aircraft. *That's like throwing gasoline on the fire*, he thought, concerning the reaction it would cause in the already highly volatile state of escalating rhetoric between Israel and Iran. He worried about what Michael was walking into over there. He was only going to Istanbul to try and find out what had happened to Ali, but Harry was uneasy about where Michael's journey would lead him. Harry was confident Michael knew how to take care of himself, even if it had been ten years, but the forces at play here could swallow up even the most skilled operator. Hopefully Michael would be able to connect with his former contact in Istanbul and get his—or was it her?—assistance. He would, of course, do whatever he could to support Michael from back here in D.C. He never would have imagined that, at age sixty-five, he would be involved in what might turn out to be the most complex and far-reaching intelligence operation of his life. He thought he had left all that when he'd retired from the Agency. *Funny the curveballs life throws you*, he thought.

The breaking news scrolling along the bottom of the screen caught Harry's eye. *Hezbollah launches massive missile strike into northern Israel. Massive casualties reported in Haifa. Stay tuned for further news.*

"Oh, crap. I hope you still can bring your A-game, Mikey. You're going to need it," he said aloud.

Chapter 12

Breakfast, consisting of two pitas and a few slices of white cheese, was placed through the slide at the bottom of Ali's cell door. It lay there untouched for the rest of the morning. Ali lay on his cot, trying to understand what had happened to him. He didn't think he had gone crazy. He was aware of his surroundings. He knew where he was and how he'd gotten there. He could recall everything that had happened since last Friday night. But then, most crazy people didn't know they were crazy. Perhaps he was just mentally exhausted. He had been through a lot the past few days, and maybe it was just catching up with him; that was why he was confused about who had questioned him a few hours ago. At least he hadn't been physically harmed or threatened. To the contrary, his questioner had actually seemed to be trying to help him come to terms with his situation. Whatever was going to happen to him would happen, and there was really nothing he could do to change that. His destiny was no longer in his hands. If he was going to die, then it would all be over anyway, so there was nothing more they could do to him. He knew he would suffer physical pain, quite severe, he imagined, but all he could really do was continue to tell them the truth. He felt a sense of resignation to his circumstances. Strangely, it was a rather peaceful feeling.

He lay there thinking about his life. He missed Janet terribly since she had succumbed to the cancer two years ago. They had grown very close in the months prior to her death. The times he would sit with her, holding her hand while she was connected to the bottle dripping the highly specialized poison into her body that was supposed to kill the cancer cells and leave the healthy ones alone, had been precious. In the end, the cancer cells had won the battle, but the last six months they had spent together were a blessing to both of them. They had shared their deepest thoughts, fears, regrets and joys with each other, more so than during any of the past twenty-nine years of their marriage. The day she died, he was next to her, holding her hand, with Roxanne standing on the other side, doing the same. He remembered her looking at them, giving a slight smile and saying goodbye one last time before she left them. They had made their peace together and were ready for what was to come, but the pain of that final separation was crushing. As the months passed, he had slowly gotten on with his life. Roxanne had gone off to college and he had focused on his work at the State Department. Life was slowly getting back to a certain sense of normalcy, falling into a rhythm, and then this had happened. It was difficult to make sense of it all. He had trouble understanding why his whole life was filled with loss. From a young age, he had lost his parents, his country, his life. He had eventually made a new life, adopting a new country, marrying a loving wife and having a beautiful daughter whom he cherished, only to have it all taken away from him again. He felt heartache for Roxanne, knowing that she would never see him again and probably never find out what happened to him, much like what he had experienced with his parents. He didn't want her to have to carry that for the rest of her life, like he had.

If he had only taken his chances and turned himself in to the Turkish authorities, maybe he would have been able to convince them of his story. He should have, rather than thinking the Iranians would believe him. It was a foolish mistake on his part, a mistake that would end up costing him his life. He saw the irony in meeting the same fate as his parents, after they had made the ultimate sacrifice in sending him away so he could escape their fate. In a strange way, it gave him a sense of closeness to them. They might have even been in this prison, perhaps even in this very cell. He wondered if they had been tortured. It would have been better if they had just been killed in the streets, amidst the chaos of the revolution. That way, they would have been spared the horrors he knew many others had experienced in Evin Prison. He hated the Iranian regime for what it had done to his parents. It was the reason he had so willingly helped Michael Blackstone all those years ago in Athens. He had wanted to get back at the regime for everything they had taken from him. He had gladly done whatever Michael had asked of him. Unfortunately, things hadn't gone as expected. He had to stop thinking about his life. It was gone. It no longer belonged to him. The only life he had now was inside these prison walls, for however much longer that might be. Dwelling upon the past wouldn't change a thing. He was ready to accept whatever lay ahead for him.

Just as he had finished that thought, he heard a key being inserted into the lock. He sat up on his cot and saw a guard appear and motion him over. Ali stood up and walked towards him.

"*Salaam*," he greeted the guard as he walked over to him.

"*Salaam*," the guard answered back with a displeased look on his face.

"How are you, brother?" Ali asked with genuine concern.

The guard glowered at him, "I did not tell you to speak. Just shut your mouth and come with me."

"I will do whatever you ask. I know you have a difficult job and the pay is not sufficient for what you have to deal with each day. We all wish we could provide more for our families. I see you are married. Do you have children?" Ali asked him as he walked out of his cell and stood in the hallway, waiting for the guard to shut his cell door.

"Why are you asking me these things? You are a prisoner here, I am the guard." He turned and pointed down the hallway, motioning Ali to move.

"I know you are my guard and I am your prisoner. But I am asking you not as my guard, but as my brother. I do not know you and you do not know me, other than from the current roles we find ourselves in. I do not hold any animosity towards you because you are my guard. You are not responsible for bringing me here to this prison. You are just doing your job, trying to provide for your family. I do not know how much time I have left in this life, so I will not waste any of it with anger, resentment or fear towards others. I can only try to show some kindness. Otherwise I will not be able to face what awaits me without losing my sense of being. I will depart from this world intact spiritually, if not physically," Ali answered as he started walking in the direction he was instructed.

As the guard walked silently behind him, Ali wondered why he had said that. After a few steps, Ali heard from behind, "I have a five-year-old daughter and a three-year-old daughter. They are the jewels of my eye."

"May they live many years," Ali replied, a traditional Persian greeting.

"*Mamnoon*," the guard thanked him. "My wife and I had wanted to try and have a son, but it is already difficult enough to raise two children on my pay. I love my precious daughters, but I would have liked to have had a son, so I could pass on my family name. I am the only son of my father. I have three other sisters. My family's name will end with me."

"I am afraid it is the same with me, brother. I was an only child. I have only one daughter. She will marry someday, and my family name will be no more."

"I am sorry to hear that, brother," the guard said unexpectedly.

"It is all right. Those types of things are not as important in America. When I am gone, the only thing Persian left with my daughter will be her eyes," Ali replied with a slight hint of melancholy.

"You are from America?" the guard asked in surprise. "I have a cousin who lives in America. I have never seen him. He was born there shortly after my aunt and uncle fled during the revolution in 1979. My uncle was a senior officer in the Shah's military. They fled along with many of the others who were in the government. My cousin has a family also. His wife is Lebanese. They have two children, a boy and a girl. He is a software engineer in California. He works for Apple. They have never visited here, but I have spoken with him on Facebook. It is technically still illegal in Iran, but if you go through a VPN, you can access it. Everybody does it. He has invited me with my family to come visit him and has even offered to pay for the tickets. Unfortunately, because of my job, I would never be allowed to leave Iran and visit America. I hope someday, they can come visit us here in Iran."

"That would be nice if relations could be normalized someday between Iran and the United States, so families could travel back and forth freely."

"Yes, that would make me very happy. It would also bring great joy to my mother to be able to see her sister's son. My mother and her sister were very close. I remember when I was young, they would write letters back and forth very often. My aunt's letters would always arrive resealed from having gone through the censors, but that did not stop them. They continued writing until the very end, when my aunt died in a car accident. Someone who had been consumed with alcohol driving a big American truck drove through a red light and hit her at high speed. She survived a few days, but they were unable to save her. Now my uncle lives with my cousin and his family in Palo Alto. I know that is close to San Francisco, where the Golden Gate Bridge is. I have seen it on television. I would like to go see it someday."

"I hope that will happen for you," Ali told him as they reached the interrogation room from the previous day.

The guard opened the door for Ali and motioned him inside. "I hope you will be able to see your daughter again one day. Do not lose hope, brother. Not everyone is swallowed up by this prison."

"*Mamnoon*, brother. May you someday have a son," Ali said.

"*Enshallah, enshallah*," replied the guard, leaving Ali in the custody of the IRGC colonel who was waiting to interrogate him.

Ali turned and faced Hamed, who was standing next to a table, looking at him in bewilderment. "*Salaam*." Ali nodded his head respectfully.

Hamed stood in silence for several moments before finally saying, "*Salaam*. Now sit down."

Ali walked over to the table and sat down. He noticed a large metal case on the floor over by the wall, the kind used to store equipment or instruments. He turned and faced Hamed standing across from him, making eye contact with him deferentially and waiting for him to speak.

"You are making friends with the guards, I see," Hamed said mockingly.

"He is not my enemy, Colonel. I had just asked him about his family," Ali replied.

"And you are concerned about his family because he has been so kind to you?" Hamed asked with a hint of sarcasm.

"No. It was the first time I have seen him. He has not been kind or unkind to me. He is merely doing his job, what is expected of him. I cannot have ill feelings towards him for that. I was merely trying to show some kindness to the man. That is all I can do under my current circumstances."

"Will you show me the same kindness when I am merely doing my job?"

"Colonel, I know what is expected of you and the power you have over me. I have no control over what you will choose to do to me. I can only accept my fate and, with whatever time I have remaining, live in a way that will prepare me for what awaits me after I depart this life. I do not want it to be in anger, fear or despair. I have no animosity towards you. I do not even know you. I can only wish the same blessings to you and your family, if you have one. I know you have your responsibilities and duty to perform. You will do what is required of you," Ali told him.

"You can be certain I will perform my duty. My family is not your concern. Your concern at this moment should be to tell me the truth about why you came to the Iranian consulate with your preposterous story."

"I realize the story sounds preposterous. It is hard for me to believe at times. But it does not change what I heard and what happened to me afterwards. I can only tell you the truth. To tell you otherwise would be a lie."

"Why is it you did not go to the American authorities? If what you are saying is true, your FBI would have conducted an investigation."

"I did not think I would get a chance to tell anyone my story. That man Canton would never have permitted it. If I had turned myself in to the Turkish authorities, they would have contacted the US government and handed me over to them. Going to the Iranian consulate was the only chance I thought I had for someone to believe me and do something about it."

"Ah. So what is it you would like us to do about it?" Hamed asked, getting to the real reason Ali had approached them.

"I do not know, Colonel. I just had to tell somebody the truth. I realize what the possibilities are if individuals with power start making decisions and taking actions based upon misinformation and lies. Many people will get killed."

That was not what Hamed wanted to hear. There was a reason the Americans had sent Ali to them with such an outlandish story. They wanted Iran to react a certain way, take an action that would put them at risk, give the United States and its Zionist ally a justification for attacking them. That was what General Bardari had told him, assigning him personally to uncover the truth, by all means necessary. He had been adamant about that. He wanted a confession.

If he couldn't get Ali to tell him the truth, then he would force a confession from him, one way or another, that he had been sent by the CIA to mislead them. That would satisfy Bardari. But then, what would be accomplished if he was wrong about the prisoner? What if what Ali was telling him was the truth, by some unlikely chance? Would it make any difference in how his country reacted? More importantly, would it make a difference in how other countries acted against Iran? He had to be sure. The future of his country depended on it.

"I told you last time that I would not hesitate to use extreme measures if I did not believe you were telling me the truth. I do not believe you are. There is something you are hiding. Since you choose to continue with your deceit and withhold the truth, you leave me no choice but to extract it from you." Hamed walked over to the door, opening it and motioning to the guard standing out in the hallway. "Secure the prisoner to the wall."

The guard who had escorted Ali from his cell came into the room and walked over to Ali. He looked at Ali with a sorry face, as if saying he wished it were not him having to do this. Ali stood up, looking him in his eyes and letting him know he understood, then walked over to the shackles bolted to the wall.

The guard followed him, then turned to Hamed asking, "How do you want me to secure him, Colonel?"

"What do you mean, how do I want you to secure him? With the shackles, of course."

"I mean facing towards or away from the wall?"

"Towards the wall, and strip him completely."

The guard looked at Ali and murmured, "Sorry, brother, your clothes."

Ali nodded slightly, let out a sigh and began to unbutton his shirt. After taking off his shirt, he removed his shoes and unzipped his pants, taking them off also. He looked at Hamed, hoping that had satisfied him.

"Everything," Hamed instructed.

"Your socks and underwear, brother," the guard said softly.

Ali removed his socks and pulled off his boxers, then looked at Hamed, awaiting his fate.

"Turn around, brother," the guard told him.

Ali turned and faced the wall. The guard fastened the leg irons to each ankle, then secured each wrist, before pulling the slack out of the chains until Ali was spread eagle against the wall. Ali began to tremble. He knew he would soon be experiencing pain. He would scream, that was just an uncontrollable physical reaction, but he hoped he would be able to maintain some semblance of dignity and not break down into a sobbing heap. He had accepted that they would break him physically, but he wanted to endure psychologically, emotionally, spiritually.

Ali heard the sound of latches being undone and a lid being flung open. There was the clatter of metal, then the hissing of gas, followed by a few short scrapes of gritty metal, and finally the sound of a flaming torch. He heard footsteps approach him as the intensity of the torch grew louder. His forehead leaning against the wall, he whispered a prayer. "Allah, give me strength to endure what lies ahead. I am frightened. Forgive me for not turning to You before now. Please have mercy upon me." He heard the sound of the torch by his ear and could feel the heat from its flame against his face. From his other side, he heard Hamed whispering in his ear.

"Are you praying for Allah to spare your life?"

"I am praying, but I am not asking Him to spare my life. He will decide if that is what He wishes. I am just asking Him to forgive me for not living up to His expectations. Asking Him to have mercy on me."

"You believe you deserve mercy?" Hamed asked cynically.

"I do not know if I deserve it, but if I cannot get it from Allah, then who can I get it from?"

He stood silently next to Ali, staring at him, holding the propane torch next to his head. A feeling of irritation came over Hamed as he observed that Ali didn't appear to fear losing his life. From interrogating hundreds of prisoners, he had learned to detect fear pouring out of men just as clearly as he could see the sweat dripping from their faces and, in many cases, witness them losing control of their bodily functions. Ali was sweating, but there was something different about him. He had an air of fearlessness. It wasn't some valiant attempt to display bravery or show defiance, but from some deep sense of inner peace. He had not witnessed this before with other prisoners. Did Ali not realize how much pain he could inflict on him? Over the years, he had perfected his methods of breaking even the most defiant men.

"Do you know the temperature of this flame?" he whispered in Ali's ear while holding the torch in front of his face. "It is two thousand degrees centigrade. I could cut off each of your fingers in a matter of seconds and they would not even bleed, but the pain would be unimaginable."

"And yet there is nothing I can do about it," Ali told him matter-of-factly.

"You can tell me the truth," Hamed yelled at him, losing his composure.

Ali looked at him for a few seconds before saying, "I am telling you the truth. You are not my enemy, nor are the people of Iran. I was born here. I lived here. You are my people. I do not like many of the things the government is doing, because they do not allow Iran to flourish. I have lived in the United States for close to forty years now. I am grateful for all the opportunities it has given me to make a new life for myself after my parents sent me there during the revolution. It has been very good to me. But I have no misconceptions about all the ills that plague America. There are costs that come with having an open and free society. America is not perfect, but it allows its people to live free according to their conscience, good or bad. There are evil men everywhere, both here and in America. Each one of us can only decide for ourselves what type of man we will be."

Hamed lowered the torch from Ali's face and stepped back, his anger dissipating as Ali's words sank in. He shut off the torch, walking over to the table and setting it down. He looked at the guard standing by the door, their eyes catching, as he observed the look of relief on his face.

"Release him," he ordered the guard.

The guard walked over to Ali and began unlocking each of the shackles. As he freed Ali from the last, he whispered, "Allah has shown favor upon you, brother."

Ali turned and faced Hamed. He stood there waiting for him to speak.

"Get dressed and sit down," Hamed instructed Ali.

Ali quickly threw on his clothes, then walked over and took a seat at the table. He sat silently looking at Hamed, waiting for him to speak. Oddly, Hamed did not feel challenged by Ali's stare. It was a look as if from a friend or family member, waiting to hear what he had to say. He walked over to the table and sat down opposite Ali.

"Go bring some water and two glasses," he ordered the guard.

"Yes, sir," he replied and left the interrogation room.

Hamed studied Ali's face. He looked for some sign of deception, some indication that he was attempting to manipulate him. He couldn't find any. He hadn't experienced this kind of situation before. In all his years of interrogating prisoners, there had always been some fear, some vulnerability, some aspect of each subject that he could take advantage of to obtain the information he was after. It was the reason he had been promoted so rapidly, the reason General Bardari had assigned him to handle the interrogation personally. How would he tell Bardari that he had been unable to learn anything more than what the prisoner was claiming—that he was convinced Ali's implausible story was true? He would think him a fool. Yet something inside him told him Ali wasn't lying.

What was he to do? He thought about what Ali had said about the intended reason for the foreign minister's assassination—bring destruction and chaos to the Middle East. That would mean the death of thousands, perhaps millions. His family wasn't immune to that risk. If Israel was backed into a corner, it would be forced into using its nuclear arsenal against Iran. He knew that was a very real possibility if things escalated out of control. They were already moving in that direction with the missile attack on Israel, ordered by Bardari through the IRGC's Hezbollah surrogate in Lebanon. He hadn't been briefed on the attack, but he knew Hezbollah didn't act on that level without a directive from the IRGC—in other words, from Bardari himself. Even if he were able to somehow convince the general that Ali's story was the truth, would it make a difference in how Iran responded, or were things already set in motion that couldn't be turned around?

"Assuming you are telling the truth, what is it you expect?"

"I do not know. I did not go to the consulate knowing what to expect. It was the only option I had at the time. I had to tell somebody the truth."

"So you did, so you did," Hamed repeated as he pondered what to do now.

***

Michael felt the thud of the landing gear touch down at Istanbul Atatürk International Airport, then heard the Airbus A-340's reverse thrusters engage as the large aircraft began to slow down the runway. This was it, he was finally here. Michael looked out his window at the terminal. Somewhere in there, Asya was waiting for him. He wouldn't quite call it butterflies, but he certainly felt the anticipation he had managed to contain finally overwhelm him. He would be facing her shortly. He didn't know what to expect. Would she be excited to see him? They had been close, but many years had passed since then. He told himself not to have unrealistic expectations. She was just doing a favor for an old friend. She might even feel uncomfortable about what he had asked of her. He would find out soon.

The plane turned off the runway and taxied to its gate. When it came to a stop, the dual jet ways moved forward, positioning themselves onto the left side of the aircraft. The flight crew disarmed the doors, then pulled the lever, opening doors in both economy and business class. Michael stood up and grabbed his carry-on and backpack from the overhead. He moved forward and crossed through the galley towards the forward door, where his flight attendant addressed him one final time as he exited the aircraft. He had just stepped onto the jet way when he felt someone grab him and pull him off to the side. He turned and saw Asya staring directly at him. Michael's face lit up as they made eye contact, a feeling of elation sweeping over him.

"*Salaam*," he greeted her, keeping his voice muted.

"*Salaam*," she answered him, her smile bursting out through her eyes. "Here, put this on." She handed him a dark blue Turkish Airlines tarmac jacket, like the one she was wearing. He placed his backpack on the floor and threw on the jacket. "Follow me," she instructed him as she turned and opened the door that led to the stairs outside.

He followed her down the stairs, keeping pace with her as they walked under the jet way towards the terminal, where a midnight-blue Audi A7 with a blue police light on the roof was parked. She popped the trunk release for Michael to throw his backpack and carry-on inside, then got into the driver side. He sat in the passenger seat and closed his door, turning to face her. She looked at him with her radiant smile. She looked older, but in some respects was even more attractive than he remembered. Her natural beauty had been enriched with an air of sophistication. She still wore her jet-black hair the same way, the almost boyishly short style accenting her high cheekbones and almond-shaped green eyes, and two large diamond-studded earrings added a touch of elegance.

She reached across the center console, giving him a quick hug and the traditional Turkish kiss on each cheek. "It's so good to see you, Michael. You look the same. You haven't aged a bit."

"You look great. Better than great. I mean, you always looked great, it's just you look... vibrant," he finally let out, transfixed by her presence.

"Oh, stop it. The wrinkles under my eyes say otherwise. But thank you, you're sweet," she replied as she pushed the engine start button, bringing the supercharged V-6 to life. "You can take that jacket off now. I didn't want to attract any attention to you while you were walking on the tarmac," she told him, shifting into first gear and pulling into the painted lanes for the ground support vehicles.

She drove around the terminal to a service gate manned by Turkish military. She rolled to a stop and lowered her window, showing the sentry her ID. The young conscript came to attention and saluted, then lowered the vehicle barrier, letting them pass through the checkpoint and exit the airport.

"I'm impressed. Snap to attention and a salute," Michael commended her. "You must be someone important."

"Well, having the rank of colonel gets you some respect."

"You're in the military?" Michael asked.

"No, I'm still with MIT. I have the equivalent rank of colonel, so we are issued military IDs to access restricted areas without attracting attention."

"Colonel? What is it you do at MIT?"

"I'm chief of counterterrorism for Istanbul Province," she told him, pulling onto Rauf Orbay Drive and heading back towards downtown Istanbul.

"I'm really impressed now. You've come a long way. Chief of counterterrorism."

"It's been seventeen years, Michael. I hope you thought I had it in me to get somewhere in my career. Did you think I would settle down, stay at home and have babies?" she teased.

"No, I always thought you had what it takes to do whatever you chose. I'm just surprised, knowing the macho male mentality here, that your agency would let something like that happen. That means you'd be giving orders to a lot of men working under you." He grinned as he gazed at the side of her face.

She glanced back and forth at him several times, her smile growing on her face as she made her way through traffic. "Are you staring at me?" she laughed.

"I guess I am. It's just hard to believe I'm looking at you again so many years."

"I know, Michael. It feels like half a lifetime ago. It's all I have been thinking about today. Do you know what it was like trying to fall asleep last night after you called?"

There was a short period of silence as Michael reflected on her statement. Why wouldn't he expect her to have trouble falling asleep after he'd dropped in on her life unexpectedly after all these years? She was obviously happy to see him again. After all, they were old friends. Of course, she would share that with him. She was always straightforward when she spoke, never one to play games about what was on her mind. He always knew where she was coming from. He liked that about her.

"Nice car. This can't be standard MIT-issue, even for a colonel," Michael said, finally breaking the silence.

"No, it's mine. I have a Fiat for work."

"Well, I guess MIT colonels must get paid pretty good, then."

"It was the one thing I always wanted to do—how do you say, splurge on a nice auto. I have a good salary, but not enough to afford a car like this. My father died three years ago and left me some money. He never remarried and hardly spent anything on himself after my mother died. He was married to his career in the military."

"Sorry to hear that. He was a general in the Army, if I remember correctly?"

"Yes. He retired five years ago as the deputy chief of staff. He didn't know what to do with himself. He would just sit at home and smoke two packs of cigarettes a day without going anywhere. He had a heart attack. He died alone at home while drinking his coffee and reading his morning newspaper. I found him later that evening when I stopped by his home because he was not answering my calls. I would call him every evening to check on him," she said sadly. "So, tell me, Michael, how has your life been since your days here in Istanbul?"

"Where to start? Well, I don't work for the CIA anymore, as you've probably figured out from me asking for your help. Karen and I divorced in 2005. I was assigned to Athens, and she decided to stay in the US with our daughter, Samantha. Things had already deteriorated between us. Athens was just the last straw. I met someone while in Greece and married her in 2008. We divorced recently. Actually, just yesterday it was finalized. I left the CIA in 2008. That's a story unto itself. I've been working as a real estate agent since then. There's a lot more in between, but I won't bother you with the details. How about you? Are you married? Do you have a family?"

"I guess you can say I am married to my career. I was in a long-term relationship with someone. He was an army officer with career ambitions, just like myself. We both seemed to be focused on our careers more than on each other. We both recognized that and eventually parted as friends. He is a good man, just like you."

"I don't know if I'm a good man. I've managed to ruin two marriages, so I'm obviously not doing something right. A lot has changed with me, Asya. I'm not the same man you remember."

She looked at him, studying his expression. He knew she sensed something was different with him. One thing had been answered for him—Asya wasn't married. After all these years, she had chosen to remain single. It didn't surprise him that she had been in a relationship with a military officer. Asya was a self-assured person. She would naturally have been attracted to an equally strong and confident man. He wondered if she had any regrets about never marrying or having children.

"I would expect much has changed for you after all these years, just as much has changed with me. That is just life, is it not?"

"That it is. Anyway, I just want to thank you for helping me out at the airport. You're probably wondering what I'm involved in, asking for a favor like this. It's not the Turkish authorities I'm concerned about knowing about my presence in Turkey—in other words, you. It's my previous employer I'm trying to avoid. I don't want to inconvenience you any more than I already have. You've already done enough, but I'm sure you want to know what I'm involved in, especially considering your position with MIT. You're obviously in the thick of things with the Iranian foreign minister's assassination. The reason I'm here is related to that, possibly even more than you could imagine. I'd rather wait to fill you in when I have your full attention, because what I'm going to tell you is going to blow you away. Is there someplace we can go and sit down and talk in private?"

"I hope you're hungry for some dinner, because I'm taking you to a special place where we can talk and get a bite to eat," she told him as she merged onto Kennedy Boulevard, running along the waterfront of the old part of Istanbul. "Whatever it is you have to tell me, you have piqued my curiosity, but I'm also looking forward to catching up after so many years. You have always remained a very special person to me, Michael Blackstone."

"So have you, Asya," Michael answered, feeling the connection between them still there.

***

Canton was in his office with his door closed, tapping a pen on his desk in an irritated mood. He'd woken up that morning planning on heading back to Istanbul on the heels of Blackstone, but Payton had called him and told him to be at his office at 2:00 p.m., despite his objections that he had to leave immediately. He could have disregarded Payton's order and gone anyway, talking to him on a secure link from the plane. He didn't work for the Secretary of State, that he could give him an order like that. Canton knew, however, that when it came to the pecking order of their conspiracy, he was at the bottom, below Payton and the President. He wasn't foolish enough to openly defy Payton. He would have to head to the airport immediately following their meeting. Istanbul Station would keep tabs on Blackstone until he got there. He looked at his watch. It was 1:00 p.m., 8:00 p.m. in Istanbul. Why hadn't he gotten a call from the chief of station, telling him they'd picked up Blackstone? His flight had left on time from D.C. He would have landed over three hours ago. He should have cleared customs by now and been picked up by the surveillance team. Maybe there were just a lot of arrivals during that time of day and things were backed up. Something wasn't right. He sat for several more minutes, waiting impatiently.

He would have to leave for Payton's office soon. It would take him a good half hour to get to Foggy Bottom, where the State Department was located. He was about to pick up his phone and call Istanbul Station when it rang. He snatched up the receiver before a second ring.

"Canton."

"Hello, Jonathan. This is Bob in Istanbul. Thought you'd be on your way over here."

"I got held up. I should be in the air within a few hours. Have you picked up Blackstone?"

"Your boy is nowhere to be found."

"What?"

"The surveillance team has been posted at arrivals and he hasn't come out. I had a female officer pose as his wife and inquire with Turkish Airlines if he was on the flight. They told her he boarded at Dulles and should have been out by now. Unless he's been held up at customs for some reason, he's not here."

"Did your team miss him? Do you have his photo?" Canton yelled hysterically over the phone.

"Of course we have his photo, and my team did not miss him. I am telling you that he did not come out with any of the other passengers from that flight. I don't know how to say it any simpler. I could make some inquiries with customs, but that would draw unnecessary attention. If he's not on their radar, he will be if we start asking questions about him," the COS warned Canton.

"I don't care what you have to do. Find out where the hell he went. He didn't just disappear!"

"I'll see what I can find out."

"Don't see, do!" Canton demanded.

"I'll call you if I have something."

"Shit! Shit! Shit!" he shouted to himself. *That's impossible. Somehow, he gave them the slip. Maybe he put on a disguise and they didn't recognize him. No, that's stupid. How would he have gotten through immigration looking different than his passport photo? How could they have missed him? He still looks pretty much the same as his photo from the Agency. Someone must have helped him.* He looked at the time. It was 1:25 p.m. *I'll deal with this as soon as I'm done with Payton,* he told himself as he headed out of his office to the parking garage.

***

Michael was enjoying the view of the illuminated Bosphorus Bridge from the rooftop terrace restaurant where Asya had taken him. It was a calm night, and gold and purple lighting reflected a mirror image of the bridge on the tranquil waters below. They were alone on the terrace, the other customers choosing to stay indoors. It was still a bit cool in the evenings this early in the year, but Asya knew the restaurant owner and had him light the overhead propane heater, which took the chill out of the air. Michael had just finished relating to her everything that had happened since he had received the voicemail from Roxanne, except, of course, the part about his failed attempt to take his life. It wasn't something he was ready to share with her, nor did it have any relevance to his reason for being there. She sipped her wine as she silently considered what he had just told her. When she finally broke her silence, it was clear she was deeply disturbed.

"Michael, what you've told me is almost too bizarre to believe. If it was anyone other than you, I would think they were crazy. What is even more disturbing is that your former associate Canton came to my office the day before yesterday, asking for assistance in locating Ali Shiravi. Without coming out and exactly saying so, he seemed to imply that Ali may have somehow been involved in the foreign minister's assassination. He was definitely concerned with finding him at all costs. We have put out a stop-and-detain directive with his photograph to all ports and border crossings, along with distribution to the national police, but so far there have been no reports of him. The one thing we found reviewing the video from the Four Seasons immediately prior to the assassination is an individual exited the elevator in the lobby at twelve fifty-seven a.m. It shows the back of his head, but looking at the photograph Canton gave me of Ali, it is possible it could be him. The individual was balding with dark hair and wearing a light-colored sport jacket. Unfortunately, there was no other video of this person after that."

"Canton is not to be trusted. I know Ali, and if he says Canton is involved, I believe him. Canton is more than a former associate. He assisted me on one of my operations. I believe he intentionally compromised the operation, risking the lives of the asset and the target. Ali was that asset."

"That I don't have trouble believing. He did not leave me with a very good impression when he came to see me. I found him to be unprofessional. I think women in America would call someone like him a creep, is that correct?"

"It didn't take you long to figure him out. He's not the most brilliant operator, but he can be dangerous. There's no limit to how low he will stoop to get what he wants. He is a treacherous narcissist with absolutely no principles. Does that give you a better idea of what type of person you're dealing with?" Michael warned her.

"How did someone like that become a deputy director in your CIA?"

"That's a good question. When I knew him, he was one of the laziest case officers I had ever encountered. He had a real chip on his shoulder about not getting the recognition or respect he thought he deserved. If the Secretary of State is involved in this also, I wouldn't be surprised if he has something to do with Canton being in the position he's in. Who knows how high this goes?"

"What are you saying, Michael, that the President of the United States is also involved in this?" Asya asked in disbelief.

"I don't know. I don't see how the Secretary of State could be involved in something like this without the President knowing. It just doesn't seem possible. If the Russians are involved, there's no way that can happen without Markov calling the shots. Nothing happens in Russia without him. I don't see how Secretary Payton could be coordinating with Markov and President Steele not be involved. Either way, it's treason."

"But what if it is a sanctioned operation?"

Michael remained silent while considering Asya's question. Could the assassination of the Iranian foreign minister actually have been a sanctioned operation by the US government? That sounded too incredible to be possible. Just like the operation that went after Osama bin Laden, even the most highly classified operation of that sort would have a handful of the administration's national security team involved, such as the Secretary of Defense, the DNI and the DCI, among others. Michael could not imagine all of them approving the assassination of a foreign country's leadership, even if it was Iran. It seemed inconceivable that they would let Russia know about something like that, let alone be involved. Iran was one of Russia's few allies in the world. Most importantly, Canton wouldn't be playing a central role in such an operation, that was a certainty. Michael couldn't conceive of any possibility it was a sanctioned operation.

"No, Asya, I think that's almost an impossibility, unless everything I know has been completely turned upside down since I left the CIA. None of it makes sense. There's no way we would have the Russians involved with something like this. Even if it were sanctioned, are you all right with the United States government assassinating foreign leaders in your country?"

"You are right, Michael, it does not make sense. And, no, I am not all right with any country using Turkey to commit terrorist acts, which is what this was. As I'm sure you realize, I am centrally involved in the investigation. So far, we have not been able to uncover any substantive leads on who was responsible for the assassination. The obvious suspects would be the Israelis, but we have no indication of Mossad or any other Israeli special operations forces being involved. We keep a pretty tight watch on the Israelis operating out of both their embassy in Ankara and their consulate here in Istanbul. The consequences of something going wrong and them getting caught do not seem worth the risk. What would they hope to gain?" Asya asked.

"What would anyone hope to gain? Consider the consequences so far. Iran and Israel are pointing fingers at each other, and tensions in the entire Middle East are starting to heat up. If one side or the other makes a foolish move, things could spiral out of control very quickly. The whole region could fall into chaos. Who would benefit from that? It could put the whole world into crisis mode."

Asya looked out at the view of the Bosphorus Bridge off in the distance. Michael studied her face in the subdued lighting. He could see how the weight of her responsibilities had taken its toll on her. She was still incredibly attractive, even with the slight wrinkles starting to form under her eyes, but Michael sensed the seriousness in her. The young woman he had met twenty years ago had had an almost naïve enthusiasm about intelligence work, thinking any challenge could be overcome with enough determination and ingenuity. Michael could see she had experienced things since then that had tempered that enthusiasm to a disciplined shrewdness.

She turned and looked at him square in the eyes. "Why do you think Ali told his daughter to contact you? Did he not know you were no longer in the CIA?"

"He knew, and he knew why. I don't know why he told her to get a hold of me. I guess he thought I was the only one he could trust, especially with Canton involved. I don't know if he made a wise choice. I don't even have any idea of where to go from here. You guys have the country locked down looking for him, and he's nowhere to be found. Unless he's lying dead somewhere, it's like he's vanished."

"I think he made a wise choice. Who else would have dropped everything and come looking for him halfway across the world?"

"I didn't exactly drop everything. I had pretty much cleared my calendar before any of this even happened."

"Still, Michael, there are not many people who would do what you have done for someone that was not even family or a close friend."

"Well, I kind of consider him a friend. At least I consider I have a responsibility to try and help him."

"He is fortunate to have you as a friend, then."

"We'll see about that."

"Considering what you have told me, it looks like Ali may be our only possibility of proving this conspiracy. If we don't find him, we may never be able to prove anything. Do you have any idea what he would have done in this situation?"

Michael was about to answer her when the waiter came back out onto the terrace to check on them, asking if they wanted anything else. Asya looked at Michael. He shook his head.

"*Hesap lütfen,*" she said, asking the waiter to bring her the bill. He gave a nod and headed back inside.

"This was great, Asya. Fantastic food and a great view."

"I'm glad you liked it."

"As far as what Ali might do in his situation? I don't know, that's tough. He obviously felt he was in danger, calling his daughter the way he did, so I'm assuming Canton at the very least suspects that he knows about the conspiracy. In that case, his boss, the Secretary of State, also knows, so Ali probably felt he had nowhere to turn. You would think his only recourse would be to contact the Turkish authorities, you guys, but he hasn't done that. It's been four days now. I don't think he could be on the run on his own in Turkey this long and not attract somebody's attention. He's either dead and his body hasn't been found, or"—Michael paused as the expression on his face changed to one of uncertainty—"or, he might have turned to the Iranians."

"You think he would do something like that?"

"Well, just think about it a moment. He's Iranian. I mean he's a US citizen, but originally from Iran. He has personal knowledge of a plot to assassinate their foreign minister, he can't turn to his own people because he's scared, he didn't turn to you, probably thought the Turkish authorities would just turn him back over to the Americans because no one would believe his word over the Secretary of State's. They may even be trying to implicate him in the plot."

"Canton did go out of his way to lay that innuendo during our meeting."

"If I were in his shoes, that's where I would turn. He probably felt he had no other choice. Isn't there an Iranian consulate here in Istanbul, if I remember correctly?"

"Yes. On Ankara Street."

"I'd be willing to bet that's where he went. Would you happen to know if there are any traffic or security cameras by the consulate?"

"I would not call them traffic cameras. There is video surveillance of all diplomatic missions. If he went to the consulate, we would have it on video. I will arrange to have you review it first thing tomorrow morning when the technical people are in. If I call them in now, it will raise eyebrows, especially bringing you in this late, unless you think it is necessary to do it immediately."

"No, it can wait until tomorrow. I'm not even certain about my hunch. There could be other possibilities that aren't so readily apparent."

The waiter brought the check and handed it to Michael. Asya grabbed it from him. "Unless you brought lira with you, I have this," she told Michael.

"Okay, this one's yours. Thanks." He looked at his watch. It was 9:45 p.m. "I need to find a hotel. Any suggestions?"

"Yes, I do. You can stay at my place."

"Asya, you don't have to do that. I don't want to invade your privacy and inconvenience you. Just a decent, cheap hotel close to you. Doesn't have to be anything fancy."

"My place is cheap, it is free, and having you stay with me is in no way an inconvenience. Before you arrived, we were getting nowhere with our investigation. Ali may be the only lead we have, and you are the only connection to Ali. Having you stay with me is actually a convenience. I don't have to waste time dropping you off and picking you up. If you check into a hotel, you will have to give them your passport, and there will be a record of your stay. I don't know where all this is going to lead, but you keeping a low profile while you are here is probably the wise thing to do. And also, it gives me a chance to spend more time with an old and dear friend. I have a spare bedroom, so don't worry, you won't end up spending the night on the couch."

"You have a point. I'll take you up on your offer. Which reminds me, I didn't have my passport stamped coming into the country. That's going to give me problems when I have to leave and enter the US."

"Don't worry about that. I will take care of your passport. Let's head back to my place, then. We will get an early start tomorrow and see where things take us."

"Sounds good. I'm really happy to see you, Asya. Apart from you being my only chance of helping Ali, you are a special friend. To tell you the truth, I was a bit nervous about seeing you again after all these years," he confessed.

"Nervous? Why would you be nervous?" she asked him, surprised.

"I don't know. I wasn't sure how you would feel about seeing me again, especially under these circumstances."

"That is the most ridiculous thing I have ever heard. I owe you my life, but apart from that, I know the type of person you are. You are one of the few people in this world that I completely trust. You are very special to me, Michael Blackstone."

"Well, I guess I can stop being ridiculous, then, since we have that straightened out," he replied with a big grin.

"Michael, there is no other person I would rather have by my side under these circumstances, especially with that ridiculous grin to keep me cheered. I missed it."

"I didn't know my grin kept you cheered."

"There are many things you do not know," she said as they got up from the table to head back to her apartment.

"Hmm, I didn't realize you were holding back on me all those years we worked together. There must be more to Asya Tarhan than meets the eye," he parried her playful banter, recalling how she could go toe to toe with anyone when it went to wit. But this felt different, almost as if she were flirting. *Okay, stop it. She's just an old friend and former colleague. She's just happy you're here because you both have been through some tight spots together. She knows she can count on you. Don't make any more out of it than it is,* he told himself as they made their way through the restaurant out to her car.

As he sat in the passenger seat next to Asya, it hit him. Four days ago, he'd tried to kill himself because life had become so hopeless. He had fallen into a bottomless pit of depression. Now, he felt rejuvenated, like he was walking on clouds. He realized the magnitude of what lay ahead, trying to find and help Ali, not to mention exposing a plot that could rattle the entire world, but he hadn't felt this alive in a very long time, since before everything had unraveled in Athens twelve years ago. Did he feel this way because he now had a purpose, a challenge, or was it because of Asya? Whatever it was, he never wanted to go back to the place he had just left. He finally felt like himself again, the Michael Blackstone he remembered.

***

Canton had been waiting outside Secretary Payton's office for close to twenty minutes. He was fuming inside. He did his best to mask his irritation from the Secretary's receptionist, but his frown and pursed lips made it clear he wasn't happy. The fifty-something receptionist, her hair pulled back in a tight bun and reading glasses hanging on the edge of her nose, glared at him with a look that made it clear his displeasure wasn't her concern. Finally, he saw the door open and heard Payton laugh, thanking the British ambassador for coming by and expressing his prime minister's concerns about the rising tensions in the Middle East.

"You can reassure the prime minister that we have made it clear to the Israelis that we will not tolerate any unilateral action by them. Despite the shocking missile attack by Hezbollah on Haifa, if they proceed with any type of attack against Iran without our concurrence, they're on their own. We won't back them in the Security Council," Payton told him with one hand on his shoulder as he walked him through the reception area to the other door.

"Very good, Mr. Secretary. I will relay that to the prime minister. I have confidence that the United States is doing whatever it can to keep things from slipping out of control. Bloody shame about all those casualties in Haifa. I suppose it could have been much worse if the Israelis didn't have their Iron Dome air defense system. From the accounts I've heard, it appears to have been reasonably effective, knocking down most of the incoming missiles, but it just takes a few to slip by and cause devastation in a populated area."

"Yep, real tragedy, all those innocent victims. We'll certainly do whatever we can to keep that from happening again. Have a great day, Mr. Ambassador." Payton led him out the door. "Sorry to keep you waiting, Jonathan. Hope it didn't inconvenience you too much. Been in nonstop meetings since I've gotten back. Come on in. Hold all calls, Betty, unless it's the President of course," he instructed his receptionist.

Canton followed Payton into his office and closed the door. "Have a seat, Jonathan. So, I hope you have some news for me regarding Shiravi. Have you located him?"

"No, Bill, I haven't. That's what I would be doing right now if I hadn't been summoned by you," Canton replied sarcastically.

"I don't know who the hell you think you are, but don't ever come into my office with an attitude like that. I summoned you here because I spoke to the President last night. I can't overstate how disturbed he is about having Shiravi dangling out there as a loose end, threatening to compromise the entire operation. I assured him you were personally handling the matter and he needn't be concerned. I don't want to have to tell him you weren't able to take care of the problem when he asks again. You need to pull out all the stops and find Shiravi. I don't care what you have to do. You have the entire US intelligence apparatus at your disposal, you should be able to find some peon interpreter. Do I make myself clear?" Payton admonished him, eyeballing him for an indication his demeanor had changed.

Canton took a deep breath before answering. "Yes, Mr. Secretary, loud and clear. I'll do whatever is necessary to clean up this mess."

"Good, I'm glad we understand each other. Just remember that, and everything will be fine between us. This isn't about you or me. There's a bigger picture here. We have a chance to rid this planet of a whole bunch of savages that just can't figure out how to live in a civilized manner. It'll be better days again for this country, the whole world as a matter of fact. You get it?"

"Yeah, I get it. Is there anything else, or can I get back to taking care of our loose end?"

"That's it. You can show yourself out," Payton dismissed him.

Canton stood up and left Payton's office. He glanced at the receptionist as he walked by. She glared back at him, letting him know he was in her territory. He didn't need to be told what needed to be done. He was already thinking about what he would do to Blackstone. He would learn the consequences for crossing him. He and Shiravi would meet their demise soon enough, along with whoever else was helping him.

***

They drove down a quiet, tree-lined residential street off one of the main boulevards not far from the Four Seasons, where the foreign minister was assassinated. Asya pulled her car partway onto the sidewalk where the driveway entrance to her apartment was and aimed her small remote towards the electric vehicle gate. She drove onto the complex, which consisted of two five-story concrete buildings standing side by side amidst other similar apartment buildings on her street. She parked her car under the cover of what would normally have been the ground floor of the building but instead was an open area with parking spaces in between the building columns. Michael noticed most of the cars parked there were BMWs and Mercedes, with a few Japanese and Italian makes.

"Looks like a nice complex," Michael remarked.

"It is. There are ten apartments in each building, two on each floor. My father purchased it twenty years ago when it was newly built. He gave it to me for my twenty-fifth birthday. Insisted I needed to live in a secure place when I started working for MIT. I think he just wanted to spoil me because he still thought of me as his little girl. He did everything for me after my mother died. Other than the army, I was the only other thing he lived for. I think he always felt guilty that his career somehow contributed to my mother's death, even though that is nonsense. I know his career prevented him from spending as much time with me as he wanted while I was growing up without a mother, so he tried to compensate by always making sure I lacked nothing. I am extremely grateful to him, but he sometimes overdid it. I guess I should be thankful he always paid for me to have the best gymnastics coaches. I think that's part of why I trained so hard. I never wanted to disappoint him considering all he did for me."

Michael followed Asya into the small lobby of her apartment. In all the years they had worked together, he had never been to her home. Along with Michael's carry-on and backpack, they squeezed into the small elevator common to apartment buildings in Europe. She hit the 5 button and with a slight jolt, the elevator began moving. He watched the wall in the elevator shaft, separated by a door for each floor, pass by them as they ascended to the top floor. They exited onto the small landing at the top of the marble stairwell, where there were two doors, one to each apartment. Asya inserted her key into the deadbolt, turning it several times, then did the same with the key for the door handle, opening the solid wooden door. She flicked on the light switch next to the door and entered her apartment. Michael stepped into the large open area that was her living room and dining area. Asya slipped off her heels and walked across the cherry hardwood floors to the couch, setting her bag down. From there, she walked over to the long vertical blinds and pulled them open, revealing the large sliding glass doors that led out onto the balcony. Michael set his bags down and took off his shoes, placing them next to the door, and walked over to her.

"This is a nice place," he commented as he looked around.

"Thanks. It's home."

Michael could tell she tried to make it as warm as possible. The décor had an elegant but feminine quality to it with Italian leather furniture and a full-size lithograph of Gustav Klimt's *The Kiss* hanging on the wall, but felt like not much time was spent in it. Michael stood next to her and looked out at the city lights.

"Want to go outside?" she asked.

"Sure!"

Asya depressed the latch and slid the large glass door open wide enough for them to slip through out onto the marble tiled balcony, which ran down the length of the building and around the corner. Rolled-up awnings lined most of the balcony. There was a glass-top patio table with four chairs and a couple of loungers. Along one side were various ceramic planters with inverted water bottles stuck into the soil, providing hydration to the plants, something that indicated the occupant spent time away from home. Michael looked at the tiny thong bikini hanging from a drying rack and turned to her, smirking with raised eyebrows.

"I'm on the top floor, I can sunbathe in privacy," she proclaimed with a hint of cheekiness.

"Hmm, I wonder how many of your neighbors are dirty old men with binoculars?" he taunted her.

"What makes you think they are old men? You don't think I can attract the attention of thirty-year-olds anymore?"

"Asya, you could attract the attention of any man any age," he blurted out before he realized how it sounded.

She shot him an amused smile. "Thank you for the confidence boost, but the reality of forty-seven is not flattering. I'm not a young woman anymore and I can feel it, despite trying to stay fit. There are some aches and pains that remind me of that every morning when I step out of bed."

"I'm certainly no spring chicken myself. I know exactly what you're talking about."

"Spring chicken? That is an expression for being young?" she asked, amused.

"You got it. You must not watch many American movies."

"I can't remember the last time I have watched any movie. It seems like I am always busy."

"All work and no play is not good," Michael scolded her.

"Look who is talking. I remember you working eighteen-hour days, six days a week when you were here."

"Yeah, I did, and that foolishness cost me my marriage. Make that two marriages," he uttered, leaning forward and resting his arms on the balcony ledge.

She did the same next to him, their arms touching as they stood side by side, quietly looking out over the city lights. Asya finally broke the silence. "This work can be very unforgiving for any relationship. At least you shared part of your life with someone—well, two someones. Look at me, all these years by myself. Even if the man I was with for a while had not been as ambitious as

I was with his military career, what man in their right mind would put up with someone like me, always out, not being able to tell them where I am and what I am doing? It can be lonely at times."

"If you could do it over again, would you go into the same type of work?" Michael asked.

"That's a hard question to answer. I know myself and what attracts me. I have always wanted some challenge, something that makes me look forward to getting out of bed in the morning. I think that is why, after I won the medal in the Olympics, I searched for something I could do that would be equally exciting and challenging. I've had excitement and challenge, but it has come with a cost. But you know all that. I suppose you are asking me if it was worth the cost. I don't know, Michael. Never having had someone to share my life with, I have nothing to compare it with. Would you?"

The question put back to him made him recount the price he had paid for his choices. There was Karen, Sam, Eva. Were those costs worth it? From where he stood now, he would have to answer in the negative. Yet here he was, in Istanbul, Turkey, standing intimately close to one of the most attractive and intelligent women he had ever met, his equal and then some. He had traveled to exotic foreign locations, chased terrorists and jumped out of airplanes—but all for what? Where had it all led? An attempt to end his life was the answer to that. He had to consider that cost also. It wasn't something he wanted to bring into the equation answering her question. He felt ashamed having to disclose something like that to her. She had always regarded him as being capable, resolute, a solid man whom she could always rely on in a tough situation. What would she think of him now, if she knew how low he had sunk? He wasn't ready for that.

"I don't know if I can answer that either. I've paid a big price as a result of my choices. I know I'm not the same person now that I was back then. I guess it depends on whether I like the person I've become. I hope I'm still a work in progress," he said, hedging his answer.

"Hmm, sounds like we both have some regrets."

"Yeah, it does, doesn't it?"

There was another moment of silence between them. He hadn't felt this emotionally intimate with anyone in a very long time. He wanted so badly to put his arm around her, but resisted the impulse. She was his former partner, his friend, but he could sense a connection, a certain electricity between them. The attraction had always been there when they had worked together, but neither of them had ever overtly acknowledged it, suppressing it amidst their daily contact on the job together. Something felt different now. It wasn't anything in particular she had said, just a feeling he had. He was reading too much into things, he admonished himself. It was a bad idea. He had just divorced, just tried killing himself. He was in no emotional condition to become intimately involved with her, or anyone. He didn't want it to be a rebound reaction on his part. She might not even react the way he expected. Better to just keep things the way they were and not bring any awkwardness into their friendship. There was too much that needed to be done to risk any complications.

"Well, we better get some sleep. We have an early day tomorrow. Let me show you the extra bedroom. I'll grab you a towel in case you want to take a shower after your long flight," she said, turning to head back inside.

"That sounds like a great idea. I'm sure I'll fall asleep like a baby after that." He followed her inside and down the hallway to his bedroom.

She pulled a towel out of the large built-in wardrobe in his room and handed it to him. "The toilet is in there." She pointed to the door across the hallway. "There is soap and shampuan in the shower, and toothpaste on the counter. Just help yourself to anything that you need while you are here. There is not much in the refrigerator. Sorry, I'm lacking on the domestic side. There is a wonderful bakery café just down the street. We can grab some breakfast and coffee in the morning."

"Sounds good." He took the towel from her. "Thanks again for everything, Asya. It was a wonderful evening."

"We didn't do much, but you are welcome. It was wonderful for me also. It is so good to see you again, Michael. Sleep well," she told him, giving him a peck on the cheek before turning and going to her bedroom down the hallway.

He stood there for a second, savoring the softness of her lips and the whiff from the scent of her perfume before heading to the living room to retrieve his bags. The thought of Asya being down the hallway in the next room was on his mind. He hoped a hot shower and the effects of jet lag would allow him to fall asleep when his head hit the pillow. It was going to be an interesting few days—more interesting than he realized.

***

Canton returned to his office at Langley following his meeting with Payton. He was stewing over the way he had been admonished, as if it was his fault Shiravi hadn't been found yet. He resented the fact that he was at Payton's beck and call when the problem was clearly a result of Payton's own carelessness. Now, if he didn't manage to find Ali, the President would attribute the entire mess to him. He was certain Payton had diverted the blame to him. His entire future depended on finding and eliminating Shiravi, as well as Blackstone now. He also had Shiravi's daughter to deal with. He would take care of her later. He had enough problems for the time being. He knew where he could find her in Boston. His only objective for now was to figure out where Blackstone was.

He logged on to his computer and, using his deputy director access, he retrieved Blackstone's personnel file. He began going through it, starting from Michael's initial hiring and training at the Farm. He read through the evaluations by Michael's instructors, becoming increasingly annoyed the further he read. One evaluation after the other commented on Michael's performance across the spectrum of different skills and tradecraft taught to the trainees: "Exceptional aptitude in problem solving…nonstop effort in overcoming obstacles…ability to consider a variety of alternative solutions." He resented Blackstone even more. He recalled his time at the Farm, three years before Blackstone had gone through. It was a challenging ordeal for him. He had made it through, but it had been touch and go. He had the misfortune of having a few old-school instructors, relics who had outlived their usefulness in the field. They had been sent to the Farm as instructors in order to bust the chops of new recruits, telling them how they wouldn't have survived in Moscow in the days of the Cold War. There was one instructor in particular who had singled him out, riding him continuously for unpreparedness in practical exercises. He had made no more mistakes than any other of his fellow recruits. One asshole had made his life miserable for nine months. Blackstone must have lucked out with some decent instructors to get comments like that.

He read further through Michael's file, noting his first assignment after graduating as an assistant desk officer at Langley, a standard for most newbies. He scanned through Michael's performance reports, becoming irritated once again at the exceptional evaluations and recommendation for overseas assignment after only twelve months. It had taken him two years to get out into the field. The female desk officer he was assigned to had developed a dislike for him, through no fault of his own. He had even offered to buy her dinner several times. She had declined despite his best efforts in convincing her it would give them an opportunity to improve their working relationship by getting to know each other better. She must have been one of those man-hating lesbians, sticking it to him with mediocre performance evaluations such as "meeting expectations" and "completes tasks when directed." Well, he had shown those who had tried to screw him throughout his career. He was a deputy director, more than what any of them could claim.

Canton looked at the next page and found what he was looking for, Michael's first overseas assignment, Istanbul Station, Turkey, August 1998–June 2002, MIT Liaison, Counterterrorism. He knew it. Blackstone must still have some contacts there. That's how he'd managed to slip the surveillance team waiting for him at the airport. His personnel file, however, wouldn't disclose anything about who those contacts might be. He would have to search through Istanbul Station's Intelligence Information Reports, or IIRs as they were known in the intelligence community, for that period. He indexed the database for Istanbul Station reports written by Blackstone, Michael, the first one beginning in October 1998. He scanned through the subject lines of each report, noting the variety of terrorism-related intelligence Blackstone was obtaining from his participation in supporting MIT's counterterrorism efforts. He was about to move to the next, when something caught his eye—a name in the body of the report under SOURCE: TARHAN, ASYA, MIT COUNTERTERRORISM LIAISON OFFICER. Canton stared at the name before moving to more of Blackstone's IIRs. There she was again: SOURCE: TARHAN, ASYA, MIT COUNTERTERRORISM LIAISON OFFICER. He spent the next hour and a half looking through the entirety of Michael's IIRs. Of the two hundred eighty-seven IIRs Michael had written during his four years at Istanbul Station, ninety-one of them had Asya Tarhan as the source. That had to be his contact in Istanbul who had helped him at the airport. It made sense. He might have even had something going on the side when he was working with her. He was probably sleeping with her. How else could he have written so many IIRs?

He had been right about her during his visit to her office a few days ago, when she had been a cold bitch to him. Michael had probably already spoken to her and told her about him. That was why she had only been lukewarm in agreeing to assist him. It explained everything. He had to get back to Istanbul as soon as possible. He couldn't have the MIT chief of counterterrorism assisting Blackstone in finding Shiravi. But what was his next move? As much as it made sense that Tarhan was Blackstone's contact, he had no proof, other than circumstantial evidence from the IIRs. Maybe Blackstone had another contact that wasn't mentioned on any official report. After all, he had cultivated contacts throughout his career who had assisted him in ways that would not be officially documented. There was no way he could know for sure, so he would have to focus on Tarhan. He would learn if she was Blackstone's contact, one way or another. He looked at the clock on the wall. It was 7:30 p.m., 3:30 a.m. in Istanbul. He wondered if Blackstone was in bed with her right now. He was almost certain she was the one helping Blackstone. She had made the wrong call. *MIT or not, she's messing with the wrong person. She'll find that out firsthand*, he vowed to himself.

He picked up his phone and dialed the CIA's aviation department. As a deputy director assigned to one of the CIA's priority cases, he had at his continuous disposal one of the CIA's small fleet of Gulfstream G450s and G550s to transport him wherever the needs of his current responsibilities required.

There were always two complete flight crews on one-hour standby, living in quarters situated within the hangar where the aircraft were housed. Whenever an aircraft was needed, a crew went out and another on-call crew was called in to replace them. In this way all eight of the CIA's Gulfstreams were deployable within just a matter of a few hours. It necessitated maintaining a robust flight department in order to support an immediately deployable fleet of aircraft, but it was just another part of the overhead costs that gave the CIA its ability to be anywhere in the world in less than twenty-four hours.

The trip to Istanbul from D.C. would take just under ten hours. If he left for the airport now, he would be in the air in just over an hour. That would get him there around 3:00 p.m. local time. Once there, he would figure out for certain, one way or another, if Tarhan was the one helping Blackstone. Even if it turned out that she wasn't, it wouldn't be possible to allow her to remain alive, since she would then know Blackstone was a person of interest. It would be an unacceptable risk to their plan; she would have to be eliminated. *Such a waste of fine eye candy*, he thought. It was unfortunate that he hadn't had a chance to enjoy himself with her, but there would be plenty of others. Once they were past the point of no return, the President would have no other choice but to appoint him as the new DCI. He would be one of three individuals directly involved in the greatest restructuring of the international order since the end of World War II. There was no way he would allow anyone to ruin their grand endeavor, and his place in history. He would probably go down as one of the most powerful directors of the Central Intelligence Agency. There would be no shortage of women willing to jump into bed with him then.

Chapter 13

Michael woke to the filtered light streaming in through the blinds in his room. He was momentarily disoriented, until he recalled the previous evening with Asya. He sat up in bed, emitting a large yawn and arching his back as he stretched his arms above his head. He could hear a drawer opening and closing, then the sound of running water coming from somewhere in the apartment. He stood up and stiffly hobbled across the room to his carry-on, pulling out a pair of gym shorts and a T-shirt and throwing them on before heading out of his bedroom. He went across the hallway into the bathroom, going through his morning routine, then back out to the hallway and headed towards the kitchen and living room area. The smell of coffee filled the apartment. He walked into the kitchen and found Asya standing in front of the stove in a flowery red silk robe and fuzzy slippers. He stood there momentarily, trying not to stare, but couldn't help noticing the curvature of her toned calves and the outline of her athletic back through the thin fabric. She was still in fantastic shape. From that angle, she could have easily passed for a thirty-year-old. She sensed his presence and turned toward around.

"*Günaydın*," she greeted him with a smile. "How long have you been standing there staring at me?" she laughed.

"Staring at you? What makes you think I was staring at you?" he replied, slightly embarrassed.

"I don't know, you stood there for a few seconds and didn't say anything. I guess you've never seen me in a robe and, how do you say, furry slippers?"

"I think you mean fuzzy."

"Yes, fuzzy," she giggled. "I'm making espresso. Would you like some?"

"Sure," he answered her, walking over to where she was hovering over the stove.

"What is Seahawks, some bird?" she asked, looking at his T-shirt.

"I don't know if it's an actual bird, but the city I live in, Seattle, has a football team, as in American football, called the Seahawks."

"I see. It looks good on you," she said, glancing down to his Adidas running shorts and back up at him. "You still keep in great shape."

"I don't know about great, but I try to run a few times a week and go to the gym. That way I can still enjoy an occasional beer and pizza. You obviously keep in shape. Do you still hold the pull-up record at your office?" he asked her.

He remembered twenty-one years ago, not long after he had started his assignment as the MIT counterterrorism liaison, being at an after-hours celebratory party at Asya's office, after the successful completion of a counterterrorism operation. After an hour of drinking shots of Raki, a few of her male colleagues began ribbing her regarding her celebrity of being the only female serving on an MIT counterterrorism team. Trying to have a little bit of fun at her expense, they asked her how it felt to work around so much testosterone. Upping the ante, she replied that she didn't know, but if someone could beat her in a pull-up contest, she might have an idea. This had elicited a raucous response, and all nine male team members of her unit accepted her challenge. Attempting to pressure her further, they specified she would have to wash and iron the clothes of every team member who beat her for one month. She had agreed under the condition that each male member she beat would have to shave his legs outside the main entrance of their building on different mornings when everyone was arriving for work. Not wanting to chance any of their macho male egos being bruised, they upped the ante, making it an all-or-nothing contest. If just one team member beat her, she would have to wash everyone's clothes and none of them would be required to shave their legs. She had accepted their terms.

Michael remembered following the rowdy bunch down the stairs to the basement gymnasium, where they found a pull-up bar. They agreed she would go last. Each team member took his turn at the pull-up bar. The majority managed somewhere in the range of eight to ten pull-ups. Two managed to swing themselves up fifteen times. Finally, the last one to go before Asya, who had served in the Turkish special forces, jumped up and began cycling through his pull-ups. He passed through fifteen effortlessly, twenty, then began to slow at twenty-five, struggling through thirty and managing to eke out his thirty-second pull-up, before letting go of the bar and jumping down, to the cheering of his male colleagues. Asya stood there and watched everything, unfazed. Finally her turn, she unbuttoned her blouse, taking it off and exposing her athletic shoulders and arms through the gray ribbed tank top she was wearing underneath, to the jeers of her male colleagues. Michael stood towards the back of the raucous crowd, waiting to see if she would end up washing dirty laundry for a month straight or watching a different male team member shave his legs each morning in full view of their fellow MIT colleagues arriving for work. Asya walked up to the pull-up bar, squatting down to rub some dust from the floor onto her palms, then leapt up and grabbed the bar. With the rhythmic swing of a gymnast on the uneven bars, she began to pull herself up and down in what looked like an effortless display of athletic performance. She maintained a steady rhythm through twenty, then her fatigue began to show as her pace slowed, until by thirty she was struggling. She kicked up thirty-one with a grunt, then readjusting her grip, she swung herself up one more time for thirty-two. Barely hanging onto the bar, with an intense grimace, she swung her body slightly forward, then up, clearing her chin above the bar before coming back down and letting go. She stood there with a big grin of satisfaction across her face amongst the moans of her male team members, knowing that she earned the right of being able to remind them of their humiliation, should any of them ever attempt to give her a hard time in the future.

"Ha-ha, you remember. No one has challenged me to a contest since then, so I suppose I still do hold the record. I don't know that anyone today even knows about it. For some reason, my colleagues back then were never eager to keep that record documented."

"They should have known better than to challenge an Olympic gymnastics medal winner to a pull-up contest. They must have missed your performance on the uneven bars."

"Yes, those were fun times. I miss those years. I missed working with you. I always appreciated the respect you showed me. You always treated me as an equal," she told him as she turned down the flame under her Bialetti espresso maker.

"You were one of the best intelligence officers I've ever worked with. MIT is lucky to have someone like you. I know you would have gone a long way if you were an American citizen working for the CIA."

"Thank you, Michael, that means very much coming from you. It looks like we will have a chance to work together once more. It seems strange after so many years to work a case with you such as this. We are not the same young operatives anymore, chasing terrorists through buildings and across rooftops. Now it seems I spend more time in a business suit and heels, behind my desk or briefing some minister, than doing any fieldwork. I just want you to know that I will have to treat you as a source for official purposes when I take you to my headquarters today. I cannot make it appear that you are an official representative. I hope you will understand."

"Of course, Asya, that goes without saying. I'm already in your debt for just helping me at the airport. I didn't expect anything beyond that."

"Don't ever say that again. After what you did for me, you will never be in my debt," she told him emphatically. "Besides, you are the one helping me. We are at a dead ending without the information you have from your friend Ali. Helping find your friend will answer many questions."

"I think you mean dead end," he corrected her affectionately. She was still fluent with her English, but her occasional literal translation from Turkish to English made him smile each time he heard a slip in her sexy accent. He had never thought about her in that manner. It wasn't that he had not recognized her femininity in the past, but it had always been through the filter of their professional relationship. Standing next to her in her silk bathrobe and fuzzy slippers cast her in an entirely different light to him now. It was a nice feeling that he could imagine himself getting used to.

She gave him a smile just as the last of the espresso began spurting out through the top of the metallic tube of the Bialetti. "Would you like sugar or milk with your espresso?" she asked.

"Do you have any sweetener?"

"You mean aspartame?"

"Yeah, fake sugar."

"Sorry, I don't. Those are all chemicals. They are not good for your health. You should not use them," she cautioned him.

"Okay, sugar will work," he responded, wondering what she would think of all the sugar-free Monster energy drinks he consumed like water while working out.

She filled two espresso cups halfway, handing Michael one, along with a crystal jar full of sugar. Michael plunged the small spoon into the sugar, scooping up a heaping spoonful and dumping it into his cup. She pulled a small container of milk out of the refrigerator, adding a shot into her cup, making herself a macchiato. They stood in the kitchen sipping their espresso across from each other as they prepared for their day.

"If it turns out Ali went to the Iranian consulate, that would change the dynamics of the entire situation. Assuming he has told them the information about the assassination plot, their government's response should be different from what they have shown so far with the accusations against Israel and the United States," she told Michael.

"You would think, but maybe it's too much for them to believe something so incredible. They may even think it is some sort of provocation. Who knows? There's probably a lot of confusion in Tehran right now. I'd guess there's a power struggle going on between hardliners in the IRGC and whatever moderate elements are left, urging a more cautious approach. With all the rhetoric flying back and forth between Israel and Iran, things start to take on an inertia of their own. Slowing things down becomes harder and harder despite any evidence that may point to the contrary. Things can quickly get out control like a runaway chain reaction."

"It is already becoming a volatile situation. Not only are Iran and Israel's militaries mobilizing to high alert, but their neighbors are also increasing their readiness levels. Our air force is flying increased patrols along the border with Iran. One miscalculation on the part of any of the actors can lead to disastrous results," she said, voicing the same concern that was on Michael's mind.

"Whatever their endgame is in killing the foreign minister, they had to have factored the reactions of both Iran and Israel. You couldn't have come up with a better scenario to bring instability and chaos to the Middle East. It's just like the assassination of Archduke Ferdinand in 1914, that set off the beginning of World War I. In this case, however, there isn't any common denominator that's apparent between the conspirators," he remarked.

"I can understand some elements in the US government thinking that it would be a way to weaken Iran, however irrational, but what motivation would the Russians have bringing this on? Their interests do not coincide with those of the United States when it comes to Iran or the rest of the Middle East."

"I know, it doesn't make sense."

"Let's see what the latest is coming out of Iran and Israel this morning." Asya walked into the living room and grabbed the remote for the television.

He followed her in and sat next to her on the couch as BBC World came on the screen. She turned up the volume to hear the correspondent, who was reporting in front of rubble and emergency crews still at the scene of an apartment building in what could have been Afghanistan or Syria that had obviously been hit by some large bomb. They quickly realized they were looking at an apartment building in Israel as they listened to the news correspondent's report, "...as the death toll currently stands at fifty-seven and will likely increase as more bodies are pulled from the rubble. Another missile hit a primary school nearby. Fortunately, it was after the school day had ended and there were no children present. A custodial worker and two teachers who were still at the school were killed in the attack. From the scale of the damage to the apartment building and the school, it is obvious that the missiles used in yesterday's attack were of a much larger and more powerful type than previously used by Hezbollah in attacks against Israel. This is Brian Richardson, reporting from Haifa, Israel, for the BBC." They both looked at each other with troubled expressions on their faces. It looked like the situation was beginning to spiral out of control, just as they had feared.

***

Prime Minister Akerman sat with a grim look on his face in his hardened war room, located three stories underground. On one side of him sat Defense Minister Rozen, with Lieutenant General Ehud Levi, the chief of staff of the Israeli Defense Force, next to him, and on the other side, Mossad Director Schimmel. The remainder of the security cabinet filled the rest of the conference table. The mood was subdued as everyone waited for the prime minister to speak.

"Gentlemen, you all have seen the carnage from the missile attack on Haifa yesterday afternoon. The fatalities thus far stand at sixty-three, and over one hundred wounded. It is a miracle there were not more casualties considering the magnitude of the explosions. This was like no other missile attack launched against us by Hezbollah. Of the ten missiles that were launched, two of them hit major structures and caused significant damage. One of them was a grade school—thank God it was after the children had been let out—and the other was an apartment building, where most of the casualties were sustained. Our Iron Dome missile defense system worked well, but eighty percent is not acceptable when it comes to missiles of this size. General Levi, tell us about the missiles used in yesterday's attack," the prime minister said, handing it over to the IDF chief.

"The missiles used in yesterday's attack were not of the type that have been used in past indiscriminate rocket volleys aimed in the general direction of towns and cities, but which just as often land in vacant spaces outside of populated areas. Those typically contain a forty-five-kilogram warhead, enough to cause serious damage to vehicles and smaller structures such as homes, but nowhere near enough to cause the damage sustained by the large concrete apartment building that was hit yesterday. The missiles used in yesterday's attack were Iranian-made Fateh-110 guided missiles, each carrying a six-hundred-and-fifty-kilogram warhead, roughly the equivalent of the two-thousand-pound GBU-10 guided bombs dropped from our F-15 Strike Eagles. We suspect that starting in November 2014, Hezbollah began receiving deliveries of the Fateh-110 from Iran and may have up to seven hundred missiles currently in their inventory. With a three-hundred-and-fifty-kilometer range, they can hit targets anywhere in Israel all the way down to the northern Negev. Yesterday's attack originated from a mountainous region around the Bekaa Valley in northern Lebanon, one hundred and seventy-five kilometers from Haifa. As the prime minister mentioned, our Iron Dome did well, bringing down eight of the ten missiles launched, but they have enough in their arsenal to potentially overwhelm our defenses, with dozens getting through," the IDF commander briefed those present.

Aaron Levin, the minister of public security, interjected, asking, "If you know where they originated from, why doesn't the IDF launch an attack and take out the remaining missiles?"

"It's not that easy, Minister. They are on mobile launchers and easy to conceal. Even if we had accurate intelligence and were to take out a significant number of them, they would still be left with enough to launch a significant attack."

"If they have had them since 2014, why have they waited until now to use them?" Yitzhak Rubinstein, the information minister, asked.

"That, I cannot tell you," the general replied.

"Perhaps Benjamin can shed some light on that," Akerman said, referring the question to the Mossad director.

"We have a source inside Hezbollah that has told us that, although Iran is Hezbollah's primary weapons supplier now that Syria is in shambles, it is with the stipulation that operational control of larger weapons such as the Fateh-110 remains with the IRGC. In other words, they can only be launched at the direction of Major General Mohammad Bardari, the commander of IRGC. That is why we are confident the order for yesterday's attack came straight from Tehran. What we do not know is whether it was done with the knowledge or approval of President Rostami. We would not put it past Bardari to go forward with something like this without first advising Rostami, but we consider it unlikely he would take such bold action without first consulting Mahdavi. It would be very brazen even for him to risk inviting the ire of the Supreme Leader. He may be able to divert attention away from himself by claiming to the rest of the world it was Hezbollah who was behind the attack, but both Rostami and Mahdavi know it is only he who has that ability."

"That is exactly why we cannot risk Iran developing a nuclear weapon and the missile technology to deploy it. They have shown with this attack that they will not hesitate to strike civilian areas with unrestricted military weapons. It is unthinkable that we can allow a nuclear capability in the hands of those fanatics so they can threaten the existence of Israel. If they are so bold to strike us like this, you can be certain they will not continue to abide by the terms of the nuclear agreement and resume their nuclear program. We have no choice but to go ahead with Operation Yem Sevp," the prime minister declared to his cabinet.

"What about the United States, Ehud? Will we notify them that we are striking the Iranians?" asked Defense Minister Rozen.

"No, we will not! The Americans did not notify us when they struck the Syrians with their cruise missile attack. We are under no obligation to inform anyone when it comes to defending the security of our nation. We cannot rely on the United States to protect us if Iran develops a nuclear weapon. They were not even able to exercise any leverage with the Russians in preventing them from selling their S-400 Missile System to the Iranians, which was just announced yesterday. Do you believe that was just coincidental? Once they have that system in place and operational, it will make any attack against them much more difficult and riskier for our pilots. They will learn about it just like the rest of the world. Are there any other questions?"

No one spoke.

"Then it is agreed, we are moving forward with Yem Sevp. General Levi, are we prepared to launch the attack on Friday, before the Sabbath?"

"We are on seventy-two-hour standby, Prime Minister. We will not be ready until Saturday. Once the order is given, our units will be briefed and make the necessary preparations to execute the attack. They have trained for all the logistical and tactical components of conducting such a strike but have not been briefed on the specific target for security reasons. We are also incorporating our eight new F-35s in the attack, since the squadron has just completed all its readiness trials and they are now combat-ready. They will be virtually invisible to any of the air defense systems the Iranians have currently protecting their airspace, including the S-300 at Fordow. If you wish to wait until after the Sabbath, we can launch this Sunday, four days from now."

"Then that is what it will be. We will take whatever necessary steps our ancestors have also taken throughout our four-thousand-year history, to safeguard the Promised Land God has bestowed upon us, to live as a free people in our own land, the land of Zion and Jerusalem."

***

Hamed yawned as he sat waiting outside of General Bardari's office. The general's secretary had just offered him sweet tea, which he accepted gratefully. It had been an early morning for him. He had risen at 5:00 a.m., before even the morning prayer, to sit in the silence of his living room. He liked the time right before sunrise. There was a certain quiet and calmness before the day came to life, during which he could meditate on the things that were troubling him. It was at those times he would ask Allah for clarity, so that he could fulfill his duty in protecting the Islamic Republic as faithfully as possible. There was a certain heaviness that came with that duty. In order to extract the truth from those he interrogated, he would sometimes have to use harsh measures that caused trauma to his subjects. That trauma, often leaving both physical and psychological scars on the victims, was something he knew was unavoidable. It did not give him pleasure, but his duty was to protect Iran from its enemies, and the way he did that was to ensure the information he obtained for his leadership was the absolute truth. He knew Allah could see his heart, could see that he did not do this out of hatred or anger, but as his sacred duty to protect his people from infidels who wished them harm. Just as it was a soldier's duty to kill the enemy, it was his duty to seek the truth, and sometimes that involved inflicting pain on the enemy. He tried to find solace in the fact that none of his subjects had ever suffered death as a result of his methods, something that couldn't be said for all of his colleagues. Nonetheless, it troubled him. He often wondered if killing a man in combat was an easier burden to bear than systematically administering significant discomfort, and in some cases torturing a fellow human being until they could stand it no longer and broke.

The clarity he had sought from Allah this morning was the certainty that what Ali was telling him was the truth. He had interrogated enough prisoners during the course of his career to be able to detect deception and misdirection. That ability had served him well in knowing when he needed to continue pushing further with his subjects, until he no longer detected deception. In Shiravi's case, he was at an impasse. As incredible a story as it was, there was a certain peace he had sensed in Ali, which made him believe he was telling the truth. He realized the implications for his country. If the United States and Russia wanted Iran to believe the Zionists were behind the foreign minister's assassination, it had to be for the purpose of goading Iran into reacting a certain way. A way that was intended to do Iran harm. That would be the only purpose for such a deception.

The meeting with Bardari this morning was to brief him on the results of his interrogation of the prisoner. He had a strong feeling Bardari wouldn't like what he had to tell him about Shiravi. He knew only one man could have authorized the Hezbollah missile attack on Israel, and that was Bardari. What would he think when he was told Israel wasn't responsible for the assassination, after he had already ordered the retaliation against them? The Israelis would obviously not let the attack on them go unanswered. He knew Bardari would have to answer to the Supreme Leader for his misstep, but better he had the truth now, so that they could alter their strategy and avert an all-out war with Israel. They would find ways to punish the United States and Russia for this treachery. They could make Shiravi's testimony public, bringing it to the world's attention and discrediting both nations. Perhaps it would even lead to the downfall of the American administration. Iran would now be the one seen as the moral nation in the eyes of the international community, while America was exposed as the corrupt Great Satan it truly was. Bardari would be thankful he had uncovered the truth for him, before any further miscalculations were made as a result of this contemptible deception.

Through the door, he could hear Bardari shouting to someone over the phone. He could tell Bardari wasn't pleased. Although he had never had the brunt of Bardari's anger directed at him, he had witnessed his boss take out his rage on other subordinates who had displeased him. It wasn't something he wanted to experience. He had heard rumors that Assad, the foreign minister's security chief, had been stripped of his rank by Bardari when he had reported to him following his return from Istanbul with the foreign minister's body. He knew Assad. They had both completed the IRGC academy together. He was a good man, although perhaps a bit rough around the edges. He knew he would never have been derelict in his duty to protect the foreign minister. Finally, he heard the smashing of the phone back down on its cradle and then silence from the other room.

The phone on the secretary's desk rang. She picked it up, said yes twice, then put it back down and turned to Hamed. "The general is ready to see you, Colonel."

"*Moteshakeram*," he thanked her as he stood up and headed to the general's door. Stepping inside, he found Bardari sitting behind his desk staring at the wall in front of him with a scowl on his face. He paused by the door waiting for Bardari to acknowledge him, not wanting to interrupt his thoughts. After a few moments had passed, Hamed finally broke the silence. "General?"

Bardari turned his head, shifting his gaze onto Hamed standing there waiting for him to speak. "What do you want, Colonel?" he asked in an irritated tone.

"I had an appointment with you this morning, sir. I am supposed to brief you on what I have learned from the prisoner."

"The prisoner? Yes, yes, come sit down." He motioned Hamed to one of the two chairs on the other side of his desk.

Hamed walked over to one of the chairs and sat. "General, I have thoroughly interrogated the prisoner, and as incredible as his claims are regarding a conspiracy by the Americans and Russians to assassinate the foreign minister, I believe he is telling us the truth." He finished his initial statement and paused, waiting for it to sink in with his boss.

Bardari remained silent, staring out over his desk at Hamed until finally interrupting his silence and breaking out into laughter. "Oh, Hamed, you had me there for a moment. I needed a good laugh. I have been on the phone all morning, first with that fool of a president, and then with the Supreme Leader, having to explain myself for retaliating against the Zionists. Rostami infuriates me. Somehow, he believes I have to answer to him for my actions. It wasn't even our military who launched the attack. I am the one who is responsible for directing Hezbollah to act on our behalf, not the president!"

Hamed sat silent for a moment, thinking of how to respond to Bardari's obvious misunderstanding of what he had just told him. He could understand why the general would have difficulty believing Shiravi's story. Even he had thought it preposterous initially. Nonetheless, he had completed his interrogation and was convinced he had obtained the truth. It was his duty to advise Bardari on what he had found out, even if the facts were inconvenient.

"General, I believe you have misunderstood me. I was not attempting to be humorous. I am convinced that the prisoner's claims are true. It was the Americans and Russians who assassinated the foreign minister. The prisoner is their Secretary of State's interpreter. He overheard the secretary speaking with a CIA officer about the assassination plot, which also involved the Russians, the ones who actually carried out the assassination with one of their Spetsnaz teams. He even knew that shell casings from Israeli ammunition would be found at the scene, something no one else outside of a small select group of individuals, including yourself, knew about. He would have no reason to fabricate such an unbelievable story."

"Colonel, have you all of a sudden become a fool? It is an obvious attempt to mislead us in order to disrupt our relationship with the Russians. I assigned you to interrogate the prisoner personally rather than having one of your men do it, because you have always been exceptional in performing your duties. I expected you to have a confession from the prisoner regarding what the Americans were hoping to accomplish with such an outlandish story."

"With all due respect, General, the prisoner was not sent to us as some sort of ploy. He is genuine in his intentions in turning to us with the information that he overheard. I am not claiming that he came to us out of some desire to help us. I do not believe that was his motivation, but rather that he had no other options available to him. They had made an attempt on his life. He had nowhere else to turn."

Hamed could see that Bardari was not pleased with him. His neck had turned beet red as he sat behind his desk, stewing on what he had just been told. Despite Bardari's displeasure, there was nothing Hamed could do about it. The truth was the truth.

"I want you to listen to me very carefully, Colonel. You are going to go back and you will obtain a confession from the prisoner concerning the true nature of this obvious ploy to mislead us. I don't want to hear any more of this nonsense about Russian Spetsnaz teams assassinating the foreign minister. We have already established it was the Zionists who were responsible, and the appropriate response has been taken. Are you questioning my judgment in this matter?"

"No, General, I am not. I am just providing you the facts according to what you assigned me to investigate. I have no control over how those facts influence your judgment. If you choose to act in a manner contrary to what the facts indicate, that is completely your prerogative and not something for me to question."

"I will not tolerate insolence from you, Colonel. How dare you attempt to lecture me? You have no idea what the facts are. You think in your limited capacity, you have insight into everything that affects the security of the Islamic Republic? If you did not have such an exemplary record, I would relieve you from your post and have you reassigned to an infantry unit. I thought you had ambitions to progress in your career. Now, I do not want to hear any more nonsense about this conspiracy. I order you to go back and interrogate the prisoner until you get a confession from him. I don't care what means you have to use in order to accomplish that, just get it done. Is my order understood, Colonel?"

Hamed knew it was unwise to push things any further with Bardari. It wouldn't make any difference and possibly risked the future of his career in the IRGC. For now, he would just acknowledge his superior's order.

"Yes, sir, I understand completely."

"I knew you would comprehend the importance of this matter. I will expect a full report from you as soon as you obtain the prisoner's confession. And one other thing, Colonel, no one is ever to hear about the prisoner's ludicrous story. Is that understood?" Bardari warned him.

"Yes, sir."

"Good. That is all, then. I have to leave now to meet personally with the Supreme Leader. I sense the old fool is beginning to vacillate on responding firmly against the Zionists. Someone needs to counter what Rostami has been telling him about exercising restraint and remind him he once had a backbone, back during his days in the revolution. I don't trust Rostami or that son of a whore who advises him, Karbashi. You are dismissed."

Hamed stood up from his chair and saluted his commanding officer before turning and walking to the door. Things hadn't gone as he'd expected. He would have to figure out how to resolve his predicament. Perhaps Bardari was correct, that in his position, he was not able to see everything.

***

Michael was back in the passenger seat while Asya navigated her A7 through the busy streets of Istanbul as Turks began their workday. She was wearing a formfitting olive-green business suit that highlighted her figure while still giving her an air of confidence and authority. He couldn't help but notice how elegant she looked. She had always made heads turn when he had worked with her two decades ago, but back then she would just as often be dressed in tactical gear taking down a terrorist cell, or blending in wearing jeans and a clingy T-shirt, like half the cosmopolitan Istanbul females in their late twenties. Now, she had blossomed into a middle-aged beauty with an air of sophistication. It was a concerted effort to keep from glancing at her too often as she drove. He was already self-conscious about admiring how great she looked. He didn't want her to think he was gawking at her.

"I can't believe how crowded it is. It was crowded when I was here twenty years ago, but nothing like this," he commented on the traffic.

"I know. Istanbul has grown very much since you were here. Back in 2000 the population was around eight and a half million. Now, it's somewhere close to fourteen and a half. It takes twice as long to get anywhere."

"And I thought Athens was congested. This is even worse."

"When were you in Athens?"

"It was 2004 through 2007, my last assignment before I left the Agency."

"Michael, can I ask why you left the CIA?"

He sat silently while thinking of how to respond to her question. At this point, there was no reason to withhold from her some of the details of the operation. She knew Ali was Iranian. Who else would a double-agent operation using an Iranian-American asset target, other than Iran? He didn't have to tell her Karbashi had been the specific target, but at this point, considering they were pursuing the conspiracy to assassinate the Iranian foreign minister, did it really matter if he disclosed classified information to her about a twelve-year-old CIA operation that had gone bad? That wouldn't truthfully be answering her question anyway. The operation being blown wasn't why he'd left. It was the judgment call he had made during the operation, and the end results because of that call; that was the real reason.

"It's a complicated story. Maybe we should leave it for when we have a bit of time."

"Okay, whenever you want. For today, I'm not going to sign you in as an official visitor. I don't think it's a good idea to be documenting the fact you are visiting MIT. I'm going to give you a visitor's badge to get you into our headquarters, but I'm going to treat you the same as a confidential source.

In a way, you are. Your information is assisting with our investigation of the assassination. No one will ask any questions since you will be with me."

"Of course, I'm with the boss lady."

She turned and glanced at him, giving him a smile. After another ten minutes of driving, they finally arrived at MIT Headquarters. It wasn't what Michael remembered from his time working with Asya. This was a modern five-story black cubicle glass building, in the northern part of Istanbul by the Golden Horn Bridge, along the waterfront of the Bosphorus.

"This is a new building?"

"Yes. You remember the old location closer to the center. We moved here seven years ago. It is quite a bit larger and much more updated technologically. The old headquarters was in a seventy-five-year-old building from right after World War II," she told him as she pulled up to the security gate.

Rolling down her tinted window, she flashed her ID to the sentry, who waved her through. They proceeded down a ramp to the underground parking garage, where she pulled into one of the reserved parking spaces next to the elevators and stairs.

"Rank has its privilege," Michael commented.

"It's nice to have some of the benefits that come with being in charge, but life was much simpler and more fun when I was just one of the guys, as you Americans like to say. I'm not saying I don't enjoy the challenge of the position, but it can be very lonely at times when you are the one in charge. You have to keep a certain separation from those who work for you, especially being a woman in a man's world as things are in Turkey."

"Well, you just shattered my misguided beliefs about what it's like to be the top dog," he kidded her.

She shot him an inquisitive glance, not sure if he was being serious or joking with her, as they walked to the elevators. She scanned her ID, opening the elevator doors, then placed her thumb on the fingerprint scanner and hit the number 0 button. The elevator took them up one level to the main floor, where the security office was located. They walked into the office, where she was greeted by the security personnel. From what Michael could remember of his Turkish, he heard Asya ask the young male security officer to issue her a visitor pass under her name, at which he handed her a badge and a logbook for her to sign. She handed Michael the badge and said in Turkish, "İşte, *bunu koyun,*" telling him to put on the badge.

"*Sağ olun,*" he thanked her.

They exited the security office and entered the elevator again, Asya hitting the 5 button this time. "You remember some of your Turkish," she remarked.

"Well, I made out most of what you said about the visitor pass, and I still remember how to say thanks, but don't expect much more. It's been a long time. I'm just happy your English is so good. Otherwise there would be a lot of awkward silence."

"I have my father to thank for that. He stressed the importance of learning it like a second language. He told me it would open so many additional opportunities, and he was right. I could even have an intimate conversation with you while we walk, and most people in this building would have no idea about what we were speaking of. Do you speak any other languages?"

Michael didn't know what to think about her use of word *intimate*. Her English was fluent and proper, but there were occasions when she would use a word or phrase out of context. By the matter-of-fact expression on her face, he was fairly certain she meant "private," but those little humorous slips of hers always captured his attention unexpectedly. He wondered what it would be like to be in a romantic relationship with her, and those were intentional little playful comments. He had always felt a natural comfort being around her when they had worked together. Even though he had always recognized she was strikingly attractive, it was never in a romantic or lustful way. She had been so much his equal, both physically and intellectually, that he almost thought of her as a great male partner who just happened to be very good looking. The fact that he was married and interacting with Asya in her official capacity as the host nation intelligence service suppressed any crazy idea to even think otherwise. He had heard stories and read case files during training of CIA officers who had foolishly crossed that line with a member of the opposite sex from a foreign intelligence service. It never ended well. Now, however, those considerations no longer existed. He wondered what it would be like to add that intimacy to the close friendship they had developed all those years ago. His logical side snapped him out of his momentary fantasy back to reality. The possibility of pursuing any type of relationship with Asya was just as out of the question. She lived in Turkey and was a senior career officer with the Turkish intelligence service. He lived in the United States and was a real estate agent who had just tried to kill himself. Was he smoking crack, thinking there could ever be any type of relationship between the two of them?

"Michael?"

"Huh?" Hearing his name caught his attention.

"I asked if you spoke any other languages."

"Oh, sorry, I was daydreaming. Well, other than Turkish I once knew, I was pretty fluent in Greek at one time and not bad in some basic Farsi."

The elevator doors opened, and Michael followed Asya down the hallway. Colleagues greeted her as she passed by. Michael noticed that, other than secretaries sitting behind desks in their bosses' offices, all the other senior personnel on the top floor of MIT Istanbul Headquarters were males. Michael walked a half step behind Asya, showing deference to her in front of her male peers. She had certainly come a long way in her career with MIT. Michael knew that many foreign intelligence services, especially in the Muslim world, were almost exclusively male-dominated, especially in the upper echelons of its leadership. Although Asya wasn't quite in the Front Office, as agency directors and deputy directors were referred to, the fact that she was the chief of counterterrorism for a major population center such as Istanbul was an almost unprecedented achievement. They turned a corner and headed to an office door on the outer side of the building. They walked into the waiting area, where Asya's secretary was sitting behind her desk.

"*Günaydın, Bayan Tarhan,*" her secretary greeted her.

"*Günaydın, Aynur. Tüm görüşmelerini beklet,*" Asya said, returning the greeting and instructing her to hold all her calls.

"*Evet, Bayan Tarhan,*" her secretary acknowledged.

They walked past the secretary to the second door that led into Asya's office. As they entered, Michael's attention was drawn to the view of the Bosphorus along the floor-to-ceiling exterior glass wall. Rank certainly did have its privileges.

"Not bad," he commented.

"Yes, it is a phenomenal view. I sometimes take it for granted now, but I always remind myself of my initial impression the first time I took this office two years ago. It is even more spectacular at night when the bridge is illuminated. Sit down a moment while I check my messages and call the technical department to prepare the video footage of the consulate for us to review. Would you like anything to drink?" she asked him as she slipped in behind her desk.

Michael shook his head as he sat down on the brown leather couch on the other side of her desk. He glanced around her office as she listened to her messages. It was professional in its appearance, with various large maps and prints of early Ottoman art hanging on the walls, but absent of any personal touches that said anything about its occupant, not even a family photo. Michael wondered if Asya purposely kept any aspect of her personal life from her work environment because of her unique position as a female in the traditional male hierarchy of her agency. He guessed any hint of femininity would make it that much more of a challenge to assert authority over her predominately male subordinates. Her male peers at MIT probably looked for any reason to claim that she wasn't tough enough for the position she occupied. He guessed it was a pretty lonely place for her when it came to sharing any aspect of her personal life with her colleagues at MIT. It was different years ago when Michael was working with her. Then, she was just a junior member of the MIT Counterterrorism Unit in Istanbul. She had earned the respect of her team by being able to go toe-to-toe with her male counterparts both physically and intellectually. She had been accepted as one of the guys. Now things were different. She couldn't afford to do so in her position. Michael had witnessed her abilities and toughness firsthand. Having been to her home and seen her in her silk robe and fuzzy slippers had been the first time he had seen the feminine side of her. Having experienced both sides of her now, he found her that much more appealing.

She went through her messages, then made a call. From picking out words of her conversation, Michael could tell she was talking to someone about preparing the video of the Iranian consulate. She paused, placing her hand over the mouthpiece, and looked at Michael. "Video coverage from 8:00 a.m. Saturday to start with?"

"Yeah. If he went there, I don't think it would have been before they opened for business."

Asya removed her hand from the mouthpiece and finished giving instructions to the person on the other end. Hanging up the phone, she directed her attention back to Michael. "Okay, it will take them a few minutes to compile the video and then they will let me know. All the feeds from the various consulates and other locations we keep track of are stored in a secure data bank here in our monitoring facility. It's amazing, just rows and rows of servers on shelves in a large air-conditioned room. You will be able to review the video here in my office." She pointed to the two large monitors on the side of her desk.

"I'm impressed. MIT has certainly come a long way in their technical capabilities."

"We went through a very big modernization during the time we moved into this new building. It was desperately needed in order to keep up with the increasing technological sophistication of terrorist groups and our adversaries."

"I'm sure I would be amazed by all the new capabilities and gadgets. It almost feels surreal to be sitting here in the office of the chief of counterterrorism for MIT, in Istanbul, Turkey, after being away from all this for so long. It's as if I've instantly stepped into this strange new reality from some dream, but at the same time it feels so familiar. It's a challenge getting used to it, because sometimes I think I'll wake up and it will just have been one of those really wild and vivid dreams. You know what I mean?"

"I'm sure it has been quite an ordeal from what you've told me so far. If it is a dream, do I look like what you imagined I would after all these years?" she asked.

Michael thought about how he should answer her question. Had she purposely put him on the spot to see what he thought of her, or was it just an innocent question? Either way, it didn't matter. He was going to answer it truthfully. There was no reason not to.

"Asya, you look better than anything I could have imagined. It's not that you didn't look great twenty years ago. It's just that now, despite being older, you look more beautiful than ever."

She tilted her head slightly and gave him a smile, with a slightly surprised expression on her face. "You think I'm beautiful?"

"Ah, yes. Of course, you're beautiful. You always have been."

"Hm, I didn't realize you thought your partner was beautiful all those years you worked with her."

"It's not something you really say to your partner, but I certainly noticed from the first time I met you. Considering that I was married, and that you worked for MIT and I worked for the CIA, it was something I made a conscious effort not to focus on. I even remember telling myself to think of you as my very attractive sister, but I quickly dropped that line of thought because of the even stranger places that led," he said, trying to be funny.

"I didn't realize I was making it so difficult for you to do your job. I'm so sorry. I hope you never have to think of me as your sister again," she shot back with a mischievous laugh.

Well, it was out in the open. If she couldn't sense how he felt about her before, she certainly was aware of it now. He couldn't leave things as they stood, with her knowing about his feelings, and he not hers. He would put her on the spot now. He didn't want to continue being around her, for however many more days, without knowing what she thought about him. Better to be clear about where things stood, so he could concentrate on what he was there for, to help Ali.

"So, what did you think about me when we worked together as partners?"

She paused to consider his question, her lips pursed with a slight smile.

She was about to answer him when her phone rang, causing them to break eye contact as she answered. He heard her say "Yes, okay, thanks" in Turkish.

"The video is ready. I'll pull it up on my computer and you can begin looking through it," she told him, turning to her computer screens and grabbing her mouse. She clicked on a file, which opened a program that brought up HD video from what looked like across the street from what he assumed was the public entrance of the Iranian consulate. "Come here and I'll show you how to use the program. It's easy," she told him as she stood up from her chair.

He walked around her desk and took a seat behind the twin monitors. He looked at the one on the left with the video. She stood slightly behind him and leaned over next to him, her neck inches from the side of his head. He could smell her perfume as she clicked on the mouse to explain the different functions of the program.

"You can see down here is the date and time, right here is how you zoom in, this is how you can increase the speed to 2x, 4x, 8x and 16x, and this is how you freeze the image and go frame by frame. You can adjust the brightness and contrast here. Even though it is HD resolution, the camera is about fifty meters away across the street and up three stories. You will see, when you zoom in, you will have to get a pretty clear shot to make out a face. The security window is on the side, so it will be a profile of the individual unless they turn to the side and look across the street."

"It looks pretty straightforward. I think I'll be able to figure it out. It may take a while to go through the entire day, even at 4x speed. That's fifteen minutes an hour. Won't I be interfering with your work sitting here in your office?"

"Don't worry. I have a meeting with one of my teams in a few minutes that will take about an hour. I will be able to work around you. What you are doing is more important than anything I can do at the moment. Ali may be our only real chance in finding out exactly what happened with the assassination. If there is anything you need, just ask my secretary, Aynur. Her English is fair, enough to understand anything you might need," she reassured him.

"Okay, I'll get to it. We could be just grasping at straws, but this is all we have for the time being."

"I'll be back in about an hour, then," she said, heading for the door.

"See you in a bit," he replied, then turned his attention to the video. It was a long time since he had examined surveillance video. On one hand, it felt very strange to be sitting there, yet on the other, he felt at ease with the wild direction his life had abruptly shot off in over the past few days. He wondered where things would lead if Ali turned up in this video. He knew the further he ventured down the road he was on, the more unpredictable things could get. Just how unpredictable, he had no idea.

***

Captain Engil, the communications and maintenance officer of the 140th Squadron of the Israeli Air Force, also known as the Golden Eagle Squadron, looked at the operational order his commanding officer had just handed him and shook his head incredulously. They wouldn't be able to integrate with the rest of the Israeli Air Force aircraft involved in Operation Red Sea. The battle plan called for the use of the M'sanver Ma'or, the Blinding Light jamming system, against Iranian air defenses or any others who could challenge them there and back. The jamming system was deployed using six modified Boeing 707 aircraft, flying at forty thousand feet and staggered two hundred miles apart. On board each aircraft was a fifteen-hundred-kilowatt generator that powered broad-spectrum jammers which completely saturated the battle space with high energy, causing a communications and air defense blackout through a corridor one hundred and fifty miles wide by nine hundred miles long, from Israel through Syria, Iraq, and into Iran all the way to Qom, where the Fordow nuclear facility was located. The Israeli attack force would maintain their communications through the use of constantly rotating encrypted tactical frequencies that were synchronized to the Blinding Light system, allowing all the mission aircraft to communicate with each other and the two Gulfstream G550 Airborne Warning and Control System (AWACS) aircraft that would be coordinating the attack. Although the eight new F-35 Lightning IIs of the Golden Eagle Squadron had just been certified combat-ready, they were still waiting for the Lockheed Martin technicians to update the communications software so they could integrate with the Blinding Light system. They were scheduled to do that in two weeks. That was a major problem.

"What are we going to do, Colonel?" Captain Engil asked his commanding officer.

"That's why I showed you the operational order. It's scheduled for Sunday. I have to put together our strike package and forward it to General Bachman so he can incorporate it into the overall mission plan. I haven't told him yet about our problem. I wanted to wait until I checked with you. How long will the update take?"

"Once the technicians are here, they can do it in a few hours for all of the eight Lightnings."

"Okay, I'll let the general know. You contact Lockheed Martin and get those technicians here ASAP. I don't care what you have to do to make it happen. Update me as soon as you have an answer from them."

"Yes, sir. I'm on it." Engil saluted his CO and turned to leave his office.

Lieutenant Colonel Janner picked up his encrypted phone and dialed the direct line for Major General Havi Bachman, Commander Israeli Air Force. After the second ring, he heard the other end being picked up and the gruff voice of the general.

"Bachman."

"General, this is Lieutenant Colonel Janner down at Nevatim," he said, referring to Nevatim Air Force Base, located near the town of Be'er Sheva, southwest of the Dead Sea on the northern periphery of Negev Desert.

"Shalom, Colonel. I'm assuming you are calling regarding Yem Sevp."

"Yes, sir. We have an issue regarding our F-35s being able to integrate communications with the rest of the aircraft."

"What! What is the issue? You were certified combat-ready two weeks ago," Bachman shouted, causing Janner to pull the receiver away from his ear.

"We are, sir, but we were waiting for Lockheed Martin to come and perform a software update on our avionics so we can sync with the M'sanver Ma'or system. They were scheduled to be out here in two weeks. We weren't given any warning regarding deploying M'sanver Ma'or during operational training with the other squadrons. I have my communications officer contacting Lockheed Martin right now to see about getting their technicians out here immediately, but I wanted to notify you directly without wasting any time getting up through the chain of command. From the mission plan I just received, I felt you needed to know immediately, sir."

"Dammit, Janner, that is unacceptable! We have orders to execute the mission in four days! How long will it take to do the update?"

"Once the technicians arrive, just a few hours, but we'll need a day to test communications between the squadron and an AWACS with the M'sanver Ma'or deployed, to make sure everything is working as it should. The other option sir, is that we fly in ahead, beyond the range of the M'sanver Ma'or, and take out the air defenses around Fordow with our HARM missiles. I seriously doubt there is anything between here and Fordow that will be able to detect us. We will be able to maintain standard encrypted communications amongst ourselves and command elements outside the range of M'sanver Ma'or."

"Out of the question! We are not going to risk any complications with this mission. There are already too many moving parts. We're deploying nearly a third of our air force to pull this off. We are certainly not going to take any unnecessary risks. I want you to apprise me the moment you know how soon your Lightnings will be ready to go. Is that understood?"

"Yes, sir. I hope to know something later today," Janner replied as he heard Bachman hang up abruptly.

Chapter 14

Michael was sitting behind Asya's computer screen on the other side of her desk, staring intently at the pedestrian traffic walking by and stopping in front of the Iranian consulate, at 4x speed on the video playback. It was the fastest he could go and still be able to keep track of faces moving in and out of the video. He had been at it for close to two hours, stopping on occasion and moving the video back, then advancing at half speed, anytime he saw someone that caught his attention. He kept having to remind himself to blink his eyes and relax his neck, as he felt his body begin to stiffen from fatigue. He didn't know how security personnel that monitored cameras could sit behind a screen for eight hours straight, day after day. He would lose his mind. Asya had come back from her meeting and was sitting behind her desk, reviewing reports that her secretary had printed out for her. That was one thing they shared in common. Although Michael was tech-savvy and comfortable behind a computer screen, he needed to read something on paper to fully absorb the content of the material. There was just something about holding it in your hand and reading it on ink and paper that allowed his brain to process the information more thoroughly. He paused for a moment to rest his eyes, glancing over at Asya. He smiled at the sight of the stylish reading glasses resting slightly down her nose as she was immersed in one of her reports. There was something captivating about how attractive she still looked even with the reading glasses that revealed she was well into middle age. She looked up sensing he was looking at her.

"Are you smiling at my reading glasses?"

"Not at your reading glasses, you in your reading glasses."

"Oh, is that so? And I suppose I look more humorous than you do in yours," she hit back while he looked at her over the top of his own reading glasses.

"You don't look humorous one bit. It actually makes you look kind of sexy in a strange sort of way."

"I never imagined starting to look like a grandmother was sexy."

"I've never seen any grandmothers look like you."

"Well, to be a grandmother, you have to be a mother first. My life didn't take that path," she remarked with a sense of resignation.

"This line of work doesn't make it easy to be a parent, let alone have a normal marriage. I experienced it firsthand," he replied, attempting to allay her notion of having missed out on part of life.

"I suppose you're right. That was something Ercan and I fortunately realized before we almost made the mistake of getting married."

"Do you ever have regrets?"

"No, not regrets. We still remain close friends, even though we do not see or speak to each other often. We dated for five years. We considered getting married, but we both realized that would not end well with what each of us wanted in our careers. He would have wanted to have children, as any man would, and expected me to assume the conventional role of a stay-at-home mother. That was not for me. He knew that and respected what my ambitions were. He met a very nice woman five years ago and they married. He has a two-year-old son and his wife is expecting again. I am very happy for him. I would rather have that than having gone through a difficult ordeal and having it end in heartache with bad feelings towards each other."

"Yeah, that kind of pain can really mess you up. Cuts straight through to your soul, worse than any physical pain."

"I can see that in your eyes."

"I didn't realize it was that obvious."

"It's not, but I can sense something is different in you from when we worked together all those years ago. I don't know what it is, just some feeling I have."

"Hm, that's interesting," he said, interrupting the course of their conversation as he turned back to resume his search through the video.

She lingered, looking at him briefly before turning back to her report. Michael sat quietly scanning through the video for another ten minutes before clicking the pause button, rewinding slightly, then slowly moving forward frame by frame as he looked at the individual approaching the window at the consulate's entrance. He clicked on the magnification button, zooming in on the individual's profile standing in front of the window. He zoomed back out and moved forward at half speed, watching the person stand there as he spoke to whoever was behind the window. There was a pause as the person stood waiting in front of the window without speaking, then there it was—he turned to the side, glancing across the street towards the direction of the camera. Michael hit pause, then zoomed in towards the man's face. He advanced frame by frame until coming across a sharp image of his face. He looked a bit older, but it was definitely him.

"There he is," he uttered, attracting Asya's attention.

"Ali?"

"Yep," he said as he turned the screen towards her.

She studied the image, comparing it to the photo of Ali she had been given by Canton. "It looks like it could be him."

"I know it's him. I spent close to two years with him on a regular basis. He's aged a bit, but it's definitely him," he declared confidently.

He jotted down the time from the upper right corner of the video, 15:17, before resuming watching at 4x speed. He hit pause again at 15:21, when he saw Ali open the door and enter the consulate.

"Well, we know he went in, now let's see if he comes out." Michael hit play and increased to 8x speed, now that he had identified Ali in his beige sports jacket and dark pants. Asya wheeled her chair around her desk to watch the video alongside Michael. They sat staring at the front entrance of the consulate as the time stamp on the video passed 16:00, then 16:30, 17:00, 17:30, then finally 18:00 until it started becoming dark as dusk arrived. The only other individual they had seen was a middle-aged woman who had come to the consulate window a little after 4:00 p.m., but no Ali.

"What time do you think they close for business? I'm guessing they wouldn't be open past six," Michael asked.

"Let's see," she said, reaching across him, grabbing the mouse and clicking on the browser, then typing in "Iranian consulate Istanbul" in the Google search bar, which brought up a window showing their business hours were from 8:30 a.m. to 11:30 a.m.

"He was definitely there after hours. Let's go through to at least ten p.m., to see if he came back out," he suggested.

They sat side by side focused on the video for thirty minutes, as it moved past them at eight times normal speed. Other than an occasional pedestrian pausing in front of the consulate, they didn't see anyone come or go from the consulate through 10:00 p.m.

"Looks like he may have spent the night," Asya commented.

"Yeah, but just to be certain, let's run it through Sunday morning at 10:00 a.m. I'll bump it up to 16x speed. That should get us through it in, what, about forty-five minutes."

Michael resumed the video, hitting play and clicking the speed button up to 16x. She scooted in closer to him. He smelled her perfume as they sat shoulder to shoulder looking at the video flying past them. It would have been a tedious ordeal under normal circumstances having to concentrate that long, but the forty-five minutes spent in close proximity to her seemed to have flown by. He wouldn't have minded watching the video for the remainder of the day, but stopped it as soon as the time stamp reached 10:00 a.m.

"So, what do you think?" he asked, turning to face her.

"He did not come out the same way he went in, assuming he is no longer there."

"Is there any video coverage of any other exits from the consulate, a vehicle exit?"

"I don't believe so, but I can check. In the meantime, I'm going to assign someone from the technical division to review the rest of the video feed up until the present to see if they spot Ali exiting," she told him as she reached for the phone on her desk.

He listened to her talk to the person on the other end. His Turkish was coming back to him as he picked up Asya instructing them to search for the male that was captured on the video last Saturday entering the consulate at 15:21 until the present time and report back to her immediately. He heard her ask about other video, then an "uh-huh" and "thanks" before she hung up the phone.

"No video coverage of any other entrances or exits," she told him.

He thought for a moment, then said, "I doubt he's still there. If he went there to tell them what he knows about the assassination, they would have thrown him out fairly quickly if they thought he was some kind of crazy person. Otherwise they would somehow have to get him back to Iran to further evaluate him. That's what I would do under those circumstances."

"You just gave me an idea," she exclaimed. She picked up her phone, dialed her secretary, and spoke briefly to her before hanging up and looking at him. He returned her gaze, waiting for her to say something, finally giving her one of those "what?" looks. She was just about to say something when her phone rang. She quickly snatched up the receiver, and a male's voice came over the other end. Michael heard a hello from her, then something about the airport and a diplomatic flight to Iran. There was silence, then the male voice came back on the line and spoke rapidly as she scribbled something on a notepad while responding with several "uh-huhs." She thanked him, disconnected, then quickly dialed another number. Michael heard her talk about the airport, an Iranian flight, Sunday and again about video. There was a pause, then a familiar-sounding male voice on the other end. He guessed she was back on the phone with her technical department. "*Harika!*" he heard her exclaim—"fantastic"—followed by a thank-you before hanging up the phone.

She looked at him and gave him a smile, then said, "There was an Iranian diplomatic flight from Istanbul to Tehran on Sunday. All the diplomatic flights use the VIP terminal at the airport, which is in a different section from the regular commercial flights. There are extensive security cameras there, covering the terminal area as well as the aircraft that are parked there. There are no jet ways at the VIP terminal, so the passengers deplane the aircraft down the stairs and walk the thirty or so meters to the terminal. They do that so they can roll out the red carpet for visiting dignitaries. I've asked the technical department to get me the video coverage of the Iranian aircraft. That way we can see who boarded the plane. We will have it shortly," she said excitedly.

He smiled at seeing the same enthusiasm he remembered from working with her all those years ago. Once she got an idea and started pursuing it, the energy she emitted that was contagious to everyone around her. Michael could envision how she had turned out to be a motivational boss as the chief of counterterrorism. He guessed that was how she had been able to rise through the ranks of MIT and earn the respect of her male colleagues. To be successful operating in the secret world of spies required one to have intelligence, talent and good instincts, which Asya had plenty of, but it also required a drive to push beyond the conventional limits that separated the competent from the exceptional. Asya was certainly one of those exceptional intelligence officers that were far and few in between. Her phone rang, and she snatched it up.

"*Evet. Taman, sağolun*," she said, thanking the technician for informing her the airport video was uploaded to her computer. "That was the technical department. We can look at the airport video."

"Well, let's see what there is to see," Michael said as Asya grabbed the mouse and clicked on the folder that had just appeared on her desktop.

The video playback program opened back up, only this time they were looking at the image of a Boeing 727 with "Islamic Republic of Iran" painted on its fuselage. It came to a stop on the tarmac, and all the service vehicles came bustling in towards the aircraft. The time stamp said 11:00. They watched the stair truck pull up to the aircraft's front door and a conveyor truck pull up to a larger cargo door located just forward of the wing. After the stair truck had positioned itself, the forward passenger door was pulled open and a crewmember dressed in Iranian Air Force uniform hustled down the stairs holding a folder, where he was met by an airport official. The crewmember pulled out some documents and handed them to the official, who looked them over. The official handed him back one of the papers and shouted something into his ear as the aircraft's auxiliary power unit came on. The crewmember then turned around and climbed back up the stairs and went inside the aircraft. Asya hit the 4x speed button as they waited to see who would arrive to board the aircraft. A fuel truck pulled up on the other side of the aircraft and the driver connected its hose to the underside of the wing. They saw another crewmember, perhaps the captain, come out to the top of the stairs and smoke a cigarette in the bright sun of the late morning.

Asya increased the speed to 8x. Finally, just as the time stamp passed 12:00, they saw a black Mercedes E300 pull up to the aircraft, followed by a black Mercedes Sprinter van. Asya hit the normal speed button just as a dark-haired male with a few days' beard growth wearing a light gray suit exited the passenger side of the E300. Another man in a beige suit, also with several days' beard growth, exited from the passenger side of the Sprinter, walked to the rear of the van and opened the two back doors. Both drivers also got out and made their way to the rear of the van. It was evident by his hand gestures as he walked to the back of the Sprinter that the man in the gray suit was in charge. The four of them hopped into the van, then slowly made their way back out, carrying a wooden casket, each of them holding on to a rope handle on either end. They carefully carried it a few steps to the conveyor belt, where they gently set it down. The conveyor belt operator moved the casket to the top of the belt, by the aircraft's open cargo door. The four of them then walked back to the Sprinter, and repeated everything again with a second casket, this time straining some as they carried it to the conveyor. After laying it on the belt, they made their way up the stairs into the aircraft, reappearing by the cargo door. They lifted the first casket, taking it into the aircraft, then returned for the second as it made its way up the incline. Upon reaching them, they each grabbed hold of a corner and lifted it off the belt. For an instant, it almost looked as if they would drop it, as one of them stumbled while straining to bring it into the aircraft.

The crewmember who had initially exited the aircraft appeared by the cargo door, giving the conveyor belt operator a thumbs-up. As soon as the conveyor was pulled away from the aircraft, the crewmember lowered the cargo door, pulling it shut. The two drivers exited the aircraft down the stairs to their respective vehicles and drove them away out of the camera's view. The aircraft crewmember then appeared by the door and gave the stair truck driver a thumbs-up, signaling him to pull away as he closed the aircraft door. A few moments later, the fuel truck operator unfastened the hose from the underside of the wing, retracted it into his truck, then pulled away from the aircraft. In another few minutes, the Boeing 727 slowly began moving forward, leaving the camera's view.

Asya hit pause as they both looked at each other. "That was a quick turnaround," she commented, looking at the time stamp, which showed 11:18.

"Yeah, they didn't waste any time. I'm guessing the two guys who left with the aircraft were part of the foreign minister's security detail, along with the occupant of one of the caskets."

"That's correct. He had three security personnel with him, one of whom was also killed along with the foreign minister. No Ali, however." She looked at him, waiting for his response.

He sat there, wondering where this left them. Could Ali possibly still be at the Iranian consulate after this many days? Could they be holding him there against his will? That would be highly unlikely. A consulate wouldn't be set up to hold a captive for any prolonged period of time. Nor would they have the proper personnel to debrief or, depending on their approach, interrogate Ali.

"Do you know if any other Iranian diplomatic or security personnel have arrived at the consulate since the assassination?"

"No, not that I am aware of. I do not have any contact with Iranian intelligence or security personnel regarding our investigation. Everything is done through the foreign ministry with the Iranian ambassador in Ankara."

"Hm. I thought for sure they would have had to get him out of Turkey and back to Iran," he said, pausing again in silence while he thought of other possibilities. "Let's run the video again."

Asya hit the rewind tab, bringing the time stamp back to 11:00, then hit play again. "Wait, go back to where they're loading the second casket onto the conveyor belt," he told Asya. She reversed, then hit play again, showing the four Iranians struggling to carry the second casket from the van to the conveyor. "Now go back to the first casket."

"It looked like it was much easier for them with the first one, doesn't it?" she commented.

"It sure does. Was the foreign minister a big man?"

"No. He was tall, but slim. About a hundred and eighty-five centimeters."

Michael tried to do the conversion in his head, attempting to divide 2.54 into 185. "That's, um…"

"Almost seventy-three inches—six one as you would say."

"Thank you. I'm impressed. And you just happened to know there were two point five four centimeters in an inch?"

"Well, of course, don't you?" She smiled at him.

He returned her smile, amused at her obvious attempt to show him up with her ability to out-think him. There had always been a friendly rivalry between them, whether it had been in physical performance or mental ability. It was something he had always found appealing about her, and although he had been physically stronger and faster than her, he had always acknowledged and respected her ability to think quickly on her feet and come up with solutions.

"He must weigh at least a hundred and eighty pounds. That's, what, about eighty kilograms?"

"That would actually be closer to eighty-two kilograms, but you are correct. It didn't appear that they struggled with the first casket as much as the second, almost as if one was much heavier than the other. That is odd, because the foreign minister's security guard who was killed was slightly shorter than him, but of similar stature. Why would one be so much heavier than the other, then?" she asked.

"That's a good question. Would you go frame by frame until you find a sharp image of the second casket still lying on the belt?"

She advanced the video frame by frame, until coming to a sharp image of the second casket. They sat there next to each other, studying the image of the casket on the conveyor belt with the aircraft in the background.

"See how far you can zoom in on the casket," Michael requested.

Asya clicked on the zoom feature, each time dragging the casket back to the center of the frame, then zooming in again. She zoomed in to 16x before the image began to get grainy. They studied the top of the casket, noticing something unusual.

"Do you see that?" she asked.

"Yeah, it's some kind of pattern. Go back to the first casket."

Asya reversed the video to when the first casket was being placed on the conveyor belt and zoomed in. "No pattern on the first one, the lighter one. I'm going to see if our technical department can enhance the image of the second casket," she said, picking up her phone and dialing. Michael caught enough of her conversation to understand her instructions to the technician. "It will take them a few minutes. Are you thinking what I'm thinking?"

"Are you asking if I think there were two bodies in the second casket?"

"Yes."

"We're thinking the same thing, then. Why else would the casket appear so much heavier? I think Ali may have been in that second casket. The only question is alive or dead," Michael said with uncertainty.

"It wouldn't make sense for them to kill him. They would want to question him back in Tehran."

"No, it wouldn't, but who knows what could have happened back at the consulate? Mohammedi's security personnel could have been so angry and full of rage that they took it out on Ali and went too far."

They sat in silence, both knowing the implications if Ali was dead. Michael realized he was their only link, their only proof of the conspiracy to kill Mohammedi and bring about the destruction of the Middle East. There would be no way for them to prove the President of the United States had plotted with the President of Russia to undermine the entire world order. No one would believe such an absurd accusation without a witness. Everything depended upon Ali being able to declare firsthand what he had heard and allow the world to judge the veracity of the allegation. Apart from the uncovering the conspiracy, Michael hoped he would be able to help Ali reclaim his life and reunite with his daughter. He dreaded the thought of having to return to the United States and face Roxanne with the news that her father had been killed. The phone on Asya's desk rang, breaking the silence, as she snatched it up before the second ring.

"*Evet. Sağolun.*" She hung up the phone. "They were able to enhance the image some. Let's take a look."

She turned back to her computer and clicked on the image that had just been sent to her from the technical department. Enlarging it back up to 16X, they stared at it, then turned and looked at each other.

"Those look like air holes to me," he declared, with a sigh of relief.

"I think you are correct."

"Well, they wouldn't have bothered with air holes for a dead body, so I think we can assume that's how they smuggled Ali out of the country. I know it's only conjecture, but nothing else makes sense. What do you think?"

"I agree. That is the only plausible explanation. Under the circumstances, who else would they try to smuggle out of Turkey in such a manner? So, now that we are fairly certain Ali is alive and in Tehran somewhere, where does it leave us?" she asked.

Michael pondered the situation for several moments, then turned to Asya and said, "I'm going to have to go find him."

Asya remained silent. The look on her face said everything. Michael knew what he had just said sounded crazy, but what other choice was there?

***

Hamed sat in his office located in an undisclosed industrial complex in the northeast of Tehran. It was a fitting place, since the IRGC controlled a significant portion of Iran's economy. It had become a multi-billion-dollar conglomerate invested in all sectors of the Iranian economy, from the defense industry, to oil and gas, petrochemicals, and major infrastructure construction. It would be like Lockheed Martin, Exxon Mobil, Dupont and Bechtel all wrapped up in one organization.

Hamed was troubled by his meeting with his boss. He couldn't understand why General Bardari was dead set against considering that Shiravi might be telling the truth. He had told the general he was convinced Shiravi was being truthful. Bardari had never previously questioned his judgment. He had rarely failed to extract the truth from any of his subjects. Whether it was through the use of psychological pressure or harsher methods, sooner or later, every man had his breaking point. Hamed was a master of his trade. The years of interrogating prisoners made him an expert in distinguishing between truth and lies. Most prisoners had something to hide and made some effort to mislead, foolishly attempting to avoid punishment. Little did they understand their punishment was unavoidable. The interrogation was simply to ascertain the facts about why they were being punished. With Shiravi, however, it was a different case.

He sat there thinking about Shiravi's last interrogation. Even under the immediate threat of extreme pain, he hadn't cowered like most subjects. He had been at complete peace with himself. Some hardened terrorists had been able to withstand showing fear initially, but it was out of a sense of defiance. He had even on some occasions had to interrogate some so-called men of faith, mostly Sunni clerics who had been involved in anti-government activities. Hamed had never detected any hint of reassurance or strength that they drew upon from their faith. Most of them trembled in fear and broke into sobs, pleading to be spared pain. Ali, on the other hand, had displayed an acceptance of his circumstances and a certainty in what he was saying and what awaited him. Hamed hadn't encountered that before. He was certain that he had gotten the truth from Ali.

It did not appear, however, that General Bardari wanted to hear the truth. It seemed he had already decided his course of action, regardless of what the truth was. So where did that leave him now? Was he going to inflict so much pain on Ali in the hopes that he changed his story? He did not think that would happen regardless of how much torture he endured. What would it even accomplish if he did manage to do so, other than make General Bardari look favorably upon him? Hamed knew what it would mean if he did not. He would remain a colonel for the rest of his career, however long that was, and most likely be transferred to a remote IRGC base in some desolate corner of Iran. It was the kiss of death for one's career in the IRGC. It would also be a difficult blow to his family. His wife would stand by his side, silently trying to make the best of it, but his two sons would suffer the most. In Tehran, they attended the best schools and were afforded opportunities to excel in ways that wouldn't be available in some remote outpost.

Hamed was torn by the dilemma facing him. Should he remain steadfast in what he believed was the truth regarding who had assassinated the foreign minister and risk General Bardari's wrath, or should he protect his future and pressure Ali into changing his story? He needed to seek guidance from Allah as to which path he should take. He looked at his watch. It was 11:06 a.m., almost an hour until Dhuhr, noon prayers. He stood up and walked around his desk to his prayer rug in the corner of his office. He knelt down, placing his forehead on the rug, and closing his eyes, he began to pray.

"O Allah, Great One, Most Magnificent, who sees all and knows all, who through Your Prophet Mohammed revealed the truth to all his servants. I praise you. Glory be to Allah, glory be to Allah, glory be to Allah. Allah hears the one who praises Him. I ask You, O Great One, reveal the path I should take forward. Open my eyes so that I may have clarity to see the truth. I have tried to keep my heart pure as I live my life. You have kept me from falling into darkness, despite the pain I have at times inflicted on others to discern the truth. I am convinced I have obtained the truth from this man, but I do not want my pride to blind me from considering I may have been fooled by the enemy. Perhaps the enemy has attempted to deceive me into believing this man is under Your control, when he is actually a servant of his. Shaitan is a deceitful beast, who is always attempting to distort Your truth through his evil ways. Allow me to hear Your voice. Reveal to me the way forward."

Hamed finished his prayer and continued kneeling in silence, waiting to discern Allah's voice from his own thoughts. The seconds turned to minutes as he waited for some indication. He slowed his breathing, attempting to clear his mind and allow Allah to steer his thoughts. The longer he remained in that position, the more he felt a sense of being alone. Why was Allah not speaking to him? He didn't expect to hear an actual voice but was hopeful Allah would guide his thoughts to show him how to proceed. There was nothing. Just random unconnected thoughts without any clear picture. He remained there patiently for several minutes longer, not wanting to appear demanding that Allah respond to his request.

He had lost track of how much time had passed when the ringing of his office phone broke the silence, causing him to flinch at the interruption of his time with Allah. He attempted to ignore the ringing as he remained in his prostrate position, waiting for the caller to hang up. After the tenth ring, he finally stood up in frustration and walked over to his desk, picking up the phone.

It was his wife. She was calling from the emergency room at Akhtar Hospital. Reza, their youngest, had been taken there after being hit by a car while chasing after a ball that had been kicked over the fence of the schoolyard. He was unconscious and on oxygen. They were preparing to take him for a CAT scan to determine the extent of his head trauma. The doctors had told her Reza had suffered significant brain trauma, and they were not sure if he would survive. She hadn't finished speaking when Hamed put the phone down and rushed out of his office to his car. He pleaded with Allah to spare his son, asking for forgiveness for anything he might have done to have brought this tragedy onto his precious child.

***

President Martin Steele sat at the small round table in the kitchen of the private residence, located on the second floor of the White House. He sipped his coffee and ate his toast as he read through his daily briefing. Prepared every morning by the DNI, it was a top-secret document that briefed the President on world events with intelligence from the CIA and the rest of the US intelligence community. Alexandra Kinkaid-Steele walked into the kitchen wearing her White House bathrobe, her face concealed behind an exfoliating facial mask, leaving only her eyes and lips exposed through the avocado green. He glanced up and gave her a forced smile, thoughts of aversion crossing his mind at the sight of her. At fifty-two years old, the First Lady was past her prime, the wrinkles and saggy breasts not offering an appealing sight for several years now. They were civil to each other, both knowing one needed the other to sustain their positions in the upper echelons of America's rich and powerful, but there was no intimacy between them. He had needed the wealth of her father, Endicott Kinkaid, which had helped him win the 2016 presidential election. It wasn't that Martin Steele wasn't a wealthy man. He had been the founder and CEO of Steele Investments, with a net worth of 397 million dollars, but his father-in-law was the chairman and major stockholder of Nordak Petroleum, with a net worth of seven billion dollars. He had practically bankrolled Martin Steele's entire campaign, funneling money through his daughter, the First Lady.

Martin Steele hadn't come from money. He had earned a scholarship to Harvard, where he'd met Porche Hamilton, the heiress to the Hamilton Hotel chain. After graduating with a degree in finance, they had married, and he had gone to work for Goldman Sachs. He had done well there, earning close to twenty-seven million dollars in fifteen years, but it was his wife's family's wealth that had allowed him access into the upper echelon of society's ultra-wealthy.

Upon the death of Maxwell Hamilton, Porche had inherited her father's share of ownership in the hotel empire, worth roughly 290 million dollars. Two years later, while vacationing in the Cayman Islands, Porche had met her untimely death while they had been scuba diving together. Her death was ruled an accidental drowning due to a defective regulator, the diving company being found negligent despite maintaining that all their equipment had been regularly inspected and that they never had a mishap in their seventeen years of operation. With his newly inherited wealth, he had left Goldman Sachs, venturing out to start his own investment firm, Steele Investments. He had grown it into a respectable firm and established a name for himself, finally being able to step out from behind his deceased wife's shadow.

Years later, while traveling to North Dakota to meet with Endicott Kinkaid about investment opportunities with his firm, he had met Alexandra. Endicott had thrown a dinner party, and in addition to all the wealthy and influential guests who had been invited, his daughter Alexandra, a former assistant United States attorney who had just been elected to her first term as a Republican congresswoman representing the district Nordak Petroleum was located in, was also there. They had immediately been attracted by each other's intense ambition for accomplishment and success. Ten years his junior at forty-two, she was still able to make herself look attractive with a daily regimen of high-end cosmetics and designer business suits, but he wasn't pursuing her for her looks. He knew that her father's wealth and her ambition to advance her political career would give him additional access to the upper echelons of wealth and power in the United States. Recognizing what each of them could bring to the table, they had decided marriage would be a mutually beneficial venture for both of them. Endicott's approval reassured them they were making a shrewd decision. Alexandra Kinkaid-Steele had been a capable congresswoman, but her father's wealth and influence, along with her husband's, had swayed the Republican House leadership to bestow her with the chairmanship of the House Intelligence Committee in 2014, during the last two years of President Andrew Walker's second term. It was then that Martin Steele, with the financial backing of his father-in-law and other wealthy Republicans, had started his campaign for president. An unlikely candidate with no political experience, he had successfully defeated establishment candidates with the campaign slogan of "Making America Strong as Steele." During his campaign, he promised to bring back the good times that American manufacturing had once enjoyed, before the ravages of globalism had devastated it. With the last-minute release of unsubstantiated rumors on Facebook that Vice President Sam Russell, the Democratic challenger, had been involved in child sex abuse thirty years ago as a foster parent with his wife, Martin Steele was able to pull off an upset victory, stating afterwards that he didn't believe those rumors to be true.

A year into his term, he was now consolidating his power with the help of his party, controlling both houses of Congress. His bold and aggressive style, along with his ability to paint the establishment politicians in Congress as do-nothing hacks, had gained him wide popular support among his base. Despite filling most of his cabinet and senior White House staff exclusively with Wall Street and corporate executives, he was coming off a good first year with a fifty-three percent approval rating. His hard line with Iran in bringing them back to the negotiating table again had also garnered him support from the foreign policy hawks in his party. Economic growth, however, had been flat, despite promises that the recent tax cut he'd pushed through Congress for those making above half a million dollars would create growth. He had a vision to change all that, however, and restore America's status as the unrivaled economic superpower of the world. He would realize that vision by taking control of the world's energy supplies, with the help of the Russians, and bringing back the global stability enjoyed during the Cold War. The fact that a few million Persians and Arabs, along with a few thousand Israelis, would lose their lives was unfortunate, but inconsequential in the grand scheme of things. History was riddled with examples of great death and destruction when any great empire had consolidated its power. There was Alexander the Great, the Romans, the Ottomans, and Great Britain, just to name a few. The world was in turmoil. It needed a strong and dominant America to bring back some order.

"Your boy Canton has really made a mess of things, Alexandra," Martin Steele mentioned as he continued to read through his briefing.

"Oh, really, what did he do?" she responded while turning to the next page of her paper.

"It appears that Bill Payton's interpreter overheard them discussing the operation. Canton was supposed to eliminate him but failed."

"Why did the interpreter overhear them discussing the plan in the first place? It would seem it was Bill who is responsible for the mess, since it was his interpreter."

"Bill is the Secretary of State. It's not his responsibility to clean up mishaps, which there will undoubtedly be on occasion in such a complex operation. Wasn't that the whole purpose of having Canton involved, to take care of the unseemlier side of things? You recommended him, said he could be counted on to keep things discreet. There is nothing discreet about some State Department interpreter running loose with information that could jeopardize the plan and implicate all of us."

"How will this affect everything now?"

"It won't. We're moving forward as planned. If he happens to turn up somewhere, he'll be eliminated. Things are moving too quickly to worry about some interpreter who may or may not be alive."

"As long as you feel confident it doesn't create any problems. I know my father is looking forward to doubling production of Nordak's Parshall Oil Field operations. His good friend, Governor Dennison, just got the North Dakota legislature to approve a forty-year lease to Nordak, so now they can invest heavily in expanding their hydraulic fracking and horizontal drilling capabilities. Once OPEC crumbles, Nordak will become the thirteenth-largest oil producer in the world. That should easily double our, I mean his, holdings in Nordak. He's eighty years old. He won't be around that much longer."

"You think I'm doing this for the money? I have more than enough money to last me the remainder of my lifetime. This isn't about money, Alexandra. It's about power. It's about reasserting America's dominance in the world."

"We are the dominant military power in the world, Martin. There is no other country that comes close. You of all people should know that. I'm just saying that this is going to be good for our business interests as well as the rest of corporate America."

"Alexandra, we can't sustain our military power at the current rate, continue non-discretionary spending and pay on our increasing debt unless we wrestle back our lost share of the world economy. In 1968, we made up thirty-seven percent of the world's GDP and now we're down to twenty-one. Our GDP is roughly nineteen trillion dollars and China's is twelve. Ten years ago, they were at five trillion. At the current rate, they will have passed us by in ten years if we don't do something about it. Once our plan has come to fruition and we have control of the world's oil supply, we'll be able to keep them on a tight leash. Anytime we want, we can starve their economy to death and unleash social chaos over there—they'll be getting around Beijing on bicycles again."

"Won't the Russians be able to sell them all the oil they need?"

"The Russians will sell to the Europeans as well as the Chinese, but that won't be enough to sustain all their energy needs. The Russians don't want a strong China, one that's ever increasing their military in size and capability right on their border. Despite not being happy about a strong Europe and NATO encroaching on their borders, they know no European country is going to invade them. It's in their interests to eventually mend their relationship with Europe and integrate into the EU economy for the long-term benefit of their economy. Despite Markov putting on a bold face, the sanctions are putting a stranglehold on any growth, and he knows Russia's inability to produce anything other than oil and gas will forever keep them as a third-world economy, a Venezuela with nukes. Even places like the Emirates and Saudi Arabia are starting to surpass Russia in diversifying their economies. We will be the only major economy to be completely energy independent, while everybody else will be feeling the pinch. China's energy costs will be going up and ours will be going down. With our extra energy revenues, we'll be able to upgrade our infrastructure to take us well into the twenty-first century and make us that much more efficient. That's how we're going to get back our unrivaled dominance in the world."

"Well, I'm just glad you have it all figured out, Martin. My father was right in supporting you getting elected, even if he was motivated by what your presidency would do for Nordak."

"And I'm sure that never factored into you encouraging me to run," he commented sarcastically.

"Oh, forgive me, I didn't realize your motivations were so altruistic in running for President, all in the best interest of serving the average joe," she snapped back.

"I came from average joes. Unlike you, I wasn't born with a silver spoon in my mouth. I had to earn every dollar I made."

"Don't lay that bullshit on me, Martin. You know and I know if it wasn't for your ex-wife, you would still be working at Goldman Sachs, maybe as a senior vice president, pulling in two or three million a year. I always thought it was so unfortunate she died while the two of you were scuba diving."

"And what are you implying, Alexandra?"

"Just saying. I don't think I would ever go scuba diving with you if you asked."

"Don't worry, if I ever want to get rid of you, I'll think of something much more creative," he answered her as he stood up to begin his day. He had a busy schedule, including a press conference on the current state of affairs in the Middle East.

***

Harry had just pulled his Cadillac CTS into the parking lot of Lockheed Martin. It was a sunny spring morning in Bethesda, Maryland. The cherry blossoms were in full bloom in the D.C. area, temporarily giving it an aura of purity, amongst all the politicians, lobbyists, contractors and other special interests entangled with each other, constantly trading money for power and vice versa. There was something nauseating about it all that didn't sit well with Harry. He had always told himself when he retired from the CIA he would get as far away from this place as possible. Somehow, the allure of his corporate salary as vice president of international risk mitigation, almost three times what he'd made as a chief of station, was enough to scuttle any plans he had for a nice quiet retirement back in Reno, Nevada. His wife, Rose, also deserved more than what his adequate government retirement would provide him. He wanted to make sure she didn't go without anything she desired. He knew she loved him, but he wasn't fool enough to believe she was attracted to him solely because of his youthful good looks. Guys in their mid-sixties with wives over twenty years younger than them usually had better than middle-class incomes. Apart from wanting to be able to provide Rose with a very comfortable lifestyle, he really didn't know what he would do in retirement. He realized after a year or two of trying different hobbies to keep him occupied, he would begin a gradual mental and emotional decline without stimulus from the challenges that had become an integral part of his identity with his career throughout the CIA. He wasn't running spies, but his job kept him involved in the international fray of corporate espionage by foreign intelligence services against the largest defense contractor in the world. He had become just like so many of the other upper-level bureaucrats who had retired from government service and couldn't escape from the trappings of the corporate military-industrial complex that had become the fourth branch of government in Washington, D.C. It was his life, and he was content with it.

He walked the short distance to the front door from his reserved parking spot. He pulled his security badge from the retractable holder hanging around his neck, swiping it through the security turnstile, and headed towards the elevators that would take him to his office on the seventh floor, right below the executive offices of the CEO and the rest of corporate upper management. His thoughts were with Michael and what was before him. Harry knew what the odds were of Michael being able to find Ali, let alone get him back safely to tell his story about what he had heard the Secretary of State discussing with Canton. It was hard for him to believe the President of the United States and the Secretary of State could be involved in such a vile plot with a thug like Markov to destabilize the world. Steele probably thought that he was doing just the opposite, bringing some sort of order back to the world with Russia, like things were during the Cold War. Little did he realize the Pandora's box he would be opening up. The world had changed since the Cold War had ended. There were no longer two monolithic superpowers in which the world was aligned with one or the other. The world had moved on. There were new major powers in the world, including China, India, a united Europe, and the myriad of other independent actors who saw no reason to align themselves with the United States. Like it or not, the United States was no longer the helmsman controlling the direction of the rest of the world. The genie was already out of the bottle when the Cold War ended and there was no putting it back.

He hadn't heard from Michael since he had left his home Monday morning. He knew Michael could take care of himself, but he also knew the odds were stacked against him. It had been twelve years since Michael had operated in the world of deception, misdirection and high-stakes danger. It was a long time for someone to be away from that type of environment and suddenly be thrust back into it. He hoped Michael could rely on whoever was helping him in Istanbul. For his part, he would stand by and wait to render whatever assistance he could from his end. In his position as head of counterintelligence for Lockheed Martin, he had many assets and contacts at his disposal that he could tap into to help Michael in some way if he needed it.

He walked into his secretary's office. She was sitting behind her desk, sipping her tea while immersed in whatever she was looking at on her computer screen.

"Good morning, Barb. That's a pretty dress you're wearing," Harry complimented her, knowing she was the one who made his life easy.

"Good morning, Harry. Why, thank you. You know how to charm a woman. There's a fresh pot of coffee brewing. You're going to need it when you see all the messages waiting for you. There's some General Bachman with the Israeli military who has been trying to get a hold of you. He's already called twice this morning, asking when you would be getting into work. I told him you didn't come in until nine, at which I think he said something not too nice in Yiddish."

"That would be Havi Bachman. He and I go back a long time. I knew him when he was a captain in the Israeli Air Force when I was stationed in Tel Aviv back in the mid-nineties. Their Air Force was helping us with some electronic surveillance intel on Hezbollah munition sites in Syria. He was a top-notch officer. I'm not surprised he made it to general."

"Well, he sounded pretty anxious. He asked me to tell you to please call him as soon as you got in. His number is on your desk. He said it rings to an STE," she told him, referring to a secure terminal equipment telephone for encrypted communications, developed by the National Security Agency for the US government and its close allies.

"Okay, thanks, Barb."

Harry walked into his office and sat down behind his desk. He looked at the seven messages that were left for him and shook his head. This was supposed to be his retirement job. A few trips overseas every so often, liaising with his contacts at CIA and other foreign intelligence services and periodic security briefs to the senior executives upstairs. Some days it felt like he was just as busy as when he was a chief of station. Maybe he was just older and his motivational level wasn't what it used to be. He figured he would hang in there for a few more years until he had everything paid off and had put away a cozy nest egg to get him through his remaining years. Unless he lived past ninety, he had more than enough for him and Rose to live comfortably. One thing was for sure, he wouldn't hang around D.C. He would sell his home in Bethesda and move back to Reno. It had changed significantly in the forty years since he had left, but he still considered it home, as much as any career CIA officer could think of any place as home.

He poured himself a cup of coffee from the coffeemaker on his credenza next to his desk. He smelled the fresh aroma of the Starbucks French roast that Barb would have brewing each morning and took a sip. Rose would normally not allow him to drink coffee for breakfast, instead squeezing him fresh grapefruit juice each morning with his toast. She would lovingly tell him it was because she didn't want to become a widow before the age of forty. He wondered how upset she would be if she knew how much coffee he drank at work. At least he took his Losartan blood pressure medication diligently.

He punched in the combination of his safe, then placed his thumb on the fingerprint scanner. He heard the click of the lock and turned the handle, unlocking the main drawer. He pulled out his Fortezza crypto card and stuck it into the slot in his STE. He looked at the message with the 972 country code telephone number for Bachman and dialed.

After a brief moment, Harry heard it ring on the other end, then a familiar old voice from the past. "*Shalom.*"

"*Shalom*, Havi. It's been a long time. How've you been?"

"Harry! I'm doing well. Still in the Air Force, but unfortunately, I don't get to sit in a cockpit anymore. The only place I sit now is in my government-issued office chair. One of the unfortunate rewards of staying in long enough to be promoted out of flying. How is everything with you? Still in the game, I see, but I imagine the compensation is much better in the corporate world." Bachman sounded happy to be speaking with him finally.

"I have no complaints about the compensation but dealing with these corporate types can get old after a while, if you know what I mean. Sounds like things have gone well for you, even if you don't get to experience the rush of flying Mach 2 in F-15s anymore. I'm surprised to hear from you after all these years. How did you know where to find me?"

"I obtained our points of contact for your employer, and to my surprise you were listed as security liaison. I need to discuss a technical matter with you. Can we go secure?"

"Sure, I'll hit it," Harry told him, pressing the SECURE button on his STE to initiate encrypted communications between them. "Okay, shows we are secure. So, what can I help you with, Havi?"

"We have a bit of a predicament with a communications issue with our F-35s. Our squadron just recently became operational, but they are unable to communicate securely with the rest of our aircraft through our jamming systems. Your technicians are scheduled to be here in a few weeks to install the integration software, but we have some exercises scheduled in a few days and our Lightning IIs will not be able to participate. It was an unfortunate oversight by the squadron's communications officer. The war games were centered around our new F-35 squadron. I was wondering if you might be able to help me with that?"

"Havi, that isn't my department. Have you contacted the technical folks here to see if they can help you?"

"The squadron is working on that, but I was wondering if there was anything you could do on your end to exert any influence with the head of that department to get the technicians out here immediately. The defense minister and the chief of the General Staff are supposed to be present to observe the F-35s in action, so you can imagine what a headache and embarrassment it would be if we had to delay things. I was wondering if you could pull some strings and see if we could get those technicians here immediately? I would greatly appreciate it, my old friend."

"Well, I suppose I can see what I can do to help move things along a bit. I know the F-35 program manager, so I'm sure he could authorize anything. When is the exercise scheduled to start?"

"Sunday."

"You mean as in this Sunday, four days from now?"

"Yes, Harry, this Sunday. We really need them here by Friday at the latest."

"Holy cow, Havi. I don't know if that will be possible, but I can ask and see what I find out. Must be a pretty important exercise if a general is making calls to get techs out on such short notice," Harry baited him.

"The defense minister is very interested in seeing how our new squadron performs, so I don't want him to be disappointed. I'm not ready to retire just yet, if you know what I mean."

"Well, you don't want to disappoint the defense minister. I'll see what I can do and get back to you. It's almost sixteen thirty there. I may not be able to get back to you until sometime tomorrow your time, before I can find out anything."

"Call me anytime, even if it is the end of your day there. I'll be in my office until very late."

"Okay, Havi, I can't make any promises, but I will try to help you out if it is possible."

"Thank you, Harry. I'll wait to hear back from you. *Shalom.*"

"*Shalom.*" Harry ended the secure call.

That was strange. Havi sounded pretty desperate to get those technicians out there for it being just an exercise. Even if the defense minister was interested in seeing how their new F-35 squadron performed, it was very unusual for the head of the Israeli Air Force to be making calls for technicians. Something didn't smell right, Harry thought to himself. This was more than just an exercise. The Israelis were planning something big, and soon. Things were going to spiral out of control very quickly if they struck Iran. Iran would certainly retaliate massively and openly, not bothering to hide behind the cover of Hezbollah, and then the Israelis might feel forced to resort to their nuclear arsenal.

Their attack was scheduled for Sunday, then. He would have to let Michael know. Finding Ali might not have any bearing on stopping what had already been set in motion, but he was their only shot at bringing this plot out into the open. Perhaps if the conspiracy was made public, there was a chance, however small, of putting the brakes on what was quickly becoming a runaway train.

He turned to his computer and found the number for the F-35 program manager. Although he was calling for the purpose of expediting the technicians to Israel, the longer it took, the better.

***

Asya didn't know what to say about Michael's decision to go into Iran in search of Ali. It was so extreme that for a moment, she thought he might have been joking. The look on his face, however, told her otherwise.

"Michael, did you hear what you just said? Even if you were able to get into Iran without drawing the attention of the authorities, how do you intend on finding where Ali is being held? If you somehow managed to do that, what would you do then?"

Michael didn't immediately respond to Asya's questions. He realized the enormity of what he was proposing and was also aware of the risks involved. At the very least, he could be captured and imprisoned as a spy. He could also be killed, but considering he had just tried to do that to himself less than a week ago, that possibility didn't worry him as much at this point. His greatest concern, besides helping Ali, was what would happen if this conspiracy wasn't brought out into the open for the whole world to see what was really happening. He didn't have everything figured out yet, but he had an idea of who might be able to help him, despite how unlikely it might have seemed to any rational person.

"I may know someone who can help me find Ali, but I'll need some help finding him. I'll also need some help getting into Iran discreetly, and of course getting out. I know it puts you in a difficult position, but do you think you can help me with that?"

"Yes, Michael, of course I will help you any way I can. Besides owing you my life, it is a top priority for my government. I would not hesitate to do whatever I could for you. Getting you into Iran will not be a problem. Getting you out may be a little bit more of a challenge, depending upon what you are planning. I know someone who is very good with that sort of thing. Who is the person you need to find?"

"He's someone who knows Ali fairly well from ten years ago. At the time, he worked for the MOIS in the Iranian embassy in Athens. I don't know if he's still with the MOIS, but maybe you can run some checks. His name is Farzan Karbashi."

"Karbashi? Why does that name sound familiar? Hold on, let me query our system and see what comes up." She started typing on her keyboard. A few seconds later, she got the answer to her question. "Of course he sounds familiar—he's the director of the MOIS. Do you know him?"

"Yeah, I know him, although we met only once, very briefly."

"Does he know you?"

"I'm sure my face is etched into his memory, but he doesn't know anything about me other than any suspicions he may have of me being associated with Ali in some way. Karbashi and I got a brief look at each other right before the operation ended under less-than-ideal circumstances. Karbashi was my target in the double-agent operation Ali was involved in. Over the course of two years, they established a fairly close relationship with each other. It's been twelve years since then, but I have no doubt Ali has not faded from his memory. Their relationship didn't end the way I'd planned, but I'm almost certain he would hear me out about Ali and even consider helping him out if he could. I just need to track him down so I can approach him in private, without landing in an Iranian prison. I'm guessing I could still recognize him, even after all these years. He may have only gotten a brief look at me, but I studied his face for over two years. My best shot of tracking him down is coming out of MOIS headquarters, wherever that is. If he's the director, he shouldn't be too hard to spot heading home each day in some large Mercedes."

"For as strange as it sounds, it actually makes the most sense to try to make contact with him. But do you realize how many things could go wrong? Between getting into Iran, making your way to Tehran, then attempting to surveil MOIS headquarters, the risks are enormous. You are more likely to be caught or killed before you could somehow manage to get Ali and yourself out of Iran. I just want to make sure you have thought this through before I help you."

"I know what the odds are, Asya. I'm under no illusions of what my chances are of pulling that off, but at this point, what other options are there? I'm open to any suggestions," he answered with a look that told her he was committed to seeing his decision through.

"No, I don't have any suggestions. I know where things stand. I know getting Ali out is the only possibility we have to expose the plot and stop this madness. But how is it that it all falls on you having to risk your life? Two days ago, I heard from you for the first time in seventeen years. I'm overwhelmed to see you again after all this time, and now you are telling me I have to help get you into a situation from which I may never see you again?"

"You're overwhelmed to see me?"

"What? Well, yes, I am. You are a very special person to me, Michael. You drop back into my life out of nowhere and now I have to help you possibly get yourself killed. It is a bit much to deal with."

"Hm. I would almost think you have some feelings for me," he suggested jokingly, trying to lighten the moment.

"Do not joke." She gave him a light shove to his shoulder. "I do have feelings for you. I have always had feelings for you. It is just that our lives had never left any possibility for anything to happen between us. You never acted inappropriately or said anything when we worked together all those years, you were too much of a gentleman, but I could always sense an attraction, a connection between us. It was something I always wondered about, even years later after you had left. Do you know the thoughts that have been racing through my mind since we spoke over the phone two days ago? I have had to struggle just to stay focused on my work."

He studied her face as he took in the sincerity of her confession to him. If she only knew how much she had occupied his thoughts. It was the first time he had ever witnessed that vulnerable look on her face. Their eyes locked as they bared their emotions to each other. He wondered what she was seeing in his face. He had never looked at her in that way before. During the years they had worked together, he had never considered her as anything other than a close and trusted friend. They had shared private moments together, but never with the emotions he was experiencing now. They continued looking into each other's eyes, their faces a foot apart. They slowly started moving toward each other. Michael took in the whiff of her perfume as their lips neared. Just as they were about to touch, the phone on her desk rang, interrupting the intimacy of the moment. She shot him a frustrated look as she turned to pick it up.

"*Evet,*" she answered her secretary, then Michael heard her say to put him on, whoever "him" was. "*Merhaba Müdür*"—"Hello, Director"—which Michael took to mean she was speaking with her boss, the director of MIT. Michael attempted to follow her side of the conversation, but his proficiency in Turkish had dropped after so many years. He could tell she was talking with him about the investigation but couldn't understand any of the details. She glanced back at him, smiling, while her boss rattled on, growing louder and louder on the other end. After a bit of back-and-forth, the conversation finally ended and she put the phone back in its cradle.

"He sounds like an excitable guy," Michael commented as she stared at him, her mind still on the conversation.

"Yes, he is."

"Everything okay? He asking why you haven't finished the investigation yet and found out who was responsible for killing the foreign minister? Colonel Mustard in the library with the candlestick?"

"Colonel who? In what library? I don't understand."

"Never mind. You would have had to have grown up in the United States in the seventies and been into board games to get it."

"I see. You are talking about a game you played as a child?"

"Something like that. So, what's your boss have to say?"

"The usual. Asking how things are going and what we have learned so far. I told him we were making progress and pursuing some new possibilities, but I did not mention anything about Ali or you. I think it is best to keep it confined to a very small circle, basically you and me and the person I am going to ask to get you in and out of Iran. If somehow you manage to get Ali out, I will worry about what I am going to tell him at that time. If you do not succeed, there is no point in drawing attention to the fact that a former CIA officer entered Iran illegally with the assistance of Turkish intelligence and the military in an attempt to break out a prisoner of the IRGC. The fewer people who know, the better and safer for all of us."

"I agree. I don't think that would go over well with your boss's boss,

President Ocsilan."

"No, and he would not hesitate to have us all imprisoned, suspecting it was some sort of plot against him that did not go as planned."

"Yeah, that would be ironic, me stuck in an Iranian prison the rest of my life, and you in a Turkish prison. Do you think they would allow us to exchange letters with each other?"

"I see you haven't lost your sense of humor when facing danger."

"What? And show how scared I am? Who's going to take care of my transportation? I'm assuming it's someone in the military."

"Yes, he is a colonel in our special forces. There are only a few people I trust as much as I trust you, Michael. He is one of them. Once I tell him what has happened, he will not hesitate to help, especially since I am asking."

"Sounds like you two are pretty tight. He's the one you were in the relationship with?" Michael caught himself feeling somewhat jealous. That was strange, he thought. Why should he feel jealous about Asya being so close to another man she would trust with her life? Who was he to have any exclusive claim to Asya's trust?

"Yes, it is him. He is the commanding officer of MAK, our version of Delta Force. We still remain very good friends."

"It's nice to have someone in your life you can trust and count on."

"He's not really in my life anymore, but I understand what you are saying. Let me see if I can track him down. Hopefully he is not deployed on a mission and I will be able to get hold of him," she said, picking up her cell phone and dialing a number from her contacts. She held the phone to her ear as it rang several times, until a male's voice finally answered on the other end. "Asya."

"*Merhaba, Ercan. Nasılsın?*" she greeted him and asked how he was.

"*Iyiyim. Sen?*" he said, answering that he was well and asking about her.

"*Iyiyim,*" she replied and continued speaking.

"Uh-uh," Michael heard him acknowledge when Asya finished speaking, then paused before saying something else. The conversation went back and forth several times, too fast for Michael to fully understand what was being said, especially hearing just one side of it. The conversation finally ended with Asya telling him she would see him tomorrow.

"We are in luck. His unit is actually conducting training by Mount Ararat in eastern Turkey. I did not tell him any details since we were speaking over our mobiles, but he understood enough to know that I need his assistance. I told him I will be flying into Agri tomorrow, the closest airport, with another individual. He will meet us there."

"Yeah, we couldn't have asked for any better luck than that," he said, trying to sound encouraged. Michael knew that Mount Ararat, the tallest mountain in Turkey, was located near the Iranian border. Although it was extraordinary good luck that Ercan's unit was in the area to assist them, the reality of what awaited Michael was beginning to settle in. He felt butterflies in his stomach.

"We need to come up with some type of plan once you get into Iran. Have you given it any thought?"

"Let's take a look at a map of western Iran near the border," he told her.

She turned to her unclassified computer and clicked on Google Earth. They studied the area along the Turkish-Iranian border and zeroed in on the small city of Maku in Iran, just over the border.

"That is right by the Gurbulak border checkpoint. It is the main border crossing for that area into Iran. There is an Iranian customs inspection station there, but if we can insert you in past that, you should be able to make your way to Tabriz and on to Tehran. I think that is your best chance to blend in. What do you think?"

Michael studied the map. "Can you zoom in on the terrain just south of Maku? Keep going. Right there, that small valley or ravine just on the outskirts of town to the southeast. That looks like a good spot to infill. It's about ten to fifteen kilometers over the border, so it wouldn't attract attention if he skirted through the valleys in the dark. I'm assuming his unit flies with night vision. If he can get me into that valley, he can set me down right before first light, then I can hike the four or five kilometers down that wash into town. I have a satellite phone I brought with me, but I'll need a GPS and some Iranian currency. I can go in under the cover of being some mute peasant farmer making my way to Tehran by bus. I'll need to get some old baggy pants and a shirt, a blanket, old shoes or sandals, and an old rusty farmer's knife, just in case, and some sort of large basket to fill with dates and some stinky goat cheese. I can hide my sat phone and GPS in the basket under the cheese and dates."

She stared at him with a look of disbelief. "Had you already thought that out, or did you just come up with that?"

"I just came up with it. Why?"

"How do you just come up with something like that?"

"I don't know. It just makes sense, considering what the situation is. Got any better ideas?"

"Not at this moment. I suppose I should not be quite as concerned about your chances of actually pulling this off, if you can improvise and come up with a plan that quickly."

"I'm glad you're not, because I'm terrified," he said, in a half-hearted attempt to be funny while being half-serious.

"I will get you a GPS and Iranian rial. We can go to the bazaar and get you some clothes, dates, panir, goat cheese and a basket. We'll go over your plan with Ercan tomorrow once we get to Agri."

She went to the Turkish Airlines website and checked flights.

"There's a flight that leaves from Istanbul at eleven tomorrow morning and arrives in Agri at three, with a connection through Ankara. We will buy two separate tickets tomorrow at the airport ticket counter. The flight is not even half-full. What were you thinking as far as your passport is concerned? Will you take it with you? I do not know which would be worse for you if you were to get caught, to be with a US passport or no identification at all."

"I've been thinking of that. I don't know that either would be any worse. If I have no ID, they will never be able to definitively prove I'm an American, even though they will be able to eventually get it out of me. I have no illusions about what I'll be in for if I get caught. Having the US passport isn't going to cause them to go any easier on me. At least it will give everybody some plausible deniability of having nothing to do with any of it."

"Who is everyone?"

"Everyone, other than me. You, the Turkish government, the US government, UPS, FedEx, Colonel Sanders, everyone. Let's just hope that doesn't become an issue. I don't think I'd come out of something like that looking as good as I do now. I'd probably need some dental work and a little cosmetic surgery."

"You have a strange way of making jokes when your life is in jeopardy."

"Yeah, it's a bad habit I picked up somewhere along the way."

"Wait here while I get you the GPS and some rial," she told him, finally breaking eye contact with him as she stood up and walked out her door.

Michael sat in the silence of Asya's office, thinking about what lay ahead for him. The butterflies in his stomach were beginning to feel like bats. At fifty-four years old, he had been out of this line of work for too long. During his prime, a mission like this would have been a daunting endeavor, even with the support of everything the CIA had at its disposal. Now he was doing it pretty much on his own, other than catching an unsanctioned ride with a foreign intelligence service into a hostile country, with no in-country contacts or support, other than the remote possibility of the director of the MOIS, whom he had targeted in a double-agent operation over a decade ago. It was the definition of insanity.

Chapter 15

Hamed walked through the emergency room doors of Akhtar Hospital, located near Reza's school. He found Laleh sitting in the waiting room with a distraught look on her face that caused a sinking feeling in the pit of his stomach. She looked up at him, searching his face for some sign of reassurance that everything would be all right, but it was all he could do to keep tears from welling up in his eyes at the thought of his child dying. She stood as he approached her and wrapped his arms around her. She started sobbing. He felt her grief overwhelm him as he held her. He tried to think of something to say but could only continue to hold her close to him, reassuring her with his presence. When she finally released all the emotions she had been holding inside her, he looked into her eyes. "Allah will protect our child," he whispered, trying to convince himself as much as her.

"I know He will," she replied as she tried to bring her sobs under control.

"What have the doctors told you?"

"He has a broken leg and arm, along with three broken ribs and a collapsed lung. He is unconscious and may also have suffered brain trauma, but the doctors do not know the extent of his injury. He had a CAT scan, but they are waiting for the neurologist to look at the results," she told him, trying to keep her voice steady.

"Where is the neurologist? Why haven't they done this yet?"

"I don't know, Hamed. They have not told me."

"How did this happen?"

"From what Reza's teacher told me, the children were on their break, playing outside in the schoolyard. Reza was playing soccer with some of his classmates and the ball was kicked outside of the schoolyard into the street. He chased after the ball, and as he entered the street, a car sped by very fast and struck him, sending him flying into the air. When they ran out to him, he was lying in the street unconscious."

"And who is the driver of the car who struck him?"

"I don't know, Hamed. The car did not stop. It continued on."

"What do you mean, it continued on?" Hamed repeated in disbelief.

"It just continued driving without stopping to see if Reza was hurt."

Fury welled up within Hamed. *What kind of person could be so callous as not even to stop? What kind of person would do such a reprehensible thing?* He seethed at the thought of someone hitting his child and continuing on as if they had merely struck some stray dog in the street. He would find out who had committed such a wicked act and be just as merciless to them as they had been to his child.

His attention was drawn back to his wife. He saw the fear and uncertainty in her face. For the time being, he suppressed his rage. He would deal with the driver later. His main concern now was his son's life. He looked around and spotted a nurse behind a counter. He strode up to the counter, catching the nurse's attention. The nurse didn't know who he was but recognized from the way he carried himself that he was someone of significance.

"*Salaam.* May I help you?" the nurse acknowledged him.

"*Salaam.* My son Reza was brought here. He was struck by a car. I would like to speak to his doctor."

Realizing he was a man used to giving orders, she politely told him, "Please wait one moment and I will find him."

He waited for what seemed like an eternity until he saw a doctor in a white lab coat walking towards him with the nurse following.

"*Salaam.* I am Dr. Farahani. You are Reza's father?"

"Yes, I am Colonel Ahmadi," Hamed answered, using his rank to let the doctor know he expected straight answers.

"Your son has sustained significant injuries, Colonel. Apart from several broken bones and a collapsed lung, he has suffered traumatic brain injury. We have performed a CAT scan, which has disclosed he has a contusion on the left side of his brain that shows signs of bruising—in other words, bleeding—in the region which is responsible for motor skills. He is currently in a coma, which is not unusual for this type of injury. At this point, there is no way to determine the extent of the injury. The broken bones will heal, but if and how he will recover from his head trauma, only Allah knows."

Hamed took in the doctor's words, trying to come to terms with what he had just been told. His precious Reza might be taken away from him or, worse yet, left to endure as a vegetable for the remainder of his life. How could this have happened? What had his sweet innocent child done to deserve this?

"I don't care what has to be done. I don't want any expense spared. I want you to do whatever is possible for his recovery. Do you understand me?" he demanded.

"Rest assured we are giving him the best care possible. For now, only time will determine how he recovers. We will keep you updated with any change in his condition."

"My wife and I want to see him."

"Colonel, I do not think that is a good idea. Your son is in critical condition in the intensive care unit. It will be traumatic to see in him in such a way, especially for your wife."

"Then I will see him alone. Take me to him," Hamed ordered the doctor.

"Very well, follow me," the doctor acquiesced and turned back in the direction he had come from.

Hamed followed him down the hallway, around the corner and through the double doors that led to the hospital's intensive care unit next to the emergency room. Hamed walked past the large window, peering into the first room, and saw the form of his youngest son lying in the bed, connected to a myriad of monitors with a plastic tube coming out of his mouth connected to a respirator. A rush of emotion at the shock of seeing his precious little Reza in that condition washed over Hamed, forcing him to do his utmost to keep tears from welling up in his eyes. He followed the doctor into the room, where a nurse was standing next to the bed, monitoring the young child's condition. The doctor walked over to her and asked to see the latest chart notes, pulling her just outside the door in the hallway, allowing Hamed some privacy to be with his son.

Hamed walked over and stood next to the bed. The pain that hit him at the center of his core was overpowering. He couldn't contain himself any longer. Tears streamed down both cheeks. He wanted to grab his child's hand, but his arm was in a splint. He couldn't even place his hand gently on Reza's head. It was completely bandaged. His little face with closed eyes peering out through the narrow opening of the bandages, along with the intubation tube protruding from his mouth, made for a disturbing sight. He was relieved Laleh hadn't come in and seen Reza this way. It would have overwhelmed her to the point of no longer being able to function. He needed her to remain strong, if only for Tahmin's sake. He wouldn't be able to take care of an emotionally incapacitated wife and his nine-year-old son and be there for Reza, not to mention his work during such a time of risk and uncertainty for his country.

Hamed carefully placed two fingers in Reza's cupped hand and gently squeezed with his thumb, taking in the tenderness of his injured child's flesh. He stood there in silence amidst the faint beeping of the monitoring equipment, gazing at Reza's distorted face. Everything seemed surreal, as if it were one of those dreams in which one knows they are dreaming but are helpless to escape.

It felt like all the energy had been sucked out of him. He experienced such an enormous sensation of weight on him that he felt he was about to be crushed. He shut his eyes to block the disheartening sight of his battered child and began to pray softly.

"Most Merciful Allah, hear my prayer as a cry out to You. You see everything and know everything. You are most powerful and most merciful. I plead with You now and ask that You spare my child's life. Heal his broken body and restore him. He is just an innocent young child. He has not even had a chance to sin against You, Allah. He is a blessing to us from You. I know he is Your child first and is Yours to take when You please, Allah, but I beg that You leave him with us longer. Let him grow up, experience the joys of finding love, becoming married, having children. I beg You, do not bring this sorrow onto us. You are most merciful, Allah. *Allahu Akbar, Allahu Akbar, Allahu Akbar.*"

At some point, he sensed the presence of someone behind him and slowly let go of his child's hand. He brushed the moisture from his face and turned to face the doctor, who was standing inside the doorway.

"I know it is disturbing to see him like this. We will do everything in our power to save your child's life. The best thing you and your wife can do is try to maintain your peace as best as possible under the circumstances and pray to Allah to be merciful to your child."

"Yes, yes, we will do that. Thank you, Doctor." Hamed's words slowly drifted away as he turned and walked past the doctor into the hallway and headed back to his wife.

Their eyes met as he approached her back in the waiting room. He tried to maintain his composure but felt a tear begin to trickle down his right cheek. He tried to give her a reassuring smile but could tell from her reaction that she could read his face.

"He is in Allah's hands," he told her.

"Allah is merciful, my husband. He will protect our son," she managed to get out.

"He is merciful, but the man who did this to our son does not deserve Allah's mercy, nor mine. I am going to find out who he is, and there will be retribution for what he has done."

"Hamed, let Allah bring whatever justice this man deserves. Do not let this darken your soul."

"Allah will bring judgment, but it is I who will exact justice for what he has done to our child," he replied, making it clear that whoever was responsible would face his wrath.

"However Allah guides you, my husband," she responded dutifully.

He managed to give her a smile, letting her know he cherished her devotion to him. "I am going to Reza's school to speak with his teacher and see what more I can find out about the vehicle that struck our son. What of Tahmin?"

"My sister has picked him up from school and taken him to their home. Fortunately, his class was not outside for him to see his brother under those circumstances. He knows that Reza has been taken to the hospital, but that is all. I will stay here for a little while longer, then go to my sister's to check on him."

"Very well, my beloved wife. I will see you in a few hours unless we hear something from the hospital. You have my love."

"You have mine also, my esteemed husband," she told him, returning a faint smile.

He turned and walked out of the waiting room, exiting the hospital and heading towards his car. He would find out who this vile creature was and make him pay for what he had done to his precious child.

***

Asya returned to her office holding a Garmin hand-held GPS, a Samsung smartphone and a thick stash of Iranian currency, which she handed to Michael.

"Holy geez, how much is this? What, am I going to buy a car?" Michael exclaimed, looking at the wad of cash.

"It's sixty million rial, roughly the equivalent of one thousand five hundred US dollars. There are several different denominations. The one-hundred-thousand-rial bill is about two and a half dollars, just to give you an idea. That's all I could pull out of our currency vault without drawing attention, but it should be enough to cover incidental expenses and any emergencies, which you will hopefully not have," she answered him.

"Thanks, Asya, I really appreciate it. What's the mobile phone for?"

"You are welcome. It is a clean phone, with a Turkish number through Turkcell. It will work in Iran, through the Iranian mobile company MTN Irancell, if you need it. Assume that when you register on their network, the IRGC's signal corps will know that a Turkish mobile phone is roaming on one of their mobile networks. How closely they monitor foreign mobile phones, I cannot tell you, but you will have it available should you need it. It is a two-SIM mobile phone. If you can somehow obtain an Iranian SIM card, you will also be able to use it with this phone. Now let me get the coordinates of MOIS headquarters in Tehran and program them into your GPS. Besides the fact that you have the coordinates of MOIS headquarters, just getting caught with a satellite phone and GPS will be enough to land you in Evin Prison." She sat back down next to him and turned to her classified computer.

"I'll just tell them I got separated from my tour group from Israel and I'm trying to find my way back."

"I don't think it would go over well."

"What, Iran is no longer a holiday destination for Israelis?"

She shook her head in disbelief, trying to ignore his sarcasm as she pulled up the geographic coordinates for MOIS headquarters and entered them into the GPS.

"And finally, let's take a look through our classified database to see if we have any current photographs of Karbashi." She typed a few keystrokes through several screens until a color photo of a man, obviously taken through a telephoto lens, popped up on her screen.

Michael instantly recognized him. It was Karbashi. His trimmed beard all white now and perhaps ten pounds heavier, but it was him.

"That's him," Michael declared assuredly.

"This photograph is from eleven months ago, taken in Lebanon when he traveled there for some type of meeting with Hezbollah representatives," Asya informed him.

"I won't have any problem recognizing him if I catch sight of him."

"Okay, let's head to the bazaar to pick up what you will need for the mission. There is nothing more we can do here. We can get a bite to eat there and afterwards go back to my apartment and prepare for tomorrow. Are you hungry?"

"To be perfectly honest, I have so many butterflies in my stomach right now, I don't have much of an appetite. I'll force something down, though, just to keep my strength up for what lies ahead. I'm certainly starting to feel my age today." He gave her a smile, trying to look reassuring.

She studied his face. She realized just how dangerous the mission was that he was about to undertake. It would have made any seasoned intelligence officer or special operations operative at the peak of their career extremely anxious. She knew Michael must have been experiencing some doubts about his ability to find Ali and then free him. He had been away from this line of work for more than ten years and was well into his fifties, even if he still looked like he was in good physical shape. For some reason, however, she sensed that he was not concerned about his life. It wasn't that he was attempting to appear cavalier or feign bravado, but more as if he had nothing to lose. She wanted to say something to him, make a comment, ask him a question, but didn't know exactly what. It was a strange feeling. Perhaps later that evening, when they were back at her place, she could entice him into sharing whatever it was she was sensing.

"You do a good job hiding it." She gave him a concerned smile. "Let's go." She stood up and grabbed Michael by both hands, pulling him up from his chair.

"I'm just a good faker." He smiled back, liking the feeling of holding her hands.

They exited her office, Asya advising her secretary on the way out that she would be out for the remainder of the day and would probably not return until sometime on Friday. Her secretary acknowledged with "*Taman, Bayan Tarhan,*" remaining focused on the letter she was typing on her computer. They walked down the hallway to the elevator and took it back down to the parking garage. They exited the elevator and walked towards Asya's Audi. Asya broke off and headed towards the passenger side, tossing Michael the keys.

"You drive. I remember how much you liked the challenge of seeing how fast you could make it through Istanbul traffic. By now it's starting to thin a bit for a few hours. You should have fun taking it down the Otoyol 1."

"You still remember some things about me," he commented to her.

"I remember a lot of things about you," she replied as she opened the passenger-side door and slipped into the seat beside him.

Michael dropped the key fob into the cup holder in the center console, then pressed the start button, bringing the supercharged V-6 to life. He slowly pulled out of Asya's reserved parking space and made his way to the parking garage exit and out onto the street. He headed west towards the Otoyol 1, one of the main expressways running through Istanbul. Pulling onto the on-ramp, he accelerated, winding out the Audi's supercharged engine in third gear as he shot onto the "One," as the locals called it, in what was fairly light traffic for Istanbul during the early afternoon. He shifted into fourth gear and let up on the accelerator as he merged with the flow of traffic. For as much as he would have liked to test the limits of the Audi's capabilities, he figured being pulled over by the Turkish police would probably not be the wisest situation to find himself in at the current time. He would have plenty of other opportunities in the coming days to get an adrenaline rush. He took in the whiff of Asya's perfume, aware of the butterflies in his stomach. He didn't know if the butterflies were because of the upcoming mission or having Asya sitting in such close proximity to him. He settled back in his seat, trying to relax while relishing the presence of Asya next to him.

They sat in silence as Michael made his way down the One towards the ancient part of the city. It was a comfortable silence he remembered having shared with Asya during such times as extended surveillances together. It was almost as if they were tuned into each other's subconscious, as sometimes happens with rare friendships in which both know what each other is thinking without having to say a word. He glanced over at her and took in her profile as she looked forward into the traffic. She sensed his gaze and turned, making eye contact with him with a warm smile. It almost seemed like old times, Michael thought, yet he was also keenly aware of how different things were. Beyond the close bond of friendship and trust they had always felt for each other, now Michael was feeling something more. It was obvious Asya was also having similar feelings. He struggled to make sense of how he had found himself in this situation with her after so many years had passed since they had last seen each other—less than a week after he'd tried to kill himself. Now he was being deluged by a tidal wave of intense feelings for her, less than forty-eight hours before going on a dangerous mission that there was a very good chance he wouldn't come back from. The rational side of him knew it wasn't a good thing to be feeling what he was for her at the present time.

A voice inside Michael was telling him he should pull back. He had already opened himself up to her far more than what was the wise thing to do. That would make him vulnerable as he prepared for the mission. He didn't need emotions clouding his judgment. The same applied to Asya. He didn't doubt her ability or professionalism, but he knew her emotions could also affect her judgment. He didn't want to leave her hanging with any thoughts or expectations for anything beyond the mission. He didn't want to cause pain again to someone he cared for very deeply. Someone he thought he might even already be falling in love with. It was ridiculous. *Pull yourself together, dude. You're acting like a damn selfish fool. It wasn't enough you destroyed the lives of two women you supposedly loved, now you think you feel something for Asya, and you're willing to bloody her heart also. Suck it up and focus on what you came here for.*

"What's wrong?" she asked.

"What do you mean?"

"I don't know, I sense something is troubling you."

"Well, considering what I'm about to step into, I'm guessing you sense all the trepidation that's oozing out of every single one of my pores right now," he said, trying to put up an emotional wall of defense.

"No, it's not that. I know you are aware of all the risks and have come to terms with them. It's just that I see a vulnerability in your eyes. Not fear, just something I haven't seen before."

"I'm fine, Asya, really."

She realized Michael wasn't ready to share whatever it was she had picked up on. She wasn't going to force it, and she didn't want to step over his boundaries. He had come back into her life unexpectedly out of nowhere, and the rush of all the intense emotions she was experiencing had thrown her off balance. She had resigned herself to the direction her life had taken as a result of her decisions. She fully expected to remain single, finish out her career with MIT and retire as one of those old spinsters, never having found any intimacy with someone to grow old with. She had consciously given up that chance several years ago. Now a man from her past, a trusted friend that she had always wanted to be so much more, was suddenly back into her life with no ties to another woman. He still looked youthful for his age, but there was now a sense of maturity and wisdom, along with some emotional scars, signs of how some of that wisdom had been gained. She found herself yearning to keep him in her life a little while longer, just to see if there was any possibility for a future together. She told herself that she was opening herself up to be hurt. Asya the spy master knew the chances of ever seeing him again were not good. Asya the woman who yearned for the intimacy of someone in her life hoped the story would somehow have a happy ending. It was a struggle she wasn't prepared to deal with, especially as she faced the most high-profile assignment of her career while at the same time illegally helping a former CIA officer compromise the sovereignty of one of Turkey's neighbors. Had she gone completely crazy and lost her ability to think rationally? She wasn't sure. What she was sure of was that, despite the odds, Michael's plan was the only chance they had of bringing this insanity to an end and saving the lives of tens of thousands, if not millions, of people. Any possibility of a future with Michael wasn't something she should be thinking of, at least not now. She didn't know why, or even realize exactly when, she had placed her hand across the top of Michael's, which was resting on the center console.

Michael felt Asya's hand come and grasp the top of his. He didn't turn to look at her. He continued driving, their hands touching like it was something completely natural as they faced the greatest challenge and danger they had faced since working together. His thoughts went back to that unspent .45-caliber round. How was it that he was here in the car with Asya at this moment, when all the laws of probability should have him lying lifeless in a dark frozen drawer in the morgue at Harborview Hospital?

***

Hamed walked through the front doors of Tahmin and Reza's school. He made his way to the office, walking past the secretary and barging into the headmaster's office without announcing his intentions.

"Sir, sir, you cannot go in there!" The secretary stood up and attempted to intercept him as he made his way past her.

Mr. Turani, the headmaster, looked up with surprise at the man who had barged into his office. "Can I help you?"

"I am Colonel Ahmadi, Reza's father." He directed his glare at Turani.

"Colonel, I am very sorry for what happened to Reza. Everyone here is very shaken. Do you have any news of his condition?" the headmaster inquired, standing up and showing deference to an enraged parent who also happened to be a colonel in one of the government's security services.

"He is in a coma, in critical condition. He may not survive. I need to speak with everyone who witnessed what happened. Adults first, then children if necessary," Hamed stated plainly, not wanting to mince words or waste time.

"Yes, yes, of course. I have already spoken with Mr. Ghasemi, who witnessed what happened. I can tell you what he told me, but I assume you will want to hear it firsthand from him."

"You are correct. Send for him now. I will speak to him in your office," he instructed the headmaster.

"Right away, Colonel." He looked past Hamed and nodded to his secretary, who was standing at the door to his office with an anxious look on her face. She turned and shuffled hurriedly out of the office down the hallway to Mr. Ghasemi's classroom. She returned shortly, with Mr. Ghasemi following behind her.

"Mr. Ahmadi, I am Mr. Ghasemi, Reza's teacher. I am so sorry. We are all praying for him. I was told you wanted to speak to me."

"That is *Colonel* Ahmadi. I was told you witnessed what happened?"

"Yes, I did, Colonel," Ghasemi answered anxiously. "I am still in shock from what I saw."

Hamed looked at Turani, giving him a nod towards the door. The headmaster clearly understood what was expected and made for the door, closing it on his way out of his office.

"And what is it that you saw?"

"I had the students outside for morning recess. Some of the boys were playing soccer on the playground. The ball was kicked high towards the fence, going over the top and into the street. Reza was the closest and immediately ran towards the exit and into the street before I could even shout for him to stop. I do not know what possessed him to do that. All the children know they are never permitted to go beyond the confines of the schoolyard. A large silver Mercedes was coming down the street very fast. Reza did not see it. The car struck Reza just as he ran into the street. Reza was thrown into the air over the hood and onto the side. The driver did not stop, did not even slow down, like nothing had even happened. I ran out into the street and found Reza lying unconscious. He was bleeding from the head, and his one arm and one leg looked like they had been broken. He was still breathing. I did not want to move him. I yelled at the children to call for help. Other teachers came out. We put a blanket over him and waited for the ambulance to come."

Hamed glared silently at Ghasemi, rage welling up inside him again. He had to force himself to remain calm and not let his emotions prevent him from thinking clearly. He tried not to direct his anger towards Reza's teacher. It wasn't his fault Reza had run out into the street. Hamed needed him to be able to recall as much as possible of what he had observed.

"What else do you remember about the vehicle? How do you know it was a Mercedes?"

"I saw the Mercedes symbol on the back of the car as it drove off."

"What else? Was it a newer or older style? Did it have any identifying markings, anything unique or unusual about it? You said it was large. Did you see what model number?"

"I do not remember seeing any model number. Everything happened so quickly. It looked like a newer model, perhaps only a few years old. I do remember one thing, however. It had one of the blue-and-white government license plates on it, the kind that ministers and senior military officers have."

"Did you see the driver and occupants?"

"I only saw a driver. I did not get a good look at his face, but I was able to see that he was wearing a uniform and had a gray beard."

"What color was the uniform?"

"It was dark green."

"And what else can you remember about it?"

"The hat. The hat." Ghasemi hesitated. "It had gold oak leaves all across its bill."

Hamed realized why he had hesitated. All Iranian males served in the military and knew what the gold oak leaves, or scrambled eggs as they were referred to in militaries around the world, signified. Their wearer was a flag-level officer, a general or admiral. In this case, the fact that the uniform was green ruled out naval forces.

"Was the uniform camouflage or solid?"

"It was solid."

"You are sure?" Hamed demanded certainty.

"Yes, Colonel, I am sure about that," Ghasemi answered reservedly but firmly.

Hamed stood in silence, taking in what he had just been told. His stare was causing the already nervous teacher to begin perspiring profusely, sweat running down his temple. He knew the implications of what he had just been told. A general had hit his child and driven off without stopping to see how badly he was hurt or to offer help.

"Have you told anyone else about the driver? Your headmaster? The police?"

"No, I did not tell the headmaster about the driver. I knew that was not something that should be discussed freely. I have not spoken to the police. Headmaster Turani spoke to them and told them what I had witnessed. They have not asked to speak to me," Ghasemi explained.

"And you will not tell anyone else what you just told me about the driver. Is that understood?"

"Yes, Colonel, of course!"

"That will be all." Reza's teacher headed towards the door. "And, Ghasemi, thank you for taking good care of my son. He has spoken fondly of you. He says you are strict with them but they enjoy being taught by you."

"It heartens a teacher to hear that. Thank you for telling me. Reza is a bright boy and has great potential to become something special one day. I will pray and ask Allah to be merciful and restore him back to health," he said, opening the door and exiting the headmaster's office.

Hamed contemplated what he had just learned. The perpetrator of this savage act against his child was a senior military officer. The thought of someone in that position acting in such a vile manner made his blood boil. He didn't care if he was a flag-level officer. He would find out who it was and make him pay dearly for his cowardly act. He stood there motionless, staring straight ahead but not noticing anything in front of him.

His mind wandered back to his prisoner. He had been foolish to believe Shiravi was telling him the truth about everything. Was he going soft? Since when had it not been necessary to inflict some physical pain in order to ensure a prisoner was being completely forthcoming? He would make certain Shiravi was telling him the entire, unaltered truth. He didn't notice the headmaster, who had wandered back into his office, standing there waiting for him to say something. Hamed decided he was finished and started walking out of the office, glancing at the headmaster and saying nothing as he passed by him. His thoughts were on Shiravi and his duties, but his emotions remained connected to the perpetrator who had hurt his child.

***

Michael parked the Audi on one of the side streets a few blocks from the east side of the Grand Bazaar. They walked the short distance and entered through the same doorway Ali had entered four days earlier. The familiar feeling he remembered from many years ago immediately returned to him. The Grand Bazaar had always fascinated him, despite the dozens, perhaps even hundreds of times he had visited it while stationed in Istanbul. There was something magical about walking through the world's oldest and largest indoor market. It wasn't only its vast size, with over sixty streets and four thousand shops; it was the cornucopia of sights, smells and sounds that created such a unique sensory experience. Everything from Turkish and Persian rugs, pottery and ceramics, lamps and glassware, polished brass, silver and gold sold there, to the exotic scents of incense intermingled with the mouthwatering smell of lamb, beef and chicken kabobs and shawarma, with the cacophony of over two hundred and fifty thousand daily visitors haggling over prices and making deals with the vendors and merchants, made it like no other place Michael had experienced anywhere else in the world. No wonder it had been used as a venue in two James Bond 007 movies, along with a host of other films. It was also an excellent location to meet clandestinely amidst the myriad of narrow alleyways separating the thousands of booths and shops. Michael and Asya had done so often when obtaining sensitive information from contacts and assets with ties to terrorist organizations. It was a place Michael felt a certain connection to.

They walked together side by side in no particular hurry, gazing at the various merchandise and wares. It wasn't as if they were tourists fascinated by the first experience of visiting the Grand Bazaar, but to anyone looking at them, they appeared like an ordinary couple in no particular hurry, just enjoying each other's company. Perhaps on a certain subconscious level, that was exactly what they were doing. It was difficult for either of them to acknowledge at the present moment that, in a little over twenty-four hours, Michael would be going on a dangerous covert mission he might not be returning from. For now, they were content just to enjoy each other's company, as if they were a couple who had all the time in the world together. It was a mutual feeling both of them shared without either having to say anything to the other.

"Want to get a bite to eat before we get your supplies?" Asya asked.

"You read my mind. I wasn't hungry earlier, but the smell of the shawarma is causing my salivary glands to go crazy." His butterflies momentarily let up at the thought of biting into one of those delectable pleasures he remembered from years back. He had eaten shawarma back in D.C. and Seattle, but there was something about the real thing that couldn't be replicated anywhere else.

"You miss your shawarma, I see." Asya recalled how he never tired of eating the same thing each time they had to grab a quick bite to eat on the job.

"I could eat one five days a week," he replied enthusiastically.

"Yes, I remember," she laughed.

They walked up to the first shawarma shop they came across, and sat on two stools at the small counter across from the grill and rotating rotisseries. They were greeted by a fat middle-aged man wearing an oil-stained white T-shirt, a couple of days' stubble on his unshaven face and a cigarette hanging from his lips.

"*Merhaba,*" he grunted, blowing smoke into their faces.

"*Merhaba,*" Asya replied, slightly annoyed, moving her face away from the cloud of smoke.

"Ahh, *afedersiniz,*" the shop owner apologized, embarrassed at his blunder. He pulled the cigarette out of his mouth, placing it on the edge of the counter.

Michael looked at the cigarette and glanced at Asya with an amused look on his face. Nothing had changed in Istanbul.

"What can I get you?" he asked them.

"I will have a chicken kebab and a Çoban Salatası," Asya said, ordering a traditional Turkish salad, consisting of finely chopped tomatoes, cucumbers, green peppers, onion, and parsley, with lemon juice, olive oil, and salt dressing.

"Two lamb shawarmas and a plate of hummus for me," Michael said, managing to spout out his order in Turkish.

"To drink?" the fat Turk asked.

"*Gazlı su*," Asya said—sparkling water.

"Coke light."

The shop owner turned to the column of sizzling lamb slices rotating around the orange-hot electric burner. He picked up a long knife from the counter and began slicing thin pieces of lamb, which fell onto the foil draped around the bottom of the rotisserie.

"You are hungry," Asya commented.

"It may be my last good meal," Michael half-joked.

"Let's go sit over in the corner." She gestured towards the small booth towards the back of the shop.

They sat across each other on the pillow-cushioned benches a few inches above the floor, sliding in cross-legged under the low table. The fat Turk brought over their drinks, then returned a few minutes later with their meals. Michael tore off a piece of pide, the Turkish equivalent of pita bread, dipped it into the plate of hummus and tossed it in his mouth.

"Mm, mm. Just as I remember it. I've tried so many different ways of making it, but I can never get it to taste quite the same."

"I didn't realize you liked Turkish food so much."

"In general, I love Middle Eastern food. Who knows, I may have some Turkish blood in me. After all, your people did subjugate my people for four hundred years."

"Oh, don't start the Greek-Turkish guilt trip with me. For all you know, you may be more Turkish than Greek depending on where your ancestors were from. Didn't the Byzantines control most of modern-day Turkey at some point in history?"

"If you put it that way, you may even have some Greek in you. I'll start calling you Asya Papadopoulos," he laughed.

"Speaking of which, what kind of Greek name is Blackstone? I had always meant to ask you. That is not your true family name, is it?"

"That's a long story. It happened to my grandfather when he first came to the United States back during World War II and he was drafted into the US Army. They couldn't pronounce his name in Greek, so it was translated to its English equivalent."

"So, what was your family's actual surname?"

"It was Mavropetrakis, which means black stone or rock in Greek."

"Mavropetrakis. It is not too difficult to pronounce," she said.

"Well, maybe not for you, but I guess it was for some hillbilly eighty years ago."

"Hillbilly?"

"Like an uneducated village person."

"Oh, you mean a *köylü*."

"A what?"

"A *köylü*. How do you say in English? Yokel?"

"Yeah, that would be a good characterization from what I remember of my grandfather's story. It was even funnier hearing him tell me how my grandmother tried to pronounce Blackstone when he went back to Greece after the war and asked her to marry him. Forty years later, it still sounded funny every time she said her last name in her Greek accent," Michael recalled fondly.

"Are your parents still living?"

"Yep. They're in Florida. That's down in the southeast corner of the US."

"Where Miami Beach and Disney World are located. Correct?"

"That's right. You know your geography."

"Of course. Did you not learn all the countries and their capitals when you went to school?"

"No, geography isn't one of the subjects they emphasize in American education."

"That is surprising."

"You would be surprised by a lot of things about the education system in the United States. There's a reason why Americans are some of the most uninformed people regarding what's going on in the world around them. Most kids getting out of high school can't even name ten states, let alone ten countries."

"That is a shame to have such a poor educational system in the richest country in the world. It is very surprising, considering there are so many great universities in the US."

"Higher education is a different story, but even then, there are some college grads that don't know how to write a proper sentence or do basic math, like division or percentages."

"Your daughter—Sam, isn't it? Is she still in school?"

"Yeah, she's in her second year in medical school at the University of California in Los Angeles. She's a real go-getter."

"Do you see each other often?"

"No. We don't have that close a relationship with each other. I tried to be a part of her life after I left the CIA and returned to Seattle, but it wasn't something she cared to pursue. Kind of hard when it's one-sided. I saw her once last summer when she was up visiting Karen. We had lunch together."

"I am sorry, Michael. I remember how much you treasured her when you were here in Turkey. I can still picture her with her little ponytails when I saw her that time you had me over for dinner to meet your wife. She must have been four or five years old. She was such a cute little girl."

"Oh yeah. I remember. Actually, how could I forget? It was probably one of the most nervous days of my life."

"Nervous? Why were you nervous?" Asya asked, amused.

"Considering I had been working up the courage for over a month to finally break the news to Karen that my new Turkish partner, who I had been doing all-night surveillances with, was a beautiful former Olympic gymnast, I would say I had good reason to be a little bit concerned about how the evening would go with the two of you sitting down over dinner together. Things actually turned out better than I had expected with how the two of you clicked pretty well. That's not what I was expecting to happen the entire day leading up to it."

"Oh, Michael, how did you think it would go? That your wife would take one look at me and assume there was something going on between us? I remember Karen to be an intelligent and self-confident woman with good intuition. She would have been able to sense something right away if there was anything between us beyond our work. I was not a threat to her. That is why we got along so well. She also knew you would never betray her."

"I guess it depends what you mean by betray. In the end, I did, just not with another woman. I chose my job over her and Sam. I don't know if that's any better. I'm sure it must have hurt her just as much."

"Don't be so hard on yourself. This work of ours, of mine now, is not easy on marriages and family life. I am guilty of making the same choice you did, career over love. It is not any easier. It is just that I do not have to carry the guilt of having caused someone pain, other than maybe to myself. But I'm the one who made that decision and brought it on to myself. I'm sure you did not marry Karen with the intent of bringing sorrow and pain to her and then divorcing her when you got tired of being with her. No, you truly loved her. Things just happen in life. We grow older with someone and we realize we are not the person we thought we were and our spouse is not the person we thought they were. Most people try to work things out and make the best of life together, for others there are just too many unresolvable differences. I am not trying to make light of what you went through, just trying to give some perspective."

"Geez, you could have your own daytime show and rival Dr. Phil. You trying to make me feel better?"

"Michael, we have not seen each other in over fifteen years, but I can sense something is troubling you. I don't know what it is, but you are carrying some burden that is weighing on you. There is something wiser about you. That is very captivating in an older man who is still quite attractive. But you have also experienced much pain, perhaps while picking up some of that wisdom. I can see it in your eyes."

"Older man? What are you getting at? I don't mind the captivating part, however," he joked.

"I see you do not want to talk about it. Maybe you will later. I told you how surprised, happy, and amazed I have felt since you suddenly reappeared in my life. I don't want you leaving for this mission with something weighing on you. I want there to be some chance I will see you again. I do not want to settle for just forty-eight hours after seventeen years and then never to see you again. I do not mean I expect anything, even if you do make it back—which, I mean, you will come back, it is just, I wanted there to be a chance for us to spend some time together as friends. Do you understand what I just tried to say? I do not even know if I understand," she said, flustered.

He looked in her eyes and saw a vulnerability he had never seen before. Even though she was older and wiser now and had reached a position of responsibility and power, she had revealed to him the feminine side of her that yearned for the companionship of a mate, a lover, a partner in life. Although he had always been aware of her physical beauty, he had dealt with that part of her as if she had been his sister or cousin. It was the only way in his mind to compartmentalize any desires that could have progressed into a physically intimate situation that would have been disastrous on several levels. Instead, he had developed a friendship with her that in some ways had been more intimate than any physical relationship. It was a close friendship of trust, of sharing each other's thoughts, laughing at each other's sense of humor, enjoying each other's company, much as if it had been with many of his guy buddies from Special Forces, yet different. She was a woman, a beautiful, intelligent, confident woman. He wasn't looking at her as his sister or cousin any longer.

"I get what you're saying, Awsh," he told her with a gentle smile.

She returned the smile. Their eyes locked, searching the deepest recesses of each other's being. He could feel it, the emotional tug that was drawing them together. It was something he could never have imagined less than a week ago, even in his wildest, most bizarre dreams. A week ago, intimacy with anyone had been the last thing on his mind. Through something beyond his control, his intention to take his life had been thwarted in a manner that didn't make any rational sense. It defied the laws of probability. Those things just didn't happen, not in the normal world. He couldn't explain it. Now, it was hard for him to remember what had been so terrible, what had weighed so heavily on him, that he had called it quits. He had never been a quitter his entire life. Perhaps that was what Asya had picked up on. How could he tell her that he had tried to take his own life, that he had been so weak? What would she think of him?

"Awsh, a week ago, I could never have imagined seeing you again. Now, all of a sudden, we're sitting across from each other, and I can't even begin to explain how it feels to see you again, talk to you, be in your presence. On one hand, it feels so natural, like no time has passed and we've always been together. On the other, it almost feels like some cruel joke, because I know the reality of what lies ahead for me. You've always been a very special person to me, even after all these years. I can tell you feel something for me also, more than what we had just as friends before, but I'm not the same man you knew. My life hasn't gone the way I thought it would go. There are some things about me that would make you see me differently."

"Hm. So, you think that I'm the same person I was, the same person you remember? I know you have changed. Both of us have changed. We all face struggles in life. Whatever you are carrying that is making you believe I would think any less of you, you are wrong. At least give me the benefit of the doubt, as your friend, that I know the type of man you are, Michael."

He struggled with the idea of revealing the truth to her about just how low he had sunk, the truth about what he had attempted. Without giving much thought about exactly what he would tell her, the words began coming out of his mouth, "Awsh, less than a week ago, I…"

The Iridium satellite phone in Michael's coat pocket rang, interrupting him. Surprised, he reached in, pulling it out and looking at the number calling him. He recognized it immediately. He had memorized it, the only number that would be calling him. It was Harry's Iridium. He pressed the answer button. They were alone in the restaurant, and the owner was busy watching his small television as Michael put the oversized mobile phone up to his ear.

"Hello." He waited to hear Harry's voice. "Hello." Nothing. He looked at the signal strength, which was barely registering. Being under the cover of the indoor market, it was surprising there was even a signal to get through for it to ring.

"Awsh, this is important. I need to get it. We need to get out from under cover." He stood up.

He was about to reach for his wallet, when he remembered he hadn't had a chance to exchange any dollars for lira since arriving in Turkey. He looked at Asya, who was reaching into her purse for her wallet. She laid down sixty lira, the equivalent of eleven dollars, onto the table as they made for the door, the restaurant owner thanking her for the generous tip she had left over and above the cost of their meal.

"It's my contact back in D.C. The only one I have that can be of any help to me. If he's calling, it's important," he told her as they made their way down the crowded street.

Michael glanced at his watch. It was 4:17 p.m., 8:17 a.m. back in D.C. Harry had just started his day. He wondered what Harry had needed to tell him to break operational silence. It wasn't that Michael had any concerns that their communications via his Iridium would be monitored. It was just a practice in intelligence operations to keep communications minimal—only when absolutely necessary—meaning it must be something significant. They finally found an exit on the west side of the Bazaar across from the Beyazıt Mosque and made their way to the other side of the street and into the large courtyard of the mosque. They walked towards a less crowded area, where Michael dialed the number and listened while it connected, then began to ring.

Harry, who was sitting on a bench in one of the outside courtyards of the Lockheed Martin headquarters campus, hit the answer button and put his Iridium up to his ear. "How you doing, pal?"

"All is good. Connected with my friend I was telling you about, and she's going to help me with my travel plans from here. She's got some connections and has arranged a lift for me without drawing much attention. Will probably be heading out in about thirty-six hours or so. Hoping I can track down my old buddy and get him to come back with me. How are things with you?"

"Just busy as always, you know how it is. I got an unusual call from an old contact of mine who works at the Kirya. He's the senior guy in charge of their air assets. He was calling to ask if I could help him out by pulling some strings and getting some technicians out to them ASAP to work out a technical problem they're having with some equipment, some very advanced hardware they've gotten from us recently. Would only be calling and asking for a favor like this if they had something pretty significant on the horizon. Thought you might want to know, not to put any more pressure on you."

Michael pondered what Harry had told him. He clearly understood Harry was giving him a warning that something big was about to take place, but he was drawing a blank about what he meant by the Kirya. It sounded familiar, but he was having trouble placing it. He glanced at Asya with a questioning look and mouthed, "Kirya?"

Asya thought for a moment before it came to her. "IDF headquarters," she whispered.

Michael nodded in acknowledgment, recalling the name of the compound where the General Staff of the Israeli Defense Force was located in Tel Aviv.

"I see. Do you have a timeframe when this might take place?"

"Realistically, I don't think we'll be able to get anyone out there until Friday. I imagine it will take the techs at least a day to fix the problem and test the system, so I would bet on Monday, but it could even be Sunday at the earliest. My pal gave me some lame excuse for the rush, but he wouldn't be asking for a favor like this unless they were pretty desperate. I'm going to touch base with the program manager and have him keep me updated real-time on when his techs actually complete the work. This is too important to let slip through the cracks. If my pal's outfit goes ahead with what I think they're planning, it could be the start of something that may quickly spiral out of control. That's the last place you want to be if that happens. You know what I mean?"

"That's not good. Doesn't leave much time."

"No, it doesn't. You sure you're up for this? You know you might not make it out of this," Harry asked, voicing his first sign of concern.

"If you're asking whether I think I can pull this off, the answer is, I really don't know. If you're asking if I still want to go through with this, I've come to terms with what could happen to me. Either way, it's not like we have any other choice. If I manage to get him out so he can go public with what he knows, maybe we can put the brakes on this and save lives. If I don't make it, then what's one more life going to matter, apart from it being mine?"

Neither of them spoke as they both silently acknowledged the reality of the situation Michael was facing. Asya looked at him with concern. Just hearing one side of the conversation was enough for her to understand the seriousness of what had been said.

"Okay. I'll do whatever I can on my end. Maybe you should give your friend there my contact info. She can call me directly on my cell if she needs to."

"Awsh, can I give my friend your number?" he asked her.

She nodded her head in the affirmative, reciting it into the phone's mouthpiece as Michael held it out to her.

"Did you get that?" Michael asked.

Harry repeated it as he wrote it down. "Don't forget to give her my number. And might I say, she has a sexy voice."

"I'll make sure she has it. You can verify it's her by the name of our favorite rooftop bar in Athens. And I'll let her know you like the sound of her voice."

"Okay buddy, be safe. Make smart decisions. Don't take unnecessary risks. Weigh the odds and play the percentages. You gotta come out of this so we can pound a few beers and spin tales about how you saved the world," Harry told him, the sound of his voice revealing his concern.

"Yes, Dad, I'll try to stay out of trouble," Michael assured him, trying to lighten the mood. "I'll definitely take you up on the beers. Out here."

"Talk to you soon, pal. Out." Michael heard the other end disconnect.

He turned to Asya. "Did you get most of that?"

"Enough to understand something is about to happen rather soon. What are the Israelis preparing to do?"

"He's not sure. He's an old trusted colleague and good friend of mine. Now he works for Lockheed Martin in their security department. He said an Israeli contact of his, high up in the IDF General Staff, called him and asked him for a special favor." Michael related to her the details.

"If that is the case, it could very well be for their F-35 fighters. They had taken delivery of them from the United States over the past year. I remember reading some intelligence reports that stated they may have already activated their first squadron."

"I didn't realize you were also involved in foreign military intelligence?" Michael commented, somewhat surprised.

"It is just something I read in one of our general intelligence briefings. Keeping track of what our neighbors in the region are up to militarily is one of my organization's primary roles."

"You could be right. An air strike of some sort against Iran would be pretty risky, even for the Israelis, but the way things are going, I wouldn't rule anything out. If that happens, the Iranians will be forced to retaliate. Between their missiles in Lebanon under the control of Hezbollah and their long-range missiles in Iran, some will probably get through Israel's air defenses. If the casualties are high enough, the Israelis may feel they have no other choice but to respond with nukes. If that happens, you know what will happen in the whole region. That very well may have been the reason for the assassination of the Iranian foreign minister, to provoke a tit for tat, causing chaos and destruction throughout the Middle East."

"What would that accomplish? It would take out a huge percentage of the world's petroleum supplies and cause an international economic catastrophe. It would not be good for anyone, including the United States or Russia."

"It would certainly kill the stock market. Things could be even worse than what they were in 2008. It doesn't make sense economically."

"Not economically, but geopolitically, if you think about it."

"How so?"

"Russia and the United States would collectively control most of the world's petroleum supply. They would wield much more influence in the world than they do now. Think of the added leverage the United States would have on China."

"Yeah, but think of the added leverage Russia would also have, especially on Europe. I don't think the US would ever go for that."

"Michael, whatever additional leverage Russia would get would be nothing compared to what the United States would gain. It would amplify each country's influence in the world equally, but the United States is so much larger and stronger, both militarily and economically than Russia. It would be an exponential increase for the United States over Russia."

Michael thought about Asya's argument. The more he considered her reasoning, the more he realized what she said made sense. Although there were a lot of variables and unknowns in what could happen when the international community was hit with such a traumatic jolt to its long-established order, when all the dust had settled, the United States would ultimately be in the driver's seat as far as its position of unparalleled influence on the world stage. China's economy would certainly be held hostage by the US and the other oil-producing countries aligned with it. Even Venezuela, who would be the largest remaining OPEC producer, had finally returned to the US's geopolitical orbit, following the ouster of its nationalist president as a result of the economic collapse because of gross mismanagement and the collapse of oil prices. Russia alone, even with all of its oil production, would not be able to do much even if it wanted, in supplying China with all of its petroleum requirements. Michael was impressed with Asya's intellect and her ability to look beyond the obvious. He'd always recognized she was smart, but this was impressive even for her.

"Wow. Do you happen to play chess?" he asked her.

"No. I have never tried it. I have always wondered if I would like it. Why do you ask?"

"I think you would like it. Let's hope we don't have to find out if your theory is correct. I'd rather find out what they were hoping to accomplish when they're on trial and on their way to prison. If we can get this crazy plot stopped, maybe all those responsible will be exposed and held accountable, but that's not going to happen if I can't get Ali out. This is definitely not the direction my life was headed a week ago," he uttered.

Asya wondered what he meant by that. What direction had Michael's life been heading than a week ago? He had been about to tell her something when they had been interrupted by the phone call. She didn't want to pry into Michael's personal life, but at the same time, she didn't want him to go off on what he was about to face if there was something he wanted to get off his chest. She felt a connection to him, as if they had not been separated all those years. She wondered if he was experiencing similar feelings. She felt something, as if he was wanting to draw closer to her, but something was holding him back. Maybe he would tell her later, back at her place.

"Let's go back into the bazaar and get your supplies, then we can head back to my apartment and relax some. You have a big day tomorrow; you need to get some rest. It may be some time before you will have a chance to again."

"Sounds like a plan," he told her as they headed back towards the entrance of the bazaar. He grabbed her hand as they walked side by side across the street. It felt natural to both of them, something neither of them could have imagined seventeen years ago.

"By the way, what is the code word I will need to use if I contact your friend?"

"It's the rooftop Galaxy Bar."

"Rooftop Galaxy Bar. I am guessing there are some stories associated with that place?" she stated more than asked.

"Oh, there are always stories with Harry," he replied.

***

The unmarked white G550, with a tail number that showed it was registered to a holding company in the Cayman Islands, touched down on runway 17L, then taxied its way to the pad by the VIP terminal, where all the other corporate jets dropped off their passengers. Whether it was other countries' government officials or CEOs doing business in Turkey, privacy away from the commercial airline terminal was something that was afforded to those with power and wealth. The chief of station waited outside with the ground crew and a Turkish immigration official as the Gulfstream taxied to one of the drop-off spots and stopped, cutting its engines as the door opened and the aircraft's stairs extended to the ground. The COS walked up to the ladder with the immigration official as Canton made his way out of the aircraft and descended the stairs. Upon reaching the ground, Canton pulled out his black diplomatic passport and presented it to the immigration official, who, after examining it and comparing the photograph to Canton, handed it back, gave a slight nod, then turned and headed back towards the terminal.

"Jonathan, how was the flight?" Bob, the chief of station, walked up and gave his hand.

"Never bad when you have your own plane to fly in," Canton boasted.

"That's us over there." The COS gestured towards the dark blue BMW 550i with the discreetly tinted armored windows.

As the second most important US official next to the ambassador, the chief of station was entitled to the added protection of an armored vehicle. Unlike the ambassador, who had the latest Mercedes 560 S Class, keeping a low profile was the chief of station's priority. Although the body of the 550i was from the previous BMW model line, under its skin was the latest technology BMW had to offer, married with the some of the most advanced in custom vehicle armoring. Other than an RPG or direct hit from a sizeable IED, the BMW, with its run-flat tires, was designed to survive an attack long enough to be drivable out of the kill zone to safety.

Canton and the COS walked over and got into the rear of the vehicle. The driver and a CIA security officer were sitting in the front. Bob handed Canton a Glock 26 subcompact 9mm pistol.

"Thanks." Canton took the gun.

"Where to, Jonathan?"

"The Ritz-Carlton. And I want a clean rental delivered there. Either a BMW 650 or an Audi 8, preferably black, but I'll settle for graphite, or even dark blue, in that order. You can charge it to the Mohammedi operation, Nile Diamond. Whoever drops it off, just stick the key and the contract in a sealed envelope addressed to me. You can leave it at the front desk, they'll get it to me. And by the way, make sure it's a new model, not like this old heap."

"Nothing like advertising your presence," the COS commented.

"Sometimes blending in with the movers and shakers keeps you from being noticed when you're hiding in plain sight. That's the problem with a lot of the old conventional way of thinking in this agency. Makes you fail to take an aggressive approach and get anything done."

Bob didn't bother to comment, wondering to himself how Canton had made it to the position of deputy director. "You heard him, Sam, the Ritz-Carlton," the COS instructed his driver.

"So, Bob, give me an update on what progress you've made so far on locating Shiravi or Blackstone."

Doing his best not to show his annoyance at Canton, Bob answered, "We're still working on it. We haven't been able to find any info on either of them. We've reached out to all our assets and sources. No one knows a thing. I'm in continuous contact with the director of MIT, and the Legat is in communication with the minister of the interior. They don't have anything either, at least nothing they've shared so far," he said, referring to the FBI legal attaché assigned to the embassy.

"That's unsatisfactory, Bob. You haven't found out anything. You're supposed to have this country wired. Doesn't look that way to me," Canton said condescendingly.

"That's the situation at the moment. Sometimes that's just how things go. Being able to exercise patience while diligently continuing to work all the angles is what it takes to get things accomplished out in the field. At least, that's what every successful case officer knows." Bob couldn't resist putting Canton in his place.

Canton noticed the slight grin on the security officer's face in the front seat. How dare the COS humiliate him in the presence of two junior officers. He would give Bob his payback when he was appointed as the new DCI. He'd never cared much for Bob in the first place. He was one of those career old-timers who had served as a chief of station several times over the course of their careers. They thought they were the authority on all intelligence matters, yet many of them had never held a senior management position back at headquarters. When he became director, old Bob here would be putting in his retirement papers after being assigned to a go-nowhere liaison position at some other agency like NRO or NSA. This would surely be Bob's last chief of station posting.

"I don't want any more excuses, Bob. Don't try to justify your failures by lecturing me about intelligence matters. Just remember, I'm a deputy director.

You're just one among a hundred or so other chiefs, and a washed-up one at that. You really think you have much of a future when you can't produce anything in your own backyard when the Agency needs it most? How's that going to look?" Canton sneered.

"Jonathan, there's a reason why you've never had a COS posting, or even a deputy COS posting. It's because you're a pompous fool who's never accomplished anything of significance as a case officer. Believe me when I tell you, I'm not the only one in this outfit with that opinion. I don't know how the hell you ever made it to deputy director, but don't come into my country, tell me I don't know what I'm doing, and try to intimidate me with your pathetic insinuations that you hold any leverage over my future. I can retire anytime I want, and although I'll stay as long as the work is still challenging and rewarding, I got a lot of other plans I'm waiting on when all this is over. So, if you need my assistance while you're doing whatever you're doing in my country, I'll help you any way I can. Otherwise, you know what you can do with yourself." Bob stared him in the eyes after he finished making clear what he thought about him.

Canton felt the rage boil inside him. With all his effort, he tried to focus his anger towards meeting Bob's stare, but he couldn't help but notice out of the corner of his eye that the young security officer in the front seat was barely containing his smile. Although he couldn't see the driver, he was sure the same was happening with him. His rage continued to escalate to the point where his right eye began to twitch.

Bob finally broke the tension. "You need to chill out and get yourself under control or you're going to implode. The last thing I need to be dealing with right now is a headquarters weenie that had a meltdown out in the field. Do what you need to do while you're over here, then go back to headquarters, where you're obviously of some use."

His eye still twitching uncontrollably, Canton turned and faced the window, feigning observing the passing scenery. His eye continued to twitch uncontrollably. His thoughts were muddled by his anger. He knew he had to pull himself together and think clearly, but he had been thrown off balance by the unexpected clash with the COS. He couldn't let that happen again. He had to maintain his composure. Otherwise things could slip out of his control, and he would lose the ability to keep them moving in the right direction. Bob was an insignificant factor in the outcome of his situation. He needed to find out if Tarhan knew anything about Blackstone and Shiravi, then silence her, and then make sure Blackstone and Shiravi were also silenced. How that happened, he really didn't care. He didn't need Bob's assistance for that; he had Rostov to assist him. He needed to track him down. That would be his first order of business after he got to the hotel. He watched the passing scenery in silence as his eye continued with its uncontrollable spasms. *How much further is the damn hotel?* He would exact retribution from all who had slighted him. He would have the final satisfaction.

Chapter 16

Asya drove her Audi through the opening electric gate of her apartment complex around the corner of the building and pulled into her covered parking spot. Michael got out, carrying sacks filled with his peasant clothing disguise. They had decided it would be more practical to obtain a basket, dates and goat cheese in Agri rather than take them on the plane. Ercan would be able to help them with that. Asya got out, clicking her key fob to lock the Audi, and joined Michael as they walked to the foyer of her building.

"Stairs or elevator?" he asked her.

"I would normally say stairs, just so I could kick you in your butt, as you used to say, but I don't have it in me right now to take on five flights of stairs in heels and a skirt. I think it would give you an unfair advantage," she laughed.

"Oh, so you think you could kick my butt? I'm carrying bags. That evens things up."

"You really want to race me?"

"Not really. I just wanted to watch you run up the stairs in a skirt and heels, something I don't remember ever having seen you in."

"I suppose you are right about that. Working on a team with all men, I wanted to blend in and not attract attention. I always wore slacks and functional shoes. The last thing I wanted was to have my colleagues gazing at me never take me seriously."

"Good that you did. Otherwise I would have been gazing also. That would have been very bothersome to me, considering how much time we spent together."

"Bothersome to you? How do you think it would have been for me, having you staring at my legs?"

"I think you would have liked it," Michael needled her as they got into the tight elevator.

"Oh, you think so? So why is it you are gazing at my legs now, Mr. Blackstone?" she asked with an amused smile.

"Rats, you caught me," he admitted.

"I will forgive you this time, only because I know it is such a new experience for you to see me in a skirt."

"So, what happens if I'm caught again?"

"I'm not sure. It depends if I start liking it," she replied coyly as they looked at each other across the bags in Michael's arms.

It hit him as they stood there waiting for the elevator to reach its destination that they were flirting with each other. They had always enjoyed the back-and-forth banter, trying to one-up each other as partners who spend long hours together often do. This was different, however. This had definitely crossed over into flirting, something he never could have imagined in the past. Of course, then, he had been married, and the relationship with Asya had been professional, something he never would have considered violating. They had become good friends as well as trusted partners, but the boundaries defining their relationship had precluded anything like this. He liked it. It felt natural. He felt comfortable stepping into Asya's sphere of intimacy and allowing her into his. He sensed the same on her part. On one hand, it was wonderful; on the other, there was a cruel irony to it. In twenty-four hours, he might never see her again.

He needed to put the brakes on his emotions. He needed to keep his head clear. He wouldn't stand a chance of succeeding with his mission if he was preoccupied thinking about her. Spending tonight with Asya was probably not the wisest thing to do. The way things were heading, there was a good chance of physical intimacy between them, especially after one or two glasses of wine. That would be a major mistake. He was certain both of them would regret it later. Maybe he should check into a hotel for the night. They could meet up tomorrow morning on the way to the airport. That would ensure nothing would happen. Then again, they would be lying in their separate beds, thinking about each other as sleep escaped them. That was the last thing either of them needed with what lay ahead. How would he even bring up the idea of staying in a hotel? What would she think? Would she be relieved, or feel completely rejected? That was the last thing he ever wanted her to feel. He would have relished a chance to spend some time with her, the opportunity to experience a completely different side of her, a chance for both of them to share in each other's intimacy. Less than a week ago, he had been in such a dark place, he'd tried to kill himself. Now, the thought of being able to spend some time with Asya, if for no other reason than to explore any possibility of a future with each other, made him feel like he had just awakened on a bright summer morning to the sound of birds singing outside. There truly was a cruel irony to his situation.

The elevator came to a sudden stop as it reached the fifth floor, jolting Michael away from his thoughts back to Asya. He was taking in as much of her as he could, with however much time they had left together, until they would have to part ways, perhaps for good. There was no way he could go to a hotel tonight.

"What are you thinking?" she asked him, studying his face.

"What am I thinking? Hm, I don't know if I should tell you. It might freak you out," he said, pushing open the elevator door with his back and stepping out into the fifth-floor landing.

"It's that terrible?"

"No, it's not terrible."

"Why do you think it will, how did you say, freak me out? I take it you mean overwhelm me. Is it overwhelming you?"

"Yeah, in a way it is."

"So, are you going to talk to me about it, or just leave me wondering, feeling overwhelmed because you will not share your thoughts with me at a time like this, when we may never see each other again? Are you going to keep whatever you are feeling about us to yourself?" she asked, looking him straight in the eyes.

Michael didn't expect the directness of her question. It wasn't so much what she said, but rather the emotion behind it, her body language, the chemistry that was developing between them. Acknowledging that would break down the last barrier keeping them from openly declaring their feelings for each other. He just couldn't do it. It would be the most foolish and selfish thing he could do under the circumstances. Foolish because everything he had been taught in the CIA stressed the increased risk and vulnerability to case officers operating in hostile environments if their head wasn't clear, preoccupied with personal issues that clouded their judgment. Selfish because he would be bringing about a vulnerability in Asya's heart that she hadn't had just two days ago. It was something she didn't need, especially when the odds of his ever seeing her again weren't in his favor. It would be a cruel thing to do to someone he cared for so much. *Stop playing games with her. You just tried killing yourself a few days ago. It wasn't bad enough all the pain and hurt you caused Karen and Eva, now you're going to do the same to Asya, just because she makes you feel better about yourself. Don't put her through that, you selfish bastard,* he chastised himself.

"It's just something I'm struggling with. I don't want to bother you with it. You're dealing with enough right now with all your responsibilities. You don't need to hear my issues."

"It sounds like you do not want to tell me. It's okay, I respect your privacy. I know you have a lot on your mind about what lies ahead. Of course it's overwhelming. I know how it would make me feel, if I were in your situation. I do not want to make it any more stressful for you. I will make us some dinner, we can have a glass of wine, relax a bit, and go to sleep early. We will have a long day tomorrow, especially you. You will have many long days ahead of you. You need to be as well rested as possible."

He could tell her feelings had been slightly hurt. Her words made sense and expressed her thoughtfulness towards him, but he could hear the disappointment in her voice that he had chosen not to trust her with his feelings. They would have dinner, enjoy each other's company, reminisce about the good old days together, and call it an early night.

She pulled out her key and inserted it in the high-security lock, turning it three times until the dead bolt slid out from the metal frame securing the steel reinforced solid oak door. In her line of work, her personal security was something she didn't take for granted. Living on the top floor of her building offered the added safeguard against entry from the exterior, unless of course access was gained via one of her neighbor's balconies. Her final safeguard was the Sig Sauer P290 subcompact 9mm she carried in the quick-release holster built into the interior of her black leather purse. The purse, made by a custom leather designer whose clientele included some of the ruling elite class in Turkey, didn't sport the Gucci name, but the quality of the craftsmanship equaled anything the luxury Italian brand had on the market. Both had been gifts from her father when she had been promoted to her first supervisory position.

They entered her apartment, where she kicked off her heels and slipped on her fuzzy slippers she had left just inside the door. Michael took off his shoes and left them by the door.

"I'm going to get out of this and put on something more comfortable," she informed him as she walked down the hallway to her bedroom.

"Okay," he replied as he walked over to the tan leather couch and plopped down. He looked around at her apartment. It had a comfortable warm feeling to it. It wasn't just the décor, it was the way it reflected her personality. You could tell right away it was a woman's place. It had a softness that reflected a feminine touch to it, but it also revealed the assertiveness and self-assuredness of its occupant. It would have been nice to spend some more time here, he thought, aware that this might be the last night he would find himself in such a comfortable environment. The possibility of finding himself in an eight-by-ten-foot cell in Evin Prison made him want to take it all in, while he could. He pictured himself spending evenings sitting on this couch with Asya leaned up next to him, both of them sipping a glass of wine, enjoying each other's company. Part of him wanted to escape from what was awaiting him. Why was it his responsibility to save the world? He was just one man. A washed-up former intelligence officer who had been selling real estate for the past twelve years. The odds he faced were incredible, astronomical. Did he really believe deep inside that he stood any chance of succeeding? He would more than likely be captured or killed before he even got to Tehran. Even if he did make it to Tehran, how would he get Ali out? Track down the director of the MOIS and convince him to break Ali out of prison? That was insanity. He would be wasting his life for nothing. He had a second chance now. A chance for a new beginning. A chance to do it right this time. A chance with Asya.

Stop it! Just stop it! You are such a fool. What chance do you think you would have with Asya if you turned tail and ran like a coward, after everything that has happened? What would she think of you? You think she would have the slightest bit of respect for you? You wouldn't be able to look yourself in the mirror. Better you should have succeeded in ending it all last week than to back out now. It's not like anything is being taken away from you. For all practical purposes, you made that decision for yourself five days ago. Suck it up and be a man. There's no other choice now. You know what needs to be done.

He closed his eyes, placing his forehead in the palm of his hand as he came to terms with his future. He knew the second thoughts were being brought about because of his feelings for Asya. Two days ago, he had had no doubts about what needed to be done or any fears. It wasn't because of any misconceptions about what could likely happen to him, it was just that any of those possibilities didn't make him feel as he was giving up anything in his life. He had come to terms with the fact that his life had already been forfeited. He no longer had any claim to it. Its sole purpose now was to rescue Ali and save as many lives as possible. If he somehow survived, maybe then he could reclaim it for himself once again. The sooner he came to terms with that, the sooner he could clear his mind of all the confusion and doubt and be able to focus on what lay ahead.

He looked up at Asya, returning to the living room in black Lycra tights and a loose lavender sweatshirt that hung partly down her arm, exposing her neck and shoulder. He was mesmerized by her presence. His thoughts returned to the image of her snuggled up next to him on the couch, her head leaning against his shoulder as they sipped their wine and shared each other's company. This wasn't going to be easy.

"You look comfy." He smiled at her as she walked over to him and stood in front of him.

"I feel much better."

"It's funny seeing you in a tailor-made woman's business suit that highlights in what great shape you're still in. Different from what I remember seeing you in seventeen years ago. I mean, don't get me wrong, not funny as in ha-ha, just unusual seeing that side of you. I mean, not unusual. I always thought you were a beautiful, attractive, woman, I'd even go as far as to say sexy, but I never thought of you in that way, back then, I mean. What I mean is, I like seeing this side of you also," he fumbled with his words.

"You do? Well, I guess you have never seen me comfy like this in my home either. I would never have allowed you to spend the night at my apartment back then, unless of course you were in some danger. I don't think you would have ever been able to take me seriously if you had seen me in my fluffy slippers," she giggled.

"You had fluffy slippers back then?"

"I have had fluffy slippers all my life. I remember when I was nine or ten, the first pair of slippers my father had to buy me after my mother had died. They were some pink fluffy rabbit or mouse slippers, I don't remember, but I have had fuzzy slippers ever since. Just not rabbit or mouse anymore." She gave him a smile.

"That's a funny thing to learn about you now. I can't ever picture having a conversation about your fuzzy slippers seventeen years ago. Imagine what it would sound like having a discussion about fuzzy slippers with your counterterrorism partner," he laughed. "You know, Awsh, I like seeing this other side of you. It just really sucks when things are finally lined up in both our lives where that could happen, but fate has it completely out of our control." He gave her a melancholy smile.

The smile remained on Asya's face but began transforming from one of exuberance to one of fading warmth, like a late afternoon during an Indian summer. "I know, Michael. Trust me, I know. It has been tearing at me all day. I am not going to pretend like everything is just normal with me. We have always been completely honest and trusting with each other all the years we worked together. I am not going to change that because I feel something different, something more about you now. Two days ago, my life had been on the path that it found for many years now. I had made my choices and had resigned myself to the fact that I probably would be finishing off my remaining years alone. I do not know if I would have ever met some man as a friend, someone to share company with, but never someone who I would have such a strong emotional connection with, like I feel with you. All those years we worked together as partners, I treasured you as a friend and admired you as an example of the type of man I would want to have in my life. Ercan came close to that, but you know the story. It was a choice, a sacrifice that I was not willing to make. Now you have dropped back into my life, when there is no reason for us not to be with each other, but there is something beyond our control that makes it impossible again. It is like the world is pulling you away from me, and there is nothing that I can do to change that. It feels maddening, like I just want to scream at the top of my lungs. I feel completely lost, disoriented, as if I cannot even think about tomorrow. So, does that give you an idea of how I feel? I can't believe I told you all that. It was not what I was planning on telling you when I came back out in my fuzzy slippers. I was going to tell you that I was going to order some food to be delivered, because I did not want to waste time cooking when I have such little left to spend with you. Much less than what I just overwhelmed you with," she confessed, her smile melting away into sadness.

Michael studied her. She looked wounded, not physically, as when she had been stabbed and he had saved her life, but emotionally. She had always kept her guard up. It wasn't that they didn't sometimes have deep discussions during the long hours while on a surveillance in order to pass the time, but the discussions had centered on some topic of debate, never about themselves or each other. Now she had exposed her innermost feelings to him. She had answered any doubts he might have had about whether to stay the night or go to a hotel. How would it turn out? Would they stay up all night and just talk? Would she tuck in next to him on the couch as he put his arm around her, holding her close to him? Where would that lead? He had never felt unsure of himself around a woman. Now he felt like a nervous teenager on a first date. It was ridiculous. He was a grown man. It was Asya, after all. As much as a woman could be, she had been one of his best pals, a trusted partner, closer in some respects than even some of his SF buddies. Now he was unsure of how he should be around her. How would he maintain his composure in a little over twenty-four hours from now, when his life would depend on it? He wasn't ready for any of this. What was he thinking?

"Awsh, sit down." He patted the couch next to him.

She slid in next to him, close enough that it would have felt awkward and uncomfortable if he didn't place his arm around her. His hand came to rest on her bare shoulder. He felt her take in a deep breath and a long exhale, followed by a slight shudder that traveled through her body. The touch of her soft skin, the scent of her perfume, and the proximity of their bodies had an intoxicating effect on him. He didn't want to move, didn't want to ever have to leave this place. He remembered he wanted to tell her something, wanted to tell her what he had tried to do a few days ago. He wanted to try to explain how he had reached such a low point in his life. He wanted to try to make her understand what he felt like now, make her understand what he felt about her, about them. He wasn't sure if he could find the right words.

"You know, you've always been a very special person to me. Even though it's been all these years since we've seen each other, there aren't many people I've felt as close to as you. Part of me almost feels guilty about that. It makes me question whether I should have felt this way about Karen and Eva. I did love them, at least as much as I thought I could, but obviously not enough. Otherwise I would still be with one of them. I don't know why it is that I should feel this way about you. I mean, we always got along really well. You appreciated my strange sense of humor and understood my warped way of looking at the world, most of the time. And you...you had something about you that always made me look forward to spending time with you, even if it was chasing down terrorists. Our paths unexpectedly crossed for a while, and then just as suddenly split apart and we went our separate ways. It was one of those sad times that sticks with you, but you just tell yourself that's just the way life is and there's nothing you can do about it. You just go on, from time to time recalling some of the fond memories you shared together, but never thinking you'll ever see that person again. A week ago, I could never have imagined that I'd ever see you again. Those memories of you were still with me, but they had faded beneath everything else that had passed through my life since then. I wish somehow I could wipe clean a lot of what's happened to me since then, because it's changed me, and I don't know if you'd recognize me, or even think the same about me, once you got to know me again."

Asya sat silently cradled next to him, taking in what he had just told her. He could feel the rhythm of her breathing as they sat looking out at the lights of the city. He had just opened himself up, spilling his guts about how he really felt about her. He wanted to turn and gently kiss her on the neck but forced himself not to. A kiss right now wouldn't be a good idea. If he did, any semblance of control he still had remaining would come crumbling down, leading them towards a situation that wouldn't be good for either of them. He was content at the moment just to sit there in silence, feeling her presence, waiting for whenever she was ready to say something.

"Michael, I've changed also. Did you somehow believe that I went into suspended animation while you lived your life? I am not the same person you remember. I don't know what you would think of me either. We all make decisions we regret later in life, but hopefully we learn from those mistakes and they make us into a wiser person, shape us into a better version of ourselves. I know it doesn't always happen in the timeframe we would expect, but we just keep trying. I don't know how else to continue waking up every morning and face each day. I don't have a secret formula for getting through life. If you know of someone who does, please tell me, so I can quit my job, sell everything I own, and go follow them."

Michael felt the tenderness of her words, the message she was trying to convey to him. He searched for meaning in what the last twelve years of his life had been about, what purpose had they served. How had they made him a wiser person, a better version of himself? It was difficult to answer that from where he was now, but he was hoping Asya's words were somehow true. He realized he was gently rubbing her shoulder with his thumb. He couldn't remember when he had started doing that. She placed her hand on his knee. He instinctively reached for it with his other hand, placing it over hers, grasping it gently.

"There's something I need to tell you," he finally let out, tilting his head towards her face. "Something I've been wanting to tell you but couldn't seem to find the right words to explain it, so you could understand. I don't even know if I understand. It's something you need to know about me. I don't know if we'll ever see each other again, Awsh, but I can't leave without you knowing. If I somehow get through this and there's any hope of a future, a chance for us, I need to know whether you could ever want me, with all my failures, all my weaknesses, all my scars. Either way, then I would be able to face whatever lies ahead for me without constantly wondering. You understand what I'm trying to say?"

"Just tell me, then," she replied, twisting to face him.

He slid his hand off her shoulder and placed it with his other, grasping hers. He paused as he looked at her. She was beautiful, in some respects stunning with her mix of Mediterranean and Central Asian looks. With her athletic body, she could easily have been a descendant of one of the nomadic tribes from the days of the great Genghis Khan Empire that had reached as far as the Mediterranean and into parts of Europe. But despite her physical looks, what captivated Michael, what drew him to her, was a quality about her. There was something very plain and straightforward when she spoke to you, almost an innocence in the way she let you know what she thought about something, how she felt. She was a strong-willed person, intelligent, as tough as any of the SF soldiers he had served with, but she had a genuineness that was at odds with her sophisticated intelligence officer persona. He found this dichotomy about her mesmerizing. It was something that he could take a lifetime exploring. He could imagine spending evenings sitting on this couch, or any couch, holding her in his arms. If it could ever be, he had to tell her everything.

"Last Friday, I tried to kill myself. I put a gun to my head and pulled the trigger. I can't explain why I'm still alive. It doesn't make any sense to me. I know it sounds so extreme, so cowardly, so uncharacteristic of the person I believed I was. I thought I was stronger, had more fortitude, wouldn't quit so easily, but I guess I was wrong. Now I'm sitting here next to you, having all these feelings about you that I never knew existed, a day before I'm going on an impossible mission that I most likely won't come back from. I don't understand any of it. That's about as short as I can make it so you understand where I've been, what I've done, how I feel, what's been going around inside my head. I'm sure you have a lot of questions, but at least now you've got an idea of what kind of basket case I've become. I don't want you to get too attached to the person you think I am. I don't want you to be hurt if you never see me again. That's what I've been wanting to tell you."

She saw in his face the pain of everything he had shared with her, confessing his shortcomings as a man, the doubts about himself, the hopelessness of his situation. She squeezed his hand, wanting him to know she felt his anguish, knew what he was going through. She searched for how to respond, what to say, what to ask him. It jarred her to hear that Michael had tried to take his life. It was hard for her to process that of all the people she had known, he would be the one to attempt suicide. He had been such an optimist. Despite the situation, despite how bad things looked, whatever the problem, Michael had always been the type of person everyone turned to for reassurance, some words that would give confidence that everything would turn out all right. It wasn't that he was fearless or recklessly brave; he just had a calmness about him that allowed him to think through all the better possibilities and avoid dwelling on everything that could go wrong. He seemed to understand that one had no control over those things, so better to focus on all the things one could influence. What had happened to shake that confidence about life? What was it that had gotten the better of him? She knew the kind of man he was. Whatever it was, it had to have been extremely formidable.

"Do you want to tell me about it?" she finally asked, not knowing if he needed a prompt to continue with anything more he might have wanted to tell her.

"I'm assuming you're referring to me trying to pop a cap in my noggin?" he said, reverting to his unconscious habit of trying to bring some levity into a serious situation.

"If that's your way of saying putting a bullet in your head, yes, but everything else also, if you want. What led you there? How you feel about that now? How you feel about me?"

"Sounds like you want to hear everything."

"As I said, Michael, only if you want."

"Okay, well, where to start? Sometime over the past few months, I somehow arrived at the decision that life wasn't worth living anymore. I can't remember exactly when that happened or what I was thinking at that moment, but somehow it took on a life of its own, and everything I did from then on was to move closer to taking the final step. What was so terrible about my life? I don't know that I can give you an answer you'll understand. Anybody looking in from the outside would have said I had things pretty good. I was making good money with real estate, far better than what I made working for the government. I had a nice home, nice car, a very pretty wife, but despite all that, I had somehow fallen into this dark hole that I felt helpless to get out of. No matter how hard I tried, told myself I had nothing to complain about, reminded myself how well I had it compared to so many others, I just couldn't see the sunshine. It seemed like there was nothing to look forward to, no reason to get out of bed, like it was a gray rainy winter morning, day after day. Eva cut me a lot of slack, tried to be understanding, but it got old. Year after year, it just wore her out. She couldn't take it anymore, so she filed for divorce. I don't blame her. It was devastating her emotionally, spiritually, every which way. I'm surprised she hung on as long as she did. I went to see a doc, tried all the different happy pills to see if it was some kind of chemical imbalance, messed-up serotonin levels, seasonal disorder from living in Seattle, something medical that I wasn't the cause of. Nothing seemed to help. Most people didn't have a clue that anything was wrong, other than Eva, and probably my parents. I got pretty good at faking it. Everyone just knew me as Mike Blackstone, the real estate broker, the guy with some mysterious past that he didn't talk much about. They saw someone who looked like he had everything he wanted. I guess that's because everyone who knew me had only known me since after I'd left the Agency and moved back to Seattle. They really didn't know anything about me, my experiences, what I'd been through, who I really was. At first, I tried to make that best of it, starting over in a new place, new wife, new career, a new chapter in life. I don't know exactly when I started thinking things weren't the way they should be, or even if it was a conscious thought, but at some point, I started feeling like my life didn't have any meaning, direction, sense of purpose. Everything I did seemed superficial and insignificant. It was like I was just going through the motions of living my life. I remember thinking to myself one day, you went from being a secret agent to a real estate agent. It wasn't that I thought selling real estate was beneath me, like I was someone special. It just got to the point where I couldn't stand having to take some couple from one house to another until they could finally make up their mind what they wanted to buy. I began to feel like a glorified used car salesman. Meanwhile, I'd watch the news and see what was going on around the world, remembering some of the things I was involved in, thinking I used to be a small cog in all that, making a little bit of difference, doing my small part in trying to make this a better world. That would then take me to the reality that I'm not any longer, and the reason for that. I think maybe that's part of it, the fact that I was responsible for letting that happen. Whether I really had any control over that or not, I don't know. I've asked myself that question so many times over the years, replayed everything in my head, over and over. I've never been able to come up with a satisfactory answer to put it to rest. I tried to get past it, but somehow it just stayed with me. I just couldn't let it go, until it gradually began to define the way I saw myself, the way I interacted with the world around me, the people closest to me. At some point, I just came to the realization that there wasn't anything I could do to change things. I couldn't go back in time to do things differently, undo everything I put Eva, Karen and Sam through, have a different outcome in life, so I decided to call it quits before it got even worse. How's that for some psychoanalysis?"

He had done it. Everything was now out in the open. He waited for her response, studying her face as she took everything in. What would she think of him now? Surely, she wouldn't look at him the same way. He had let her see past the thin veneer of courage, fortitude and character, into his damaged core. He knew he needed to tell her something about the person he had become, but he hadn't planned on baring his soul to her. Now she knew the true extent of how bad things had gotten, the depth of the pit he had fallen into. How could she ever want to be with someone like that, someone so flawed? At least he had finally gotten it off his chest. He felt relief, even if it meant the end of any possibility with Asya. He wouldn't be left agonizing over that distraction while he was on his mission, wondering if they could have had a future together.

"That is a lot of weight you have been carrying, Michael. It must have been slowly crushing you all those years. I am sorry you have had to suffer through so much pain. It sounds like you blame yourself for much of what has happened. Sometimes it is blame that causes most of the pain when things are not as we would like. In life, there are some things that are just beyond our control to change. Even if you could go back in time and do something different, it does not mean there would be any better outcome. Things just turn out the way they do, and it is difficult to understand why, until maybe long after in the future, if ever. There is nothing I could tell you that would help you make any sense of why your life has taken the course it has. It sounds like you have blamed yourself for many things that were beyond your control, and it made you think you had to pass judgment on yourself. No one can do that except God. What I will tell you is that He has some purpose for you, because you are alive despite your best effort at attempting not to be, a monumental task has been placed before you, and our lives have crossed again, this time in a much deeper and more meaningful way. I know the type of man you are, Michael Blackstone. There are not many men who would be willing to face what you have decided to take on. You are a courageous, selfless and compassionate man. You do not have many shortcomings, but one of them is that you think you can control everything, fix things, make them right. There is a fine line between confidence and arrogance, self-assuredness and pride. When the realities of life rudely remind you may have crossed over the line a bit, it causes you to doubt yourself, look for blame that you have not measured up to the person you thought you were. None of us can measure up to our ideal of the person we want to be. We can only learn from our experiences and continue to strive towards that ideal. Don't let feelings of guilt deceive you into believing otherwise. I don't know if your purpose in life includes me in it, but if it is something I have any control over, I would like that to be. It is something that I will be praying for."

He wasn't expecting that kind of response from her. He didn't think she would be judgmental, but at least that she'd start backing away some to put a little distance between them once she realized the extent of his issues. It was just the opposite. She had embraced his circumstances, encouraged him to embrace them also. She had bolstered him by making visible some of his weaknesses. She had turned what he perceived to be his greatest failure in life into proof that he had been given the opportunity to find his real purpose. She made it clear to him that she wanted him in her life, so much so that she would be praying for him. It was a surprise to hear her say that. He grabbed her other hand, holding one in each.

"I don't know what to say, Awsh. I don't even know what to think. A week ago, I thought my life was over, had reached the end. It didn't faze me that much. I had become someone I didn't recognize anymore, so it didn't seem as if it was the life of Michael Blackstone that was coming to an end. It was like some stranger you see in the street that looks familiar from somewhere but doesn't mean anything to you. Now suddenly everything has been turned upside down. It's as if I've come out of a coma and I found you waiting by my bedside, but the doctors walked in and said that I'm not in the clear yet, I have to have an operation that I may not pull through. Tell me how I'm supposed to deal with that."

"Michael, you are asking me a question that I don't have an answer for. I am just as confused. All that I do know is that you have suddenly come back into my life, carrying an enormous burden you have to see through. I just want you to know how I feel about you, that I want you in my life, and I am going to do whatever I can to help you get through this if there will be any chance for us afterwards. But only God knows how it will all come out in the end."

"I never realized you were religious."

"I'm not. What makes you say that?" she asked.

"You said that you will be praying for us and that only God knows how everything will turn out."

"Yes. I do believe in God or Allah, as we call Him, and I do pray to Him, but I am not religious in the sense of attending mosque or reading the Quran as part of my daily routine. I had read it many years ago and am familiar with the teachings of Mohammed, as I have read the Bible and am familiar with its teachings. You seem surprised."

"I just never heard you talk about God before, that's all."

"No, I suppose I had not. It was not that I did not believe in God, I just did not consider Him as playing a central role in my life. I was preoccupied with other things that I thought needed my attention, my focus, like proving to myself and everyone else I had the ability to succeed in whatever challenge was in front of me."

"So, what's changed now in your life, as far as God's concerned?" he asked her, intrigued by this new discovery about her.

"What has changed? I'm not quite sure that anything has changed. I have just become more aware of His presence in my life, in everything around me."

"What do you mean?"

"I mean, I see the way things take place in the world, the way things happen in life, in my life. A lot of people believe in chance or coincidence to explain why things happen the way they do. But if one really examines things closely, they would realize the odds of things turning out the way they do time after time are simply astronomical. I can certainly say that about my life. So, I have a choice. I can believe in chance, in random improbability dictating how things happen in life, or I can believe that there is a higher presence with us that is actively engaged in this world. I choose the latter. That is why I pray, because He will hear my needs, my desires, hear the questions and uncertainties I have about my life."

"Has he ever answered you?"

"If you are asking if He has spoken to me, if I've ever heard some voice from above? The answer is no, but He has answered me in other ways that are just as clear."

"Oh yeah, in what ways?"

"He has answered me in my thoughts. You will ask how I know it is Him and not just my own thoughts. I will tell you. I know myself, my fears, my strengths, my weaknesses, and what my intellect is capable of. Many of the answers that I have gotten to my prayers, I know are beyond the capability of my intellect. I just didn't have it in me to come up with such an answer. The other way He has spoken to me is by how He allows things to unfold in my life. There are things that have happened to me at different times in my life that felt unfair, disheartening, overwhelming, and at the time I couldn't see any good solution to the situation, no matter how hard I tried. Then a series of events that I never could have foreseen started unfolding, in such a way that this once unsolvable problem went away or in some cases turned into a blessing. You know me, Michael. I am a realistic person, someone who sees things as they are, logical, someone who can make a rational decision. I have either gone crazy as I have gotten older or am finally seeing things more clearly as they are."

Michael had to pause and digest everything she had told him. He had been caught off guard. He wasn't expecting a metaphysical discussion on the principles of communication with God. This new dimension of Asya had caught his curiosity. He always knew she had a good core as a human being, but he had never seen this spiritual side of her. She was one of those people who radiated light. Everyone liked being in her company, both men and women. She had a way of bringing those around her up. He realized she had depth, but this was surprising.

"So, my only two choices are you're crazy or you actually talk with God?" he half-joked.

"I communicate with Him. He hears me. He just doesn't always give me His answer when I expect to receive it. Sometimes, at first, it may be a challenge to clearly understand what He is trying to tell me. Sometimes it is not the answer I want to hear. But He always gets back to me one way or another."

"You sound pretty certain about that, Awsh."

"That is the only thing I am certain about in this life."

"Hm. So, what are you going to pray for when I leave?"

"I am going to ask God to watch over you, protect you, keep you safe, give you the strength to endure whatever lies in your path and guide you in the right direction. I am going to tell Him how I feel about you, even though He can already see it in my heart, and ask Him, if it is His will, to bring you back to me."

"Wow. If I have that much cover, who needs anything the CIA's got to offer?" he said, trying to interject some levity into a topic he was uncertain about. "I'm just kidding. Actually, that means a lot to me, Awsh. You know, it's not that I don't believe in the existence of God, or some higher power, that's somehow responsible for everything around us, bringing order to the universe and all that, but it seems so detached from the reality of everyday life."

"You are saying that you have never experienced anything in life that is unexplainable, something that makes you stop and wonder how that happened, why that happened? You said it means a lot to you that I will pray for you, but how do you mean that? Do you just appreciate my gesture of how important you are to me, or could you use a little help from God?"

"That's really putting me on the spot. Let's see, how do I answer that? I suppose I mean it both ways. It's very touching that you care so much about me that I'm on the top of your request list for God. I don't know that anyone has said that to me, or if they have, not in the way you mean it. I could certainly also use as much help as I can get, for what I'm about to face. I just don't know if I'm on the top of God's priority list."

"Do you really believe that? How is that you are sitting here in front of me right now, alive, breathing, not a scratch on you, when you just tried to take your life? You did not tell me the details of how it was you were unsuccessful in that effort, but I know what your capabilities are with weapons. It was not some random chance. You know the odds better than me." She paused. "I am still waiting for the answer to my first question."

Michael sat there silently, trying to give himself time to consider any alternative rational possibility. The obvious answer to her question stood out in plain sight, like an unspoken elephant taking up all the space of her living room. Of course, Michael knew the odds of a misfire happening like that. It defied all laws of probability—even more remarkably that it happened to be the one bullet on the one occasion that his perfectly maintained Glock had been pointed at his head and hadn't performed its intended function. What reasonable explanation could he come up with to challenge the certainty of her belief?

Their eyes locked, the windows of their souls open for each other to see, knowing this might be their last chance to do so. They could feel the deluge of each other's emotions, like the giant waves hitting the beach right before a big storm. The worst thing that could happen to him now wasn't death or imprisonment; it was passing up the chance to bare his soul to her, and her living the rest of her life always wondering. He couldn't hold back on her. He had to lower every last bit of defenses that regulated how far people were allowed into his life. If he didn't, it would haunt him through the entire mission, and however long afterwards without her.

"Awsh, I know everything points to the fact that something beyond the physical laws this universe is responsible for me being alive right now, but why should I jump to the conclusion that it's me that God needs for whatever his purpose is, and that's why he intervened with some kind of miracle? He could have found a million other ways of stopping some evil that is about to happen in this world. He doesn't need me."

"Is that what this is about? You think God needs you. Of course He does not need you. He does not need any of us. He wants you. He wants us all. Why else would He have created us? He does not need us for anything. There is nothing we can do for Him or give Him, other than return His love and give Him our attention. He chose you for whatever His reasons are to address this wrong that is about to happen in the world. He did so by giving you a glimpse of His power by actively stepping in and suspending the laws of nature, and you believe you are not important to Him. Then He brings you and me together right before you face the most formidable challenge in your life, and you think He does not want to bless you with as much as He can give you. What kind of an impersonal God treats you like that? Why is it so hard for you to consider God as something more than just a concept, as someone actually in the room with you?"

It felt like he was swimming in rough seas of emotions, with the tops of waves breaking over his head. Part of it was from the enormity of what Asya was trying to convince him of. Part of it was from the intensity of her feelings for him. It was disorienting, but at the same time an unexplainable feeling of peace washed over him, as if some blanket of uncertainty had been lifted off him. Her words echoed in his head. *What kind of impersonal God treats you like that?* Could she be right? Had God directly intervened to save his life, and just happened to fit him into his overall plan for handling matters in this world of His? He felt a buzz of energy coming up from the back of his neck into his head. The feeling was astonishing. Everything around him appeared so clear, so sharp, as if his senses had been hyper-sensitized. He saw detail, heard sound, sensed the energy in his surroundings. It was similar to what he had experienced before when coming to in his living room, but more intensely now. Maybe the combination of travel, time difference, excitement and uncertainty of what was to come had finally caught up with him. Had his nervous system released a flood of dopamine into his brain that was causing this sensation? If he was having some kind of seizure or mental episode, it wasn't a bad feeling. He just needed to let it run its course and he would hopefully soon feel normal again. Otherwise, he might be asking Asya to take him to a doctor.

"Are you okay?" she asked him.

Michael paused before answering, "Ah, yeah, I think so."

"What's wrong?"

"Mm, nothing. Nothing's wrong, I just feel a bit weird."

"What do you mean, weird?"

"I don't know how to describe it. It's like I'm on some kind of drug. I mean,

I don't feel bad, it's just that everything around me seems, feels, different. Like everything's more pronounced."

"Okay," she let out slowly, observing him closely.

"We didn't even have any wine yet. Maybe I could use a glass right now."

He let go of her and ran his hands through his hair. What was happening to him? Here he was, sitting with a beautiful woman, an old friend that he hadn't seen for years, having one of the deepest conversations of his life, twenty-four hours before going on a suicide mission. It was almost too much to handle. He wondered if maybe he actually had shot himself but somehow survived and was now in a coma, his body lying in some hospital bed back in Seattle with his mind trapped in this surreal dream. How would he know it wasn't real if he was in a coma? His reality would be limited to the confines of his damaged brain. His only chance of escaping would be his body finally giving up its struggle and cutting the power on the movie projector of this bizarre film.

He pulled his hands from his head, reaching and gently grasping Asya's face. She was momentarily startled as he gazed into her face, as if searching for something. He drew slowly towards her until their lips came into contact. He kissed her softly, transforming any feeling of surprise into tender delight as their lips lingered with each other. His heart raced. The sensation wasn't something that could be manufactured in a subconscious dream. This was real.

He finally pulled away while continuing to look into her eyes. She smiled at him, conveying what no words could say. There was something wholesome about who she was as a person, something untainted by the world she lived and worked in. It came out with a subtleness that was overshadowed by what most people noticed about her extraordinary beauty and impressive abilities. He had always known this about her, but being with her had never been an option until now. What would it be like to have her in his life? It felt so real, yet still beyond his grasp.

"I don't know where that came from. I just wanted to make sure this was real, you and I, everything. I hope I didn't cross the line. If I did, I'm sorry, Awsh. I'm just not myself."

"That was nice. I always wondered what it would feel like to kiss you. It is even better than what I imagined. You did not cross the line, and do not say you are sorry. I am not sorry."

He resisted the urge to grab her and kiss her all over again, this time longer and more intensely. He knew where things would lead, of course, and although he could think of nothing he would enjoy more, deep inside he knew it would be a mistake for both of them. The resulting feelings of attachment between them, would only lead to deep emotional wounds if he didn't make it back. He had already done that to others. He couldn't allow that to happen again. If he didn't make it back, of course she would grieve, but she would eventually recover and move on with her life. It wouldn't be good for him either. She would be constantly on his mind and distract him from what he needed to do. For as desperately as he yearned to experience the intimacy of making love to her, he knew he couldn't. If there was any possibility of a future for them, he needed to survive first, and he could only do that without anything interfering with his focus and clouding his judgment. He had to buck up and do what he knew was necessary. It was hard, but being a real man was never easy. But what to say to her? Was she hoping, wanting, the same from him, as he was from her?

Why don't you just tell her the truth? Don't you think she'll understand? You're underestimating her. You think she can't figure it out, maybe even be thinking the same thing herself, hoping you can resist, because she knows she might crumble the instant you touch her one more time.

"Awsh, there is nothing I would rather do at this moment than make love with you into the early hours of the morning. And I mean that in the way of being able to do that every night, as long as our old tired bodies can keep it up. But if we do this right now, you know how much it will mess with both our heads. I have no illusions about what I'm going to face, but if there's any chance of me making it through this, I need to have my head clear and not have my emotions clouding my judgment. You're my only lifeline to make it back out, so I need to have you sharp and disconnected from me emotionally. I need you to understand why I'm not all over your lips this very second. I need you to know that I love you, that I can finally love you the way you deserve."

She reached with her right arm and placed her hand on Michael's face, holding it like it was precious irreplaceable china. "My dear, gallant Michael, I hope you can feel how much I wish that right now, how much I crave to have you. You do not need to explain. I know. I do not want to settle for experiencing that with you just one time and never again. I am selfish. I want you every night. I want to share my thoughts and feelings with you, see your smile, feel you next to me over and over again."

"I don't know how we're going to get any sleep tonight. What are we going to do, sit here on the couch, my arm wrapped around you until we pass out from exhaustion?" he said, making the first effort at backing out some from the intimacy of their situation.

"Why the couch? I want to fall asleep in your arms, but lying in my comfy bed," she replied, letting him know she didn't want to waste one minute of their remaining time together away from his presence.

"Okay, but you have to wear some flannel pajamas or sweats. It would be cruel to torture me with anything slinky that you'll be wearing to bed when I come back to you," he enthusiastically cautioned her.

"I suppose I will have to go shopping while you are gone to update my sleepwear. When you live by yourself, you choose comfy over sexy."

"Just that thought alone will keep me going through the most insurmountable situation," he told her as he grabbed her hands and pulled her up.

"I'm not really hungry. I'd rather spend it lying next to you, until the rhythm of your breathing lulls me to sleep."

"Mm, that sounds enticing. So much for me staying focused while I'm on the mission."

She took his hand and led him down the hallway to her bedroom. They knew the hazards of crossing the line they had mutually established, but that wasn't going to keep them from sharing the intimacy of each other's presence on the last night they might have together. Both of them hoped they would be able to fall asleep before their passions overcame their better judgment. It was going to be a difficult road ahead; they didn't need to make it more so.

***

Canton had gotten settled into his suite on the thirty-second floor at the Ritz-Carlton. Also known as the Suzer Plaza, it was a modern thirty-four-story glass-exterior high-rise situated two kilometers south of the Four Seasons. Although not directly on the water, its upper floors offered phenomenal views of the Bosphorus. Where the Four Seasons' classic elegance reflected the grandeur of the Ottoman Empire, the Ritz-Carlton was a state-of-the-art example of Istanbul's status as a modern international city. At the equivalent of nine hundred euros a night, it had a phenomenal view of the Bosphorus Straits. It certainly was nice traveling as a deputy director with a plane at his disposal and plenty of operational funds allocated for him to use in furtherance of a priority investigation. His car rental and hotel bill would just be a small drop in the bucket that he could bury somewhere in the expense appendix of the final operational report, which he would be authoring. And what could be better than to pick up a hot Russian hooker each night and bring her back to his luxury hotel? He could drag this thing out and have a different Slavic beauty every night of the week. At a couple hundred euros a night, he could easily write it off his operational cash expenditures as inducements to sources providing him information. He would make sure to ask each one of his "sources" if they had ever been with an Iranian client.

He knew all the ins and outs of writing properly worded reports. His writing ability had served him well throughout his career. As long as you kept submitting operational proposals to establish a funding code, you just needed to be able to write creative operational reports to justify expenditures. If things didn't work out after a couple of years of developing your source, it was unfortunate, but no one could criticize you for not trying. You just wrote up another operational proposal and submitted it, opening up a new funding code. He had become very proficient, always cycling in a new operation to maintain a steady caseload. As one shut down, a new one went active. No one paid enough attention to notice they all had run their course after a couple of years without producing any results. There were many operations within the Agency in their early stages that hadn't yet begun yielding results. His just got lost in the numbers.

He pulled out the clean mobile phone for communication with Rostov and dialed the number he had memorized. It rang several times, until he finally heard a familiar heavy Russian accent answer in Turkish, "*Evet.*"

"It's me, your twin brother. How is the goat herding, Yakov? Do they keep you good company at night?" he responded laughingly.

"I'm surprised to hear from you this late. I thought you would be occupied caressing some young boy while taking a bath together," he replied with a deeper slight, making Canton bristle. "What is it?"

"We need to talk. Are you still in Istanbul?"

"Is that right? It seems we always need to talk when you are unable to take care of something yourself."

"I don't need any of your sarcasm. Can you meet me in the same place as last time in forty-five minutes?"

"I will meet you in two hours."

"Two hours? Really? That's the earliest you can meet me?"

"I do not work for you, nor am I at your disposal whenever you have a problem. I said two hours."

"Fine! I'll see you in two hours." He ended the call. "Russian asshole!" *Who the hell does he think he is? Somehow, he must have forgotten that he's just some SVR hack who was sent here to take care of coordinating the wet work. Maybe someone needs to remind him where his place is*, he thought, despite knowing he wasn't going to be the one to do so. His room phone rang. He picked it up.

"Mr. Canton, this is the front desk. A package that has been left for you here."

"What kind of package?"

"It is a bubble envelope."

"Have it delivered to my suite immediately," he directed, hanging up the phone just as he heard the front desk person begin to say something.

He felt irritable. Everything was getting on his nerves. Perhaps it was the jet lag catching up with him. The COS and Rostov not showing him the respect he deserved, didn't help his disposition either. He needed not to take it personally. They were nobodies. He was going places. Not too long from now, he would show them. He would show everyone when he was the new DCI. He checked his watch. It was 9:17 p.m. He wouldn't be meeting with Rostov for another two hours. That had completely messed up his plans for this evening. Now he would have to wait until after midnight to find a decent working girl to bring back to his room. By then, all the choice selections would already be taken for the night and he'd have to settle for some third-world Middle Eastern whore, which didn't sound appealing to him. It would also be too late for him. He needed to get some decent sleep tonight in order to be sharp tomorrow. He couldn't let himself lose control of the situation. Otherwise any dreams of being the DCI, or even staying out of prison, would be dashed. It all depended on making sure Shiravi was permanently silenced, and Blackstone, along with his Turkish piece of ass, was eliminated. He would need Rostov's assistance with that.

He was startled by the knock on his door. "Concierge. You have a package."

He silently walked over to his door and looked out the peephole. A young male in a black Ritz-Carlton uniform with gold trim stood there holding a white package. "You can set it down."

"Leave it in the hallway, sir?"

"Yes."

"Very well, sir. Good day." The concierge placed the envelope in front of the door and turned, leaving his field of view.

Canton waited for about thirty seconds before slowly opening the door and cautiously peeking out. He saw the young employee standing down the hallway, waiting for an elevator. The employee glanced in his direction. Spotting him standing partway out his door, he acknowledged Canton with a slight nod. Canton, caught in his trepidation, returned the nod and picked up the package, quickly retreating into his room and closing the door. Through the bubble wrap, he felt a set of keys. Of course it was keys. He had been expecting them. He really needed to chill out, he told himself. The concierge probably thought he was some paranoid freak. If he let small things rattle him all the time, how would he be able to take care of everything on his end? He just needed to contain three people until things were set in motion, and the bombs and missiles started falling. Once that happened, there was nothing anyone could do or claim that would make the smallest bit of difference. The changes on the world stage would have been set in motion, and the current DCI would be eventually fired because the CIA didn't have a clue about any of this happening.

He turned around and headed back into the living room of the suite, tearing the plastic package open, reaching in and pulling out a key fob. He looked at it in the palm of his hand, the five white letters progressively increasing his blood pressure the longer he stood there looking at them. He pulled out two folded pieces of paper and opened the first one. It was the rental agreement paperwork, listing the fictitious name of the customer. In the unlikely event he was pulled over by the Turkish police, he would have to develop a plausible explanation as to whose vehicle he was driving, but that wasn't his concern. He opened the second piece of paper to find a valet parking ticket inside a handwritten note. *Sorry, rental place didn't have any of your requested models. This was the best I could do. Enjoy. Bob.* He took a second look at the rental contract again. *Volvo V60. That son of a bitch.* He turned his attention back to the Europcar plastic tag attached to the key fob, reading it over and over again: *V60 wagon, alpine green.* His hands started trembling, the tremor quickly growing to a full-on shake as he read the handwritten note one more time. *This was the best I could do. Enjoy. Bob.*

In a fit of rage, he hurled the keys at the wall, hitting the large gold-framed mirror. He heard the sharp clink of an object hitting glass, then saw the crack reaching from the upper right corner through the middle, and down to the lower left corner. He looked at the reflection in the bifurcated mirror and saw twin images of a distorted face staring at him. He was momentarily startled, not recognizing the enraged person staring back at him from the other side of the wall. It almost looked as if something was twisting his face into some deranged individual you would see in any of the latest sci-fi or horror movies. He pulled away from the front of the mirror. He was getting too jumpy, letting an insignificant annoyance get under his skin once again. So Bob wanted to stick it to him and try to mess with his head. Okay, he wasn't going to let it bother him. It was just transportation. He would sit back and relax until it was time to head out for his meeting with Rostov.

He walked over to the well-stocked mini-bar and looked at the selection. Johnnie Walker Blue Label. At least he wouldn't have to settle for second-rate scotch. He glanced at the price list. *Fifty euros for a one-ounce bottle! Those Turkish shysters. Pff, what do I care? Uncle Sam's paying for it.* He cracked the seal on one of the bottles and poured himself a drink. If he was going to have to wait for that Russian flunky, he would at least enjoy the moment.

He plunked down on the sofa and looked for the remote for the large flat-screen that was sitting atop the long mahogany cabinet. He looked on the lamp table next to the couch, then the coffee table in front of him, finally walking over to the television cabinet, nothing. *What the hell? What is going on?* he thought in a heightened state of annoyance. He plopped back down on the couch with his glass of Blue Label and took a swig of perhaps the smoothest blended scotch whiskey on the planet. He savored it in his mouth for a moment and then let its smooth warmness coat his throat as it made its way into his system. It would shortly start taking the edge off his mood. He looked over at the cracked mirror, and any momentary pleasure he received from the scotch evaporated at the thought of what the hotel would charge him for the damage. He threw down what remained in the glass and got up for another. He twisted open a second Blue Label, pouring it into his glass and downing it with one clean shot. He reached for a third. Just as he was about to pour it down his throat, he caught himself and suppressed the urge to lose control of his self-restraint. He sat back down on the couch and took a lingering sip from his glass. Blue Label wasn't intended to be consumed like some cheap shot-guzzling bourbon.

He felt the pleasant sensation of the alcohol take its effect throughout his body. When he had finished his work here, he would take a week of leave so he could recover from the hectic pace of the last week. Perhaps he would make a quick trip to Thailand for several relaxing days of Thai massages and whatever else was negotiated on the side. He was certain that would restore his sense of calm. He wondered if there were some way he could take the G550 there. He would have to think on that one. Maybe he could fabricate some lead that he had to follow up on which would justify flying to that part of the world on the Agency's dime. That might be his only option if it was after the bombs started dropping. Commercial air traffic would obviously be disrupted for a while, much like during the weeks following 9-11. He let his mind wander off lazily to pleasurable thoughts of sitting in a bubbly hot tub with one Thai beauty massaging his shoulders and another massaging his feet, each working their way towards one another.

Without warning, his focus suddenly turned to Blackstone. His neck muscles immediately became tense as his blood pressure spiked again. How could he let his mind be hijacked like that? How could his thoughts have gone from two beautiful young playthings to the person who had become the biggest thorn in his side since—since ever? Why was it he hated him so much? It was more than just the fact that Blackstone had stuck his nose into something that was none of his business and had disrupted their well-laid-out plan. He could have handled making sure Shiravi had been permanently silenced one way or another, but Blackstone's sudden appearance in the middle of this relatively minor unexpected problem had created a headache he didn't need. He told himself not to overreact to the risk posed by Blackstone. After all, he had been out of the arena for over a decade. At the same time, a small voice inside him warned him to be cautious. He remembered how capable an operator Blackstone had been back in Athens. He had come so close to actually pitching an Iranian intelligence officer, closer than any other CIA case officer had ever come. Members of the MOIS and IRGC had always been considered very hard targets for recruitment. Unlike during the Soviet Union days, when KGB and GRU personnel could be targeted ideologically, knowing from within how rotten and hollow the communist ideology of the state had become, the Iranians were a different story.

The rift between Iran and the United States wasn't based on differences in political ideology. Despite the internal struggle in Islam between the Shia and Sunni sects, the Iranian regime looked at itself as the vanguard of the Muslim world's struggle against the morally bankrupt West, led by the United States. It was a similar moral and ideological battle to the one the United States had faced against the Nazis during World War II. Good against evil. The MOIS and IRGC were Iran's soldiers against that perceived evil. Not one of them had ever been recruited to spy for the CIA. Blackstone's would have been the first. The thought of having to witness Blackstone's smugness at his success would have been too much for Canton to handle. He had made sure he didn't have to endure such a slight. Instead, he'd witnessed the great Michael Blackstone face defeat and disgrace in the worst way possible for a case officer. He had been recalled to headquarters before the end of his tour, a most certain way to derail a career in the Agency. The thought of what he had done to Blackstone gave him satisfaction. This time he would seek to completely destroy him. First, he would have to take care of that insolent little Turkish whore. That was enough! He needed to get his mind off Blackstone, even for just a short while. Otherwise, he would go crazy. He coerced his thoughts back to the hot tub with the two young Asian beauties. It was the last thing he remembered thinking.

He wasn't quite sure how long his mobile phone had been ringing as he fumbled, trying to pull it out of his pocket. He was momentarily disoriented as he looked at the number that was dialing him. He quickly snapped back into full awareness of what had happened as he recognized who was calling him by the unregistered number showing on his mobile. It was 11:27 p.m.—he had fallen asleep waiting for the time to pass until his meeting with Rostov. Shit! What excuse was he going to come up with as to why he was late for an operational meet. He couldn't say he had fallen asleep. It would make him look like an unprofessional amateur. He could never allow that, especially in the eyes of that Russian flunky. His mind raced trying to come up with a plausible excuse as he hit the answer button on his mobile and raised it to his ear. "Yeah."

"What do you mean yeah? You are late." Canton heard the disdain through that heavy Russian accent.

"Something came up. It was unavoidable. Sorry, couldn't call you, but I'm on my way."

"What do you mean you couldn't call? Is this also how you run your intelligence operations? It is a wonder you have made it to the position you have within your organization. I suppose it is the same in every organization. Some advance by knowing the right person to be *wooshes* to. How do you say in English, cocksucker?"

"I was talking to the director of the CIA. You really think I'm going to break out of a call with him to let you know I'm going to be a little bit late? I would have done the same if I was on a call with your director, just so we're clear on who's running the show operationally out here. I told you, I'm sorry you've been inconvenienced. I'll be there in twenty minutes." This time of night without traffic, he could easily make it to their meeting site on the other side of the Bosphorus if he left right away.

"Don't waste my time with your excuses. Be here in twenty minutes, or you will not find me here waiting."

He tucked the car keys and the parking voucher into his pocket as he grabbed his jacket and headed for the door. The elevators being free this time of the evening, he rapidly made his way from the thirty-second floor down to the lobby. Hurrying across the ornate lobby and out the front door, he spotted the concierge and walked up to him, handing over his parking voucher and car keys. "Make it quick, I'm in a hurry."

"Yes, sir. It will be a moment while I have one of the valets retrieve your vehicle," the concierge said, maintaining his politeness despite Canton's tone. He had grown accustomed to the rudeness of some of the guests who stayed there. After all, many of those who could afford to stay at the Ritz-Carlton were also used to giving orders to those working for them, either as employees or servants. That was just the way life was in his part of the world. He was fortunate to have such an impressive job compared to most of his siblings. His older brother had his own cab, but he was the one who wore the black blazer with the gold Ritz-Carlton insignia to work, being the first to greet the distinguished guests who arrived daily. He grabbed the small gold whistle hanging from his neck and gave a short blow, signaling one of the young valets to make haste over to him.

"The gentleman's vehicle. *Chaboojak!*" he said, telling the valet to hurry.

The boy, who didn't look over twenty, grabbed the keys and briskly trotted back into the lobby and over to the service elevator that would take him to the parking garage in the basement of the building.

Growing impatient after what seemed like five minutes had passed, Canton finally spotted a green Volvo wagon approaching. Irritated already that it had taken this long to get his car, the sight of it brought on a feeling of overwhelming anger inside him. The thought of attempting to pick up some hot young Slavic beauty in that alpine green family sports wagon was almost more than he could bear. He felt the acid in his stomach start churning and the twinge of heartburn come on suddenly. He had to forcibly keep himself from lashing out and screaming obscenities at the COS. He couldn't be seen losing his cool in the presence of the concierge and the valet, even if they were merely hotel personnel. He had just finished telling himself he needed to stay in control and not let inconsequential things rattle him.

The valet parked it in front of him, got out and stood by the door waiting. Canton walked around to the driver side, got in and yanked the door shut. Not giving the valet a chance to step away from the car, Canton put it in first, popping the clutch and squealing the tires as he sped out from the covered driveway. He slammed on the brakes, almost ramming head-on into the hydraulic security barriers, which were in the raised position. He blasted his horn in annoyance. *That idiot concierge. What the hell is wrong with him? He saw I was in a hurry heading out. I'll have to talk to the night manager when I get back*, he told himself. A few seconds later, the barriers dropped, allowing him to race out of the driveway onto the street. He glanced at his watch and saw the time: 11:35 p.m. He had already wasted seven minutes. That left him thirteen minutes to make it to his destination. If he didn't hit any traffic, he could make it across the bridge in five minutes and make his meet on time. He just hoped he didn't attract the attention of any Turkish police that happened to be out on patrol along his route. He would have to exceed the speed limit by even more than what was typical for Turkish drivers.

Fortunately, traffic was light as he made his way north on Çırağan Boulevard to the Bosphorus Bridge. Once on the bridge, he floored it, shifting through all five gears until the Volvo's speedometer passed one hundred twenty kilometers per hour before letting off the accelerator. He made use of all three lanes, weaving his way rapidly through the sparse traffic crossing the Bosphorus over to the Asian side of Istanbul. He was halfway across the long expanse when a Turkish police car passed him going in the opposite direction. The bridge was lit brightly enough that he could see the faces of both officers look at him as he sped by them. He looked in his rear-view mirror and saw the flashing blue lights of the police car turn on. He hadn't seen any speed limit signs, but he knew by how fast he was passing traffic that he had blown through whatever the posted speed was. Whether the blue lights were intended for him as a message to slow down, it didn't make a difference. If they were considering chasing after him, they wouldn't stand a chance. He would be off the bridge before they had even gotten across their end and turned back around to pursue him. In thirty seconds, he was off the bridge and heading south on Paşa Limanı Avenue. Another glance at his watch told him it was 11:40. He had eight minutes to make it the twelve miles to the location where they had met previously. It wasn't the best practice to use the same site twice in a row, but the port had several advantages. It was easy to spot anyone attempting to follow you in, and it offered many secluded areas, making it a secure and expedient location.

He sped past the pier for the tour boats and ferries that made their way up and down the Bosphorus on a daily basis. They were all tied up until they started their daily runs in the morning. As he entered the industrial area of the harbor, he realized that he would likely make his time down to the minute. He was lucky there was virtually no traffic, allowing him to make full use of the Volvo's 240-horse turbo-charged four-cylinder motor. Coming around a curve as he was getting near, he was surprised by a truck exiting the port pull out directly in front of him. He slammed on the brakes and felt the ABS struggle to bring his car to a halt. Coming to a full stop a foot from the semi, he breathed a sigh of relief. The relief was short-lived, however, as the rear tire of the large trailer caught the front corner of the Volvo. He felt his car jerk and heard the sound of scraping as the truck turned onto the street and made its way past him.

"Ah! I can't believe it! You idiot! Don't you even see where you're going!" he screamed at the top of his lungs. He felt his eye begin to twitch, the same way it had earlier. He strained to control his breathing as he tried to recover his composure. *It's no big deal, it's just a rental. It's not my problem, it's Bob's. It's actually good it happened. I can get rid of this piece of crap*, he tried telling himself. He didn't even want to look at the damage. From what he could see, it didn't look that bad, maybe just a slight scrape to the bumper. He put it into first and slowly released the clutch. Nothing. He looked at his instruments and saw that he had stalled it. He depressed the clutch and turned the ignition, bringing the engine back to life. He gunned it, driving the last kilometer before turning into the warehouse complex. He hadn't bothered doing a surveillance detection route. He didn't have the time. It really didn't matter because he was positive no one could have followed him at those speeds and gone unnoticed that time of night.

He turned to his watch: 11:52. He was four minutes past their meet time.

Rostov would still be there. He would probably have some derogatory remark waiting for him, but he would certainly not be so foolish as to risk something going wrong with the operation just to spite him. He knew his masters back in Moscow wouldn't tolerate such impertinence. He drove down the dimly lit area, illuminated by the glow of the yellow streetlights, until he spotted the familiar-looking warehouses sitting side by side. Switching off his lights, he pulled in between them and disappeared into the darkness. As he drew closer, he spotted the almost imperceptible red LED in the top corner of the windshield of a vehicle parked in the shadows—their verification method for spotting each other during a nighttime meeting. He recognized Rostov's dark blue Opel parked alongside one of the warehouses. He pulled up opposite him and rolled down his window to face an annoyed Russian glare.

"I am sure you have another very credible excuse as to why you are late again, but please spare me the burden of having to hear it," Rostov said with displeasure.

"You're so full of wit, aren't you? We have some very important business to take care of. Otherwise there's a risk of everything unraveling. If that happens, I'm certain no one back in Moscow will want to hear any of your lame excuses. You'll probably get the same kind of hero's welcome as back in the good old Soviet days with the KGB—a bullet in the back of the head in some basement cell at Lubyanka Prison. I know things haven't changed much since then. So, if you're done with your sarcasm, I'll fill you in," Canton shot back, proud of how he had put Rostov in his place.

"What is it that is so important?"

"Shiravi somehow made contact with a former CIA officer he knew from many years back. The guy's name is Michael Blackstone. Don't ask me how they know each other. Blackstone's been out of the service for over ten years, but somehow has decided he's going to help Shiravi and made his way over here to Istanbul. We don't know where he is. He gave our surveillance team the slip at the airport. He had inside help. The only one he has any connection with over here that could give him that kind of help is the current MIT chief of counterterrorism here in Istanbul, Asya Tarhan. You ever hear of her?"

"I know of her," Rostov said curtly.

"Well, I had an official visit with her a few days ago after the hit on Mohammedi. She couldn't provide me any intel, which is good for us, obviously. Since Shiravi made contact with Blackstone, we have to assume Blackstone knows everything Shiravi knows, and if Tarhan is the one helping Blackstone, we have to assume she knows everything too. We don't have access to Shiravi and Blackstone, but we do to Tarhan. We need to get her and find out anything she knows that can lead us to Blackstone and Shiravi. Obviously, once we do that, she will have to be eliminated. That's a shame, because she's a nice piece of ass, but a bitch also, so I'm not too heartbroken."

"She is also a senior officer in Turkey's intelligence service, in case you have forgotten where you are right now."

"I don't care what she is. It sounds like, despite how you like to portray yourself, you're just all talk when it comes to something challenging. Is it too much for you to snatch a female spook and extract a little bit of info from her, or don't you have the stomach for it? I don't see we have any other choice in the matter, do you?"

Rostov sat there silently while he considered what he had just been told. Canton knew he had him boxed in. Now, he just needed to set the terms of what each of them would be responsible for doing. He would leave the wet work to Rostov. That was more up his alley. He would take care of extracting the information from Tarhan, intending on experiencing as much enjoyment throughout that process as possible. It wasn't as if she would have the ability to do anything to him afterwards. She would be dead. Rostov would take care of that part.

After a few moments, Rostov answered, "I will have to confer with Moscow first, but on this I agree with you."

"Good, that's what I wanted to hear. Obviously, I can't get my local assets involved in this operation, so you're going to have to come up with the arrangements for the snatch and grab, a secure location to keep her at while I interrogate her, and then of course you will have to take care of the disposal afterwards. Think you can handle your part?"

"It appears you expect us to take all the risks, while you take none but obtain all the benefits."

"What risks? Is it too much for your boys to handle? Your Russian women have you so whooped, you're scared to take on a middle-aged piece of ass? I'd say I'm the one taking all the risk since she's going to see my face, but then again who cares, since it will be the last face she sees? Whatever I get from her, of course I'm going to share with you. We'll still need to eliminate Blackstone and Shiravi. Can't do it without your help," Canton said, trying to throw Rostov a bone after the insult.

"You seem to forget that we are in this situation as a result of your carelessness. Now you must rely on others to clean up your mess. If you were working for the SVR, you would be the one getting the bullet in the back of the head as a result of your incompetence. I will arrange for the abduction and the interrogation location. You will have to arrange a meeting with her outside her office, in the evening after dark, in a location I provide to you. Can you take care of your part?"

"Yeah, I can take care of that. How quickly can you put this together?"

"It will take a few days. Saturday or Sunday."

"Good, that will give me all the more reason to set up a meeting with her outside her normal working hours on a weekend," Canton said with satisfaction. He knew he had scored as big a victory as he could have hoped for. He still had to deal with Blackstone and Shiravi, but this was the first step. Taking care of Blackstone would give him the most satisfaction, but Tarhan would definitely bring him the most pleasure.

"I will contact you by Friday to provide the location and time."

"All right, then, I'm glad we see things the same way. I knew that despite your foolish pride, in the end you Ruskies manage to consider things rationally, unlike these senseless rag head fanatics over in this part of the world. We're going be doing both our countries a big service cutting down their numbers after all this is over and done with. After we get the Chinks on a tight leash with their oil and gas supplies, it'll be just like the good old days when it was just you and us," he patronized Rostov. *Only Russia will be a whole lot smaller and weaker than the USSR ever was*, he finished his thought. "*Dasvidanya*, comrade." Canton rolled up his window and slowly started pulling away.

Rostov keyed the mike to his concealed communications unit. "He's pulling out. Follow him. I want to know where he is staying," he ordered the surveillance teams.

"Krasnya One, understood."

"Krasnya Two, understood."

"Krasnya Three, understood."

"You can stay off him. It will not be difficult to track a Volvo station wagon with one headlight and no bumper cover," he advised his team, then released his mike. "*Dasvidanya, Doorack*," he said, bidding goodbye to the fool.

Chapter 17

Michael woke to find Asya's head nestled on his shoulder. Although it seemed a bit strange to look down and see her arm draped across his chest, the feel of her next to him was something he could very easily get used to waking up to every morning. He listened to her quiet breathing and took in the scent of her hair against his cheek. It was a wonderfully new experience, after all the years they had shared together only as friends and partners at work. They had come to her bed and lay down next to each other in the same position, eventually drifting off to sleep together. Neither of them spoke; they had nothing more to say to each other. They both knew what lay ahead and just wanted to experience the intimate presence of each other, for the short while they had remaining together. He wondered if this would be the first and last time they would ever share this experience. If it was, he had no regrets. He would at least have this memory of having been close to her.

With his other arm, he reached across and ran his fingers softly through her hair. She responded with a barely audible "mmm." He continued gently caressing her, causing her to pull in closer and rub her face back and forth into his shoulder. She opened her eyes and looked up at him, giving him a pleasing smile that said she shared the same feeling of contentment at where she found herself.

"Good morning."

"Yeah, it is a good morning," he replied.

She scooted up to him and planted her lips on his, giving him a long, drawn-out kiss. They lingered there, allowing themselves to soak up as much of each other as they could short of letting the passion take over and lead them down the path they knew wasn't possible right now. They finally broke contact and peered into each other's eyes, communicating silently what both of them wanted. It was maddening.

"Michael Blackstone, you better come back. This is not how I want to leave this. I want all of you," she told him passionately.

"I want the same," he replied earnestly. "I can't begin to explain how us coming together like this after all these years makes me feel. I just want you to know, no matter what happens, how much you mean to me, Awsh. I know it sounds strange saying it after we've been together for only two days. I don't understand it myself. I'm just happy, overjoyed, thankful it happened." he finished, his voice starting to crack.

How in the world could he tell someone he had just met less than forty-eight hours ago that he felt that way about her? They had known each other for almost four years, during which time they had become very close, but it had never been personal. They might not have been physically or emotionally intimate; that aspect of their lives had been separated by a giant wall of mutual respect and professionalism, but they had shared other parts of themselves. Even though they hadn't seen it, they knew that personal side of each other's lives existed. Now that that barrier had been torn down, it was all that was needed to fill in the missing pieces of their relationship. He knew their lives had taken such different trajectories, but for whatever reason, they had crossed paths once again. Where anything could lead, he had no idea, but he knew he couldn't leave to go on this mission, without having told her how he felt about her.

"*Seni seviyorum*, my sweet," she answered, telling him she loved him also.

"For as much as I hate the idea of moving one inch from where I'm at, if I don't get up and hop in the shower this minute, I may not be able to maintain my self-control any longer," he told her, the torment clearly evident in his voice.

"I think that is a good idea, because my self-control at this moment is almost nonexistent. If you do not get out of this bed, I am going to attack you," she cried out in frustration.

Michael jumped out of bed, sparing them both from further agony. He stood at the side of the bed, looking down at the outline of her body behind her flannel nightie that went down to just above her knees. He was mesmerized by how good she could look in granny sleepwear. Who needed Victoria's Secret? She lay on her side, with one leg in front of the other and her head propped up in her hand, looking back at him. He noticed her smile increasing and her eyes drifting back and forth from his midsection. He looked down and spotted what she was looking at, causing him to blush.

"See? I did a tactical retreat just in time, or we would have lost complete control of the situation," he laughed.

"Hmm, you have a similar effect on me. It is just we women can hide it longer, up to a certain point," she toyed with him.

"Okay, I really have to get to the shower. Otherwise I'm going to jump back in bed and do some unthinkable things to you." He turned and headed towards the door. Short of being surrounded and captured by a platoon of IRGC special forces, he would do whatever it took to get back to this woman.

***

Hamed arrived at his office after stopping by to visit Reza at the hospital. His condition remained unchanged. He was still on a respirator in a deep coma. Hamed wanted to sit there next to his bedside holding his hand all day, but his duties called, and he had forced himself to leave after forty-five minutes. After speaking with Reza's teacher yesterday, he had returned to his office in order to prepare for his next, and for all practical purposes last, interrogation of Shiravi. This time around, he had planned on employing some enhanced interrogation techniques that would create significant physical discomfort. Although he might require some light medical care afterwards, there would be no lasting physical disabilities. With psychological disabilities, however, Hamed couldn't be so absolute. Each man had his own breaking point. Some could bounce back and live a normal life; others were not so lucky. It was an unfortunate and sorrowful thing to do to another human being, but Hamed's first duty was to his country and people. What was the price of a few hundred men, compared to the safety of his entire nation?

He had sat behind his desk for nearly three hours trying to organize his line of questioning but found that he couldn't concentrate on anything for more than a few seconds before his attention was focused back on Reza. His precious child was fighting for his life, and Hamed was helpless to do anything to save him. He would periodically get up and walk around his desk to his prayer rug and bow down to Allah in prayer, asking for the same thing each time.

"Most Merciful Allah, I humbly ask You to spare my precious child. Please do not take him. Restore his body and mind and allow him to return to us." At this, he would break down sobbing.

He had finally left his office when he realized it would be useless to try to stay any longer and actually accomplish anything. He was in no condition to develop his interrogation plan. In his state, all he could do was return home and sit in the dark silence of his living room. His wife had returned from the hospital and collapsed in bed early from the emotional exhaustion of the day. Her sister had offered to have Tahmin stay at her home, so that they could focus on Reza. He had sat in his chair throughout the night, dozing off occasionally for a few hours, then waking to have his mind race through countless thoughts about all the possibilities of how he could track down whoever had so heartlessly mowed down his child. He didn't care if it was a senior IRGC officer. He would find a way to return the cruelty to this vile man, so he could experience the same pain he had inflicted on his child. His expertise in that field would allow him many options on how to drag it out in order to ensure complete retribution for his evil. Of course, Hamed would have to find a way of disposing of the body afterwards, but he had many avenues available to him as an IRGC colonel in his special division.

Working directly for General Bardari granted him authority to make use of virtually all of the extensive facilities and locations under the IRGC's control. Disposing of a badly disfigured body wasn't an everyday practice, but it didn't raise eyebrows with anyone when it was occasionally necessary. After all, they were the IRGC. The extended absence of an IRGC flag officer would eventually come to the attention of the command, but by then there would be no way to connect it to Hamed. There would be an investigation, but it would remain unresolved. Hamed was too professional to leave any evidence connecting him to it. Besides, he knew the IRGC unit that would investigate such a disappearance. The level of expertise of his colleagues didn't impress him. There was a reason one was sent to the Internal Investigations Department. It was usually because they had a reputation for laziness and a lack of motivation. The commander of the department was Colonel Ajabari, who himself was at a dead end in his career. The challenging part would be gaining access to his subject, being a flag-level IRGC officer. Hamed would have to arrange something, most likely at his victim's residence.

It saddened him to think he would be forced to eliminate the two men who would assist him in that endeavor. It wasn't possible to allow anyone to remain alive that could implicate him in kidnapping an IRGC general. It would be unfortunate, but they were enlisted conscripts assigned to the IRGC, expendable when necessary. Although they would be assisting him in seeking personal retribution for the brutal assault inflicted on his son, the IRGC would be better off without such a contemptible senior officer. How could any man claim to worship Allah, yet lack the most basic conscience? Their sacrifice, however, wouldn't be in vain. He would ensure the families received their medals for heroism while serving their country, along with a survivor's stipend.

It was the part of his duties that he didn't care for, having to exercise discretion over life and death, but he had grown accustomed to that responsibility. He had hoped it wouldn't harden him to the point where he would lose his humanity. In many ways, he detested what the system they lived under had done to their society, how it devalued individual life. Having to defend their way of life against the continuous attack from the West necessitated a certain level of insensitivity in order to be able to defeat their enemies. He hoped his sons would choose another direction in life. Perhaps they could become doctors or clerics, so they wouldn't have to sully themselves with the coarser things of life.

After hours of this relentless cycle throughout the night, he finally got up from his chair and took a hot shower, attempting to work the soreness out of his stiffened neck. It was still dark, and his wife remained asleep in their bedroom. He quietly made his way in and gently kissed the side of her head before leaving their apartment. He made his way back to his office, having a prisoner he still needed to deal with. He arrived while the building was still mostly empty. He made himself a pot of hot sweet tea to help him shake off the cobwebs and think clearly. He had just begun sipping his tea when he heard the call for sunrise prayers. He got up from his desk and made his way to his prayer rug, kneeling down and bowing his head.

He remained there in silence, searching his mind for his prayer to Allah. He finally opened his mouth, beginning, "Allahu Akbar. Glory be to Allah. Praise be to Allah. There is no God except Allah. Allah is the greatest and there is no power and no strength except with Allah. He hears the ones who praise Him. Most Merciful, I ask You to forgive me for my sins. I have not lived up to Your expectations. I have, at times, been a hard man, failing to show the same mercy to others that You have shown to me. I have tried to live my life righteously, teaching my children Your instructions received through the Prophet, and protecting our faith from the evil attacks of the infidels. I have always served You, my Lord, if not always correctly, always full-heartedly. I have sought Your guidance but have never asked You to reveal anything to me that was beyond your wishes. Now, my Lord, I ask You to reveal to me the one who has done this to my child. Grant me this wish, so that I may bring Your justice to the evil man who did this wicked act with such cold-heartedness. Please allow me this, Allah. *Allahu Akbar, Allahu Akbar, Allahu Akbar.*"

He rose from his prayer rug and returned to his desk. It was time to return his focus to Shiravi. He needed to resolve this outstanding issue once and for all and provide General Bardari with a final report. He would offer his professional opinion regarding the veracity of Shiravi's information, backed up by the assurance that it had withstood the trial of his enhanced interrogation techniques. If Bardari didn't like his results, he could get somebody else to try, but he knew there was no one with a better track record than him in extracting the truth. He went over Shiravi's confession in his mind, pondering where the most critical part of his story was, the part that would leave him the most vulnerable, along with what tools would be most effective in breaking down any resistance. Electrical current was unpleasant enough that most individuals could resist it for only a very short period of time, long before very much intensity was required. He didn't want to cause Shiravi any more pain than was necessary, especially since he was fairly certain he was already telling the truth. Perhaps it would be traumatic enough for Shiravi to disclose something else he might be holding back. Something that Hamed could hang his hat on as certainty he had obtained the complete truth. He would see how things went. If it was apparent Shiravi had nothing else to provide, he wouldn't continue to unnecessarily subject him to pain. He harbored no personal animosity towards the man. He would reserve the agony for the man who had harmed his child.

He sipped his sweet tea while he rubbed the back of his neck. Having spent the night in his living room chair, even if it was oversized and deeply cushioned, wasn't the wisest thing for his body. Besides the stiffness, he hadn't gotten enough sleep and felt the first signs of a headache coming on. He didn't like going into interrogations not being in tip-top mental shape. He would prepare the rest of the day, leave early to spend time with his son beside his bed, hold his small hand and pray to Allah for him. Perhaps he could even convince the staff to find him a small cot so he could sleep in the presence of his son all night. That would give Laleh the opportunity to go back home and get a good night's sleep after spending the entire day at the hospital, with the peace of knowing he was next to their son. He would probably even sleep more restfully there himself, rather than spending another sleepless night in his living room chair. His mind needed to be clear tomorrow. It was his against his subject's. He needed to be as sharp as possible in order to maintain complete control of the situation. He was the one who dictated how the interrogations went, keeping his subjects off balance and constantly uncertain about their immediate future. His complete control over his subjects' fate, coupled with assistance from his enhanced interrogation tools, made it an uneven playing field. But since when was interrogation supposed to be fair?

***

Michael pulled Asya's A7 into the parking garage at Istanbul Atatüurk International Airport. He found it amusing that she tossed him her car keys when they were preparing to leave her apartment for the airport. It wasn't that he didn't enjoy driving her performance Audi through the distantly familiar streets of Istanbul. It brought back some exciting memories of chasing down bad guys during the heyday of his youthful past. He didn't know if she did it out of some Turkish code of conduct that had been bred into the DNA of Turkish women over the centuries, or if she also wanted to revisit some of those same memories. But the irony and humor of the head of Turkish counterterrorism in Istanbul interacting with him like she was his college sweetheart while at the same time helping him undertake one of the most incredible hostile country penetration operations in history as an amateur wasn't lost on him. It all seemed so surreal. As his thoughts drifted back and forth from questioning if all this was real, he wondered if in fact he had shot himself and was trapped inside his damaged brain as it was taking him through some wild never-ending dream. He noted, however, he had called himself an amateur. Too self-possessed a thought for all this to be a dream. It was real enough—and sobering.

He had at one time had received Special Operations training and had run intelligence assets in real life, but that had been a long time ago. Things had changed since then. He had changed since then. It wasn't that he doubted his ability to still be able to think quickly and clearly. He had also maintained his fitness pretty well for a fifty-some-year-old. It was more an issue of confidence in himself. Or had it just been cockiness in the past? Some feeling of foolish invulnerability. He had found out the hard way just how vulnerable he had been. Whether it was genuine unease or the butterflies felt before the first snap of the game, he knew the period before the kickoff was always the worst. He wondered if that was how all those thousands of young GIs felt leading up to the D-Day Normandy Invasion during World War II.

Asya had decided to leave her car at the airport garage, waiting for her return tomorrow. There was no reason for her to stay in Agri. She could be no help to him there. Istanbul was where she had all her resources. They would have to wait to discuss what exfiltration support Ercan's unit could provide Michael. Dropping him off in the dead of night was risky enough. Illegally encroaching on a country's sovereignty for a second time, when you no longer controlled the timing, could be suicidal, or could at a minimum land the colonel in a military prison for life if they were detected. There were a lot of risks for everyone, but what was the alternative if they didn't act? Asya realized the magnitude of what she would be asking of Ercan. She was also sure he wouldn't hesitate once he learned of the details and the consequences if nothing was done. The only two men who had ever mattered to her, were both putting their lives on the line. It didn't surprise her that neither would hesitate to do so. She knew what kind of cloth both of them were cut from. They weren't perfect, but they were both principled and courageous men who didn't shrink from fear when they knew what was required of them. She wondered if that was what had drawn her to both of them, despite their handsome looks.

They grabbed their bags from the trunk and headed across the elevated pedestrian platform to the terminal. As planned, they purchased their tickets separately, but requested the two adjoining empty seats they had found on the Turkish Airlines website. The mere fact that they would be sitting together wasn't an issue. An electronic record of having purchased tickets together was. The flight was scheduled to depart at 1:30 p.m. and arrive in Agri at 3:35 p.m. It would give them just enough time to grab a cup of coffee before their flight started boarding in forty-five minutes. They found the Starbucks along with an empty table and sat, sipping their coffees while watching travelers rush by them to their gates. To anyone who happened to see them, they appeared like a typical couple traveling together on holiday. Michael looked at Asya dressed in her brown leather jacket, clingy black skinny jeans and designer Italian boots. She looked amazingly attractive. He was sure other men, traveling alone or accompanied, also noticed her. She was hard not to notice. He liked the thought of traveling with her sometime in the future on their way to a place like the island of Santorini for a summer holiday. For now, he had to settle for the staging area of their mission. Their entire situation was one big paradox. She looked at him over her cup as she sipped it. Her eyes smiled at him with affection. He returned a slight smile, wondering if she was having similar thoughts.

They heard the boarding announcement for their flight and made their way to their gate. It would only be a little over a two-hour flight, just long enough to enjoy a refreshment and take a short power nap. He would need to get as much sleep as he could leading up to the mission. He didn't know how much opportunity he would have once he had gone in. He prepared himself for the likelihood it would be only a few hours here and there, as was usually the case on these types of missions. There was a reason special operation units were issued amphetamines prior to extended missions; sleep was a luxury in very short supply.

They boarded when they heard their section called and took their seats in row seventeen of the Turkish Airlines Airbus A318. They were fortunate in that the flight was only half-full and the seat next to them was vacant. After fastening their seat belts, they grabbed each other's hand, as naturally as any other couple flying somewhere together would. He looked at her hand in his. *Guess we're a couple*, he thought and smiled, *at least for a few more hours*. A few moments later, the aircraft backed away from its gate and taxied promptly to the number two position at the end of the runway. Michael closed his eyes and put his head back as he had done so many times in his past. He felt the aircraft move forward and take the turn onto the runway. Thirty seconds later, he heard the engines come to full throttle and felt the thrust of the plane gradually beginning its acceleration down the runway. He remembered the sensation of lifting off the ground, then the sound of the landing gear retracting back into the plane, before he drifted off to sleep. Asya looked over at him in amazement and gave a big smile. He hadn't changed in seventeen years.

***

Canton had slept in, waking late in the morning in the plush king-size bed of his suite at the Ritz-Carlton. He was thankful he hadn't pursued getting some female companionship on his way back from his meeting with Rostov last night. He had gotten a good night's sleep, which he had desperately needed. He knew if he had brought back company, he might have gotten to sleep by 3:00 a.m. if he was lucky. Then he would be dealing with the headache of a hangover while having to kick some Russian whore out of his suite a few hours later. He knew he would have felt miserable. He would have time to indulge later.

While he waited for room service to bring him the coffee and poached salmon he had ordered for brunch, he organized his thoughts about what he needed to accomplish today. His first priority was to get things set up in order to lure Tarhan into a situation where they could abduct her. He was sure he would thoroughly enjoy every aspect of her interrogation; that would make a night with a Russian whore pale in comparison. He would take his time with Tarhan and ensure he had completely broken her, both physically and emotionally, before they would dispose of her. He couldn't wait to see the expression of helplessness on her face, begging him to let her go, telling him she would do anything if he would just spare her. He would have the satisfaction of totally humiliating her, stripping her of all her dignity before her end. The thought of having so much power and control over another's life excited him, giving him a feeling of potency. He knew in order to defeat your enemies, you had to be completely ruthless in how you dealt with them. It had always been that way throughout history.

He pulled out his official government-issued mobile phone and dialed Tarhan's office, getting her secretary.

"This is Jonathan Canton with the US embassy. I'd like to speak with Ms. Tarhan."

"Hello, Mr. Canton. Ms. Tarhan is not available currently. Would you like to leave her a message?"

"This is important. You need to get a hold of her right away," he instructed her brusquely.

"If you leave me a message, I will attempt to get it to her as soon as it is possible, Mr. Canton," she answered politely.

"This is an important matter to both our governments. I should be able to get a hold of her at a moment's notice. Do you know when she will be available?" he asked annoyed.

"I do not know, Mr. Canton. She keeps her own schedule. But I will attempt to contact her if you would like me to do so."

"Why don't you give me her mobile number and I will contact her directly?"

"I am sorry, Mr. Canton, I am not authorized to give out her number. Only she does," Asya's secretary parried him once again, politely telling him he could piss off if he thought he could intimidate her. In this case, he was dealing with the doorkeeper for Tarhan, and all doorkeepers knew they were the ones with the power when it came to accessing their principal.

"All right, just tell her to contact me immediately. She has my number," he finally relented.

"I will do that, Mr. Canton. Is there anything else?"

"No, I'll just be waiting to hear back from her promptly," he finished and abruptly hung up in the middle of the secretary telling him to have a good day.

He looked at his watch. It was almost 12:30 p.m. That annoyed him. He should have set an alarm. He had wasted half the day, but he finally felt clearheaded and told himself the extra sleep was worth the time. Besides, there was nothing he could do until he had made contact with Tarhan. In the meantime, he would get a hold of Bob and tell him to have someone come and exchange his rental car. This time, he would order him as a deputy director to provide him with a car that met his requirements, and that was not a Volvo sports wagon. It might have been Bob's country as far as operational authority went, but he outranked a chief of station and expected his orders to be followed when it came to logistical support for this priority investigation.

He heard a knock on the door and the announcement of room service from the other side. He would sit and enjoy his coffee and poached salmon while he caught up with the news on BBC World and CNN International. Classified briefings were certainly important, but the mainstream international press had correspondents stationed throughout the world that often picked up on events that fell beneath the radar of the intelligence community. Not always as critical as the collection priorities of the CIA, but no less valuable in filling in the backdrop of what was going on in the world.

***

Michael woke from his slumber as the flight attendants came by for the last trash collection before the flight began its descent into Agri. He twisted his head to stretch his neck as gave a big yawn attempting to bring himself back into the present moment. Asya smiled at him.

"You fall asleep like hitting a switch," she told him.

"Yeah, it's something I picked up through all the training in the military. You grab sleep when you can get it, so you learn how to turn it on and off pretty quickly. It's stayed with me ever since."

"You will certainly need that for what is coming up. How are you feeling?"

"I'm doing okay. You know how it is before big operations, all the anxiety of not knowing what to expect. You try not to let uncertainty and doubt get the better of you, while trying to stay calm and clearheaded. I know it'll be different once I'm in-country and actually have to operate in whatever the environment is," he confided.

She squeezed his hand and continued rubbing it with her thumb. He liked her soothing touch. Once they had landed, they would be in the presence of Ercan and his unit for the hours remaining until he would infill into Iran. There would be no more tender contact between the two of them. He hoped he would be able to feel her soft touch again someday.

As the landing gear opened beneath, Michael looked out his window and saw the magnificent sight of the snow-covered Mount Ararat off in the distance towards the Iranian border. In approximately twelve hours, he would be hiking in on foot on the other side of that border. He tried to convince himself he was prepared to face whatever awaited him. If he kept his cool and thought clearly, with a little bit of luck, he might somehow survive this undertaking. He tried not to focus too much on how everything was going to come together, especially breaking Ali out of wherever he was being held. He would just take it one step at a time and see where things led. For this mission all the planning in the world would be useless. There were too many variables and unknowns. He would have to improvise along the way. He hoped he was up to the task. It was a constant battle fighting back the doubt that he wasn't.

The Airbus touched down, the reverse thrusters roaring to life as they helped bring down the speed of the braking aircraft. The pilot made a hard right catching the ramp so he wouldn't have to taxi back down the field to the terminal. He pulled into the small apron next to the terminal building. It wasn't a large airport, just enough room for four medium-sized jetliners to park. There were two daily flights into Agri. One direct from Istanbul, the other one making a stop in Ankara. Michael watched as the ladder truck approached the side of the aircraft and positioned itself next to the front door. He saw the flight attendant slide the door latch and push it open. The passengers stood up and began making their way to the front of the aircraft. Michael and Asya grabbed their bags from the overhead bins and fell in, shuffling up to the door. Descending the covered stairs, they walked towards the terminal building. They passed by the baggage carousel and the two Turkish policemen with their Heckler & Koch MP5 submachine guns slung across their shoulders. They gave Asya a long stare as she walked by, not out of suspicion, but clearly taking in the most noteworthy sight they had seen thus far in their day. Michael wondered if they even noticed him walking next to her.

They walked out through the entrance of the terminal to the curbside. There was the usual line of taxis out front that had shown up hoping to catch a fare from one of the arriving passengers, the drivers voicing "taxi" to each of the passengers as they came outside. Asya looked down towards the front of the drive and spotted a tall dark-haired man with a mustache in a green sweater and camouflage pants, standing next to an olive-green Toyota Land Cruiser outfitted with a deep-water air intake and exhaust kit. He noticed her and gave a nod as they made their way towards him. Asya walked up to him, giving him a kiss on each cheek, followed by a brief hug, which he returned. He was a handsome man who looked very well kept for a man close to Michael's age. As a colonel in Turkey's elite commando unit, he obviously had to maintain superb physical condition. Not that he would be leading missions at his age and rank, but as the leader of the unit under his command, he had to set the example to his men. Michael forced himself not to let the subconscious reaction of jealousy get the better of him. Of course she would give him a kiss and a hug. She had once intended on marrying this man. It was natural she still had some lingering feelings for him. Part of him still felt the sense of loss of Karen and Eva in his life. Those were emotions you couldn't completely divorce from your memories.

"*Merhaba,*" she greeted him.

"*Merhaba. Nasılsın?*" he said, asking her how she was.

"*İyi,*" she answered, telling him she was doing well. "This is Michael, an old friend of mine from seventeen years ago. We worked together in Istanbul. He was with the US embassy, assigned to work with us on the counterterrorism unit back when I first started. Michael, Ercan," she said in English.

"Nice to meet you Michael," Ercan said in perfect English.

"Nice to meet you also. Asya's told me some about you. I know how highly she thinks of you. Thank you for being willing to help us out with this situation."

"All right. Let's head back to our base and you can fill me in on the way," he told them as he opened up the back of the Land Cruiser for their bags.

"We need to stop and pick up a basket. Something that looks local and that Michael will be able to pack with him for some distance," Asya told Ercan.

"Okay, I know where we can find that in Agri. The markets should be opening back up soon."

They got into their seats, Michael insisting Asya ride in the front with Ercan when she attempted to get into the backseat. He smiled at her and told her it would be easier for her to fill Ercan in on the details rather than himself, since she knew everything he did and could switch to Turkish if needed.

"I can assure you, Michael, I can understand everything you may want to tell me. I spent two years at NATO in Napoli, Italy, where the utilized language was English. It was a prerequisite that you had a good command of English to even be considered, which I had from studying it while in university, but having to speak it daily for two years made me learn it very fluently, particularly after hours in social situations."

"Wow, that's impressive. I'd say you even have one up on Asya, even though her English is pretty good."

"Oh, she did not hesitate to correct me when I said something that made me sound like some peasant from a village in eastern Anatolia, but she certainly spoke it much better than I did prior to living in Napoli."

"When were you in Italy?"

"I went there for my first staff assignment as a brand-new major fourteen years ago. You can imagine as a 04 at NATO, I was assigned as the aide to one of our generals on staff there. A glorified gofer, if that is the correct term I am remembering. It was not bad for two years. Not very challenging, just keep the general on time, his uniforms cleaned and pressed, and warn him discreetly if it looks like he will embarrass himself, especially if he is heading back home with lipstick on his face. It helps one's career to have an appreciative general, especially one who managed to survive the leadership purges our military has been going through. Besides that, I had the opportunity to learn much about other NATO members' militaries and made some very good friends that I still remain in contact with," Ercan related to him.

"That's the same time as I was in Athens, Greece, which is indirectly related to our current situation. I'll let Asya fill you in. Just a heads-up, it's going to sound pretty incredible," Michael warned.

Ercan pulled out from the curb and headed around and out of the airport. They traveled down a secondary two-lane highway, through rural agricultural areas, as they made their way towards Agri. Asya began by relating the story in reverse, filling him in about Ali and what had happened to him following the assassination of the Iranian foreign minister. She explained about sighting him on the video going into the Iranian consulate, then the crates being loaded into the Iranian aircraft, and their belief that he had been smuggled out of Turkey into Iran. Finally, she told him about Michael's decision to go in and attempt to liberate Ali, and the ad hoc plan they had come up with to accomplish that. When Asya had finally finished her briefing, Ercan sat in silence while he drove. Michael could tell by the look of his eyes in the rear-view mirror that he was still taking it all in.

"You were certainly correct, Michael, it sounds beyond incredible. The leaders of the United States and Russia conspiring to commit such a heinous crime. If I did not know Asya the way I do, and the fact that she vouches for you, I would think you were some unbalanced person or provocateur of some sort. But how will you be able to locate this man and, even if you do, break him out of prison and escape from Iran?" Ercan asked in disbelief.

"Both very good points, and I don't know that I can provide with any rational answers, other than there is one very highly placed person in the government of Iran who might have a vested interest in helping Ali. I will attempt to locate this official and convince him to help me get Ali out. That's basically my only hope, but under the present circumstances, I can't think of any other options. If you have any ideas or suggestions, I'd be all ears."

"I am speechless. I do not know if that is the most insane plan I have ever heard or the boldest. What support do you have?"

"Pretty much Asya here, an old trusted friend back in D.C., and whatever you can offer."

"And how do you intend to get to Tehran? It is over one thousand kilometers from the border."

"By bus, just like every other Iranian."

"I see," said Ercan, then fell silent again, contemplating Michael's request.

"I realize what we're asking of you, Ercan. It could mean the end of your career or even worse if something goes wrong or it is found out. I know you're being considered for brigadier. This could mean the end of that," Asya said, breaking the silence.

"It is not that, Asya. I understand the significance of what Michael has to do. I also understand what is at risk for the entire world if something is not done to stop this madness. What I risk, is insignificant by comparison. I will do whatever is required to assist you, Michael. I am just thinking of how I will do this. We will discuss this back at our camp and come up with a plan. I am assuming you will want to go in as soon as possible."

"Yes, there's really no time to waste. Asya and I were considering some possible locations. I'd like your opinion on our idea and what would be possible as far as a nighttime insertion. Do you have rotary aircraft available with that capability?" Michael asked.

"I have four Black Hawks with night vision capability, which the unit under my command has been training with. Getting you in over the border will not be too difficult. The challenge will be getting you back out, if that is part of your plan."

"Yeah, that's the big unknown with all of this. I certainly don't expect you and your men to wait around here indefinitely in the hopes of getting Ali and me back out. I can't tell you if or when that could actually happen, and the risk for your men may be unacceptable. Calling it a plan is really stretching the meaning of the word."

"We were scheduled to remain here conducting training until Monday. If necessary, I can extend it for a longer period. We will just have to plan an extraction point and communications procedures for when you will be there. As I said, Michael, I understand the significance of what may happen if nothing is done to stop this. I do not want my children growing up in the world that will exist if this is allowed to progress to the point that nuclear weapons are used. Turkey shares a border with Iran. It will greatly affect our country and the entire region. I am in, for as long as is required."

Michael was impressed with Ercan's fortitude. He realized why Asya had been attracted to him. He seemed to be a man of principle who didn't quit when things got tough. He couldn't say the same about himself. He wondered if this was his way of trying to redeem himself, putting himself in an impossible situation filled with so much danger. Whatever his true motivation, there was no other choice. No one else could do what needed to be done. He would either succeed and save Ali and the lives of millions of others, or fail and fade into oblivion, forfeiting any meaning to his life, just as he had nearly done a few days ago.

"Well, here we are. It is not much. I would not call it a city, but it is a large town with a few restaurants, three hotels and all of the basic necessities. I send some of my men in every morning to the bakery for some fresh pide," Ercan informed him. "The stuffed dough is baked for about ninety seconds in an extremely hot brick oven and comes out as a flat bread that is slightly crispy on the outside, but very light and tender on the inside. They make it quite delicious here, stuffed with goat cheese and spinach. It is one of the few luxuries we indulge in when we are out here training. It is true what Napoleon said: 'An army marches on their stomach.' Keep good soldiers fed, and they will do anything you ask of them."

Ercan turned down a secondary street lined with various shops and small warehouses. He parked the Land Cruiser in front of a storefront attached to what appeared to be a small workshop. All three got out and entered. Hanging from hooks on every wall were a variety of hand-stitched leather bags and a selection of different baskets scattered throughout the store. An old Turkish man wearing a knitted vest was sitting in the back-corner puffing on a water pipe filled with flavored Turkish tobacco.

"*Merhaba*," they greeted him in unison.

"*Merhaba*," he replied, nodding as he continued to puff on his hookah.

They walked around looking at the various bags and baskets. One hanging on the wall immediately caught Michael's eye. He walked over to the beige bag, pulled it off its hook and examined it. Made of tightly braided hemp, it was in the shape of a canister, about two feet deep and eighteen inches in diameter, with two sturdy handles that wrapped around the bottom of the bag.

"This looks like it will work," Michael commented. "I just need something to attach to the handles to sling it over my shoulders." He looked around the shop and spotted a worn three-inch-wide canvas strap hanging over by the old man smoking his tobacco. He walked over to it and grabbed it.

Ercan walked over, grabbing the bag and strap, and asked the old man the price. "*Bu kach para?*"

"*Iki yüz,*" the old man replied. Two hundred lira.

"*Cok pahalıydı. Altmış,*" Ercan said, offering sixty instead.

"*Yüz,*" the old man said, countering with one hundred.

"*Altmış,*" Ercan insisted.

"*Yok hayır,*" the old man told him—no.

Ercan hung the bag and strap on an empty hook and turned as if to walk out of the store.

"*Taman, taman. Altmış,*" the old man relented.

Ercan pulled out three twenty-lira banknotes and gave them to the old man.

"*Teşekkürler,*" he thanked Ercan.

"*Rica ederim,*" he replied, turning and heading towards the door with Michael and Asya following.

"Quite a bit of haggling. That was sixty lira, if I remember correctly. How much is that worth these days?" Michael asked.

"About fifteen dollars," Asya answered.

"I do not know what the old man was smoking in his hookah, thinking he could get two hundred lira for this bag and old strap," Ercan commented with slight annoyance. "I certainly do not look like a tourist."

"He's just trying to make a buck." Michael reached into his wallet and pulled out a twenty-dollar bill, attempting to give it to Ercan.

"No, Michael, please do not insult me. It is nothing."

"Thanks. This will work perfect. I can bury the sat phone and GPS in the bottom of the bag under a pile of dates and pide instead of goat cheese, if the bakery is open. That will provide me with a good supply of food and lighten my load a little," he said as they got back into the Toyota, this time Asya getting into the back.

"I will drive by on our way back to the camp," Ercan said as he started the vehicle and put it into gear, pulling away from the curb.

"Good that you have not shaved in a few days, Michael. Once you put on the clothes we purchased, you will blend right in," Asya commented from behind.

"Yeah, hopefully I'll look like your average Iranian peasant heading into the big city."

"Do you speak any Persian?" Ercan inquired.

"*Shawshawalaaam*," Michael muddled out of his mouth barely decipherable, tapping his ear.

"Ah, very good, feigning to be deaf. That will provide you with some temporary cover if you are questioned by anyone. You will have to be careful not to react to any sounds that will give you away. I am sure in your previous line of work, you had some experience in blending in with indigenous populations."

"Between Special Forces and the CIA, I had plenty of training, but I never had to do it in a real-world situation. Talk about baptism by fire."

"You were Special Forces also?" Ercan asked, surprised.

"Yeah, I had a short career before getting injured and being forced out."

"What happened, if I am permitted to ask?"

"I had a very hard landing on the last jump I made while stationed in Germany. It did a number on my spine. They wouldn't let me stay in SF. It was a choice between pushing a desk in the regular Army or starting a new career. A desk would have been the end for me. I chose the latter."

"Hm. I would have done the same in your situation. The two years on the NATO staff assignment pushed me to my limits of boredom. Did you retire from the CIA? You do not look old enough for that."

"Not quite. I left under less than desirable circumstances. Without going into all the details, that's how I'm connected to Ali and the Iranian official who I'm hoping will help me get him out."

"I see. It sounds like you have had quite an interesting life. You will have to make use of everything you have learned from both your careers for this mission. I am certain it is unlike anything you would have encountered before in Special Forces or the CIA," Ercan said, trying to sound encouraging.

"You're right about that. It's been twelve years since I've been out. It feels like I'm in way over my head."

"It would feel overwhelming for anyone, even if they were active and in their prime."

"Yeah," was all Michael could say as they pulled up to the bakery, which was still open.

Ercan left the motor running and ran inside. A few moments later, he returned holding a large plastic bag filled small loaves of fresh pide and another with bottled water. He handed them to Michael through the window, then ran into a small market a few doors down. He returned a quickly with two plastic bags of dates and got into the driver's seat.

"Throw these, along with the pide, in your bag and your disguise is complete," Ercan said, handing the dates to Michael. The mouthwatering aroma of the pide filled the inside of the vehicle. After grabbing one for Michael and one for himself, he handed the bag of pide to Asya in the back.

Michael tore off a piece and tossed it in his mouth. "You were right about these being good. They'll definitely get me by for a few days. A kiosk selling these in Manhattan would make a fortune."

"That's what my men line up for each morning. I have an arrangement with the bakery for them to bake an extra four hundred of them every morning at six a.m. That gives each man in the company at least three loaves each day to supplement their military rations. It is amazing the impact such a relatively minor thing can have on morale. They will be disappointed when the training is finished, and we have to return to the mess hall of our base," Ercan laughed.

They drove through some more countryside down rural two-lane roads, then turned off onto a dirt road and drove for another three kilometers until they approached a structure off in the distance that Michael recognized from many years ago. As they got closer, Ercan slowed the Land Cruiser as he approached the sentry posted at a checkpoint outside a large encampment protected by a wall of HESCO barriers. They were two-meter-thick collapsible wire mesh containers with heavy-duty liners, that could be filled with sand, dirt or gravel using a front-end loader to form a ready-made fortification out in the field. Able to withstand machine-gun and RPG fire, along with other explosive attacks, they were used extensively by the US military for forward operating bases in the remote regions of Afghanistan and Iraq.

As the Toyota came to a stop, Ercan rolled down his window to receive a smart salute by the sentry when he recognized his commanding officer. Ercan returned the salute and proceeded through into the large compound. Michael observed seven large green tents pitched on the gravel surface, two

Conex boxes, a row of eight outhouses, and an assortment of various military vehicles, ranging from HUMVEEs to transport vehicles on one end, with four Blackhawk helicopters, a Conex box and fuel truck on the other, anchored in the center by a six-meter-tall sandbagged wooden guard tower looking out over the three-meter-tall walls.

"This is a semipermanent training camp that my unit and other Turkish Special Forces units use. We pack everything in and out, but the HESCO barriers. It makes for rustic accommodations, but with Mount Ararat close by, it is an ideal location for our mountain training."

"Wow, it's been over two decades since I was in a place like this. Brings back a lot of good memories. In addition to the challenge and excitement that came with SF, there was a lot of comradery and close bonds made with fellow comrades. I still miss that sometimes even after all these years," Michael reminisced.

"I always sensed the soldier in you," Asya commented from the backseat.

"How's that?"

"Just the way you carry yourself. The way you think also, very disciplined and organized."

"Hmm, maybe that's why I never really liked real estate," Michael joked.

"Real estate?" asked Ercan.

"Selling property, houses. You know, a salesman. Not that there's anything wrong with that for the right type of person. It just wasn't my thing."

"What do you do now?"

"What do I do now? I don't know. Up until a few days ago, that wasn't something I needed to think about." He turned and looked back at Asya. "I guess play James Bond for now and hope everything turns out with a happy ending, just like in the movies."

"For all of our sakes and so many others, I hope that is the case, Michael," Ercan affirmed.

They pulled up next to the last tent, which had a small portable eight-foot tower with three small satellite dishes attached to it. There was a generator humming quietly inside a plywood enclosure and various cables running into the tent.

"This is our command center, where we plan and coordinate the training missions. The tent next door is our briefing tent and mess hall, and the remaining tents are for my men and accompanying flight personnel," Ercan explained as they got out of the vehicle and walked to the entrance of the tent.

They followed him through the entrance of the tent into the command center. Inside there was a beehive of activity, with soldiers sitting on stools with several long folding tables in parallel rows that had a myriad of laptop computers, communication equipment and other electronic gear on them. A row of LED shop lights attached to a two-by-four wooden beam ran across the span of the tent, supported by stands on either end, provided lighting. A large flat-screen hung on another stand along the opposite wall displaying satellite imagery of terrain with small multicolored unit designators at various locations, a white-board next to it with lists scribbled in Turkish and arrows drawn across. A large terrain map, spread across two tables, was being studied by a young captain and a salty sergeant major.

"*Dikkat!*" the captain yelled as soon as he noticed his commanding officer enter the tent. Everyone immediately stood at attention.

"*Rahat,*" he said, calling them to ease, reverting their attention to what they were focused on.

"Just got goose bumps walking into this place. Makes me feel like a young man again." Michael smiled.

"Yes, I enjoy being out in the field. It is something I will miss if I am promoted. Those days will be over for me then."

He walked over to the captain and sergeant major hovering over the terrain map and engaged them in a short conversation. Michael and Asya stood off to the side. From what Michael could make out, he was asking them about how the current training evolution was progressing. He nodded as he listened to their update and dismissed them when they finished. He turned to Asya and Michael and signaled them over.

"So, tell me what you had in mind," he said, directing his attention to Michael.

Michael studied the map a moment, orienting himself. "This is us, somewhere in this vicinity?" He pointed just east of what he assumed was Agri.

"Yes, right here." Ercan placed his finger on the map. "This is Ararat, and this yellow line here designates the border."

"This, then, must be Maku, just over the border."

"Correct."

"All right, then. See this wash right here, about a klick just over the border?"

Michael pointed. "If you could put me down somewhere in there about an hour before dawn, I could make my way down that valley and into town. The terrain looks remote enough in that area that it should provide good sound cover for the helo."

Ercan studied the terrain. He pulled up a stool and sat down, placing his elbows on the table and resting his chin on his folded hands. He sat there thinking for several moments as Michael and Asya waited for him to say something. Finally, he turned and directed his attention to a lieutenant sitting at one of the tables and fired off a short burst of commands. The lieutenant popped up, replying "yes, sir" in Turkish, and ran out of the tent.

"I told him to go get the commander of the aviation unit. He is a major. I am going to tell him that I have received orders from the General Staff to insert you into Iran across the border. I will have him, along with his executive officer and senior crew chief to fly the mission. I will advise him this is a highly classified mission. He will have the flight plan and drop zone coordinates and that is all. They will not ask any questions, and you will not have to say anything to them unless it is necessary. He speaks fluent English also."

"Okay, looks like this is actually going to happen," he said, the realization hitting him as he looked at Asya.

She gave him as encouraging a smile as she could muster. He made a similar effort in return, seeing from the expression on her face that the reality of what he was about to undertake in a few hours had also hit her. Ercan observed the exchange between them. It was subtle. She wasn't one to allow her emotions to be revealed openly, but he had known her intimately for several years. He could tell Michael was very special to her. In a few minutes, a prematurely balding major in his mid-thirties entered the tent, followed by the lieutenant that had summoned him.

He walked up to Ercan and saluted, addressing him by his rank. "*Albay*."

"Major," he said in English, "I need to brief you on a highly classified mission. I have just received orders from the General Staff. This gentleman is from one of our close allies, and this lady is with the ministry. I have been directed to insert this gentleman into Iran just over this range here, an hour before dawn." He pointed to the insertion point. "You will fly this mission, along with your executive officer and senior crew chief. Based upon the terrain, can the insertion be made without attracting any attention?"

The major glanced at Michael and Asya, then turned his attention to the map. He went over to one of the notebook computers that had a monitor connected to it and zoomed in on the satellite imagery of the insertion point.

He returned to the terrain map and studied it some more before turning his attention to Ercan.

"Yes, Colonel, it can be done."

"Good! Prepare your flight plan, and get back to me to brief it as soon as you are finished."

"Yes, sir!"

"And, Major, you are to discuss this with no one else other than your executive officer and crew chief. Advise them of my order. Is that understood?"

"Yes, sir, understood, Colonel."

"Very good, then, you are dismissed."

The major saluted, then turned and exited the tent in search of his XO and crew chief to begin mission planning.

"Sunrise is at approximately six thirty, which makes astronomical dawn at five. We will need to insert you no later than then to ensure the Blackhawk is completely invisible. It is a little over one hundred kilometers to the drop zone from here, approximately twenty-five minutes' flight time. We will plan for a four thirty liftoff. I will need you back here for a preoperational briefing at three thirty." Glancing at his watch, he continued, "That gives you a little over nine hours. I would suggest you use that time to rest and prepare mentally for the mission. I understand what you are undertaking, my friend. I call you friend, because I know you are a special person to Asya, and that makes you my friend." He shot her a smile. "I have known her long enough to recognize that, and I have only seen that one other time. I will do whatever I can on my part to help you succeed in your mission. Not only for Asya's sake, but also for all the other lives that are at stake. My unit will remain here. I have determined their mountain combat skills are unsatisfactory. We will continue our training until I am satisfied we are at the level we should be. I assume you have secure communications with Asya. If you can make it back anywhere near the border, she will contact me, and we will come and extract you and your friend," he told him with an intense sincerity while looking him in his eyes.

Michael felt a deep gratitude towards Ercan. He admired his boldness and certainty. He saw why he had risen to the position as the commanding officer of Turkey's most elite special operations unit. For the first time, he felt as if he actually stood a chance, however slight, of pulling this off. He hadn't been fatalistic about it. It was just that he was a realist and knew what the odds were based on his circumstances. The odds were still stacked against him, but at least now he had the support of an elite special operations unit to get him out, if he could make it back to the border.

"Thank you, Ercan. I can't begin to explain how grateful I am. You're risking a lot. So is Asya." He looked at her warmly. "I suppose we all are, but there's no alternative, is there? It would be having to carry a lifelong burden, knowing you could have tried something but didn't because of the risk."

They stood there in silence, the generator humming in the background, as the other soldiers in the tent went about whatever they were doing. The gravity of the situation was evident on their faces, as if each of them was experiencing the same reaction concerning how their lives had been brought together at this very moment, without any prior warning or say in the matter. They would either succeed and save the lives of thousands, perhaps even millions, or fail and find themselves in prison, or worse. Even if they did succeed, it didn't rule out the possibility they could face consequences for their unauthorized breach of another country's sovereignty. They might end up saving the world, yet still end up in a prison cell.

Asya finally broke the silence. "Michael will have a mobile phone and a satellite phone with him. He will contact me when he needs to be taken out. I will relay that to you with all the relevant information. Better we keep the telephone numbers Michael will have to a minimum, if the worst-case scenario happens. No reason to implicate any more people than necessary. And I will always have access to my mobile." Asya looked at Michael, the fear of what she had just said apparent on her face.

"That is fine. Since you will be providing him intelligence support, better that you also manage all communications."

Ercan pulled a set of Toyota keys out of his pocket and handed them to Michael. "Take my Land Cruiser. You and Asya go back into town and get something to eat and a hotel room so you can rest. There are four or five of them in town. Just be back here by three thirty. The sentry will be briefed that you will be returning in my vehicle."

"Thank you, Ercan." Asya gave him an appreciative smile.

"Yes, thank you for everything, Ercan," Michael seconded.

"Go now, I have preparations to make," he told them as he ushered them outside the tent to his vehicle.

Michael and Asya took Ercan's Land Cruiser back into town. After locating and driving by a few of the hotels, they settled on one that, at least from the outside, looked like it might have acceptable accommodations. Other than adventurous tourists or climbers coming to conquer nearby Mount Ararat, Agri wasn't anything close to a tourist mecca. Finding a hotel with a decent bed and bath, working Internet and an acceptable restaurant that offered room service, wasn't something they were counting on. They finally settled on the Grand Cenas Hotel just outside of town. It was a narrow seven-story white stucco building with small balconies that looked out over the surrounding dirt fields and sparse homes of the outskirts of Agri. They entered the relatively small lobby, which had the reception counter desk to one side and the entrance to the restaurant across the other side. Asya checked in using her fictitious national identification card that she used for work. She paid the bill for one night up front with cash, and after obtaining the key to their room from the elderly gentleman behind the counter, they headed for one of the two European-sized elevators, having just enough room for two persons and their luggage. They got in and rode to the top floor.

"Seems like a quaint little place. Reminds me a little of some of the small boutique hotels in Rome," Michael commented.

"I have not been there. I have been to Athens, Paris, Vienna and Prague, but never to Rome. It is one of the places that has been on my list to visit," she sighed.

"That would be a place I would love to go with you, someday," he told her wistfully.

"Someday," she replied with a reserved smile, taking his hand.

They exited the elevator and walked down to the end of the short hallway to their room. Asya stuck the key in and unlocked the door, putting the electronic tab of the key into the wall slot to turn on the lights. What they saw surprised them. It was a large room with thick wall-to-wall carpeting, contemporary European styling and a king-size bed, which was virtually unheard of in Turkey, other than in the luxury five-star hotels of Istanbul. What made their jaws drop, however, was when they turned on the light in the bathroom to find a spacious room with black granite throughout and a large glass-walled walk-in tiled shower with dual shower heads and thick white bath towels hanging from hooks.

"Wow! You gotta be kidding me."

"I was not expecting to find this in Agri," Asya agreed.

"Look at that shower. This is so unfair." He shook his head in disbelief, throwing her a flirtatious smile.

"What is wrong? You can take a nice long hot shower. It will make you feel good and relax you. You may not have that luxury for quite some days again," she responded coyly.

"That wasn't what was on my mind. It would have almost been better if this were some run-down dive with two twin beds and a tiny shower over the sink instead of the honeymoon suite."

"You can rest and recover here when you return from your mission. I will give you a much-needed shoulder massage under a hot relaxing shower then."

"Is that a promise?" He placed his hands on her waist.

"It is, if it will give you a reason to make it back," she responded, putting her hands around his neck.

They drew close, their lips making contact as they kissed softly and slowly. It was a long tender kiss yet kept in check from progressing to the point of no return. Both of them ached to fully experience each other's unrestrained passion but realized the harm it could cause at this time. Their lips parting, they continued to embrace, holding each other tightly as minutes rolled by. It was as if they feared letting go of each other, the possibility they would never have the opportunity to hold each other again looming in the background of their thoughts.

Forcing themselves to finally part, Asya suggested, "Why don't you take a long hot relaxing shower and lie down for a few hours? I'll take one after you and come and join you. I'll set my alarm on my phone for two o'clock. That will give us plenty of time to get back to Ercan's base by three thirty."

"How about you take a shower first? I'll just stay here and wait for you to finish and then jump in afterwards," he suggested.

"Yes, then you will need a cold shower, not a hot one." She grabbed one of the thick white bathrobes off its hook and tossed it over his head as she headed out of the bathroom, shutting the door behind her.

"Can't blame a man for trying," he said through the door.

He opened the glass door, turning on one of the shower heads to full hot as he took off his clothes. Finally seeing steam develop, he stepped into the shower and pulled the glass door closed. He stood under the hot water, letting it drench the top of his head and run down his neck and back. Asya was right. The feel of the hot water reinvigorated him and brought relaxation to every muscle in his body. This was it—the best he was going to feel for quite some time. If he was very lucky, and somehow everything went perfectly to plan, there was a slim possibility he could be in and out in less than a week, he thought. The key word there was plan. He had no plan. No intelligence. No locations. He had nothing. He was going in completely alone against one of the United States' most ardent adversaries. A country that had even been a challenge for the CIA to actively penetrate. There had been successes, but they had usually been through assets and proxies developed outside of Iran, who had ready access themselves. He wasn't aware of any Western intelligence officer having operated clandestinely within the borders of Iran. It was a suicide mission. Who was he trying to kid? This was going to be the last decent shower he would ever take, and he would never have the opportunity to experience what it would be like to have a life together with Asya. This moment would be the high point of his remaining life.

Stop thinking that way. You just tried to kill yourself a few days ago, and now you sound like a whining baby because something is going to be taken away from you, he chastised himself. He had known the reality of what he would be facing. He chose to do this, knowing there was no other alternative, not for Ali or all the other lives that depended on him. It was hard for him to come to terms with. How could it be that he was now responsible for all those lives? He didn't know if that was a burden he could carry, especially if he failed. It would have been one thing if it had been about the life of a single person, even if it was a friend. Even though Ali was no longer his asset, relieving him of the responsibility for his safety, in some unconventional way, he was his friend.

Then there was Asya. He had given up any hope of ever being intimately close and sharing his life with anyone again. He had written that out of his life when he had finalized the decision to end it. Even though there was no assurance of any future with Asya, he felt intense heartache at the thought of having to part with her. He had only been with her for forty-eight hours. *Am I losing my mind? That's all I need right now distracting me when I already don't stand a chance.*

He took several deep breaths, exhaling slowly, allowing the soothing hot water to calm him. Everything was just beginning to catch up to him. He needed to keep his cool and think clearly. As long as he logically evaluated the situations he encountered along the way and took a wise course of action, he had a chance of making it back. It was slim, but it was there. No matter how hard he tried to believe his self-administered pep-talk however, the logical side of his brain took him back to the odds of being able to get Ali out and put a stop to the looming humanitarian disaster. He vacillated back and forth as to whether he was an optimistic fool or a condemned realist. He wondered how he would feel if he made it back alive, but without Ali. He wondered how he would feel upon seeing news reports of the hundreds of thousands of deaths brought about by the evil plot he had failed to halt. What kind of life could he have with Asya after something like that? It would be better if he didn't come back without Ali. There would be no purpose. Much as there hadn't been when he had tried taking his life.

Okay, okay. Stop it man. You're going to freak yourself don't stop trying to over-think it. Just be positive. Think positive or you're going to lose your mind. A basket case won't be able to help anyone. Was he having some sort of panic attack? He had been in tight spots before. He certainly didn't remember losing it like this years ago when he was in his prime. Had he just turned in to your average joe, whose idea of a little excitement amounted to a tandem jump during a summer vacation in Cancun? After all, he had been in Special Forces and the CIA. He had all the tools and training he needed to accomplish this. Did he just lack the courage? Was he scared? Scared to die? Scared to fail? He slowly slid down the shower wall, sitting down with his back in the corner, his arms wrapped around his bent knees, while the warm spray from the oversized shower head rained down on him. He closed his eyes and attempted to clear his head by focusing on his breathing. For the time being, he didn't have to face anything.

"Michael." He heard a knock on the door. "Is everything all right?"

He opened his eyes, momentarily confused to find himself under a tropical waterfall. He heard another knock, then his name again.

"Yeah," he shouted. "I'll be out in just a minute." He popped up and quickly lathered himself up with the bar of soap provided by the hotel that smelled of jasmine. *I'll be the sweetest-smelling deaf and mute country peasant in all of Iran,* he thought. He passed on washing his hair. He might smell pretty for a day, but he certainly didn't want to look it. He rinsed, then shut off the water, reaching out and grabbing one of the thick white bath towels hanging on the rack. He dried off quickly and threw on one of the hotel bathrobes. The large mirror over the sink had a thick layer of condensation over it. He wiped a clear spot in the mirror and looked at himself. With the two days of dark stubble on his face, he could pass for someone who didn't regularly groom himself—just what he was after. He passed on brushing his hair, instead just pushing it to one side with his fingers, adding to his scruffy look. A couple days of not bathing, and he would blend right in, he thought. Well, at least he was a little less despondent now. Perhaps he had just needed to purge those feeling of hopelessness. An emotional release. It was something he had to go through so that he could get back to the way of thinking that was needed, the way that had always given him the confidence that somehow, he would find a way to accomplish whatever was needed. That was the Michael Blackstone he remembered. A long-lost face from the past.

He opened the door and found Asya sitting up in bed with her legs crossed, watching the television. She turned down the volume, turning her attention to him as he walked out of the bathroom.

"You were in there for quite some time. Around forty minutes. Did you fall asleep?"

"Actually, I did, but I think it did me some good. I was struggling with a lot of thoughts and doubts, so it helped me clear my head some."

"Come here." She tapped the bed next to her.

Michael walked to the opposite side of the bed and plopped himself down next to her, holding his robe together and keeping it from turning into an embarrassing situation.

"What are you struggling with?" she asked, placing her hand on his.

"You know, the usual. Do I have what it takes to actually do this? Will I ever see you again? Does the rec room at Evin Prison have cable TV or satellite?"

"Okay, at least I know you are all right when you can still joke at the most serious moments," she told him, rubbing his hand.

He turned his hand around, grabbing hold of hers. "It just feels a bit overwhelming, that's all."

"I can only imagine, my sweet. Just know that I will continuously be praying for you. I will be asking Allah to protect you and guide your way."

"You really believe he listens to you, don't you?"

"Of course I do. I told you so."

"What makes you so sure?"

"I do not know. It is not something you can prove by this world's physical laws. There is no physical evidence. It is all circumstantial. It is seeing Him act in your life and feeling Him in your soul."

"Hmm. Well, I can use all the prayers I can get. Are you on Facebook?"

"Do not joke about that, Michael. Allah did not allow this to be placed before you for no reason. Whatever may come of all this, He specifically chose you to accomplish His will."

"Well, then, what difference does it make whether you pray for me or not?"

"Because, there is power in prayer. Allah brings blessings to those who ask and believe. There is nothing beyond His ability to accomplish. He has created everything in this universe. How can He not do whatever He wishes?"

"I'm glad you have that much faith. That's something I can't match. Not that I don't believe he exists, just that I haven't experienced what you have?"

"You still have time." She squeezed his hand.

"We'll see." He squeezed back. "Your turn to get in the shower. Hurry up and come back here. I want to get under the covers with you and feel you next to me for the few hours we have left."

"Hurry up? Coming from the gentleman who spent forty minutes in the shower."

"If you're not back out here in twenty minutes, I'm going to come in there for you. Whatever may happen after that is not my responsibility," he warned her.

"Is that so? Maybe then I will stay twenty-five minutes," she said, calling his bluff.

"That thought alone will keep me going, regardless of whatever challenge I encounter."

"Good, because I will hold you to it," she said as she got up from bed and walked slowly towards the bathroom, unbuttoning her blouse and letting it slide off her shoulders, then unfastening her bra and letting it drop in front of her, exposing her back to him as she walked towards the bathroom door, finally undoing her slacks and letting them fall to the floor as she stepped out of them into the bathroom, kicking the door shut behind her.

She slipped out of her panties and turned on the shower, sticking her hand in the spray, waiting for the hot water before stepping in and closing the door. She noticed another valve to the side of the shower valve and turned it, to be surprised by steam that began belching forth from an opening below the faucet. She let the hot spray hit her face as the steam filled the shower stall. She leaned her hands up against the black granite shower wall and let the hot water run down her back while she stretched her neck back and forth. The hot steam felt good to her tired body. How much she wanted to have him right now, beneath the hot water, holding her close to him. She sobbed silently in the solitude of the steam as she thought of the possibility of that never happening. From the beginning, she had no illusions about what Michael was going to face; it was just now that the finality of it was hitting her. He had popped back into her life just a few days ago out of nowhere. She hadn't thought about him for many years, but he had always remained one of those few special people one keeps in a special place of their heart the rest of their life. She remembered the sadness she had felt when his tour had ended and the accompanying sense of loss after he had left Istanbul. His wife and daughter had left the country a month earlier to prepare their daughter for the beginning of school in the fall. Asya had seen him off at the airport when he was departing. She remembered the flood of emotions she'd felt when she told him her last goodbye. She was certain he had seen it on her face. She also remembered the emotions she felt from him, as he struggled to conceal the sadness he was also feeling. She had never expected to see him again. He would go on with his life, she would go on with hers. When they had worked together, she had coped with her feelings towards him with the fact that he was a married man, trying to look at him as an older brother, one whom she highly admired and who was extremely good looking. He was someone she could trust to have a close and trusting friendship with, yet maintain that well-defined line that could never be crossed.

She had expected and prepared to spend the remainder of her life alone. A career woman with a very small tight-knit circle of other women as friends, mostly older than her. She was still very aware of her looks as an attractive middle-aged woman and disciplined herself to stay trim and look after her appearance, but the female sexuality of her identity, was something she had been steadily drawing inside her with the passing of each year since she had split up with Ercan. A woman of her position and age had very limited possibilities of finding a kind and trusting man of character, especially one that still had all his hair and could see his toes, in Turkish society. There were very few Ercans still left unmarried, looking for someone themselves at that point in their lives. She had come to terms with the fact she would grow old as a spinster. Now, within a matter of a couple of days, all that had been turned on its head. It felt like her life had been pulled out from under her. Those suppressed emotions and desires had been awakened and were screaming within her. She realized that she still yearned to have the presence of a loving companion in her life. And for some unbelievable reason, that was Michael.

Allah, most merciful, I am so confused. Why has this happened to me at this time in my life, and why Michael? Even though he had been such a distant part of my life, You know how I have always felt for him, how I confessed to You my struggles of thinking anything beyond what was possible between us so many years ago. Why drop him into my life like this now, yet keep him just beyond my grasp? I know the reality of the dangers he faces. I accept that I may never see him again. Why bring back to life all those feelings You had allowed me to bury these past years? I know we all are created to serve Your purpose, my Lord. I just ask that You watch over him, allow him to see things clearly and guide him, protect him and keep him safe. I see that he is not convinced about You, uncertain that You listen to our prayers and are active in our lives, but please allow him to feel Your peace in whatever circumstances he finds himself. I humbly ask that You bring him back to me. I put my faith and trust in You, my Lord, she prayed. She remained in the solitude of the hot mist, allowing the hot spray beating against her body and the sputter of the steam to slowly release the angst that had grabbed hold of her. She stepped back until she felt the opposite wall of the shower, then lowered herself, sitting on the tile floor with her back against the thick glass wall.

An overwhelming sense of exhaustion washed over her. The steam was almost too hot for her to bear that close. She took shallow breaths, bending her knees and pulling her feet towards her. She looked down at her body and fixed her sight on the two-centimeter scar next to her belly button. She remembered nineteen years ago, when she and Michael had driven out to an abandoned steel mill in the industrial area of Istanbul, following up on some intelligence that was obtained from an unproven source regarding a possible meeting site for terrorist operatives. There was no reason to believe it was an active site, so Asya and Michael had decided to do some cursory reconnaissance of the location. They had gone there in the late morning, parking their car outside the compound, entering quietly through a back entrance. As they made their way past the abandoned buildings, they were surprised to come across two vehicles parked inside one of the larger metal factory buildings. Upon silently entering through the open bay door, they heard voices somewhere in the depths of the building, which was a maze of ladders, catwalks, stairways and empty rooms. They had drawn their firearms and slowly made their way through the building, carefully clearing each successive area, as they advanced towards the voices. They eventually discovered the source of the conversation when they came across a meeting between three individuals in what appeared to have once been some sort of control room. They were standing around a heavy wooden table with a small black suitcase on it. All three were armed. As Michael and Asya surreptitiously listened to their conversation, they realized they hadn't stumbled into a terrorist meet, but rather a heroin deal that was going down in front of them. They observed another open doorway across the other side of the meeting room. Michael signaled to Asya that he would make his way around to the other door and surprise them, forcing them to drop their weapons. Asya would cover from the other side and engage anyone who foolishly tried to draw on Michael.

As she stood there waiting for Michael to make his way around, her Sig Sauer P228 trained on the three drug dealers, she heard one ask what was taking Emin so long with the money. Just as soon as it registered that there was another individual involved in this meeting, the hair on Asya's neck stood as she sensed the presence of someone behind her. She turned quickly, bringing her 9mm around to counter the threat, but felt a sharp pain to the right of her belly button. She managed to fire a round off as she cried out in pain, but she missed her assailant as she was thrown off balance by the knife thrust into her abdomen. The noise of the fired round caused the three men around the table to draw their weapons. They heard another two rounds fired and then the sound of a body slumping to the floor. Michael had just made his way around to the other side, rounding the threshold of the doorway as he aimed his Glock at the three who were looking towards the open door on Asya's side.

"*Silahlarınızı bırakın!*" he shouted, ordering them to drop their weapons.

Foolishly, rather than obeying his command, they turned their weapons in his direction. The one holding a Bulgarian-made Shipka 9mm machine pistol began spraying rounds in his direction, but Michael fired off two rounds that immediately found their mark in his chest and head, causing him to drop his weapon and slump to the floor. Another, firing off a burst from his Glock 18 with its thirty-three-round magazine, was immediately neutralized from behind as Asya fired through the doorway from her position lying on the floor. The last gunman fared somewhat better, grazing Michael's left shoulder, but met the same fate as his associates when another two rounds from Michael stopped him in his tracks. Michael ran into the room, kicking the weapons away from the three assailants who lay motionless on the floor in growing pulls of blood. He saw the fourth individual lying on the floor behind Asya, clearly dead from the two entrance wounds in his right cheek and eye. Asya was doubled over in pain, clutching the right side of her lower abdomen. Michael ran to her and knelt next to her.

"Awsh! You've been shot. I need to stop the bleeding."

"I was not shot. I was stabbed. In my abdomen," she gasped.

"I need to see," he told her. He gently rolled her over, pulling back her black leather jacket and lifting her bloodied blouse to expose a small puncture wound that was oozing dark red blood. "It's not an artery. You're going to be okay. Just hang in there," he reassured her.

He took off his jacket and laid it on the floor next to her. Taking off his T-shirt, he laid it down on his jacket, then pulled out the Spyderco knife from his waistband and cut out a large square of material, folding it over several times to form a dressing. He placed it against the cut by her belly button, telling her to keep pressure on it, as he cut additional long strips of material from the T-shirt, which he then wrapped around her torso several times, bandaging the dressing against her wound. He threw his jacket back on and gently lifted her up off the floor.

"Can you stand?" he asked her.

"Yes, but it is painful." She did her best to hold herself up.

"Can you walk?"

"I will try." She attempted to take a few steps but doubled over in pain.

"Okay, okay, Awsh. I'm going to have to carry you. I just need you to hold on around my neck as best as you can. Can you do that for me?"

"Yes," she panted.

He hoisted her into his arms, grabbing his wrist and forming a cradle to carry her back to their car and take her to a hospital. He made his way through the passageways, then walked as quickly his legs would take him back to their car, a good kilometer away. He raced her to the nearest hospital, where they found that the knife had penetrated a section of her small intestine. Fortunately, she hadn't lost a lot of blood thanks to Michael's quick battlefield first aid. The surgeon was able to repair the wound without any complications. A course of antibiotics and a month of recovery at home had left her with no lasting injuries, other than the permanent reminder of the two-centimeter scar next to her belly button.

It turned out, the drug deal they had interrupted involved twenty kilograms of heroin and one million US dollars in cash that was found at the scene. The four dead included two Turkish mobsters and two Russian Chechens with connections to Afghanistan. Michael ended up having to do some creative writing when authoring the incident report to Langley as to how a CIA counterterrorism liaison officer had wandered into the middle of a major heroin deal with his female Turkish MIT liaison officer. Fortunately, a supportive chief of station and an award he received from the director of MIT for saving the life of one of their officers had spared him any negative consequences from CIA headquarters. He had earned the unquestioned trust and respect of the members of the MIT counterterrorism team he was working with as a result of his brave actions. Asya had never forgotten how he had valiantly saved her life. The special bond that was established between was something she had treasured all these years.

She had reached the limit her body could endure from the steam and hot water she had immersed herself in as she processed her emotions about Michael. Standing up, she turned off the steam, washed and rinsed quickly, then reached for the bath towel to dry herself off. She dried her hair with the hair dryer mounted on the wall, then donned the remaining bathrobe before opening the door to join Michael. She was about to tell him how relaxing that had felt when she saw that he had fallen asleep on the bed. She paused, standing there looking at him with a bittersweet smile, hoping it wouldn't be the last time she would see him. Walking over, she quietly lay down in bed next to him. She placed her arm across his chest as she lay there listing to his breathing, taking in as much of this tender moment she had left with him before drifting off to sleep.

Chapter 18

Michael heard the repetitive ringing of the alarm from Asya's phone as he opened his eyes to find her nuzzled up against him in her bathrobe. She started to stir, then opened her eyes to find him looking at her. She gave him a warm smile and tightened her hold around him. He pulled his arm out from between them and slid it under her head, shifting towards her as he continued to peer into her eyes. She returned his gaze, their eyes remaining locked, each searching to connect with the deepest, innermost being of the other, as if it would be their last chance ever to do so.

"What are you thinking?" she asked him.

"I don't know. Nothing. Everything. I'm just taking in as much of you as possible," he told her.

She reached towards him, kissing him tenderly, then pulled away, reconnecting her gaze with his.

"You know, I've been thinking about everything you said about God. Him listening to your prayers and you being able to see how he answers by how he acts in your life, or something along those lines. I've never asked him for anything or talked to him about any of my problems, so I can't really say whether or not he's spoken to me, one way or another. The one thing that I can say for sure is that, looking back over my life, especially most recently, things have happened that I don't fully understand. Things that blow away the laws of probability—more than mere coincidences. It's like a series of unrelated events that somehow come together to form this pattern or picture that's continuously morphing into something else, but I can't make out what it is. If God is in the picture turning my life this way and that way against my every expectation, then I'd really like to know why he's brought us here together the way he has. I don't know what to think, what to feel, Awsh. The feelings inside me that have been stirred up so suddenly have left me completely disoriented. On one hand, it feels so wonderful, so right, to be lying here, feeling you next to me. On the other, it's like some cruel joke, to both of us, giving us a taste of what we may never have again. How can you be so sure he really exists, or if he does, that he really cares about what you or I want?"

"The only way that I can explain it that might make some sense is, when I was a little girl and my mother died, I felt completely lost, like I was alone in the world. I had my father, but he was a military officer, always gone other than brief periods when he would be at home. I always knew he loved me, but was never a steady presence in my life. After my mother died, he was all I had.

He became an active part of my life. He was still not always at home because of his career, but we had a nanny to take care of me until he would return at night or the next day. All his spare time he would spend with me. It was like he had no friends or anything else outside his work. I was his sole focus. He took me places, showed me things, taught me things, encouraged me, picked me up when I failed or was hurt, surprised me with things I never expected. Even when he was not with me, I always knew he was thinking about me and would always be there when I needed him. God has always been there for me in the same way. He may not have always answered me as quickly as I have wanted, or in the way I expected, but He has never failed me. If anything, I have discovered that His way of answering my prayers turned out to be much more apparent than anything I could have imagined. I believe that is how He is with everyone, but you have to be willing to honestly look for Him acting in your life, otherwise how can He ever reveal himself to you?"

"You trust Him with everything?"

"I trust that He knows what he's doing."

"Even if you don't understand how or why?"

"Yes."

"And why's that?"

"Because He is God and I am not."

"Kind of a circular argument, isn't it? No way to really prove it, one way or another."

"You are right my sweet, that is why in the end, it comes down to faith. Something inside you either believes or does not."

He had nothing left to counter her with. She was right, it did come down to faith. He had experienced and witnessed things in life that he couldn't find plausible explanations for. Taken on their individual merit, they could be chalked up to a mere coincidence or one of those unexplainable phenomena in life, like single socks that go missing in the dryer. Taken together, however, over the course of a life, they formed a definite pattern, albeit not always clearly distinguishable. Could what Asya believed really have some truth behind it? Did God have a specific purpose for him? Would he reveal it to him? Would he reveal himself to him? As he continued peering into her eyes, from somewhere inside him came, *God, if you're listening, I would really love to have this woman in my life.* He thought about what he had asked for and realized that request had already been fulfilled. She was in his life. How much longer that would continue, however, depended on what course his life would take. That yet remained indistinguishable to him.

"Tell you what, you keep praying for me while I'm gone, and I'll also try to have a conversation with him any chance I get when I'm not looking over my shoulder for anyone who's on to me. If he's listening, then at least he has the both of us bugging him to give us a chance together. If he allows that to happen, then I'll assume he'll also help me with everything else he's put in front of me."

"I know the type of man you are, Michael. You have been blessed with so many good qualities and abilities. God has a specific reason He has selected you for this. If you put your trust in Him, He will show you the way. He has brought you this far. He will not abandon you," she reassured him.

"Trust, you say. Hmm, that's a tough one. I've been burned before. There aren't many people I give that to. You are one of only a handful. I guess if you have that much trust in him, I should also."

She gave him a smile, placing her hand on his temple and running her fingers through his hair. They lay there for a few more moments, trying to soak up every last second together before they realized there was no more time left. They had to get dressed and make their way back to Ercan's camp. In a few hours, before dawn arrived, Michael would be dropped off in the remote mountainous countryside of Iran to begin a journey whose ending was unknown.

"We need to get ready," he finally forced out.

"I know," she acknowledged unhappily.

"We'll be together again."

"We will."

He moved towards her, finding her lips one last time, conveying as much of his feelings to her as he possibly could in a kiss. He felt her emotion flowing back to him. They finally parted, their eyes remaining locked together, not wanting to lose contact.

"Okay, we need to get up." He forced himself from the bed, grabbing her hands and pulling her up with him.

He went to his bag and pulled out the peasant clothes they had bought back at the Grand Bazaar in Istanbul. He turned away from Asya and dropped his robe as he put on a clean pair of underwear.

"Mm," he heard Asya say.

"Tit for tat for that tantalizing glimpse you gave me going into the shower," he teased her. He put on the baggy gray farmer's pants and the ugly burnt-orange checkered shirt, then glanced at himself in the mirror. "How's this for sexy, woman?" He did his best impression of a hick, rubbing his two days of stubble.

"You are the most attractive *köylü* I have ever seen. You will need to be careful around the old peasant women. They will try to steal you as a husband for their daughters," she joked.

"Especially when I bring them gifts of dates," he laughed.

They finished packing their things, Michael arranging his newly purchased hemp bag with the GPS and satellite phone on the bottom, then the dates, the old rusty knife with the wooden handle and finally the bag of pide. He knotted each end of the leather strap to the handles and slung it across his shoulder.

"There, how's that?" he asked.

"Like a *köylü* on his way to the city," she answered.

"Perfect." He picked up his carry-on and they headed out the door.

They made their way to the elevator, then down to the quiet lobby and out the door to the Land Cruiser. Placing their bags in the back, they got in, and Michael started the engine.

"And so it begins," he declared as he put it into gear and pulled out of the parking lot onto the road.

Asya placed her hand on the back of his head and began running her fingers through his hair, maintaining physical contact with him for whatever time they had left, until it would no longer be possible once they had arrived back at the camp. The feel of her touch made Michael want to slow down and stretch out the drive for as long as possible. He stared at the beams of the headlights as they made their way through town and back out into the dark countryside. It had a mesmerizing effect on him. An old familiar feeling from long ago returned to him. It was what he remembered feeling as mission time approached: anticipation, excitement, focus. There was a certain comfort in it. The entirety of what awaited still felt overwhelming, but he gradually began settling into that old familiar mindset, tackling one challenge at a time until he eventually made it to where he needed to be. Sounded easy, he thought, just that he hadn't come close to facing anything like this in a very long time. The emotions he was experiencing ranged from one end of the spectrum to the other, from fear and uncertainty to sheer exhilaration, along with the ache of having to leave Asya all mixed together. It was a challenge keeping all his emotions in check so that he could keep his mind focused on what needed to be done.

"Awsh."

"Yes," she turned towards him, looking at his silhouette in the glow of the instrument panel.

"I just want to tell you that no matter what happens, I'm so grateful for these two days we've spent together. I can't begin to explain how much it has meant to me. How much you mean to me. You always will, no matter what. I want you to know that. Okay?"

Tears streamed down her cheek. She was glad he couldn't see her in the dark. She wanted to say so much more, but she had told him enough. She had told him how she felt, how much it had meant that he had come back into her life. There was nothing more she could say to express the anguish she was feeling at the thought of never seeing him again. She stretched across the center console and laid her head down on his shoulder. He tilted his head against hers, reaching across with his hand and caressing her face. He felt the wetness of her tears.

They finally arrived at the turnoff for the dirt road that would take them to the camp. Michael slowed the SUV and turned down the bumpy road. They were close, just minutes away. The urgency of their imminent separation hit them both like the crashing waves of rough surf preceding a forthcoming storm. The guard post for the camp entrance finally appeared in the distant glow of the headlights. Michael let go of Asya's face and turned off the headlights, leaving only the driving lights as he approached the sentry. Asya scooted back over to her side, wiping her face dry with the back of her hand and removing any trace of the emotions she had bared. She put on her game face. She needed to keep herself clearheaded if she was going to be of any help to Michael. She knew what she had to do.

Michael came to a rolling stop, rolling down his window and allowing the sentry to shine his flashlight inside their vehicle.

"*Merhaba. Albay Gültekin bizi bekliyor,*" Asya greeted the sentry, telling him Colonel Gültekin was expecting them.

The sentry, holding his flashlight in the left hand and his H&K MP-5 in his right, shined the light on each of them, then walked around the back of their vehicle, illuminating the rest of the interior, coming to a stop next to Asya in the passenger side. The sentry activated the mic of his radio, notifying his commanding officer that his two guests had arrived in his vehicle. Upon receiving a response, he waved them through.

Michael put the Land Cruiser into gear and slowly pulled into the camp, turning and driving towards the tent they had been at several hours earlier. They saw Ercan waiting for them outside the entrance. Michael pulled up next to the tent, turning off the driving lights and shutting down the engine. Ercan walked up as they got out of the vehicle.

"*Merhaba,*" he greeted them.

"*Merhaba,*" they replied in unison.

"I hope you had a chance to get some rest," he said as he shook Michael's hand.

"Yes. We found a pretty nice hotel just outside of town. Had plenty of hot water and comfortable beds." Michael caught himself altering the truth, using the plural when referring to their sleeping accommodations. He wondered why he had said that. It wasn't as if it should have made any difference to Ercan. He was married, and there hadn't been anything between him and Asya for years. Did he subconsciously do it out of respect to Asya, not wanting to bring any dishonor to her in the eyes of the man who had almost married her?

"Good. You will need to be clearheaded and at full strength. There will be many challenges ahead."

"I'm as ready as I can be. I'll just take them one at a time."

"Spoken like a true Special Forces soldier." Ercan gave him an encouraging slap on the back. "Let's go in and have our briefing with the crew." He led them inside to the command center, which was now illuminated in battle-red lighting so as not to interfere with anyone's night vision.

There were three men in green flight suits, one of them the major from earlier, sitting at the table by the white-board and the large terrain map, which was now hanging on its side.

"Gentlemen, this is Mr. Jones from one of our ally's services and Ms. Öztürk from the ministry," he introduced them, using a common Turkish surname analogous to Jones or Smith to protect Asya's identity. "Major Balik, Captain Yilmaz and Chief Kartal," Ercan introduced the flight crew. They exchanged hellos and shook hands. "Everyone here understands English but not Turkish, so we will brief in English. Major," he said, turning it over to the aircraft commander.

"In analyzing the terrain, the best location for an insertion within the general area you provided earlier is this small bluff, halfway down this wash between these two ridges." He indicated on the terrain map with a laser pointer. "It is fairly level with no surrounding trees, from what I could tell by looking at the satellite imagery. We will fly over the border at this point here, a saddle in between these two ridges, and make our way down this valley, keeping below one hundred fifty feet until we get to the LZ. It will be a hot landing, so we will touch down just long enough for you to dismount and then it is wheels up immediately. Our flight time is twenty-three minutes. Approximate time in Iranian airspace is ninety seconds. I'm assuming you have flown on a Blackhawk before, Mr. Jones?"

"Oh, once or twice," Michael responded with a smile to the major's question.

"As soon as we touch down, you will be given the signal from the crew chief to dismount from the left side of the aircraft so that I have eyes on you when you exit. As soon as you are clear of the rotors, I am on the throttle and we are out of there. Understood?"

"Roger that."

"You will sit in the middle of the aircraft facing to the rear, so that you have eyes on both the chief and the colonel on the mini-guns."

"Roger. Did you say the colonel?" Michael and Asya both turned and looked at Ercan.

"Yes, Colonel Gültekin advised he was going on the mission."

"Okay," Michael replied, glancing at Ercan. While on one hand, he was surprised to hear the commanding officer would be going on a risky single-aircraft mission such as this, on the other, he wasn't. Michael realized he wouldn't put his men at risk while he stayed back in the safety of his command center. It was just the type of leader he was. Michael admired him.

"Are there any questions?" the major asked.

No one responded.

"Wheels up is at four thirty. I need everyone on board and ready to go by four twenty-five. We'll start engines as four fifteen. Colonel."

"Thank you, Major. Mr. Jones, meet me back here at the command center at four fifteen. We will head out to the helo together and get situated. That leaves just over twenty-five minutes. You are dismissed," Ercan said, releasing the flight crew so they could start their preparations for the aircraft.

The major, captain and senior crew chief stood up and exited the tent, heading towards the LZ where the four Blackhawks sat parked. Michael and Asya followed Ercan out of the tent. They walked a short distance away from the hum of the generator into the darkness of the early morning.

"What made you decide to go on the mission?" Asya asked Ercan.

"Why do you ask? Does it surprise you? I cannot expect my men to take such a risk and not myself, when it is I who am putting them in danger. Even if they are following my direct order, if something should go wrong, they will be facing the consequences, whether it is death, capture or court-martial. I could not allow that. If something unforeseen should happen, then their commanding officer will also face those consequences," he declared.

It was the type of answer Michael expected to hear from him. He understood why Ercan had been given command of Turkey's most elite special operations unit. He would have excelled as the commanding officer in any US Special Operations unit, whether it was CAG or DEVGRU, more commonly known as Delta Force and SEAL Team 6.

"The noble warrior. Why does that sound like the kind of answer I expect to hear from you?" She gave him an admiring smile in the dark.

"It is what it is, my *dişi aslan*. I will go to prepare my equipment and weapons." He glanced at his watch. "Meet you back here in twenty-two minutes," he told them, then headed away towards his tent.

"What did he call you?" Michael asked her.

"Lioness."

"Lioness?"

"It was a term of endearment he used to call me when we were together," she said, somewhat embarrassed.

"Oh, really? Why is that? Are you ferocious?"

"Make it back, so you can find out for yourself." She grabbed him by the shoulders and pulled herself towards him, kissing him passionately one last time in the privacy of darkness.

They stayed like that for as long as they dared, separating before any of Ercan's soldiers happened to stumble across them. It would certainly make its way through the camp that the two mysterious strangers who suddenly showed up for some secret mission were caught with their lips locked together. It was something neither of them wanted making its way back to Ercan, despite no one else knowing who they were. It was obvious he was aware they had feelings for each other, but they didn't want to put him in the awkward position of having to comment on the scuttlebutt being talked about by his men.

When they ended their passionate embrace, they stood side by side under the stars. It was a clear sky, with a crescent moon. Under any other circumstances, it would have been a perfect setting for a quiet walk side by side in some romantic getaway. Instead, they were inside an army camp, surrounded by military hardware. Both of them were painfully aware of each passing minute as the time approached for Michael to depart. They each felt the tightening around their chest, the dull ache growing as the seconds counted down. They stood there in silence, looking up at the night sky. There was nothing more left for either of them to say. The hum of the portable generators was interrupted by the sound of the twin turbines of the Blackhawk spooling up, and the swoosh, swoosh of the main rotor beginning to rotate.

"Well, it's time," Michael said, breaking the silence. "Need to meet up with Ercan. Here, hold onto these." He handed her his US cell phone, wallet and passport, having decided it would be more of a liability than a help if he was captured. "Better take this also." He unclasped his Omega Seamaster Professional and handed it to her. "It might look a little conspicuous for a peasant to be wearing a watch like this." He put on the cheap Chinese watch they had purchased in the bazaar.

"I will hold everything for you for until you return." She forced a smile.

They turned and headed back to the command center, arriving just as Ercan was walking up with his battle gear on and his M4 slung across his chest. They followed him inside the tent. Michael grabbed his hemp bag and did one final equipment check. He pulled the satellite phone, GPS and spare batteries out from underneath the concealment of the dates and pide. He turned them on, verifying they were functioning, then repacked them, leaving the handle of his old knife within easy reach should he need quick access to it.

"Everything good?" asked Ercan.

"Everything's good," Michael answered.

"Okay, let's head out to the helo. Asya, wait here in the command center until I return. You can sit next to the lieutenant over there, who will be monitoring communications. You will be able to track us on his mission status monitor," he told her, pausing momentarily to give them a chance for their final goodbyes.

They locked eyes with each other, relaying as much as they could in that brief moment before Michael picked up his bag and slung it across his shoulder, turning towards Ercan and following him out of the tent. They walked towards the flashing red beacon of the idling Blackhawk on the other side of the camp. Michael felt the goose bumps erupt over his entire body as the reality of the moment set in. He recalled that same sensation many years ago, walking in the darkness towards a waiting Blackhawk, to be transported somewhere out in the middle of nowhere for a night training mission. This, however, wasn't a training mission, nor did he have his M4. His sole weapon was a rusty old farmer's knife.

They approached the Blackhawk, its twin turbines at full idle. The kerosene exhaust smell from the JP-8, mixing in with the main rotor's wash, whipped Michael in the face, causing him to shift his balance forward. Everything felt surreal. It was something he had experienced countless times many years ago, but it seemed like it was all just a dream now. The crew chief wearing his bulbous flight helmet with its cable running inside the aircraft greeted them by the open door next to the M134 mini-gun. Ercan stepped to the side, letting Michael enter the Blackhawk first, the crew chief pointing him to the center seat facing aft. Michael swung his hemp bag to his side and sat down, buckling himself into the four-point harness. He put on the headset that had been left for him and heard the pilot and copilot communicating with each other. Ercan hopped in next, removing his Kevlar helmet and securing it to his side, and made his way across to the opposite side, donning the flight helmet and manning the mini-gun on the starboard side of the aircraft. He glanced at Michael, giving him the thumbs-up. Michael replied in kind, letting Ercan know he was set.

The crew chief jumped in the aircraft and positioned himself on his M134, advising the pilot in command that everyone was in. The major conducted a comm check, going around to each one of them, finally calling out Mr. Jones, to which Michael responded with a "Lima Charlie," loud and clear. A moment later, Michael felt the pilot increase the throttle to the powerful turbines, as they lifted off the ground into the night sky. A feeling of exhilaration came over him. He looked down at his legs as that initial wave of adrenaline gave him the sensation that his legs were shaking. It had always annoyed him, from when he was a teenager waiting for the start of a football game. At first, he had confused it with fear, but later he had come to recognize it as an overwhelming release of energy throughout his body in anticipation of some challenge or threat. He had conditioned himself to let it pass through him. He imagined it was similar to the feeling a heroin user experienced with the initial wave after shooting up. In his case, it was an involuntary injection of adrenaline from his adrenal glands into his bloodstream. He took a deep breath and exhaled slowly, trying to slow his heart rate. He needed to calm down and get his energy under control so that he could think clearly. The hike down the wash into town would burn off some of that excessive energy and level him out, he thought. Until then he just needed to enjoy the twenty-three-minute ride as the pilot flew with night vision goggles, hugging the terrain one hundred and fifty feet above the surface at a hundred and forty knots. It was better than any amusement park ride Michael had ever been on.

The minutes sped by as Michael glanced out either side into the starlit sky, the only other sensations being the cold night air rushing through the cabin and the constantly shifting centrifugal force against his body as the Blackhawk banked left and right while lurching up and down. It wasn't long before Michael felt the pilot pull back on the cyclic and reduce the throttle, slowing the aircraft as it descended towards the LZ. Michael prepared himself and looked towards the crew chief. He felt a tap on his left shoulder and turned to see Ercan giving him a good luck thumbs-up. Michael returned the gesture and turned his attention back to the crew chief. He felt the helo touch down and heard the pilot announce over the intercom, "You are good to go, Mr. Jones. Good luck." Michael removed his headset, hit the release for his safety harness and stepped towards the door. The crew chief scanning the terrain through his night vision goggles behind the mini-gun, gave him a quick thumbs-up as he exited the aircraft. Michael stepped out and ducked as he walked forward away from the Blackhawk. He heard the turbines increase their pitch and felt the powerful wash strike his back as it lifted back off the ground and accelerated away from him into the dark sky.

He crouched down in the darkness, holding still as the sound of the helicopter grew fainter until it was all quiet. There wasn't much he could see yet, other than the outline of the surrounding ridges with the starlit sky in the background. He looked out of the sides of his eyes, where the greater concentration of the black-and-white light-sensitive rods were located, for any sign of movement. His main receptors for any possible danger, however, were his ears. He remained motionless, scanning his surroundings for any sounds to determine what was normal versus what was cause for concern.

He heard a faint sound off in the distance and strained to make out what it was. Finally, hearing the slight ting of a bell, he realized it was a flock of goats or sheep somewhere down below him. The question was, was it a tended flock? If he could hear them off in the distance, it was certain some shepherd down there would have heard the sound of the helicopter, however brief it might have been. If someone had heard, hopefully they assumed it had been passing by, rather than setting him down in their country. Of all things to start off having to be concerned about, why did it have to be a flock of sheep? He would remain there for another half hour, until the sky began to lighten enough for him to be able to make his way down the wash and head into town. He figured it would take him about an hour and a half, which would put him there somewhere between 6:30 and 7:00, just as things were starting to come to life.

He tried to think ahead and picture how he hoped things would progress as he waited for the sky to lighten. He would casually wander through town until he came across the bus office and purchase a ticket to Tehran. He just needed to make it onto the back of a bus and patiently wait out the long, and hopefully boring, nine-hundred-kilometer drive to Tehran. With any luck, he would get there sometime tomorrow morning. Saturday, being the start of the work week in Iran, would be perfect timing for him to scout out the location of MOIS headquarters and hopefully figure out some way of tracking down

Karbashi, following him to his home, and then cold-pitching him into assisting an ex-CIA officer in breaking Ali out of an Iranian prison. That sounded like a well-laid-out plan, he thought sarcastically. It would be impossible for him to succeed. He needed to be realistic. Did he really think he would just happen to stumble across the director of Iranian intelligence, then convince him to commit the high crime of treason against his country?

He looked up and saw slight brightening to the east across the horizon. It was a welcome sight. He silently chastised himself for starting to slip into a negative attitude. He knew it would be the beginning of the end if he allowed that to happen. It was going to be an adventure full of challenges, but he would take them as they came. He knew that. Why was he allowing himself to forget it and let uncertainty creep in? He had always thrived on that type of excitement, the thrill of not knowing what would happen. It was the reason he had left Wall Street for the Special Forces and then the CIA. He had always had a positive attitude back then, eager to go out and overcome any challenge that confronted him. He was still that same man. He had just been away from it for too long. He had let the relative safety and comfort of mundane civilian life soften him. He needed to suck it up some and put a sharp edge on his thinking if he was going to have any chance of succeeding in his quest. He would find Ali and get him out. He had to. There was no other choice. Things would be all right, he tried reassuring himself.

The sky had become light enough to begin illuminating the ground in front of him. The terrain was mountainous enough that the only vegetation was brush and a few scraggly junipers here and there, making it fairly easy for Michael to spot a path leading down the wash to the valley and farmland below. Despite the scuffed-up appearance of his boots, they fit him well and still had a good amount of tread left on the soles. The strap of his bag was wide enough that it didn't cut into his neck and shoulder. He was in good shape and ready to begin his hike into town. He just needed to watch his footing and not take a fall or twist an ankle. That wouldn't be good. The early-morning mountain air felt cool against his face as he carefully chose his steps, working his way down.

He hiked for about half an hour, the unmistakable sound of the flock growing louder the closer he got to the bottom. From the number of baas and behs, along with the clanging of bells, it sounded like it a sizeable flock. He eventually walked into a dry riverbed that made its way through agricultural fields on either side. He stayed within the relative concealment of the riverbed until eventually coming upon the outer stragglers of what turned out to be a large herd of goats. It had become light enough by then that Michael could see about ninety to a hundred goats milling about in the riverbed ahead, snacking on the brush that grew up and down its banks. He slowed his pace and looked for any signs of anyone tending the herd. He wondered if goats had shepherds, or was it only sheep? Coming upon the bulk of the herd, he slowly made his way through the throng of grazing goats, as they milled about feeding themselves. The pungent smell of the goats and their droppings made him take shallow breaths. Any lingering smell sticking to him would add to his disguise, hopefully keeping others from wanting to get too close to him. He would smell pretty ripe by the time he had a chance to bathe again. If he did manage to track down Karbashi, he could only imagine what initial impression he would make on him. He looked up at the banks as he made his way by, searching for anyone watching over the goats. He had the advantage of being in the shadows of the riverbank, while the backdrop of the lightened sky illuminated everything up above. He eventually made his way through the herd without seeing any other living creatures with two legs. He breathed a sigh of relief. A chance encounter with anyone before he made it into town wasn't something he wanted to risk. It would have seemed as somewhat unusual for a vagrant such as him to be wandering around out in the middle of nowhere at that hour of the morning. He would definitely have drawn attention.

As the riverbed shallowed and widened out into the surrounding farmland of wheat fields and pistachio orchards, off in the distance, he could see the town of Maku, his destination. He headed towards what looked like the main road up ahead, about a kilometer away. Once he made it there, he would fit in more naturally. Things were going pretty well, at least for the time being, he thought. His newfound optimism put a spring into his step as he headed in the direction of town. He would be there in under thirty minutes.

***

The two Iranian teenagers with their wool blankets had been leaning against the juniper tree on the bank above the herd, as they typically did every long and boring night while they tended their family's goats. They watched as Michael made his way out of the riverbed towards the road. They had heard the sound of the helicopter earlier that morning in the mountains above them. Now some stranger was walking out of the riverbed, coming from the direction of the wash while it was just getting light. This had been anything but a typical boring night. Something strange was going on. The older brother told the younger to stay with the herd while he followed the stranger from a distance to see where he was going. He would tell him all the details when he returned in a short while.

***

Asya had been waiting outside from the time she heard the pilot radio to the communications officer they were returning to base. She knew there was nothing more Ercan could have told her regarding Michael, but she wanted to at least hear from him that they had set him down without incident and now he was on his own. After what seemed like an extremely long twenty-three minutes, she heard the faint sound of the Blackhawk off in the distance, growing louder with each passing second as it approached the camp. She finally saw its outline in the brightening sky as it came in over the HESCO barriers and set down next to the other three helicopters. She waited by the command center tent until Ercan made his way over.

"Well, he is down," he told her.

"Everything went smoothly?" she asked, trying not to show any concern.

"Yes."

"Good. It is in Allah's hands now."

"It always is, Asya, but he will also have to rely on his abilities. He seems like a true professional. I assume that was your experience when you worked with him?"

"Yes, he was, and still is. He was the one who saved my life when I was stabbed years ago. The scar, by my belly button."

"Ah, yes. I remember you telling me about that. That was him? It does not surprise me. He is a tremendously brave man to attempt what he is doing. He knows the risks and danger he faces yet is still willing to do it."

"We both know what he faces. Yes, he is brave, but it is something more than that. He knows there is no one else in a position to do anything. It is only him. He is the only one who can help his friend, the only one who can possibly save so many lives. It is a heavy burden to carry."

"He means a lot to you, doesn't he?"

"You can tell, can you?"

"I have known you very well, Asya. I can tell you have feelings for this man from the way you carry yourself around him. Nothing obvious, just small subtle things only I would catch." He shot her a smile.

"You think so?"

"I know so. He would be a good man for you."

"What makes you think I have any desire to have a man in my life now?"

"I do not know if you have any desire, only you do. I just told you what I see in you and what I think about him. I will do whatever is in my power to help him get back out. You can be certain of that."

"Thank you, Ercan, it means very much to me. Otherwise, his chances would even be worse than they already are. You know if something goes wrong, not only will it be the end of our careers, but we would more than likely be hanged if this becomes known."

"I am well aware of that, Asya, but I do not see that we have any alternatives either. I have one child and another one on its way. I do not want them growing up in the aftermath of what will result if nothing is done to stop this evil. What is the value of your life or mine when compared to how many other lives are at stake?"

"Yes, I know, and I am not questioning your willingness to face anything when you know you are doing the right thing. The magnitude of this, however, is like nothing we have ever faced before. You and I are such insignificant players in the greater scheme of things that we can be crushed if it is found out that we have crossed the wrong people."

"Then let us be careful in everything we do. There may be others who can wield much more power than anything we have, but that does not mean they are smarter or wiser than us. If at some point we will need to become more active, then we will need to plan carefully how to cover ourselves. I would think you would have the expertise in that area, my *dişi aslan*."

"You still insist on calling me that?"

"Why shouldn't I? You are just as fearless. I do not know of any other woman who would come close to doing the things you do."

"That does not say much about my feminine side."

"I know that feminine side firsthand, have you forgotten? You just keep it well hidden except from those you choose to reveal it to."

"Good, that is how it will stay. It is difficult enough to keep all my male subordinates in line. That last thing I want is for them to think there is anything tender about me. I think they are all scared of me."

"Asya, you would have most of my men scared of you. It is intimidating to any man when they encounter a woman who can match or surpass them in what they took for granted as their Allah-given ability as a man. Most do not know how to react."

"Why did I not intimidate you, when we first met?"

"What makes you think you did not? I just enjoy a challenge. Perhaps that is part of the reason Michael is drawn to you."

"That has just recently happened. There was never anything before.

Whatever his reason, I hope he has a chance to find out if that is what he really wants. But enough with trying to work out my love life. How about that ride back to the airport?"

"Give me a minute to remove my gear and I will be right back," he told her, turning and heading to his tent.

She watched him as he strode away. He was right about her. She did have a desire to have Michael in her life.

***

Ali woke to the sound of the metal slide in his door being opened and a breakfast tray with two pitas, several slices of goat cheese, dates and hot sweet tea coming through the opening. He heard the familiar voice of the guard from the other day.

"Good morning, brother. *Salaam.* I have brought you your breakfast. How are you today? Did you sleep well?"

"*Salaam*, brother." Ali sat up in bed, then stood and walked over to the door. "Thank you, thank you, especially for the dates and tea. This is the first time I have been given tea. I am well, praise Allah. I did not see you for a few days. How are you? How is your family?" Ali asked as he grabbed the tray.

"I was off for the past two days. I am well and so is my family. We went to our country house. It is one hour from Tehran. We had a wonderful time. The dates are from there. It is not much of a house, just a bedroom and another room that has the kitchen in the living room, with an outdoor toilet, but we have water and electricity. I built it myself with the help of my friend slowly over the years. It has a little bit of land where my wife plants a small garden. We go there often in the summer to escape the heat of Tehran," he told Ali through the opening in the door.

"It sounds wonderful."

"It is our little private paradise away from all the weight of living in Tehran. I don't know how long I could continue to do this job if I did not escape to the serenity of the country every once in a while," the guard told him poignantly.

"Thank you again, brother." Ali bent over and looked through the opening.

"You are welcome. Perhaps someday I can take you to show you our country house," the guard said optimistically.

"*Inshallah*," Ali responded, using the traditional Muslim phrase for "If God wills it."

"May Allah protect you."

"You also, brother." Ali ended the exchange as the guard closed the slide and continued with his morning rounds.

Ali took his tray and sat down on the edge of his cot. He studied his breakfast before setting it down on the small stand next to him. He didn't have an appetite just yet, but he gratefully took the tea and sipped it. He thought about everything that had happened to him. It hadn't even been a week yet, and his life had gone from uneventful and secure, if not a bit mundane, to being turned completely on its head. He looked around at his walls and closed his eyes. He imagined what it would look like if he opened them and he was sitting on his living room couch back at his home in Alexandria. He kept his eyes shut for fear of forgetting what that looked like. It had only been a little over a week since he had been there, but it seemed like an eternity. He wondered if he would ever see it again. He didn't think that in a despondent way, more just as a matter of wondering what lay ahead for him in his life, however long it might be. Although he had accepted and come to terms with the possibility that he would more than likely die, he was still hopeful Allah had other plans for him. If not killed, then what? Spend the rest of his life in Evin Prison? He much preferred that Allah would spare him that fate and just take him, hopefully with the least amount of pain necessary for leaving this world. He was under no illusions; he knew the Iranian regime. Eventually they would run out of patience with his failure to tell them what they wanted to hear. They would go to their standard practice of inflicting torture until the prisoner was completely broken. Only then would they be sure nothing had been concealed from them. He wondered how much useful information they got that way.

What else could he tell them? Make up a story? Tell them about some intricate plot the CIA had concocted to mislead them? What would it accomplish, even if that was what they wanted to hear? They would still kill him at a minimum, but more likely use him for some propaganda victory by parading him around with his revised story. Even if they unexpectedly released him after his usefulness to them had diminished in some sort of prisoner swap, where did that leave him? He would be returned to the US as a traitor for having fabricated such a story. That would leave him a pariah in society at best, more likely an inmate at some federal penitentiary. How could Roxanne live with that, knowing her father had betrayed his country? He had no option other than to stick with the truth and hope that they would mercifully take his life in a quick and painless way.

Somehow, he hoped they would believe him. The truth about this treacherous act needed to be revealed for the world to see, before millions of people were unnecessarily killed. He thought about the millions who had been murdered by Hitler's Nazis. It seemed history just continued to repeat itself, generation after generation, when it came to man's savagery. It fascinated and horrified him at the same time as he thought about the man's capacity to inflict violence on his fellow man, with more viciousness than the fiercest predators in the animal kingdom. It was going to happen again, on a large scale. He knew how many of the fanatics in the regime thought. If the Israelis attacked, it was all they needed to justify a massive retaliation against them. If that happened, Israel would unleash their nuclear arsenal on Iran. They would have no choice.

Perhaps that was how he would die, with millions of others in Tehran. In that case, he wouldn't die alone. Far from being comforting, the thought of being included with so many souls being extinguished all at once disturbed him. He wondered what it was like for Allah to sense the pain simultaneously crying out from so many of His children. How did something like this fit into His plan? How did he fit into Allah's plan? And speaking of Allah, how was it all of a sudden that he was reaching out to Him for guidance and reassurance? Since when did he start believing in the existence of the Almighty? Was it that delusion he had right here in this very spot two days ago? He thought about the experience, taking himself back to that moment, trying to recreate exactly what happened. He remembered everything, but now he questioned his mental state at the time. He had probably been in a mild state of shock from the experience of the past few days. Of course, it was understandable that he could have suffered from a delusion, as he had. He was searching for answers, and his subconscious was doing its best to accommodate him. He needed answers as to why he had found himself in this horrible situation. Why had he been cursed with having been the sole witness to the truth about this evil plot? What could he do about it now, behind these prison walls? Was he just some expendable pawn that had been swept off the board, to be forgotten as ever having existed? He wanted to know.

"Why me?" he whispered, slowly opening his eyes again.

At first, he thought something had happened with the lights. Everything was so bright. He couldn't make out anything in his cell. He stood up and looked around, left, right, up, down. Everything was just bright white. He looked at his hands and arms, or where they should have been out in front of him, but there was just whiteness. The same when he looked down, searching for his legs and feet. As bright as it was, it didn't hurt his eyes. He just could not see anything. He tried stepping forward and walking towards the opposite wall of his cell, but it seemed as if he was unable to reach it. It wasn't as if he had lost his self-awareness. It was as if everything around him had been removed from his present sphere of existence, or perhaps it was the other way around.

"Why not you?" he heard a voice answer. It was the same voice from the other day. Once again, Ali couldn't make out if he was speaking English or Farsi.

"Who are you?" Ali asked, bewildered.

"I am."

"You are who?"

"I am."

"You are who? What is your name? Where are you?"

"I go by many different names."

"So, what shall I call you?"

"You have already called me by my names."

Ali was avoiding saying what he was thinking. It was too much for him to come to grips with. This couldn't be happening again. It couldn't be real. He had obviously been drugged by his captors and was hallucinating. He wasn't in fear or distress. On the contrary, he felt calm and at peace. It was just a giant chasm for the logical and rational part of him to step across.

"Why are you struggling with what you are thinking? You have referred to me for the past several days, have you not?"

"How do I know it's You? Maybe I'm just imagining all this," Ali said, attempting to talk himself out of his delusion.

"You know you are not imagining this. Why can you not say My name, Ali?"

Ali remained silent, searching his innermost being and preparing for his next words.

"Are You God? Allah?" Ali finally let out.

"I am, however you choose to call Me."

"May I see You?"

"You are in My presence. That is enough. It is not necessary for you to see Me with your physical eyes. They would not survive. You will still need them."

"If I cannot see You, then how do I know You exist outside of this encounter?"

"You have always been able to observe My actions. I am all around. As far as hearing from Me, have you ever asked?"

"You are answering me in riddles. I am just as confused," Ali cried out in desperation.

"Yes, you are confused. It is because you never had expected to have an encounter with Me."

"Of course I never expected to have an encounter with You. Who goes through life expecting something like that to ever happen?"

"You called out to Me just a few days ago. Why did you do so? Do you not believe in Me? You went to a mosque regularly for over a year more than a decade ago. Did you not believe in Me then?"

Ali didn't speak. After a long silence, he finally replied, "No, I don't. I mean I didn't. Now"—he paused—"now I must. I have met You face-to-face, for lack of a better word. I am not meaning to be disrespectful, I am just overwhelmed. When I went to the mosque to pray, I just repeated the words I was taught must be said. I did it for another purpose, not to really pray to You. I called out to You now because I am desperate. I did not expect to hear from You. I don't know if I can even trust my own senses. I have lost all control of my life. Everything has been taken away from me. I am not scared of dying. I have come to terms with that. It is just that I feel helpless. I do not know what to do. Please forgive me for doubting You."

"You are forgiven, Ali. You are not the first who has not believed. Some of My most beloved children started out that way."

"I have never had any reason to turn to You before. I was told You were only something the mullahs used to fool the ignorant and gain control of the country. It is they who are responsible for killing my parents, all in Your name."

"I see. So, it is the God of the mullahs you do not believe in. What about the God of all My other children?"

"Your other children? I'm not sure what you mean. Are you talking about Christians?"

"Yes, I am their God, but I have many more children."

"I'm confused. Do you mean the Jews also?"

"They are My children, but I have more."

"Who? Buddhists, Hindus? They don't believe in You. I mean, they don't believe in just You," Ali asked, confused.

"They are My children. You are all My children, even those who choose not to believe in Me. Not all My children may understand My true essence and honor Me in the same way, but that does not make them any less My children."

"I have never thought that way. I have never thought about You. I just lived my life the best way I knew how, tried to love others as much as I could and do what I thought was right."

"Where do you think that comes from, Ali?"

"Where what comes from?"

"That inner guide that steered you in life."

Ali sat, stood, whatever position he was in, and remained silent while he thought. Why was God drilling him with such deep questions? He was forcing him to dig into the deepest recesses of himself, searching to answers for His questions. It was as if He was pressing Ali to discover a side of himself that had thus far been unknown to him.

"I guess it must come from You."

"You know, then, how I have created you live in this world."

Ali thought about what he had just been told. Of course, if God in fact existed, He was responsible for creating everything in the universe, including him and all the other humans living on this planet. But if that was the case, what would explain all the violence in the world, explain how man could do some of the vicious things he did to his fellow man?

"Why, then, do we do the things we do to each other? Look at what is going on this planet. How is it we can do the horrible things we do to each other?" Ali asked in despair.

"You asked the big question. You want to know what went wrong if I made you so perfect. Why did My children start behaving the way they do now? The answer is both simple and complex. I have designed and created every single aspect of every one of My children, each in their own beautifully unique way. Along with all your abilities, I have also granted you the freedom to choose. That is a gift that I have jealously guarded in how I bestow it upon My creation. The freedom to follow the ways I have designed for your happiness and joy or the freedom to disregard them. The freedom to choose to love Me or to reject Me. The freedom to choose to be in My presence or be absent from My presence. These are choices each one of you has to make for yourselves, because I have also bestowed another quality upon each one of you. Your temporary nature in this world is very brief, just long enough for you to make those choices. Your eternal nature will be determined by what you each decide. So, you see, the explanation is quite simple. Each one of you has been given the freedom to do as you please. What happens to each of you as a result of those choices, is as complex and unique as anything in My creation."

Ali again remained silent while he pondered the meaning of what he had just been told. He marveled at its simplicity, yet at the same time he struggled with its implication. *Each of us can choose, but the choices of some bring pain and suffering to others.* Where was the justice in that? He hadn't chosen to be a captive in an Iranian prison. Millions of people would not have chosen to be victims of a nuclear attack. Some of God's children were making choices that were affecting the lives of so many of His other children, and not for the better.

"You are troubled by what you have learned." Ali's thoughts were interrupted.

"Yes, I am, Allah. You may have given us freedom of choice, but it doesn't matter, because the choices of others affect our lives, and there is nothing we can do to change that. Look at me. I didn't choose to be in the situation I'm in. Others made decisions to do what they want, and the rest of us have to suffer because of them. Where is the justice in that?"

"Ah, you are saying there is no justice. You seem to have confused freedom and justice. The freedom of choice I have given you is not for the purpose of allowing you to control what happens to you in this life. It is to control what happens to you after this life. I have never bestowed to My children the power of dispersing justice. That is one of the choices you have taken upon yourselves, apart from Me. You do not have the capacity to exercise justice, no more than you have the capacity to know what is in each other's hearts. Only I have that ability. The justice that you attempt to dispense upon each other is but a corrupted and misguided distortion of My justice. Only I can dispense justice to My children, when the time comes. Each one will receive the justice they are due. I tell you this as one of My beloved children, despite whatever pain and suffering you may experience during this very brief part of your existence, it will seem insignificant afterwards. It is like when a small child falls and skins their knee. At the time, they scream and cry out in pain, as if it is some unconceivable suffering they will experience forever. Yet years later when they are older, the pain has long gone and the only reminder is but a small scar. That is how it will be with all My beloved children who chose to be with Me. They will forever be removed from the pain and suffering of this world to experience all the joy and happiness found in the light of My presence. Those who have chosen not to be with Me, sadly, will have to endure the suffering and anguish of my light departing from the world they have chosen, leaving them forever in darkness."

More silence as Ali processed God's words. Had he been confusing his freedom to choose the direction of his life with the apparent lack of justice in this world? The more he thought about it, the more he realized he had no control over what was just and not just in this world. The only control he really had was over where he wanted his life to go after he left this world. It was something he realized for the very first time in his life. When that would be, however, he didn't know. Could he ask God for that answer? Did he even want to know? If he was going to die in this prison, he could at least prepare himself for that until he departed. Why would God have chosen to speak to him then? Did He just want to wake him up and let him know He existed before he left this world? Did He have some other purpose for him?

"You are wondering why I have chosen to speak to you now."

Ali was surprised to be told what he was thinking.

"I am, Allah. I don't think You do this very often, that is, talk to people directly. Why me? Why now? Will I die soon?"

"That is a question I cannot answer for you. If I revealed to you when your time was, it would affect your every decision in such a way, that it would take away any real freedom of choice you had. I have chosen you, Ali, because the path of your life intersects with the paths of other of My children who are playing a part in My plan for all of you. You also have a part to play. That is why I have chosen to speak to you."

"So, what do You want me to do, then, Allah?"

"You will know when the time comes."

"How will I know? I am stuck in this prison."

"You have everything that you will need."

Ali paused again, uncertain of where things would go from here. He felt the same sense of peace as following his first encounter with God, but it didn't reassure him he had the answers he needed. He needed help. He couldn't do it on his own.

"Will you continue to talk to me, answer my questions?" Ali asked.

"What is it you would like answered?"

"What do I want answered? There are a lot of things."

"Such as?"

"Like, what am I supposed to believe? Should I worship as a Muslim or as a Christian? Is the truth found in the Quran or in the Bible? Is Jesus truly who he says he is? Was Muhammad right? How will I know the truth when I hear it? How will I know the truth about You?"

"All those questions have already been answered. I have revealed Myself to this world. If your heart is pure and you truly seek the truth, you will find it, because I will guide you. If there is darkness in your heart and you look only for answers to satisfy your own will, then you will be misled by the Liar. You will know the truth when you weigh it against My nature, not man's."

"But there are so many things I still do not understand. Why do things happen the way they do? How am I supposed to do the right thing if I do not understand everything about Your plan?"

"You cannot understand everything. My thoughts are not your thoughts, neither are your ways My ways."

"So, will I continue to hear from You?"

"You will hear from Me if you truly seek Me, but not in this way."

"But why did You speak to me a second time, then?"

"Did you believe after the first time?"

"I don't know. I wasn't sure if I was losing my mind then."

"Do you believe now?"

"Yes, Allah, I believe."

"Then it is not necessary to speak to you in this manner any longer."

"How then will I communicate with You?" Ali asked anxiously.

"In the same way that all of My children do who seek Me. They observe Me acting in their lives. They sense the direction I am guiding them in. They feel the peace of My presence with them wherever they are. It is as unmistakable as this conversation we are having now. Most of My children have not received this blessing to hear from Me in such a direct manner as you have. For this reason alone, your faith in Me should never be in question any longer. Do you believe all that I have told you, Ali?"

"I do, my Lord! I will never lose faith! I thank You so much, Allah!"

"Then open your eyes and look for Me throughout your life, my child."

Ali was momentarily confused. His eyes were open. He had opened them while sitting in his cot into this blinding brightness. Checking to make sure they were still open, he gave them a quick squeeze shut, then flicked them open to find himself staring at the walls of his cell.

"Allah? Allah? Are You still here?" Ali waited for an answer.

There was just silence, but he knew the answer to his question. Of course God was still here. It was just that Ali's ears could not detect His voice any longer. A momentary feeling of sadness came over him at the realization he would not hear God so directly, so concretely, again. But it quickly passed when he felt the joy of finally having experienced Him for the first time in his life. He wanted to continue feeling that joy for the remainder of his time in this life, whether it was days, weeks, months, or perhaps even years. However long it was, he knew what awaited him afterwards. Until then, he would just try to live his life without expectations and watch God's plan unfold before him. When he had to make decisions along the way, he trusted that God would guide him in the right direction. That's what he would be asking for when he prayed. He just hoped that he would be able to understand God's answers as clearly as he had now.

Chapter 19

Michael walked on the shoulder of the main road in and out of Maku. One direction headed towards the nearby Turkish border, the other direction towards Tabriz and eventually on to Tehran. It was 6:45 a.m. and he could see things were starting to come to life up ahead as he made his way towards Maku. With a population of around forty thousand, it wasn't a large city, but it played a significant role in the daily trade between Iran and Turkey. Being the first major population center across the border, with its variety of offices and businesses, it had a steady flow of people and vehicles coming and going. There were several bakeries, butchers, grocery stores and eateries, various import and export offices, branch offices of all the main Iranian banks and even a shopping mall. It also had a customs office that was co-located with the Iranian national police in the same building. In addition to all the legal trade, an ample amount of smuggling took place across the border, especially cigarettes, which was the tightly regulated monopoly of the state-owned Iranian Tobacco Company.

Already there was steady traffic moving in and out of town, everything from trucks, farm tractors and pickup trucks to peasants leading their mules in with burlap sacks strewn across them. The highway turned into the main street going through town. As was the case with most rural areas in third-world countries, the main highway was the lifeblood of every town it ran through. Although the road going through town remained wide, delivery trucks double-parked as their drivers made their morning deliveries gave it a sense of disorder and chaos. Michael felt relief at being able to blend into the morning commotion, just a poor peasant enduring a hard life like so many others in rural Iran. No one paid any attention to him, except for the older of the two brothers who had followed him into town, himself also blending into the hustle and bustle.

Michael was certain he would come across the bus office somewhere on the main street. He just needed to take his time and not appear to be in a hurry. With his nervous system on high alert and adrenaline pumping throughout his body, his mind was racing in high gear. During any intelligence operation, especially in a hostile country, it was a natural reaction to want to do everything much faster for any given situation. It was a conscious effort to force himself to slow things down. The other aspect of working undercover was the natural paranoia that everyone around you was looking at you more than they actually were. He fell back on his old training, reminding himself that most people were so preoccupied with their own immediate situations they didn't even pay much attention to the person right next to them. Small kids, however, were a different story. Their natural curiosity made them lock in on someone or something in unpredictable ways, without rhyme or reason. Hopefully he looked unpleasant enough to dissuade even a child's curiosity.

He kept his head tilted slightly down, hiding his eyes as he scanned his environment back and forth. He wondered when the first bus was scheduled to leave. He thought about how he was going to buy a ticket, how he would communicate. He couldn't remember any of the Persian he had learned while in Athens, so he couldn't write down the word for Tehran. He would have to do his best acting as a deaf-mute, uttering something that could pass for Tehran. He was hoping most people's proclivity for uneasiness around disabled people would prevent any suspicion. It was a far-fetched cover, but what other choice did he have, not being able to speak the language? If this had been a CIA operation, it could have been used as training material at the Farm for new recruits. He wasn't sure, however, how it would be used—as an example of extraordinary resourcefulness, or as a monumentally foolish approach that resulted in a disastrous ending.

As he entered town, he got a whiff of the aroma coming from the open door of a bakery, making him aware of the hunger pangs in his belly. He reached into his bag and pulled out some pide, tearing a piece off and stuffing it into his mouth. It wasn't as tender and scrumptious as yesterday, but it would quell his hunger. His supply of food would last him at least a couple of days. He could always buy more food later from a street vendor. The less interaction he had with shop owners, the better.

He eventually made his way into the heart of downtown, where he caught sight of a bus parked along the curb up ahead. As he approached, he saw it was a Mercedes that looked at least thirty years old. It was parked outside what Michael recognized to be a small bus terminal. He peered in and saw rows of old plastic seating and an overweight balding man in a gray sweater vest, sitting lazily behind the glass counter, sipping his morning tea and reading a newspaper. Michael would have been thrilled that he had so easily located his means of transportation to Tehran, except for what he saw next to the bus station in front of a beige three-story concrete building with the Iranian flag hanging outside. Parked diagonally against the curb were several police vehicles. Milling around outside the building, smoking cigarettes, were two Iranian police officers in their dark green uniform with their MP-5s dangling sloppily off their shoulders. *Oh crap, just what I need*, he almost let out audibly, while doing his best to maintain his composure. *Okay, no big deal. You're still just the same pathetic peasant to them as you are to everyone else around you. Just stay in role and do what you were going to do anyway. This doesn't change a thing*, he told himself.

He looked back inside the bus office at the ticket clerk. This was it. He focused as he prepared himself, the same way he imagined play actors did just before they walked out onstage. He was about to step through the door when an elderly lady in her headscarf and chador holding a cane appeared out of nowhere, heading for the door to go inside. Out of instinct, Michael reached for the door and opened it for her.

"*Moteshakera*," the old woman thanked him in her crackly voice.

For a second, Michael felt like a deer caught in the headlights. He wasn't expecting to have to interact with a sweet old grandmother. His natural tendency was to respond, but he kept his mouth shut. Finally raising a hand next to his ear and turning it back and forth, he gave her the biggest smile he could muster. She hobbled up to the clerk, who glanced at her and put his paper down.

"*Salaam*," the clerk greeted her.

"*Salaam*," she replied, began speaking to him.

Michael stood behind her at a respectable distance, trying to look as dimwitted as possible, scratching his head and turning it, looking around, not focusing on anything for more a few seconds. He could hear their conversation, but he only picked up the word Tabriz and a few words that sounded vaguely familiar, any Persian he had learned years ago having evaporated from his memory. Finally, the old lady pulled a wallet out of her purse and counted out rials, handing a stack of bills to the clerk, who handed her a ticket in return.

"*Moteshakera*," she thanked him, bowing her head.

The clerk gave a slight bow and turned his attention to Michael. Michael walked up to him, slightly dragging one foot and gave him an enormous face-distorting smile.

"Tewan," he blurted out, managing to send some spittle out into the air in front of him, a few drops landing on the counter.

The clerk glanced down at the counter, then looked back up at Michael and started saying something to him. Michael returned a blank stare, raising his hand to his ear and turning it back and forth, and once again belted out, "Tewan!"

The old lady, who had taken a seat in the waiting area, looked up at the clerk and shouted, "Tehran!"

The clerk looked at the old lady. Michael turned his attention towards her also and gave the elderly grandmother his biggest smile, then turned back to the irritated clerk, who started speaking to him again. Michael returned him the twist of his hand and a huge smile, then motioned him to write it down. The teller, getting more annoyed by the second, grabbed a copy of the bus schedule and jotted down on the back "600,000," momentarily throwing Michael off balance when he saw the size of the figure. He quickly rebooted his brain, remembering the figure was in Iranian rials, reaching for the wallet they had bought, along with his other clothing in the Grand Bazaar. He turned away from the clerk, adding to his cover of being slightly off-balanced, and searched through his bulging wallet, pulling out six hundred-thousand-rial notes, then turned and handed the equivalent of fifteen dollars to the teller. Of the fifteen hundred dollars in rials Asya had given him, he could only fit one-quarter of the bills in his wallet and still be able to fold it shut. The years of rampant inflation as a result of the economic sanctions that had been imposed on Iran because of their nuclear program had caused massive devaluation of the rial. Even after the Iran nuclear deal had lifted the economic sanctions, foreign banks were still hesitant to do business with Iran, unsure if they would come under future US sanctions. The clerk handed him a ticket which Michael stared at, then looked up at the teller and tapped his left wrist, searching for the departure time. The clerk impatiently grabbed the ticket and pointed to 09:00 printed on the ticket. Michael looked around for a clock, spotting one on the wall above the old lady. It was 7:51 a.m.; he had over an hour to wait. He looked back at the clerk and raised both his hands, gesturing and looking around. The clerk, thoroughly exasperated by now, pointed to the other side of the room. Michael nodded his head, doubling down on his big toothy smile, then turned and walked across the room, taking a seat a few chairs away from the old lady.

He sat there quietly, looking at the floor, slightly rocking his head, staying in role. He wasn't quite sure who he was trying to imitate, a deaf-mute person or someone with a mental disorder. A little bit of both, he figured, would be that much more effective at keeping people from wanting to engage him. He was glad just to sit there in silence while waiting for his bus. It gave him a chance to collect his thoughts following his first interaction since arriving in-country. It had just been a simple transaction to purchase a bus ticket, but it had challenged him to maintain his composure and keep his cool. How was he going to make it all the way through tracking down Karbashi, if something like this had felt so stressful? He did his best to reassure himself. He thought that he had actually played it off fairly well. He had managed to buy a bus ticket in a foreign country without having to utter a word, other than an unintelligible grunt. *Small steps, small steps*, he told himself. A steady trickle of passengers started coming into the bus office, purchasing tickets, then taking their place in the waiting area.

It seemed like everything was progressing uneventfully, until he saw the young boy of about fourteen years of age step inside the ticket office, followed by two policemen. There were enough passengers sitting in the waiting area to make it difficult to easily spot anyone. The two policemen stood behind the boy with a look of impatience as he scanned the waiting area. Michael, looking down at the floor, kept eyes on what was going on with his peripheral vision. The boy started slowly wandering through the room, glancing from person to person. As he drew near, he paused in front of Michael. Knowing he was on the spot, Michael raised his head and gave the boy a big distorted smile, then shifted it towards the two policemen. The boy was momentarily surprised by Michael's reaction, but then regained his composure and turned, nodding to the officers. Michael maintained his smile, shifting his gaze back and forth from the child to the policemen, picking up that the officers were confused. One of them fired off something to the boy in an exasperated tone, but the boy replied back, sounding sure of himself. Michael continued smiling, bobbing his head back and forth at the three of them. Finally, one of the officers turned to Michael and uttered a short command. Michael raised his right hand next to his ear and twisted it back and forth, causing the officer to repeat what he had said even louder. Michael continued smiling, keeping his hand next to his ear, until the old woman sitting two chairs down from him interjected herself, informing them Michael was deaf. The officers turned their attention back to Michael, then to the boy, firing off another annoyed comment to him. The boy, however, unwilling to back down, continued pointing at Michael, maintaining his story.

Keeping his smile and bobbing his head was all Michael could do to appear calm on the exterior, while inside he could feel his heart begin to race as the first signs of concern began setting in. *Stay calm, keep focused, you have the advantage. You know what's going on. They're still confused. Slow it down. Slow it down. Deep breath.* He did his best to keep from becoming unnerved. He was unprepared for this sudden encounter that had snuck up on him without any warning. He had just recovered from his ticket-buying experience, and now he was having to deal with an official arm of the Iranian security establishment and this unrelenting kid that had some kind of issue with him for some unknown reason. *Who the heck is this kid, and what's his connection to me?* He tried to make sense of what was going on.

Clearly not sure of themselves, one of the officers pointed to Michael's bag, indicating he wanted to look inside it. Michael continued smiling and bobbing as his mind raced to come up with various options for the predicament he found himself in. He could refuse to let them examine his bag. If they decided to seize it, emptying its contents and finding the satellite phone and GPS, he was finished. There would be no way to explain himself. Continuing to feign deafness would likely result in the butt of one of their guns across his face. On the other hand, he could take the chance and willingly display the top contents, offering them some pide in the hopes it would dissuade them from wasting any more of their time on whatever this boy was claiming. Seconds were ticking by; he had to decide. He had to either willingly open his bag for them or make a break for the door. First, he had to get up off his chair and gain some positional advantage. He stood up slowly, swinging his bag off his shoulder and setting it down on his chair, attempting to draw their attention away from him to his bag. As they stepped forward to look at the contents of his bag, Michael noticed the end of his knife's wooden handle protruding out from the dates under one of the pieces of pide. It also attracted the interest of the officer closest to the bag. Reaching for the pide, the officer took a few of them out of the bag and set them down on the adjoining empty chair, then returned his attention to the wooden handle.

Michael realized he had to react before the officer got any further into his bag. He took a step back as he reached for the sidearm of the officer standing next to him, drawing the Sig Sauer P226 9mm from its holster and pointing it at the head of the officer, before either of them realized what had happened.

"*Ta!*" came out of Michael's mouth unexpectedly, commanding the two police officers to raise their hands. How he had dived into the depths of his memory and somehow retrieved the Persian word for "up," was just as much a surprise to him as it was to the two officers hearing a deaf-mute suddenly give a such a sharp and clear command. Caught completely off guard, both officers slowly raised their hands above their heads as the young boy stepped back in fear. Michael reached with his left hand and removed the sidearm of the other officer and tucked it into his waistband. Without missing a beat, he kicked out the back of the knees of one officer, then the other, causing them both to buckle and drop to the floor. Michael followed up immediately by pushing one, then the other, face flat on the floor, planting his shoe on the middle of one's back as he pointed the end of the Sig against the head of the other.

"*Aqamt!*" he ordered them to stay, surprising himself again by remembering another Persian word. He stepped back from the officers and grabbed his bag from the chair. He glanced around the waiting room, pausing as he looked at the young boy who had caused him all this trouble, noticing his wide-open eyes and the look of terror on his face. The other twenty or so bus passengers, along with the clerk, were staring at him in bewilderment with their mouths hanging open, struggling to come to terms with what they had just witnessed. Michael hastened through the waiting area to the door, tucking both Sigs into his bag, then stepped outside and turned back in the direction he had come from. He wanted to run but forced himself to walk quickly instead, not wanting to attract any unnecessary attention until he had no other choice. He had made it about fifty meters when he heard the blast of a police whistle somewhere behind him.

He turned his head over his shoulder and saw the two police officers come running out the bus station, continuing to blow their whistles as they scanned the street in every direction, looking for him. They spotted him in a matter of seconds, but rather than come after him, one continued blowing his whistle as the other got on his radio.

Michael had their two 9mms, and they were unarmed. He considered drawing down on them to force them back inside the bus station but decided against it, realizing all the attention a man brandishing a gun on two policemen would attract. Instead, he decided to make a break for it, taking off running down the sidewalk. It was an obstacle course around all the pedestrian traffic that had filled the street by that time in the morning. He knew he couldn't stay on the main road much longer before other police units would be in pursuit. It would be just a matter of minutes before the area would be swarming with them. His only chance to evade capture would be by heading down side streets and finding some cover until he could regroup and figure out what to do next.

Turning the corner at the next intersection, he made his way down a narrower street with small shops, that eventually transitioned into tightly packed three-story apartment buildings. Clotheslines hung across most of the small balconies, some of them covered by rolled-out awnings that provided shade from the scorching sun of the summer and the occasional rain during winter. There weren't as many pedestrians on the street, mostly children carrying their bags on the way to school. Both sides of the street were lined with one parked car after another, giving Michael some cover as he continued heading away from the direction of the police whistle blaring off in the distance. Reaching another intersection, he turned a corner, putting more distance and additional streets between him and the disturbance. He continued the left and right turns at each successive intersection, moving in a diagonal pattern away from the station and the main street. Off in the distance, he heard the start of sirens as other police units began responding to assist their two comrades, who had been disarmed by some crazy vagrant.

He couldn't stay on the streets for too much longer. It would only be a matter of time before enough police units joined the search that they would eventually come across him on foot. He had to find a temporary location where he had a chance to figure out his next move. This wasn't a good start to the mission. He hadn't even managed to begin his journey away from his infiltration location before having the Iranian police in hot pursuit of him. So much for keeping a low profile. Somehow, he had been compromised from the very beginning. Who was that kid? There was a reason he avoided kids when it came to operating undercover. They tended to be a bigger hazard than adults. His immediate concern was to avoid capture. If he could make it out of town, perhaps he had a chance to escape. There was no reason to believe they suspected he was some kind of foreign agent. He hadn't given anything up to them. He had just uttered two short commands to them in Persian, perhaps not with a perfect accent, but he doubted they would have picked up on that in the midst of their shock at having their weapons taken away from them and pointed at their heads. If anything, it was more likely they thought he was some drug smuggler involved in transporting heroin over the border to Turkey, Iran being the main transit route from Afghanistan on Iran's eastern border. Whatever they thought, it didn't change his precarious situation. If he was caught, the truth would eventually be discovered.

Searching his surroundings looking for a place to hide, Michael heard the sound of a siren growing louder and closing in on his location. He only had seconds to find cover before he would be discovered. Noticing a space between the buildings just ahead, he dashed into the narrow passage, just moments before a police car came screaming by. He continued down the narrow passageway, finding an open door that led into an interior stairwell. He ducked inside and quickly climbed up the three stories of concrete steps to the rooftop. He stayed inside the small landing at the top of the stairwell, peering out through the open doorway at the surrounding rooftops of the adjacent buildings. The residential area he was in was composed mostly of tightly spaced three-story flat-roofed concrete buildings, with an occasional four-story building here and there. Other than the thru streets on every other block, most buildings had narrow alleyways separating them, barely wide enough to allow a compact car to squeeze through. Most rooftops had clotheslines strung across them, some with laundered clothing and sheets hanging on them. It gave the rooftop landscape the appearance of orchards of galvanized metal trees with strange large multicolored leaves fluttering in the wind on a high mountain plateau of concrete rectangles. Most of the roofs also had a small enclosed stairwell on them, similar to the one he was hiding in.

He remained inside his little hideaway for the time being, giving himself a chance to catch his breath and pull himself together so he could come up with his next move. He made a deliberate effort to slow his breathing and force out any thoughts of what would happen to him if he were caught. Worrying about that wasn't going to help him think of solutions to his current predicament. He couldn't stay hidden in this little rooftop room indefinitely. Eventually someone would come up to hang some clothes. Despite this unfortunate setback, he knew if he could get out of town and put distance between him and the police, he stood a chance of making it to Tehran, where he could get lost in its population of eight million residents. The bus option was out. He couldn't go back there. He couldn't make his way out of town on foot either. His description had obviously been communicated to all police units, so any man on foot matching his description would immediately catch the attention of those who were out searching for the man who had disarmed two of their fellow officers.

He pulled out one of the Sig Sauers and inspected it. He removed the magazine and saw that it contained fourteen rounds, the fifteenth being chambered. An inspection of the other Sig revealed the same thing. That gave him thirty rounds. The last thing he wanted was to get into a gunfight with the Iranian police. If that happened, it meant his mission had completely failed. It was almost a liability to hold on to the guns, but it was against his nature to give up weapons he had in his possession, especially when in enemy territory. For the time being, he would hang on to them, until he was sure he had become anonymous once again, when they would lose any usefulness to him.

He could try to wait it out where he was until evening, then venture back out after it had become dark. That would make him harder to spot, but he still would need to find an alternate method to get out of town. He would be easy to spot on the main road even at night. Also, he didn't want to waste any more time trying to find Ali. The ten hours he would lose until nightfall was too long. Besides, some housewife in her hijab might wander up there any second with a basket full of clothes. He had to find another solution soon. Waiting there wasn't a viable option. Did he go back down and start wandering his way through neighborhoods, looking for some means out of town? Was he going to steal a car? Even if he did, he was sure the police had already set up checkpoints heading out of town in both directions. He could steal some type of enduro motorcycle and ride out through the countryside. There was plenty of mountainous terrain just beyond the outskirts of town. He stood a better chance that way than by car on the highway. Even that, he realized was too risky. There wasn't enough tree cover. He would be out in the open for anyone to spot him. He needed to somehow discreetly smuggle himself out. He needed to find a truck heading out of town and hitch a ride hidden away inside, past any police checkpoints. That made the most sense. It was his only viable option under the circumstances. But how was he going to find a truck? He couldn't just aimlessly wander the streets looking for transportation while the entire police force was out searching for him.

Michael peered back outside, across the sea of rooftops. He decided he needed to maintain the high ground. Although there was a chance he could be spotted by someone, it was safer than being out on the street. He would jump his way across one rooftop at a time and seek cover before moving onto the next. That would give him a better vantage point than being down on street level. Hopefully he would be able to spot a possible escape vehicle to stow away on.

He cautiously stepped outside the cover of his small room and did a reconnaissance of the rooftops in every direction, looking for any threats. It was still early enough that no one was out hanging laundry yet. The laundry scattered on various rooftops had obviously been left out from the night before. He estimated he was three to four blocks west of the main street. He had lost count of how many lefts and rights he had made during the heat of his escape. He looked to the south, the direction he wanted to head out of town, and decided to move in that way across the rooftops. He wasn't so concerned about the six-to-seven-foot space in between each rooftop. With a running leap, he would easily clear that distance, assuming he didn't stumble and break his neck in a fall. It was the landing on the other side that he was concerned about. With the injury to his back that had forced him out of Special Forces, one leap was bad enough. Having to jump his way across several rooftops was going to do a real number on him. What he wouldn't have given for his bottle of oxycodone right now. He knew the pain he was going to suffer. He just hoped it wouldn't cripple him.

He cautiously walked over to the edge of the roof and peered down the gap between the two buildings. He pulled his head back as soon as he caught sight of a fat white-haired old man wearing a white T-shirt, who was holding a hose and cleaning the walk in between the buildings. As long as he didn't look up, Michael would be fine during the split second that his body would appear in the sky overhead. *Okay, piece of cake. You can do this. Just keep your legs bent when you land. Don't take the brunt of the impact on your back*, he thought, visualizing it before taking a few steps and leaping across onto the other rooftop. He came down on his right foot and ran a couple steps to slow himself down, then quickly made his way to the small stairwell room. Fortunately, the door was open and he popped inside. He felt the slight ache in his lower back from the impact of the landing, but it wasn't too bad. He had felt worse when he had gotten off the plane in D.C. after flying coach for five hours. He knew it would get a little worse with each successive jump.

He glanced back outside. Not seeing anyone, he studied the next rooftop in his direction of travel and observed that all was clear. Once again, he repeated his previous routine, casually venturing out while surveying the surrounding rooftops as he made his way towards the edge, then taking a few steps and launching himself across the gap to the other roof. He relaxed his knees as he landed, but still felt the jarring on his lower back as he ran for the cover of the stairwell. He rested there for a moment to recover his breath and slow down his heart rate. The physical activity of a couple running steps and a leap were not that strenuous. It was the psychological effect of leaping across a chasm with a forty-foot drop, along with the risk of being spotted by someone, that had gotten his heart rate up, the way it was a week ago when he had been out running just before attempting to take his life. He continuously needed to remind himself to stay calm and think things through clearly, one step at a time. If he didn't make any foolish mistakes, with a little bit of luck, he would be able to get himself out of his current situation.

He peered across the horizon of rooftops. From what he could see up ahead, the rooftops were beginning to spread out, with larger open areas between them. He could tell he was gradually moving away from the center of town towards the outlying areas. It looked like he had four more rooftops until he reached what looked like a sizeable open area. It could be a field, or an area with smaller buildings, perhaps even single-family homes. That made for three more jumps. He flexed his torso, stretching his spine left and right and hearing a few pops. His lower back didn't feel that bad. He could certainly tell he was giving it a beating, but the general dull ache he was feeling instead of a sharp pain told him that he was still physically undamaged. He just needed to keep doing what he was doing and make sure he used good form on each landing. He went back outside and repeated his leap twice more without any mishaps.

He was about to launch again but stopped short just as he was about to take his first step, when a woman carrying a laundry basket suddenly appeared on a roof several buildings to his left. He nonchalantly began looking down onto his roof as if he was studying something, slowly tracing his footsteps to the stairwell. As he walked back, out of his peripheral vision, he saw the woman glance over at him, noticing that someone else was out on a roof. He went back inside the small room, keeping himself out of her line of sight while observing her from around the corner of his doorway. Although she was wearing a hijab, he could tell from her face and the toddler clothes she was hanging out to dry that she couldn't have been more than twenty-five, close to the same age as his daughter.

He studied the young mother performing her traditional domestic duties. It occurred to him that he considered her a potential threat, along with every other Iranian whose life he was actually trying to save from the horrible fate that awaited them if Israel resorted to using nuclear weapons against Iran. He imagined that any nuclear strike would initially be limited in scope, most likely targeting the Iranian military command structure and the IRGC, but most of those assets were located in, and around, Tehran. Any nuclear attack in a densely populated urban area would result in tens of thousands of deaths and even more injuries. He was certain if Iran suffered even a limited nuclear attack, it would respond by unleashing every missile in its arsenal, along with Hezbollah's, against Israel, only to invite a follow-on nuclear strike once again by Israel, undoubtedly even greater in scope. It would snowball into a humanitarian nightmare and put the entire Middle East into turmoil, thus accomplishing whatever warped strategic goals President Markov and President Steele had intended. Although he didn't have proof either president was involved in this depraved plot, he was certain something like this couldn't take place without their direct involvement, especially in Markov's case. The thought of what awaited all these innocent human beings if he failed bolstered his resolve to do whatever was necessary to succeed in his mission. He wasn't scared of the possibility of dying as much as failing, but he knew in order for that not to happen, he had to stay alive.

Another five minutes and the young mother finally finished hanging her laundry, disappearing back into her building and leaving the coast clear for Michael to resume his unorthodox journey across town. He slowly made his way back out onto the roof. Seeing that the coast was clear, he didn't waste any time running and then leaping once more into the sky before landing onto the adjacent rooftop. From this new vantage point, he could finally see what the open space was next to his building. Across a much wider alley of about ten feet was a two-story warehouse or plant of some kind, with a paved lot on two sides of it. What caught Michael's attention, however, was the three trucks parked adjacent to the building, and the cargo being loaded by a conveyor belt into their open beds. One truck was already filled, while another was under the conveyor belt, with its bed almost full. He recognized the reddish-green olive-sized nuts as raw pistachios, their soft exterior husks still covering the inner hard shell. They had obviously just been harvested from the nearby orchards and were being taken somewhere else for processing. He quickly realized this was his way out of town, at least the best opportunity he would get. He had nowhere else to turn. He had made his way as far as his rooftop hopping would take him. Now, it was either the trucks, or moving back onto the street and looking for another option. He knew that was no option at all. It would just be a matter of time before he was caught.

He glanced around once more and saw there were no other individuals on any nearby rooftops that could see him. He surveyed the leap from his roof across the wide alleyway and down one story, onto the roof of the warehouse. This was a significantly wider gap than his previous jumps. There was quite a difference between jumping a six-to-seven-foot span compared to the ten to twelve feet that was now before him. He would have to commit to a full sprint and an all-out leap to come even close to clearing that distance. The ten-foot downward drop would help him gain some additional distance, but he risked breaking an ankle or leg, not to mention what it would do to his back. He peered over the edge of the roof and saw that if he didn't make the jump, the drop to the ground wouldn't be survivable. Even if it didn't kill him, he would likely be paralyzed, with multiple broken bones, internal injuries, and most likely a fractured skull. He pulled back from the edge as a wave of fear washed over him. He went back inside to the cover of the small room and sat down on the hard concrete floor, resting his back against the wall and taking slow, deep breaths. He looked at his hands and saw they were trembling. That was strange. Why was he having such a reaction? He had jumped out of the back of C-130s from fifteen thousand feet dozens of times. He had never had any fear of heights before. Had he lost his nerve after all these years?

Michael realized that if he didn't take advantage of this opportunity, the odds that something else would present itself were virtually none. This was it. He had no other choice. He would either make the jump to his escape and continue on with the mission or hopefully not survive the fall. It was definitely going to be comparable to a hard skydiving landing due to a misjudged flare during gusty conditions. Perhaps not as hard as the landing that had incapacitated him and gotten him medically discharged from the Army, but hard enough to significantly hurt him. The human body wasn't designed to sustain repeated crashes without it eventually taking its toll. He had already sustained a lifetime's amount. Another major one like this might be enough to seriously re-injure his lower back enough to prevent him from being able to go on with the mission. That was what he feared. He had to compose himself and just do what needed to be done.

He had practiced his hard landing technique at jump school hundreds of times from five feet on soft grass or in a mat room. It was high enough to fully deploy the technique without causing any injuries, unless someone wasn't paying attention to what they were doing. He recounted it in his mind. It had been a long time ago, but it was one of those things that had been etched in his memory. Feet together and knees springy, contact with the ground in the following order: balls of feet, side of calf, side of upper leg, side of butt, side of back, behind the arm, hugging elbows tightly to the side and slightly front while keeping the upper arms against the chest to prevent wrist and hand injuries, all in one smooth flowing motion. He knew the steps by heart; it was just that his body hadn't put itself through that coordinated series of movements for over a quarter of a century. It was like asking a fifty-four-year-old ex-Olympic gymnast to perform the floor routine that had won them the gold medal at age twenty-two. He had the steps in his head, he just didn't know if his body would be able to do what his brain told it. He hoped he could. It was the only way he would survive the jump without injury.

He took the hemp bag off his back and opened it in front of him, repackaging the GPS and satellite phone in the middle of the dates to protect them from damage. He re-secured the bag tightly across his back, then crouched down by the stairwell doorway with his eyes closed. He pictured himself leaping off the building, keeping control of his body through the air, then making contact below, meeting the surface in one smooth roll and displacing all the energy from his instantaneous deceleration. *As they say, it's not the fall that kills you, it's the sudden stop at the end*, he joked with himself. He realized Asya had been right about his nervous habit of making jokes when there was danger. He repeated the sequence over and over in his mind, his body flexing as he visualized himself going through the roll. This was it. He had to go now. No more stalling.

He stood up from his crouch and started loosening up, shaking himself like he was a boxer preparing to go into the ring. He slowly made his way toward the edge and stopped right before it. He started pacing backwards, focusing on his strides. When he had taken the five steps he had calculated were enough to get him to full acceleration, he paused for a moment before committing to his next action. *Feet together, knees springy. Feet together, knees springy. Body awareness, stay in control*, he repeated to himself. Suddenly springing forward, he accelerated as fast as his fifty-four-year-old legs would propel him and leapt into the air. His legs and arms rotating to steady his body, he brought his feet together and tucked his arms against his torso a split second before he came into contact with the rooftop below. The balls of his feet touched down simultaneously next to each other, and his knees compressed as he shifted his body sideways to redirect his forward momentum. He rolled along the front of his shin, side of his knee, side of his thigh, upper arm and continued around for a second roll as the abrasive surface of the concrete scraped his knees, his wrists and the side of his face.

When he finally came to a stop, he remained motionless in a fetal position, taking slow, deep breaths, assessing whether he felt any significant pain anywhere in his body. He felt the sting of the abrasions on his knee, wrist and face, but there was no indication of pain anywhere else. He slowly extended his legs, seeing that they still functioned, next his arms, then he slowly sat himself up. He had made it. It wasn't pretty, but he had survived and wasn't paralyzed or badly injured. He looked at his torn trousers and the chewed-up skin on his arm, slowly turning his hand to make sure he hadn't broken his wrist. It was just skin that would scab and eventually heal. He dabbed the side of his face with his sleeve and saw small dabs of blood. His arm and face stung, but all things considered, it wasn't too bad.

He looked around at the surrounding buildings to make sure no one was looking down at him as he slowly stood up. He took a few steps. Nothing hurt, and he wasn't limping. Other than a little dull ache, even his lower back didn't feel that bad. He looked back up from where he had jumped. He was amazed that he hadn't injured himself. Perhaps Asya had already started praying for him. He thought in disbelief about how many times he had defied all the odds during the course of the past week. Perhaps he did have an ever so slight chance of accomplishing this suicide mission.

He made his way over to the side of the building, where the trucks were being loaded with their cargo. He crouched down as he approached the edge and looked below him to the conveyor belt dumping raw pistachios into the bed of the second truck. He saw a group of three men standing next to one of the trucks, smoking cigarettes and talking with each other. He guessed they were the drivers, waiting for their trucks to be filled until they could depart for wherever they were taking the pistachios. Where was their destination? Michael wondered. If he stowed away on one of the trucks and they happened to be going to Turkey, it would be a disastrous setback. He might make it safely back over the border, but having Ercan reinsert him into Iran again was unlikely. There was too much risk involved, especially since the Iranian authorities were now on high alert, searching for someone who had been feigning being a deaf-mute and had disarmed two police officers. He thought it was more likely the trucks were heading somewhere in Iran. The pistachios were being taken to some other facility for further processing. Wherever they were going, his immediate concern was getting out of town undetected. He would worry about where that was afterwards. He continued to observe the scene down below. The second truck was just about full. From the rate at which the conveyor was filling the cargo bed of the second truck, he estimated it would take around thirty minutes to fill the last truck.

Another man suddenly emerged from inside the warehouse and shouted at the drivers, causing two of them to head to the cabs of their trucks just as the conveyor belt stopped. One got into the truck that had just been filled, the other into the empty one. They started their engines, and the truck under the conveyor pulled away, making room for the empty truck to back in and take its place. The driver of the truck that had been just filled backed up to the warehouse and parked, then got out and walked back over to the other two drivers, resuming conversation as the conveyor belt came back to life.

Michael didn't have much time. He needed to get into the back of one of the two full trucks before the third was filled and they left the warehouse. He looked at how the filled trucks were positioned. Both of them had been backed up against the warehouse. It wouldn't be a difficult jump, about twelve feet down, much more forgiving into a mound of pistachios than the hard concrete surface he had just landed on. The only problem was how to make the jump without being noticed by the drivers. He would need something to distract them. He looked around and spotted something that got his attention. On the other side of the roof, underneath some solar panels, were what looked like two metal paint cans.

He walked over and picked up the rusty cans, which, to his delight, were half-full of liquid. With both cans in hand, he walked back over to the side of the trucks. He cautiously peered over the edge, searching for a distraction that would be heard over the noise of the conveyor discharging the pistachios into the back of the truck. He spotted what he was looking for. To the far side of the lot was a large metal dumpster. He couldn't see into the dumpster, but he hoped it was empty, which would serve his purpose well. He crouched as he walked over to one of the full trucks that was parked next to the truck under the conveyor belt. The drivers were just below him and to his left. He judged the distance to the dumpster at around thirty meters.

He lined himself up with his target truck, then took a few steps back while still keeping sight of the dumpster. Setting one of the cans down, he swung the other back and forth with his arm, accustoming himself to the feel of it. Finally, with an overhand swing, he launched the can into an arc towards the dumpster. He watched the can sail through the air towards its target, then saw it miss its mark, landing just beyond the dumpster, without even a slight reaction from any of the drivers. He picked up the remaining can and gauged the feel of it in his hand. Once again, with an overhand swing, he released the half-full can into the sky and watched it as it made its way towards the dumpster. Its trajectory looked good, finding its mark and causing a loud clang as it landed inside the dumpster. Michael saw the drivers suddenly turn their attention towards the noise, so he quickly took a couple of steps and leapt off the roof into the bed of the truck, planting himself into the mountain of pistachios.

After dislodging his legs, Michael pulled off his shoes and poured out the pistachios. Fortunately, they been recently picked and their outer husks were soft. Otherwise, it wouldn't have felt pleasant experiencing the hard edges of partly opened shells tearing at his already stinging abrasions. He listened for any movement outside but could only hear the noise of the pistachios pouring into the truck next to him. He was pretty sure he hadn't been spotted making his jump. He wanted to peek over the top of the truck bed but decided it was too risky.

An idea came to him. He opened his bag and reached in past the pide, in between the bags of dates, and pulled out the smartphone Asya had given him. He opened the back, carefully removed the SIM card, and placed it in his new wallet, knowing if it fell into the sea of pistachios, it would be lost forever. He reinserted the battery and powered it on, no longer concerned about it registering with the Iranian cellular network. He activated the phone's camera, switching it to the selfie lens, then carefully raised it up until he could see over the top of the truck bed. He slowly moved the phone around, surveying the area outside. He saw the three drivers engaged in conversation, as if nothing had happened. He breathed a sigh of relief, knowing that he had made his jump unseen.

He considered what the police would be doing to track him down. He realized two officers having their weapons taken from them would bring about a dramatic response, especially in a country like Iran, where such a brazen act against the police was virtually unheard of. A similar situation in the United States would result in an army of various law enforcement agencies swarming the area to locate the perpetrator. They would most likely be setting up checkpoints, inspecting all vehicles leaving town. He had to prepare for that possibility. He moved to the front of the cargo bed and began digging out an area of pistachios that he could bury himself under. He hoped they didn't use police dogs. After clearing an area six feet long and three feet deep, he sat down and did the only thing left for him to do. He waited.

After about half an hour, the conveyor belt finally stopped. He sat motionless, straining to pick up any sounds. He could hear the faint chatter of voices he assumed were the drivers, along with a variety of other indistinguishable sounds, but no sirens. He knew that didn't mean they had given up the search for him. On the contrary, they had likely gone from the reactive mode to a more deliberate and methodical search mode. Michael heard a new voice enter the conversation, then some silence, followed by the door of the cab opening and closing, then the engine coming to life. The same thing was repeated by the two other trucks next to him. Finally, there was the sound of the transmission being jammed into gear and a lurch forward. Hopefully this would be Michael's escape from what had almost become a disastrous situation just as the mission had gotten under-way.

Michael made himself as comfortable as possible on the mound of pistachios. They were still soft and small enough to conform to the shape of his body, almost like a bean bag chair, just with larger beans. He thought how much fun it would be for young children to be able to climb around in the back of the truck that was acting as his escape vehicle. The three trucks had pulled out of the warehouse compound and made their way through the neighborhood. Michael sat with his back against the front of the cargo bay wall as they passed by each apartment building, hoping no one would look down from a balcony or window and notice a man sitting in the back of a truck full of pistachios. He didn't bother trying to use his cell phone to see where they were heading. He knew there was only one way in and out of town. They were making their way towards the main street. Which way they would turn, he would find out soon enough. If they were heading back into Turkey, they would be going through the border checkpoint, where he risked being discovered by customs officials inspecting the cargo. If they were heading the opposite way, then hopefully it was his way out, giving him a chance to complete his mission if his luck held out. He glanced at the shallow grave he'd constructed. He was prepared for whatever police checkpoint they had to go through. He just wanted to get it over with quickly and get as far away from this town as possible.

They made it down to the main street and turned in the direction heading into Iran. A non-eventful drive through the middle of town and back out onto the main highway came to a sudden halt shortly after they had cleared the last home on the outskirts of town. Michael realized they had arrived at the checkpoint. Should he begin his self-burial process and prepare to slip through the checkpoint, he wondered, or should he turn on his mobile phone once more to get a visual and better idea of what he should prepare for? He decided having more information was worth the slight risk, so he powered it back on and activated the selfie camera, raising it slowly above the top of the cargo bay wall. He slowly moved the phone back and forth, scanning the terrain. He saw the police checkpoint off in the distance, but what he saw between them and the checkpoint surprised and dejected him at the same time. In front of them was a line of cars and trucks stretching close to two miles long, waiting their turn to go through the checkpoint. The Iranian police had no intention of letting anyone so brazen as to disarm two of their officers escape from their clutches. They were searching every vehicle with a fine-tooth comb, and it had brought traffic leaving town to a standstill. He might as well make himself comfortable, he thought, as he scooted himself into his grave and moved around pistachios, adjusting his formfitting recliner. He was going to be there a while before it would be their turn. He placed his head back on his hands as he looked up at the billowy white clouds lit up by the bright sunshine in the deep blue sky. It was a perfect day, despite how his morning had started. He had a lot to be thankful for.

***

Asya's flight back from Agri arrived in Istanbul at 10:30 a.m. Not wanting to waste any time, she drove immediately back to her office from the airport. It wasn't that she expected to be able to find out anything about Michael's progress, but being close to all her intelligence resources at such a critical time, would make her feel as if she were in the position to be able to support him if he needed help. As part of her responsibility in investigating the Iranian foreign minister's assassination, she had immediate access to all signals intelligence collected by the General Staff Electronic Systems Command, more commonly known as the GES, which was Turkey's version of the NSA. One of the GES's primary responsibilities was keeping tabs on all communications of their neighbors, including Iran to their east. Formerly a branch of the Turkish military, the GES had been transferred under the control of MIT a few years ago as part of President Ocsilan's effort to strip power from the Turkish military and solidify his position as president.

She walked in and greeted her secretary. "*Merhaba, Anyur*. Any calls?"

"Oh, *Merhaba*, Ms. Tarhan. Just the director wanting an update, and Mr. Canton from the US embassy asking you to call him back."

The hair on her neck stood up. It was a subconscious reaction from knowing Canton's true involvement in the conspiracy and the warning Michael had given her about him. She wondered what he wanted. He was probably calling to see if he could get any information that might help him track down Michael. She assumed that he knew Michael had made it to Istanbul and had somehow slipped through CIA surveillance efforts to pick him up at the airport. He would probably give her some false story about Michael and ask for her assistance in tracking him down. Perhaps she could turn the tables on him and use it as an opportunity to see what information she could gather from him. Whatever he wanted, she knew that caution was called for when dealing with him.

"*Teşekkür ederim, Anyur*," she thanked her secretary and walked into her office, shutting the door. It was already 11:30. *Half the day already gone*, she thought. She wondered what she was in such a rush to accomplish. Knowing the truth about the assassination of the Iranian foreign minister, yet not being able to officially report it up her chain of command and on to the president, for whom all of MIT's intelligence collection efforts were ultimately intended, put her in an awkward situation. In a way, what she was doing could be considered treasonous, especially in the eyes of President Ocsilan, who was already paranoid about any potential enemies challenging his power. She couldn't just come out with an intelligence report, however, with everything she had learned from Michael and how they had discovered the whereabouts of Ali Shiravi. How would she explain who her source was? The man she had just arranged to have infiltrated into Iran by the commander of Turkey's elite counterterrorism unit? Both she and Ercan would immediately be imprisoned and be completely useless to Michael. If Michael somehow were even able to get Ali out of Iran and bring the conspiracy out in the light, it wouldn't change the situation for Ercan and her. Even if they were eventually released, both their careers would be over. And all for what? Because they had the courage to do what was necessary to save their country from the chaos and devastation that would occur on one of its borders, not to mention all the human life, whatever its nationality was. She just had to let things play out and stand by to help Michael out any way she could. Everything was in his hands now. She would worry about how all this would impact her when they were able to get Michael back out with Ali. In the meantime, she would have to brief her director that there had been no new developments in the investigation.

Her thoughts returned to Canton. The more she thought about him, the more disgusted she became. She had already observed that he was a chauvinistic pig, the way he'd leered and come on to her during their meeting. But the additional knowledge she had gained about him from Michael brought to light just what an evil man he was. She dreaded the idea of having to be in his presence again but knew it was to her benefit to see what she might be able to learn from him. She wasn't in the mood for seeing him anytime today. It was the weekend tomorrow. What did it matter? She would just be standing by her office all day. Probably just sleep on her couch. She had a small bathroom with a sink and toilet in her office. A personal perk for senior MIT department heads. It was a status symbol in the male-dominated Turkish culture to warrant such privileges. She was one of the few women in the Turkish military and intelligence establishment to have risen to that level. She knew some of her Turkish male counterparts might resent having a female among their ranks, but they all respected her abilities and accomplishments.

Before she called Canton, she wanted to freshen up and change her clothes, since she most likely wouldn't be going back to her apartment tonight. She walked over to the tall wardrobe in the corner of her office and pulled the doors open. Hanging on a clothes rod were several changes of clothing, everything from a business suit to Lycra running tights so she could go for a run during lunch. She shuffled through the hangers and pulled out a pair of black Calvin Klein gabardine slacks and a fitted white cotton-silk blouse with black polka dots. *That's good*, she thought, *still looks professional yet as comfortable as workout clothes.* She opened a drawer and riffled through a tangle of socks, stockings and underwear. She looked at her selection. If Michael made it back and decided to stay a while, she would definitely need to go shopping for something more like she would have worn ten years ago. She was still an attractive woman in great shape and she wanted Michael to notice. The realization that she was thinking about Michael and her underwear selection wasn't lost on her. She couldn't believe herself. She was acting like some college-aged schoolgirl. That was foolish. She was setting herself up to experience a lot of sorrow if he didn't make it back, and she knew what the odds were. Besides, if she was going to be of any help to him, she needed to be able to think clearly and not be distracted by her emotions. She stripped off her clothes, gave herself a quick sponge bath with the packet of baby wipes she kept in her office, rolled on some deodorant and threw on her change of attire. She rummaged through her closet and picked a pair of black suede ankle boots, classy yet comfortable.

After applying some lipstick and spraying a wisp of perfume on her neck, she sat down in her chair behind her desk. She picked up the business card Canton had left her during his visit. Jonathan Canton, Deputy Director, Counterproliferation, Central Intelligence Agency. She looked at the sideways eagle on the CIA seal. She wondered how someone like Canton had become a deputy director within the CIA. She knew that every intelligence agency had its share of misfits that had somehow managed to sneak through the initial screening, but they were eventually figured out after they had been out in the field for a while, once their performance, or lack thereof, became evident. They were normally marginalized for future assignments, with no real possibility to make it beyond a field agent. How was Canton able to rise so high? He either had to be very devious or willing to stab anyone in the back who got in his way. Michael had warned her about him. She shouldn't underestimate him.

She picked up her office phone and dialed Canton's US mobile number, waiting momentarily for the call to work its way through the international mobile network until it found his phone roaming in Istanbul before it started ringing. After the fourth ring, she heard "Canton" on the other end.

"Mr. Canton, this is Asya Tarhan returning your call." She tried to sound cordial and not let any indication of disdain show in her voice.

"Ms. Tarhan, thanks for getting back to me. I called because I would like to brief you on some recent developments from our end that I believe will significantly assist you in your efforts regarding the matter we spoke about during our meeting. Would it be possible to meet so we can discuss this matter?" Canton attempted to sound as businesslike as possible.

He had to manipulate her to come to him, for Rostov and his men to capture her. He would set things in motion, making an appointment at her office, then changing plans at the last minute to throw her off and having her meet him at another location under some false pretext. He needed to control the situation. Once she was his prisoner, she would be completely helpless. Then he would be able to break her and force her to tell him everything she knew about Michael. He would take pleasure in that process. She was never going to be released. Rostov would dispose of her body when they were through with her. He would call Tarhan's secretary on Monday to find out why she hadn't shown for their meeting, just to cover his tracks. He would be completely unaccountable.

"I see. I don't have any time today. Can it wait until tomorrow?" she proceeded cautiously, trying to feel him out.

"It's time-sensitive. I'm sure you'll want to review the information as soon as possible. I'm tied up myself at the moment, but I'll be free later today. Would you have time to meet late this afternoon at your office?" he asked her, lying on the bed back at his hotel suite.

She paused a moment before answering him. He was obviously attempting to force a meeting without trying to sound pushy. What was he up to? Did he know something, or was he just on a fishing expedition? There was only one way she could find out, and that was to meet with him. She would have him come by at 4:30 p.m., while it was still regular business hours and her secretary was still there.

"Will four thirty work for you, Mr. Canton?"

"Four thirty is perfect."

"Very good, Mr. Canton. I will have a guest pass waiting for you and have someone escort you to my office just like last time."

"See you then, Ms. Tarhan."

"Yes. Goodbye, Mr. Canton." She hung up her phone.

She didn't know why she had such an adverse reaction to him. Talking to him made her skin crawl. He sounded completely professional over the phone, but there was a certain insincerity in how he expressed himself that she picked up on. She understood why Michael believed Canton had compromised his operation with Ali. Perhaps Canton wasn't a good intelligence officer, but he was dangerous nonetheless. She would have to think about how she would deal with him if he was still in Turkey once the plot was exposed. Would she have him picked up as a terrorist? Even if he was a deputy director in the CIA, that didn't give him any immunity if he was involved in a terrorist act perpetrated in her country. She wondered what Canton would tell her when they met in a few hours. She would have the advantage in that he was unaware she knew Michael, while at the same time she knew everything about him. She would control the situation, not Canton.

***

As soon as Canton hung up with Asya, he dialed Rostov on his other mobile phone. By the fourth ring, Canton was becoming annoyed. By the fifth, he caught himself tensing his shoulders, and after the sixth, he heard the automated female Turkish voice sending him to voicemail. "Call me now!" Canton left his message, the irritation apparent from his tone.

He ended the call, then sat up, got off his bed and walked over to the glass door that led out onto the large balcony that came with his luxury suite. Apart from the hot tub that could comfortably hold four people, the balcony was large enough to have a small party on it, with four chaise sun loungers and the wicker rattan furniture. After he had ensured Blackstone and Shiravi had been eliminated, he would be sitting in this hot tub one evening with three Russian—no, make that a Russian, a Turkish and a Central Asian whore. He might as well go all out and celebrate the occasion of his success. He pictured it. The Middle East would be in flames, and he would be frolicking naked with three beautiful whores in this hot tub, guzzling bottles of Dom Perignon with his three sex mates, knowing he would be returning to D.C. to soon become the new DCI. It would be much harder for him to continue his exploits with call girls, but as the director of the world's most powerful intelligence agency, he was sure he could somehow manage to secretly satisfy his sexual appetites. At fifty-seven, he was still in his prime. He had put on a bit of weight around his midsection, and the bald spot had become more pronounced despite his stylist's best efforts with a comb-over, but women could still sense his virility. They could tell he was someone of significance.

His daydream about his future celebration was interrupted by the ring of his clean mobile phone. He recognized the number that was calling him. There were only two people who would call him on that mobile, Rostov or Victor Petrovich.

"Why didn't you answer when I called?" Canton wasted no time asserting himself.

"How do you say in English, *yebat' sebya*?"

"I don't speak Russian."

"Maybe you should learn."

"Have you completed what I directed you to do?"

"You do not direct me to do anything. I told you it would take a few days, Saturday or Sunday."

"I need everything set up and ready to go by tomorrow evening. I want you to call me by tomorrow afternoon to show me the secure location and run me through where I'm going to meet her for you to do what you're supposed to. Is that understood?"

"You will hear from me tomorrow." Canton could detect the contempt in Rostov's tone.

"Good. I'm sure you understand what would happen if you were unable to fulfill your responsibilities and it resulted in certain people becoming exposed. I don't think there is anywhere you could hide and stay safe. You could try London, but I've heard it's had its drawbacks for some of your former colleagues," he threatened before ending the call on his terms. He wasn't going to let some Russian SVR hack address the future DCI like that.

Well, he wouldn't be meeting with Asya Tarhan tonight. He would call her at 4:15 p.m. and cancel the meeting, telling her something urgent had come up and that he would get back to her as soon as possible. That left tonight open for him to have a soak in his hot tub. Perhaps he would have a trial run with only one naked beauty the first night. The car rental agency had delivered the replacement vehicle for the wrecked Volvo, so he was all set to go and cruise for an evening companion. This time he would be driving a shiny black BMW 650i, much more in line with what he'd expected in the first place. Some hot Russian whore would be more than eager to jump in. After all, whoever was driving a car like that must be someone who could afford her all night.

He went back in and poured himself a Johnnie Walker Blue Label on the rocks from the mini-bar and walked back out to the balcony. He looked down at the amazing view of the Bosphorus as he let the velvety smoothness of the Blue Label slide down his throat. His room bill would be charged as operational expenses for a temporary command post for the CIA. Payton had told the DCI that he wanted to leave Canton in charge of the investigation in Istanbul, since he had been there when it all happened. The charges for the BMW 650i, the luxury suite and whatever associated mini-bar charges listed on the hotel invoice would all go into the classified file that he would maintain control of, until it was all over and he was made the new DCI. In that position, he would be in control of the file and make sure it was classified Eyes Only for a select few individuals at the seat of government, such as the President and a few select cabinet secretaries. No one would be looking at the operational expenses appendix. He had it all figured out. Istanbul was going to be his DCI pre-appointment bachelor party. Having to deal with Tarhan would just be icing on the cake.

He thought about his approach on how he was going to break Tarhan when he interrogated her. She was obviously not your ordinary woman, having made it to her position in Turkey's intelligence service. But she was still a female who would break when she was de-humanized enough. He would start by having her stripped, her ankles and wrists bound to the wall, with high-intensity spotlights shining on her continuously to fatigue her physically and psychologically. He would sit back in the shadows where she couldn't see him past the blinding lights and question her. She would resist at first, but the feeling of vulnerability from her complete helplessness would eventually take its toll on her, and she would crack. Once he found out what he needed about Blackstone, he would help himself to Tarhan in her weakened and exposed position before handing her over to Rostov's men to do what they wanted with her before disposing of her. If they snatched her tomorrow evening, he estimated he would have things wrapped up with her by Monday evening. He highly doubted she could hold out for more than forty-eight hours. If needed, he could hasten the process by dehumanizing her even further in order to break her mentally. With women, physical torture or beatings were never necessary when there were other means of breaking them emotionally. He was confident he would find out everything Tarhan knew about Blackstone by the time he was done with her.

***

Hamed had spent the entire morning and most of the afternoon in his office, going over his interrogation plan, to include what enhanced interrogation techniques he was going to use in order to ensure Ali wasn't holding anything back. By the time he was done, Hamed would be certain he knew everything Ali was thinking. He would then be able to assure General Bardari that what the prisoner had initially told him remained true. The general would then have no choice but to turn his attention away from Israel and focus on the true culprits, the Russians and Americans. Hamed knew how an all-out war with Israel would end. Iran could inflict heavy damage on Israel with all of the missiles at its disposal, but the Zionists had nuclear weapons and could completely obliterate Tehran and most other major cities. Once the truth was revealed, there would be no reason to continue escalating the situation with Israel.

It was almost 3:00 p.m. and he wanted to get to Evin Prison before the beginning of rush-hour traffic. He figured by the time he had finished interrogating Shiravi several hours later, traffic would have subsided, and he would head back to the hospital to check on Reza. He was tempted throughout the day to call his wife, who was at the hospital, to check on him, but he forced himself not to. Laleh had gone to the hospital at 8:00 a.m. after stopping by her sister's house to get Tahmin off to school. He knew she would have called if there was anything to tell him. She tried her best to remain positive, but Hamed could sense that fears of what might happen to their child were starting to get the best of her. He also knew the reality of the situation, but he shut out any thoughts of having his sweet child taken away from them. It would be impossible for him to conduct the interrogation if he allowed any vulnerable thoughts to enter his mind.

He walked over to his closet and took out the case that held the electrical current apparatus. It was one of his preferred enhanced interrogation instruments because, if used properly, it was a very effective tool, even without having to utilize high amounts of current to get a subject's cooperation. Unlike the sadists that Western films often portrayed torturing prisoners with car batteries, Hamed rarely found it necessary to increase the level of intensity to where it would leave even the slightest burn marks. The immediate discomfort from just a modest amount of current traveling through the body was often enough to break even the most hardened prisoners, especially if applied to sensitive areas. He would try to make it as least painful as possible for Shiravi, while still being ensured he was being told the complete truth. There was a fine line between ensuring one was obtaining the truth from the subject and being fed fabrications to avoid discomfort. It was a science. Used by an untrained amateur, the device was as useless as the water boarding the foolish Americans used at their Guantanamo Bay. The prisoner would say anything to stop the torture of the sensation they were drowning. When it came to interrogation, he was a surgeon, not a butcher.

Hamed wondered what would eventually happen to Ali. It wasn't his concern officially, but he felt a certain sympathy for Ali's situation. He seemed like a sincere individual who was doing what he believed was right. He had voluntarily approached the Iranian government, even though, in light of his circumstances, he didn't have any other choice. On the surface, it seemed like such an implausible story, but Hamed was good at his trade, and he knew when men were lying or telling the truth. He was almost positive Ali had told him everything. He would be certain in a few hours. What would his government do with him then? He was born in Iran and technically an Iranian citizen, but what if it was found out that his country was holding prisoner a member of the foreign ministry of the United States? How would his country handle that situation? But how would anyone ever find out? That would mean they would have to keep him as a prisoner the rest of his life or kill him. That didn't sit well with Hamed, but it wasn't his place to concern himself with such matters. His duty was only to discover the truth and provide it to those above him who were in the position to make those decisions.

He grabbed the handle of the case that contained his interrogation device and headed out of his office, past his secretary's desk to the hallway. He walked towards the rear exit of the building, where his government vehicle was parked. As he walked through the parking lot towards his car, he heard his mobile phone ring in his coat pocket. He set down his case and reached for his phone, glancing at the number and recognizing it immediately as Laleh's mobile phone. He quickly touched answer, bringing the phone to his ear and acknowledging his wife, "Bale," as she said his name and began sobbing.

He listened to her through her sobs, but what she was saying didn't register with his brain. She was telling him their Reza had been taken from them, but it was as if he couldn't understand the meaning of her words. He ended the call and stood in the middle of the parking lot, staring off in the distance. He couldn't remember where he had been heading or what he needed to do. He stood there frozen in time and space, unaware of anything else around him.

Chapter 20

It had been longer than Michael had anticipated. The line of traffic advanced painfully slow through the late morning and into the afternoon. It was the same routine every five minutes. The driver of his truck would jam the transmission into gear and lurch the truck a few feet closer to the checkpoint. He was comfortable enough in his custom pistachio recliner, with the vibration from the motor of the truck adding a relaxing massage feature. He had lain there looking up at the sky, thinking about how he had been brought to his current situation. It almost felt like he was in the middle of some bizarre dream, the kind so vivid it seemed like you were actually living the experience, but at some level, you were aware that you were in a dream. Only in his case, there was too much detail, physical sensation, solidity to his existence, to let him entertain that thought for more than a few seconds. Between Special Forces and the CIA, he had had many challenging and adrenaline-filled moments, but nothing like his current situation. He was struggling just on how to process everything so far. Cognitively, he fully understood his circumstances. He was able to evaluate the events taking place around him and react with a coherent response for each situation. It was his psychological reaction to everything that was the real challenge.

A week ago, he had been sitting in his luxury condominium, staring out at the magnificent view of the Seattle waterfront while gulping a handful of opioids down with vodka, smoking a joint, and putting a gun to his head. How had he ever arrived at the point in his life, in which he had sunk to the level of attempting suicide? What had been so miserable in his life to have reached such an extreme? What was he lacking that had caused him to make the judgment that it was better to end it all and have nothing—no one, no future, just darkness? He had things, plenty of nice things, in fact. Despite the tough economic times, he had hung in there and had done well enough in the booming Seattle real estate market to afford a nice BMW and his condominium, and he had managed to build the investment portfolio he'd maintained from his days on Wall Street. He wouldn't receive a government retirement since he had quit the CIA, but his partial disability from the military and his investments would be enough for him to live comfortably into old age. But it wasn't the lack of material possessions or money that was the cause of his emptiness.

There was no intimacy in his life, with anyone. He was alone. No one was to blame. He had caused it. He was the one who had pushed everyone away. First with Karen, by closing her out, letting them become strangers. Then it was Sam after the divorce. Despite his efforts, they'd slowly grown apart. What had he expected after he'd allowed their family to break apart? Things would stay the same? Finally, there was Eva. After he had quit the CIA and they had moved to Seattle, things were never the same. The trajectories of their lives had slowly diverged, to the point where, in the end, they were just strangers inhabiting the same dwelling. If he was completely honest with himself, he knew he was responsible for letting that happen also. Had he even tried with her? Was he capable of having intimacy with anyone? What was wrong with him? Did he really think he had any chance of a future with Asya, even if he did survive this mission?

In both cases, with Karen and Eva, had he not been one hundred percent committed to each of them? He couldn't honestly say he had never noticed a pretty woman who had come across his path, but he hadn't once flirted, let alone acted inappropriately towards another woman. He was certain neither Karen or Eva had ever been unfaithful to him. He did love them both. Were they not the most important person in his life at the time? What had gotten in between them to change that? That question made him pause. He thought about his marriage with Karen. He tried to look back over the twenty-one years they had been together. He searched for the culprit that had pulled them apart. The harder he looked, the more he realized what it was. He could no longer deny that he had chosen his ambitions over her, first with making a fortune on Wall Street, then with Special Forces, and finally with the CIA. He had expected her to tag along with him on his journey through life without really knowing, or bothering to ask, what she wanted out of life. He expected her to follow him, in his pursuit of…of what? What was he pursuing? Money, adventure, accomplishment? Was it just blind ambition that had pushed him to believe he had to accomplish something significant, meaningful in life? What was he trying to prove and to whom? That he had to amount to something? Was he that unsure of himself, or was he just self-centered and selfish?

Then there was Eva. Michael had met her shortly after the finality of Karen being permanently out of his life had set in. It was a strange time in his life. He had just experienced several years of an extended emotional trauma with the slow breakup of his marriage, but he had never come to terms with his feelings about how it had affected him. He had been so preoccupied with the success of his double-agent operation targeting Karbashi that he had compartmentalized all the pain and loss from the divorce. Eva had come into his orbit after the operation had been up and running for quite a while. He finally had some time to spend with someone else outside of his work, and so, their relationship developed. He had found her physically captivating the moment he laid eyes on her at the beach. He was also attracted to her personality and her way of looking at life. Born and raised in communist Czechoslovakia during the Cold War, she had grown up in a completely different society and culture than what Michael had experienced. That and her sexy foreign accent, along with her attractiveness, were enough to hook Michael into wanting to pursue her, before he had even come to terms with the breakup of his first marriage. Living in Greece with a beautiful lingerie model while being the CIA case officer of a promising double-agent operation against Iran provided Michael a steady supply of excitement, intrigue and adrenaline. He was burning his candle on both ends, but it didn't faze him. He woke every morning looking forward to what the day would bring him. He was hooked. It was his narcotic.

Everything had been going great. It had felt like Michael was on top of the world. That is when it happened. The operation had been approaching a critical milestone. Ali had begun regularly attending the mosque near Omonia Square for the Friday evening prayer service. He had eventually drawn the attention of the gray-bearded man in his late forties who also regularly attended that service. It was after six months, on one of those evenings after prayers had ended, that the gray-bearded man had come up to Ali as he was exiting the mosque and addressed him in Persian.

"*Salaam*, brother."

Ali turned to the polite gentleman, whose face had been etched into his memory from the photographs Michael had had him study, and returned the greeting. "*Salaam*."

"Ah, you are Iranian. Do you attend this mosque regularly?" Karbashi asked, knowing full well Ali had been there every Friday night for months.

"Yes, I was born in Iran, but I live in the United States. Well, I live in Athens now, but I mean I am an American citizen. I have been attending prayers here for a few months on Friday evenings. And you?" Ali dangled him an opening.

"Yes, brother, I am Iranian also. My name is Farzan."

"I am Ali. Nice to meet you, Farzan."

"Very nice to meet you, Ali. I also live in Athens. I had been looking for a place to worship for quite some time. It is difficult in Athens to find a mosque. The Greeks are good people, but the Orthodox church is intolerant in allowing us, Allah's faithful, to worship openly and freely. I believe it is because they still harbor hostility against the Turks for having subjugated them for four hundred years. So, you are American. I have a cousin who lives in New York City. He and I grew up together. We lived next to each other and played every day together. When the revolution started, my uncle and aunt left for the United States and that was the last time I have seen him. We were very close. Maybe you knew him. Did you live in New York?" Karbashi baited him.

"I doubt that very much. I grew up in Virginia with my aunt and uncle," Ali continued, leaving Karbashi a trail of bread crumbs. He had practiced endless hours of role-playing with Michael during his six-month training leading up to the operation. Michael had played Karbashi, exposing Ali to an ever-changing mix of conversations and questions to prepare him for his first encounter with Karbashi. Michael had taught him to release small snippets of relatively insignificant personal information while still appearing reserved. Whenever the time came, the door would be open for Karbashi to enter, confident that he was in control of the situation. That time had finally arrived.

"Ah, Virginia. Is that not where Washington is located? I have always wanted to travel to the United States to see the Statue of Liberty and travel to the Grand Canyon, but unfortunately that will never be possible. Your government does not issue many tourist visas to Iranian citizens. It is really quite a shame. I know many of your fellow Americans think we Iranians hate them, but the problem is between our governments, not the people. So many of us have family living in the United States, like myself. Do you still have family in Iran? You said you lived with your aunt and uncle. What happened to your parents, if I may ask?"

"They sent me to the United States during the time of the revolution, like your cousin. They were supposed to follow shortly after. I never heard from them again." Ali kept it short, while still making its impact apparent.

"Oh, I am very sorry. They were chaotic times. I remember them all too well. I was at the university in Tehran at the time. There were many tragedies that took place. Where in Iran were you from?" Karbashi asked, pleased with how the conversation was going.

"What a coincidence. I grew up in Tehran. I was attending the University of Tehran in 1979. I was studying architecture." Ali felt he was doing well bringing Karbashi along.

"Yes, that is quite a coincidence." Karbashi let out a laugh. "Perhaps we may have even seen each other. Did you become an architect?"

"No, things did not turn out that way for me when I went to the United States. I ended up working for my aunt and uncle, cleaning offices after they were closed for the day. In other words, a janitor. I eventually went back to school and learned computers, but I have always wondered what would have happened if I could have continued my schooling for architecture."

"Perhaps you would have become a famous architect and have designed some skyscraper in America. Are you involved with computers now that you live here in Athens?"

"Not really, although I use them at work. I work at the US embassy. I am pretty much just a clerk, dealing with paperwork." Ali waited patiently until the right moment came to offer that up.

"Oh, Ali, our lives are connected with one coincidence after another," Karbashi belted out with a hearty laugh. "I work at the Iranian embassy in the consular section, a glorified passport clerk myself. I am so very happy we ran into each other. Do you have time to join me for a meal? I know a very good Persian restaurant not too far away."

"Well, I suppose I could. I don't have any plans. My wife and daughter are back in the United States visiting her parents."

"Wonderful, wonderful. You will very much enjoy the food. Come, my new friend, let us go then to the metro," Karbashi placed his hand on Ali's shoulder and gestured towards the direction of the metro station.

"It has been a long time since I have tasted Persian food. My aunt passed away ten years ago, and my wife is an American girl. She knows meat-loaf and mashed potatoes but is ignorant when it comes to kabobs and tadeeg." Ali threw in a bit of Persian male chauvinism. He had Karbashi hooked.

"Looks like Swordfish has taken the bait." Michael remembered calling out Karbashi's code name to the surveillance team that evening. It was the beginning of a yearlong relationship between Karbashi and Ali before it had ended unexpectedly. It was something that Michael didn't see coming.

Michael's attention was drawn back to his present moment. He had just gone through another one of the seemingly endless cycles of his driver forcing the transmission into gear, lurching forward a few feet, then coming to a jolting stop, but this time he heard sounds of doors opening and voices shouting commands. Pulling out his mobile phone and powering it on, he hit the camera app and switched it to selfie, then slowly raised it to see over the wall of the cargo bay. What he saw startled him. They were third in line at the checkpoint, behind a passenger bus and a car up front with a family of five standing outside as a police officer checked their documentation while a police dog went through their vehicle with trunk and doors wide open. *Great, a dog.* A moment of panic hit Michael. He immediately switched off his phone and stuck it in his pocket. He quickly positioned himself into his shallow grave, worming his body back and forth into the pistachios, trying to get as deep as possible. He laid his bag next to him on his left, but before he began burying himself, he pulled out one of the 9mm Sigs from the bag, verified a round was chambered, and set it next to his right hip. He then started with his feet, sweeping the piled pistachios from either side down on his legs and working his way up, making sure all the pistachios looked even. As he got to his chest, he chose to set his right hand on the Sig and finished his burial with his left hand. His head and face took some time, while he adjusted his head to be looking towards the back of the truck, then covering his face with a shallow layer of pistachios so that his eyes were barely peeking through. Amongst the millions of small green and red nuts, he wasn't as worried about having his eyes spotted as he was about leaving any visible sign that he had disturbed the mound of pistachios. What he really feared, however, was the German shepherd being unleashed in the back of the truck and immediately sniffing him out and exposing his position. What was his plan of action then? Would he shoot the dog, the dog handler, and any other officers at the scene? He did have thirty rounds between the two Sigs and the cover of the truck's steel walls, but how did he think that was going to end? No, resorting to the guns would ensure the end of his life and his failure; he'd be letting everyone down. Ali, his daughter, Asya, and a great number of innocents who had just happened to be born and living in this part of the world. It was a nonstarter, a fatalistic option. The odds of somehow escaping capture and successfully completing his mission were astronomical, but at least better than the first alternative.

The driver forced the transmission into gear and lurched the truck forward one more time. The next time it would be them. Michael knew he shouldn't let his current circumstances surprise him. What did he expect he would encounter? Was he that naïve or foolhardy thinking he actually stood a chance of pulling this off? Perhaps deep inside, he really didn't believe he could, but living with not having tried would have been intolerable. Either God had plans for him somehow getting the world out of this mess, or it was just one last cruel joke he would experience in this life. *Okay, stop thinking that way. It's not going to help or change the situation.* He tried to keep positive. He remembered what one old crusty sergeant major instructor at Ranger school used to say to him. "Let's not over-analyze it, sir. If you're gonna die, you're gonna die, and there ain't nothing you can do about that." In a very simple and profound way, there was a lot of wisdom in the sergeant major's statement. God had his plans of what was going to happen, whether you liked them or not.

Strange that he was thinking God was directing his life in some way. He had always believed that what happened to him in life was nothing more than the direct results of the decisions he had made. He had come to believe that he had either not been able to see things clearly or had made some terrible decisions. Maybe that was his problem, he was always trying to respond and control the situation, rather than just trusting. Trusting in what? God? Was he now thinking about God out of sheer desperation, because there was nothing left in himself that he could believe in any longer? Asya obviously had some pretty strong opinions about that. Well, he hoped she was right and that she was throwing in a little prayer for him. He needed all the help he could get.

Enough time had passed, as Michael contemplated the direction his life had taken while the police thoroughly checked all the passengers on the bus ahead, that the truck lurched forward once again and came to a halt. Michael heard an officer shout at the driver, then heard the truck engine go silent. Next the sound of the cab door opening, the driver stepping down and an officer questioning him. What Michael heard next gave him a sick feeling in the pit of his stomach. Even in Farsi, Michael recognized commands of a dog handler guiding his canine around the truck as it sniffed for any—what? Was it a drug dog? An explosives dog? Whatever it was, if they let it in the back of the cargo bay, it would certainly head straight for him. Then Michael saw something that made him cringe—what looked like the platform of aircraft type stairs being rolled up against the back of the truck. It was just seconds later that Michael saw the head and shoulders of a tan-and-black German shepherd appear at the top, waiting attentively for its handler to join him. When the Iranian police officer appeared on the platform, he examined the truck's cargo before giving a command that launched the canine into the truck. Michael tensed himself and instinctively grabbed firm hold of the Sig in his right hand as he waited for the dog to run towards him and expose his hidden location. What happened next caused him to relax the grip on his weapon as he witnessed the poor shepherd begin to yelp as it became bogged down and immobile with its legs buried in the pistachios. Michael saw the dog's handler shake his head in disbelief before jumping down himself and sinking ankle deep in pistachios to hoist his dog out and help push him back up onto the platform. Following behind his canine partner, the officer pulled himself back up onto the platform, then pulled off each shoe and shook out pistachios with his relieved shepherd sitting next to him, before they both retreated back down the stairs.

Michael breathed a sigh of relief. Once again, he had escaped. Was it just good luck, or was there something more at play? As the driver started the engine and forced it into gear, lurching the truck forward and pulling out of the checkpoint, Michael wondered what the likelihood would have been evading detection if he had been stowed away in any other vehicle. Of all things, pistachios? It was something he never would have come up with, regardless of how much thought and planning he put into it. He didn't know what to think. How everything had been transpiring in his life since last Friday was disorienting yet reassuring at the same time. He didn't want to falsely get his hopes up, but he was beginning to believe that he might actually have a chance in rescuing Ali. What happened after that, he didn't have a clue. He guessed that if God was somehow involved, he wasn't going to show him the entire play-book all at once. He just needed to focus on dealing with things one at a time as they occurred. Strange how his life had changed so drastically. He never saw it coming.

***

Asya had been sitting behind her computer all afternoon. She had reviewed all the reports her subordinates had submitted regarding the progress of the investigation to date, and there was no information indicating any additional progress had been made. Her people were following up on all the typical leads, reaching out to all their sources, but they had come up with nothing pointing to who may have been responsible. Other than the physical evidence of the Israeli shell casing discovered at the scene of the crime, everything else was a complete zero. She had known that would be the case. It was all in Michael's hands now.

Doing the only thing she could think of that might be useful, she began searching all Iranian communications intercept traffic from the GES, along with whatever shared NATO member intercepts she could find. It was tedious sifting through the raw feed before it had been processed and analyzed by GES analysts, but it was the only thing available for her to do that might give her any indication of how to help Michael. She had looked through whatever Iranian diplomatic and military traffic had been intercepted and deciphered but had come away with nothing. By chance, she decided to take a look at the routine unencrypted police radio frequency communications that had been swept up by the GES antennae arrays along the Iranian border, which were ignored by the analysts but translated into Turkish by linguistic algorithms on the GES mainframe. Something she almost passed over but redirected her attention to was an intercept from earlier that morning on the police band, regarding two Iranian police officers being disarmed at the bus station in Maku and a manhunt called out for the perpetrator. Asya read through the transcripts, searching for additional details, but the translation left empty gaps that the computer was unable to process. From what she was able to determine, she was almost certain the perpetrator they were searching for had to be Michael. What were the odds that two Iranian police officers had been disarmed in the town Michael had infiltrated into that morning? The realization alarmed her. If the Iranian authorities were searching for Michael, something had seriously gone wrong.

Asya continued scrolling through the translated transcripts, looking for any updated information on the search for the man who'd disarmed the police officers. She read that checkpoints had been set up going out of Maku and that police units had been conducting searches throughout town, but no communications regarding having captured a suspect. That was a good sign. Asya felt the trepidation that had suddenly come over her begin to lift. She knew Michael could take care of himself if he got in a tight spot, but she hadn't expected he would have such conspicuous contact with the Iranian authorities so quickly. The thought that she should have infiltrated into Iran with Michael, posing as his wife in order to help him, ran through her mind, but she quickly dismissed it. She knew it was just her feelings for him talking. She needed to be exactly where she was, so that she might be able to give him the support he would need when the right time came. She stayed focused on the police intercepts, keeping her eyes glued for any additional transcripts as they became available on her screen. It was a challenge keeping track of all the different locations the communications were being collected from, but she would know what was relevant when she saw it.

Her concentration was interrupted by the ring of the phone on her desk. She snatched the handset before the second ring and answered with a quick yes. It was her secretary, informing her Jonathan Canton from the US consulate was on the line. She glanced at her watch; it was 4:25. She had lost track of time. Her meeting with Canton was in five minutes. Why was he calling her? She told her secretary to put him through.

"Hello, Mr. Canton. Are you almost here?"

"Hello, Ms. Tarhan. You'll have to excuse me, but I won't be able to make our meeting. Something unexpected has popped up at the last minute that I need to deal with. It has to do with the matter which we are both very concerned about. I would like to postpone our meeting until tomorrow if that is possible. I have some important information to pass onto you, especially in light of what just came up."

"I understand. I can meet with you tomorrow. Were you thinking about morning or afternoon?" Asya asked.

"It would have to be late afternoon or early evening. I will be tied up most of the day. Does that work for you?"

"Our office just had minimal essential personal present on weekends, but I will be there. I can meet you at the security office."

"How will I get in contact with you? Do you have a mobile?" he asked.

"You can reach me through my office phone. I will be here all afternoon. If I am not, you will be put through to my mobile number." She avoided giving him her mobile number.

"All right, then, I look forward to seeing you tomorrow evening." He tried to sound as congenial as possible.

"I will see you then. Goodbye."

"Have a wonderful night, Ms. Tarhan," she heard him say as she was hanging up the phone.

She felt the same feeling of repulsion again. What was it about that man that created such a visceral reaction within her? She knew he was a manipulative snake, but she had dealt with other similar detestable individuals over the course of her career in the intelligence field. Canton, however, had a knack for making the hair on her neck stand every time she talked to him. Perhaps it was a subconscious response to the fact that he was trying to harm the man she greatly cared for, the man she was hoping would come back into her life for more than just a couple of days. She wondered what was so important that he had to urgently meet with her. He was someone to be concerned about, but as long as Michael was in Iran and away from his reach, he didn't pose any significant risk. She would listen to what he had to say and try to figure out what he was up to. Maybe she would be able to catch him in a lie and turn the tables on whatever he was scheming. For now, she would focus on trying to figure out what else she might be able to discern about Michael's situation from the Iranian police intercepts. It would be a long night, but she had a comfortable couch in her office and a pillow and blanket in her closet. She picked up the phone and buzzed her secretary.

"Anyur, can you go down to the canteen before they close for the day and get me a pot of French coffee? I am going to be staying late tonight."

"Yes, Ms. Tarhan, right away."

"Thank you, Anyur. You may finish your day after that and get out of here a little early. Do I remember correctly that your boyfriend is supposed to take you out for dinner tonight?"

"Yes, Ms. Tarhan, it is our one-year anniversary from when we first met."

"Well, I hope he takes you somewhere nice," she told her secretary, wondering if she and Michael would ever be celebrating any anniversaries.

Hamed didn't remember anything about the drive from his office to the hospital. He didn't remember the route he chose, how long it took, or the city bus he almost collided with, blowing through the red light at a major intersection. It was almost as if he were trapped in a terrible dream, trying to make it through until morning arrived, when he would finally be able to escape from his horrible ordeal. He sat in his car at the hospital parking lot, his hands hanging onto the steering wheel as he stared out the windshield at the parents with their teenage son in his school soccer uniform, hobbling out of the hospital on crutches and a cast on his left ankle. He would never have the chance to see his precious Reza play soccer in his school's uniform. He and Lelah would never be able to share in the joy of witnessing Reza graduate from school, marry, give them a grandchild someday. All of that was gone. There would just be emptiness now, a void in their lives filled with sorrow.

He thought about poor Tahmin, having to live the rest of his childhood with the scar of his little brother being taken away from him so young. Hamed had also experienced death at a young age. His older brother had been martyred during the Iran-Iraq War at the age of fourteen, clearing minefields with thousands of other young children for the Iranian military's counteroffensive against Saddam Hussein. Hamed had been only eight years old at the time. He remembered crying when his father told him the news, but also remembered how proud he felt at how his older brother had bravely fought for their country, protecting them against that evil dictator, Saddam, and the Great Satan America that had been supplying him the weapons with which he was bombing Iran. In Reza's case, however, what would he tell Tahmin? Would he tell him that his younger brother had been run down like a dog by one of their country's own senior IRGC leaders, someone who was supposedly dedicated to protecting them against the immoral and wicked ways of the West? What would he say to Laleh? That it was Allah's wish to take their son from them? That the person responsible for committing this atrocity would go unpunished by Allah? That would never happen. He would be Allah's instrument for finding this devil and dispensing the just punishment for his sin.

Getting out of his car finally, Hamed made his way across the parking lot to the main entrance and walked numbly down the hallway towards the ICU. As he passed through the two automatic doors, he saw Laleh sitting in one of the plastic chairs next to the nurses' station. He saw the pain that had distorted her beautiful face, making it seem like she had instantly aged twenty years, her eyes swollen from the river of tears she had cried over the past hour. She raised her head and looked at him as he approached, her eyes revealing the grief she was feeling. She stood up and grabbed him, beginning to sob as he took her into his arms. He held her close to him, trying to console her while her entire body convulsed in sorrow. He could feel the raw emotion from her pain pouring out. It permeated his entire being, ripping through his heart, feeling like it would overwhelm him.

After holding on to each other for what seemed like ten minutes, Hamed pushed away from his wife and walked towards Reza's room. He paused by the door before going in, trying to regain control of his emotions before having to gaze onto the lifeless body of his precious child. Forcing his feet to take the final steps and enter the room, his eyes caught sight of Reza's motionless body on the hospital bed. They had removed the breathing tube and all the IV lines and wires his little body had been connected to just an hour ago, and now he looked like he was just sleeping. Hamed walked over to his bedside and looked down at his child's peaceful angelic face, picking up his little hand and holding it tenderly. It was completely limp and felt cool to the touch, revealing that all life had passed from his small body. Hamed took in a deep breath and tightened his jaw, trying to keep from breaking down in front of his dead child. Not being able to control himself any longer, he reached down and picked up his son, holding him tightly in his arms as he began to sob uncontrollably. He held Reza's head against his shoulder while he nuzzled his face into his, savoring each second of this one last chance he would have to hold his child.

As he held his son's limp body, Hamed said a prayer. "Most Merciful Allah, I raise the soul of my son up to You and ask that You take him into paradise with You. Comfort him in the peace of Your presence. May he always know how much we love him and how much joy he has brought into our lives. May the memory of that joy always dwell within us, until we are reunited when we join him in paradise. Console us from our pain and grief, so that bitterness and darkness do not overwhelm us. Reveal the one who is responsible for committing this merciless act, and may they receive Your just punishment for their evil. You see into my heart, Allah. You can see the anger and vengeance it seeks. Guide me so that I may fulfill your will and not my own. You are all-knowing, Most Merciful Allah. You are all-powerful, Most Merciful Allah. Allahu Akbar. Allahu Akbar. Allahu Akbar."

With that, he kissed his child's forehead and gently laid him down back onto the bed. He took care in positioning him as if he were sleeping on his side, placing one arm under his head and the other across the pillow, the way Reza normally slept. He stood there for a few more moments looking at his child, tears streaming down his face, not being able to force himself to leave. Digging deep to find the strength, he managed to say his final goodbye, briefly placing his palm against Reza's face before turning and wiping the tears from his face as he left the room.

***

Canton had just finished showering and was sipping on another Johnnie Walker Blue while he stood naked in front of the bathroom mirror, preparing to go out and pick up his evening's company. He looked up as he leaned his head forward and combed his graying hair across the bald spot on the top of his head. He took a step back and looked at his naked body. He had put on an extra twenty pounds over the past ten years, principally around his midsection, back and chest, giving him somewhat the appearance of a Shar-Pei. His sucked in his gut and expanded his chest, admiring himself in the mirror. He wasn't concerned with what any of the women he went with might have thought of his physique; they were paid to satisfy him, not the other way around. He was trying to decide what nationality he was in the mood for tonight. He was feeling a bit adventuresome and considering something other than his standard Eastern European beauty. Perhaps he would get a little wild and bring an African girl back to his room. He would look for a young one with light skin, no more than eighteen years old. He didn't want any merchandise that had had a lot of use. Of course, he would be safe and use double condoms. Who knew where these girls had been? He would be able to be a little bit rougher with an African girl than what the European whores were comfortable with. It would be a little appetizer for what waited for him with Tarhan, when he was through with her and had obtained what he needed.

He was splashing cologne on his face and other parts of his body when one of his mobile phones began ringing. He could tell by the ring tone which one it was. Rostov was calling him. *What could he want Friday night?* Canton wondered. He walked into the bedroom and grabbed the ringing phone from the top of the dresser.

"Yeah," he answered.

"Where are you?" he heard Rostov's heavily accented voice ask.

"What do you mean, where am I? I'm in Istanbul. Where else would I be?"

"Can you meet me at our location?"

"Right now?" Canton asked, annoyed.

"Within an hour."

"I have plans."

"Are your plans more important than what we need to accomplish tomorrow?"

"Can't it wait until tomorrow morning?"

"No, it cannot. You said you wanted things quickly. This is quickly. Preparation is required. If you would like to take matters into your own hands, that is fine with me. Your decision."

Canton stood there naked, trying to think of options. It was already 8:00 p.m. By the time he would be finishing with Rostov, it would be close to midnight, and once again he would have missed the window for the prime selection of whores to choose from. Rostov had a knack for rubbing him the wrong way, but he knew he had no other choice. He couldn't risk any screw-ups, and he certainly couldn't allow Rostov to hold it over him that he was the one who hadn't followed through with what needed to be done. His African adventure would have to wait.

"Okay. I'll see you there in one hour."

"One hour. No repeat of last time. You will not find me waiting for you."

"Don't give me ultimatums, and definitely don't make threats you can't back up. You know what your job is, and I know mine. My job is to give you direction, and your job is to follow that direction. Don't forget that."

"One hour." Canton heard the other end go dead.

"Slavic asshole!"

Canton went over to his suitcase and pulled out a clean pair of white BVD briefs, then threw on a pair of black trousers, a black button-down shirt and a black sports jacket. He would cruise by the red-light district when he was finished with Rostov, and hopefully find something that was still available for him to bring back to his suite for the night.

After putting on socks and shoes, Canton called the concierge and told him he needed his car ready out front in ten minutes. He had left his keys with the valet, so that he wouldn't have to wait for his car again like the other night. Lately, it seemed, he always felt agitated and impatient. Tonight, he would have plenty of time to make his way to their meeting without having to rush, enjoying the drive in his replacement BMW 650i. He wouldn't let anything get under his skin, not even Rostov. He casually made his way down to the lobby, stepping outside to find his shiny black luxury sports coupe waiting for him at the end of the red carpet under the brightly lit covered driveway. Walking over to the same valet from the other night, standing next to the open driver's-side door, Canton handed him a five lira note, the equivalent of one dollar, as he climbed into the plush interior. The valet gave a nod of appreciation as he closed the door for him. *Now this is more like it*, Canton thought, grabbing onto the steering wheel and looking around at the black-and-tan leather interior. He would be cruising in style. With his DCI salary, he would be able to afford the eighty-five-thousand-dollar price tag of a car like this. He would gain the respect and admiration of all the CIA employees working for him. And who knew what lucrative opportunities awaited him in the private sector after his stint as DCI was over? That was where the real money was.

He fastened his seat belt and pushed the start button, to be startled by the loud screech of the starter telling him that the car was already running. He glanced up at the valet looking at him with an amused look on his face. Canton slammed it into gear and stomped on the accelerator, squealing the tires and making the valet jump back as he sped out of the hotel driveway. Three seconds later, he slammed on the brakes as he came up to the security gate at the hotel's entrance. He laid on the horn at the security attendant, who hadn't lowered the hydraulic barrier quick enough. He waited impatiently for five seconds, then stomped on the accelerator once again, shooting out onto the main road in front of the hotel. He let off the gas when he realized he was weaving in and out of traffic, passing every car. He realized he was being foolish, risking being pulled over by the Turkish police and issued a ticket, creating a documented record of his identity on some Turkish national police database. Those things occasionally happened to intelligence officers stationed overseas, but it wasn't a smart idea to attract unnecessary attention, especially a day before a senior Turkish intelligence chief would go missing. He was letting himself get sloppy. Events were moving quickly now. He couldn't afford to misstep when he was so close to obtaining everything he had always wanted. He would never again have to deal with menial dogs like Rostov. Soon, he would be at the pinnacle of power in the intelligence world.

He drove north up along the Bosphorus, crossed over the Bosphorus Bridge and headed back down south along the waterfront. It was a strange night. There was a fine mist, almost like a heavy fog, that cast a surreal yellow glow around each streetlight as he made his way towards the industrial port area. He wondered what Rostov had come up with to capture Tarhan. He would have to make it very clear to him that he was only responsible for capturing Tarhan and ensuring she would be constantly under guard during the extent of her usefulness to them. He would be the one exclusively interrogating her, without Rostov or any of his men present. The information she had was solely concerning an internal US matter that had nothing to do with Russian involvement in the operation. Rostov and his men were just providing logistical support. He would tell the Rostov that once he was done interrogating her, Rostov and his men could do whatever they wanted with her before disposing of her body. It didn't matter. Once he was finished with her, she would be in no condition to tell Rostov anything. Even if there were no physical indications of trauma, she would be psychologically and emotionally broken, and maybe just a little bruised, depending on how hard she resisted.

He arrived at their previous meet location. He pulled into the same complex of warehouses and turned down the streets they had prearranged for the primary and alternate meeting locations between warehouses. He drove slowly keeping it in first gear, avoiding having to use his brake lights until he caught sight of a parked car with a faint red LED in the top corner of the windshield. He looked at the time. He was five minutes early, leaving nothing for Rostov to try to use against him. It probably drove the Russian crazy being in the subordinate position. That was why the Russians had always resented the West. They knew that, despite their bombastic rhetoric, they'd always been in the subordinate position. Too bad. He would have to make sure he also put Petrovich in his place when he became DCI. No way the director of the

SVR should ever have the misconception he was on equal footing with the Director of Central Intelligence. Even the director of Britain's Secret Service, MI6, understood that.

Canton turned off his parking lights and rolled slowly towards Rostov. As he pulled up next to the Opel, he spotted Rostov along with three other burley-looking men in the car with him. A slight twinge of fear came over him. He had been expecting to meet with Rostov only. Who were these other three? He slowly rolled down his window, looking at Rostov while trying to maintain awareness of what the passengers in the car were doing.

He gave Rostov a nod. "Who are these three, Moe, Larry and Curly?"

"Follow me," he instructed Canton, rolling up his window, putting his car into reverse and slowly backing his way out from between the warehouses.

Canton sat there for a moment, surprised at Rostov's unexpected command. Who did he think he was, pulling a stunt like this? He wasn't going to just follow Rostov with a car full of strangers, without knowing where he was taking him. He pulled out his phone and dialed Rostov's number. A moment later, he saw Rostov's car stop at the end of the warehouse and heard his voice come over the phone.

"What is it?"

"Where the hell do you think you're going, and who are the three goons with you?" Canton demanded, not disguising his annoyance.

"Do not worry, we are not going to do what men like you do to each other—how do you say, sodomize. If we wanted to do that, we would have done that here." Canton heard laughter in the background.

"Screw you! Don't pull this shit with me. You either do as you're told, or you can answer to your boss as to why you've failed."

"If you want to see what we have come up with follow me. Otherwise, you are on your own," Rostov answered him curtly.

Canton heard the other end go silent and saw Rostov's car back out and face in the direction of the exit. He angrily shifted his car into gear and began moving forward. He followed Rostov out of the warehouse complex back out onto the street, heading further south along the Bosphorus, then turning onto an expressway. They drove another twelve minutes southward, then exited onto a boulevard that ran along the water, leading them to the vast Istanbul shipyard that was home to twelve shipbuilding and repair companies. With multiple dry-docks, piers, construction barges and giant cranes, it was a sprawling industrial complex, twenty miles south of Istanbul. They turned off the street and entered the complex, driving past large open lay-down yards containing everything from massive piles of structural steel and stacks of pipping to partially cut up rusting hulls of ships. The complex was fairly quiet on a Friday night. Each company had its own sectioned-off area of warehouses, piers and dry-docks along the horseshoe-shaped shipyard facility, with their own security. They headed towards the south end of the yard along the main access road, passing several dry-docks, until they came to a group of dimly lit large two-story structures on the opposite side of the active shipbuilding area. They pulled down a road that had fallen into disrepair with large potholes and finally arrived at a group of older wooden buildings that looked like they hadn't been used for several decades.

Rostov stopped his car, turned off the engine and exited with his three companions. Canton pulled up several yards behind them and turned off his car. He took the Glock 26 he had gotten from Bob out of his jacket pocket and discreetly checked that a round was chambered before returning it to his pocket. He got out of his vehicle and stood by the open door, looking at Rostov and the three other men who were with him.

Rostov looked at him impatiently. "Are you coming?"

"Where to?" Canton asked, glancing around.

"Over there." Rostov gestured towards the buildings.

"What is this place?"

"It is an abandoned sell factory."

"A what factory?"

"Sells. Sells, for old selling ships before they had oil."

"Oh, sails. I couldn't understand what you were saying. So, what are we doing here? And you still haven't answered me who these three gentlemen are." Canton asked less rudely, realizing he was exposed and outnumbered in his current situation.

"They are my team. Who do you think they are? And this is where you will bring Tarhan tomorrow night to capture her."

"What do you mean, bring her here? You expect me to bring her all the way out here?" Canton asked incredulously.

"Where did you think we would do this? In central Istanbul?" Rostov replied sarcastically.

"No, but this is pretty out of the way. How am I going to get her to come out here?"

"I do not know. You are the one who has been dealing with her. Tell her you have someone she needs to meet, that this person will only agree to meet here. This is a safe place to do this."

"This is really lame, Rostov. What kind of a half-ass believable story do you think I can come up with to convince her to come all the way out here by herself?"

"That is up to you. Are you not a CIA division chief? How did you reach such a position if you cannot even come up with a simple ploy to lure her here?"

Canton was furious he had been put in this position. How was he going to convince Tarhan to come all the way out here? She would be suspicious. Rostov did have a point, however, about it being a safe location. No one would have a clue to even begin looking for her out here. It was remote, and it would make it easier to dispose of her body at the end.

"Tell me the plan," Canton conceded.

***

Reclined in his contoured bed of pistachios, Michael had dozed off in the back of the truck as they headed southeast away from Maku. The vibration of driving down the road and the warmth of the afternoon sun brought on waves of drowsiness after hours of adrenaline pumping through his system. He was exhausted, especially not having gotten a full night's sleep before being flown in over the border before first light earlier that morning. Everything was starting to catch up with him, and he felt it. If he didn't get sleep whenever he had a chance, he risked making mistakes, especial at critical moments. The last thing he remembered was his eyes slowly closed as he drifted off to sleep with the sun shining down on him.

Michael's eyes slowly opened to a darkening sky with the first of the brighter stars beginning to make their appearance overhead. A waxing crescent moon was beginning to rise, providing a faint light. He was momentarily disoriented while his brain kicked into gear before he realized where he was, the events of the past few hours coming to the forefront of his thoughts. How long had he been asleep? He glanced at his watch, barely making it out in the dim light; it was almost 7:30 p.m. He had slept for over three hours. The truck was lumbering down the road at what felt like a fast speed. He wondered where they were. It was dark enough for him to carefully have a peek over the wall of the bed. He rolled over and crawled to the front of the cargo bay, where he slowly raised his head until he could see. There were no vehicles close enough behind them whose headlights would expose the outline of his head. He turned facing front and raised his head until he could see over the cab of the truck. He could tell from the lack of buildings and streetlights they were somewhere in an unpopulated area, but up ahead off in the distance, Michael could see the lights of a good-sized city. He also spotted the green-and-white beacon of an airport and the runway lights. Despite it feeling like they were gradually climbing in elevation, the city ahead looked like it was higher still. What he saw, or didn't see, was what really caught his attention. There was a black void in a big section of the night sky to the south of the city. There were no stars, just the faint outline of darkness in the heavens. That had to be a large mountain, Michael realized. From the amount of time that had passed and what he recalled from the map of Iran he'd studied at Ercan's camp, he guessed they had to be approaching Tabriz.

Michael reached into his bag and dug under the dates. They were beginning to get sticky, and he decided to dump them and replace them with the much tidier pistachios. Removing all the contents of his bag, he laid the other Sig, the satellite phone and the old rusty knife down, then switched on the GPS and waited for it to cycle through its start-up as it locked on to enough satellites to give him a fix on his location. As soon as three satellites had been acquired, his assumption was confirmed when the map appeared on the screen, pinpointing his position. He was just outside Tabriz. He switched off the GPS to save battery life. Lining the bottom of the bag with pistachios, he laid the satellite phone and GPS inside, then poured a thick layer of pistachios over them. He looked at the two 9mms and tried to decide whether he should keep both of them, or at least one of them. It went against his basic instinct to give up weapons in his possession, but in the end he realized there wasn't any situation he would come out on top of if he ended up having to resort to using them. He grabbed one, released the magazine, threw it as far as he could off the side of the road, ejected the round from the chamber and did the same with it, then disassembling the slide from the receiver and hurling each of them off into the darkness on either side of the truck in thirty-second intervals. He repeated the same sequence with the other Sig. *Well, that's that,* he told himself, hoping he had made the right decision. He filled his bag with more pistachios, tucked his rusty blade inside, leaving the handle sticking out, then filled the top with his remaining pide. He had enough to last him another day, but he would need to replenish his food supply eventually.

Michael rested his arms along the top of the cargo bay wall and stared at the city lights. He thought about briefly turning on the satellite phone and giving Asya a quick cryptic call letting her know he was all right but forced himself not to. Even though the chance of being intercepted was minimal, he didn't want to risk a call for anything other than a critical reason, such as his exfiltration. He questioned his motivation for wanting to call her. Did he just want to hear her voice for reassurance? Was he feeling lonely, on his own? He was completely on his own, and he needed to come to terms with that, he reminded himself. *Just focus on what you need to do next and nothing else, and no one else. Don't lose your edge or you won't make it through this.* He knew better than to let his emotions distract him. He had become soft having been away from this type of life for so many years, despite trying to convince himself otherwise.

Michael guessed the destination of the pistachios was Tabriz. There was probably some pistachio processing plant there, which removed the skins, then dried or roasted the shells, packaging them for sale. He decided he would wait for the truck to stop or slow down at the right location once it got to Tabriz, and he would jump out. Where the right location was, he had no idea. He didn't want to wait too long and risk being spotted. The deeper he went into Tabriz, the greater the possibility. He wasn't so much concerned about being seen from above. There was enough shadow that it would be difficult to spot him, unless someone was shining a light directly on him. It was just that the further he went into the center of the city, the more people would be out who might spot him jumping from the truck. He didn't want to risk two encounters with the Iranian police in the same day.

As the truck drew closer to the outskirts of the city, they occasionally passed industrial-type complexes along the highway, until they came upon the airport on their left and a large industrial complex on their right, which marked the beginning of Tabriz's suburbs. It wasn't late yet, so there was a fair amount of traffic still out on the streets. Michael kept his head raised just enough to be able to see over the wall. It was becoming significantly brighter from all the city lights, but he was hidden in the shadows of the cargo bin. He had no choice, however, but to keep his head exposed as he looked for the right opportunity to jump from the truck the moment he spotted what he was after. He didn't want to ride the truck to its final destination of some processing plant. He didn't know what he would find there, and in doing so, he would be giving up all his options of controlling the situation. He needed to position himself in the optimum way so he'd be able to quickly continue his journey onto Tehran. He racked his brain for follow-on transportation possibilities. Did he try his luck again with a bus? He imagined in a bus terminal in a large city such as Tabriz, it would be easier to blend into anonymity amongst the hundreds of passengers who were waiting to depart. Was there rail service to Tehran? That was one thing he'd failed to investigate while putting together the mission plan, if you could call it that. He had assumed he would board a bus in Maku and keep with bus transportation all the way to Tehran. He knew there was no train station in Maku. It was an understandable oversight during the frenzy of throwing together a last-minute plan, but a costly one nonetheless. It wasn't something he would have let slip through the cracks ten years ago.

They had just passed the airport, heading straight toward the brightly lit metropolis, when the driver veered to the right as the highway split, taking what appeared to be a bypass route that skirted the city. They drove south along the outskirts, which remained an industrial area. *Well, that made sense*, he thought. Had he expected to find a pistachio processing plant in downtown Tabriz? Their current heading concerned him, however. He knew that the bus station would be towards the middle of the city, and where they were heading didn't put him anywhere close to that. Tabriz was a big city, with well over a million inhabitants. If he jumped off the truck out here and hiked in, it would take him all night and well into the morning to make it to the center and locate the bus station. He agonized over what to do.

Suddenly, Michael's eyes caught sight of a universal symbol recognizable in any part of the world. He saw the green sign with the white outline of a train. *A train station! Somewhere close.* His was suddenly hopeful. As they drove further, the topography began changing from the factories and industrial yards to residential sections with apartment buildings. The road they were traveling remained three lanes but changed from a fast-moving highway to a three-lane city boulevard, with traffic pulling off and stopping on the side, picking up and letting off passengers. *Where is this guy going?* Michael wondered. He looked up ahead and could see that the residential section they were driving through began transitioning back into commercial and industrial space. Where was the train station? He had to make a decision soon. He scanned the road all around him until once more, on the right side, he saw a green railway sign with an arrow pointing to the right. That was it. The sign was pointing him to a train station or railroad of some sort. He had to get off the truck now. He slung his bag over one shoulder and made his way to the right side of the truck, positioning himself so he could swing over the cargo bay to make the leap down onto the road. Hanging from the side, the distance would only be about three feet down to the asphalt. If he could land perfectly and roll, maybe he would survive the jump without any major injuries, just some bruises and scrapes on his arms and legs to add to his collection. He wondered how he'd ever found this kind of stuff exciting. He was older now and had outgrown the foolishness of youthful invincibility.

He looked down at the quickly passing asphalt beneath them. The truck must have been traveling at least thirty-five miles per hour. No, that was crazy. He would definitely hurt himself, probably even break an ankle, he thought, when he was suddenly surprised as the driver slammed on the brakes and brought the truck to a stop, just as it gently tapped the back of a passenger car in front of them. This was his chance. Michael grabbed hold of the top of the cargo bay and swung his legs over, momentarily hanging on before releasing and landing on the road. He heard the driver open the door on the other side and climb down, but by then Michael was headed towards the sidewalk. He nonchalantly looked around to see if anyone had spotted him jumping off the truck, but any pedestrians in the area were unaware of his presence.

Michael couldn't believe his good fortune. After taking off his shoes and emptying them of pistachios, he turned and headed back towards the direction of the railway sign. They had only driven half a mile past it, so he was back to it within about eight minutes, turning left down a main street, following the direction of the arrow. He continued walking down the road on the sidewalk. There wasn't much pedestrian traffic, which surprised him. He wondered if the rail station was some distance away. A city bus full of passengers drove past him from the direction he was heading. That was a good sign, he thought. Perhaps it was coming from the train station. He continued walking another block until he turned the corner to face a brightly lit railway station. It was a large, prominent building, with three-story-tall angled white columns lining the length of it and a bright yellow illuminated overhang giving it a postmodern neoclassical look.

As Michael approached the main entrance, he saw people going in and out, and passengers being dropped in cars that were coming down another street. *Must be several ways in here*, he thought, understanding why he hadn't observed much traffic going down the street he had come from. He came up to an old steam locomotive display sitting on top a pedestal outside the entrance, staring at it as he walked past it. By all appearances, it looked just like any other display one would see at a train station while traveling throughout various parts of the world. What was so unusual about Michael's situation was that he wasn't in just any other part of the world. He was in Iran, and everyone around him was a potential threat if he was careless. He prayed his attempt to purchase a train ticket would go better than his try with the bus earlier that day. *If you want me to succeed, help me out with this, God.* He gathered himself mentally as he walked up to the main doors and went inside.

The interior of the train station was a cavernous hall, with small shops lining its perimeter and a row of ticket booths on the far side. People were milling around talking, some eating or drinking while standing, others looking at the large electronic display depicting the departures and arrivals of trains, which alternated the times and destinations between Farsi and English, fortunately for Michael. He looked at the next scheduled departure for Tehran and spotted a train arriving from Ankara, Turkey, at 10:00 p.m., then departing at 10:15 p.m. and arriving in Tehran at 6:25 a.m. the next morning. He looked at his watch. It was 8:43 p.m. That was perfect. It would be leaving in an hour and a half. He would find some corner and lie low, blending into the busy big city train station until it was time for him to board his train for Tehran. Now came the hard part—buying the ticket. He dreaded this part but knew it was unavoidable.

Michael looked across the large hall to the ticket booths and spotted three of them that were lit and open. He started walking towards them, looking to see who was in each before deciding which one to walk up to. Behind the glass of the first one, Michael could see an older gentleman who looked like he was in his sixties, reading a newspaper. He was out. He reminded Michael too much of the bus terminal clerk back in Maku. At the next open ticket booth, he saw a heavyset older woman wearing a black hijab with a scowl across her face. Not getting a warm and fuzzy feeling, he decided to pass on her also. He shifted his attention to the last open ticket window, and what he saw lightened his spirits. Behind the glass was a pretty young woman in her late twenties to early thirties, her hair covered with a brightly patterned floral hijab. She was busy talking on her mobile phone with an animated demeanor, intermittently laughing in between pauses in her conversation. Michael headed over to her. He approached the window and waited, not wanting to disturb her conversation. She turned her attention to him as she continued speaking, waiting for him to tell her what he wanted. Without going into his deaf-mute impersonation, in as much of an accent-free voice as he could muster, he uttered, "Tehran."

The girl behind the window paused her conversation and replied to him in English, "You want sleep?"

Michael, surprised to hear her speak in English, responded, "Ah, yes. How much for private cabin?" He pronounced his English with a slight foreign accent this time.

"No private cabins, but you can have empty cabin. No other passenger. Express train from Ankara. Only one other stop, Zanjan. One million, four hundred thousand rial."

Michael did the math in his head. That was roughly thirty-five dollars. Getting a good night's sleep in his own cabin was worth it. Even if he did end up sharing the cabin with someone, it was better than being stuck next to someone in a seat. He would take it.

"Yes, I want," Michael responded.

He pulled out his wallet and counted fourteen one-hundred-thousand-rial notes, then handed them to the girl, whose attention had turned back to the person on the other end of her mobile phone. She typed on the keyboard in front of her while cradling her mobile phone between her ear and shoulder and carrying on her conversation.

A moment later, the girl slid a ticket to him under the glass and pointed to the left, telling him, "Track three, ten o'clock."

"Merci," Michael thanked her, using the common term in Persian as well as French.

Her attention had turned completely away from him and back to her conversation now that she had provided him with his ticket. He turned from her and casually made his way across the great hall towards some chairs positioned along the wall. Thank goodness twenty-something-year-old girls were the same in Iran as they were in the United States when it came to preoccupation with their social life. Even at this hour, there were hundreds of people milling around, some waiting for their trains to depart, others waiting to meet family or friends who would be arriving. He was comfortably anonymous as he sat in the crowded station, waiting to board his train and make it to Tehran, hopefully without any further surprises. He felt cautiously optimistic that he had escaped the dragnet now that he was a few hundred kilometers away, here in Tabriz. He was fairly certain the Iranian police had put out a national alert regarding the incident, along with a description of Michael, but the more distance he put between himself and Maku, the less intense the search would be for him, as local police were preoccupied with other priorities. Since he was dressed as a vagrant in old faded clothing, any description of him would be fairly nondescript, but he would try to change his attire as soon as the opportunity presented itself.

Michael looked across the station at a line of small shops that were still open. Next to the convenience store selling the typical cigarettes, newspapers, snacks and beverages for travelers, Michael spotted a small shop displaying various blankets and linens. He stood up and walked across the large hall to the other side, where all the shops were located. His attention was drawn to a blanket with geometric designs in brown, burnt orange, beige and blue, that was hanging from a wooden rod in front of the shop. When he got to it, he saw that it was a wool blanket, about four feet wide by seven feet long. He examined it closely and noticed it was a pigment-dyed hand-woven blanket. It had probably come from one of the local mountain villages surrounding Tabriz. The quality of the wool and craftsmanship was excellent. He spotted the small white tag pinned to it, which had 800,000 written on it. That was roughly twenty dollars. He couldn't believe it. He had seen similar Native American type Pendleton wool blankets cost over two hundred dollars back home, and they were machine-made. He decided to buy it. He could throw it over him to change his appearance, and it would also come in handy in keeping him warm. It was only March, and the nights were still chilly, especially in Tabriz, which was at an elevation of over four thousand feet. He wasn't sure how well heated the trains were either. The blanket would be a good investment and come in handy. As he reached for his wallet and pulled out eight hundred-thousand-rial notes, he spotted the proprietor walking towards him from inside the shop. Not wanting to engage him in conversation, Michael pulled the blanket down from the dowel it was hanging on and stood there with the cash in his hand. When the shopkeeper reached him and started saying something in Persian, Michael held out the blanket for him to see the price tag with one hand and the rial in the other. The shopkeeper glanced at the price, then took the money and counted the bills, finishing with a smile and quick nod. Michael returned the nod and smiled before turning and heading back in the direction he'd come from.

As he walked back across the marble floor, he was relieved at how easy that transaction had been. The shop owner had probably been pleasantly surprised he'd received full price, not even having to haggle on the price of the blanket, something that was unheard of in that part of the world. Michael was also pleased. He hadn't expected to be finding great buys on rare handmade Persian wool blankets. He wasn't on vacation, after all. He wondered about the possibility of hanging on to the blanket through the mission. What a souvenir it would make if he somehow survived and made it back with it. He could imagine sitting in a rocking chair next to Asya thirty years from now with the blanket draped across him, keeping his old, tired bones warm, as a reminder of a strange and remarkable life long ago. It was strange, he thought, imagining some sort of future after where he had come from just a week ago, and what still lay ahead for him. Then again, if things turned out otherwise, maybe he would be allowed to keep the blanket, and it would keep him warm in his Iranian prison cell.

He found an unoccupied seat in an area over in the corner of the terminal that was littered with passengers on the floor, leaning against the wall and slumped back in chairs, catching some shut-eye while they waited for their trains. Michael sat down and made himself as comfortable as possible. His was starting to feel the soreness in his body. The day's feats of leaping across rooftops and outrunning the Iranian police were starting to take their toll on him. He needed to get some rest, and not on a bed of freshly picked pistachios. He looked at his watch. It was 9:03 p.m. He threw his newly purchased blanket over him and leaned his head forward, leaving his eyes open ever so slightly to monitor his immediate surroundings. He was starting to feel sleepy, but he needed to stay alert for just one more hour until he boarded his train, and then he would have eight hours of relatively safe uninterrupted sleep.

His thoughts drifted back to Asya. He wondered where she was and what she was doing right now. Knowing her, he guessed she was probably back in her office, standing by in case he needed anything. He was lucky to have her to support him if he needed help. He hoped Canton wouldn't trouble her anymore with trying to track down Ali. He knew she could handle him, but he didn't want her to have the aggravation of having to deal with a conniving vermin like him. He was also thankful he had his trusted friend Harry Barso to count on. He wasn't exactly sure how Harry would be able to help him, but the fact that he had such an experienced operator back in the nation's capital gave him a sense of reassurance. He knew if he was able to get Ali out of Iran, he would need all the help he could get leveraging Ali's knowledge of the conspiracy to expose the plot.

Harry was a good man, and one of the sharpest operators Michael had encountered during his time with the CIA. As a boss, he was a straight shooter and expected results. He had an innate ability to see through bullshit and didn't hesitate to call anyone on it. He also did everything he could to support his people and help them succeed, offering his wisdom and guidance from years of experience of his successes and failures. As a friend, he was as loyal as they came. It wasn't the type of conditional self-serving loyalty that was conveniently given when things were going well, but the kind that persevered even when times became tough. Michael had never forgotten how fiercely Harry had defended his decisions and actions to Langley's second-guessing after the disastrous outcome of the operation against Karbashi.

Michael also knew that Harry had suspected it had been Canton who was somehow responsible for compromising the operation, but there was no way to prove it, not even circumstantial evidence pointing in his direction. There was no other logical explanation, however. Ali had been thoroughly debriefed by Michael in the presence of Harry, as well as having passed several polygraphs afterwards, indicating that he hadn't disclosed anything about the operation to anyone. Only four individuals knew the specific details of the meet: Michael, Ali, Harry and Canton. The problem with attributing the compromise to Canton was that there was the whole other aspect of the meet that was beyond Michael's and the CIA's control, which involved Karbashi. There was no way to prove that Karbashi hadn't somehow been compromised. The only problem with that possibility was that there were no intercepted Iranian communications by the NSA indicating Karbashi would be meeting with Ali. As part of the operation, Michael had coordinated with the NSA to receive any intercepts of Iranian embassy communications concerning Ali. There were none. From everything Michael had observed during the course of the operation, Karbashi was a careful operator.

Despite all of Harry's efforts to defend Michael, the resulting circumstances had made it impossible for Michael to remain in Athens. Michael had known it, and his immediate transfer back to Langley wasn't a surprise. What transpired afterwards was what had finally sealed Michael's fate with the Agency. A follow-up internal headquarters investigation resulted in the finding that Michael had exercised poor judgment in the action he took, which had resulted in what had gone tragically wrong with the operation. He was given two weeks of unpaid leave and reassigned to an administrative support position for coordinating the CIA's network of couriers, which hand-carried some of the Agency's most sensitive classified information via diplomatic pouch to and from Langley and its overseas stations.

Michael had seen the writing on the wall when he made the fateful decision of resigning from the CIA and starting a new life. He thought that change, along with marrying Eva, was something he was ready to handle, but it hadn't turned out that way. It seemed like it had been a twelve-year journey through no-man's land, like he had been treading water in rough seas, trying to stay afloat while searching to find some sort of meaning in life to cling on to, but not finding any, until he finally had become too tired to continue trying. The thought that he had just given up like that made him feel ashamed of himself. He wasn't a quitter. How had he let himself fall into such a deep and dark hole? It was a question that he had been struggling to find an answer to for several days now. What made it that much harder to come to terms with was how he had also suddenly been snatched out of that dark hole. The thought of where he currently found himself after everything that had happened to him over the past week, felt overwhelming at times. He couldn't logically explain it. Where was life taking him? Did he even have any say or control over his destiny? He was obviously serving some purpose. He just couldn't see it and had no idea where things would eventually lead.

Michael's thoughts were interrupted by a loud announcement of the PA system that echoed through the large station and was completely unintelligible to him. He checked his watch and saw that it was 9:55. He looked up at the large electronic display. It still showed a 10:00 p.m. arrival from Ankara and 10:15 departure for Tehran. His train would be here in five minutes. He stood up, draped his blanket across his shoulders, and made his way towards the doors which led to the platforms. He followed the sign for track number three, leaving the huge hall and walking out onto the platform, which had begun filling with passengers. Michael looked at his ticket and saw that he was assigned to car number four, cabin number seven, bunk number one. He wondered how many bunks were in each cabin. He hoped the girl who had sold him the ticket was right and he wouldn't have a cabin-mate. He didn't want to have to feign being a deaf-mute for the entire journey to Tehran. He would spend most of the time sleeping, of course, but it would be a much-needed break if he could allow his alert level to drop for a few hours and let his nervous system unwind some. It had been a stressful day.

He looked down the track and saw the front of a blue-and-silver locomotive coming down the track toward him. The brakes squealed as the train slowed coming into the station. When it finally came to a stop in front of him, the doors opened and a crowd of passengers began to disembark, dragging their bags and suitcases, pausing on the platform to look around before continuing on towards the main terminal. Michael counted the fourth car from the locomotive and made his way toward it. He paused at the doorway and let a young mother pass. She was dragging a large suitcase, accompanied by her two young sons, who looked like they were between the ages of six and seven. He wanted to help her with her bag but stood back and gave her space, not wanting to risk any unnecessary encounter, despite how noble his motivation. After she was on board and began making her way down the passageway of the sleeper car with her two boys in tow, Michael stepped on and followed behind at a distance, looking at the numbers on each door until he came upon the number seven. He slid open the door and looked in. Both bunks were empty. Maybe it was his lucky number seven. He slid himself into the tiny cabin. There was barely enough room for two people to stand side by side next to the two bunks, but for now it was all his, and that was all that mattered.

Michael sat down on the lower bunk and set his bag next to him. He looked around the cabin and spotted two plastic bottled waters on the small nightstand below the window. He reached for one, breaking the seal as he twisted off the cap, then raised it to his mouth and took a long swig. That was just what he needed. He still had a sufficient supply of pide to get him through for another day, but he needed water. He had drunk the two bottles he had brought with him, and had been beginning to get thirsty. He sat there and waited patiently while the remaining passengers boarded, until he heard two short blasts from the locomotive's whistle, then felt the jerk of the brakes being released and the train beginning to roll out of the station. It looked like the cabin was all his. He could finally let his guard down some and get some much-needed rest to prepare him for whatever lay ahead when he arrived in Tehran.

Michael glanced at himself in the small mirror mounted on the opposite wall. His hair was uncombed, his face unshaven, and he had smudges on his face. He poured some water into his right hand, splashed it on his face, attempting to wipe away some of the grime, then dried himself with the edge of the sheet on his bunk. No wonder the girl at the ticket window had wanted to get rid of him as quickly as possible. He looked like some sort of derelict. He thought about the initial impression he would make on Karbashi if he managed to track him down and confront him. He imagined it would take some convincing on his part before Karbashi would begin to sense of this wild man's crazy story.

Michael finally heard what he had been waiting for, a knock on his door. He slid it open and saw the conductor standing there, waiting to see Michael's ticket. He handed his ticket to the conductor, who glanced at it, gave it two quick stamps with his hole punch, then handed it back to Michael before moving quickly on down the passageway to the next cabin. Michael slid his door shut and turned the lock, securing his cabin from any unexpected intrusions. He could finally relax and get some sleep. He threw his bag on the top bunk, then lay down on top of the covers of his bunk, throwing his newly purchased blanket over him. The pillow was hard and the mattress left much to be desired, but the motion of the train, combined with his sheer exhaustion, had him drifting off to sleep before his next thought had even begun to form in his mind.

Chapter 21

Asya woke on her office couch. As far as couches went, it had comfortable cushions and was long enough, but she was a stomach sleeper who made full use of her queen-size bed, with an arm reaching to one corner and a leg to another. Being forced to sleep on her back didn't sit well with her body. She looked at her watch. It was 6:10 a.m. She looked towards the windows and saw that the sky was starting to become light. She kicked the blanket off and sat up on the couch, arching her back and stretching her arms as she tried to get the kinks out of her neck. For a forty-five-year-old woman, she was in fantastic shape. She had maintained a consistent fitness routine going back to her teenage years as a gymnast up through the present. Having to continuously prove herself in the male-dominated world of Turkey's intelligence service, she had always been able to go to toe-to-toe with any of her male peers, fitness-wise if not in sheer strength, as Michael had recalled of her feat in pull-ups. That had been twenty years ago, however, and her body now was so much more aware of all the aches and pains of old injuries and the gradual wear and tear from all of the exercise that kept her as fit as she was. The worst was the running. Over the past few years, she had limited it to twice a week for thirty minutes, preferring to swim laps three days. She supplemented the running and swimming with her own yoga and pilates routine with some dumbbells, but her favorite gym exercise was with suspension straps that used her own body weight as resistance. Perhaps it was because it reminded her of her days as a gymnast on the uneven bars, having to maintain control of her body at different angles, but it had maintained her core strong as a piece of spring steel. She could also still knock out a respectable fifteen pull-ups. Some mornings, every once in a while, she just felt like a tired old lady, and having slept on the couch made it one of those mornings.

She stood up and walked to her bathroom in her red-and-yellow Galatasaray soccer club jersey and yellow sweatpants, which she wore as pajamas. She turned on both taps and waited for the warm water before splashing her face several times to fully wake up. Grabbing her toothbrush, she squeezed a strip of toothpaste onto the bristles and stuck it in her mouth, brushing her teeth and freshening her mouth from the staleness of morning breath. She ran a brush through her hair, smoothing out her bed-head, then twisted open her lipstick and applied some color to her face. She was fortunate to still have a youthful complexion, partly due to genetics and partly due to forgoing excessive exposure to the sun over the years. Her olive skin gave her all the color she needed to augment her striking looks. She walked over to the wardrobe and pulled out a clean pair of panties from the drawer. Slipping out of her soccer jersey and sweats, she put on her bra and grabbed the black-and-white polka-dot blouse she had changed into yesterday afternoon. She sniffed it before putting it back on along with the black slacks. Planning on spending the day in her office until it was time to meet Canton, she stayed in her comfy gray-and-yellow Mahabis slippers.

She went to her desk and sat down in front of the computer screen, nudging the mouse and bringing her computer back to life. She needed a cup of coffee before she dove back into searching through the Iranian intercepts. Opening the lid of the carafe on her desk, she looked inside and saw that there was still some coffee left inside. She poured the remains of yesterday's coffee into her cup and took it over to the small microwave on her credenza. Entering ninety seconds, she hit start and watched as the coffee rotated in circles, her thoughts returning to Michael. He had been in-country for just over twenty-four hours. She wondered where he was, whether he was safe, captured, injured, or even still alive. She felt powerless, unable to actively help him. She asked herself how long she would be willing to wait to hear from Michael until having to accept he wasn't coming back. Was it two days, three, an entire week, before she had to give up hope and come to terms with reality? It was a question she wasn't ready to answer just yet. She had to maintain her faith and trust that Allah had a specific purpose for Michael. She couldn't believe Allah would miraculously save him from taking his own life, just to have him face a meaningless death in Iran. Her last thought swung back around and smacked her hard upside her face. Who was she to think Allah's plans for Michael didn't include death, albeit meaningful and for a specific purpose? She was being presumptuous in thinking she could understand Allah's ways.

The microwave signaled that it had finished warming her coffee, but Asya ignored it, instead dropping to her knees in front of her desk and laying her forehead down on the Persian carpet. She remained motionless in that position for several minutes, not being able to bring herself to pray. She felt a touch of guilt at bringing her selfish request before Allah, knowing that what she wanted for herself might run contrary to the Almighty's plan.

Finally, she let out, "Most Merciful Allah, I humbly ask You to watch over Michael and keep him safe. Protect him from those wishing to do him harm, and most importantly continue to protect him from the evil one, who wants nothing more than to destroy him, just as he has already attempted a few days ago, except that You had other plans. Sustain him with Your strength, guide him with Your wisdom and enable him to see things clearly, so that he may fulfill whatever Your plans are for him, whether they include me in his life or not. That is all I ask of You, my Lord."

Asya stayed on the floor silently for a few moments. She didn't know what she was waiting for—a sign, a feeling, a thought, something to reassure her. She had lost track of time when, at some point, she felt a refreshing breeze blow over her that caused her to sit up and look around for its source. She looked at her door. It was closed. She looked at her two windows. They were closed. That was the oddest thing, she thought. Perhaps she had nodded off and had suddenly come to, thinking she was outside. Whatever it was, she felt a sense of well-being, a feeling that everything was the way it was supposed to be.

She stood up and walked to the microwave to grab her warmed coffee. She opened the door and carefully reached for the coffee so as not to burn herself on the heated ceramic cup. When she grabbed the cup, she was surprised to find that it was cold. That was strange; she could have sworn she'd hit ninety seconds for the time. She stuck it back in, hit ninety once more and start. She waited for it to finish and opened the door once again to find the coffee steaming and the cup hot to the touch. She carried it over to her desk and sat back down behind her computer screen, which had gone dark. She nudged the mouse, waking her computer again. She looked at the bottom of her screen and was surprised by what she saw. It was 9:30 a.m. She looked at her watch. It said the same. Three hours had passed that she couldn't account for.

***

Michael had slept through almost the entire train ride from Tabriz to Tehran. He didn't even wake during the stop in Zanjan, and fortunately wasn't disturbed by having to share the cabin with another passenger. He woke to the sound of the tracks and the gentle rocking of his bed. He tilted his head back and looked out the window and observed the early signs of dawn in the orange sky. He let out a big yawn as he arched his shoulders. He felt well rested, despite the aches and pains that permeated his body. Although he certainly felt the consequences of leaping from building to building yesterday, all things considered, he was so thankful he hadn't injured himself. That would have been catastrophic. More than likely, he would be lying on a prison cot in an Iranian jail cell right now, or even a refrigerated drawer in a morgue, instead of his private cabin.

Just the thought of what he had done made him shake his head in disbelief. He was a fifty-four-year-old middle-aged guy who had spent the last twelve years selling real estate, jumping his way across the Maku skyline like he was some kind of James Bond. What the heck had he gotten himself into? Sure, he had been in Special Forces and a CIA officer, but that was years ago, when he was a young man. And even then, he wasn't leaping across rooftops while being chased by police in a hostile foreign country. Nothing in Special Forces or the CIA had prepared him for something like this. It was almost too bizarre for his rational mind to come to terms with. Yet, here he was on a train about to pull into Tehran, where he was going to attempt to stake out MOIS headquarters in the hopes of spotting its director, and then approach him and ask for his help in breaking out an Iranian prisoner. Was he crazy? It was one thing to have evaded the police back in Maku, but this was something on an entirely different level. Did he even stand the slightest chance?

His thoughts were interrupted by the squeal of the brakes as the train began to let off speed. He glanced at his watch and saw that it was 6:25 a.m. He was surprised. Right on time. He stood up from his bunk and looked outside his window. He could see they were running parallel to a major thoroughfare, through the intermittent glimpses between the shops and the commercial type buildings they were passing by. It was light enough for him to see the signs of Tehran beginning to come to life for the day, as there was already a fair amount of traffic on the busy road. He wondered about how the life of the average Iranian compared to that of the average American. Apart from the cultural and religious differences, he figured they were probably more similar than different. Despite what the news back home portrayed, with the fifteen-second clips showing marchers holding Death to America signs during government-staged propaganda parades, hostile thoughts towards Americans were the last thing on the average Iranian's mind. Daily life in Iran was probably very similar to most other places in the world that weren't inundated by conflict or abject poverty. Men and women going to their jobs, couples struggling to make ends meet, parents trying to do their best raising their children, worried about what the future held for them. Michael knew what the not-too-distant future held for them if he failed in getting Ali out. That thought was enough to bolster his resolve that he would somehow manage to accomplish what he had come here to do.

The passing scenery was suddenly interrupted by darkness as the train entered a tunnel, taking it below the city surface. Michael grabbed his blanket off the bed and folded until it was short enough to hang over his bag, then slung it across his shoulder. He looked at himself in the mirror one last time before getting ready to step out and face what awaited him next. Between his matted hair, the four days of beard growth, his clothing and the peasant bag and blanket, he looked like someone who only lacked an empty can to look pathetic enough to fit in sitting comfortably on some busy street corner, waiting for the charity of passersby. Well, that was the effect he was after. Maybe by some crazy chance, he would be able to plant himself somewhere outside near MOIS headquarters and not look obvious. But then what? Stay there for hours, days, on the off chance of catching sight of Karbashi leaving work? Who knew how many different entrances there even were? He could spend a week there and never catch a glimpse of him. He didn't have a week. He knew that for certain.

One thing at a time, he told himself, once again catching himself falling into the same thought pattern. He became annoyed that he was allowing himself to focus on all the obstacles that lay ahead. He had never been a negative person when there was a challenge before him. He always counted on his ability to assess a situation clearly, consider all the options, calculate the odds, then put together a plan and execute it. In this case, he was completely blind to Ali's situation, knew the odds for all options were terrible, and was completely winging it with absolutely no plan at all. It made him feel helpless. It wasn't a matter of not having resolve; he just couldn't see any logical way he would be able to get by all the insurmountable hurdles that lay ahead. He struggled with that reality. He had to make himself believe he somehow would. Otherwise, he was doomed. He knew others had faced insurmountable odds in the past, but somehow had miraculously survived and managed to accomplish the impossible. His grandfather was a testament to that. He hoped what Asya had told him was true, because only God would be able to get him through what looked like the impossible from where he was sitting.

They came out of the tunnel into daylight. The train, having dropped all of its speed, split off onto one of the numerous tracks as it pulled into the Tehran Central Railway Station. Michael looked through his window, surveying the outside to see what he would be walking into once he got off the train. They pulled up slowly alongside a platform that had another train across from it. It looked like it had also just pulled in, its passengers disembarking onto the platform with suitcases and small children in tow. The train came to a jolting stop, its doors opening a moment later, then passengers swarming out, adding to the chaos already on the platform. Just what Michael wanted. He would blend into the anonymity of the crowd making its way down into the terminal. Michael slid open his cabin door to find the young mother from the night before making her way past him, herding her two young children in front of her while tugging her large suitcase behind her down the narrow passageway. She gave Michael one of those looks typical of mothers with young children, appealing for patience. Michael returned a smile of understanding and instinctively reached for her suitcase, picking it up and carrying it for her so she could tend to her children. She returned his kind gesture with a smile of appreciation. They made their way down the three steps out onto the platform, where Michael handed back her suitcase to her.

"*Merci, merci Agha!*" she thanked him repeatedly.

Michael nodded and stepped into the crowd of passengers making their way towards the terminal, leaving her with her two young children and suitcase. For as much as he wanted to carry her bag the rest of the way, he knew it was an act of kindness fraught with risk he couldn't afford to take. Hopefully she had someone who had come to meet her and the children. It was probably not wise to have helped her as he had. She could have had a husband waiting for her on the platform. It would have been an uncomfortable and awkward encounter to say the least, especially in a conservative Muslim society such as Iran.

Michael made his way amongst the throng moving down the platform. His appearance didn't dissuade those around him from crowding next to him. He thought about the reaction he would have received looking the way he did in a large city back home. What a difference in cultures. Iranians were obviously not as preoccupied with physical appearance as the average American, or maybe they were just more accepting of the inequities of life. Michael knew that mentality was similar to other parts of the world where materialism hadn't yet become the measure of how a society judged fulfillment and happiness in life. Although the Iranian people didn't have real freedom to determine their leaders, as in other countries where a small group of elites maintained an iron grip on power, they seemed to have a certain pragmatic understanding of life. Unlike the principles of democracy in the United States, which valued the individual's ability to determine their position in life, Iran was an ancient civilization that had experienced millennia of having one's role in society determined by others. The concepts of democracy and individual freedom, weren't part of the organic makeup of the Persian psyche as it was in the American, despite the apparent hypocrisy in how those ideals were actually implemented, as countries readily reminded the United States when they were the object of its criticism on human rights.

Michael looked around at the sea of people he was engulfed in. They were going on with their daily lives, accepting their fates. While he felt sorrow for them, at the same time, he had an admiration for the Iranian people. Their seeming lack of self-determination, hadn't stifled their zeal about living life to the fullest, with family and friends being the bond that held them together as a people.

As he entered the terminal, Michael's attention was drawn to the huge concrete relief of locomotives and classic Persian art that adorned the entirety of the large station along its tall walls. He hadn't expected to see something so modern. It was an impressive piece of architecture, he thought as he walked towards what appeared to be the main entrance. Once outside, he would have to find himself some transportation to get him to MOIS headquarters. He knew from the intelligence imagery Asya had shown him that it was a nondescript high-rise building next to the Tehran University of Technology in the northeast section of the city, where many other government ministries were located. He seemed to recall the train station was somewhere in the south-central part of the city, but he would have to rely on the coordinates programmed into the

GPS to get him where he needed to go. GPS devices were illegal in Iran. It would be a challenge using it. Although it was compact, it certainly couldn't pass for a mobile phone. He would have to look at it intermittently and keep it hidden from view while he attempted to zero in on MOIS HQ. It was highly risky, but he had no choice in the matter.

On his way to the exit, Michael made a stop at the men's restroom. He hadn't had a chance to use the toilet aboard the train, and nature was calling. He dreaded what he would find in the public restroom of the central train station in Tehran. He remembered the one in Istanbul, and it hadn't been a pretty sight. As he entered the tiled passageway into the men's restroom, he was surprised to find a brightly lit and fully tiled spotless restroom with modern Western toilets and urinals. It was a welcome relief after having to take care of business in the back of a pistachio truck. It gave him a chance to wash his face and rinse his mouth afterward. He was surprised to even find working rotating towel dispensers to dry his hands and face, until he saw a man of close to sixty wiping the counters. He noticed the man's prosthetic left leg as he hobbled by carrying his broom and dustbin. Michael realized he was more than likely a veteran of the Iran-Iraq War from over thirty-five years ago. The government had probably given him this restroom attendant job for life to make up for the sacrifice of his leg while defending the Islamic Republic from the secular devil Saddam Hussein. Michael saw the plate in the corner on top of the counter with a few bills on it. Michael pulled out his wallet and removed two ten-thousand-rial notes, leaving them on the plate, attracting a "moteshakeram" from the man to let Michael know he was very thankful. Michael nodded and smiled as he exited the restroom and headed towards the main doors to the outside. He exited the terminal to a spacious square and a large traffic circle connecting five major arterials that funneled the morning traffic around the park at its center. He looked around, searching for some transportation options. He figured he would stick with his original idea of commandeering a scooter or motorcycle. It would be the best way to blend into traffic while tailing Karbashi, if he was ever able to spot him. Despite the heavy traffic starting to build in front of the station, it was too out in the open for him to risk stealing a motorcycle. He risked being spotted. Although he would be able to make an escape through the traffic, the last thing he wanted was to draw attention by having its angry owner running after him down the street. He would look for a more discreet place, perhaps down some alleyway or other concealed location. He made his way around the traffic circle to the other side and headed down one of the main streets. Coming upon various scooters and motorcycles parked on the sidewalk as he walked by, he nonchalantly tried to see if any had keys left in them. He continued down the street, passing various tea shops and small restaurants that were beginning to open their doors for business. It was too crowded and out in the open, he thought, for him to try lifting a scooter or motorcycle around here. He would have to wait. As he came upon a small grocery store and pharmacy next to each other, he heard the buzz of a small motor come up behind him. He turned his head and saw a young man in his mid-twenties ride up onto the sidewalk on an old Vespa scooter, forcing Michael to quickly step out of the way to keep from being run down. He stopped his scooter in front of the pharmacy and hopped off, leaving it running while he ran inside.

Michael looked at the scooter, then looked into the pharmacy, where the scooter owner was standing in front of the counter, talking to the pharmacist. He couldn't believe his luck. He hesitated a moment, trying to decide what to do. It was out in the open and certainly not discreet, but he didn't know if he would get such an easy opportunity again. On impulse, he hopped on the scooter. Pushing it off its center stand and walking it off the curb onto the street, he gassed the throttle and brought the Vespa's small engine to life. Catching a glimpse of the man in the pharmacy turning to look, Michael started moving as the scooter began accelerating down the street. He glanced in the rear-view mirror to see the man run out into the middle of the street, stunned as he watched his scooter disappear in front of his eyes. It was exactly what Michael had wanted to avoid, but at least he hadn't been chased after. He felt a twinge of guilt at having stolen the poor soul's transportation out from under him, especially in light of the fact he might have been getting medication for someone. He hoped that sparing his and the lives of his fellow Iranians from the devastation he was trying to prevent would make up for his loss. With any luck, the scooter would eventually be recovered for the owner by the police after he was finished with it. He would try to be careful and not damage it, but where it finally ended up, Michael didn't want to venture a guess.

There were a fair number of vehicles on the street as the morning commute began to build, but it was easy for him to weave his way in and out of traffic on the nimble little Vespa. Small and quick and as easy to park as a bicycle, it was the perfect transportation for what he needed to accomplish. He made a left at the first intersection he came to, then throttled it, serpentining through traffic to the next intersection, where he made a right and repeated the maneuver in reverse. After a series of three turns in each direction, he finally let off the gas and blended back in with the traffic, feeling comfortable that he had put enough distance between him and the scene of the crime. Between all the turns he had made and the adrenaline that was pumping through him, he had no idea what direction he had taken off in. Other than the lightness of the sky indicating east, where the sun would be rising, he had completely lost his point of reference of where he was in the city. Now that he could slow down some, he needed to get his bearings and figure out what direction he needed to be heading in to find MOIS headquarters. It was time for the GPS. It would hopefully lead him exactly to where he needed to go, if the intel for the coordinates was correct. First, he needed to pull over. He decided the best way to use it without drawing attention to himself was to pull over every so often and check if he was going in the right direction. Little by little, he would eventually make his way to where he would hopefully find Karbashi. If not, the mission would in all likelihood be a failure.

Michael had no illusions. It was Karbashi or nothing. He had no other options. There was no plan B. For that matter, there was no plan A. He was making it up as he went along, hoping for the best outcome each time under ridiculous odds. He had never operated that way before. He had always prepared thoroughly, tried to anticipate every possibility, weighed each option carefully, done everything possible to always maintain control of the situation. Now, he had control over nothing. He didn't like that feeling. He needed to have some control, to be able to shape the course of events. He couldn't let another Athens happen.

Athens? He wondered what made him think of Athens now. Athens was a completely different situation. The operation in Athens was one of the best planned and executed double-agent operations in the Agency at the time. Even Harry had been impressed with how quickly he had been able to bring things along to the point where Karbashi was going to be pitched. Michael had been flawless in how he had played Ali in his double-agent role. Karbashi believed that it was he who had been manipulating Ali, cultivating him to provide classified information, while all along it had been Michael who had been anticipating Karbashi's moves and using Ali to lure him in further. Michael had been the one controlling the situation. That was, until betrayal had wrenched all that out of his hands. He knew who was responsible for that betrayal; he just had no way of proving it.

Michael focused his attention back on what he was supposed to be doing when he suddenly spotted a small gap between parked cars on the side of the street next to a small city park. He quickly pulled out of traffic and pulled in between the parked cars. A tree planted in the sidewalk gave him some additional concealment. Swinging his bag around in front of him, he opened the top, and shoving his right hand inside, began digging around underneath the pistachios while trying not to squish his last two remaining pieces of pide or cut himself on his knife. He found what he was searching for and unburied the GPS, setting it on top of the pistachios and turning it on. As he waited for it to lock onto a minimum of three satellites, he scanned his surroundings to see if he had drawn anyone's attention. Looking to his right in the direction of the park, he saw a four-year-old little boy, both hands grabbing onto the chain-link fence, staring curiously at him. Michael gave him a quick smile and looked around to see where his mother was. *Darn little kids*, he thought, *they're always staring at you for no particular reason.*

Michael looked back inside his bag and saw that the GPS had finally locked onto the minimum number of satellites to give a fix of his location on the small screen. He zoomed out and discovered that he had headed off in a northwest direction away from the train station. He scrolled to saved waypoints on the menu and highlighted the only one that had been programmed into the device, the coordinates for MOIS headquarters. If it wouldn't be bad enough to get caught with a satellite phone, the GPS with those coordinates would be enough to keep him locked up in an Iranian prison the rest of his life, if not get him executed as a spy. He selected the waypoint and waited as the GPS calculated a route to get him to his destination. He saw it was thirteen kilometers, about eight miles, northeast from where he was. He figured driving that distance in the city while stopping every so often to check the GPS would take him close to an hour. Darkening the screen of the GPS to preserve battery power, he closed his bag, swinging it around to his back as he looked to his left, waiting for a break in traffic to pull back out onto the street. The moment he saw his chance, he gunned the little scooter and pulled in behind a small bakery delivery truck. The mouthwatering aroma of its freshly baked goods swirled around in the air behind the truck, reminding Michael how hungry he was. He would scarf down one of the last two pides he had left. He would need to replenish his food and water supply if he was going to spend the next several days attempting to track down Karbashi. Other than finding a spot to take care of the call of nature, he would have to stay put and keep his eyes peeled. It would only take fifteen seconds to miss Karbashi if he went by. He didn't have the luxury of time to spot him, as he had in Athens.

***

Captain Engil, the maintenance officer of Golden Eagle Squadron, stood outside the arrivals doors at Ben-Gurion International Airport in Tel Aviv, holding a cardboard sign in his hands with the names of the two Lockheed Martin techs written across it in black magic marker: "Jackson/Peters." He had been waiting there since 8:00 a.m., sent by his commanding officer to personally ensure the technicians were picked up immediately after clearing customs and escorted to the Israeli Air Force Blackhawk waiting for them on the tarmac just outside the VIP lounge. Bill Jackson and Sam Peters finally came walking out through the automatic doors, each of them wearing their khaki Lockheed Martin polo shirts, with large sand-colored backpacks hanging on their shoulders and large black Pelican cases in tow behind them. They paused and searched the crowd, spotting the man in the Israeli Air Force uniform holding the cardboard sign with their names scribbled across it, at the same moment he made eye contact with them. They walked around to the end of the waiting mob and met the Israeli officer, Bill Jackson asking, "Captain Engil?" in a Texas drawl.

"Yes. Mr. Jackson and Mr. Peters, I assume?" Engil responded.

"That's us," Sam Peters answered enthusiastically, extending his hand.

"Thank God you are finally here. What took so long for you to get out. Your flight arrived one and a half hours ago," Engil said with a hint of annoyance.

"Well, your customs folks were pretty interested in all our electronics we got packed up in our cases here and were asking a whole lot of questions about them. We tried being as straightforward as possible without telling them any details about what we were here for. It took a while for them to track down the right person back at your air force HQ to get us cleared through. Guess there must have been some kind of mix up, 'cause the air force person in charge of coordinating our arrival was saying we weren't expected till two weeks from now," Bill Jackson, a retired US Air Force senior master sergeant, informed the irritated young Israeli officer.

"I see. Well, follow me, gentlemen. There is a helicopter waiting to transport us immediately to Nevatim Air Base."

The captain led the two technicians outside the arrivals area, where an olive-drab Toyota Land Cruiser was parked in a restricted zone. An Israeli Air Force airman stood leaning against the vehicle looking as if he were bored stiff, but became alert when he saw his officer walking towards him with two civilians in tow. He walked to the back of Toyota and opened the rear door, assisting the two Americans hoisting their baggage into the back of the SUV. They climbed in the back, the captain getting in on the passenger side in the front, and the young airman shutting the back door and quickly jumping into the driver's seat and starting the engine. They drove out of the arrivals area towards the exit of the airport, turning off onto a service road that took them to a gated checkpoint manned by an Israeli soldier holding a Tavor X95 assault rifle. The airman and the captain showed the soldier their IDs, the captain saying something to the soldier in Hebrew, who then walked to his guard shack and lowered the hydraulic vehicle barrier. The Land Cruiser pulled through onto the tarmac and headed towards a waiting Israeli Air Force UH-60 Blackhawk that was starting to spool up, its twin turbine engines coming to life as its large main rotor slowly began to rotate. The crew chief waiting outside the helicopter helped Jackson and Peters transfer their Pelican cases onto the chopper and secure them, then seated them on the nylon webbing seats facing forward, assisting them with their safety harnesses and headsets. Engil took a seat across from them facing backwards, securing his four-point harness and donning a headset. The crew chief jumped back outside and conducted a cursory check of the exterior of the aircraft before collecting the cable connecting his helmet to the Blackhawks communications system as he climbed back inside, signaling the aircraft commander they were all secured for takeoff.

Requesting permission from the control tower for departure, the pilot received an affirmative response a few seconds later. Sam and Bill felt the twin turbines surge with power as the pilot twisted the throttle, increasing the "whup, whup, whup, whup" sound of the main rotor as Blackhawk began rolling forward, then lifted off the ground. Gaining altitude as it flew past a large aircraft maintenance hangar, the UH-60 banked to the right and continued climbing as it left the confines of the airport. Turning once again, they headed out over the Israeli countryside as they flew southwards towards Be'er Sheva, the closest sizeable town to where the air base was located on the northern edge of the Negev Desert.

"It is about twenty minutes' flight time to the base," Captain Engil told them over the Blackhawk's internal communication system.

The two technicians nodded at him in acknowledgment, giving him a thumbs-up. Flying one thousand feet above the surface, Sam and Bill were able to look out through the open doors on either side at the small Israeli settlements interspersed between tracts of irrigated, of otherwise arid land, that made up much of Israel's sprawling agriculture industry of citrus, avocados, bananas, plums, nectarines, grapes, dates and various specialty produce, such as the world's sweetest cherry tomatoes.

"I had hoped your company would have sent more than just two technicians. We are in somewhat of a hurry to get our communications equipment updated in time for training the squadron is scheduled to participate in very shortly. It was an oversight on our part not to realize ahead of time we had an incompatibility with the rest of our aircraft. How long do you think it will take you to complete the work?" Engil interrupted their viewing.

"Well, let's see now. We're talking eight aircraft, about three to four hours for each, so let's just figure on thirty-six hours to play it safe," Bill Jackson advised the young Israeli captain, despite knowing full well each software update took no more than two hours.

"Thirty-six hours! That puts us well into tomorrow evening before the squadron is ready to go." The squadron's maintenance officer knew he would bear the brunt of the IDF senior command's outrage, even if his commanding officer defended him. Operation Yem Sevp's delay would be attributed to the squadron's unpreparedness. Despite having been caught completely off guard by the news that their newly activated squadron would be needed as the primary strike team for the greatest mission in Israeli Air Force history, his name would be on record as the maintenance officer associated with the squadron's operational non-readiness. This wouldn't be good for his career. He hoped that, despite the delay, the destruction of the Fordow facility and success of the mission would erase any memory of why the mission had taken place a day or two later than what was originally planned.

"We'll work as fast as we can, but I'm sure you want us to be careful everything is working one hundred percent with no hiccups. Wouldn't want to be in the middle of a mission and lose comms and navigation because things were rushed instead of done properly," Sam Peters said, trying to appease the distressed junior officer.

The F-35 program manager had called them into his office yesterday, informing them they were being diverted from their previously scheduled trip to Sydney for avionics updates to the initial order of twenty-four F-35s, which had recently been delivered to the Aussies. Instead, their trip to Israel, scheduled in two weeks, was being moved up, because of an urgent request directly from the IDF General Staff. The strange thing was that they were being rushed out there as soon as possible but had been instructed by their boss to take their time performing the updates, telling them to take twice as long as was normally required to finish the work. They were also given the name and number of Harry Barso in Lockheed Martin's security department and told to discreetly call him securely after they had arrived at Nevatim Air Base. They were both used to having their schedules changed last minute, but calling someone in their company's security department was something neither of them had ever been asked to do before. It was an unusual instruction, but they also worked for the world's largest defense contractor on the most secretive and expensive weapon's program in history. Unusual things that were outside the scope of their knowledge were par for the course when it came to the F-35 program.

It seemed like a quick twenty minutes before they arrived at the sprawling air base located on the northern fringes of Israel's Negev Desert. As the Blackhawk came in over the outer perimeter of the base and set down on a landing zone where other UH-60s were parked, they could see a flurry of activity going on throughout the base. Two squadrons of F-15I Raams, the Israeli Air Force's version of the Strike Eagle, were parked on their aprons, with ground crews and mechanics scurrying around them, inspecting engines, servicing components and preparing them for what the former US Air Force senior master sergeant recognized was some kind of major operation.

"As I mentioned, we are scheduled to have a major training exercise soon, which is why we need the Lightnings ready to go so quickly with the other aircraft," Captain Engil said, attempting to explain all the preparations that hadn't gone unnoticed by both of the techs as they got out of the Blackhawk and headed with their cases in two towards the hangar with a large Golden Eagle painted on the open doors. They could see the eight F-35s parked inside, with a similar gaggle of service personnel bustling around the aircraft.

"Must be one hell of an exercise," Bill Jackson commented as he walked by an F-15I that had a crew handling a five-thousand-pound GBU-28 bunker buster bomb. "You guys planning on doing a live-fire exercise with that baby there?" He gestured at the intimidating eighteen-foot bomb being mounted underneath the Strike Eagle.

"It is all part of the training exercise. The ground crews must practice arming and disarming the aircraft," Engil said, doing his best to downplay the obvious preparations.

"Hm" was Sam Peters' only comment.

"We will go to our squadron's offices first. Lieutenant Colonel Janner, the commanding officer, wants to meet you before you get started with your work." He led them past the hangar to a two-story rectangular concrete building. "You can leave your cases here"—he indicated to them as they entered the front door—"the colonel's office is upstairs."

They followed the hurrying captain up the stairs and down the hallway to a door that had a placard on it with two silver leaves, signifying the commanding officer's rank. Engil gave a quick knock on the door and waited.

"*Nikhnas*," said a brusque voice, instructing them to enter.

"Colonel, Captain Engil reporting with the two technicians from Lockheed Martin." He saluted his commanding officer.

"It is about time." Janner stood up and welcomed Jackson and Peters, shaking their hands. "I very much appreciate you being able to come last-minute like this to update the communications of our Lightnings. I assume Captain Engil has advised you of the predicament we find ourselves in. This is the first time since we have activated the squadron that we are participating in a training exercise. With the defense minister anxious to see how well our new F-35s will be able to integrate with the rest of our aircraft, it would be quite unacceptable if we could not show off our capabilities. How quickly can you perform the updates and have the aircraft ready to go?"

"Well, as we told the captain here, it's gonna take around four hours each aircraft, so I'd say thirty-six hours just to be safe." Bill Jackson's answer was definitely not something that sat well with Janner from the reaction on his face.

"I see. Let's not waste any time, then. Captain Engil will get you started and take you to the hangar. He is at your disposal for whatever you need. Do hesitate to ask. Forgive me for not extending any pleasantries to you, but as you can see, we are under the gun as you say in the United States. Now, is there anything I can do for you to make your job easier?" Janner asked.

"I sure could use a restroom, Colonel, I gotta piss like a racehorse," Jackson replied matter-of-factly.

"Ah yes, the toilet. Captain Engil will show you and get you also something to eat and drink. If that is all, I will leave you to your work." The squadron CO shook their hands as his maintenance officer ushered them out of the office.

After making a stop at the toilet on the ground floor, Engil led them to a small canteen in one of the nearby buildings, where he purchased them several bottled waters and four orders of fried matzo balls. "These should keep you going, so you can get started. There is a toilet in the hangar if you need to use it. Here is a mobile phone with my number programmed into it. You see here where it says Engil." He handed Jackson the phone and they walked back over to the hangar with their Pelican cases in tow.

"It's only eleven. This is supposed to hold us over until dinner?" Jackson asked.

"I will bring something by for dinner so you do not have to stop working," Engil replied as they entered the large hangar where the eight new F-35s were parked. He walked them over to a gruff-looking bald man who looked like he was in his late forties. He had a heavy five-o'-clock shadow and was dressed in blue overalls. When he saw the captain approach, he gave him an obligatory salute, waiting to hear what the officer, young enough to be his son, wanted.

"Gentlemen, this is Senior Chief Sergeant Gellner. He is the senior enlisted of our maintenance crew. Senior Chief Sergeant, this is Mr. Jackson and Mr. Peters. They are from Lockheed Martin, here to update the communication modules. Assist them with whatever they need to complete their work. I will return periodically to check on things. I expect to see progress. I leave them in your care."

"*Ken adonee*," Gellner said, acknowledging the captain's instructions, but Engil had already turned and was walking away, leaving them facing each other in the hangar.

"Well, he sure as heck has a bit of an attitude, don't he?" Jackson commented to the senior chief sergeant.

"He's not a bad kid, just starting to feel the pressure we are all under to get the squadron fully operational. Like all captains, he wants to make major someday. Gentlemen, are you ready to get started on the first aircraft?"

"Sure thing, just need to make a quick call back to my company to let them know we are on location and we're good to start the updates. I'm gonna need to go outside the hangar for this sat phone to work," Jackson advised the senior chief sergeant.

"Do whatever you need to begin your work. I will be in the hangar if there is anything you need," Gellner told them, then walked away to one of the F-35s his maintenance team was working on.

"I'm gonna give our pall Mr. Barso a call and fill him in on what's going on here. They're definitely getting ready for something big. I spent twenty-five years with squadrons when I was active-duty, and this don't look like just some training exercise to me," Bill Jackson declared.

"Yeah, sure seems like it's more than just an exercise. I wonder who this Barso dude is and why he's so interested in what the Israelis are doing," Peters replied.

"Don't know and don't care. Above my pay grade. I'm just gonna do what the boss asked us to do and let the big wigs back at corporate worry about the what and whys. Let's just finish this job here, so we can get back on track and head to Sydney when we're done. Bottled water and matzo balls out in the middle of nowhere don't compare to sitting by the water in downtown Sydney sipping a cold beer," the senior tech answered his younger partner before walking out of the hangar and placing a secure call to Harry Barso back in Bethesda, Maryland.

Michael had lost track of how many periodic stops he had made to check the GPS, but he was making steady progress towards MOIS headquarters, even if it was taking longer than he'd expected. With close to nine million people and surrounded by mountains to the north and east, Tehran was the second-largest and most densely populated city in the Middle East, outdone only by Cairo. Even on the agile little Vespa, Michael found it slow going amongst the sea of automobiles, trucks, taxis and other two-wheeled vehicles that crowded the streets. The morning traffic had suddenly materialized like the flash floods that filled the dry washes during monsoon season in Arizona. Trying to spot a good place to stop each time, then maneuvering out of traffic and pulling over, discreetly studying the GPS for a few seconds, then maneuvering back into traffic to repeat the procedure over again in half a mile had eaten up all of the morning into the afternoon. It seemed once rush hour started in Tehran, it continued nonstop all day, until whenever the workday ended in this part of the world.

He was getting close, the GPS on the last stop showing only half a mile away, as he made his way north on Shariati Street. From the imagery he had studied at Asya's office, the multistory office building would be on the right, with a large open-pit construction site next to it, just prior to the road crossing under the six-lane Resalat Expressway, which cut across Tehran east to west. As he closed in on his target, his attention was drawn to a nine-story office building surrounded by a six-foot concrete security wall that had a six-foot steel picket railing on top of it, the top of each picket angled out towards the street. It was definitely designed to make it very difficult for anyone to breach. Michael noticed a high-security sally port pedestrian entrance as he passed by the building. He looked for a vehicle entry but only saw a long driveway going down along the side of the building, between it and the construction site next to it. He continued flowing along with traffic past the construction site but was unable to see anything, because of the eight-foot-high plywood wall that surrounded it. As he came to the corner, he turned right down the city street which paralleled the expressway overpass above it. He rode down another block and turned right again, doing the same once more, until he had turned back onto Shariati Street, heading back to make another pass by the building.

As he moved along in the sea of traffic, this time he focused his attention to the opposite side of the street, looking for any possible locations he could set up a surveillance of the building. What he saw sparked his interest. Across the street from what he hoped was MOIS headquarters and the adjoining construction site was what appeared to be some sort of museum or exposition hall, which took up the entire length of the block. What looked even more promising was that side of the street was tree-lined and its wide sidewalk was filled with people milling about outside the entrance of the building. Once more, Michael continued on down the street with the flow of traffic. He needed to figure out the best position for him to be able to surveil vehicles coming and going from the building. It would be the only chance he had of spotting Karbashi, however bad the odds were. He needed to make another pass or two, this time coming from the opposite direction in order to change his vantage point. He wasn't too concerned with the frequency of riding by a few more times. The volume of traffic, along with the number of scooters and motorcycles, would disguise him, making him virtually invisible. When he came to the expressway again, he turned left, riding one block, then making a U-turn underneath the overpass, heading back and turning down Shariati Street in the opposite direction this time. As he passed the construction site on his left this time, he was able to look down the driveway running in between the site and the MOIS building, catching sight of a car coming out of a vehicle gate behind the building, heading towards him out in the street. He turned to his right and saw that the drive was almost directly across from the museum's entrance. Next to the museum on one side was a restaurant and on the other a travel agency. It looked like an ideal set up for what he needed. He made his way down the street again, making a series of right turns until he found himself back on Shariati Street. As he passed by a restaurant on the corner, he spotted an opening between two parked cars and guided the Vespa to the curb, lifting it up onto the sidewalk and parking it beside a large elm tree across the street from the drive leading towards the rear of the MOIS building.

Michael hopped off the scooter and nonchalantly glanced around his surroundings, finally spotting where he wanted to go. First, he needed to find a prop that would complete the image he wanted to portray and hopefully allow him to remain in place for several hours. He walked down the sidewalk towards the museum doors, where there were a class of high school students waiting with their teacher to go inside. As he walked past the entrance, he looked above the door at the green sign. Under the Persian script, it said in English, "Reza Abbasi Museum." Next to the entrance was an ATM. Michael continued down the sidewalk, heading towards a metal waste receptacle in between two trees. He looked inside, poking around, his appearance giving credence to his scavenging. He finally found what he was looking for, pulling out an empty can about the size of a small can of Folgers coffee. Rather than coffee, its former contents appeared to have been tea, from the images of tea leaves on the outside. He reached for his wallet inside his buttoned pocket and pulled out two ten-thousand-rial notes, worth about twenty-five cents apiece, and threw the bills in the can.

He walked back in the direction he came from, passing the group of students who were making their way into the museum, then stopped and unfolded his blanket, laying it down on the sidewalk. Sitting down on the blanket with his legs crossed and his back against the wall, he set the can down in front of him. He reached inside his bag and turned off the GPS, shoving it back under the pistachios and placing one of the two remaining pieces of pide on top. Grabbing the other piece, he took a bite from it as he looked across the street down the driveway. He couldn't have asked for a better option under the circumstances. The museum entrance with the ATM close by, along with the tall trees providing him shade and the continuous flow of passing traffic providing him cover, made it a perfect location for a sidewalk beggar to set up for the day. He would have to play it by ear and see how long he could stay there before his presence attracted any attention. He could always resort to his deaf-mute act if he was approached by anyone. In the meantime, he would gut it out having to sit in that position hour after hour as he kept his eyes on the driveway. He was close enough that he could make out the faces of the drivers pulling out into the street from the driveway. The shade from the trees prevented any glare off the windshields.

This was it. Michael was laying it all on the line right here. He was hoping Asya's intel was right, that across the street was MOIS headquarters. He was hoping that Karbashi was somewhere in that building, hoping that today or tomorrow at the latest he might be able to spot Karbashi leaving in his car, hoping that he could tail him all the way to his home, break in and somehow convince him he wasn't some madman, asking him to break Ali out of prison and help them escape back to Turkey. He thought about the odds he was facing. His conclusion almost made him feel like a fool for sitting where he was, hoping for the nearly impossible to happen. But what other choice did he have? He wondered what he would do after two, three or four days of having sat there and not seen Karbashi? At what point would he decide to pack things up and try to make his way back towards the border? He knew he only had a very limited amount of time to find Ali and get him out. Otherwise, there would be no chance to stop the events that had been set in motion. Maybe he would still be sitting in this spot a few days from now and suddenly see a blinding light, followed by a millisecond of intense heat before everything went dark for him and millions of others around him.

Well, God, if you're there listening, here I am. Don't know what else to do. Don't know how or why I've ended up where I am. Don't know how I'm going to accomplish this insane task in front of me. I don't even know if you're really there or I've just lost it and talking to myself. I don't know anything, actually. He bit off another piece of pide and chewed it, as an old lady paused in front of him, dropping a two-thousand-rial note in his can. He looked up at her and gave her a great big smile and grunted something that vaguely sounded like, "*Mamnoon!*"

***

Hamed stood next to Laleh with Tahmin in between them as they watched the pallbearers lift the little body shrouded in white out of the coffin. They handled it like precious cargo as they gently turned him sideways so that he was lying on its right side facing the Kaaba at the Muslim holy city of Mecca in Saudi Arabia. Hamed stood there in a trance, aware of his wife and son, the imam, and all the other family members and friends around him, but as if they were only apparitions and it was just he and his little Reza, all alone with each other. He imagined catching sight of him hiding behind one of the monuments across the cemetery, like when they played hide and seek together with Tahmin. He pictured himself sneaking up behind Reza and surprising him, causing him to shriek with excitement and laughter. The realization that he would never see his sweet little smile or hear his loving laughter again made him feel completely numb inside. The imam stooped down, placing his hand on Reza's shoulder. With his mouth next to Reza's ear, he gently shook his little body while reciting the Talqin, the Muslim burial prayer, one last time, then turned to Hamed and nodded sympathetically, letting him know he was finished. After the knots of the burial shroud were untied and some soil was placed under his cheek and head, Hamed closed the lid of the coffin and the pallbearers carefully lowered the small coffin down into the grave. Grabbing the shovel, Hamed stepped forward and began shoveling dirt, covering his child as he said goodbye one final time, with Tahmin standing next to him holding his mother's hand, watching his little brother disappear forever.

When he had finished, Hamed tossed the shovel to the side and stood there staring at the freshly dug earth that had just been returned to its original place. He knew Reza was now in paradise experiencing the joy of being in Allah's presence, but Hamed's joy of experiencing his child's presence had been forever taken from him. He wasn't sure if he would ever see his child again. He didn't know if Allah would find him worthy of paradise when his time to leave this world would come. Unlike his little child, who hadn't yet had the chance to submit to sin, other than perhaps a little disobedience to his mother, Hamed's soul wasn't pure. He had sinned extensively, bringing pain, anguish and causing harm to many, all in the name of defending his country. He had never killed anyone in the performance of his duties—he was too much of a professional to allow that to happen—but he was certain some of his subjects had probably wished for death by the time he was finished with them. Perhaps those types of sins couldn't be forgiven. Perhaps he would be separated from Allah and all his loved ones for the rest of eternity.

As family members and friends slowly began to leave, heading to Hamed's brother's home for a meal, Hamed instructed Laleh to take Tahmin to their car and wait for him. When everyone had departed, Hamed squatted down next to Reza's grave and placed his right hand on top of the fresh dirt. He remained in that position, not wanting to allow any distance between him and his child. Tears welled up in eyes as he tried to maintain control of his breathing, until he could no longer contain himself, finally breaking into sobs. He didn't know how long he had been there, allowing all the emotions that had bottled up inside to finally pour out of him. When there was nothing more left to come out, he patted the earth over his child's body.

"I will find who did this to you, my child. I will find him and he will be made to answer for what he has done. I promise you that, my child, I promise you. I will always remember you tenderly in my heart, my child, until we will hopefully be together again someday if Allah finds me worthy," he said as he grabbed a handful of dirt and let it run through his fingers before standing up and turning towards his car, where his wife and other child were inside looking at him. He studied their faces as he walked towards them. He saw the sorrow in their eyes. It stabbed him in his heart like a knife. He would inflict greater pain on the man who had done this to his child, before casting him out of this life into whatever Allah had awaiting him afterwards. Hamed knew that he was infringing upon Allah's sovereignty when it came to decisions concerning life and death. He hoped Allah could forgive him for taking that into his own hands.

***

Asya had spent the entire morning and most of the afternoon in her office, other than a quick run across the street to a small coffee shop for two double espressos and a baklava. She hated doing that to her body, but for the time being, straight sugar and caffeine was what she needed to keep her focused. She spent the entire time behind her computer, monitoring the feed from GES headquarters of Iranian police intercepts and any other Iranian military and diplomatic traffic GES was able to pick up. Her military also had access to NATO Top Secret intelligence, which the United States and Great Britain both contributed to, but she also knew the NSA and GCHQ were very selective in what they released to their supposed equal partners. She had even resorted to tracking whatever was available on Iranian media outlets via the Internet through a VPN on her unclassified computer, in the unlikely chance she might be able to spot something useful. There was nothing. Other than the initial police intercepts regarding the incident in Maku over twenty-four hours ago, she was in a complete blackout regarding any information about Michael.

She had known that was going to be the case before he'd gone in, but it didn't keep her from feeling helpless and frustrated just standing by waiting to receive a communication from Michael, if one would ever come. She realized the latter was a possibility. Actually, it was more than just a possibility, it was more than likely. Why was she letting herself become naïvely hopeful she would see him again? After all, she was a professional intelligence officer. She knew the reality of what Michael was up against, the odds he was facing. How long would she wait before giving up hope? Yet what else could she do? She had prayed to Allah and asked Him to protect Michael, but beyond that, who was she to question His plans? As agonizing as it was, she would just have to stand by and be patient, trusting that He would reveal to her what she was supposed to do when the time came.

She looked at her watch. It was already 5:20 p.m. No wonder she was feeling hungry. She hadn't heard anything from Canton. Maybe he wasn't going to call. Although she was curious to find out what he was up to, her priority was to be available whenever Michael might need her. She thought about what to have for dinner. She could run out and bring something back to her office and settle in for the night. No, she wouldn't spend another night on the couch again. She would feel doubly miserable tomorrow. Abusing her body like that wouldn't serve any purpose. She also needed to take a shower. Besides needing to freshen up, she knew standing under the hot water for thirty minutes would make her feel so much better. She would get into bed early, maybe read her book some, then get a good night's sleep so she could get back to the office bright and early and wait some more. She didn't know why she had a preoccupation with being in her office. Michael was going to contact her on her mobile phone, which she would constantly have with her, whether at her home or in the office. She guessed it was having instant access to all of her agency's assets that were at her disposal that gave her a sense of reassurance. She didn't want to risk a delay of even a few minutes if Michael called for assistance.

She got up from her desk and gathered her dirty clothes from yesterday to take back to her apartment. Grabbing her jacket and purse, she was just about out the door when the phone on her desk rang. She almost jumped turning to get to it, until realizing it would be her mobile phone ringing if it were Michael calling. She looked at the screen on her desk phone and saw that it was a Turkish mobile number that didn't look familiar. She thought about whether to answer it. It probably wasn't Canton, and she didn't want to waste any more time. If the call center had put it through, whoever was calling must have sounded convincing enough for the call to be forwarded to her desk. She picked it up.

"*Merhaba*," she answered.

"*Merhaba*, Ms. Tarhan. This is Jonathan Canton."

"Oh, Mr. Canton, I was beginning to think you might not call."

"My apologies for keeping you waiting so long. As I told you yesterday, something suddenly came up that had to be addressed immediately. It has taken all day. I have just now finished, and it is something that I believe you will find very useful to your investigation. Would it still be possible to meet? It is very time-sensitive."

She paused a moment, considering how to respond. What was it that was so time-sensitive? Was he somehow trying to play her or did he really have something that could be useful to her? She had to find out. It was something she could do while she waited to hear from Michael. Maybe she would be able to discern what Canton was really up to.

"Yes, we can still meet. When can you be here?" she answered.

"Actually, I was hoping you might be able to meet somewhere else. There is someone I believe you will be very interested in meeting. I'm afraid, however, there is no way I would be able to convince them to come to your office. They are very paranoid as it is about having any official contact with anyone in the government. It was difficult enough for me to get them to agree to meet with you at all." He tried to sound as enticing as possible. There was some truth in what he was telling her, after all.

She didn't like where this was going. He was trying to steer the conditions of their meeting, and it didn't sit well with her. But then again, she knew that if he did actually have some asset or source with information, they would naturally not feel comfortable walking into an office of the Turkish government's intelligence service. She would see who this person was and what they had to offer. She wouldn't waste much time if it looked like Canton was playing games with her. She started thinking of possible locations to meet with them. She glanced at her watch again. It was 5:40 p.m.

"I see. Would you be able to make it by seven somewhere in the vicinity of the old city? That is in a little over one hour," she offered. It would give her enough time to scout out a location and call him back giving him the specific location.

"Seven would be fine. However, you would need to come to the location of this person. They are very limited in how far they can venture, and it would be quite impossible for them to come to that part of the city. They are actually located across the Bosphorus on the other side all the way down by the commercial port."

The hair on the back of her neck was beginning to stand up. A little voice inside her was telling her not to let him dictate the location. It was a cardinal rule in intelligence work never to let a source determine the location. She knew better than that. All her instincts told her so. Canton wasn't a source, however. He was the senior CIA liaison with her agency for the most high-profile terrorism investigation ever conducted. It was Canton's source. She hoped he was at least competent enough to have thoroughly checked the location. She would just have to exercise extreme caution and not assume Canton had taken all the proper precautions.

"May I have the location?" she finally replied after a brief pause.

"Yeah, sure, I can meet you in a place not too far away, because I'm not really sure of the area myself. I'll use my phone to get there and then you can follow me the rest of the way in your car. It's not that far away. Do you know where those helicopter landing pads are up on the hillside across the road from the main port area?"

"Yes, I do, Mr. Canton."

"Well, there's an access road that cuts off the main road and runs parallel inside the port for a short bit. I'll be waiting for you there. I'll be in a black

BMW."

"Very well, Mr. Canton. I will meet you there at seven."

"Seven it is. I look forward to it, Ms. Tarhan. You won't be disappointed, I promise you."

"We will see. Goodbye then." She ended the call with him.

Wonderful, she thought, he wasn't even that familiar with the location. Was he as incompetent as Michael had claimed when it came to work? He had warned her to be cautious when dealing with him because he was slippery as a snake. She would use caution, of course. She would have liked to have had backup with her, at least a countersurveillance unit in another vehicle to make sure they weren't being followed, but she didn't want to yank a couple of her subordinates out of their homes on a Saturday evening with their families, especially with only just over an hour's notice. She could have insisted on pushing the meeting back a couple of hours, but she wanted to get home at a decent hour, so the quicker she got it over with, the better.

She went back to her closet and pushed through her hangers until she found the one that had her black leather Bianchi shoulder holster for her Heckler & Koch P30 9mm and two extra magazines. The holster fit comfortably and snugly under her leather jacket, allowing her to draw quickly and make full use of the forty-five rounds. It was better than the fourteen rounds she had available with her little subcompact Sig P290, which she had to draw from her black leather tactical purse. She assumed Canton would be armed also, regardless of what his proficiency with firearms was. She still had an uneasy feeling about the whole thing.

She looked at her watch. It was 5:50 p.m. This time of the evening on a Saturday, it would take her no more than half an hour to get to the port. There was no time to eat now. She would grab something in a few hours, when she was done with Canton and on her way home. In the meantime, she knew of a Starbucks on the way to the bridge. She would pop in and pick up a French coffee and a pastry to eat while driving over there. It would at least give her a shot of energy and hold her over until she could eat something more substantial and healthier a little later. She grabbed her black Italian leather jacket that she had purchased several years ago when she had traveled to Italy on holiday. Along with her jacket, she dug through her closet and grabbed a pair of over-the-ankle Italian leather boots, which she had purchased on the same trip. She had left for her Italian holiday alone with half an empty suitcase and had returned with it full, with one additional suitcase she had purchased there. Cramming in as much as she could in two weeks, she had visited archaeological sites, museums and churches and was fascinated by all the history. But she was still a woman, and shopping had of course been a major part of her Italian holiday.

Pulling back slightly on the slide, Asya checked to verify a round was chambered in her H&K P30, then holstered it back under her left arm. She threw her leather jacket on and zippered it slightly, concealing any sign she was armed. She glanced at herself in the mirror on the inside of the wardrobe door. She was dressed in appropriate business attire, she thought, for working out in the field. Unlike the fitted ladies' business suits, high heels and stockings she had gotten used to wearing since she had become a senior leader in MIT, she still felt more comfortable in her street clothes, even as her look had become more sophisticated over the years. She wasn't the young and aggressive agent kicking down doors and apprehending terrorists any longer, but she still missed the days of dressing down and blending in with the crowds on the streets. Dressed all in black, she looked like she was ready for business. That was the message she hoped Canton, and whomever they were meeting, would get loud and clear. She wasn't in the mood, nor had the time for any foolishness. She grabbed her mobile phone, switched it to vibrate, and placed it in the interior zippered pocket of her jacket, before she headed out of her office to her car. She glanced at her watch one more time—almost six o'clock. Maybe if she was lucky, she could be home by 10:00 p.m. She hoped Canton wasn't wasting her time.

***

The sun had gone down and would be setting soon, just as the attendee had let the last few visitors out before pulling the steel gate across the front of the main doors and closing the museum for the day. The pedestrian traffic on the sidewalk had also thinned out, making Michael's presence there stand out. He didn't know how vagrants were treated in Tehran, but he didn't want to push his luck. He hadn't been harassed by anyone nor had any police approach him in the close to six hours he had sat in his spot begging. He had been able to keep track of every vehicle coming down the driveway in between the MOIS building and the construction site but hadn't spotted anyone who looked like Karbashi. It was an ideal location, since the vehicles had to stop before pulling out into the street, giving him an opportunity to look at the driver and front passenger, then see into the back when it turned to go in either direction.

He was tired and his body ached from sitting on the unyielding concrete sidewalk, even with his blanket folded beneath him. On top of his physical discomfort, he felt worried and anxious. He knew he couldn't stay there any longer. Besides risking an encounter with the authorities, it would soon be dark and he would no longer be able to see inside a vehicle. It was all he could do to hold back feelings of despondency from creeping inside his head. If he was even at the right location, positioned in the only vehicle exit from the building, it didn't matter. If Karbashi was in his office somewhere inside there on the top floor, what were the odds of Michael spotting him? For all he knew, Karbashi might stay late every evening. He might even be pulling out in thirty minutes, and Michael would be long gone. He had always been an optimist, but these were hopeless odds, and the rational side of his brain knew it. So what part of him was trying to encourage and keep him going, trying to make him believe some miracle would occur?

He almost felt like a fool for even having decided to go through with such a hopeless and foolish mission. So why had he? Did he feel he owed it to Ali to at least try, even if it meant his likely capture or even death? Was it that he would have thought himself a coward if he didn't? That he wouldn't be able to live with himself? He had just tried to kill himself because he had reached a point where he couldn't live with himself any longer. How ironic, he thought. No, he wasn't scared of dying. He was scared of failing. He knew that was what it was. Not only failing, but failing again, for a second time that would have far greater consequences than the first. It wasn't fair for him to have to bear those consequences, all the death and carnage, just because he had been handed impossible odds. Ten years ago, all the odds had been in his favor, he had been in control of the situation, and yet it had ended disastrously for him. Did he really expect to find Karbashi and convince him to break Ali out in time to stop the pending cataclysm? It didn't matter, he told himself as he stood up off the sidewalk and picked up his blanket, draping it across his bag as he slung it around his shoulder and walked towards his scooter. He would at least go to his grave, whether it was by a bullet or after a long prison sentence knowing that he had tried, did everything within his power, everything that anyone could have asked of him. He could find consolation in dying that way, much more so than in the manner he had attempted just over a week ago.

Michael knew he had to find a place to bed down for the night. He could feel the temperature dropping, and he wouldn't have a cozy private cabin to sleep in tonight. At least he had his wool blanket and a bag full of pistachios for a pillow. He just needed to find a secure location to spend the night before returning in the morning to spend another day on the sidewalk, just so he could go to his grave in peace. He sat on his stolen scooter and came down with his right heel on the kick starter, bringing the small engine to life. He walked it off the sidewalk onto the street and waited for a pause in the traffic before gunning the throttle and shooting out in between two parked cars into the traffic. Cars had their lights on as the last glimmers of daylight faded and dusk arrived. Michael didn't expect to find so much traffic out on the road at 7:00 p.m. Tehran was definitely a busy and bustling metropolis with a population that congregated into the evening despite being under a theocratic government. There were cars full of families and younger people who were out socializing in addition to those commuting home at the end of a long workday. If he hadn't known any better, he would have thought he was in some crowded European city.

Michael thought about what kind of location he was looking for as he headed south on Shariati Street. He hadn't ridden far, maybe only a quarter mile, when to his right, he saw trees instead of buildings. He remembered riding by there several hours earlier, but it hadn't registered with him since he had been focused on trying to locate MOIS headquarters. He turned right down one of the narrow streets that headed into the greenery and found himself in the middle of what appeared to be a city park. There were lighted walkways and park benches amongst the trees and shrubbery interspersed throughout small patches of lawn. Families and groups of young adults, both male and female, were walking or passing through in their cars and on scooters. Michael knew the Persian people were a very social society going back thousands of years, but even this surprised him. He slowly cruised through the park, taking in all the activity as he considered the possibility of making this his overnight venue. It wasn't as if he would find anything else this close and convenient to where he needed to return the next morning. The soft ground was surely better than a corner tucked behind some building on a hard concrete surface. It almost seemed too good to be true, he thought.

He circled around once more, making another loop through the park before he spotted what he was looking for. There was a small rise that led up to a knoll with a cluster of bushes surrounded by trees that overlooked the main lighted areas of the park. He maneuvered the Vespa up onto an unlighted walkway that ran along the bottom of the knoll and hopped off, killing the motor. Other than a young couple that had walked past, coming out of the shadows in what was their only opportunity for some intimacy without being caught by the infamous Morality Police, that section of the park was deserted. Iran's Morality Police patrolled the streets, enforcing Sharia law when it came to dress, particularly among young women, and social contact between males and females. The younger generation of Iranians had grown tired and impatient with the Shia clerics' intrusion into every aspect of their lives. Iran, unlike most other autocratic Muslim countries, hadn't restricted access to the Internet, so that younger tech-savvy generation knew what life was like in other parts of the advanced world, and they wanted the same individual freedoms for themselves.

Michael pushed his scooter up the knoll towards the bushes. When he reached the top, he found a dense cluster of juniper bushes in the midst of a stand of cypress trees. He walked around the bushes, trying to see if there was a spot that would work for him to spend the night. There was just enough ambient light for him to notice a shadow in between two bushes, drawing him towards it. As he approached, he discovered a narrow passage in between the bushes leading into a dark area where none of the ambient light penetrated. He laid the scooter down on the ground beside the bush and ducked, cautiously making his way through the small opening. As he passed in between the juniper branches, coming through to the other side, he froze when he saw two yellow eyes staring at him in the darkness. It was some small animal that had been just as surprised by Michael's unexpected visit as he had been to find it staring at him in the darkness. Michael heard a small growl, then a hiss, before it took off through the bushes in the opposite direction from him. Slowly making his way forward, he found himself in a small circular opening surrounded by a thicket of juniper bushes. The ground was fairly level and layered with a bed of dried juniper needles. Unlike the spiky juniper shrubs he was accustomed to back home, this variety of junipers was not prickly but rather soft to the touch. Through gaps in the branches, he could see the lights below him, but inside this thicket was as dark as one could find in the heart of this busy city. He couldn't believe his luck.

Michael crawled back outside his protected refuge and picked up the Vespa, pushing it back through the narrow passage. There was just enough room to lay the scooter down and for him to lie next to it on his natural sleeping pad. He took out his last remaining pide and situated his bag behind him. It wasn't the same as his down pillow back home, but it was better than nothing. He left the GPS and sat phone buried underneath, not wanting to risk the unlikely chance of being discovered with his contraband exposed out in the open. He lay down on the juniper bed, placing his head on his pistachio sack and spreading his wool blanket on top of him. He was surprised at how comfortable he felt. His pistachio pillow conformed to the back of his head and provided just enough support so that he could look comfortably up at the sky through an opening in the trees. He tore off a piece of his last pide and shoved it in his mouth, eating his dinner as he stared up at the crescent moon that had come into his line of sight in the night sky.

He hadn't spent a night like this underneath the stars since his days in Special Forces. Those occasions were usually in the mountains, forest, or deserts, in the heart of the wilderness many miles from any towns or populated areas, where he remembered being able to see the endless stars that lit up the night sky. This wasn't the heart of the wilderness, but Michael felt the same calm and serenity he remembered from spending nights out on some ridgeline in the German Alps. This was certainly not what he had been expecting. He recounted the past thirty-six hours as he lay there gazing at the moon. Except for his surprise run-in with the police at the beginning, everything else had actually worked out amazingly well, other than the fact that he still hadn't found Karbashi. Maybe there was some absurd chance he would actually be able to accomplish what he had come here to do, despite what his better judgment told him.

God, if it's you pulling the strings here, thanks. This is way beyond anything I'm capable of. I just wish you'd show me what to do next, because I'm completely in the dark. I have no clue if I'm even heading in the right direction for that matter. Do you hear me, God? You even there? He listened to the distant sounds of the city surrounding him as he drifted off to sleep.

***

Asya was munching on the almond croissant and sipping the French coffee she had picked up at the Starbucks. The sun had just set, and the violet and yellow lights illuminating the Bosphorus Bridge cast a beautiful reflection on the waters below as she sped across to the other side of Istanbul. Her mind was on Michael, wondering if he had made it to Tehran yet. She knew the next few days were critical. If he wasn't able to locate Karbashi and convince, or force him, if necessary, to get Ali out soon, each passing day significantly increased the risk he would be caught or even killed. She also knew Ercan couldn't indefinitely keep his unit in Agri waiting to extract Michael. As some point they would have to return to their garrison headquarters back in Ankara. Otherwise, his commanding general would start to ask questions. Waiting to hear anything from Michael was excruciating. It was the hardest exercises in patience she had ever had to endure in the over twenty years she had spent working intelligence. Everything was beyond her control. All she could do is wait. Perhaps she would gain something useful from whatever Canton wanted to see her about. Fortunately, she had the advantage over him, knowing what he was really all about from Michael. She would still be cautious in dealing with him, not wanting to disregard Michael's warning.

She down shifted the Audi as she came off the bridge and circled down and around to Paşa Limanı Street. She glanced at the Omega Constellation she wore on her left wrist and saw that it was 6:40. Perfect, she thought, it would get her to the Haydarpaşa port area twenty minutes early, giving her just enough time to do a reconnaissance of the area to see if she could detect any surveillance on the meet location. She knew he was in a black BMW of some sort, but he didn't know her vehicle. She would do a drive-by, then turn into the port and backtrack past their meet site to see if she could spot anything suspicious. She wasn't concerned about surveillance from the helipads on the hillside above, across the other side of the street. That was the headquarters of 1st Army Command. There would be no possibility for a CIA surveillance team to enter there. She couldn't think of any reason Canton would want surveillance of their meeting, but it was just a force of habit to always exercise caution and conduct a surveillance detection route when she was going to a meet.

Dimming her headlights, she drove north back up through the port. It was quiet, other than two giant cranes that were operating offloading containers from a large container ship that was docked along one of the piers of the terminal. Truck traffic in and out of the port had ceased for the evening, and other than an occasional utility vehicle driving through, it was dead quiet as she passed by the meet location. She stopped the Audi in between some containers that gave her some cover yet allowed her to observe the area. She looked at her watch again. It was 6:55. She would remain there until a black BMW pulled into the access road and stopped at the meet site, then drive out of the port onto the access road and pull up behind him. Five minutes passed, and no black BMW. *Well, he's not punctual,* she thought, *nor professional.* Finally, at 7:04, she saw a shiny black 6 series BMW pull into the access road and come to a stop at the meet site. *That must be him.* She drove out through the port and circled around back down the access road, pulling up and stopping ten meters behind him. She would wait for him to come to her. A few seconds later, she saw the driver-side door of the BMW 650i open and Canton step out and walk towards her. He was dressed in blue jeans and wore a dark brown leather racer jacket that was unzipped. As he approached, there was enough light from her orange parking lights for her to catch sight of what appeared to be a low-profile holster on the right side of his waist. She wondered if the weapon had been declared to the Turkish government. It had probably been handed to him by the CIA chief of station when he'd arrived in-country. She didn't know whether to be comforted by the knowledge that he was armed or concerned about his ability to use the weapon proficiently if the need arose. She lowered her window as he approached her driver-side door.

"Well, good evening Ms. Tarhan. How nice to see you again. I hope you are doing well since we last met. You were a bit late." She detected a slight tone of sarcasm in his voice.

"My apologies, Mr. Canton. Sometimes my duties cause me to lose track of time. So, what is the information this source of yours has to provide, and where are they located?" Asya didn't wish to waste time with niceties and get straight to business.

"Although I couldn't go into any details over the phone, I'm certain the information they have will be extremely useful to you. The information concerns who was responsible for the Iranian foreign minister's assassination." He stopped short, wanting to entice her further.

She paused a moment to think about what Canton had just told her. What was his play here? Did this source actually have credible information, or was Canton trying to manipulate her somehow? She didn't know enough to make an informed judgment. She would have to engage him further and try to figure out if what he was telling her was legitimate.

"Is that so? That would be extremely useful. How do you know this source of yours is reliable?" she baited him.

"Oh, trust me, he's reliable. He has been thoroughly vetted, and I can honestly say he knows firsthand who killed the foreign minister," he told her with confidence.

"And who is this source of yours?" Asya was thrown slightly off guard by the audacity of Canton's claim. She knew what Michael had told her about the cryptic message Ali had passed to him through his daughter. It was Canton who was somehow involved in this insane plot. How was it that he was now coming to her, claiming to have information that contradicted what Ali's message implied?

"Ms. Tarhan, you know I can't disclose a CIA source's identity to a foreign intelligence service, but I can tell you they have direct knowledge of the entire plot. After you hear what they have to say, you can judge for yourself if their information is true or not. It won't take you long to figure out who they are, even if you don't get their true name. Trust me on that."

Trusting Canton wasn't something that came without great reservation. Before Michael had even informed her about him, a voice inside her had told her to be wary of him. Now he was claiming a source could provide the answer to what her agency's investigation was trying to uncover. If it was truthful information, wouldn't it naturally implicate Canton? After all, that was Ali's claim. Maybe Canton was trying to misdirect her with some type of false flag operation. But then again, she couldn't be totally dismissive of his overture. The investigation was her responsibility, and if there was any possibility that Ali's message had been inaccurate or mis-conveyed, she couldn't just ignore it. Despite the fact that Ali had clearly gone to the Iranian consulate and had almost certainly been taken to Iran against his will, it didn't necessarily prove his information was correct. Maybe Ali himself had misunderstood or was confused about the truth. Had she just completely accepted Michael's assertion implicating Canton, the US Secretary of State and the Russian government in the murder of the Iranian foreign minister? It had been twelve years since Michael had last seen Ali. How was he so certain Ali hadn't somehow gotten involved in something improper and as a result gotten himself into the current predicament he found himself in? For that matter, Michael could be risking his life for nothing. She couldn't assume that whatever Canton was up to was just some sort of ploy.

"So, who does your source say is responsible for killing the foreign minister?" she asked, getting to the heart of the matter.

"You know, it's better if I let you hear it directly from the source's mouth, because if I try to tell you, you're not going to believe me, and I don't know enough about the details to answer all the questions you're going to have. I just met with him yesterday for the first time and it took me a while to accept what he was claiming. But let me tell you, by the time I was done hearing him out, I was convinced what he was telling me was the God's honest truth."

"And why are you so certain? What kind of history of reliability does this source have? You said you met him for the first time just yesterday. What is his access?"

"Yes, I did. But his access is right in the heart of the conspiracy. Unless he is completely lying, which he would have no reason to, he would be the one to have intimate knowledge of the entire plot." He knew she would have to pursue his enticement. He was drawing her in. Now he just had to get her to follow him into the trap.

She looked at his eyes trying to spot any indication of deception. It was dark, and she could only see the faint outline of his face, making it difficult for her to make an assessment. Her gut was telling her he was up to something, but the logical side of her was telling her she had to follow up on where this was leading. She would stay sharp and keep on alert. If it turned out Canton was playing her, she would play it cool and wait for her opportunity to take Canton's source into custody and have him interrogated. This was her country, and she wasn't going to allow any misinformation attempts to take place, regardless if it was anyone from the CIA behind it.

"All right. Where is your source?" she finally agreed.

"He's just south of here, down by the shipyards," he told her.

"The shipyards? You said it was close by. That is almost twenty kilometers from here," Asya replied with a hint of annoyance.

"Actually, I said it wasn't too far from where we would meet. It will only take fifteen minutes to drive there. Just follow me in your car. It will be well worth it. You'll see." Canton laid out his final piece of bait.

"I hope you are correct and not wasting my time, Mr. Canton. I will follow you," she told him, raising her window to indicate she was ready to go.

Canton turned and walked back to his car with a smile on his face. She had taken the bait. He got back into his BMW and pushed the start button. He loved the smell of the inside of this car. It reminded him of power, sex and money. Soon, he would soon have plenty of all three. Until then, he would do what needed to be done and enjoy doing it. In less than half an hour, Tarhan would be his captive and he would have his way with that Turkish bitch. He would get out of her, one way or another, how he could find Blackstone, and hopefully Shiravi, finally being able to tie up all the loose ends and wait for the rest of the grand plan to fall into place. He put the 650i into gear and drove down the access road. He looked in his rear-view mirror and saw Tarhan was following in some type of Audi. *Well, the bitch has taste*, he thought as he pulled out onto Paşa Limanı Street and headed south towards the shipyards.

Asya turned on her headlights as she pulled out onto the road behind Canton. Something just didn't feel right to her. She thought about calling one of her subordinates, maybe her deputy chief, and letting him know where she was headed and with whom. It would be the wise thing to do. No one had any idea where she was going or what she was up to. The communications center had a record of the incoming calls to her office, but that didn't tell anyone anything about her current status. She decided not to make the call. Other than Ercan, no one else knew anything about Michael or her involvement with him. She didn't want to risk drawing any unnecessary attention to what she was pursuing on her own. Everything would be all right. She would hear what the source had to say and make a determination if there was any credible information or Canton was trying to pull something. If that was the case, she would take whatever action was necessary to neutralize him. Even if she couldn't go to her director and request he take the unusual step of asking the CIA chief of station to have Canton sent back to the United States, she could effectively isolate him from having access to any information concerning the MIT investigation.

They drove a bit further, then got onto the D100 expressway, the same highway that cut all the way across Turkey from west to east, eventually ending up at the border crossing into Iran. It gave Asya a sense of connection with Michael, knowing that she was on the same road he had probably traveled on fifteen hundred kilometers east of her. In another twelve minutes, they exited the expressway onto Sahil Boulevard, which ran back along the water and the vast shipyard complex. Asya followed Canton's BMW as he turned off the road and entered the shipyard. She followed him past lay-down yards that contained large sections of cut-up rusting ship hulls, heading south around the horseshoe complex, past dry-docks that had stopped work for the night, until they came to another road that was obviously no longer used. Canton slowed down as he maneuvered the BMW around the deepest potholes, not wanting to damage the undercarriage of the car, as they made their way towards a group of older wooden two-story buildings. Asya could tell they hadn't been used for several decades from their exterior condition. It was definitely a good place for a clandestine meet, but she would have liked the chance to have checked it out first instead of going in blind without knowing what to expect. She had done so in the past. It was part of the job description when it came to intelligence work, but she had never liked not having control of the situation. It had almost cost her life twenty years ago, and would have if it hadn't been for Michael.

Asya felt the hair on her neck stand up as an uneasy feeling came over her. *Okay, calm down, Asya, everything's all right. Nothing is going to happen. You're armed, and despite your personal feelings about him, Canton is not a fool to put them in some precarious situation. His source was just being cautious, giving himself plenty of escape options should he get spooked,* she tried to calm herself. Canton pulled his car alongside one of the vacant buildings, far enough forward for Asya to pull up alongside the building. She turned her engine off, leaving her parking lights on to cast just enough light so that she could see Canton as he exited his car. She opened her door and stepped outside, staying behind the door for cover as she scanned her surroundings. She didn't detect anything, but the hair on her neck was still standing and the uneasy feeling wouldn't subside.

Canton got out of his car and turned towards Asya. "You coming?"

"Where is your source?" she asked warily.

"He's here. He's waiting inside for us." Canton tried to sound reassuring.

"Tell him to come out. We can talk out here," Asya replied firmly.

"You sure? It might be more private inside."

"Outside will be fine," Asya didn't yield.

"Okay, then, outside it is. Rostov!" Canton shouted.

Asya waited, looking towards a dark doorway in the building to her right. She saw a figure emerge from the shadows and walk towards Canton, stopping next to him.

"Well, here he is." Canton waited for her.

Asya looked around once again, seeing if she could detect any movement coming from the building. She couldn't see anything through the dark openings, most which no longer had intact windows. She cautiously stepped out from behind her door and began walking towards them. All her senses were on high alert for any signs of danger. As she approached Canton and the other man, his face came into view. He looked vaguely familiar. The blond hair and mustache, the eyes—where did she know him from? Her brain raced trying to recall where she had seen him before. He was a Russian. Now she remembered. She had seen his face in MIT's database of suspected foreign intelligence officers operating in Turkey. What was he doing here? This was Canton's source? He was the one who had intimate knowledge of the assassination? Ali's information was true, then. Why had Canton brought her here to meet with a Russian SVR officer? Things were not adding up. Something was wrong.

Rostov's man inside the building on the second floor back behind the shadows of the open window put Asya's right buttock in the green cross-hairs of the night vision scope mounted on top of his air rifle. He gently squeezed the trigger and heard the sound of compressed air force a dart down and out the barrel of the rifle as it made its way towards Asya.

Asya felt the sharp sting on her right side just as she realized she had been set up. She reached for her 9mm inside her jacket and drew it out, raising it towards Canton and Kapalov. As she tried to hold her gun steady and acquire a sight picture on her two adversaries, she felt the dizziness spread over her as her vision became blurry. She tried steadying herself, but within a matter of seconds, she found herself falling to the ground as she tried to maintain consciousness. She heard Kapalov give some command in Russian, then sensed someone run over to her before everything went dark.

Rostov's man knelt next to Asya with a stethoscope and listened to her heart for several seconds. He pulled out a syringe and injected her in her arm, then listened to her heart again. Finally, he looked up at Rostov and gave him a nod that everything was okay.

"What did your guy shoot her with?" Canton asked Rostov.

"It is the etorphine, an animal tranquilizer used to put down elephants. The dosage we administered to her was obviously significantly lower, but it can still be dangerous to humans. She was given an injection of naloxone, which is the antidote. She will be out for another five minutes before she starts coming to," Rostov explained.

"Five minutes! She needs to be out longer than that for us to get her inside and secured," Canton exclaimed.

"Do not be concerned. You see?" Rostov pointed towards his, man who was injecting Asya with another syringe.

"What's that?" Canton inquired.

"One hundred milligrams of zolpidem, a sedative. I believe you call it Ambien in your country. Only five times the amount one normally takes to help with falling asleep. She will be out well into tomorrow. My man will administer a stimulant to wake her when you are ready to begin interrogating her."

"That's pretty good. I'm impressed," Canton said, surprisingly offering a compliment to Rostov.

"Of course. What did you expect, that we do not know how to do our job? You underestimate your adversaries," Rostov replied.

"I didn't know we were adversaries," Canton said.

"There is much you have to learn."

"Well, let's get her inside and take care of her vehicle. What are you going to do with that?" Canton asked.

"That is not my responsibility. You said you wanted her. You did not say anything about her *machina*."

"What do you mean, not your responsibility? We can't leave it out here in the open."

Rostov looked around until he saw what he was looking for. "We will put it inside," he said, pointing towards a large opening to the inside of the building with a sliding wooden door.

"And then what?"

"That is for you to decide," Rostov told him matter-of-factly.

"That's great. Doesn't look like to me you know how to do your job very well," Canton sneered.

"Do your job, I will do mine. *Poluchit' yeye vnutr*," he told his men, instructing them to get Asya inside. They lifted her onto a makeshift litter.

"Oh, don't worry, I'll do my job," he replied as he watched Rostov's men carry Asya inside.

Chapter 22

Ali was awakened by the sound of the lock on his door being turned. Sitting up on his cot immediately, he waited to see who was entering. The door swung open and he saw the jovial round face of Farzan, who came in holding a tray with several plates on it.

"Good morning, brother, I have brought you your breakfast," he announced as he entered Ali's cell.

"Good morning, Farzan. I didn't realize it was morning already," Ali greeted him.

He couldn't remember how many days ago it had transpired, but they had begun addressing each other on a first-name basis. Farzan had developed the habit of delivering Ali's breakfast and lunch each day rather than sliding it through the slot in the door, sitting down with him as he ate to converse with him about life in the United States. Ali had shared with him his experiences after he had moved there, his struggles in adapting to a different culture, meeting an American girl and marrying, raising a daughter in the West. Farzan in turn shared with Ali what his life was like. What it was like to raise his two young daughters in modern-day Iran, the aspirations he had for them, the struggles he knew they would face as young women in the strict theocratic state. He was a devout Muslim, praying to Allah regularly and trying to live his life as devoutly as possible, despite struggles with food and his habit of smoking. But he believed the clerics controlling the government had taken things too far, trying to stifle any sense of pleasure and enjoyment in their society. He had told Ali about what a great cook his wife was, and how food and cigarettes had been the two vices that gave him some enjoyment in the midst of his cheerless job, where he had to observe the men he was responsible for guarding as their souls were systematically bled dry of every last bit of their humanity. They had disclosed personal information to each other, which wasn't the norm between guard and prisoner. It was a welcome break for Ali from the endless monotony and boredom of hour after hour that had rolled into several days.

"Look what I have brought you. My wife baked them last night. It is sheermal, sweet bread. Do you remember it at all from when you lived here before going to the United States?" Farzan pulled the paper towel off one of the plates, revealing three yellow rounds of pita bread with nuts and raisins baked in them.

"Oh, yes, I remember these. My aunt in the United States used to bake them during holidays. It has been over thirty years since I have had them. Thank you, brother, you did not need to do this."

"It is nothing. When my wife bakes, she bakes enough to last for a week. She thinks she is being clever because she hides them in different locations so that I do not finish them in a few days, but their wonderful aroma gives them away. When I rise early in the morning for work before she and the girls have woken, my nose and I have full run of the kitchen to find where she has attempted to conceal them from me."

"They look delicious."

"Try one. Eat, eat. You will be amazed," Farzan urged him.

Ali picked one up and raised it to his mouth, biting into the mildly sweet bread that got its rich yellow color from saffron, which, along with the ghee butter, milk, pistachios, almonds and raisins, gave it its distinct rich taste and tender buttery texture.

"Mm. Mmm! These are beyond delicious, Farzan, they're incredible!" Ali exclaimed.

"I told you. *Befarma'id,*" Farzan said, wishing him bon appétit.

"Thank you again, Farzan. If it was not for you and your kindness, things would have been very difficult for me. Your visits have brought a ray of sunshine to my soul each day. I have lost track of time in here other than when I receive my meals. I do not understand why no one has come to question me for many days now. Do you know anything?"

"I do not know. They do not tell us anything. Our job is only to guard the prisoners and not ask any questions. I have not seen the colonel in several days. Consider yourself lucky, brother. It is never a pleasant experience when the colonel is with you. Most do not leave the same person they were when they came in," Farzan answered sorrowfully.

"It just seems very strange. It has been four days now since he has questioned me. Do you think he is finished with me?"

"No. Otherwise, you would not still be in this cell without any window. These are just temporary holding cells for prisoners who are being interrogated. There are no windows so that you become disoriented and lose track of night and day. It makes it easier for them to break you."

"Is this what normally happens with prisoners who are being interrogated?" Ali asked confused.

"No, brother, it is not. Once the colonel begins with a prisoner, he is relentless, day after day, until the prisoner is broken and reveals everything the colonel wants to know. I do not know why things have been different with you. Perhaps Allah is watching over you."

"Maybe, Farzan. Many strange things have happened to me since I have come here, things that I cannot explain or fully understand. I am grateful I have not been physically harmed. It is just the uncertainty of waiting and waiting, not having any idea of what lies ahead, that makes it so difficult."

"Allah may have other plans for you. Keep your faith, brother. It is the only thing you have left to sustain you. Otherwise, you will lose yourself forever. I have witnessed this with my own eyes more times than I care to remember. This place can rob you of your sanity. I pray for you every night before I sleep, asking Allah to protect you and deliver you from this place. I do not know the details of why you are here, but I know it is not because you have done something wrong. I can sense it with you."

"Thank you, Farzan, I appreciate your encouragement and prayers. I guess I will have to wait and see what His plans are for me." Ali sighed, accepting that he had no other choice in the matter.

"Allah will not abandon you. You shall see. Now I must go. I will come by again in five hours with lunch. I will bring you some lamb stew and pita from our mess hall. The other guards know that I like to have my late-afternoon second lunch. They will not suspect anything. *Salaam alaikum,* brother." Farzan turned and headed for the door.

"*Alaikum salaam,*" Ali replied as Farzan left his cell.

Ali sipped his tea while he ate the two remaining sheermals and the goat yogurt with honey in the other bowl. He couldn't believe how blessed he was to have found some kindness in this place. Farzan didn't have to tell him what happened to men's souls here. He knew the reputation of Evin Prison and was convinced of the colonel's ability to inflict severe physical and mental pain. Yet here he had been for an entire week and nothing terrible had happened to him yet. His two encounters with Hamed had certainly been frightening, to say the least, but for whatever reason, Hamed had spared him from having to endure any torture.

Then there were the two encounters with God. He was not sure how to take that. He knew what he had experienced, what he had heard, but as the days passed and he didn't hear anything more, he began to wonder if his mind had been playing tricks on him. No, he hadn't hallucinated. He remembered how vivid the experience was. He remembered what he'd heard and felt. It was tangible. It was real. He had been just as lucid and awake then as he was right now.

He got down on his hands and knees and put his forehead to the floor, staying like that in silence. He remembered Allah had told him He wouldn't speak to him audibly any longer, but he was hoping a message would come through, disclosing something to him, anything, just some reassurance that this was all part of His plan. He waited. There was nothing, just more silence. After what seemed like half an hour, Ali finally spoke.

"Allah. Allah. Are you there?"

He heard nothing. Just endless silence.

"Allah, I know You said You wouldn't speak verbally to me anymore and I know You said I was part of Your plan, but I've been here for one week now and nothing has changed. I am locked up in here, not knowing whether it is night or day, not knowing about anything that is going on outside of this cell, not sure what I am supposed to be doing other than just waiting. Please, Allah, I ask You to tell me something, anything," Ali pleaded.

He waited, then waited some more. Still, there was nothing.

"You choose not to tell me anything, Lord?" Ali waited one more time.

"Very well, my Lord, I will continue to wait. I just ask that You give me strength and courage to keep from falling into despair. You are most powerful and all-knowing, Allah. I am not. I trust in You. There is no one else I can trust in."

Ali got up from the floor and sat back down on his cot. He thoughts went to his daughter, Roxanne. He wondered if he would ever see her again. He knew how scared she must have felt after his brief telephone conversation with her. Not having any knowledge of his whereabouts or what had happened to him must be overwhelming for her. He wondered if the State Department had attempted to contact her. What would they have told her? He had no idea if she had been able to contact Michael Blackstone and pass on his bizarre message. Even if she had, what did he expect Michael to do? Call the police? The FBI? He realized there was no one looking for him, other than perhaps Canton. He was completely on his own.

He looked around at the dingy gray walls of his cell, then up at the incandescent light hanging from the ceiling, casting a dull glow that was the only illumination in his world at the moment. He knew Allah was there with him. He could sense it from the peace he felt despite all his uncertainty. That's when he felt it. He wasn't sure what it was at first—some kind of loss, an overwhelming sadness. As he struggled to understand it, he realized it was someone else's pain he was feeling. He didn't know how to explain it; he just knew what he felt. The magnitude of the loss and sadness deeply troubled him.

It was as if some great wrong had been committed to bring about such pain. He wondered what the wrong was. Had it already started? Was the vicious tit for tat of thousands of innocent lives being killed beginning? Was the evil plan he had knowledge of finally coming to fruition? He hadn't heard any explosions or bombardments indicating Tehran had come under attack. Then again, if the worst of all fears came true, he wouldn't see the blinding flash from his windowless cell. He imagined he would just hear a brief thunderous explosion a moment before the blast wave brought tons of the prison's concrete and steel crashing down on him. He sat quietly and listened. There was just silence. Whatever was causing the unsettling feeling, he knew someone was suffering dearly, but he didn't know what it had to do with him. Why had he had been made aware of it? He hoped someone would come soon and tell him something, even if it was Colonel Hamed.

***

Michael woke to a lightening sky and the sight of sparrows flying amongst his thicket of bushes, chirping and tweeting as they chased each other from branch to branch. He sat up and looked around to see if anyone had spotted him but saw that the cluster of junipers had shielded him from any onlookers who might have been passing by. He looked at his watch. It was 6:40 a.m. He twisted his shoulders back and forth, stretching out his spine. He felt some stiffness, but considering he had slept outdoors on the hard ground, the bed of juniper needles had been kind to his back. It wasn't a very cold morning, but the night had been chilly. Fortunately, his handmade Persian wool blanket had kept him comfortably warm. Even his neck didn't feel too bad for having slept on a cashew pillow. It wasn't his king-size Sleep Number bed back home, but it had probably been the most comfortable night's sleep he had gotten of all the times he had spent nights out under the stars while in Special Forces with only what he could carry in his rucksack. He could hear some early-morning traffic in the distance, but there was a calm serenity from where he sat in the mostly deserted park. He felt ready to start the day. He wasn't crazy about the idea of having to sit on his folded blanket on the sidewalk for the next twelve hours, but the sky looked clear, and it felt like it would warm up to be a fairly pleasant day. It could always have been raining, he reminded himself. Not that he hadn't spent endless days out in the rain, miserable and cold, but that had been more than twenty years ago, and his tolerance for discomfort had diminished greatly. Even during his years in the CIA, he'd always had a warm and cozy bed to sleep in. At fifty-four, his body didn't need this kind of abuse.

Before setting back up at his surveillance point, he would first have to replenish his food and water supply. He didn't feel that hungry because the nearly constant trickle of adrenaline into his system had suppressed his appetite, but he knew he had to keep himself hydrated and nourished if he stood any chance of making it all the way through with his mission. Who even knew what kind of condition he would find Ali in? He might possibly have to assist or even carry Ali partway to a vehicle. Hopefully Ali hadn't put on a lot of weight over the past twelve years, Michael attempted to humor himself. To find food and water, he decided he would cruise around the general vicinity on the Vespa, looking for some kind of food cart. He wanted to avoid having to enter any type of establishment to replenish his supplies. It increased the risk of something unexpected happening, as he had already experienced. He would just ride down the streets in concentric blocks away from the park until he came across a food vendor and restocked with whatever he was selling, then make his way back and set up for the day. What he wouldn't have given for a Dunkin Donuts drive-thru right now, but he wouldn't have known how to order half a dozen old-fashioned glazed donuts and a large coffee in Persian. He didn't need to be drinking coffee anyway, not while having to spend the entire day on the sidewalk. He would have to take care of morning business somewhere in the park and be conservative with his water.

Michael slowly crawled through the narrow passageway leading out and peered around outside his protective thicket. He was up on an exposed knoll with open space all around him other than the cypress trees scattered around him. He also saw occasional pedestrians who had come to the park for their early-morning exercise. He reversed, crawling backwards, returning to his sanctuary. *Crap*, he thought both figuratively and literally. What was he going to do now? He looked around what had been his sleeping quarters last night and might have to be tonight also. "Oh man," he let out to himself. He didn't even have any paper. He looked around searching for trash, even leaves. He saw nothing, until the small compartment door underneath the handlebars of his Vespa caught his attention. He told himself not to get his hopes up as he reached over and depressed the release with his thumb. He pulled open the small hatch and peered inside, not knowing what to expect, to be stunned by what he found. He stared at his discovery and burst out into a subdued laugh. Lying at the bottom of the small compartment was a half roll of toilet paper. He couldn't believe his incredible luck. The owner of the scooter had probably shared a similar experience and had taken future precautions. He would tuck away some rial bills inside the toilet paper roll as a gesture of gratitude to the owner.

After taking care of business, he pushed the Vespa through the shrubs until he was standing with it outside what had been his home for the night. He hoped he wouldn't have to return there tonight, but he knew it was a possibility. He would deal with that issue if need be when the time came. He sat on the scooter and gave the kick-start lever a quick downward thrust, bringing the little motor to life. Did he have enough gas? Better to check, he thought, getting off and pulling the seat up, exposing the gas cap for the tank. He opened it and saw the small tank was almost full. He couldn't believe his luck once again. It almost made him feel like leaving a note thanking the owner, but he guessed a hundred dollars' worth of rial would make up for the inconvenience of having his scooter stolen for a few days. What else was he going to do with all his rial? He certainly wasn't going to need it to purchase two tickets on Iran Air back to Istanbul. He put the seat down and climbed back on, then gave a little twist on the throttle as he began rolling downhill towards the walkway leading out to the road.

Michael slowed as he reached the bottom of the knoll, looking for any walkers coming towards him, when he almost collided with two runners coming around the corner. He swerved hard to the right, almost going back off the walkway into some bushes as he heard the angry shouts of the runners. That was close, he thought as he steadied the scooter and his breathing. He hadn't expected to see people running in Tehran. He carefully rode down the remainder of the walkway to the street that crossed through the park back out to Shariati Street. He would turn right and head away from his target, looking for food, so as not to attract any additional attention to himself. Hopefully he would find something without having to ride too far.

Michael stopped at the intersection, looking down Shariati Street in both directions, then doing a double take just as he was about to pull out into traffic. To his left not twenty yards down the sidewalk, was a food vendor with a motorcycle-drawn cart. Michael turned his scooter and rode the short distance up the sidewalk towards the cart. When he pulled up, he saw that the vendor had a heated bin full of some type of baked rings, larger and thinner than a donut, but completely coated in sesame seeds. He had seen those before many years ago, on the sidewalks of Athens. He wondered if they were similar. There was also a small cooler with bottled water, some juices and a red-and-white can with Persian script on it, which Michael took to be the Iranian version of Coca-Cola. He saw the white piece of cardboard taped to the top of his cart that had Persian script written on it with the numbers written also in Persian. He didn't know how much it said, but they couldn't be more than forty thousand rial each. That was about one dollar. He would get eight of those and four bottles of waters. That would fill up his bag and give him enough supplies to last into tomorrow. He looked up at the vendor, who was waiting for him, and smiled, giving him a grunt and putting his hand to his ear. He motioned to the sesame rings, showing eight fingers, then to the waters with four fingers, smiling and rocking his head slightly. If he was going to play the role on the sidewalk, he figured he might as well practice. The vendor reached into his heated bin with tongs and grabbed him eight rings, throwing them into a paper bag, then pulled four waters out of his cooler, placing them into a blue plastic bag and handed them both to Michael, showing him ten, then five fingers. Michael nodded his head more and smiled as he took out his wallet and, making an obvious effort for the vendor to see him, turned to his side as he shuffled through the wad of cash stuffed into his wallet. He pulled out two one-hundred-thousand-rial bills and handed them to the vendor, who handed him back five ten-thousand-rial notes and a "*mamnoon*," thanking Michael.

Michael repositioned his bag around his back with his replenished supplies and walked his scooter to the curb, letting it down off the sidewalk in between two parked cars as he waited for an open spot to join traffic. Once again, he was mystified at his streak of luck. He wondered when the odds would catch up with him. He gunned the throttle and shot out into the street, heading back up towards the direction of MOIS headquarters. He rode past the MOIS building, scanning the area for anything unusual, then looped back in the other direction, looking to the other side of the street towards his surveillance location outside of the museum. It was still early. The museum had obviously not opened to the public yet, but there was enough pedestrian traffic in either direction as people hurried to work. It would be a natural location for a street beggar to set up for his early-morning shift.

Michael pulled over to the far right as he slowed and looked for a spot to park the Vespa close enough so he could get to it quickly. As he rode slowly past the driveway leading into the MOIS building, he sensed the sudden approach of a car behind him. He turned his head and saw an older blue Mercedes come up from the rear and nearly hit him, the driver looking up suddenly and slamming on the brakes, screeching to a stop. Michael's attention shifted from the luxury hunk of steel that almost ran him down, to the driver behind the wheel. Through the windshield, Michael saw the driver raise his hands and give him a sheepish smile in acknowledgment of his mistake, then shifted his attention to the oncoming traffic as he looked for a chance to turn into the driveway across the street. Michael stared at the driver as his brain paused with a delayed response, before the large Mercedes pulled across traffic and into the MOIS driveway. A split second later, when it registered, Michael was so stunned he almost forgot he was still standing out in the street. It was Karbashi. It was him. His beard, gray twelve years ago, had now turned to all white, but he remembered that face better than most of the people he had worked with over the years. He was certain. *Wow*, he thought, *I can't believe it's actually him. What the heck is going on this morning?*

Michael's astonishing luck was almost too good for him to believe. It reminded him of an old black-and-white movie he remembered watching as a child, where the main character had been exposed to some sort of radiation, and as he walked by rows of slot machines, he would set off jackpots one after another, spewing coins out all over the floor. It was one thing with the toilet paper, the full tank of gas and the food vendor. None of them were necessarily any indication of some type of divine intervention, just coincidences in the everyday normal occurrences of other people's lives, even when taken together in how they benefited Michael. Karbashi, however, just then, face-to-face, with a few feet and a windshield separating them, unbelievable. Trying to come to terms with the fact that Karbashi had come to him, had almost run him down, was incomprehensible. He didn't know what to think. Those types of things just didn't happen except in the movies. Part of him didn't want to believe it; the other part wanted to jump off the scooter and do a happy dance in the middle of the sidewalk in downtown Tehran. He told himself to pull it together. He still had a long day ahead of him out on the sidewalk. He had caught sight of Karbashi coming into work, but he still had to spot him leaving, follow him home and ask him to break Ali out of prison. The thought of that almost made him laugh. He knew he was still facing nearly impossible odds.

Michael heard a honk behind him and turned to see the driver of a small vegetable truck with an annoyed look on his face, waiting for Michael to pull off the street so he could get by. Michael walked the scooter in between two parked cars and up onto the sidewalk, leaving it next to one of the large elm trees lining the street. He walked to his spot from yesterday and set down his folded blanket, taking his position on the sidewalk. Placing his bag down next to him, he took out one of the sesame rings and a bottle of water. *Breakfast of champions*, he told himself as he bit into his Iranian donut. It tasted just about the same as of the ones he remembered from Athens. He wondered if the Greeks had gotten them from the Persians or if it had been the other way around. He looked up and saw the yellow rays of the sun finally appear in the sky above him. It looked like it was going to be a mild day. He leaned his back against the wall and enjoyed his breakfast ring as groups of sparrows chased each other amongst the trees. It wasn't as comfortable as the back of a surveillance van but it could have been worse. It wasn't raining.

***

Canton was in a foul mood as he pulled the BMW into the shipyard complex and made his way around the service road towards the abandoned sail factory. It was already 10:00 a.m. and his head was pounding despite the two Tylenol he had taken with the liter of water he had guzzled. After securing Tarhan inside and leaving one of Canton's men to stand guard over her through the night, Canton made his way back to the city and cruised the red-light district, looking for female companionship to take back to his hotel room. It hadn't been late, only 9:00 p.m., but for some reason the selection was in short supply last night.

The first girl he'd pulled up on to ask about availability and price had a large sore on her lip. He thought he had fared well on his second try, when he settled for an attractive taller central Asian girl with an exotic look, picking her up and heading back to the hotel, until his wandering right hand had discovered his nomadic princess was actually a prince. He had slammed on the brakes in the middle of the street, bringing the traffic behind him to an abrupt stop as he reached across and opened the passenger door, forcefully shoving his crying passenger out of the car. He hadn't been in the mood after that experience to circle back and find a replacement companion. He had headed back to the hotel instead and proceeded to clean out his mini-bar of its stock of Johnnie Walker Blue, then settled on the four bottles of Chivas Regal.

He hoped his mood would change after he had a chance to make Tarhan tremble in his presence. He would toy with her and dangle the possibility of sparing her if she told him what he wanted to know about Blackstone, but in the end, he would completely ravage her as she begged for her life. He would show Rostov and his men just how much they had underestimated him when he obtained what he needed from her. He pulled up to the vehicle entrance and slid open the large wooden door, then pulled his car into the building and parked it next to Rostov's, behind Tarhan's Audi. He saw Rostov walk out from around the corner, holding his Russian P-96 9mm pistol, standard-issue for SVR officers. He shut off his engine and got out of the car.

"*Dobrey ootra*, comrade," Canton said, mockingly, with a Russian good morning.

"Why are you so late? You said you were going to have an early start with her. We had to give her another injection to keep her sedated," Rostov asked, obviously annoyed.

"I had some things to take care of. What's the big deal? All you and your goons have to do is babysit her. Once I get what I need from her, you can do whatever you want with her."

"And why is it our responsibility to dispose of her? You are the one who has created this mess. You have put my men and me at risk because of your foolishness."

"I'll put in a good word for you with your boss Petrovich when all this is over, let him know how well you followed orders. Maybe you'll even get a promotion to head dog catcher."

"You should just worry about what will happen to you if all this comes apart as a result of your incompetence, comrade," Rostov shot back.

"Oh, don't worry, it won't be long before your boss will be calling me directly for help on a number of issues. I'll remember to ask how your new posting is in some shithole central African country is going. I don't have any time for your Slavic bullshit right now. I need to get started with Tarhan and get what I need from her. Just be ready to dispose of her body when I'm finished with her. I'm guessing you're going to dump her somewhere out in the middle of the Bosphorus where the crabs can get to her? Actually, I don't really care what you do with her, just make sure her corpse is never found," Canton instructed him.

"I will do what is required because it is my duty. I will take no pleasure in it. You, on the other hand, appear to relish it. She does not deserve such a dishonorable end. She is twice the man you will ever be. You are a contemptible coward." Rostov sliced deeply into his ego.

Canton's face turned red with fury. He was so enraged at the slight, he couldn't even find the words to respond. Then it happened again. His right eye began to twitch. He squeezed it shut, attempting to make the twitching subside, but it only exacerbated the problem. Soon, the muscle in his eyelid was in full spasm. He noticed the amused look on Rostov's face. As his humiliation incensed him even further, he made his way past Rostov and turned the corner down a long corridor past several empty storage rooms with racks of large empty shelves. The corridor emptied into a large assembly room with twelve huge wooden tables, measuring some twenty by forty feet, which decades ago had obviously been used for stitching sails together, from the outline of where large industrial sewing machines had been bolted to the tabletops. Lying on top of one of the tables unconscious was Asya, with one of Rostov's men sitting on a stool next to her. Rostov came into the room behind him.

Canton walked over and looked at her. "Where are all her things—her gun, purse, phone?"

"Everything is in her auto to be kept together. We will dispose of it when it is time to dispose of her."

"Her phone? Did you check her contacts?" Canton asked, annoyed.

"It is locked."

"And?"

"And perhaps you would like to send the mobile phone of a missing MOIS counterterrorism chief to your CIA laboratory and ask them to unlock it?" Rostov answered him mockingly. "I turned it off and removed the battery so it could not be tracked after it is realized she is missing in a few days. That is why we do not have the luxury of spending more than one or two days here, unless you are not confident in your ability to interrogate the woman."

Ignoring Rostov's slight, Canton looked around the room until he spotted what he was searching for. "I need her secured up against that cage, arms up with her wrists next to her shoulders." He directed his command at Rostov's man, who just looked at him. "*Ponimayesh pangliyski, Ivan?*" Canton asked him if he understood English.

"Do what he asks, Alexi," Rostov told his man in English.

Getting up, the big blond Russian took his stool and placed it against the metal cage that at one time must have been some type of secure storage area. He looked over at Rostov and gave him a nod, requesting his assistance. Rostov walked over, and together they lifted Asya off the table and, carrying her under each arm, set her down on the stool. As Rostov held her up, Alexi reached into his bag and removed eight industrial-size zip ties and four eight-inch-long sections of cheap rubber hose. Sliding a zip tie through each piece of hose, he proceeded to secure Asya's wrists firmly above her shoulders and each ankle about a foot from the cage, allowing her feet some mobility so that she could maintain her balance whether sitting or standing.

"Oh, give me a break. Like a little pain around her wrists and ankles is going to make the slightest bit of difference in what lies ahead for her," Canton remarked sarcastically.

Disregarding Canton's comments, Alexi removed a small zippered nylon case from his bag and opened it, revealing several small bottles and syringes. Looking at the labels on each little bottle, he selected one, along with a syringe. Inserting the needle through the rubber top, he sucked the clear liquid into the syringe, then, tapping the air bubbles to the top, depressed the plunger slightly until only liquid remained.

"What are you giving her?"

"Epinephrine. It will counter the effects of the zolpidem," Alexi informed Canton as he stuck the needle into the back of Asya's upper arm and depressed the plunger.

The three of them stood there and watched as Asya began to stir, slowly lifting her head, shaking it back and forth, then opening her eyes, trying to focus her vision. It took her a moment to understand where she was, but as the epinephrine kicked in, it finally registered who was staring at her. She stood up suddenly and thrashed with her arms and feet, struggling to free herself but fell back down to the stool, the effects of the Ambien not completely reversed just yet.

She glowered at Canton with fury as she shouted, "Do you think you will get away with this, Jonathan Canton? You have made a tremendous mistake.

You will pay dearly for this, I promise you!"

"I believe I already have gotten away with this, and it is you who will pay, Ms. Tarhan, if I don't get what I need from you," he answered her smugly.

She turned to Rostov next. "I know you. You're Russian. What do you believe you are accomplishing, working with this criminal? Do you have any idea what you are doing?"

"I am carrying out my duty Ms. Tarhan. I take no pleasure in having to work with this man nor with this unfortunate situation concerning you. I hope you understand this is not a personal matter, just business, as they say," Rostov answered as deferentially as possible under the circumstances.

"You will not get away with this. All of you will suffer the consequences, that is certain."

"I will leave you to your work, then," he told Canton. "Do as he says," Rostov instructed Alexi, then turned and left the room.

"You can leave also. Just hang tight in the other room in case I need you," Canton instructed Rostov's man, who turned and headed after his boss.

"Well, well, Ms. Tarhan, it seems we find ourselves in a very unusual situation," Canton said, standing in front of her. "You have some information about an individual who is actively working against my government— committing treason actually, in cooperating with a member of a foreign intelligence service. That would be you. I'm sure you know who I am referring to. Michael Blackstone, with whom you are very well acquainted."

"I know who Michael Blackstone is, and I also know he is not the one committing treason. You are the one who is committing treason against your country. I know all about your involvement with the foreign minister's assassination. Do really believe you will succeed with this insane plot? You are deranged if you do." Asya didn't mince words.

"Is that right? You know, Asya—may I call you by your first name since we are going to get to know each other so well? It doesn't concern me what you think about me or what you believe about some plot. What concerns me is what you know about Blackstone. I want to know where he is and what he has told you about Ali Shiravi."

"I do not know where he is, and even if I knew, do you really believe I would tell you? What he has told me about Ali Shiravi, I had already known. He is the Secretary of State's interpreter and obviously knows something of great significance since he has turned up missing. What is it that he knows that has you so concerned, Mr. Canton? Is it something that implicates you?"

"What he knows is none of your business. Your president had personally assured the Secretary of State that your government would do everything in its power to assist ours in locating Mr. Shiravi. From how I see things, that doesn't seem to be the case. Instead, the head of the MOIS counterterrorism department in Istanbul is aiding and abetting a disgraced former CIA officer who has gone rogue against both your government and his own. I wonder what your director would think about that—or your president, for that matter. I'm guessing you would probably lose your job and have a new residence in some women's prison. Oh, I'm sure the guards would enjoy having some hot former MOIS chief who is completely at their mercy. If you don't want to meet that fate, I suggest you tell me where Blackstone is and maybe some allowances can be made with your future." Canton dangled some false hope out for her to grasp onto.

"It is you who will be in prison, and I am sure you will make a nice companion for one of your fellow inmates," she fired back.

"You know, I am trying to give you every opportunity to spare yourself from a lot of anguish and pain, but you don't seem to appreciate that. Don't you realize your position? I'm the one who holds all the cards here. I decide what happens to you. I can be kind or not so kind to you. You won't like the not-so-kind side of me."

"It does not matter how you threaten me. There is nothing I will tell you." Asya stared at him defiantly.

Canton reached down and yanked the stool out from under her, forcing her to stand up. He smirked a foot away from her face, placing his hand on her breast over her blouse. She thrashed wildly, attempting to lunge towards him, the zip ties holding her back.

"You're a wild one, aren't you?" He opened his mouth and chomped his teeth together, taunting her as he withdrew his hand from her.

"You are a worthless coward. You want to have your way with me? Untie me if you are man enough."

"I'll have my way with you, you can be assured of that. Now tell me where Blackstone is. I know you have been helping him. Tell me and I will spare you. I give you my word."

"Your word means nothing."

"Oh, now why did you have to say a hurtful thing like that? You don't really know me. I think you have completely misjudged me, Asya. If you tell me where he is, you will be surprised at how much better things go for you.

You don't have to go through all this suffering for nothing. Sooner or later, Blackstone will be caught and all your sacrifice will have been for nothing. Tell me where he is. Go ahead, it's okay, I won't think any less of you," Canton said, trying to manipulate her.

"I do not care what you think of me or what you threaten to do to me. I told you I do not know where he is!"

"You have seen him recently, however, haven't you?"

"I will tell you nothing."

"That is really too bad. I was hoping to go easy on you, but you're not leaving me much choice." He placed his hand inside her upper thigh, causing her to thrash again.

"How are things going?" Canton was startled to hear Rostov's voice behind him, turning and seeing him standing across the room by the corridor.

"She's doing her best to put on a brave face. I'm finished for now. I'll be back tomorrow. I think she just needs some time to reconsider her situation and weigh her options."

"We do not have that much time. Soon it will be noticed she is missing. The longer we have her, the greater the risk," Rostov warned him.

"I will get what I need out of her. She just needs a little softening up, don't you, Ms. Tarhan?" he taunted her. "Make her stand for twenty-four hours. That will help speed the process along. Let your men know she is not to sit. I'm out of here," he told Rostov as he walked past him down the corridor towards his car.

Rostov walked over and picked up the stool from the floor, placing it back underneath her while looking at her directly in the eyes. "Do you want water?" he asked, gesturing with the plastic bottle he was holding.

Asya returned a fierce glare but took him up on his offer. "Yes, I will have some."

Rostov twisted open the cap and held the bottle up to Asya's mouth, allowing her to finish the bottle.

"If you need to use the toilet, let Alexi know. He will bring a bucket, release one of your hands and give you some privacy."

"Thank you," she told him.

He nodded his head, then turned and walked to the corridor, disappearing from sight. A moment later, Alexi, the tall blond Russian, returned, and hopping up on the closest table, took a seat as he stood watch over Asya.

Asya sat back down on the stool. She wasn't so much concerned about what awaited her as about not being able to help Michael when he would need it. Where was her mobile, her gun, her car? What was she going to do now? She was helpless, and no one knew where she was. How had she allowed herself to fall into such a trap? She had been foolish to let Canton lure her in so easily. She had underestimated how contemptible and cunning he was. Michael had warned her. Now all she could do was wait and hope that Canton would slip up somehow and she could seize the opportunity. She had no other choice.

Most Merciful Allah, I need Your help now Lord. I know they do not intend to let me live, but in the end, it is You who will decide my fate. I also know it was You who prevented Michael from taking his life, instead placing this great task before him. You brought the paths of our lives together once again for a reason I cannot see from where I am. You are all-knowing, Allah. All that I ask of You, my Lord, is to show me what it is I must do and when. It is in You that I put all my faith and trust. Give me the strength, Lord, to endure whatever it is that lies before me. Allahu Akbar. Asya prayed silently in the presence of her captor.

***

Michael had gone through two of his bottles of water and four of his sesame rings. Sitting on the unforgiving sidewalk for most of the day with nothing to do other than stare across the street, all the while trying to appear as if looking nowhere in particular, was very tiring. His body was beginning to ache substantially. He stood up every hour to stretch, but it didn't do much for his lower back. But despite all his discomfort, it was the perfect temperature, somewhere in the mid-seventies, on a sunny spring day under the shade of the giant elm. He saw that he had already managed to accumulate half a can of rial notes, even though he knew most of them were probably the equivalent of five or ten cents. Nonetheless, he was surprised at the commonplace generosity of Iranian people. He looked at his watch. It was 3:10 p.m. He had been out there for eight hours. He had known it was going to be a long day, but he had forgotten how tedious it was and how slow time passed on a static surveillance. Normally it would be in some room or the back of a van, with a partner to switch back and forth on every half hour in order to remain sharp and keep from getting fatigued. But in this case, Michael was going to have to gut it out all on his own out in the open for at least another five hours, he was guessing. He didn't expect Karbashi would be leaving work before 6:00 p.m. He knew the type of man he was from spending two and a half years observing him and learning as much as possible about him.

How ironic, Michael thought, that the operation in Athens had ended with Karbashi and him staring each other face-to-face, and now, years later, in a different country under different circumstances, they had begun this next chapter once again face-to-face with each other. He wondered if anything had registered with Karbashi when he had faced Michael through his windshield. Probably not, he guessed. After all, it was all these years later in Karbashi's own country, and Michael looked like an unshaven vagrant. It would have been the last thing to have crossed Karbashi's mind as he drove to his office at MOIS headquarters in Tehran. Michael recalled the last time they had met, under much different circumstances.

After the initial introduction to each other and dinner, Ali had continued to run into Karbashi at Friday evening prayers each week. When arriving at the mosque, Ali would acknowledge Karbashi with a nod and smile and wait for Karbashi to approach him after prayers. After their initial meeting and follow-on dinner, Karbashi had continued to ask him out for Friday night meals. In addition to sharing with Ali the various aspects of current life in Iran, he had also taken on the role as a mentor and older brother to him, explaining the facets of their religion, Ali having been raised as a secular Iranian most of his life. Ali in turn would tell Karbashi about what his life had been like in the United States, every once in a while, and always subtly, making mention of the occasional prejudice he had experienced by some ignorant Americans when they had learned he was Iranian. Michael had trained Ali to take it very slow, to be friendly but not too forward, allowing Karbashi to advance the relationship on his terms. Karbashi had also been very cautious, never asking Ali anything about his work at the embassy during the first few months. Karbashi had revealed that he was married with no children, that Allah hadn't blessed him and his wife with parenthood, but that they had still found joy in their lives. His wife, an accomplished pediatrician, worked as head of pediatrics in one of Tehran's main hospitals, the reason why he was in Athens unaccompanied.

When his, wife, Janet, and his daughter, Roxanne, finally arrived in Athens, Michael had to modify the direction of the operation so that Ali would have an explanation as to where he was disappearing to each Friday evening. After consultation with Harry and extensive discussion with Ali, it was decided to invite Karbashi over to Ali's apartment to introduce his wife and daughter. Ali had introduced Karbashi to Janet as a friend he had met through the small Iranian expatriate community in Athens. Karbashi didn't hesitate to let Janet know he worked in the consular section at the Iranian embassy, telling her if Ali ever wanted to show her and Roxanne his heritage, he could expedite visitors' visas for them. Michael remembered how much of a professional Karbashi had been, impressing and smoothing over Janet as a very social and interesting new friend of theirs. His impeccable English, spoken with an English rather than American accent, further added to Karbashi's allure. Any concerns about Ali and his family's comfort level had dissipated after the first visit. Ali's visit to the mosque for Friday evening prayers was something Janet had even encouraged, letting Ali know she thought it was a good idea he was exploring his spirituality.

Michael had been ecstatic at how well the two had hit it off. He could tell from how cautious Karbashi was in assessing Ali that he was a serious professional in his trade. The relationship nonetheless grew quickly and a bond was beginning to form between them. Ali had even started referring to Karbashi as Farzan, his first name, during debriefings with Michael. Michael could sense a connection was beginning to develop between the two of them. Ali had told him that, although he knew Karbashi had pursued the relationship purely for intelligence gathering reasons, he sensed Karbashi was developing true feelings of friendship. Michael, at least, had daily contact with Ali to monitor his mutual feelings for Karbashi, part of the normal human emotional response that often develops in any intelligence operation. It was always a challenge for an intelligence officer to keep the barrier of separation up of their emotions, while still trying to portray a level of sincerity to their asset. At the six-month mark there had still been no overt attempt by Karbashi to learn Ali's position at the US embassy, or ask him to provide any other type of information. Michael had begun to question whether Karbashi suspected Ali was a double-agent dangle, but why then had he continued with the relationship, even strengthening it as time went on? He had gone so far as to invite Ali, Janet and Roxanne to dinner multiple times at various restaurants and tavernas to show his appreciation for their hospitality to him. That wasn't a sign that he distrusted Ali. Why then was Karbashi spending so much time with Ali? What was he grooming him for?

Talking it over with Harry, Michael decided he would have Ali make an overt move to get a response from Karbashi. Ali was going to relate that his update for his security clearance was coming due, and that he was required to list all his foreign contacts. He had failed to let his boss know about their friendship, which had been established for close to six months, and now he faced a dilemma. It was taking a chance, possibly spooking Karbashi and pushing him away or perhaps drawing him in closer, but something had to be done to change what had become the status quo. Michael remembered that conversation between Ali and Karbashi at the Persian restaurant one evening. Ali had played his role perfectly, displaying how troubled he was about the decision he faced. He hadn't asked Karbashi for his advice on what to do but let slip that his boss, the colonel, needed him to complete his security questionnaire by the end of the week. After a long silence, Michael remembered hearing Karbashi's words over his ear-piece telling Ali that he didn't think it would be wise to mention him, explaining that it would make unnecessary trouble and possibly bring an end their friendship. Karbashi had asked Ali about referring to his boss as the colonel, at which time Ali revealed that he worked for the Defense Attaché's Office in a clerical support role. Karbashi hadn't reacted overtly at Ali's disclosure other than reemphasizing that disclosing him on his security clearance wouldn't be a good idea. That was when Michael knew that Karbashi had crossed the Rubicon and there was no going back.

Yet for some reason, despite Ali not bringing up the topic again, the months rolled by with Karbashi never asking anything of Ali. Other than a one-week trip back to Tehran to visit his wife, Karbashi continued his relationship with Ali and his family as if nothing had changed. On weekends, they had traveled to various of the ancient Greek ruins, even going to the Plain of Marathon twenty-six miles outside of Athens, where the Greeks had defeated the much larger invading Persian forces of King Darius the Great in 490 B.C. After another six months had passed, bringing the friendship to the one-year mark, Karbashi broke the news to Ali that his time in Athens was going to be up in six months and that he would be transferring back to Iran. He told Ali he hoped they could somehow remain friends. Michael didn't know what to make of Karbashi's lack of any attempt to ask Ali for any information. He didn't have any concerns that Ali was not being forthright about everything that had transpired with Karbashi. He trusted Ali, and along with the CIA-required polygraphs of assets every three months, he was certain that there was nothing that was eluding him concerning Karbashi's unexplainable behavior towards Ali. Michael was almost beginning to wonder if Karbashi's true intentions were only to have a genuine friendship with Ali. Considering all possibilities, perhaps the fact that they had met in a mosque somehow prevented Karbashi from going after Ali as an intelligence source. Maybe there was something Michael wasn't seeing. That was when it happened.

It was a Friday in early May when Ali and Karbashi were visiting their favorite Persian restaurant after evening prayers. After finishing their meal and discussing the imam's sermon while drinking tea, Karbashi asked something that caused Ali to react with genuine surprise. It was the exchange that Michael had been awaiting for over a year.

"Ali, you know you have become a good friend to me over the past year. I have grown close to you and your family, and I cherish our friendship. I have something to tell you about myself and a favor I would like to ask of you. I had told you that I work in the consular section at the Iranian embassy. That is the cover position I use to conceal my true position. I actually work for the MOIS, which is my country's intelligence service. I did not want to reveal this to you because I did not want it to come between us and possibly ruin our friendship. Unfortunately, however, due to circumstances that are beyond my control, I now need to ask a favor of you to help me as it relates to my position," Karbashi said, leveling with Ali and watching for his reaction.

Ali sat in silence for several moments. His reaction wasn't because he hadn't prepared for this occasion, but rather because he had grown so accustomed to

Karbashi playing the role of a friend rather than the intelligence officer Ali had been trained to anticipate. Finally regaining his composure, Ali replied, "An intelligence officer. Wow, Farzan, I don't know what to say. Why did you think telling me that would ruin our friendship?"

"Because, Ali, you would suspect me of being your friend only to use you for the purpose of getting you to provide me information about your government." Karbashi sounded sincere in his answer.

"So, what are you doing now, asking me for a favor?" Ali asked, with a hint of understandable wariness in his tone.

"Ali, all this time we have been friends, I have never asked you to provide me any information. Neither am I asking you now. The favor I need to ask of you is to arrange a meeting for me with your boss, the defense attaché."

"What, are you joking, Farzan? The defense attaché? After you just told me you are an Iranian intelligence officer? I would be arrested and charged with espionage for doing something like that." Ali's months of training with Michael in various scenarios started coming back to him.

"I know it sounds crazy, Ali, but I have legitimate reasons for requesting this. Believe me when I say to you, it is not for any nefarious reasons against your country. I have been asked by my director to explore any possibilities of establishing a back channel to your government regarding our nuclear program and the sanctions your country has imposed against us. I am close to him. He knows I have met you and have established a genuine friendship. Unlike the IRGC and our current president, who would rather drive our country into the ground economically than explore the possibility of any negotiations, my director is hoping that the establishment of an unofficial line of communication would be invaluable in preventing any misunderstandings that could allow the tense situation between our two countries to spiral out of control," Karbashi explained.

"Yes, that does sound crazy, Farzan. You expect me to just go up to my boss and tell him I have this good friend who just happens to work for Iranian intelligence, and he would like to meet you to discuss their nuclear program? If he didn't have the embassy security officer arrest me immediately, he would probably have me sent somewhere for a psychological evaluation."

"You would not have to tell him I was your friend. You could tell him that I was just an acquaintance from the mosque, and somehow I learned you worked at the American embassy and I approached you with this unusual request."

"It certainly is an unusual request. I don't know what to say, Farzan." Ali fell into his role that he had practiced over and over during the months training with Michael.

"I know, I know, my friend. I am sorry I have thrust this upon you all of a sudden. I only ask because I have trust in you, and I do it for the concern of my country, and what used to be your country at one time. Please give this some consideration."

Ali remained silent for several moments, turning his gaze from Karbashi the large glass windows at the front of the restaurant. Finally, he turned back to his friend, or the man he had thought was his friend, and replied, "I am going to have to think about this, Farzan. Needless to say, I am completely taken by surprise at your request."

"I understand, Ali, that is all I ask."

"We better call it an evening. I don't know what more normal conversation we can have after what we just discussed."

"Yes, yes, I agree. I do not think either of us would have much to talk about on such trivial topics as Alexander the Great's lasting influence on Persia," Karbashi said, attempting to bring some levity back to their conversation. "Let me get the check, Ali. The meal is on me this evening."

"Thanks, Farzan. I'll need some time to digest—that is, come to terms with—all this. Let's plan on talking about this again next Friday after prayers."

"Thank you, Ali, for not getting up and walking out. I am truly grateful."

"Don't be too grateful until I give you my answer," Ali finished, playing his part for the evening and being noncommittal, just as Michael had trained him.

The debrief of Ali after that meeting was something Michael vividly remembered to this day. The implications of what Karbashi had asked for went far beyond any of Michael's most ambitious plans of someday being able to turn Karbashi. He had requested a separate undeclared line of communication between at least some elements within the Iranian government and the United States. On the face of it, this could be a treasure trove of information regarding Iran's nuclear program and also give the President of the United States some additional options in dealing with Iran. It could also be a masterful ploy by Karbashi as some sort of misdirection or influence operation, or a plot to gain insight into possible future US actions against Iran. It was a great opportunity, but Michael would have to exercise extreme caution playing chess against Karbashi. He had already proven himself an adept professional against the Israelis. Despite any uncertainties about the authenticity of Karbashi's request, Michael was well aware of what it meant if it was genuine. He would have to see where it led.

Michael had sat down with Harry and Canton, whom Harry had assigned as the alternate case agent, to discuss Karbashi's request and plan strategy on how to proceed. Michael and Harry had both agreed that under the circumstances, they would have to move forward as if Karbashi's request was legitimate. Ali, who had personal insight into Karbashi's persona, having spent hundreds of hours with him over the past year, felt in his gut that Karbashi was being sincere, even knowing from Michael how skillful an intelligence officer he was. Ali believed that unless Karbashi was some sort of sociopath capable of completely disguising his true self and masterfully playing an alternate personality, what he had asked of him seemed genuine. Canton, on the other hand, disagreed with their assessment, citing how Karbashi had played the Israeli Air Force colonel so well just a few years ago and insisting he was doing the same thing with them now. He even went so far as to suggest Michael not waste any more of everyone's time and end the operation. Other than briefly giving Canton the courtesy of listening to him as he made readily apparent his disdain for doing any more work than was necessary, Harry and Michael continued on with their planning. It was decided from the onset they would not get Colonel Richards, the defense attaché, involved. Defense attachés, even though technically serving as the Defense Intelligence Agency's eyes and ears for other countries' military capabilities, were military officers given only cursory training in conducting espionage. Their role was more that of liaison with the host country's military, trying to establish relationships with the senior leadership and see what they could pick up. If it was a ploy on Karbashi's part, they didn't want the defense attaché becoming a target of the MOIS. If it was legitimate, a back-door line of communication with the MOIS was the CIA's responsibility to manage on behalf of the President, with the DCI briefing him directly. They would have someone else stand in for Colonel Richards.

It was decided by Harry that it would be Michael. Ali would be instructed to tell Karbashi during their next meeting that he had told his boss about the request, and that Colonel Richards had agreed to meet with him. Ali wouldn't say anything at that time about Michael meeting with him, instead counting on the element of surprise to see how Karbashi would react when it turned out it was Michael rather than Richards. Michael would cover for Ali, telling Karbashi that the switch had been sprung on Ali unknowingly, the colonel having come to the CIA regarding his offer to meet. Of course, no mention would be made of Ali knowing Michael prior to the introduction, other than as a familiar passing face within the hallways of the embassy. They would allow Karbashi to determine the location for the meeting, not wanting to appear too assertive and possibly spook him if Ali came back with terms. It was a bold plan, but if Karbashi's request was on the up-and-up, then he would more than likely feel more comfortable dealing with another professional intelligence officer. If it was a ploy, it would soon become apparent with Karbashi distancing himself from Michael and Ali, which would bring the operation to an end on its own.

The following Friday after evening prayers, Ali approached Karbashi. Karbashi was his usual friendly self, but Ali had noticed a slight trace of unease about him that he hadn't noticed in the past.

"*Salaam*, brother," Ali greeted him.

"*Salaam*, Ali. How are you, my friend? I hope you had a pleasant week," Karbashi responded.

"I did, although it was a bit anxious. I'm sure you understand why."

"Yes, yes, I can imagine, with what I asked of you. It was anxious for me also. Do you have time for tea or something to eat while we discuss things?" Karbashi asked.

"That sounds good. Let's find a place with a little bit of privacy," Ali told him.

It was a pleasant evening, so they decided to go to a small taverna with rooftop seating in the area of the Plaka, located below the ruins of the Acropolis. The waiter had just seated them at their small table, bringing them water, silverware and menus, then leaving them to decide on their choice of food. It was dusk and the lights along the perimeter walls of the Acropolis made for a magnificent view from their location. It was still relatively early for most Greeks, who normally ate dinner closer to 9:00 p.m., especially on weekends, but a variety of tourists filled some of the tables, the Plaka being one of the main tourist areas in the ancient section of Athens. Karbashi sat silently, waiting for Ali to initiate the conversation.

"I thought about the favor you asked of me for several days. I went back and forth in my head on whether I should take the enormous risk and tell my boss that an undeclared foreign contact of mine who happens to work in the Iranian embassy and just revealed to me after a year of knowing him that he is an Iranian intelligence officer would like to meet him to discuss the Iranian nuclear program. I thought about the possibility of being court-martialed and spending the next several years in a military prison. I also thought about what it could mean if this could help bring some type of resolution to this serious issue between our countries, and maybe be a first small step in eventually normalizing relations. It may not happen in our lifetimes, but maybe in the lifetime of my daughter and the younger generations in both our countries. So after much thought and soul searching, I decided I would approach my boss, Colonel Richards, the defense attaché. I went into his office on Wednesday and told him that I had known you as an acquaintance from prayers at the mosque and that you had approached me. I did not say anything about the fact that we have been good friends for over a year, telling him that you had assumed I worked at the US or Canadian embassy because you could not identify me as an Iranian citizen ever having traveled to or from Iran. I told him you identified yourself as working for the Iranian embassy without saying specifically in what section, and I relayed your request to meet with him to talk about establishing a line of communication. As you can imagine, at first, he looked at me in bewilderment, even thinking I was playing some sort of joke on him, but I persisted and he eventually realized I was serious. Surprisingly, he did not even question me on my contact with you. I gave him your name and left it up to him to check out who you were. This morning, he called me into his office and told me he would be interested in meeting with you just to see what you had to say but would not make any further commitment. That is what he asked me to relay to you," Ali said, finishing his lengthy explanation.

"Oh, that is very good to hear, Ali. Did he say where or when he wanted to meet?"

"No, he did not. I am guessing he is waiting to hear what you propose."

"I see. Obviously, it would have to be somewhere discreet. Perhaps we can meet out in Glyfada some evening," Karbashi suggested, referring to the newer upscale suburb of Athens ten miles south of the center along the seashore.

"Name the time and place, and I will let him know. I told him I would be going to prayers this evening and might be seeing you. I can tell him tomorrow."

"There is an outdoor coffee shop called Flocafe, as soon as you turn off Posidonos Boulevard going into the downtown area of Glyfada. It is on a corner of a park across the street from a taxi stand by the main church, which is called Saint Constantine and Helen. If he can meet Monday evening at 9:00 p.m. that would be wonderful. There is less public out on Monday evenings. Does that work for you, Ali?" Karbashi asked being considerate of his friend.

"That is fine with me, Farzan. I am not familiar with Glyfada, but I am sure I can find it from how you described it. I can meet you out there and have the colonel join us on his own. I would not feel comfortable accompanying him there unless he orders me to, especially under these circumstances. I will suggest to him that it will allow the option for me to leave early after introductions are made, so that the two of you can be left alone to discuss matters that I do not need to know about," Ali explained, as Michael had instructed him to do.

"That is good you understand that, Ali. The topics of discussion are something of which both your government and mine will want to limit knowledge to a very select few individuals at the highest levels. I will be forever grateful, however, for the risk you took upon your and your family's future in agreeing to arrange this meeting, my good friend."

"Okay, then. I will tell him tomorrow and call you as soon as I get an answer from him."

"Thank you again, Ali, for what you have done. It took great courage to do so. I hope our efforts may help in some small way to eventually bring about the normalization of relations between our two countries, as you said." Karbashi ended the conversation as the waiter returned to take their order.

After Michael had debriefed Ali later that night, he called Harry and Canton and asked them to meet him at the embassy the next morning at 9:00 a.m., over Canton's grumbling about it being a Saturday. When they met the next morning, Michael briefed them about the arrangements Karbashi had suggested for the Monday evening meeting. Michael had already been out to Glyfada that morning and did a reconnaissance of the Flocafe and the surrounding neighborhood. Based upon the layout of the area, being in the downtown retail and restaurant district of Glyfada across from the beach, Michael decided that Ali would arrive first and meet Karbashi at 9:00 p.m. Canton and Michael would already be sitting in place by 8:30 at a location from which they could observe Karbashi and Ali arrive. They would monitor the area for any possible surveillance for five minutes, then Michael, wearing an encrypted transmitter, would exit the vehicle to join Karbashi and Ali, while Canton remained in the car and monitored the meet. Ali would act surprised when Michael showed up rather than his boss, Colonel Richards. Michael would take it from there and introduce himself to Karbashi, telling him Colonel Richards had come to the CIA, unbeknownst to Ali, because he felt he wasn't in a position to deal with this situation. Michael would acknowledge Ali as having seen him in the hallways of the embassy, to which Ali would reciprocate. Michael believed after the initial surprise at the unexpected change of individuals he was meeting passed, Karbashi would actually feel more comfortable dealing with another intelligence officer rather than a military man. Harry had agreed with the plan, confirming both Michael and Canton would be armed, not taking anything for granted meeting with an operative from a hostile foreign intelligence agency.

On Monday evening at 6:00 p.m., Ali, Michael and Canton, with Harry sitting in, met in Michael's office to go over the plan one last time before deploying for the meet. Michael told Ali he and Canton would be prepositioned in the area by 8:30 p.m. and instructed him to arrive ten minutes early at 8:50 p.m., letting him know he would join them approximately five minutes after Karbashi had arrived. In case Karbashi was already there by the time Ali showed up, Michael would make his appearance at 9:00 p.m.

Canton and Michael headed out from the embassy at 7:30 p.m. with Canton at the wheel, leaving ample time to drive the twelve miles, which normally took just over half an hour without traffic. Ali had followed shortly afterwards at 8:00 p.m. When Michael and Canton arrived in Glyfada at 8:15 p.m., they drove around the block, looking for a good location to park the car that gave them a clear view of the Flocafe but still afforded them enough distance and cover. They finally settled on street parking behind the line of taxis that curled around the corner from the taxi stand across the street from the café. Canton parallel-parked their blue compact Fiat Punto about sixty yards down the street, and they settled in to observe the café and surrounding area until Ali and Karbashi showed up. At 8:50 p.m. they saw Ali arrive just as scheduled. He took a seat at an open table under the cover of an umbrella in the corner of the café's outdoor patio, next to several palm trees. As they sat waiting for Karbashi to show, Canton abruptly declared, "I need to use the toilet."

"Right now?" Michael asked in disbelief.

"Sorry, dude, nature's calling. I gotta go."

"You didn't bring an empty bottle? You're on a surveillance, for Pete's sake."

"A bottle's not going cut it, unless you have a dogie bag on you."

"Jesus, Jonathan, of all times to have to take a dump."

"Hey, man, I don't have any control over my bowels. Something's been bothering my gut the past couple of days and it's not pretty. When I have to go, I have to go. I'm sure I can find a place nearby. Just hang on until I get back. I'll be quick."

"Well, get going, then. Hurry!" Michael replied irritably.

"Be right back," Canton told him as he exited the car and headed down the street in the opposite direction of the café. Several yards back from their vehicle, he stopped in front of a clothing store that had closed for the day. He stood discreetly in the shadows behind one of the wide marble columns in front of the store, observing the café through a small ten power monocular cupped in his right hand. A few moments later, he saw what he had been waiting for as Karbashi arrived at Ali's table. As Ali stood to great him with a handshake, Canton reached into his pocket and pulled out a recently purchased clean mobile phone, dialing a number from memory. When the other end picked up, he heard "yes" in a heavy accent.

"He's arrived, that's him," Canton responded.

"You are certain?" the voice on the other end asked.

"Yes, I know what he looks like. It's him. We're parked about sixty meters down the street across the line of taxis. Do you know where I'm referring to?"

"Yes, I can see the area."

"I'm not in the car, it's only his handler. I'll stay back."

"We are moving now from the opposite side across the park." Canton heard the other end go silent, ending the call. He continued gazing through his monocular, observing what was about to take place.

Michael looked at his watch. It was 9:05 p.m. What was taking Canton so long? He looked at the center console and saw that Canton had left the monitor and ear-piece for the transmitter Michael was wearing. *Great*, Michael thought, *he can't even hear me on whatever toilet he's sitting on right now. Okay, no big deal, it's just a few minutes more.* He would apologize for being late because of traffic. *Don't let Canton aggravate you. A case of diarrhea is the least of what he deserves for his attitude.* Michael kept his eyes on Karbashi and Ali, watching them converse as they waited for him to make his appearance. At first, he didn't give much attention to the two men who had walked up the three stairs from the sidewalk onto the café's patio, pausing next to Karbashi and Ali's table. It looked like they might have been waiting for a waiter to show them a table, until Michael noticed they were facing Ali and Karbashi, having some type of conversation with them. *Who are these clowns? Maybe just some small talk*, Michael thought.

At sixty meters away, Michael had a clear view of all four individuals at the table, but it was difficult to make out a lot of detail. He reached into his backpack on the floor between his legs and pulled out a small pair of binoculars, putting them up to his eyes for a closer look at the situation with the two new arrivals. With their backs to him, Michael couldn't see their faces, but when he took a look at Ali and Karbashi, he realized something wasn't right. Both their faces displayed looks of concern. Michael focused back in on the two strangers, but with their backs towards him, all he could see was their jackets, one of them with both hands in his pockets and the other one holding a pistol discreetly by his side. "Shit!" Michael said aloud. *Cops?* He tried to make sense of the situation. Why would they have attracted the attention of cops? *No, they weren't cops.* Worse yet, could it be EYP, the Greek intel service? *That would make more sense*, he thought. *Maybe they've had Karbashi under surveillance for some reason and are rolling him up. That doesn't make sense either. EYP's never been known to do something like that. What the heck is going on?* His inclination was to bolt out of the car and run over there, but he knew that would be a rash move, not knowing if it was the police or Greek intelligence. The last thing he needed was to be taken into custody. *How would that look?* "American CIA

Officer Arrested by Greek Police" on the front page of every Greek newspaper wasn't something good for an intelligence officer's career. Michael knew he had to be patient, not impulsive. He would sit tight and observe the situation as it developed. Where the hell was Canton?

What happened next ratcheted Michael's adrenaline level up a notch. He saw Ali and Karbashi stand from their table and walk towards the two men, a look of alarm on both their faces. Michael could see Ali turning his head in every direction, obviously searching for him. Grabbing the car keys from the ignition, Michael jumped out of the car and locked the doors before breaking into a jog towards the café. He could see Ali and Karbashi being led by the two men across the street towards the park. When Michael reached the café, he spotted the four of them cutting diagonally through the park. Michael chased after them, coming up behind them in the dim light from the sidewalk lamps in the park. What was he going to do? If they were cops, would he try to bluff his way somehow? Better to use his Greek, he thought, even with his American accent. "*Parakalo.* Hey! *Parakalo!*" Michael yelled out, meaning "excuse me," as he closed the distance to them.

The one on the right turned towards Michael and yelled, "*Astinomia,*" identifying himself as police.

"They're not police," Michael heard Ali yell as the man raised his right hand, which held a handgun towards Michael. Reacting from instinct, Michael reached to his right side and drew the Sig Sauer P229 9mm from his concealment holster, squeezing the trigger twice and firing two rounds at his target, who had just brought Michael in his sights, but a millisecond too slow. The sharp cracks of the two gunshots were muffled by the noise from the nearby traffic on Posidonos Boulevard, but for the five of them in the park, it sounded like lightning had struck right in front of them. Both of Michael's rounds met their mark. As the first assailant fell to the ground, his partner turned towards Michael and attempted to draw his gun. He was tragically too slow. As he raised his gun towards him, Michael redirected his aim and discharged two more rounds at the second assailant, bringing him to the ground an instant later.

Karbashi, Ali and Michael looked at each other, temporarily frozen in a state of shock, until Michael's brain finally kicked back into gear. Looking at Karbashi straight in the face, Michael exclaimed, "Go!" He grabbed Ali by his back and pushed him, leading him out of the park back in the direction of the car. He fought the desire to run, not wanting to draw any attention to them from anyone in the area who had heard the rapport of the four gunshots. They made their way past the café, noticing some people looking around, trying to determine where the commotion had come from. As they walked down the sidewalk across from the line of taxis towards the car, Michael saw Canton waiting outside the car on the sidewalk.

As they reached the car, Canton asked, "What happened?"

Michael hit the unlock on the key fob, responding, "Just get in the car. Ali, sit in the front."

When the three of them were in, Michael started the car and unhurriedly pulled out of their parking spot. He drove to the corner across from the Flocafe and turned right, heading away from the park, where he could see a small group of bystanders had started to gather. Making a left at the next corner, he drove one block, then made a right, putting them onto Posidonos Boulevard, heading back to Athens.

"Where's your car parked?" Michael asked Ali.

"It's three blocks from the café, parked on the street in a residential neighborhood with a bunch of multistory apartment buildings," Ali answered, keeping his responses short, just waiting for Michael to talk.

"Okay, that's good. Far enough away and inconspicuous. What happened?"

"I'm not exactly sure. I showed up there at eight fifty and took a table in the corner on the patio. A few minutes later, Karbashi showed up and sat down. We were just talking, and the two men walked up and addressed Karbashi like they knew him, using his name and telling us both not to move our hands. They both had guns. We could see them. They told Karbashi he had to come with them for some questioning and if he didn't do exactly as he was told, they would shoot him on the spot. They told me to get up also and come with them, so we both got up and did what they told us. We were walking through the park and you showed up. You know the rest," Ali blurted out, struggling to remain calm.

"Why did you shout to me they weren't police? How did they identify themselves?" Michael asked.

"They didn't identify themselves. They spoke in English to us with heavy accents, but they were definitely not Greeks."

"If they weren't Greeks, who were they?"

"Their accent sounded more Arabic, maybe even Jewish," Ali explained.

"You're sure?"

"I'm not sure of anything, Michael. I'm still trying to process everything."

Michael kept silent for a moment, trying to think as he drove. *They weren't Greeks? Who the hell were they, then? Israelis? What the heck happened? Okay,*

keep calm, keep calm. Think this through. Keep calm? I just shot two people.
Michael's mind was racing at warp speed as he tried to keep his thoughts under
control.

"Ah, what the hell's going on, and what were those four gunshots I heard?"
Canton finally let out from the backseat.

"You heard what Ali just said. Those four gunshots you heard were me
firing at those two guys who drew down on me," Michael told Canton.

"Holy shit! You offed two guys? You are so hosed, man," Canton remarked.

"Did you not hear what I just told you? They both drew down on me.
Where the hell were you?"

"I just got back to the car when I heard the four gunshots. Then you two
showed up a minute later. Where's Karbashi?"

"I don't know. He split when we did," Michael told him, then pulled out his
mobile phone and dialed Harry. When his boss answered, he said, "You at the
office?"

"Yep, waiting to hear how your evening went," Harry answered.

"Be there shortly," Michael responded.

"Okay, see you soon."

When they arrived back at the embassy thirty minutes later, Michael briefed
Harry on what had transpired, then had Ali debrief them again on everything
he had done from when he'd left the embassy until the encounter with the two
strangers at the café. Harry asked Canton what he had observed, upon which
Canton advised about his digestive issues. The three of them stared at Harry in
silence as he processed everything.

"Did anyone see you in the park?" Harry asked.

"I don't know, Harry. We didn't see anyone when we walked out, but I can't
say for sure," Michael told him.

"Okay, Jonathan, you drive Ali home. Ali, try to be calm and act normal
around your wife and daughter. Absolutely no contact with Karbashi. If he
calls, don't answer. Let Michael know. We'll worry about picking up your car
tomorrow. Got that? Can you make it into work on public transportation?"

"Yes, Mr. Barso, I can manage that." Ali replied.

"Good. Mike, I need you to sit down right now and put everything down
in an after-action report. I'm going to get on the line with Langley and brief the
DDO," Harry told him, referring to the Deputy Director of Operations.

Michael wrote his report and cabled it to CIA headquarters. The following day, things had been buzzing at Athens Station, to say the least. After extensive communications with Langley, Harry had briefed Colonel Richards about Ali's situation without going into details about the operation and asked him to assist with arrangements in having Ali and his family transferred stateside at the earliest possible time, advising him that the DDO would be personally contacting the deputy director at the Defense Intelligence Agency to explain the situation and expedite Ali's transfer. Harry had also told Michael to close down the operation and make preparations for an emergency transfer back to Langley within a week. The station would arrange to have his household goods packed and shipped back to the US. In the meantime, he was to maintain a low profile and tie up any loose ends in Greece, including however he needed to deal with his relationship with Eva.

That last week had been the most stressful and chaotic period in Michael's life. Besides having to come up with a somewhat believable excuse as to why an economics attaché suddenly had to transfer back to the United States, he had to reassure Eva that he still wanted her to remain in his life and he would do whatever was necessary to make sure that happened. Michael had to also say his goodbyes to Ali. It was a difficult experience for both of them. Although Ali was Michael's asset and Michael was Ali's handler, a tight bond had formed between them. Ali had grown to respect Michael's expertise and appreciated his sincerity in treating him with the respect of an equal rather than as the subordinate he was. Although it wasn't friendship in the normal sense of the word, in many ways, the level of trust between the two of them exceeded that between even close friends.

What was hardest, however, was his last days with Harry. Two days after the Greek newspapers and newscasts had reported the mysterious robbery and murder of two foreign tourists in Glyfada, Harry had learned through his sources in the Greek government what they already had suspected—the two dead Israelis were Mossad. Harry and Michael had reviewed every aspect of the operation, searching for any possibilities of how the meet might have been compromised on their end, but came up empty. They considered the possibility of the compromise being on Karbashi's side, but that didn't make sense either. If the Israelis had been surveilling Karbashi to snatch him, why would they have done so during a secret meeting in Glyfada and not at his residence, where he was most vulnerable and there was the least amount of risk for them? They had ample enough reason to pick him up in retaliation for what he had done to them in Belgium with their colonel, but not the way it had gone down. There was a compromise somewhere else. The more they went over everything that had happened that evening, the more they kept coming back to Canton's coincidental absence at the time of the disastrous incident. There was nothing definitive pointing towards Canton, but both Harry and Michael kept coming back to the same conclusion. The question was, why would Canton do such a thing? Had he been compromised by Mossad somehow? Without any proof other than the circumstantial evidence of Canton's absence and their knowledge of his character, they had nothing linking him to the compromise. Yet, they both knew deep inside he was somehow involved.

Harry and Michael said their final goodbyes one last time at the Galaxy rooftop bar at the Hilton. Even after Michael had transferred back to Langley, Harry had continued being his biggest defender, insisting he had taken the only reasonable action he had available in shooting the two Mossad agents who had drawn their weapons on him. That hadn't been enough in countering the CIA's inspector general's investigation, which concluded that Michael had exercised poor judgment under the circumstances. It was the beginning of the twelve-year chapter in Michael's life that had concluded with his attempt to take his own life in his apartment a little over a week ago.

Michael's thoughts were drawn back to the soreness that was emanating throughout his body. With an exhaustive effort, he uncrossed his legs and slowly pushed himself up, his back against the side of the building, to keep him from falling as he attempted to get the circulation going in his legs. It had gone beyond extreme discomfort to pain now. He leaned over, supporting himself with his hands on his knees, stretching out his back. Another few hours and he wasn't certain if he would be physically capable of popping up and getting on his Vespa, even if he did manage to spot Karbashi leaving. He hoped his aging body could hold out for just a few more hours.

Chapter 23

Hamed had spent the day at home with Laleh and Tahmin. It had been a restless night for all of them after having buried Reza yesterday. Tahmin had asked to come and sleep with Hamed and Laleh, something he hadn't done since he had been a little child, when Reza was still only an infant sleeping in his crib next to their bed. Hamed had slept on and off throughout the night, being awakened by Tahmin crying in his sleep, giving him pause from his own nightmares of seeing Reza running out into the street and being struck by a car and his little body being flung in the air. Hamed had quietly gotten out of bed before it was light, going into the living room and kneeling down on the carpet, wanting to pray to Allah, but having come up empty when he searched for something to say. He had kneeled with his forehead against the floor, remaining in that position until the light from outside had finally come in through the windows, drawing him out of the semiconscious trance he had fallen into. Laleh had come into the living room and kneeled down next to him, breaking into a quiet sob. He had placed his arm around her, trying to console her as another round of sorrow poured out of her, knowing she would never again see their little Reza come running out of his room in the morning, bright-eyed and excited to start his day. They had allowed Tahmin to remain home from school for a few days, knowing he would need some time before he would be ready to return.

Laleh had prepared breakfast for the three of them, consisting of some flatbread, goat cheese, and apricot marmalade. They had spent the day inside their home mostly in silence, trying to come to terms, each in their own way, with the cataclysmic shift that had just occurred to their lives. At one point late in the afternoon, Tahmin had come to Hamed, who was sitting in the living room, with a question he wasn't prepared to answer in any way that brought consolation to his nine-year-old son.

"Baba, why did Allah take Reza from us? Did any of us do something to anger Him?"

Hamed had been taken off guard by the simple innocence of Tahmin's question. As he sat there searching for an answer that would make some sense to his young child, he recalled his childhood, when his father had been taken from their family as a result of the brutality that had been inflicted on him by the Shah's secret police. He remembered what he had done to the general who had been regularly raping his mother, the rage he had felt when he had stuck the knife blade in the stomach of his mother's rapist. He thought about all the men he had inflicted pain on, in the furtherance of his duties. How could he truthfully answer Tahmin when he wasn't certain himself Allah hadn't considered his sins when deciding Reza's fate? One or two seconds' difference by Allah when Reza had chased after the ball into the street could have had an entirely different outcome. He looked at Tahmin's tender face staring at him, waiting for an answer.

"My sweet child, Allah did not take Reza from us because of anything any of us did. Allah does not punish those who obey His word and keep Him in their heart in such a way. Allah is good and full of light, but there is also evil in the world that fills men's hearts with darkness that allows them to do bad things," Hamed tried to explain to his young son.

"But what about the man who killed Reza? Will Allah punish him?" Tahmin asked.

"He will be punished for his sins, just as all of us are punished one way or another for each of our sins. It is for Allah to decide how and when each of us have to answer for all the times we have not followed His ways."

"Will He punish me for all the times I don't listen to what Maman tells me to do?"

"No, my child, I believe she punishes you enough with her wooden spoon, unless you would like Allah to add to that." Hamed managed to give him a faint grin.

"No! Maman's is enough! Do you punish bad people since you are a policeman, Baba?"

Hamed hesitated with his answer. Would he lie to his young child, asking such a straightforward question, or attempt to bend the truth for his innocent young mind to understand without making himself to seem like some kind of monster?

"Sometimes, Tahmin, I have to inflict pain to bad men so that they tell me the truth about the bad things they have done."

"Like what kind of bad things, Baba?"

Again, Hamed hesitated, trying to think how to respond to Tahmin's simple question. Most of the men he had inflicted pain on hadn't necessarily done any wrong according to what the Prophet Muhammad had written in the Holy Quran as Allah's wishes; rather, they were considered enemies of the Islamic Republic, a threat to both the political and religious leadership of their country. He was doing his duty in protecting all of them, his fellow countrymen, his family, against those intending to do them harm. But what about Ali Shiravi? Was he intending them harm? Was he an enemy? He worked for the American government, after all, a declared enemy of the Islamic Republic. Hamed was again doing his duty, obtaining the truth from Shiravi, whatever the cost might be. He hadn't yet inflicted any physical pain on Shiravi, however. But did he have the truth?

"Baba, are you going to tell me what kind of bad things?" Tahmin interrupted Hamed's thoughts.

"Things that a little man like you does not need to hear about just yet. When you become old enough to understand, I will explain those things to you."

"Well, how did they become bad men, Baba? Did they not listen to their maman and baba when they were young?"

"I suppose some did not, Tahmin, but most of them had some decisions to make during their life, whether to listen to Allah and choose the right way or to listen to Sheytaan and choose the wrong way." Hamed tried to keep things simple.

"How do you know if it is Allah you are listening to or Sheytaan?"

"You have so many questions. Well, if it is Allah you are listening to, He will never tell you to do anything that would hurt another person who was not trying to hurt you. Sheytaan, on the other hand, would try to give you many reasons that person deserved to be hurt. Allah would tell you to help others who are in need, even if it brings you difficulty. Sheytaan would never tell you to do that. Sheytaan would tell you to look after yourself first and make sure you get as much as you can from others, even if you end up hurting them. Allah would never say such a thing."

"But how do you hear what Allah and Sheytaan are telling you to do?" Tahmin came back with a direct question to Hamed's complicated answer.

"Hmm. You hear them in your heart. Do you know the feeling you have when you know you have done something good, like when you found that man's wallet who had lost it and brought it home to us? He was so grateful it had been found by an honest person because it had all his money that he needed to buy food for his family. You know you did a good thing, and you felt good about that. Do you also remember how terrible you felt after you pushed Reza and he hurt his arm, because you were angry at him that he broke your toy? That is how you know you have done something wrong and it was not Allah talking to you." Hamed attempted to keep it at his level.

"Have you always listened to Allah, Baba?" his nine-year-old son was relentless with his questions.

"No, my son, I have not."

"Why not?"

"I suppose it is because when you do not listen to Allah and do small bad things, it becomes easier the next time to do more bad things. Then after that, it becomes easier yet, until doing bad things doesn't even bother you anymore. That just happens as you get older and more bad things happen to you in this world. You get so hurt and angry, you forget to listen to Allah's voice, and before you realize it, you have forgotten what Allah's voice even sounds like."

"But then do you still get to go to paradise to be with Allah if you get older and do not listen to His voice?"

"I think it depends, Tahmin. Allah can see into all our hearts. He knows it is difficult in this life to always be able to hear him and do the right thing. If there is light in a person's heart and they know the times they have not obeyed Allah and are truly sorry, I believe He will forgive them and allow them to be with Him in paradise when they leave this world. But, if all Allah sees is darkness in a person's heart, then He knows that person does not want to be in His presence, so He will leave them to be in their darkness, away from his light."

"Where do they go if they are not in paradise with Allah?"

"I don't know, my child. Only Allah knows those things, but if it is not with Him, it must not be a nice place."

"I hope Reza is with Allah. I am going to miss him, but if I know he is in a nice place with Allah, then I will not feel as bad," Tahmin said sorrowfully.

"Do not be sad, my child. Your brother is with Allah in paradise. He is so happy and full of joy, more than you can ever imagine. You will see him again someday when it is your time to join him in paradise."

"When will it be my time to go and be with Allah?"

"Only Allah knows that, Tahmin. Until then, He wants you to grow up and live your life in the way the Holy Prophet has taught us, loving and showing kindness to others no matter what bad things may happen to us in life."

"I will try, Baba. It makes me happy to know Reza is with Allah. I hope all of us will be together with Reza someday. That will make Maman feel happy again."

"Maman will be happy again someday. She just needs some time for her heart to heal. We need to be extra kind to her and help her heal. Can you do that?"

"Yes, Baba, I will do that. I will always listen to her and do what she tells me."

"I know you will. I am so proud of you. You will grow up to be a brave and wise man someday."

"Thank you, Baba, for making me feel better. I love you."

"I love you too. I will always love you, my child. Never forget that." Hamed pulled Tahmin close to him and hugged him, kissing him on his forehead. "Are you ready to go back to school yet, or do you want to stay home a little while longer?"

"Mmm, I think I want to go back to school. I want to be with my friends so I am not sad all the time."

"Okay. Go tell Maman you want to go back to school so she can get your things ready for tomorrow. Give her a big hug and tell her how much you love her." Hamed released hold of his one remaining child, remembering what it was like to hold both of them in his arms just a few days ago.

"I will," Tahmin replied as he walked off down the hallway to his parents' bedroom to find his mother.

Hamed watched him walk out of his sight. He hoped he had been able to give his child some wisdom that would guide him so that his life might take a different course than Hamed's had as a result of all the pain and hurt he had experienced at a young age. How was it that after all that he had experienced with what his father and mother had suffered at the hands of the Shah's tormentors, he had become a tormentor for the current regime, which was supposedly led by Allah's faithful? Had he deluded himself all these years that he was just a foot soldier in Allah's army, having to inflict pain at times in order to protect the faithful? Had he ever heeded the words of guidance he had just given his son, or had the course of his life been in pursuit of justice, retribution, vengeance, all in the name of Allah? He would have liked to think that, regardless of what methods were necessary to use on his subjects, it had always been for the purpose of obtaining the truth, which itself was a virtue in Allah's eyes.

So why did he feel so troubled about the current situation with Shiravi and General Bardari's apparent disregard for the implications his information presented to their country? Was he completely wrong about Shiravi? Was there something he was missing, something he didn't see? And why hadn't Bardari asked for an update on Shiravi? It had been four days since he had briefed Bardari. Did Bardari know about his son and not want to be insensitive? He needed to get back to Shiravi and put this matter to rest once and for all. What would happen to Shiravi afterwards wasn't his concern. His responsibility was to ensure General Bardari had the complete unaltered truth about what Shiravi knew. He couldn't put it off any longer. It had already been three days too long. He had buried his son: now it was time for him to get back to his duties and serve his country. After dinner, he would head back to his office and prepare for Shiravi's final interrogation. He would have his final report for General Bardari first thing tomorrow, even if it took him all night.

***

Michael had spent the last four hours in agony. His lower back was throbbing in pain. For the second day, the sun had gone down, the attendant was pulling the iron gate across the front doors of the museum and the sidewalk was beginning to thin out. His can was overflowing with bills. Not a bad haul for the day, he thought, even if the total didn't amount to more than the equivalent of five dollars in rial. It would buy him his food for tomorrow. Tomorrow, that wasn't something he hoped he would have had to consider, especially after seeing Karbashi drive into work this morning. He had been there for close to twelve hours. *How long did this guy stay at work?* Michael wondered. Could he somehow have missed Karbashi leaving? No, that was impossible. He hadn't shifted his gaze for even a few seconds all day. Unless Karbashi had left in a different vehicle. Michael knew he didn't have much more time to spare. With each additional passing day, the more likely it was that something would happen that would bring things to the point of no return, sealing the fate for millions of men, women and children in this part of the world. What could he do, though? Stay here on the sidewalk indefinitely, hoping to catch Karbashi finally leaving work? Soon it would be dark, and he wouldn't even be able to see who was driving, even if he did spot a blue Mercedes coming out of the MOIS.

For as euphoric as Michael had felt this morning when he'd spotted Karbashi, a feeling of worry and doubt was beginning to set in, as he realized the futility of his situation. He had set his eyes on Karbashi, was fairly certain he was still in the building across the street, yet once again he would escape him, and he was helpless to do anything about it. He couldn't let that happen, but he had no choice in the matter. There was no way he could go through the same routine again tomorrow. The outcome would be the same. Karbashi would show up for work, Michael would spend the day on the sidewalk, assuming he was even physically able to endure another day, then he would end up in the exact same situation he was in now. No, he wasn't going to go through that again. He would just have to stay where he was, even if it became dark. He tried to stand up and stretch and almost came crashing back down onto the sidewalk, his left foot and leg having fallen completely asleep. As he tried to maintain his balance, hobbling on one good leg, two police officers came around the corner and approached him, looking at him and his can of rial on the sidewalk with his blanket.

Michael stood where he was and faced the two officers as one spoke to him in Farsi. It was the worst possible luck, Michael thought as he tried to maintain his composure during the unexpected run-in with the Iranian police for a second time. He had no idea what the officer might have been saying to him, but his only option was to fall back on his deaf and mute routine, putting his hand up to his ear and grunting some unintelligible sounds from his mouth. Michael's efforts seemed to annoy the officer, who had no patience for an obvious sidewalk beggar. He kicked over the can with the rials, causing it to roll down the sidewalk. Michael did the only thing he could, hobbling after the can and picking up his daily earnings, something that would appear natural under such circumstances. He hoped the officers were just hassling him and wouldn't want to waste any more of their time with a homeless vagrant. He had just finished gathering the last of his bills and hobbled back over to the officers, who were standing next to his blanket, watching him come towards them. The same officer who had spoken to him had removed his billy-club and was waving it at Michael, indicating that he should gather his belongings and leave the sidewalk. Michael nodded, grunting as he picked up his blanket and bag, turning to face the officers with a big smile.

As Michael looked past the officers, he saw a blue Mercedes rolling slowly down the MOIS driveway towards the street. The Mercedes stopped and waited for a break in the traffic, then turned right, heading north on Shariati Street. Shadows had begun to settle in on the tree-lined street, not giving Michael a good look at the driver, but he had seen the flash of white beard. *That had to be him*, he thought, *it was the same Mercedes*. Michael continued with his nodding and grunting, acknowledging the officers' authority as he made his way over to the Vespa. He put down the can of bills next to the tree as he mounted the scooter, swung his bag around his back, laying his blanket across it, then gave the kick starter a quick downward thrust, bringing the motor to life. Without waiting for an opening in the traffic, he gunned the throttle and shot out into the street. As soon as he saw a small gap in the oncoming traffic, he quickly swung the Vespa around, making a U-turn and heading north after the Mercedes. As he rode past his previous parking spot, he spotted the two officers transferring his can of earnings into their pockets. Michael opened up the throttle on the Vespa, getting everything he could out of its small motor, as he passed cars in between the narrow gap of oncoming traffic. He hadn't spotted the Mercedes yet when he came upon the first intersection, where he could turn right and parallel to the Resalat Expressway or continue straight on Shariati Street, crossing underneath the elevated highway. If he made the wrong decision, it would be all over. He maintained his course, heading north, hoping he had made the right choice. It wasn't completely dark yet, but most of the vehicles on the road had their lights on, making it difficult to distinguish details of any cars until one was right on them.

Michael held the throttle wide open, weaving his way in and out of traffic as he strained to make out each car in front of him. He had almost given up hope, thinking he had made the wrong call and lost Karbashi, when he saw what he thought were Mercedes taillights. As he passed the two cars that separated them, he came up behind a blue Mercedes. He could see the white hair of the back of the driver's head, but wasn't sure he had the right car or driver. He had to be certain, or he was wasting his time. He would pass the Mercedes and try to get a glimpse of its driver. There was no other way. He opened the throttle once again and came up along the left side of the Mercedes E550. When he was next to the driver's window, he looked in and saw the profile of the man he had studied relentlessly for two and a half years over a decade ago. It was him, Karbashi. Michael continued past the Mercedes, not wanting to draw attention to himself, making it appear he was just another of the thousands of scooters and motorcycles that inundated Tehran's streets. After having passed several more vehicles, Michael pulled his scooter to the side of the street and waited for Karbashi to pass by him before pulling back into traffic, staying one car behind Karbashi for cover.

They continued north on Shariati Street, heading towards the Alborz mountains, which delineated the northern border of Tehran. Michael could tell they were entering one of the more exclusive sections of Tehran from the newer upscale apartment buildings and high-end storefronts and businesses. Assuming Karbashi lived in one of these exclusive apartment buildings, how was he going to make contact with him? Would he try to approach Karbashi as he exited his vehicle before he entered the building? What if there was a parking garage? If he let Karbashi enter an apartment building, it would be virtually impossible to track him down. After about four miles, Karbashi turned left down a secondary residential street lined with apartment buildings on both sides. Michael kept back a good distance, not having the cover of another vehicle separating them any longer. Karbashi drove two more blocks before turning left again into a narrow driveway, stopping and waiting for an electric gate to open. When Michael saw the Mercedes pull in past the gate, he came up and stopped his scooter across the street, peering down the driveway that ran alongside outdoor ground-level parking beneath a four-story apartment building. Michael saw Karbashi slowly drive past the apartment building to another gate and stop once more, waiting for it to open, then his car disappeared into a green oasis surrounded by multistory apartment buildings.

That's interesting, Michael thought. *He must live in a single-family residence tucked away among all these apartments.* Michael parked his scooter in the narrow space between two parked cars and sat there studying his surroundings.

It was almost completely dark by now, other than the streetlights and ambient lighting from the surrounding buildings. He would be easily able to hop over the three-foot hedges that lined the driveway into the apartments and get around the first gate, but he couldn't see what awaited him past the second gate that Karbashi's Mercedes had disappeared behind. *Well, here goes. This is it. I either convince him that I'm not some crazy person here to do him harm, and he helps me, or I'm on the run and most likely end up in an Iranian prison.* He climbed off the Vespa and walked across the street, up the driveway and over the hedges, continuing past the parked cars beneath the apartment building to a six-foot concrete wall and solid metal gate that Karbashi had just driven through. Michael could see the tiled roof of a house on the other side of the wall surrounded by the tops of palm trees and other varieties of tall shrubs and trees. Michael walked around to the corner of the property, took a quick glance around and, seeing it was clear, pulled himself up and over the wall and quietly landed on the other side.

He remained in a tucked position behind a juniper bush, allowing his vision to adjust to the relative darkness in comparison to the lighting of the apartment parking area. When his eyes adjusted to his surroundings, he could see the one-and-a-half-story white stucco house in the midst of the green oasis of trees and plants that concealed it from its taller surrounding neighbors. In the dim outdoor accent lighting, Michael saw Karbashi's Mercedes parked outside a sloped driveway that led to a garage door on a lower level of the house. Keeping in the shadows, he made his way around the perimeter of the sloped grounds, trying to determine his best approach into the house. He would obviously have to break in, since ringing the doorbell at the front door didn't seem likely to get him into the house. As he made his way around to the back, he saw the daylight basement with sliding glass doors that led out into a secluded patio and garden area. Through the glass doors, Michael could see a dimly lit room that was apparently a sizeable study, with two couches surrounding a coffee table, a large mahogany desk and floor-to-ceiling bookcases along one entire wall. Michael slowly made his way up to the patio, stooping behind a large planter as he peered inside. He could see there was no one in the study. From the home's exterior, he guessed the main living quarters were on the ground floor and Karbashi's study and a small garage were down below.

Michael cautiously moved forward to the sliding glass door and tried pulling it open, to discover that it was locked. He studied the lock and saw that it was a basic latch. He looked down inside the track and saw there was no stick keeping the slider from opening. He reached into his bag, searching through the pistachios until he felt what he was looking for. He pulled out the knife that was the only tool he had available. Gingerly wedging it in between the glass slider and the aluminum frame of the door, he worked the knife back and forth, taking care not to break the blade. Fortunately, the aluminum frame gave just enough that, after a concerted effort, Michael felt the lever pop up from the catch. He tucked his knife back into his bag and slowly pulled on the glass slider, hoping he wouldn't hear any alarm. To his relief, everything was silent as he slid open the door and quietly let himself inside, closing the door behind him. He looked around the study and saw several oil paintings of flowers and landscapes adorning the walls, along with what looked like various small archaeological artifacts in a display case underneath the glass top of the large coffee table. Michael walked over to the bookcases along the wall and looked at Karbashi's collection. He saw a variety of books in Farsi but was surprised to see a good number of English books also, including such classics as a full volume of Shakespeare, Homer's Iliad and Odyssey and even Hemingway. What was most surprising, however, was a King James Bible, not something he would expect a Muslim to have in his private collection. Everything Michael observed in the study indicated that Karbashi was obviously a well-read and cultured individual. It was something that, despite the two and a half years of studying him in Athens, Michael had no real appreciation of, although he knew Karbashi was highly adept in his profession as a spymaster. Sensing someone behind him, Michael slowly turned to find Karbashi pointing a gun at him.

"Hello," Michael said, slowly raising his hands while looking at the Model 1911 .45 pistol with its hammer cocked in Karbashi's right hand.

"Is there something I can help you with?" Karbashi replied in English, seeming unfazed by Michael speaking English to him.

Looking directly into his eyes, Michael declared, "I am not here to do you any harm. I am here because I need your help."

"Who are you, and why did you follow me to my home from this morning when I almost ran into you?"

"I will explain everything to you. Please, may I sit down?" Michael asked.

"Slowly remove your bag from your shoulders and set it down on the floor right there," Karbashi indicated, pointing by the bookshelves. "Sit down on that sofa and place your hands on top of your thighs. Do not move them from there or I will shoot you. Do you understand?"

"Yes, very clearly," Michael answered as he slowly made his way to the sofa and sat down as Karbashi stood across from him with the pistol pointing at Michael.

"You look familiar to me, but I do not know from where. You have a few minutes to explain yourself, so begin."

"My name is Michael Blackstone. I know you are Farzan Karbashi, the director of MOIS. I look familiar to you because we have previously run into each other, twelve years ago in Athens under just as unusual circumstances. We have a mutual acquaintance, Ali Shiravi." Michael paused as he let his words register. He could tell by the look on Karbashi's face that something clicked.

"It is you! I was wondering why I could not stop thinking throughout the day about why someone I had almost run into this morning looked so familiar to me. Now I understand. It was your eyes, even after all these years. You still have not answered my question. Who are you, Mr. Blackstone, and why are you here?"

"Please allow me to finish explaining everything. What I am going to tell you will be difficult to believe, but I will let you judge the merits of my truthfulness. I was the one you were supposed to meet in Athens with Ali. At the time, I worked for the CIA. You had an acquaintance with Ali, and you asked him to put you into contact with his boss, Colonel Richards, the defense attaché. Due to the nature of what you wanted to discuss, it was determined that I would meet with you instead. As I was on my way to meet you and Ali, I observed the two armed men force you and Ali to go with them. I realized they were not Greek police or EYP. You know the rest of what happened. The two men I shot and killed were Israeli Mossad, which I assume you must have figured out. The meeting was compromised. I believe I know who was responsible for the compromise. As a result of everything that happened, I left the CIA, and the US government altogether, shortly afterwards. A little over a week ago, I received a phone call from Ali's daughter telling me her father had contacted her and left her a very unusual message regarding the assassination of your foreign minister. At the time, Ali was in Istanbul working for the US State Department as the Secretary of State's interpreter. Ali instructed her to contact me and tell me that Secretary Payton, a CIA officer named Jonathan Canton and the Russians were going to try to kill your foreign minister. This was likely shortly before he was actually assassinated. Following the assassination, Ali disappeared. I flew to Istanbul and, with the assistance of an old friend with the MIT, we determined that Ali had gone to your consulate in Istanbul. We have good reason to believe he was smuggled out of Turkey into Iran by some of your personnel at the consulate. You may or may not be aware of that. I believe the information Ali has about the assassination is credible. I also have reliable information that the Israelis may be preparing to conduct a massive military attack against your country. I believe the purpose of the foreign minister's assassination was to provoke an escalating conflict between Iran and Israel with the intent of Israel using nuclear weapons against your country, the ultimate goal being to create chaos in the Middle East. I have come here with the purpose of getting Ali out of Iran so that the conspiracy can be exposed and this insane plot stopped before millions of lives are lost." Michael paused to let everything sink in. He had tried to keep things as concise as possible, telling Karbashi enough so that he could have an understanding without overwhelming him.

Karbashi looked at Michael while he contemplated everything he had just been told. Michael studied Karbashi's face, searching for any indication of whether he believed him or thought he was some sort of madman instead. For as much as Michael wanted to say more, he thought it better to remain silent and give Karbashi as much time as needed to digest his incredible story. *Better to let Karbashi steer the conversation from here*, Michael thought, allowing him to ask the questions he wanted in order to assess the merits of Michael's truthfulness.

After what seemed like an eternity of silence, Karbashi finally responded with, "I believe who you say you are. Otherwise you would not have known about Athens. However, I do not know if you are telling the truth about no longer being in the CIA. How do I know this is not some CIA ploy?"

"May I call you Farzan?" Michael asked respectfully.

"You may," he answered.

"Farzan, I will not insult your intelligence. I know you better than you may realize, and I know Ali very well. When I was stationed in Athens, I had an operation targeting you. Ali was my asset. He was assigned to make contact with you and establish a relationship. He succeeded in that. I don't know if you ever suspected anything, but the goal was to determine if there was any way to compromise you, wittingly or unwittingly. It never progressed to that point, since you made the first move and asked him to put you into contact with his boss. Despite working for me, Ali respected you and considered you a friend, in whatever manner a friendship can develop under those types of circumstances. I also respected you, as one professional to another. I have not spoken to Ali for many years, but he would not have attempted to contact me with such an unbelievable story if there wasn't some truth to it. He is here in Iran. I know that. I have risked my life to come here and get him out. I would not have done so if I wasn't certain of the type of man he is."

"Mr. Blackstone…"

"Please, call me Michael."

"Very well, Michael. I was never entirely certain whether meeting Ali was an innocent coincidence or some kind of CIA operation against me. As time passed and Ali had not asked for or offered me anything regarding information about either of our countries, my suspicions were appeased somewhat. His actions towards me did not appear to resemble a typical intelligence agency operation. When the opportunity presented itself to establish a back-channel method of communicating with your government, whether Ali was or was not a CIA pawn was not critical at that point. It would not have had any bearing on our intentions in reaching out to your government, whether it was through your defense attaché or the CIA. I never saw or heard from Ali after that surprising occurrence that happened to us. My suspicions were confirmed that there had been some type of operation against me, whether by the CIA or even Mossad. The Mossad would certainly have a good enough reason to go after me. Whoever it was, that did not matter, because shortly afterwards, I was transferred from Athens back to Tehran. It was never reported in the Greek press that the two men killed in Glyfada were Israelis, but I suspected it from their accents and the circumstances. There was no other explanation. Now you are telling me Ali Shiravi is in my country with information implicating your Secretary of State, a CIA officer and the Russians. You have told me your country and Russia are acting in concert against my country. What do you expect me to believe?"

"I know. I would expect you to believe this is some CIA ploy to deceive you, but I am not part of anything of that sort. I'm just a washed-up ex-CIA officer who wants to expose this depraved plot and help out an old friend who I believe was trying to do the right thing. I also know Jonathan Canton, the CIA officer involved in this, very well. He worked with me at our station in Athens. I am almost certain it was him who compromised our meet in Athens to the Israelis. Now he's after Ali, trying to silence him. I believe Ali came to your consulate in Istanbul because he had nowhere else to turn and needed to tell someone. He told his daughter to contact me because Canton was involved, thinking I would be the only one he could trust and who might be able to help him. I came to you because that was the only way I could think of helping him. I need your help to do that," Michael implored him.

"How is it you expect me to help you? You said you want to get Ali out of Iran. You are asking me to help you do that?"

"That is what I am asking."

"So, you are asking me to commit a treasonous act against my country," Karbashi asked incredulously.

"I am asking you to do what is necessary to protect your country. Iran and Israel are accusing each other of being responsible for Mohammedi's assassination. Millions of your countrymen and others in this part of the world will be killed if this insanity is allowed to spiral out of control. You must be able to see that is the directions things are heading."

Karbashi sat silently, thinking about what Michael had told him. After a few moments, he de-cocked the hammer on the 1911 and set it down on his thigh.

"Thank you," Michael said. "That's quite a rarity. I wouldn't have expected to see many of those in Iran."

"It is a rarity. It came from your embassy. I believe it belonged to the Marine guards. It was presented to me as a gift by one of the students who had occupied the embassy back in 1979, a close family friend."

"I can see you are a collector of rare things," Michael indicated, looking around his study. "Who is the artist of all the paintings? They look similar in style."

"Yes, I do like to collect unique objects that depict the culture of our humanity. The paintings are my wife's. They are what I have to remember her amazing talents by. She died several years ago from cancer. She was the better partner in our marriage. I wish I had spent more time with her instead of being gone so many years on foreign assignments. Our only child died shortly after birth. The sorrow and anguish were too much for her to bear. We never had another. So now it is just myself and my interesting little trinket collection."

"I am sorry, Farzan. I had recently learned from Ali's daughter that Janet Shiravi had also passed away from cancer not too long ago. I believe you knew her."

"I did know Janet and young Roxanne. As you must know, I had been invited to their home on several occasions. She was a very nice woman. I am saddened to hear that," Karbashi said, remaining silent again for some time. When he finally broke his silence, he asked Michael, "Even if Ali was in Iran, how would you expect to get him out?"

"If I can get to the Turkish border near Maku, then I think we can get flown out," Michael answered him.

"Is that how you entered Iran?"

"Yes."

"And if you are no longer in the employee of the American government, how is it you have air transportation in and out of Iran?" Karbashi asked.

"Remember, I told you I had an old friend from MIT. She arranged the transportation."

"You are telling me the Turkish government is involved in this also?"

"Not exactly. She is acting without the knowledge of her superiors, at great risk to herself."

"She is doing this for you? She must be a very good friend."

"She is a good friend, but she's doing it because she knows what the outcome will be if she does nothing. This heinous act took place in her country, and she has a vested interest in the truth coming out also."

After another brief period of silence, Karbashi finally let out, "I believe I know where Ali is being held. In Evin Prison."

"I figured that would be a safe bet, but you're not sure, though? I would have thought as the director of MOIS you would be privy to such information," Michael said, trying not to sound belittling.

"Michael, as I am sure you are familiar with some of the past issues between your CIA and FBI not sharing information, similar issues exist between the MOIS and IRGC, especially considering how much influence the IRGC has on every aspect of our government. I was aware that the IRGC was holding an American at Evin Prison, but I was not told of his identity or his specific position, other than a low-level employee of your State Department. Despite having tried to play me, I know Ali Shiravi, and if what you are telling me is the truth, he would not make such an accusation without believing it was the truth. I do see the direction things are heading and I am greatly alarmed, just as much by my country's actions as by Israel's. You had tried to deceive me once in the past, so I am wary of your intentions. However, you also did save my life, so I am indebted to you for that. I will help you, but I will not make my final decision until I speak with Ali face-to-face. He will have to vouch for you."

"That is all I ask."

"I hope what you are telling me is the truth, for my country's sake and all others in the Middle East, even Israel. The scale of all the death and destruction would be on the same level as what took place during World War II," Karbashi declared.

"Yes, it would, perhaps even greater. I see that you are fairly well read." Michael gestured to Karbashi's entire wall of books.

"Intentional ignorance is perhaps one of the greatest sins. Allah expects us to seek the truth, even if it causes us discomfort in evaluating our beliefs."

"I noticed you have a Bible. Not something I would expect a Muslim to own. Isn't that kind of dangerous?"

"Understanding the beliefs of others is not dangerous, unless you are not certain of your own beliefs. It is also useful in intelligence to understand the belief system of your adversary. Wouldn't you agree, Michael?"

"You know, Farzan, I always recognized and respected your abilities as an intelligence officer. Going after you was like playing a game of chess against a chess master. I always cautioned myself never to underestimate you."

"I did not have the same opportunity to familiarize myself with you so intimately, but I must tell you, what you have attempted to accomplish on your own is either the most foolish thing I have ever witnessed or the boldest. I have no doubt you are clearly aware of all the risks," Karbashi told him.

"I'm not sure myself what I was thinking," Michael confided to him.

"Very well, then. You will accompany me to Evin Prison and be present when I speak with Ali in private. The director of MOIS showing up at night to speak with a prisoner will attract enough scrutiny from the guards, but do not worry, you will not have to say anything in my presence. Perhaps we should modify your appearance first, however, so you do not look like a vagrant. You played that role very well, but it has run its course. I am sure you would appreciate having a hot shower and shaving, as well as a decent meal before we go. You still have quite a journey ahead of you."

"A hot shower sounds better than you can imagine," Michael let out, breathing a sigh of relief. Somehow, he had done the inconceivable—not only locating Karbashi but also convincing him to help. He realized how astronomical the odds were of what he had just accomplished, but he was also keenly aware of what still remained in getting Ali and himself out of the country. Perhaps somebody was looking after him. He hoped so.

***

It was 8:00 p.m., and Bill Jackson and Sam Peters were just finishing completing the final diagnostics on the communications and avionics updates they had installed on the eight F-35s. They had managed to stretch things out well into Sunday evening, but Captain Engil's hourly visits to check on their progress left them with no further opportunity to stall. All the navigation, targeting and communications frequencies had been synchronized to continuously roll over according to the encrypted tactical frequency controller on the Israeli AEWC aircraft that would be coordinating the attack. As far as Jackson and Peters were concerned, their job was finished. They had done what they had been told by their boss, dragging out the update as long as possible and calling Barso to let him know what was transpiring at the air base. The sooner they were able to get out of the sandpit of a base they were on, the better. Hopefully by tomorrow, they would be back on their way to Sydney. If not, at least they would be able to spend the night at the Intercontinental in Tel Aviv, where they could go out for a few beers and enjoy some decent nightlife. Thank goodness the majority of Israelis were secular Jews. Tel Aviv had a vibrant nightlife, which Jackson and Peters had enjoyed on previous trips to Israel for their employer.

"Here he comes again. I reckon we gotta tell him we're finally all done," Bill Jackson told his partner.

"Yep. I hope they can get us back up to Tel Aviv tonight. I don't want to spend the night on some cot in one of their barracks," Peters added.

"Don't count on it." Jackson sounded pessimistic.

"Well, gentlemen, I take it you are finished." Captain Engil clapped his hands in anticipation of hearing the answer he was hoping for.

"Yeah, Captain, we've got your birds ready. Everything checks out on our instruments, but you're gonna have to get them in the air and make sure all's in sync with your jammers. But it should work," Jackson reassured him.

"Wonderful, wonderful, gentlemen. You have earned your rest. I have set you up to share a room at the officers' quarters. Are you hungry? Yes, I imagine you would be. We can go by the mess hall. I am sure someone in the kitchen will be able to make something for you to eat." Engil almost sounded giddy with thankfulness.

"Any chance you could get us back up to Tel Aviv tonight, Captain?" Peters asked.

"No, I am sorry, that will not be possible. Not until tomorrow, I am afraid. But please, gather up your instruments, and when you are ready, I will take you over to your accommodations. I will be back in fifteen minutes, as soon as I brief my commanding officer that the update is complete," he told them, turning and trotting off out of the hangar.

"Ah, shit," was all that came out of Sam Peters.

"Told ya." Bill Jackson gave his partner a Texas head nod.

***

Michael sat in the passenger seat of Karbashi's Mercedes as they headed for Evin Prison. It wasn't far from the Elahieh neighborhood, where Karbashi lived, just a quick hop on the Chamran Highway, past the Tehran Exhibition Center complex, to the Evin suburbs of Tehran in the northern part of the city. The prison itself was located in the northernmost section, by the foothills of the Alborz mountains. The hot shower, change of clothes, and microwaved lamb kabobs from Karbashi's freezer, along with some hummus, had made Michael feel like a different man. A newfound energy buzzed throughout him.

He almost found it hard to believe he was actually sitting next to Karbashi, the man he had gone after over a decade ago, who was now the head of the Iranian intelligence service and, helping him break Ali out of Iran's most notorious prison. Yet here he was, after everything he had endured to make it happen. He knew perfectly well it wasn't because of anything he had done. He also knew it was more than just exceptional luck. How everything played out time after time was beyond good luck. The odds were astronomical for how things had worked out for him.

They sat in silence as they drove. Michael studied Karbashi from the side, wondering what made a man like him tick. He had obviously a deep sense of patriotism and duty to his country, yet he was willing to commit an act that could be considered treason. He seemed to be a man of sincere faith, yet open to examining the beliefs of others without his own being threatened. He was also obviously an educated and cultured individual.

"Why are you studying me? Are you wondering why I have decided to help you?" Karbashi asked, his eyes not leaving the road in front of them.

"That's part of it, I suppose. I'm just wondering what it was that made you decide it was worth taking the chance helping Ali and me, when you and I both know what can happen to you, even if you are the head of MOIS."

"What may happen to me, Michael, pales in comparison to what may happen to millions of my fellow Iranians if I do nothing."

"I'm not saying your alternative is to do nothing, but you could just as easily parade me around in your media in front of the entire world and implicate the US and Russia. The entire world press would pick up on that, and then you would have at least put the world on notice and forced them to play defense with denials. It would also put the Israelis in a tough spot, having to consider they had been played by their supposed closest ally."

"I am not as much concerned with whatever the Israelis intend, as with how our country responds. I do not doubt for one moment, if significant enough destruction occurs in centers such as Haifa and Tel Aviv, the Israelis will not hesitate to unleash at least one nuclear weapon in the heart of Tehran. Do you know what that means, Michael? In Hiroshima, one hundred and forty-six thousand people were killed by a fifteen-kiloton atomic bomb. Israel's nuclear arsenal includes three hundred warheads, each yielding somewhere between two hundred and fifty and three hundred and fifty kilotons each. You can do the math. They can selectively destroy us, beginning as low as perhaps five hundred thousand with just one warhead, and rapidly step up how viciously they choose to strike back at us. We may have the ability to inflict significant damage by taking out buildings and causing substantial destruction, but they can decimate all of our cities, Michael. Whatever facility they decide to strike, there are individuals in my government who would call for half our arsenal in missiles to rain down on Israel. Do you know the damage that would cause in Haifa and Tel Aviv? Our responding in that way, Michael, would be like pushing the button to launch those nuclear missiles towards ourselves."

"Must feel reassuring, living here yourself in the heart of Tehran, knowing the truth about the situation." Michael made tried to add a little bit of ironic lightheartedness to Karbashi's dire explanation of what awaited the Iranian people.

"I am not worried for myself. I am getting down to the last chapters of my life. I have been able to see fascinating places in this world, be exposed to other cultures with different beliefs, experience different parts of humanity. I could not have asked Allah to bless me with a fuller life, Michael. I just regret not having been able to have shared some of that with my beloved wife. But it was never a practice of my service to allow wives and children to accompany officers on their foreign assignments. We had a life where I was gone for three years, home for two years, gone again, back again. You understand. Nor was she able to experience the joy of motherhood. We had a child, but Allah decided to take him when he was only eight months old. My wife suffered such deep pain from that loss. Something broke inside her that she never wanted to have another child. She lost herself in her art. When I was home with her from an assignment, it was like my world was filled with joy, full of vivid color, but it lacked the intellectual stimulus, the challenge that life on foreign assignment offered. Coming and going was always a bittersweet experience for me. Should I be taken from this world suddenly, it would only bring me more quickly back to my Jazmin. Do you fear death, Michael? I ask that of someone who has knowingly put himself in a position that any rational man would realize was the same as playing Russian Roulette. For reasons only He sees, Allah has chosen to repeatedly protect you to have come this far. How does knowing that make you feel, Michael?"

Michael was taken off guard by Karbashi's last remark. In a matter of a few sentences, he had articulated the foundations of his soul, then, without a pause, asked him if he was scared of dying and what he thought about the fact that God was protecting him from any harm. *Wow, his mind works a mile a minute and reaches pretty deep*, Michael thought.

"Well, I don't know how to really answer that, Farzan. Things have been kind of less than routine over the past week or so. I'm still trying to process everything, if you can understand where I'm coming from. As far as fearing death goes, I don't know. I knew losing my life was a pretty good possibility, but I don't know if it really bothered me. Not because I'm certain about what waits for us afterwards, it's just that I always felt I never really had any control over the matter, so why let it worry me? I guess you could also say I found out from firsthand experience. Sounds like you and your wife were very close, despite you being gone much of the time."

"Our souls were connected. We may have been different people, but the connection we shared transcended our physical bodies. Have you experienced that, Michael?"

Another piercing question. *This guy just keeps hitting them deep. He's going to be able to psychoanalyze me by the time we reach the prison.*

"I thought I did, with my first wife, the mother of my daughter. At least, it felt that way in the beginning. Somewhere, somehow, that connection got lost. I just can never really pin it down, no matter how many times I've thought about it. Sometimes I think that I may have chosen the mistress of my career over her. That's pretty pathetic, isn't it? At least that's how I see it from my current perspective in life. I'm in awe of how you managed to maintain such a devoted marriage and enduring relationship through all you two have been through."

"Focusing on each other's virtues and extending grace to each other's shortcomings, is the only environment in which Allah's love may flourish. It is more easily stated than accomplished. Human beings are not naturally selfless. Our selfishness is the root of all evil in this world. It is easy to lose sight of that, whether it is amongst spouses or amongst peoples."

"Words to live by, Farzan," Michael reflected as Karbashi pulled off the main road onto a drive bordered by a dry concrete river wash on one side and a tree line on the other.

"We are here. You will follow me in, carrying my briefcase. Say nothing. Act as if you are my assistant. No one will dare address you in my presence."

They pulled up to the front of the prison. Michael saw the blue sign above the main gate that read "Evin House of Detention" below the Farsi script. "Very considerate of them to spell it out in English also. That would be for someone like me, I'm assuming. A little bit ironic I'm walking through the front door with you. If you wanted to, you could just as easily check me in at the front desk with a luxury private room, compliments of the Iranian government," Michael remarked with a touch of sarcasm.

"Do you always resort to humor when you are in perilous circumstances?" Karbashi asked him as he pulled into a spot away from the main entrance, despite the parking area in front of the prison being sparsely filled at that hour in the evening.

"Someone has brought that to my attention recently. I guess it's my way of dealing with stress. I'd much rather be going into this place pretending to be your assistant than what the other more likely possibility could have been."

"Let us hope that we both do not end up with adjoining rooms. It is not a pleasant establishment. I am fearful of what condition we may find Ali in. He has likely been here for close to a week. Prepare yourself for what you might find. He may not be in a condition to walk out under his own power and may be in need of medical treatment. This is a brutal place that has broken many men, both physically and psychologically."

"I know what Evin Prison is about." Michael kept his response short, trying not to direct any hostility towards Karbashi as a result of what might have been done to Ali.

"I pray that Allah has sustained him and will restore him from any harm that has come," Karbashi replied as they approached the fortified security booth by the front gate.

Karbashi walked up to the reinforced window that had light coming from inside, surprising the guard sitting there, whose attention was immersed in some well-worn Asian porn magazine. Covering it quickly with a newspaper, the guard looked to the two individuals standing outside his booth. From the look on his face, it was evident he wasn't sure who was showing up at 9:30 in the evening on what appeared to be official business, based on the manner in which Karbashi presented himself. Michael was surprised to hear the change in tone of Karbashi's voice as he barked an order at the guard, removing an identification case from his coat and displaying it through the window. What was even more entertaining was the guard's reaction, as he jumped to attention with eyes wide open and stammered something in Farsi. He picked up a phone and dialed, engaging in a short conversation before attempting a smile at Karbashi as he buzzed the heavy metal door open, allowing Karbashi and Michael to enter a covered vehicle courtyard, where another door that led to the main reception area.

Reaching for the door and holding it open for his boss and holding the briefcase with his other hand, Michael fell into his role as Karbashi's assistant. Despite the khaki trousers being an inch too short, the white button-down cotton shirt and navy-blue zippered jacket Michael had gotten from Karbashi fit rather well. Unfortunately, Michael's feet were a size larger than Karbashi's, making the scuffed tan boots sticking out from his short pants somewhat comical. Otherwise, he looked like some government official working late into the evening with his important boss. He hoped the guard's attention would be focused on Karbashi, and he would just fade into the background unnoticed.

After a few back-and-forth exchanges with Karbashi, the guard nervously scrambled to find something on the computer screen behind the counter. With Karbashi looking at him impatiently, he picked up a phone, dialed, and had a brief exchange with the person on the other end. They waited for a few moments, the guard enduring the uncomfortable silence, trying not to look directly at Karbashi while at the same time not turning his attention away from him. Finally, another guard came into the reception area from a door at the opposite side of the room. Making eye contact with the guard behind the counter, the new guard came to attention, facing Karbashi and uttering a short greeting. Karbashi barked a brief order, causing him to turn and head back to the door he'd just entered from, with Karbashi following him and Michael falling in behind.

Leading them down a hallway, the guard took them past several doors and around a corner to a gray steel door with a metal knob. Opening the door, the guard gestured for Karbashi to enter the sparsely furnished room, which contained a small square wooden table with four chairs around it. The other thing Michael noticed about the dimly lit gray cinder-block room was the steel shackle rings embedded in one side of the wall, along with the permanent reddish-brown stains on the concrete floor below. Michael could sense the heaviness that hung in the air from all the souls that had met their demise in this room. The guard pulled out a chair for Karbashi, gesturing for him to sit down. Michael sat in the chair next to him, setting the briefcase on the floor next to his chair. The guard said something to Karbashi, making his best attempt at appeasing his obvious impatience, then quickly exited the room.

"Sometimes it is useful to display one's annoyance as to why they have not prepared the prisoner, when they had been advised of the visit by the intelligence ministry earlier that day. Clearly indicating one's intolerance of excuses, throws them even further onto their heels, so that the only thing they can think about is doing whatever they can as quickly as possible to save their own skin from what awaits them in the morning from their superior. I assume it is similar in the United States, that prison institutions do not get the cream of the cow, as you Americans like to say, when it comes to personnel."

"Not exactly on the terminology, but close enough." Michael grinned.

"He is going to bring Ali. I am sure he will be shocked when he sees us. We will have to see what condition he is in before deciding the best course of action, but one way or another, he will be leaving with us tonight."

"It's in your hands, Director."

"It is in Allah's, Michael."

***

Hamed sat behind his desk, taking one last look through his case file before leaving for Evin Prison, where he would bring to a final resolution Shiravi's claims regarding the true culprits of the foreign minister's assassination. He had interrogated him twice, and despite not having used any enhanced interrogation techniques, something inside told him Shiravi was telling the truth. He didn't understand why General Bardari steadfast in refusing to consider that the Americans together with the Russians would plot against his country in such a vile way. Perhaps the general could not accept that the United States would betray their close ally Israel by making it look like they were responsible for the assassination. But then how had it actually been a betrayal? Strategically, they had just thrown a lit match into the powder keg of the Middle East, hoping to incite an all-out war between his country and the Zionists. The Great Satan was setting the stage for the Little Satan to destroy Iran with their nuclear weapons. Could the general not see that? Had he not always trusted his top interrogator in the past when it came to the accuracy of the intelligence obtained from prisoners. Why was Bardari doubting him now?

Hamed paused a moment to consider whether there was something he was missing. Had the death of his child clouded his judgment? No, that couldn't be it. He had done both of Shiravi's interrogations before Reza had been hit by the car. He believed that he had obtained the truth back then. So how was he going to make a difference this time in convincing Bardari he was falling right into the trap the Americans and Russians had devised? It had been four days since Hamed had last interrogated Shiravi. Much had happened to him since then. The tragedy of losing his precious child had broken something inside him. He didn't know if he still processed the hard edge necessary to detach himself from his feelings when it came to inflicting physical and psychological pain on men in order to obtain the truth for the protection of his country. Yet that was something he hadn't found necessary to do with Shiravi. Why had he felt so sure he hadn't been deceived by Shiravi? Was he so sure of his abilities to detect deceitfulness in men that he was succumbing to foolish arrogance? He would have to be completely sure of himself before he briefed General Bardari one final time in the morning. He wasn't concerned how it might affect his hopes for promotion if Bardari didn't like what he heard, but he wasn't going to stay silent if the destruction of his country was at stake. He had lost one child already.

He hoped he could find the resolve to go through with whatever was necessary to eliminate any doubt in his mind that was not being deceived. He walked over to his closet where he stored his interrogation tools to select what he thought would be most effective on Shiravi. He searched for something that would cause pain but not leave any lasting psychological scars. His eyes fell on the propane torch he had intimidated Shiravi with during the last interrogation. He remembered Shiravi's reaction when he had heard the sound of the torch beside his head. It was an effective tool for breaking the resistance of even the most hardened prisoners. He would be judicious in its application on Shiravi, not causing any significant damage to his flesh, just enough to feel the brief intensity of a little skin burning. The uncertainty of how much more burning they would have to endure usually caused a prisoner to break after only two or three applications of the torch. He had never caused any significant injury to prisoners using that technique. In many ways, he found it more humane than some other techniques he had used which left lasting psychological scars to men's souls.

He picked up the propane torch with his right hand, raising it up in front of his face. To his surprise, his hand trembled as he studied the tool of his trade. He squeezed his hand, attempting to subdue the trembling, but the harder he squeezed, the more pronounced it became until his entire arm was shaking. He stared at his shaking hand. What was happening to him? Were his nerves just temporarily shot because of all he had gone through in the past few days? How would he be able to interrogate Shiravi like this?

He walked back to his desk, the torch at his side, trying to subdue the shaking. Throwing the propane torch in his black nylon equipment case, he sat back down behind his desk and opened his briefcase. He searched under a stack of miscellaneous files until he found what he was looking for. He pulled out the blue package of Gauloises cigarettes that he always kept with him. He hadn't smoked for over ten years, but they were a useful incentive he sometimes offered to prisoners when he thought it would be effective. He pulled out a cigarette from the package, then, flicking open a Zippo with his trembling hand, he lit the end of the Gauloises hanging from his lips. He took a deep drag from the strong French cigarette and held the smoke in his lungs before letting it out slowly to form a hazy cloud over his desk. He felt the rush of the nicotine come over him and gradually start to make its way through his body. He took another drag. Grasping the cigarette between his fingers, he saw that the nicotine had started to take its intended effect, his pronounced shake having been reduced to a slight tremor. That would do, he thought.

He looked at his watch. It was already 9:35 p.m. It would take him about fifteen minutes to get to Evin Prison at this time of night. He hoped he could wrap things up with Shiravi in a few hours and return home for a few hours of sleep before heading back to the office in the morning to set up an appointment to brief General Bardari. He threw the file in the briefcase along with the cigarettes and lighter. He hoped he wouldn't get back into the habit of smoking again after so many years. He had quit because he knew it was sinful to corrupt the body Allah had given him by polluting it with the filthy toxins from cigarettes, but for now, it had served its purpose in bringing his body under control so that he could execute his duty to his country. He picked his black equipment bag, slinging it over his shoulder, and grabbed his briefcase off his desk. With the Gauloises hanging from his lips, he headed for the door. The nicotine had helped in calming his nerves, but a feeling of unease still permeated throughout him. He wasn't looking forward to having to inflict pain on Shiravi. He hoped it would be the final time he would need to meet with him.

***

Michael sat diagonally across from Karbashi at the small table, waiting for Ali to be brought in. Michael wondered what Ali's reaction would be to see him and Karbashi sitting next to each other, waiting for him. He hoped Ali would be in good enough condition physically and mentally to comprehend what was going on around him and not react in such a way that would indicate to the guard that something wasn't quite right. Michael looked at Karbashi, who returned his look, their eyes connecting with a strange sort of kinship as they both sat waiting for an old friend who neither had seen for many years. It was by far the most unusual situation Michael had ever been in his entire life. He was sitting next to the man who had been his target, his primary adversary, even his enemy all those years ago, who was now helping him at his significant risk to himself. Michael had never underestimated Karbashi, but now he had a newfound level of respect and admiration of his courage and principles. Michael knew the jeopardy he was putting himself in breaking Ali out of prison. Though his actions might make the difference in preventing the deaths of millions of his peopled and the devastation of Iran, there was a good possibility Karbashi would be shot or hanged for what would be considered treason by many. His position as director of the MOIS would hardly matter if the Supreme Leader thought he had betrayed his country. The commanding general of the IRGC would certainly do everything in his power to seek retribution against Karbashi for breaking Ali out of one of their prisons. Had their lives been different, Karbashi not an intelligence officer of one of the US's enemies, and Michael not a CIA officer, they might have become friends had they met under different circumstances.

The strange and unexplainable circumstances that life brought were something that had always fascinated Michael. Perhaps it was because he had always considered the probability, or more precisely the improbability, of so many factors having to fall perfectly into place for a certain outcome to happen. It made him marvel at the unpredictability of life. He tried to understand what had caused him to lose sight of that fact, so much that he would attempt such a desperate act as to take his life. Had he lost his wonderment for what lay around the next corner in the journey of life? What had happened to him over the past nine days had forced him to completely reevaluate all of his core beliefs. A small part of him still wondered whether his Glock had in fact actually fired a round into his brain, not killing him, but putting him into a coma, with all this just being a vivid dream he was trapped in. He knew that wasn't the case, but he was grasping for some rational explanation that would satisfy the logical side of him. These things just didn't happen.

Michael heard the doorknob turn and the creak of the hinges. He and Karbashi looked over as the guard opened the door and Ali Shiravi entered through the doorway. Both Michael and Karbashi kept any sign of emotion from their faces as they watched their old friend walk towards them. With the guard behind him, Ali maintained his composure, but his eyes said everything.

"Sit down." Karbashi motioned to Ali, pointing at the chair across from him. "That will be all for now," Karbashi instructed the guard. "I will summon you when we are finished."

The guard gave a short nod and stepped back out into the hallway, closing the door. Michael paused a few seconds before saying anything, letting Ali take in what had just been thrust before him.

With a big smile, Michael let out, "Hello, Ali. Surprised to see us?"

"Salaam, old friend," Karbashi added, directing a warm smile to Ali.

Ali sat in his chair with his mouth open. Tears welled up in his eyes as he searched for something to say.

"It's okay, everything is going to be all right. We're going to get you out," Michael reassured him, not sure if Ali was comprehending everything.

"Are you hurt?" Karbashi asked. "Can you speak?"

As Michael and Karbashi looked at him, trying to discern if he was physically or psychologically traumatized, Ali finally responded, "I can speak, and I am fine, just in a little bit of shock. I don't understand how this can be, but I am so overjoyed to see you. And you, Farzan, I am confused—how, why are you here also with Michael? Maybe I am hallucinating?"

"No, Ali, you are not hallucinating, my dear friend. I am here with Michael. He sought me out for help. He told me about what had happened to you. You have been through much. You have many questions, I know."

"So, you're not hurt?" Michael asked.

"No, I have not been harmed. I don't know what to think. Asking my daughter to contact you with my message was a last desperate reach for help. I was never expecting to ever see you, and seeing you, Farzan, is beyond my comprehension. How did this happen?"

"Our old friend is now the director of MOIS." Michael smiled. "I found that out when I discovered you had been taken from Istanbul to Iran. I knew my only chance of getting to you was through Farzan. I will fill you in on everything in between later, but now we need to get you out of here and both of us back over to Turkey. There's a lot going on you don't know about. There are things happening on the world stage that may cause a lot of people to die if we don't try to stop it. What you know may be able to accomplish that."

"I overheard Secretary Payton and Jonathan Canton talking about a plot with the Russians to assassinate Foreign Minister Mohammedi. Canton knew I heard them speaking. They tried to kill me also. They were shooting at me. I barely got away. I had nowhere to go. I knew Canton would never let me live. I went to the Iranian consulate, hoping they would listen to me. They didn't believe me. They brought me here. They still don't believe me!" Ali exclaimed.

"Remain calm, my friend. No harm will come to you. Until Michael approached me a few hours ago, I was not aware it was you the IRGC had in their custody. I needed to see you in person. Hear directly from you. I believe what you are saying about the foreign minister's assassination is the truth. I see how everything that has come to pass directly corroborates what you overheard. As Michael stated, your knowledge of this evil plot is the only thing that may be able to halt the events that have been put into play."

"How is Roxanne, Michael? Is she in danger? Canton might try and come after her," Ali asked with concern.

"She's safe, Ali, don't worry. I have her staying with my parents. He won't find her. He has enough to deal with looking for you and me. I had the pleasure of running into him again, and I really rubbed him the wrong way. I've got a good friend running interference with him back in Istanbul. Roxanne is the last thing on his mind right now."

"Thank God. I didn't trust him in Athens and now I know why that is. He is an evil man."

"That he is, Ali, and, you have the ability to get him put away for a long time. The most important thing now is to get you out of here so you can tell your story. We don't have much time because the Israelis may be planning an attack on Iran that could lead to an all-out war and the use of nuclear weapons. I don't need to tell you what that will mean for millions of people not only in

Iran, but in the entire Middle East," Michael told him.

"Farzan, you know about Athens? I want you to know that I really did value our friendship. It was a difficult situation I found myself in after I got to know you. When everything was turned upside down and I was never able to see you again, it troubled me for a very long time. I felt that you thought I betrayed you. I know I lied to you, but in the end, I thought our meeting with Michael would lead to something good for both our countries."

"Do not be hard on yourself, Ali. I know there was genuineness to our friendship. We each knew that the other worked for their country's government. You never asked me to betray my country, nor did I ask you to do the same, even if our roles required it. Allah had his purpose for allowing things to go the way that they did. My only sadness is at the news of Janet's death. I was very sorry to hear that. She was a very nice woman, always displaying great warmth and kindness to me."

"Thank you, Farzan, she was that kind of person. I am impressed you are the director of MOIS now. What happened in Athens obviously didn't set you back in your career. I am very happy for you."

"That is what Allah has set before me in life. He obviously had his purpose for that. I am certain Michael would not have had the options he did if I had not been where I am. How could any of us ever imagined what happened in Athens would lead to where we all currently find ourselves?"

The implication of what Karbashi had said wasn't lost upon Michael. Who knew how much different each of their lives would have been if that fateful evening years ago in Athens had gone differently, as expected? How could one seemingly unforeseen incident have played such a decisive role in completely reshaping their lives? Not only that, but the ripple effect had changed the lives of so many others around them, perhaps even millions of others.

"While I have been here over the past several days, some things have been made very clear to me about my life also. Had I not been here, I may not have had these things revealed to me. In a strange way, I am very grateful for that," Ali said.

"Well, I'm happy you had a chance for some self-reflection, but unless we get out of here soon, none of that is going to matter. We still have a long way to go before we're in the clear, so save that thought and you can fill me in as we make our way back to Turkey. How do you intend to get Ali out of here, Farzan?" Michael asked.

"He will walk out with us. I will tell the guards we need to temporarily take him so that he can identify some other individuals and he will be returned tomorrow. That should give you several hours lead time to make your way back to the border. I will attempt to stall as long as I can to give you as much time as possible, but at some point, I will be put in the position to have to answer to the IRGC for your whereabouts. Hopefully by then, both of you will be back over the border."

"What will happen to you Farzan?" Ali asked with worry in his voice.

"Do not be concerned, my friend, whatever happens has already been determined by Allah. I have no uncertainty about what I must do. I am at peace with my decision to help you, for you are the only one who may be able to alter the course of events. What may happen to me is of no consequence."

"Okay, it's your call how you want to play this. I'll just follow along," Michael told Karbashi.

"Very well, I will call for the guard. You will use the handcuffs in my briefcase when we walk Ali out. You will escort him from behind," Karbashi instructed Michael as he prepared to buzz the guard.

Chapter 24

Hamed pulled into the parking lot at Evin Prison, parking his white Renault Mégane in front of the main entrance. Exiting the car with his briefcase and black bag, he couldn't help but notice the blue Mercedes down at the far end of the parking lot. It was unusual, he thought, to see such a vehicle here, especially at this hour. A select few people drove those types of cars in Iran, usually only someone of significance. He walked up to the guard post and presented himself in front of the window. He didn't have to take his identification out for the guard. He had been there often enough over the years that everyone knew who Colonel Ahmadi was. The guard gave him a respectful nod and buzzed him through the gate into the covered courtyard. Hamed walked across and entered the reception area to find the guard on duty nodded off in his chair, his head slumped down onto his chest. Hamed walked over and slammed his palm down on the guard's desk, making the guard's head jerk up in surprise to face the irritated stare of the colonel no guard ever wanted to anger.

"Colonel, I, I must have dozed off for a second. I, I am…"

"It is all right," Hamed raised his hand. "How long have you been on duty?"

"Since eight this morning, sir."

"That is close to twelve hours. Where is your relief?"

"He called in this afternoon. His wife went into labor. It is their first child. I am working his shift. I will be relieved in four hours. I will not let that happen again, Colonel."

"That would be a good idea. What is your name?"

"Ghazi, sir."

"Ghazi, do you know who is the owner of the blue Mercedes parked outside?"

"I have not seen it, but I assume it would be Director Karbashi's of the MOIS," Ghazi guessed.

"He is here?" Hamed asked, surprised.

"Yes, Colonel. He is with the American, Shiravi."

"Why is he with him?"

"I do not know, Colonel. He showed up here about twenty minutes ago with an assistant and said he wanted to see the prisoner. We took them to one of the interrogation rooms and brought the prisoner to him. They are there right now with him."

"Which room?"

"The first interrogation room." Ghazi hadn't even finished his answer before Hamed was walking through the door to the hallway which led to the interrogation rooms.

What was the director of MOIS doing speaking with his prisoner? Karbashi wondered as he strode down the hallway. And why at this hour of the night? This was a highly irregular breach of protocol? Had something happened he wasn't aware of? He had only been gone four days. And to have the director himself speaking with Shiravi—there was something very unusual going on. He rounded the corner and came to the first door. He paused outside, standing silently next to the steel-gray door, straining to hear what was being said inside. He could hear voices but was unable to make out anything of the conversation, other than it sounded as if it was in English. He twisted the knob, yanking the door open to find Shiravi, the director of MOIS, and another man sitting around the table, having a conversation in English. They looked up at him in surprise, interrupted by his sudden unexpected appearance.

"What is happening here?" he asked in English with a heavy accent.

"May I ask who you are?" Karbashi asked self-assuredly.

"I am Colonel Hamed Ahmadi, IRGC Intelligence."

"I am Farzan Karbashi, director of MOIS. How may I help you, Colonel?" Karbashi didn't miss a beat.

"I know who you are. May I ask what you are doing here with my prisoner?"

"Ah, he is your prisoner, you say. Well, Colonel, since he is your prisoner, perhaps you can tell me why he is still here and nothing has been done with the information he has provided?"

Hamed was temporarily confused. How did Karbashi know what information Shiravi had provided? Had General Bardari shared this with him? Had Shiravi just told him? Why was he even here at this hour? Did Bardari know about this? Who was this other man with Karbashi? One of his people?

"Director, I am somewhat confused. Why are you here talking to my prisoner?"

"I am here because you have not done what you were supposed to do. This prisoner has valuable information on which the fate of our nation depends, yet it been ignored." Karbashi kept on the offensive.

"I find it highly unusual the director of MOIS would personally be interrogating an IRGC prisoner at this hour of the night. Is General Bardari aware of this?" Hamed asked, regaining his footing.

"I do not advise the general of my schedule, just as he does not advise me of his. Is there some issue you have with this?"

"Yes, I do. You have no authority to be speaking with this prisoner. He is under the authority of the IRGC and I am the only one authorized to speak with him," Hamed made clear.

"That is where you are mistaken, Colonel. I do have the authority to speak with the prisoner. All foreign agents fall under the authority of the Ministry of Intelligence when it comes to the security of our nation. He may be your prisoner, but the information he has falls within my responsibility."

Hamed was once again uncertain about what was going on. The IRGC and the Ministry of Intelligence were two separate entities. Karbashi might be the senior-most intelligence official in the Iranian government, but that didn't give him the authority to stick his nose into a matter that was exclusively within the control of the IRGC. Was he trying to make some kind of power play? Something wasn't right here.

"Director Karbashi, I must ask you to leave. This man is a prisoner of the IRGC and you have no authority in this matter. General Bardari has not said anything to me about you questioning the prisoner. I will speak to him in the morning, and once he advises me he has authorized it, you may come back and question the prisoner."

"That will not be possible, Colonel. It is necessary for me to question the prisoner this evening. If I were you, I would go home and get a good night's sleep. You look like you need it from the black under your eyes. When you speak with General Bardari tomorrow, he will advise you that I do have the authority," Karbashi pushed.

"I must insist, Director." Hamed refused to back down.

All this time, Ali and Michael sat silently watching the back-and-forth between Hamed and Karbashi. Michael quickly realized things were heading for a showdown. He was amazed at how well Karbashi had not only maintained his composure after they had been completely caught off guard, but also how he had gone on the offensive without even batting an eye. It was clear, however, this IRGC colonel wasn't going to back down. What were they going to do now? There were three of them against him, but they were at a tactical disadvantage sitting down around the table. Michael assumed he was also armed. He wanted to get up so he would at least be in a better position to react, but he knew any such move would put the colonel on alert. He couldn't say anything either. Otherwise he would give himself away as being an American, and then they would all be in an even more dire situation. All he could do was sit and follow Karbashi's lead.

"Colonel, you are obviously very dedicated to your duty, but there are certain things you are not aware of that have very serious implications for our nation. You must believe me when I tell you, I am doing what is necessary for the safety of our country."

Hamed stood in silence in front of them. He looked at Michael, who returned his stare, their eyes locked on each other as Hamed considered the situation.

"Why are we speaking in English? For whose benefit?" Hamed asked out of the blue, keeping his focus on Michael.

"For the prisoner's benefit, of course," Karbashi replied, a hint of unease in his voice.

"He speaks Farsi, don't you, Ali?" Hamed asked, his eyes still on Michael.

"*Baleh*," Ali said, answering yes.

"*Aya Englisi sohbat mikonid?*" Hamed asked Michael if he spoke English.

Michael remained silent, believing the colonel was still talking to Ali.

"*Aya motevajeh shodid?*" Hamed asked Michael if he understood what he had just said to him.

"Colonel, there is no need for you to speak with my aide. I am the one you will address." Karbashi was caught off guard by Hamed's questions to Michael in Farsi.

Hamed reached under his jacket and drew his PC-9 ZOAF 9mm, an Iranian version of the Sig P226, and pointed it towards them, taking a step back for some distance.

"Who is this man, Director?" Hamed asked.

"Colonel, put your gun down! You have no idea what you are doing," Karbashi ordered.

"You will tell me who this man is, or I will arrest the both of you," Hamed replied, disregarding any authority the director of MOIS thought he had in this situation.

"My name is Michael Blackstone, Colonel. I am an American. I came here to get Ali out of Iran so he can tell his story to the world about who was really responsible for the assassination of your foreign minister. It was not the Israelis. It was a plot by certain people in my government and the Russian government. They wish to start a war between your country and Israel in order to create chaos in the Middle East. That way they will have control of the world's petroleum market. Ali has told you this, has he not?"

"Who are you, Mr. Blackstone? CIA?"

"Not for a very long time. I'm just a friend of Ali's who wants to help him to expose the conspirators and keep a lot of innocent people from being killed," Michael tried to convince him.

"You are lying! You have come here to commit treachery against our country, and this traitor is helping you." He pointed his gun towards Karbashi.

"Colonel, please. These two men are the only ones who can do anything to save our people. You know in your heart I have told you the truth. Do not allow the wicked men who are responsible for killing the foreign minister to bring about the death of so many innocent people with their evil plot. I can feel how much pain you have suffered recently. I am so very sorry for your loss, but do not allow this to happen to thousands or even millions of children." Ali inserted himself into the middle of the escalating situation.

Ali's words hit Hamed like a ton of bricks. His thoughts immediately turned to Reza. A wave of emotion coursed through him, deflating all the fury that had built up inside him towards his perceived opponents. He lowered his 9mm semi-auto. How could Shiravi have known about his child? Hamed tried to return his attention to the current situation but could only see the image of Reza's lifeless little body lying motionless in the hospital bed. It was etched in his memory. Standing in front of them with an expressionless look on his face, his eyes looked past them as if they were not even present in the room with him.

"Colonel, please, sit down." Karbashi motioned to the remaining vacant chair. "We will not attempt anything. You have my word."

Hamed turned towards Karbashi as if wanting to say something, but his lips remained motionless, as he looked at him in silence.

"Colonel, please." Karbashi extended his hand compassionately towards the empty chair.

As if he no longer comprehended he was an IRGC colonel amidst three potential adversaries, Hamed walked forward to the empty chair at their table and sat down, the 9mm still in his right hand hanging at his side. He shifted his gaze amongst the three of them, not as if looking for any furtive moves, but rather acknowledging them for their gestures of kindness towards him.

"Nothing compares to the loss of a child, but I can understand your sorrow. Your child does not feel pain or sorrow any longer, only the lightness and joy of being with Allah. We are the ones who experience sorrow since we no longer have our loved ones with us, but we will be with them again someday, if Allah finds us worthy of being in His presence."

Hamed looked at Ali with a mixture of guilt and remorse. He had come here with the intention of inflicting considerable pain on Ali, yet here he was comforting him with the knowledge that his child was in paradise with Allah.

"How did you know about my son?" Hamed asked Ali.

"I do not know. I just felt a tremendous sense of loss earlier. I felt it again just now when you entered the room," Ali tried to explain.

Hamed sat silently among them in deep thought. They gave him the time he needed to process everything that had abruptly bombarded him since he had arrived.

"Is what you told me before about the foreign minister's assassination the truth?" Hamed finally broke his silence.

"Yes," Ali answered.

Directing his attention to Michael, Hamed asked, "You are not CIA? That is the truth?"

"I am not. I was many years ago. That is how I know Ali, and Director Karbashi, indirectly."

"He helped you enter Iran so you could get Ali out?"

"No, he didn't. He didn't know me until a little over two hours ago," Michael told him straightforwardly. He could tell from Hamed's reaction that he wasn't sure if he had understood him correctly. "I came to Iran on my own, over the border near Maku. More accurately, with assistance on the Turkish side from an old and very trusted friend, but I was on my own until from then until I approached the director unannounced in his home. You are the second person this evening who's had a gun pointed at me."

Hamed's confusion wasn't alleviated by Michael's explanation. "You are telling me you entered Iran on your own to attempt to help Ali escape without any assistance?" Hamed asked incredulously.

"Yes."

"How did you know he was here?"

"He was spotted entering your consulate in Istanbul. His presence here in Iran was an educated guess from circumstantial evidence. I wasn't certain until I spoke with the director a few hours ago and then saw Ali with my own eyes when we got here."

"Please, everyone, call me Farzan. Under the circumstances, my official title has no relevance," Karbashi interjected.

"That is beyond reality to attempt such an insane feat. How did you expect to accomplish it? Did you not fear you would be captured or killed?" Hamed was at a loss, trying to comprehend how Michael had managed to get as far as he had on his own.

"Actually, I expected that would more likely be the case. I had no real plan of what to do. Some things happened to me recently to send me in this direction, despite trying my hardest otherwise. I just felt I had no other choice, regardless of what might happen to me. Besides Ali, I knew what would happen to millions of others. Getting killed wasn't the worst of my fears. I don't think I would have been able to live with myself if I did not try."

Hamed turned next to Karbashi. "How could you believe or trust someone who appeared at your home with such an unbelievable story?"

"A question that any rational man would ask, as did I just a short while ago. Although I have not seen him for many years, I had known Ali very closely. If it were anyone else making such an outlandish claim about the foreign minister's assassination, I would have thought they were a provocateur or mentally unbalanced. Michael knew things about Ali that no one else could have known. As far as trusting him, although I had not met him or known him until a few hours ago, this man saved my life years ago from the Mossad. In the process of doing so, he also killed two Mossad officers. That is why I am here with him right now, Hamed."

Michael looked at the three others around the table. It was almost beyond rational thought that he was sitting next to the director of the Iranian MOIS and across the table from a colonel of the IRGC, talking about breaking Ali out of Evin Prison. Nothing in the wildest dreams since he had departed from the world of espionage and spies had come close to the bizarre nature of the situation he currently found himself in. Everything going back from the Friday over a week ago through the present moment had deviated from the normal course of reality. He imagined his three other companions had similar feelings right now, as he studied their faces.

Ali caught Michael's eye. Without having to say any words, the look on Ali's face let Michael know how much he appreciated the risk he had taken in coming here to try to help him. It wasn't anything he could have ever anticipated when he had called Roxanne, asking her to contact him for help. He didn't know what was harder to believe, that Michael had actually come to Iran to rescue him, or that Farzan, the director of MOIS, was helping Michael accomplish that. Ali saw Farzan glance at him, with the warm smile he remembered from years ago, when they had shared a chapter of their lives together.

"I do not know what to think. I believe you are all telling me the truth. No such story could be fabricated. I had come here intending to employ methods that would ensure I had obtained the truth from Ali, but now I sit here uncertain of my own beliefs."

"Colonel, you are in good company." Michael disclosed the truth about his own doubts, reassuring him that he wasn't alone.

"Sometimes we cannot fully understand the ways in which Allah acts. We can only acknowledge them and do our best to fulfill how we believe he wants us to respond." Karbashi offered as a means of dealing with the conflict each of them was facing.

"Please forgive me for the pain I have already caused you, Ali. Your motives were sincere, yet I was ready to inflict additional pain on you assuming you were being deceitful, when it was others who were duplicitous."

"There is nothing to forgive. You did me no harm. Anything I suffered was more than worth it compared to what I have gained," Ali replied.

Hamed placed his hand over his mouth and began to weep. "I have inflicted pain and suffering on many others. I have reached into their souls and torn out the last remnants that remained in some of them. I did it all in the name of protecting our country, but Allah will judge me for this. Perhaps He has already and has punished me with the same pain I have caused others."

The three of them sat silently as Hamed faced the truth about his previous actions. They all knew the type of torment he had inflicted on other men's souls, yet each of them felt a sense of sorrow for the demons he was now left confronting, along with his grief from the death of his child. It was as if the cumulative sorrow he had inflicted on others had now been unleashed on him. They could see the sincerity of his remorse as he struggled to contain his emotions.

After he had allowed his soul to purge itself of the darkness that had accumulated year after year from breaking other men, he regained his composure and announced, "I will assume the responsibility of getting Ali out from here."

"How will you explain that, especially to Bardari?" Karbashi asked.

"Do not be concerned. The important thing is that this treachery is exposed and no more innocent blood is spilled. I will wait until tomorrow morning to advise the general of my actions. That will give you approximately ten hours. I cannot prolong it any longer. Otherwise, I would be duplicitous and cowardly in disregarding my duty to apprise my commanding officer, whatever the consequences to me from my actions," Hamed answered resolutely.

"Thank you, Colonel. That's much more than we would have had otherwise," Michael said.

"It will give them sufficient time to make it most of the distance to the border," Karbashi advised.

"We haven't figured things out yet on transportation. Are there any overnight trains that leave from Tehran this late?" Michael asked.

"Do not be concerned, Michael. I will take care of that, if Hamed would be so kind as to provide me a ride back to my home."

"Yes, of course."

"I'm not quite sure I understand," Michael commented.

"You and Ali will take my car and drive to the border. Highway 2 will take you to Tabriz, which changes briefly to Highway 14 just past Tabriz, then splits off to Highway 32, which will lead you directly to Maku. It is approximately nine hundred kilometers. You will need to purchase petrol at least once to make it the entire way. The tank is almost full now. When we leave the prison, you will follow us and we will lead you to the highway to the west of the city."

"Won't that implicate you?" Michael asked Karbashi.

"I will deal with whatever may result. It is Hamed who is putting himself in the most jeopardy. Do you have a way back across the border?"

"I sure hope so. Otherwise it's going to be a long hike."

"I see it is a habit of yours to make light of difficult situations," Karbashi indicated a second time that evening.

"Caught me again. Must keep me from feeling overwhelmed."

"Let us be on our way, then." Karbashi stood up from the table.

"I will place handcuffs on you, Ali, so that nothing seems odd to the guards. It will already appear unusual to be transporting a prisoner in this manner at this hour of the night," Hamed explained to them.

The other three stood. Hamed holstered his weapon and reached for his briefcase, removing a pair of handcuffs. Motioning to Ali, he requested his cooperation, the first time he had shown such deference to one of his prisoners. Ali placed his arms behind him and turned his back to Hamed, who placed the cuffs loosely on his wrists. Hamed walked Ali to the door, opening it and proceeding out into the hallway, followed by Karbashi and Michael. The guard standing outside was caught by surprise as they all emerged with the prisoner.

"I am taking the prisoner," Hamed told the guard.

Confused, the guard asked, "Taking him, Colonel?"

"Did you not hear me correctly?"

"Yes, sir!" The guard said nothing further, not wanting to provoke the ire of the colonel.

They marched Ali down the hall and out to the reception area. Ghazi looked up at them surprised, giving his colleague bringing up the rear a quizzical look and receiving shrugged shoulders in return.

"The prisoner is coming with me," Hamed informed him.

"We have not received any paperwork to release him, Colonel," the Ghazi cautiously advised, not knowing if there was some kind of administrative oversight.

"He is not being released. I am temporarily taking him. He will be returned tomorrow at some point."

"This is highly unusual, Colonel. We always receive written notification before a prisoner leaves the prison, even if it is temporary."

"Are you questioning me?" Hamed asked in an intimidating tone.

"No, sir! I have just never seen a prisoner released from custody in such a manner."

"There is a first time for everything," Hamed snapped at him.

"Yes, sir!" Ghazi knew he had pushed the issue far enough. The prisoner was the colonel's responsibility now.

The four of them walked out of the main reception area out to the covered courtyard and waited to be buzzed out the main door to the parking lot. They walked Ali to Karbashi's blue Mercedes at the far end of the lot. Karbashi pulled the key fob out of his pocket and unlocked the doors as they approached. Stopping alongside the car, Michael handed Karbashi his leather briefcase.

"Well, looks like this is it," Michael told Karbashi with a hint of sorrow in his voice. "I wish we had more time to sit down and talk after all these years. That was the original plan."

"Yes, I would have enjoyed the opportunity to converse with you on a number of topics. You are an intriguing man to have undertaken this extraordinary endeavor. I would like to give you something," Karbashi told him, setting his briefcase on the roof of the car and opening both locks. He reached in and pulled out the Model 1911 he had aimed at Michael earlier that evening, along with two additional magazines. "I ask that you only use it as a last resort against any of my people should the need arise. Here is also a mobile phone that has my number into it in case you need to contact me for any reason."

"Thank you for everything, Farzan. I wouldn't have been able to accomplish what I came here to do if you hadn't been for you." Michael reached for Karbashi's hand.

"Let us just say it is in return for what you did for me those many years ago. I would not be here otherwise. Perhaps our paths will cross again someday. May Allah protect you, guide you, and bring you joy throughout the remaining days of your life, Michael."

"The same to Farzan. One thing I've learned lately is that life is full of unexpected surprises." Turning to Hamed next, Michael extended his hand. "Colonel, thank you. I hope you can find peace. It escaped me for a long time until I finally was forced to come face-to-face with certain things about myself that I didn't want to see."

"Go in peace, Mr. Blackstone. May your efforts make a difference in saving the lives of our people and those of others, even the Zionists." Hamed took Michael's hand.

"I will do everything in my power to make that happen," he assured Hamed. "I'll start the car while you say your final goodbyes," he told Ali, giving him the opportunity to make his peace with Karbashi and Hamed.

Turning to Hamed first, Ali faced the man who, up until half an hour ago, had intended on causing him great pain and distress. It was strange, but he felt a touch of sadness saying goodbye to his former tormentor. Despite the initial cruelty he had inflicted upon him, Ali could sense the goodness in Hamed shining through the darkness that had rooted itself in his heart. He didn't know what the future held for Hamed, but it was hard to imagine he would be able to go back to his previous duties. Something had changed in him.

"*Salaam Alaikum*, brother. I will pray for you. I hope you do not have to suffer consequences because of what you are doing to help me," Ali told him, wishing him peace.

"*Inshallah*," Hamed replied, leaving the decision up to Allah. "*Alaikum salaam*, brother. I am happy you have finally found Allah's voice in your life. May he always be your guide."

Finally, Ali turned to Karbashi. "Farzan, I never had a chance to tell you that I truly valued our friendship. I can't imagine what you must have thought after everything that happened in Athens. I struggled for a long time afterwards with feelings I betrayed your trust, which initially I did, but afterwards I hoped something good would come out of it all. I just wanted you to know that."

"Thank you, Ali. I valued our friendship also, even if my original motivations were also to determine if my relationship with you could be exploited. It was my intent also in the end that our friendship would have resulted in something beneficial for both our countries. Someday, if the relationship between our two countries changes and we are still living, I hope to be able to see you again. Perhaps I can come to the United States and you can show me some of your adopted country's culture."

"I would like that, Farzan."

"Go in peace, my friend. May you always feel Allah's presence guiding you."

"*Salaam alaikum*," Ali gave him a final farewell with the traditional contact with both cheeks, before getting into the passenger seat of the Mercedes and shutting the door.

Michael and Ali watched as Karbashi followed Hamed to his car, waiting to be led to the highway that would get them to the Turkish border. As the Renault pulled up beside them, Michael put Karbashi's E550 into gear and slowly pulled out behind them as they left the parking lot of Evin Prison.

"Well, here we go. Just like old times, huh, Ali? You going to miss this place at all?" Michael asked, not wanting to waste a chance for Ali to hear some of his sarcasm from long ago.

"I don't think the saying 'a nice place to visit but I wouldn't want to live there' applies in these circumstances," Ali shot back.

"Touché, old friend. Sit back and enjoy the ride. We have a long drive ahead of us."

***

The eight F-35s of the Golden Eagle Squadron were flying in tight formation with night vision at twenty-five thousand feet out in the middle of the Negev Desert. Fifteen thousand feet above them was a modified 707 Re'em electronic warfare aircraft with a fifteen-hundred-kilowatt generator on board powering the M'sanver Ma'or, or Blinding Light Countermeasures System. It spewed out high-energy jamming signals across a broad spectrum of frequencies, effectively disrupting all communications and active radar systems in the immediate area. The power had been decreased to limit the effective range to five miles, rather than the maximum of fifty, so as not to affect Israeli air defense systems and commercial airline traffic over the nearby Mediterranean. Another five thousand feet above it was a Gulfstream G550 AEWC aircraft, which was sending encrypted navigation and guidance information to the F-35s. Everything was being read flawlessly as the AEWC downloaded and uploaded data via a secure link to the on-board computer systems which had just been updated by the Lockheed Martin technicians.

"Gold 2, Gold Leader. Radio check."

"Lima Charlie. How me?"

"Lima Charlie, Gold 2," Lieutenant Colonel Janner said, confirming he could hear his wingman loud and clear.

"Gold 3, Gold Leader, radio check," Janner went down the line with each pilot of his squadron, verifying that communications amongst each other, and then with the AEWC, were crisp and clear. Satisfied, he gave the order to return to base. He needed to let General Bachman know that his squadron was finally fully operational and mission-ready. The mission had been delayed because of his squadron's unpreparedness through no fault of his own, but they were the star attraction, so everyone had to wait for them. The aircraft now needed to be refueled and loaded with their ordnance.

Each F-35 would be carrying two five-thousand-pound enhanced GBU-28 GPS-guided bunker buster bombs each. Between the eight aircraft, sixteen GBU-28 bunker busters, totaling forty tons, would be dropped on the Fordow uranium enrichment facility, which was built underground in the heart of a mountain and reinforced with an additional two hundred feet of pressure-hardened concrete above it. The demolition engineers had calculated sixty-thousand pounds of high explosives on the exact same spot would be necessary to penetrate the facility, but another twenty thousand pounds of munitions had been added to the strike package just to make sure. To ensure pinpoint accuracy and to obtain the maximum blast damage, each GBU-28 would be released sequentially and guided to hit the exact same spot on the mountain in two-second intervals. Although the pilots would be flying their aircraft during the bomb run, the tactical strike officer and his technicians flying up above the battle space at forty-three thousand feet in two AEWCs would be tapped into the F-35s' on-board computer systems via secure link and would be the ones actually controlling the sequential release of each of the sixteen GBU-28s.

The AEWCs would be protected by eight F-15C fighters while they maintained tactical control and communication of all the mission aircraft. The strike team itself would be escorted by an additional sixteen F-15D fighters. For the aircraft to make the two-thousand-mile round-trip mission, four KC-707 Saknai aerial refuelers escorted by eight F-15A fighters would preposition themselves over eastern Iraq, waiting to top off the strike team. At two minutes for each aircraft, the four refuelers would have all twenty-four aircraft refueled in less than fifteen minutes. With a full tank of gas, once the eight F-35s with the accompanying sixteen F-15s crossed over into Iranian airspace, they would go to afterburners and, flying at Mach 1.3, it would take them twenty minutes to travel the three hundred miles to Fordow. The bombing run would take approximately sixty seconds, then the strike team would turn around and head back to Iraq at Mach 1.6, making it in sixteen minutes, having them in Iranian airspace for a total of thirty-seven minutes. The Re'em 707s would likewise begin shifting the mission's fifty-mile-wide by three-hundred-mile-long protective corridor as all the mission aircraft began the retrograde back to Israel. Skirting along southern Syria to bypass the Russian air defense systems deployed near Damascus and the US military's in the northeast of the country, the mission time from start to finish, including refueling the aircraft, was four hours and twenty minutes. It was a long, complex mission with a lot of moving parts by any standard. The execution and timing had to be flawless for it to succeed.

After the eight F-35s landed back at their base at 12:00 a.m., Lieutenant Colonel Janner told his men to get some sleep and be well rested for their 8:00 a.m. mission brief later that morning. As they slept, the squadron's support personnel would be refueling the aircraft and arming them, preparing them for the mission later that day. On air bases throughout Israel, support personnel were preparing the seventy aircraft which would participate in the mission, almost a third of Israel's entire air force.

***

They had followed Hamed and Karbashi to the western side of Tehran, where Highway 2 left the city and headed westward towards Tabriz and eventually to the Turkish border. They would travel throughout the night and hopefully make it to Maku by late morning sometime without attracting the attention of the authorities. Their timing was less than optimal. They would have to lie low somewhere until it was dark, then ditch Karbashi's Mercedes. From there, they would have to hike it back out into the hills and wait for an extraction by Ercan. Coming in during daylight hours would be much too risky. First, Michael would have to contact Asya and let her know they were on their way out so she could give Ercan warning to be standing by.

They hadn't said much for the first thirty minutes as they drove west past

Karaj, another small city that was essentially a suburb of Tehran, until they were out in the dark Iranian countryside. They sat in silence next to each other, the blue LED lighting from the dash illuminating their faces in the darkness as they processed the events of their remarkable night. Ali had changed into the clothes Karbashi had brought him from his home. Wearing a freshly pressed white shirt and a slightly large khaki suit, Ali looked as if he belonged in the luxury German sedan. At 12:30 a.m., most of the traffic on the road consisted of trucks transporting their cargo out of Tehran.

"Hey, you okay?" Michael asked.

"Yes, Michael, I'm fine. I'm sorry I haven't said much after not having seen you for so long. I'm still trying to come to terms with everything. I didn't expect I would ever see you, let alone Karbashi. I want to pinch myself, just to make sure I'm not having some kind of episode and all this is real. It has been an unbelievable last few days for me. There were times when I thought I was losing my mind. Fortunately, I was being reassured that somehow everything would be all right, but I could never have foreseen how things turned out. Then there was everything with the colonel and his child. I don't know how I knew, I just did. There is a lot that happened to me while I was in there that I am still trying to understand."

"That's all right, Ali. You've been through an unbelievable ordeal. It's going to take a while to deal with everything. I'm in the same spot as you as far as trying to comprehend everything. There's some stuff that's happened to me that I still haven't figured out. I'm just glad you haven't been harmed. To be perfectly honest with you, I didn't know what condition I would find you in. I thought we might have to be carrying you out."

"I could very easily have been in a very bad state. When I first arrived there, I thought it was all over, that I would never leave that place the same person. But then everything changed and I felt peace. I wasn't worried about what would happen."

"How was it that the colonel never physically harmed you? He doesn't seem to be the type that would show any mercy when it came to doing his job. He obviously didn't get to his position because he was a nice guy to the prisoners," Michael asked, puzzled.

"I don't know. He threatened he would, but for some reason he never went through with it. There was nothing I could have done to prevent him from doing so anyway, other than tell him the truth, which I did. Perhaps he believed me. Maybe he could see I had no reason to lie. How in the world did you get Karbashi to help you? How did you find him? I can't believe I saw him again after all these years, and what he was willing to do for me."

"How I found him? That's an unbelievable story in itself. I'll tell you as we drive. We have plenty of time. As far as how I got him to help me? It didn't really take that much. I told him who I was, everything that had happened and what you said. I don't know why he trusted me. Maybe he just could tell I was giving him the truth. He is a very unique guy, really sharp, wise beyond just book smarts, like he can see things for what they really are. I always knew never to underestimate him in Athens, but until you actually talk to him, you don't realize just how much he's got it together."

"He is one of a kind, which is why it was never difficult to be in his company. As a person, he was very genuine and interesting. It was easy to forget sometimes that he was our adversary. There were moments when I felt a real sense of guilt that I was betraying the trust of a friendship. I didn't have any illusions about how our relationship would eventually end, but when he asked straightforwardly to meet with my boss and you were going to meet with him, I felt a sense of relief that he never asked me to betray my country or vice versa," Ali confessed.

"That's understandable, Ali. I always realized there was a bond that had formed between you two. I mean, that is the ideal situation. There's a certain genuineness amidst the background of deception and deceit. It's one of the most challenging emotions to deal with when you're planning on asking someone you've befriended to betray their country. I think that sincerity was what ultimately made Karbashi decide to help you. He could have easily thrown me in jail and have had you paraded on the international stage with your story, but he didn't, at great risk to himself. He could be hanged for what he's done, same with the colonel."

"I know. They've both risked their lives, but I believe they both know what will happen to them and all their loved ones, so any personal risk to them doesn't really faze them. After losing a child, I'm sure nothing would stop the colonel from doing whatever he thought necessary without blinking an eye. He was a different man from the first time I saw him. He would do anything to protect his wife and any other children he may have. The same with Karbashi for his wife."

"His wife has died, Ali. It's just him now. You wouldn't have known, obviously. He told me when we were having our little chat back as his place earlier this evening," Michael let him know.

"Oh, I'm sorry to hear that. I remember him telling me about her and how hard it was on the two of them being apart for so many years of their marriage while he was gone on foreign assignment. They didn't or couldn't have children, I seem to remember."

"He told me they did, but it died shortly after birth."

"That's right. Now I remember. He's had a lot of sadness in his life," Ali reflected.

"You certainly can identify with him. I was sorry to hear about Janet passing away. I remember her. She was a really nice person."

"Thank you, Michael. It was very difficult for Roxanne and me at the time, but I will see her again someday. I am certain of it now. I think that was part of the reason I had such peace despite my situation. If I was going to die, it would just be that much sooner that I would be with Janet. Although I wasn't too fond of how painful and long that process might have been before I was actually going to depart from this world, God reassured me everything would be all right."

"I didn't know you were religious. I thought I remembered you telling me your parents were pretty much secular college professors and that you never really went to mosque when you were a kid."

"That's true, and I still don't know that I'm religious, but I do believe in God, Allah, however you want to call Him, now."

"Yeah? Why now?" Michael asked, his curiosity roused.

"Let's just say, while I was in my cell, I experienced something that has no rational explanation."

"What do you mean?"

"I had a couple of conversations with God."

"Conversations? Like actual verbal, talking and hearing conversations?"

"Yes. I know it sounds crazy, Michael. You're probably thinking I was just delusional or had some type of psychotic episode. That's what I thought at the time, but it was real, I know it was. I was completely rational and coherent before and afterwards. I know it wasn't some kind of mental breakdown. I just know. I'm positive," Ali declared self-assuredly.

Michael didn't say anything as he considered what Ali had just disclosed to him. As far as Michael could remember from his days in Sunday school, only a handful of people could claim to have had personal conversations with God, Adam and Eve, Noah, Moses, and maybe you could include a few others who had visits by some of God's personal messengers. Ali was claiming membership in a pretty exclusive club. Michael knew him well enough to know he wouldn't make such a claim lightly, and despite being imprisoned for a week in a place that destroyed men's souls, he didn't appear to be psychologically traumatized.

"Well, considering the week I've had, who am I to question anything? Actually, I have lots of questions, I just haven't been able to find the answers yet. So, are you a Muslim now? A Christian?"

"I don't know. Janet was Lutheran and took Roxanne to church occasionally, but I never went with them. I didn't want to be a hypocrite. When I asked God what I should believe, He told me if my heart was pure as I searched for the truth, He would guide me in finding it. I guess I'm just going to have to trust Him and see where He leads me."

"Hm" was all Michael could say, filing away the message Ali had supposedly received firsthand from the Almighty, along with all the other unexplainable occurrences of the past ten days. "Now that we're out of town a ways, I'm going to pull over and get a hold of our travel agent that's going to make arrangements for our ride back over the border. Do me a favor. There's a bag on the backseat filled with pistachios. Shove your hand in there and dig around, you'll find a GPS, a mobile phone and a sat phone buried underneath. Grab me the mobile phone. Just be careful; there's a knife that's shoved in there also."

Ali twisted around to the back and pulled Michael's hemp bag around to the front, setting it down between his legs. Pulling out Michael's rusty knife and setting it next to his feet, he shoved his hand into the bag of pistachios and searched for the phone. Pulling out the GPS first, he set it down in the center console. His second plunge into the pistachios netted him the Iridium satellite phone. His final try resulted in the mobile phone Asya had given Michael.

"Here you go." Ali handed it to Michael.

Michael turned it on and waited for it to acquire a signal. He would pop up on the Iranian mobile network, but after his short communication with Asya, he would turn it back off and become invisible once again to any Iranian authorities monitoring mobile phone traffic within their country. The next time he would use it would be when they were in Maku, ready to have Ercan come and pull them out. When the three bars came up, Michael dialed Asya's mobile phone number, which he had memorized. There was silence for a few seconds as Michael waited for the call to go through the Irancell network and connect with Asya's mobile. Instead of a ring, he heard a recorded message in Turkish, then in English. "The customer you are trying to reach is currently unavailable. Please try again later." *That's not good*, he thought as he looked at the number he had dialed and confirmed it was correct. He was certain he had the right number. He never forgot numbers. He had drilled it into his head over and over before he had even left Istanbul. He dialed it again and received the same message. Not wanting to risk a third try while roaming on an Iranian network, he powered off the phone and handed it back to Ali.

"What's wrong?" Ali asked.

"I don't know. That's not like her not to be reachable. I'll try again in a little bit. So, we got a long drive ahead of us. Why don't you fill me in on the past ten years since we parted company in Athens? We have a lot of catching up to do." Michael tried not to sound too concerned, for Ali's sake, but he was troubled.

***

Canton was pushing his black BMW 650i through the curves on Sahil Boulevard along the eastern shore of the Bosphorus as he headed back to the shipyard complex where they were holding Asya prisoner. Following his unsuccessful attempt at breaking her earlier in the day, he had returned to his hotel, spending the remainder of the afternoon and evening stewing in his room over the fact that she had remained defiant towards him despite being helplessly bound before him. She had humiliated him in front of the Russians. Rostov had probably gotten a good laugh that he was unable to intimidate a woman in such a vulnerable position. She would pay for showing such flagrant disrespect to him. He would completely dehumanize her, then she would crumble and tell him what he wanted to know about Blackstone.

Fortunately, it was late enough at night that there was very little traffic on the road, which gave him the use of both lanes to accommodate his slightly erratic driving. He had a nice little buzz going after polishing off the restocked Blue Label in his mini-bar. He had asked room service to forgo the inferior Chivas, wanting only the premium Johnnie Walker. He had lost track of how many bottles he had gone through since he had checked in a few days ago, but today's eight had added another four hundred euros to his room bill. Oh well, the cost to the American taxpayers for advancing their interests. She would be able to smell the alcohol on his breath, which just added to the humiliation she would experience as he was stripping her of all her remaining dignity.

He came up on the last curve before the turnoff for the shipyard, unexpectedly doing one hundred and twenty kilometers an hour. Not wanting to pass by it, he slammed on the brakes and spun the steering wheel to the right, causing the 650i to break into a skid as he attempted to make the turn. As he turned the steering wheel in the direction of the skid, attempting to regain control, he over-corrected, causing a skid in the opposite direction and sending him towards the curb. His front left wheel made hard contact with the curb, launching him into a wild spin in the middle of the boulevard. Finally coming to a stop without hitting anything else, he breathed a sigh of relief that he hadn't crashed his car. When he turned the steering wheel to head back in the right direction, the car began turning in circles to the right even though he held the wheel straight. He turned the steering wheel to the right until it was at ninety degrees before he was able to point the BMW in a straight direction, having to arm-wrestle it to keep it on course.

"Ah shit! I can't believe this!" He cursed his bad luck. The second time in less than a week. He limped the BMW into the shipyard and made his way down the access road toward their secluded hideaway. He pulled up outside the white wooden building and turned off the engine. Getting out, he turned on the LED light on his mobile phone and looked at his front left wheel to find it turned cockeyed to the right, with a sizeable gouge to the alloy wheel. He shook his head in disbelief. It had been a bad day to begin with, and it had just gotten worse. That Turkish whore would pay for the displeasure she had brought him.

He pulled the sliding door slightly open and made his way inside. Tarhan's blue Audi A7 was still there with her things inside. Shining his mobile phone light inside, he saw Asya's purse, shoulder holster and her mobile phone. He grabbed her phone and was about to turn it on, but decided against it, knowing it would be unwise to allow it to register on the Turkish mobile network and identify its location. He searched some more through her purse, then looked around inside her car, not finding anything else of significance? Giving up his search in frustration, he stumbled his way to the hallway and headed towards the faint light coming from the far end.

As he entered the room where they were keeping Tarhan, he found another one of Rostov's men standing guard, two LED lanterns lighting the end of the room where she was sitting on the stool, her wrists and ankles bound to the steel cage and her head slumped forward. That was good! She looked physically exhausted. She would hardly be in any condition to resist him. It was going to be a pleasure having his way with her. Rostov's man looked up at him, jumping down from sitting on one of the tables, obviously surprised to see him at that hour.

"*Sdrasvichia*, Vasyli, Grigori or whatever your name is. You know who I am?" Canton addressed him.

"The name is Dimitri, and I know who you are. Why are you here at this hour?" he asked as Asya stirred, raising her head slowly to see Canton standing back in the shadows.

"If you know who I am, then you should know that your job is to do what I tell you and not ask stupid questions that don't concern you. I am here because this bitch has information that could sink us all, and I am going to get it out of her one way or another. Does that satisfy your curiosity?"

"I was not advised you would be coming tonight."

"That's right, you weren't. You don't get advised when I decide to come or go. Anything else you would like to say?" Canton asked sarcastically. "No? Good. How's she been?"

"Just as you see her. How do you expect her to be?" Dimitri answered him with contempt.

Asya looked up at him and in a tired but defiant voice said, "Are you back because you have nothing better to do with yourself this evening?"

"Well, well, not happy to see me? I thought, being here lonely and bored, maybe you would enjoy some interesting conversation. Doesn't have to be anything too deep. Maybe we could make a little chitchat, get to know each other a little better. You could tell me a little about yourself, your likes, dislikes, whether you like assertive men or ones who do what you tell them. How was it between you and Blackstone?" he tried to demean her.

"Whatever you may think you know, Michael Blackstone is ten times the man you can ever dream to be!"

"Oh, sounds like I hit a nerve. Were you hoping you would see him again? Hoping you would feel him next to you?"

"You are a pathetic and cowardly little man!" she responded disdainfully.

"I wonder if he would want to be with a whore like you, knowing you spread your legs anytime you strike up a conversation with someone on a first date. Okay, maybe second date, if you count this morning. I'll give you the benefit of the doubt since we didn't hit it off too well. I think our current conversation is going well, under the circumstances. Wouldn't you agree?" he taunted her from the shadows.

"You speak bravely, but you can't intimidate me. Whatever you think you can do, you will not be able to break me. You will always have to live with that. That you were not able to rise to the occasion. That you were impotent and weak," she belittled him.

Dimitri snickered at Asya's humiliating remark about Canton's manhood, which Canton clearly observed from the shadows. He stood in silence, fuming at her insult as his left eye began to twitch. He felt the rage building up inside him towards her. He would show that Turkish bitch who was weak and powerless. By the time he was done with her tonight, any trace of insolence would be completely gone. He would thoroughly and completely demean her, leaving her a broken shadow of the person she was, then let her lie in her shame and humiliation the rest of the night until they finished her off tomorrow.

"I want you to strip her down naked and turn her around facing the cage," he ordered Dimitri.

The Russian SVR officer didn't move. He glanced at Asya, then turned his gaze to Canton, standing in the shadows, the look on his face indicating he wasn't sure of what to do.

"Did you not hear me? I said I want her stripped naked and turned around facing the cage, spread eagle."

"Do not do it, Dimitri. You know it is not right. Do not lower yourself to that level. You are not like him," she pleaded.

"Save your breath, bitch. You'll have plenty of opportunity to beg me in just a minute. What are you waiting for? I told you what to do." He stepped forward out of the shadows for them to see his face clearly.

"This is not correct. Rostov would not approve of this," Dimitri declared.

"I don't care what the hell you think, and it's not up to Rostov to approve or disapprove what I do with her to get the information we need. Don't worry, you can have sloppy seconds when I'm done with her, if you like." Canton smirked.

Reluctantly, Dimitri got up, grabbed a handful of zip ties and tucked them under his belt behind his back, then slowly walked towards Asya with a look of guilt on his face for what he was about to do.

"No, please!" Asya beseeched the Russian.

"I am sorry," he whispered to her as he drew near.

Grabbing her arm, he slowly raised her up and pulled the stool away from her.

"No, no, do not do this, please!" she implored him.

He reluctantly pulled out a Spyderco knife from inside his waistband and flipped open the serrated blade. Kneeling down beside her right leg, he cut one of the long zip ties securing her to the cage as she twisted her body back and forth, yanking on the restraints on her wrists. Moving to her left side, he did the same with her other leg as she continued to resist.

"Please stop, you will just make it harder on yourself," Dimitri told her as he stood up and faced her.

He waited until she finally relented and relaxed her body, slumping down and hanging from her wrists. Grabbing hold of her right wrist with his left hand, he cut the zip tie to turn her around and re-secure her wrist to the cage as Canton had wanted. With his attention momentarily drawn away as closed his knife, tucking it into his waistband, then twisting around to grab a new zip tie from his back, he was caught completely off guard as Asya sprung up from her slumped position and propelled her knee into his groin with all her strength. As he doubled over, gasping for breath, Asya came up with the heel of her right foot, making solid contact with the side of his face and spinning him around onto his knees as he struggled to keep from falling to the floor. Without missing a beat, Asya leaped up and wrapped her leg around his neck, tucking her ankle behind her other knee as she placed him into a choke hold and brought him to his knees.

Rather than going for his knife, Dimitri grasped for Asya's leg as he thrashed back and forth, trying to escape her death grip. Asya looked over towards Canton and could see the whites of his eyes from the shock of what was occurring in front of him. As Dimitri attempted to stand up off the floor, she saw Canton draw his gun and point it in their direction, trying to aim at her. She had the big Russian in front of her as cover, but knew she only had a few seconds before Canton would eventually find his mark. With Dimitri flailing, trying to break free, she reached with her free right hand towards the gun that was holstered on the right side of his waist. Seeing her go for it, Canton opened fire, emptying the entire magazine. The only round that found a target hit Dimitri in his left thigh, bringing him back down onto his knees, allowing Asya to finally unholster his Russian P-96 9mm. She fired a round towards Canton, missed, then fired again, but the instability of the struggling Russian caused her to miss once again. It didn't matter, however; panicking from her return fire, Canton turned and bolted into the shadows and out of the room.

Asya maintained her aim in the direction of the doorway Canton had fled through as the intensity of the Russian's struggle lessened. Her choke hold, along with the gunshot to his leg, had finally begun to wear down his stamina, and he began to slide into a state of unconsciousness. Another thirty seconds and he had dropped face-down, motionless onto the floor. Asya relaxed her grip around his neck but didn't let go entirely as she attempted to pull his body back towards her where she was still attached to the cage by her left wrist, which was in excruciating pain by now. Managing to turn him onto his side, she tucked the handgun into her pants and hurriedly reached for the Spyderco knife that was tucked into the front of Dimitri's waistband. Flicking open the serrated blade, she turned to her bruised and bleeding left wrist and cut the last remaining zip tie that kept her bound to the cage.

Finally free, she pulled the 9mm back out and made her way around the room towards the door, using the large wooden tables as cover. Allowing her eyes to momentarily adjust to the darkness before entering the hallway, she stood around the corner and listened for any noise. Hearing the sound of a car door slam shut, then the start of an engine, she turned the corner and made her way quickly but carefully down the hallway until she entered a large room empty room, finding her Audi parked inside. From somewhere outside, she heard tires spinning in gravel and the roar of a car engine.

Keeping her gun trained in front of her, she made her way to the partially open large sliding door. Peeking around it, she stepped outside into the cool night air. She couldn't see anything, but she heard what she assumed was Canton speeding away in the darkness. She turned and went back inside, still alert for any other threats. She looked inside her car and saw her mobile phone, purse and shoulder holster with her H&K P30. Reaching in, she grabbed the holster and placed her arms through, settling it onto her shoulders. Grabbing her Samsung Galaxy J7, she depressed the power button to wake it, but nothing happened. She held the power button down, but again, nothing. That was odd. It was fully charged twenty-four hours ago. She pulled open the back cover to find the battery missing. Rummaging through her purse then searching around her car, she was unable to find the missing battery for her mobile.

"*Bok!*" Asya let out a rare swearword. She would have to worry about that later. For now, she had to assess her immediate situation with her unconscious Russian captor. He wouldn't stay that way for long before he started coming to. He had also been shot. She couldn't just leave him there to bleed out and die, regardless of whether that was their intention for her. She turned back down the hallway toward the room where she had been imprisoned. Entering the room, she saw fourteen bullet holes in the wall on the other side of the cage illuminated by the glow of the lanterns. It was amazing she hadn't been hit at least once. *Thank You, Allah*, she offered silently.

She walked over to the still-unconscious Russian lying on the floor, a small puddle of blood underneath his left thigh. She grabbed the Spyderco knife and sliced open his pant leg from the ankle all the way up to the site of the bullet wound. He was lucky. The round had entered the fleshy part of the back of the outside of his thigh and exited cleanly a few inches away on the other side. It was oozing dark red blood rather than squirting bright red blood. *Good*, she thought, *looks like it didn't hit an artery or bone*. Next, she sliced open his T-shirt from top to bottom. Cutting two squares of the fabric, she folded them over several times, forming two bandages. With the remainder of the T-shirt, she cut long strips and wrapped them tightly around the two bandages, securing them in place over the entry and exit wounds. He might not be able to get anywhere on his own, but at least he wasn't going to bleed to death until someone could get there to give him medical attention and take him into custody. She dragged the big Russian a few feet, and with his remaining zip ties, secured both his wrists the cage. Her priority now was to find the battery and get her mobile switched back on. Michael might have been trying to get a hold of her and coming up empty. She would deal with Canton and the Russians after she made sure Michael could contact her.

Before leaving, she searched through the Russian's pockets and found his mobile phone. Hoping against odds, she tried it, but found it was locked. That wasn't surprising. It was more than likely a clean phone, but she would take it with her anyway to see what information could be recovered from it. Making her way back to the room where her Audi was parked, she went over to the large sliding door. Grabbing onto it with both hands, she went to push it, but winced in pain from her bloodied left wrist. She guessed she had broken it or sprained it badly while she was still attached to the cage, trying to subdue Dimitri. Putting her shoulder into it, she slowly forced the large door open wide enough to drive her car through. As she let up, a wave of dizziness suddenly came over her, and she slid down to the floor to keep from falling over. The adrenaline that had given her the strength to overcome her physically dominating captor had begun to wear off, and the effects of being tied to a cage for twenty-four hours without food had finally caught up with her. She tried to stand up but slid back to the floor as another wave of dizziness overwhelmed her. Crawling on her hands and knees, she made her way over to her car and pulled herself up, leaning against it to hold herself up. She hung onto the door as she swung it open, then plopped down into the seat, clinging onto the steering wheel as she tried to recover so she would be able to drive. Looking through her purse again, she found the key fob, then pushed the ignition button, bringing the Audi's engine to life. Putting it into drive, she slowly steered the car through the building's opening to the outside, where her ordeal had begun just over twenty-four hours ago. She knew it was probably a good idea to go to a hospital to be examined, have her wrist splinted and maybe get an IV to rehydrate, but she didn't have the time to waste. She would go home to clean and bandage herself up as best as she could. She needed to find a battery or another mobile phone to slip her SIM card into. She needed to hurry; every second counted.

Canton sped north back up Sahil Boulevard towards the city, doing over one hundred twenty kilometers per hour, trying to keep from losing control around the curves with the cockeyed steering wheel. From how the BMW was handling, he could tell he had messed up the alignment pretty badly. He was trying to get his hyperventilating under control before he called Rostov to tell him what happened. Someone would need to go back to the abandoned plant and retrieve Alexi, or whatever his name was, and assess the situation. Maybe there was a chance she was still attached to the cage. His mind was racing uncontrollably, trying to figure out his options, but it was hard for him to focus his thoughts as he struggled against panicking. *Okay, I'm a deputy director in the CIA. I can claim…shit! What can I claim? I'm screwed! No, I just need to get out of the country so the Turks don't have any jurisdiction over me. I'll report the Russians had information she was involved in the plot to kill the foreign minister and they picked her up to question her, then contacted me. I can sell that. Payton will back me against whatever the Turks claim.*

The first thing he needed to do was grab his things, check out of the hotel and find a temporary safe house. He would ditch his car and use public transportation, make his way down to the central train station and check into a seedy hotel using cash. He had a good amount of lira on him, enough to get him by for a few days. Should he call Bob, the chief of station, and ask for an extraction? What would he say? The Turks were trying to kill him? No, he couldn't go to the consulate; the director of the MIT would certainly be calling Bob as soon as Tarhan had told her story. He would be trapped there and not be able to maneuver. Even if he denied everything and stuck with his alternative story, he would be powerless to do anything. He had to get out of the country first. The Agency Gulfstream that had brought him here was out of the question. The Turks would be watching the airport. His black diplomatic passport wouldn't do him any good in making his escape when it came to kidnapping one of their own senior intelligence officials. They would detain him at the airport and summon the US ambassador. He had to escape via other means. He needed to contact Payton and let him know what had happened. Maybe he could arrange to get him out of the country. Maybe Rostov could help him. He had to get himself and his men out somehow. He could just piggyback with them. What was one extra man? He could explain about having accidentally shot his man. It was an honest mistake, understandable under the circumstances.

He pulled his cell phone out of his pocket and fumbled it in his hands as he dialed Rostov's number while trying to keep from going off the road. He heard the other end ring once, then a second time, a third, then a fourth. "Answer the phone, asshole!" he screamed uncontrollably.

Finally, after the fifth ring he heard, "Yes?"

"We have a situation! She's escaped!" Canton struggled to keep calm.

"What do you mean?" Rostov replied calmly, but his tone said everything.

"I went back to finish interrogating her. I told your man Vasyli to reposition her. He was careless. He let her grab his gun and she started shooting. I returned fire but ran out of ammo. I think your man may have been shot. I had to get out of there."

"His name is Dimitri. What do you mean you had to get out of there? You left him there?" The volume of Rostov's voice increased.

"I had no choice. She would have shot me also. She had all his ammo still. What good would that have done? Someone needs to go back there and assess the situation."

"You left one of my injured men there? You useless and pathetic fool. You go back there, you coward!"

"Don't call me that. I did what was necessary to save the operation. One man is expendable when it comes to the big picture," Canton defended himself.

"Perhaps two men are also expendable," Rostov said menacingly.

"Listen, it doesn't do either of us any good to try to lay blame right now. The important thing is to limit the damage and clean up our footprint. We need to get out of the country so the Turks have no one to lay hands on. That's why it's important someone gets back to the shipyard as soon as possible to see about your man Alexi."

"Dimitri, you fool! At least get his name correct, since you so cowardly abandoned him."

"Yeah, okay, Dimitri. What contingency plans do you have to get out of the country?" Canton asked.

"My plans are not any of your concern."

"Well, I'm going to need a lift out. I can't go through my official channels at the consulate because the Turks will be all over it. Unlike you, my entire organization isn't in on the plan. I can manage things, but not from inside Turkey."

Canton waited for Rostov to respond. He must have been contemplating his escape plans as Canton waited for him in silence. He was taking his time. Perhaps Rostov had no immediate plan at the ready for such an unexpected occurrence.

"Hello? Hello? Are you there?" *Shit, he hung up on me*, Canton realized. *Okay, okay. I need to stay calm and keep a clear head. I'll call Payton. He'll think of something.* He reached for his official encrypted CIA cell phone, pulling it out of his zippered coat pocket and bringing it up in front of his face while keeping his eyes on the road in front of him, pressing the activation button with his thumb to activate the retinal scanner. Nothing happened. *What? It can't be dead.* He tried to remember when he had last charged it. "Shit! I don't need this!" He had the charger back at the hotel. He would rush in, grab his things and leave. He wouldn't bother to check out. Why give the Turkish authorities any more information about his actions? Paying his bill was his lowest priority right now. Once he was settled somewhere safe, he would call Payton, he decided as he came up on the lit Bosphorus Bridge. This wasn't anything he could have ever anticipated. Suddenly, his entire future was uncertain, but he was sure he would find a way out of his predicament. After all, he had gotten through other dicey situations in which he had been suspected of treachery.

Chapter 25

Michael and Ali had driven another couple of hours heading northwest on Highway 2, paralleling the snowcapped Alborz mountain range as they made their escape towards the border. They had skirted around the outskirts of the city of Qazvin and were back in dark countryside when Michael decided to pull over on the side of the road and try Asya again. He powered on the mobile phone she had given him, waited to get a signal, then dialed her again and hoped this time it would ring and she would pick up. He held the phone next to his ear and waited. After a brief moment of silence, he heard the same automated voice, first in Turkish, then in English, telling him the customer he was calling was currently unavailable and to please try again later. He put the phone down and hit end call. Deleting the number he had just dialed from the phone's register, he exhaled a loud sigh of concern. *What is going on, Awsh? Where are you?* He looked at his watch. It was 1:45 a.m., 12:15 a.m. back in Istanbul. Something was wrong. He knew Asya would never allow herself to be out of communications range for more than a few minutes at the most. Had something happened? Could it have been discovered somehow that she was helping him? There was no way she would leave him just hanging out in the wind, completely abandoned, with no way out.

"You look concerned, Michael. That's not a look I've seen on your face before," Ali told him in the dim glow of the instrument panel lights.

"I am, a little bit. Actually, more than a little bit. The person I'm trying to get a hold of is the one who's coordinating our transportation back over the border."

"Are they reliable?"

"No one more reliable whom I would ever entrust my life with."

"Do we have any other options?"

"Not unless you want to hike thirty-some miles through a mountain range." Michael tried not to sound dismayed, but his tone said otherwise.

"So, you're saying there is no plan B?"

"Hang in there, buddy, I'm going to try someone else who may be able to get through for us. Hand me the sat phone from the bag, would you?" Michael asked.

Michael opened the sunroof to give the phone a clear shot to one of the sixty-six geosynchronous Iridium satellites orbiting 483 miles above the earth. Michael looked at his watch again: 5:20 p.m. Sunday afternoon back in Bethesda, if he had calculated the time difference correctly. Dialing the other number he had memorized, he waited to hear the familiar sound Harry's voice.

The Iridium satellite phone sitting on the bedroom dresser rang as Harry stood in the shower after a Sunday afternoon of golf at the Congressional Country Club, one of D.C.'s most exclusive golf courses, with a one-hundred-and-twenty-thousand-dollar initiation fee and a ten-year waiting period to join. Harry was using one of the corporate passes Lockheed Martin maintained for entertaining visiting foreign government VIPs when they were in town shopping for military hardware. When they weren't being used, senior program managers and vice presidents and above had free access to them on a rotating basis, one of the fringe benefits of working for the world's largest military supplier. Harry had taken advantage of the warm and sunny early spring day to play eighteen holes. He had paired up with a Merck Pharmaceutical lobbyist who was similarly using his company's membership it had for courting members of Congress during rounds of golf at the exclusive club.

Connected to the Iridium network through the Axcesspoint Wi-Fi in his home, Harry's satellite phone could receive and make calls indoors. He had carried the phone with him religiously for the past week, even plugging it into an accessory mobile disk antenna on his car when he drove. It had been four days since he had spoken to Michael and told him about his suspicions that the Israeli's were preparing to launch some kind of strike against Iran. Since then, he had been in a complete information vacuum concerning Michael's status. He was almost tempted to call Asya Tarhan to see if she could tell him anything but fought the urge, knowing it went against his better judgment and everything he had practiced as a career intelligence officer in the CIA. If and when Michael needed him, he would make contact. If he couldn't for some reason, there was nothing Harry could do about it anyway. The same went for Tarhan. She had his number and would call him if she had any news. Until then, all he could do was go about his normal routine and wait to be contacted. After he finished his shower, he would pour himself a glass of red wine and see what Rose was planning for dinner.

Michael sat in the driver's seat, the engine turned off, as he listened to the phone on the other end ring once, twice, three times and continue, finally going to voicemail. Hanging up, Michael tried a second time with the same results. He disregarded the voicemail, leaving no recorded message on a server somewhere that could be discovered if things went south. Harry was taking a big risk for him; he didn't want to add to it unnecessarily. He powered off the satellite phone and sat quietly thinking. Now he was beyond concerned. He was outright worried. His only two contacts that could offer him any help in getting out of Iran were for some reason not answering. Was something going on that he had no idea about? Had something happened to Harry also? His mind raced with possible reasons why both Asya and Harry were out of his reach. The only other option would be to try calling Karbashi, but what more could he do? He had already given them his car, at great risk to himself. He and Ali were on their own.

Michael turned to Ali, who was sitting quietly looking at him, waiting for him to say something. "Okay. That didn't go as planned. I don't know why I can't get a hold of anyone, but let's not panic just yet. We still have a lot of hours ahead of us before we need to worry about how we're going to get over the border." He tried to sound reassuring as he started the car back up and pulled back out onto the highway.

They drove in silence for a few minutes until Ali finally said, "You know, Michael, whatever ends up happening, I just want you to know that I'm forever grateful for what you have done for me. When I called Roxanne and asked her to get a hold of you, I didn't expect you would even come to Turkey. I could never have imagined you would do something like this. I have no words to describe how much it means to me."

"Hey, don't get fatalistic on me just yet. We're going to figure this out. Save the thanks for when we're over the border. It's not like I had any immediate plans on the horizon anyway. I figured a nice little vacation to Turkey and Iran was just what I needed to reinvigorate myself. My life wasn't exactly where I wanted it to be—actually, far from it. For what it's worth, you asking for my help was probably the best thing that could have ever happened to me. It's me that needs to thank you for having so much faith in me. I just hope you didn't make a big mistake, counting on me."

"There was no one else I could turn to who would know how to handle a situation like this. I remember how you handled things in Athens. I always felt confident you knew what you were doing. I was never worried," Ali reassured him.

"Well, things didn't turn out the way I'd planned, did they?"

"You know that had nothing to do with you, Michael."

"Tell that to the families of the two dead Israelis."

"We both know who was responsible for that. Canton put them in that position. There was no other possibility. He's the one who got them killed. He's a liar, a narcissist, someone with no sense of right or wrong. He doesn't care about anything or anyone else other than himself. Look at what he's willing to do now. He's a murderer," Ali said resolutely.

"I know. I just had a hard time dealing with how everything turned out. I felt like I had failed completely. I blamed myself for a really long time. It ended up destroying my marriage and almost destroyed me."

"Sometimes, we think we control our own destinies, and when things don't turn out the way we planned, we think that we did something wrong, that we failed somehow. The one thing I've learned this past week is that we really don't have control over anything other than what we choose to believe in. I don't know if it's because of what I experienced while locked up in my cell, completely hopeless at times, but afterwards, a peace came over me when I realized my future was out of my hands. All I could do is live in the present and trust that God would reveal to me what I needed to know and what I needed to do, leaving the rest up to Him."

"You're really that sure about this God thing?" Michael asked, a little surprised.

"When He actually talks to you, then makes the unbelievable happen right before your eyes, it tends to change your outlook on life," Ali replied self-assuredly.

"I suppose that's a good attitude to have about living in the present. I certainly have no clue about anything in my future at this point. I know what you mean about unbelievable things; I've had a few of those happen to me also. I'm just not as sure about God's active role in all this. He didn't personally speak to me about any of this. I feel kind of jealous about this direct communication thing you got going. It'd sure make things a lot clearer if God would share some of his insights with me," Michael said half-jokingly.

"Have you ever asked Him?"

Michael thought about Ali's question. Had he ever asked God? He didn't know how to answer that. He had never discounted the existence of God, but he really couldn't say he had ever made an attempt to actually have a conversation with him. It seemed it would be too much like talking to oneself, surrendering touch with reality for something that was undetermined at best. Didn't that risk putting oneself in a precarious situation dealing with the challenges of life in that way. The irony of his question wasn't lost on him, considering the direction his life had taken thus far. There had been a sudden and major course correction, and he knew it wasn't because of anything he had done.

"Maybe I'll give it a try some time," was all Michael could say.

Asya stuck her high-security key into the deadbolt and turned it three times, unlocking the door and letting herself into her apartment. She went immediately into the spare bedroom and pulled open the built-in wardrobe door, then searched through a drawer filled with various cables, batteries and a variety of other miscellaneous electronic accessories, searching for an old mobile phone. She found an old Blackberry and hurriedly opened the back cover to insert the SIM card from her Samsung into the Blackberry but found the Samsung SIM card wouldn't fit properly into the Blackberry's slot, which was designed for an older standard SIM card.

"*Bok!*" she let out her frustration a second time that evening. What was she going to do now? She needed another phone or battery right now. She looked at the watch on her bruised and bloodied wrist. It was 1:10 a.m. Where was she going to find a phone at this hour? Getting an idea, she went into her bedroom and pulled open the middle drawer of her dresser, reaching back underneath a pile of sweaters for a manila envelope. Opening the flap, she hurriedly reached in and pulled out a wad of cash, counting out forty-four hundred lira, worth about one thousand dollars. Folding up the money and sticking it into her pocket, she ran back out of her apartment, locking the deadbolt three times. Not wanting to wait for the elevator, she quickly ran down the stairs out the front door through the pedestrian gate to the sidewalk. Running a block down to the corner of the street, she turned right down the main boulevard and ran another two blocks to a bar that was still open. Walking inside to loud music that was blaring in the midst of the twenty-to-thirty-some-year-old crowd, she looked around for what she was after. Spotting a group of three young women sitting next to a table of five young men who were trying to outdo each other in attracting their attention, Asya walked over to them.

"Does anyone have a Samsung phone?" she shouted, drawing all eyes to her.

Surprised at her sudden intrusion, the young adults looked around at each other in bewilderment.

"I said, does anyone have a Samsung phone?" she shouted louder.

One of the girls in the group, slowly raised her hand, unsure who she was answering to. "I do."

"May I see it?" Asya indicated with her hand, meaning it more as a command than a request.

The girl looked at her friends before slowly handing it to Asya, who quickly snatched it from her hand, opened the back cover and removed the battery, looking at the SIM card.

"I'll give you forty-four hundred lira for your phone, without the SIM," Asya told her bluntly.

Looking at her friends again with an unsure nervous smile, she turned back to Asya and said, "It's only a Galaxy S6."

"I don't care. Will you take forty-four hundred for it?" she shouted impatiently.

"Yeah, sure," the girl answered her, somewhat confused why someone was offering her three times what her phone was worth.

Asya reached into her pocket, pulled out the wad of lira and handed it to the girl. Not waiting for her to count it, she turned and headed out the door, the eight young adults looking on in astonishment as she made her exit as suddenly as she had appeared before them sixty seconds ago.

Running back to her apartment as fast as her exhausted body would take her, Asya's left wrist throbbed in pain with each stride she took. She would need to splint it on her own until she had a chance to go to the hospital sometime later. The important thing now was to get her mobile phone back on the network and available if Michael needed to contact her. Not having anything left after what under normal circumstances be a warm-up run, she took the elevator back up the five floors to her apartment. As the elevator lurched to a stop, she flung open the door and stepped out, then inserted her key into the deadbolt of her door, turning it rapidly three times, rushing inside. She walked over to the kitchen counter, where she had set down her phone, opened the back and removed the SIM card, then inserted it into the mobile phone she had just purchased from the girl, who was more than likely buying her friends a round of drinks to celebrate her good fortune.

Inserting the battery and closing the cover, Asya hit the power button and waited for the phone to connect to the network. After what seemed like an eternity, three bars finally showed. She waited another few seconds until the phone displayed she had three voicemails. Going through them, she listened to messages left by some of her subordinates, but nothing from Michael. Going to the call registry, she looked at her received calls to find three missed calls from Michael's number, all within the past three hours. She immediately hit redial, anxiously waiting to hear Michael's voice on the other end. What she heard first in Turkish, then in English, made her gut twist in knots. "The customer you are trying to reach is currently unavailable. Please try again later."

Don't panic, Asya. You know him. He's doing what he should be, turning on the phone only when necessary. He'll try again later. But what if it was an emergency, and he won't have a chance again? What must he have thought when he heard that same message every time he tried to call? O merciful Allah, please let him call again. Help him with whatever he's facing, I ask this of you, Lord.

She slumped down on her sofa, taking in a deep breath, trying to center herself and reestablish some inner peace. She told herself that she was still coming down from the traumatic experience and that she would be fine. She looked at her left wrist. It wasn't a pretty sight. Between the dark purple bruising and dried blood from some pretty nasty cuts, it was more than likely severely sprained or maybe even broken. All in all, though, she had escaped with minimal physical injury, considering what she had almost had to endure. She had no illusions about what she faced. They weren't going to allow her to live. She had begun preparing herself spiritually for what awaited her. What she hadn't prepared for was Canton returning as he had, and what he was intending to do to her. She didn't know how she would have handled it. She would have probably tried to shut herself off from the outside world, turning inward and beginning to let go of any attachment to this life. She thought about what it would have been like to endure the violation of her body by that degenerate animal, how he would be the last man to have her in this life instead of Michael.

A sudden wave of nausea came over her, causing her to almost vomit, except that she hadn't had any food in her stomach since her stop at Starbucks over twenty-four hours ago. Now because of what that revolting coward had tried to do, she might have missed her only opportunity to help Michael. Because of that repugnant monster, she might never see Michael again. She wouldn't let him get away. She needed to get a nationwide alert out immediately, instructing all ports of entry to be on the lookout for Jonathan Canton, a senior officer of the Central Intelligence Agency with a diplomatic passport. What reason was she going to give? What was she going to put down in her report? That she had been kidnapped by the CIA and SVR, interrogated, almost raped, and had just barely escaped? What would that set in motion? How would she be able to stay below the radar and continue helping Michael then? She couldn't do that just yet. Not until Michael was back in the country, or until she was certain he wouldn't be coming back. She would have to worry about Canton later.

Asya looked at her wrist again and saw that her hand was trembling; both were. She needed to get some sustenance, get cleaned up and tend to her wrist. She slowly leaned forward and unzipped her boots, kicking them off, then, with substantial effort, she stood up from the sofa and dragged herself into the kitchen. She opened her refrigerator to look for something to eat. She spotted the opened bottle of red wine in the door and was tempted to pour herself a glass to help calm down, but she decided against it, knowing that would put her out for the count. She was exhausted, but she had to try to stay as lucid as possible. There was too much at stake. Catching sight of the large bowl of green grapes, she pulled it out instead and took it with her as she headed for the shower. Walking into her bathroom and turning on the light, she startled herself when she took a look in the mirror. With black under both eyes, an abrasion on her right cheek, and hair that looked like she had just gotten out of bed, it was no wonder the eight young adults at the bar had looked at her like she was some crazy woman who had just escaped from a psychiatric institution. A hot shower and a few hours of sleep would significantly improve things.

Setting her mobile phone on the counter, Asya turned the shower lever to hot and stripped out of her clothes, tossing them on the floor. She popped a few grapes in her mouth as she waited for the hot water. When the steam began rolling out of the shower, she stepped into the tub and pulled the shower curtain closed. Mixing in just enough cold water so as not to get scalded, she stuck her head under the hot spray and let the soothing water run down her aching body. It felt both invigorating and relaxing at the same time. With her head hanging forward, she supported herself with her right hand against the tiled shower wall. Feeling a little dizzy and beginning to see stars, she gingerly eased herself down into the tub, relaxing her entire body as the hot spray rained down on her. As every muscle in her body slowly began to relax and she was finally able to let her defenses down, she slowly began sobbing. All the emotions that she had kept pent up inside her, finally came rushing out, as if the dam holding them back finally gave way. It was a much-needed catharsis. If she was going to be able to continue functioning and be of any help to Michael, she needed to get her emotions under control. The warm spray brought on a relaxing sense of calmness over her as she gradually drifted off to sleep.

***

Canton had gone back to the Ritz-Carlton, parked the BMW himself down in the basement parking garage, hurried up to his suite to gather all his belongings, dumped the contents of the mini-bar into his suitcase, just in case it was needed to help calm his nerves, and was back in his car leaving the hotel in just over ten minutes. He headed to the central railway station on the eastern end of the peninsula, where the old city was located, and found a small dive of a hotel down one of the narrow streets surrounding the station. Arriving sometime after 1:00 a.m., he stood at the empty front counter of the small lobby, ringing the bell until an irritated old proprietor, with all white hair and three days of stubble, wearing a yellow-stained white T-shirt and gray boxers, shuffled out of a back room in his slippers.

"*Merhaba*," Canton said curtly, knowing he had disturbed the old man's sleep. The quicker he got a room and the less attention he drew to himself, the better. "Doooo youuu have roooom? *Odasi?*"

"I understand English, mister," the old man said with an irritated tone. "For how many nights?"

"How about two nights for now? I'll pay you up front. How much?"

The old man eyed Canton before finally giving him the price. "Two nights, one thousand lira."

"One thousand lira? That's over a hundred dollars a night! For a dump like this?" Canton exclaimed, realizing he was being taken.

"Good location, close to train station. No passport required." The old man knew there was a reason why someone like him needed a room at a place like this one, at this hour of the night.

"Fine." He pulled out five two-hundred-lira bills from his wallet and threw them down on the counter.

The old man took the lira, put them in his pocket, then turned to the wooden shelf of small boxes on the wall and grabbed a key connected to a huge brass holder, handing it to Canton.

"It is your lucky night. Room five one seven. Top floor. Best view of train station."

Canton grabbed the key from his hand, turned, and rolled his suitcase to the small elevator on the other side of the lobby. Hitting the up arrow, he waited but heard nothing. He turned with a questioning glance to the old man, and what he heard made his eye begin to twitch.

"No worky. Must use stairs." He pointed over towards the corner of the lobby.

"You gotta be kidding. That is the only room you have available?"

"Sorry, mister. Only room. Very busy. Good location. Close to train station."

Canton wheeled his suitcase to the corner of the lobby and started up the marble stairwell, holding onto his suitcase while continuously turning right, climbing up to the fifth floor. By the time he had finally made it to the landing on the fifth floor, he was drenched in sweat and could feel the pounding of his heart as it pulsed up through his temple and right eye, which by now was in full spasm.

Making his way down to the end of the hallway, he found room 517 and stuck his key in, opening the door to a room full of warm stuffy air. He pulled his suitcase in, flipped on the light and shut the door, locking it and flipping the indoor latch. He looked around. It certainly wasn't the Ritz-Carlton, depressingly far from it, but at least he was anonymous and safe for the time being. He wasn't that concerned about having left the BMW parked down one of the side streets. It wasn't under his name. If he needed to abandon it, so be it. Bob could deal with that, since he had taken care of rental for him. He laid his suitcase down on the floor and unzipped it. Grabbing the cell phone charger and one of the small bottles he had absconded with from the Ritz, he located an outlet next to the bed and plugged it in. Plopping himself down on the bed, he connected the charger to his cell phone, then twisted open the cap of Blue Label and took a big swig.

As the familiar warmth slowly spread down his esophagus, he turned on his phone and waited for a signal. Finally connecting through Vodafone, he dialed Payton's number, which he had memorized. He took another swig, finishing it off, then reached across his bed down to his suitcase and grabbed another one of the small bottles. Lying back on his pillow, he twisted it open and took another swig as he waited to hear Payton's phone ring. Finally hearing it connect, it rang once, twice, a third time, a fourth, a fifth, then a sixth before going to voice mail.

"Answer the phone!" he shouted angrily.

Dialing his number again, he took another swig, hoping it would help calm his nerves. He heard it ring again before going through to voice mail. He ended the call and dialed again, going through the same routine. Finishing off the second bottle, he reached back into his suitcase and grabbed another, then dialed again. He lay there dialing nonstop. He didn't count the number of times he redialed nor paid attention to the amount of time that had passed, but by the time Payton finally answered the phone, there were five empty bottles laying on Canton's bed.

"It's about time you answered the phone!" Canton shouted.

"Have you lost your mind? What the hell are you doing calling me nonstop like this for over an hour?"

"Why didn't you answer? Didn't you think it was obviously important why I was trying to get a hold of you?" he said with a slight slur.

"Are you drinking?" Payton asked, detecting it in his voice.

"What? Are you my mother now? There's something we need to talk about. Do you want to press the button or should I?"

"Go ahead, if you can manage," Payton replied.

Canton hit the yellow secure button on his phone, redirecting the call through the phone's encryption program. As soon as his phone did the handshake with the encryption key on Payton's phone, he heard the chime and the digital female voice telling them the call was now secure.

"So, what's so important that you called me fifty-some times?" Canton clearly heard the annoyance in Payton's tone.

"We have a situation here. We had an unfortunate occurrence. One of Rostov's men allowed a prisoner we had in custody to escape, and now it jeopardizes us being in Turkey. I'm going to need some assistance getting out. That's why I'm calling."

"What do you mean, prisoner? What prisoner, and why does it jeopardize you?"

"The prisoner was the MIT chief of counterterrorism in Istanbul. She managed to escape while in Rostov's custody. She's seen my face."

"You're telling me the Turkish intelligence service?" Payton asked, dumbfounded.

"Yes, one and the same."

"You have lost your mind? What do you mean you had the chief of counterterrorism as your prisoner?"

"It's a long story, but she was giving assistance to an ex-Agency guy who was in Istanbul looking for Shiravi. If we found this guy, then we would find Shiravi. That's why she was captured and being interrogated," Canton tried to explain.

"That is the most insane thing I've ever heard. Who authorized that?"

"I authorized it. It was something that needed to be done if we were going to locate Shiravi."

"And what were you planning on doing with her when you were done interrogating her? Give her a ride back to her office?"

"Rostov was going to take care of disposing of her and any evidence."

"You're a damn fool! Do you know that? So what's going to happen now? You said it was a she? How the hell did she escape?"

"I told you, one of Rostov's men was moving her and she got the best of him and grabbed his gun. I was lucky. She almost shot me. I barely got away."

"You barely got away? You were there when all this was happening?" Payton asked, puzzled.

"I was interrogating her. Rostov's man was moving her, and she somehow managed to take his gun from him." Canton gave him the redacted version of what happened.

"That is the lamest excuse I have ever heard in my life, and I've heard many.

So, you're telling me you're a wanted man now by the Turkish authorities?"

"Yeah, I would say that is the case."

"So why doesn't the chief of station help you get out of the country?"

"I can't go to him. The head of MIT will be getting a hold of him anytime now and telling him what happened. I'm guessing the ambassador will be notified also."

"And Shiravi? What's become of him?"

"Don't know. That was why I was interrogating Tarhan, to find out what she knew."

"Weren't you working with her? Wasn't that the reason you were over there?"

"Yes."

"So why in the world, then, did you feel the need to kidnap her?"

"I told you, she was helping this ex-Agency guy find Shiravi."

"What ex-Agency guy? Who are you talking about?"

"His name is Michael Blackstone. Shiravi was his asset in a double-agent operation when he worked for the Agency. Shiravi must have contacted him for help."

"And why would this Tarhan be helping him?"

"She knew him from when he was stationed in Istanbul years ago. They worked together."

"And because they worked together, you think some ex-CIA officer is going to show up in Turkey and ask the head of counterterrorism to help him find the Secretary of State's interpreter, who went missing at the same time the Iranian foreign minister was assassinated?" Payton asked incredulously.

"I know it sounds unlikely, but I know this Blackstone guy. He has a way of making things happen. She all but confessed to me that she was helping him," Canton defended himself.

"Did she tell you where Blackstone was?"

"No, but I would have gotten that from her if she hadn't escaped."

"You are a damn moron. You have created a shit-storm over there for us. Do you realize that, you idiot?" Payton railed on him.

"Hey, the shit-storm started when your interpreter overheard you talking.

I was just trying to clean it up for us. Things just turned out unexpectedly. That happens sometimes with these types of things."

"Shut up! Shut up! I don't want to hear another one of your lame-assed excuses justifying your incompetence. Are you somewhere safe for the time being?"

"I am, but I'm going to need a way out of Turkey. Once I'm out, we can figure out a way to manipulate the narrative. What's she going to claim, anyway, that the CIA and SVR kidnapped her?"

"I told you to shut up. Just answer my questions. When did this happen?"

"I don't know. Around three or four hours ago," Canton guessed, the alcohol distorting his perception of time.

"Have you had any contact with Rostov since this has happened?"

"Yeah, I called him and told him what happened, but he wasn't that cooperative."

"Can you blame him? You deserted one of his men like some kind of coward," Payton belittled him, the contempt apparent in his voice.

Canton stayed silent. There was nothing he could say that would make any difference to Payton. He was a military man, so he saw things only in black and white. Payton couldn't see that he didn't have any other choice than to save himself and fight another day. He had actually done the smart thing. He had always been able to maneuver out of difficult situations in the past. It was just that he'd had a little bad luck this time. He would survive this and recover. None of this would really matter anyway when he was made the DCI. Who was going to believe the outrageous story of a wacked-out female intelligence officer who was found guilty of illegally helping an ex-CIA officer, forced out because of exercising bad judgment?

"Sit tight where you're at. Don't do anything. Don't go anywhere. I'll get back to you as soon as I figure this out. Do you understand?" Payton directed him.

"Yeah, I'll stay put. Just don't take too long. I don't have the most comfortable accommodations where I'm at, but I'll make do," he said, looking over at the remaining bottles in his suitcase. Worst-case scenario, if he was stuck there another night, he could probably walk down to the railway station and find some company to bring back to his room for a few hours. "Hey, this doesn't change anything about me becoming the DCI, does it?" He waited for Payton's answer. "Hello? Hello?"

***

The sun had just come up over the horizon in the rear-view mirror as the first signs of Tabriz came into view up ahead. Michael looked at the gas gauge and saw that the low fuel warning light had just come on, and the information display was telling him they had eighty kilometers left until empty. Ali had just begun to stir after falling asleep three hours ago at around 4:00 a.m. They had talked for several hours as they drove through the night, filling each other in on their lives since they had parted company over ten years ago. Ali had done his best to stay awake but had nodded off as exhaustion finally overtook him. For as physically tired as Michael felt after everything he had been through over the course of the last week, including the eleven-and-a-half-hour time difference with Seattle, he felt amazingly alert. The experience of driving across Iran through the night in the director of MOIS's Mercedes, then witnessing the sunrise in his rear-view mirror, sent a buzz through his nervous system. His perception of his surroundings felt distorted in some way, as if he was on some kind of drug, yet his sense of awareness had never been sharper. Everything seemed brighter, more real than he had ever experienced before in his life. It was as if he had lost perception of time, and all his senses were completely immersed in the moment. Maybe it was the constant flow of adrenaline, but whatever it was, it felt as if there was nothing that could stop them from overcoming their ultimate challenge of getting out of Iran. It was the best high he had felt in a very long time, perhaps ever.

"What time is it?" Ali asked, waking from his slumber.

"Seven twelve," Michael answered, glancing at his watch.

"Where are we?"

"Tabriz. We need to get some gas. We'll be on fumes soon. I'm going to take the next exit. I'll pull over and we'll switch seats. Better if you pull into the gas station and fill it up, while I pretend to be sleeping. I'll give you some rial."

"Okay. I think I still remember what to say at a gas station, but pulling up in this thing is definitely going to get us noticed," Ali said, stating the obvious.

"Just act like you're someone important. How would our old friend Karbashi act pulling in for gas?" Michael asked, trying to bolster Ali's confidence.

Skirting along the southern edge of the city, Michael hoped they would find a gas station fairly easily without having to drive too far into town. Coming up on the next exit, Michael signaled and took the off-ramp onto what appeared to be a main peripheral leading into Tabriz. As he slowed down looking for a place to pull over, both of their attention was drawn to what looked like an old Boeing 727 parked on the side of the road in a parking lot. Michael pulled into the parking lot as they read Chichak Airlines on the side of the white airliner, which was permanently mounted on concrete pedestals with concrete stairs leading up to its main door.

"It's a coffee shop," Ali said, amused.

"That is something else. This place never ceases to amaze me. Doesn't look like it's open, though," Michael observed.

"Must open up later in the day."

"Let's trade sides," Michael said, releasing his seat belt and getting out.

After switching places, Ali adjusted the seat, then put it into gear, stalling it as he let out the clutch. "Been a while since I've driven a stick."

"You got this?" Michael asked.

"Yeah, I think so. Just need to get used to this clutch."

"Okay, before you head out, here's some rial for you." He handed Ali a rolled-up wad of bills.

After shoving them into his pocket, Ali started the car again and revved the engine as he let out the clutch, squelching the tires and pulling back out onto the road. As they headed a little further down the street, to their left, they saw a huge modern building, which was obviously the main bus terminal.

"Should we ditch Farzan's car here and take a bus the rest of the way?" Ali asked.

"Good idea under any other circumstances, but the Maku bus terminal is the last place I should be showing my face."

"Sounds like you've been there before."

"Oh yeah, and unfortunately I made quite an impression. Not what I had planned on just after coming in over the border. Hopefully we'll a place to leave the car where it can remain unnoticed until Farzan has a chance to pick it up. You can give him a call on the cell he gave us and speak to him in Farsi, letting him know."

They drove a little further down the road until they spotted a gas station to their right. Pulling in and stopping next to a pump, Ali rolled down his window and turned the engine off, waiting for the attendant to come over. Michael laid his head back on the headrest and closed his eyes as Ali took matters into his own hands.

"Fill it up, please." Ali used his best Farsi from what he remembered his father saying decades ago when he'd accompanied him as a child.

"With what?" the attendant asked.

"Petrol," Ali replied.

"What kind—regular, super?"

"Super, what do you think with a car like this?" Ali attempted to recover from his seeming confusion.

The attendant turned and walked to the pump, lifting the nozzle, then knocking on the car, waiting for Ali to unlock the fuel door. Ali searched for a release lever but was unable to find it as the gas station attendant stood by waiting impatiently.

"Try unlocking the doors," Michael said quietly, keeping his eyes closed.

Hitting the door unlock button, Ali looked in his side-view mirror and saw the attendant push the fuel door and open it, then stick the nozzle in. When the nearly empty gas tank had swallowed ninety-three liters of fuel, the pump clicked off. After force-feeding it some more gas to round it off, the attendant removed the nozzle and replaced the gas cap, pushing shut the fuel door.

Walking back around to Ali, he told him, "A million one thirty-four."

Ali unfolded the wad of cash and counted out twelve one-hundred-thousand-rial bills and handed them to the attendant. Giving Ali his change, the attendant walked away to service another car that had pulled into the station. Ali started the Mercedes, put it into gear and gently pulled out from the bay, heading back towards the street.

"That went okay for the most part. Do you want me to drive?" Ali asked.

"Yeah, for a little bit, if you feel comfortable. I'm going to try calling again."

"I think I can manage. I had never driven before I moved to the US. This may be the only chance I ever have to drive in the country I was born in. Somehow, I don't see myself coming back here on vacation," Ali commented as he headed back towards the highway.

Michael pulled his mobile phone back out and powered it on. When he got a signal, he dialed Asya's number and waited anxiously, hoping he wouldn't hear the same dreaded message again. After a short silence, he heard it ring on the other end. Before it could ring a second time, Michael heard the eager sound of Asya's voice on the other end.

"Hello?"

"Hi," Michael answered enthusiastically.

"Oh, thank Allah. It's so good to hear the sound of your voice." Michael could sense the relief in Asya's voice.

"Not as good as it is to hear yours," he replied.

"I am so sorry. I had a little encounter with our favorite person and did not have a phone for a while." Asya kept her words vague knowing their conversation was going through an Iranian mobile provider.

"Everything all right?" Michael asked, concerned.

"Yes, now it is. I will tell you about it when I see you. How are things with you?"

"I am heading back with my friend."

"That is excellent news. Will you need a ride from the same location?"

"Yes. Should be getting into town in around four hours. It'll take another couple of hours on foot to the pickup location. We'll have to kill some time until it gets dark. I was thinking about ten p.m., if that works for your friend's taxi service?"

"I will make the call and confirm. When do you want to talk again?" Asya asked him.

"I'll call you when we get into town and figure out our final travel plans."

"Do you want me to contact your other friend and let him know you have retrieved your friend?"

"I'll do it when we are completely finished with our travels, just to be sure."

"Okay, I understand. I can't wait to see you!" she said excitedly.

"Me too!" he responded eagerly. "Talk to you again in around four hours. Bye."

"*Güle güle*," she said and ended the call.

"That is good you were finally able to get through," Ali said with relief.

"Yeah it is," Michael replied, turning off the phone and looking ahead at the traffic as Ali pulled back onto the freeway, his thoughts still back with Asya.

"She must be a pretty special friend," Ali alluded.

"What do you mean?" Michael asked, sensing Ali was hinting at something.

"Nothing. I just noticed how you spoke to her," Ali replied innocently.

"Why, what did I say?"

"Not what you said, how you said it."

"I don't get it. How did I say it?"

"Like she was a pretty special friend." Ali turned to him with a quick grin before turning his attention back to the increasing traffic as the morning commute came into full swing.

"Well, she is a special friend. Her name is Asya. You'll get to meet her. We both owe her a lot. If it wasn't for her, neither of us would be here right now."

For the first time, Michael was finally beginning to believe that he was actually going to succeed in accomplishing the impossible, and he was going to be able to see the woman who had dropped back into his life after so many years. He would have a second chance to see where things could lead. A chance to restore some happiness and fulfillment in his life again.

Dripping wet, Asya put her phone back down on the bathroom counter and stepped back into the shower. Thank goodness for tankless hot water heaters. She had obviously passed out for hours under the continuous shower of hot water. She was still sore and aching but felt rejuvenated from the few hours of sleep she had gotten and the excitement of finally hearing from Michael. Standing back under the shower, she looked at her left wrist. The dried blood had washed off, leaving only her bruised and swollen wrist and the raw cuts from the zip tie. She managed to soap herself and wash her hair using her right hand. Rinsing off, then stepping out of the tub into the puddle she had dripped onto the tile during her conversation with Michael, she toweled herself off one-handed, then headed to her bedroom for some fresh clothes. After managing to dress herself with her right hand, she went back into the bathroom and opened a cabinet where she kept a small assortment of bandages and medicines. Poking through her plastic first aid box, she grabbed an elastic bandage roll and took it into the kitchen. She went to the large ceramic jar on the counter next to the stove and sorted through the various cooking utensils shoved in it, pulling out a large wooden cooking spoon. Setting it down on the counter, she laid her left arm down on it, placing her palm over the spoon. Using her right hand, she labored to wrap the bandage around her arm and spoon, fashioning a makeshift splint for her wrist. Grabbing a roll of duct tape from the bottom drawer in her kitchen, she managed to grab the end with her teeth, unrolling some and tearing it, then wrapping it around the end of the bandage to hold it in place on her forearm. She studied her handiwork. It wasn't pretty, but it would do the job until she had a chance to have it looked at by a doctor.

Asya placed a call to Ercan's mobile phone, hoping he would answer and wasn't in some helicopter where he wouldn't hear it. She was lucky, as he answered on the first ring.

"Good morning, it's me."

"I know your number. What is happening? Have you heard from our friend?"

"I just got off the phone with him. He has located his friend and the two of them are making their way back. They will be in the same location you dropped him off in a few hours. Can you get them out tonight at ten?"

"Yes. Advise him the extraction point will be that same as where he was inserted."

"I will. I'll call you in a few hours with confirmation once I speak to him again."

"Okay."

"Thank you again. You know there is no one else I could ever trust and have faith in to do something like this. You are a special man. I always knew that."

"I'm doing it because it is the right thing to do; there is nothing more that needs to be said. It is you who are the extraordinary woman, my *dişi aslan*. That is something I always knew. I will be standing by to hear back from you."

Having addressed her immediate concern of making sure everything was prepared for Michael and Ali's extraction, Asya turned her attention to Canton. She looked at the clock on the wall. It was 6:20 a.m. He had gotten around six hours head start on his escape, but had he managed to leave the country yet? More than likely, he wouldn't have been able to fly out in the middle of the night, even if he had his own aircraft. Had he gone back to the consulate for safe refuge, or was he in hiding somewhere? She wanted to put an official alert out keeping him from leaving the country but knew she couldn't do that just yet with the way things stood. As she struggled with the possibility of him getting away, a thought popped into her head. She grabbed her newly acquired used mobile phone and plugged it into her USB charger to charge the almost-depleted battery. She looked at the call registry but saw that the calls made to and from the phone were those of its previous owner. Huffing in frustration, she had another thought as she went into her living room and turned on the laptop sitting the coffee table. Waiting for it to connect to her Wi-Fi, she logged into her mobile phone account and searched through it until she located what she was hoping to find. Scrolling down her incoming and outgoing calls, she located the US number and dialed it on her mobile. It was an outside chance, but it was all she had right now.

Listening in anticipation, Asya heard it ring. It rang a second time, a third, then a fourth. Thinking she had wasted her time and expecting it to go to voicemail, she was surprised when it picked up. There was no answer, only silence, but Asya knew he was on the other end.

"I know you're there, Jonathan Canton. You think you will be able to get away with what you have attempted? You think you will not pay for your despicable actions? If that is what you think, you are severely mistaken. I will hunt you down, and when I find you, I will personally interrogate you. You will experience what it is like to be without any power, without any control, what it feels like to be completely helpless. You will be like a frightened animal on the run, but you will not escape. Do you hear me?"

There was silence on the other end, but Asya could tell her words had found their intended recipient.

"You have nothing to say? No, cowards usually do not when they are confronted with how pathetic they are. It will give me such satisfaction seeing you face-to-face again under different circumstances. It is all over for you, Jonathan Canton. That you can be sure of," she declared confidently.

Asya heard the line go dead. She guessed there was a good chance he was still in Turkey, since he had remained silent. If she had played her cards right, her bold step in calling Canton and confronting him might make him panic and make a mistake. In the meantime, she would head back to her office, where she had all the assets of MIT at her disposal, standing by to help Michael and Ali in any way she could. She would call Ercan from there, letting him know to be ready for Michael and Ali's extraction later that evening after dark. In the meantime, she needed to think how they would bring Ali back into the picture and use his information to bring the conspiracy into the light of day and put a stop to this insane plot.

***

Hamed had returned to his home after leading Ali and Michael to Highway 2 and dropping Karbashi off at his home. It had been a relatively quiet ride, neither of them saying much as they processed what had occurred that evening. Both of them knew they had crossed the Rubicon and there was no going back. Once it was discovered they had released the American prisoner, both of them would most likely be arrested and imprisoned. Yet each of them felt at peace with what they had done. They knew there was no alternative. It was the only way of stopping the escalating conflict that would eventually lead to the devastation of their country. Even if their leadership believed Shiravi's story, it would be seen as some sort of Iranian deceptive ploy if they were to parade him in front of the international community. The Americans would naturally claim Shiravi had been coerced by the Iranians into fabricating such an unbelievable story. It would still be a hard sell to the international community, but at least his testimony would be bolstered by the ex-CIA officer and whoever else was helping him. Hamed hoped when everything had run its course, the truth would come out and he might be vindicated for his actions.

He quietly crawled into bed with Laleh and tried to fall asleep, but between the tragedy of the death of his child and the events surrounding Shiravi, his mind wouldn't cease thinking. Realizing any attempt to sleep was useless, he got back out of bed and went to his chair in the living room. Sitting in the stillness of the early-morning hours, he pondered why Allah had brought this current upheaval into his life. What was he supposed to do now? What direction would his life take? His future with the IRGC was more than likely finished. Bardari wouldn't allow such treachery from one of his own senior people to go unpunished. What would happen to Laleh and Tahmin after he had been arrested and prosecuted for his betrayal? They would lose everything. They would be treated as outcasts by their circle of friends and acquaintances from the upper echelon of Iranian society. Perhaps Laleh and Tahmin would be able to live with Laleh's sister family. Jawed, Laleh's sister's husband, was an honorable man. He would take them into his household. Whatever the cost, he knew he had done the right thing in Allah's eyes. Had he done otherwise, how would he have been able to live with himself when the Zionists had unleashed a nuclear weapon against his country causing the death of so many?

He had decided to go straight to General Bardari's office first thing in the morning and tell him exactly what he had done and his reasons why. He wouldn't make any mention of Karbashi's involvement. There was no reason to implicate him. Karbashi was at least in a position to influence the country's leadership regarding everything that had occurred in light of Ali's revelations. What, if anything, Karbashi would disclose concerning his role in releasing Shiravi was up to him. They hadn't discussed amongst themselves what either of them was going to say. Hamed respected Karbashi for the wisdom and courage he had exhibited in going to Evin Prison and getting Ali out at great risk to himself. It was a shame that Bardari hadn't displayed similar judgment when it came to his understanding of what Shiravi's information meant for their country. Hamed hoped his admission of what he had done would finally lead Bardari to realize that the course he was pursuing against Israel was misguided and would lead to ruin for their country. That was the most important thing. What Bardari decided about his fate was secondary.

Prior to leaving his home, he quietly went back into their bedroom, where Laleh was still sleeping, and gently kissed her on her lips. He stood there looking at her as she stirred, taking in as much of her as he could, knowing full well it could be the last time he saw her in quite a while and in much different circumstances. He then went into Tahmin and Reza's room and sat down on Reza's empty twin bed across from Tahmin. He looked at Reza's empty pillow and patted it gently with his hand, biting his lip as tears began streaming down his cheek.

"Why are you crying, Baba? Are you as thinking about Reza?" Hamed was startled to hear Tahmin.

"I thought you were asleep." Hamed evaded his son's question, wiping the tears from his face.

"I couldn't sleep, Baba. I was just thinking about what Reza might be doing now that he is with Allah. Do you think he is sleeping?"

"Maybe he is, or maybe he is thinking about you, wondering what you are doing," Hamed answered as he moved, sitting down next to Tahmin on his bed.

"I hope he knows that I miss him."

"I'm sure he does, my child."

"I can't wait to see him again. Will he look the same, or will he grow up and look like an old man, like me when I die and go to Allah?"

"I don't know. I'm curious about that myself," Hamed answered, putting his hand on Tahmin's forehead and gently stroking his hair.

"Do you think you will see him before I do, Baba?"

"I hope so, Tahmin, but only Allah knows these things. Remember what I told you about always listening to what Allah says to your heart. If you do that, you will see your brother again someday. Until then, you need to always listen to Maman, respect her, and take care of her as you grow up to become a man."

"Where will you be, Baba? Will I take care of you also when you are old?"

"I want you to always remember that I will always be with you, even if I am not physically present with you. You will always be able to feel me in your heart." Hamed fought back the tears that were beginning to well up in his eyes. "I have to go to work now. I love you, my son."

"I love you too, Baba."

Hamed bent down and kissed him on his forehead, before getting up and heading out the door, the tears finally letting loose, streaming down his face. Somehow he knew that would be the last time he would see his child like this. Grabbing his holster with his 9mm, he ran it through his belt, securing it to his waist, then grabbed his jacket and briefcase. He would more than likely be relinquishing very shortly. Better to have it with him and turn it in than to have IRGC personnel barging in on his wife and child to retrieve his weapon. He looked around his home one last time before stepping out the door. It was 7:30 a.m. With the morning traffic, it would take him about forty-five minutes to get to General Bardari's office at IRGC headquarters. He was going in unannounced and without an appointment, but he would wait in the secretary's office until Bardari had time to see him. The general would be annoyed at him unexpectantly barging in on him, but that would be inconsequential once he had told him the reason.

As he made his way through the rush-hour traffic, his thoughts fell back to Ali. He remembered his first meeting with him, the initial interrogation. He had detected the fear in Ali then, the uncertainty about his future, his well-being, his life. He hadn't even had to use any enhanced interrogation to bring terror to Ali. Hamed was used to having the upper hand over all his subjects. Knowing that he was in complete control of their fate, there was nothing he couldn't obtain from them. Some had started out brave, willing to endure significant pain, but everyone succumbed eventually once they were broken psychologically. Hamed had detected the opposite with Ali. Something had changed within Ali the second time Hamed had interrogated him. He had actually grown stronger psychologically and spiritually. Whatever had happened, it seemed as if Ali had found inner peace regarding whatever awaited him. The fear he had previously shown, was completely gone. Hamed had never seen that happen with any other prisoner.

Then there was shock Ali had administered to him last night, telling him he somehow knew about Reza's death, sharing with him that Reza was in the joyful presence of Allah. Hamed didn't know how Ali knew, but he had no doubt that what Ali had told him was the truth. It was something he could feel deep within. He felt peace knowing he would someday see his child once again—that was, if Allah found him worthy. Whatever the outcome of his decision today, he knew he would no longer be interrogating prisoners, inflicting physical and psychological pain, destroying men's souls. He hoped there would somehow be the chance in his life now to redeem himself from all his sins.

Hamed pulled into the security checkpoint and displayed his ID to the guard, who motioned him through. That was likely the last time he would be waved through any checkpoint. He slowly drove through the parking lot, searching for an open spot. It was past 8:00 a.m. and most IRGC headquarters employees had reported for work. Finally finding an empty space towards the rear of the parking lot, he pulled in and turned off the engine. Glancing around the interior of the car to make sure he didn't forget anything, he stepped out and threw on his jacket, then grabbed his briefcase before locking the doors. He made a note of where he had parked to let whoever was going to take his keys know where his vehicle was located. Even though he would likely be treated like a prisoner soon, he still felt a sense of duty to conduct himself professionally up to the very end.

As he walked across the parking lot towards the front entrance, he searched to see if Bardari's car was in its reserved parking spot by the main door. He spotted the big silver Mercedes, telling him that Bardari had already arrived. It was a bright sunny morning for early spring. It looked like it was going to be a nice day. He wondered if this was the last time he would be seeing the outdoors as a free man, before being transported to Evin Prison. The irony was not lost on him. He had just been there not twelve hours ago as an IRGC colonel, and he would be heading back there shortly as an inmate. If nothing else, he would be an equitable trade for Ali. He had no regrets as long as he knew his actions would save his country. He hoped that the truth would come out someday. He might even be vindicated for his actions and possibly be released from prison. But he knew his days with the IRGC were over. Bardari would never accept such defiance of his authority. He was prepared to accept his fate, whatever it may be.

Approaching Bardari's Mercedes from the rear, he walked up beside it, heading for the building entrance. His eye caught sight of the crinkled front quarter panel on the passenger side. As he walked past it, his head continued turning until he slowed to a stop. He stood there and looked at the cracked front headlight and buckled sheet metal on the hood and quarter panel. He couldn't tell if it was thirty seconds or three minutes that he had stood in front of Bardari's Mercedes, staring at it. Finally turning and continuing towards the doors, he walked without consciously being aware of how his body was moving him forward. He saw his hand reach for the door and pull it open for him to enter and show his ID to the security personnel as he walked past them, but he didn't have any recollection of his journey from the front door up to the eighteenth floor and down the hallway to General Bardari's office. He walked into his secretary's office and saw her look up at him as he entered.

"Good morning, Colonel. I didn't know you had an appointment with the general this morning. You are not on his schedule," she said, surprised.

"I do not have an appointment, but I have an urgent matter to discuss with him. Is he available?" The words came out of his mouth without him consciously aware of what he was saying.

"Oh, that is somewhat unusual, but I shall ask him. One moment." She got up and walked to the general's door and tapped softly.

"Yes!" she heard a bark from inside.

Opening the door partway, she slipped in quickly, shutting it behind her. Hamed remained standing where he was, staring at the secretary's desk as he waited to see the general. There were a few seconds of silence, then a loud "Ahmadi?" from Bardari, followed by a brief pause, then an annoyed "What does he want?" another pause, then a final, "Fine, fine, send him in."

The door opened again, this time all the way, the secretary looking at Hamed, announcing he could come in. Turning, he walked past her towards Bardari as he sat behind his desk, immersed in a document, disregarding his approaching presence. The secretary closed the door as Hamed walked to the front of Bardari's desk and stopped in front of the chair he normally sat in while briefing the general. Instead of sitting, this time he stood erect facing Bardari, waiting to be acknowledged.

His head remaining immersed in the document, he finally let out, "So, Colonel, what is it that brings you to my office this morning unannounced?"

"I have released the prisoner," Hamed answered in a monotone voice.

Bardari glanced up. Startled to see Hamed standing over him, his attention was drawn away from his document and focused towards his subordinate. "What do you mean? What prisoner? The American? Do you mean you are finished interrogating him?"

"I have let him go. He is no longer in Evin Prison," Hamed explained unambiguously.

"Have you gone mad, Colonel? What do you mean you have let him go? By what authority did you let him go?" Bardari shouted, as he became livid.

"I let him go because I am convinced he is telling the truth, as I briefed you last time. If the world does not learn the truth about who is really responsible for assassinating the foreign minister, then the situation between us and the Zionists will continue to escalate until great destruction will be unleashed on our people. I told this last time, yet you continue with your escalation against the Zionists when that is exactly what the Americans and Russians want. Do you not see that, General?"

"How dare you speak to me that way, Colonel," Bardari yelled with a mixture of anger and bewilderment.

"What happened to the front of your car?"

"What?"

"How did the front of your car get damaged?" Hamed asked again sharply.

"Colonel, I do not like your tone this morning. I do not know what has happened to you, but for the time being, you are going to be relieved of your duties and will be held in custody until this issue with the prisoner is resolved. You could be court-martialed for what you have done, do you realize that?"

Hamed was so nonchalant in responding to his boss's tirade that it took a moment for it to register with Bardari that a gun was being pointed at him.

"I asked, how did the front of your car get damaged, General? If I have to ask again, it will be after I have put a bullet through your knee," Hamed asked in the same manner he used during countless interrogations.

"Colonel, what is the meaning of this? What has happened with you?"

Expecting a response from his unbalanced subordinate, Bardari was stunned when Hamed fired a shot at him, the bullet missing his head by inches as it passed by and shattered the gold-leafed porcelain horse statue on the shelf behind him. A moment later, out of the periphery of his vision, Hamed saw Bardari's secretary crack the door open and peek inside, her eyes bulging wide, before slipping back out and shutting the door.

"I will ask you one last time, General. The next time, I will not miss. How did the front of your car get damaged?"

"What? Yes. I will tell you. Some little careless mongrel ran out into the street when I was driving. He did not even look. It was not my fault. I did not have time to stop. Otherwise, I would have, just so I could get the information about his parents so they could pay for the repairs to my car. Did you see how much damage was done?"

"That little mongrel you are referring to was my son, General."

"Your child? Well, I am sorry for that, Colonel, but as I told you, there was nothing I could do. Did you not teach your child not to run out into a busy street?"

Hamed fired another round, missing him again by only inches, shattering an ancient Persian vase and spraying small ceramic fragments all over Bardari's back. The general sat there motionless, his eyes wide open in fear, anticipating the next round would be directed at him.

"You have no morals, no values, no sense of what is right or wrong. That is why you do not want to acknowledge what the American is saying is the truth. You do not care about the truth or what happens to millions of other little mongrels. It is too late. Once the American tells the world the truth, you will no longer have a justification to provoke a war with the Zionists. You will not be able to bring our country to ruin and kill so many of our people just to satisfy your sadistic hunger for death. You are a merciless monster. You are the one who deserves death, not all our innocent children."

Just as Bardari thought Hamed was going to pull the trigger on him, his office door burst open and two IRGC security officers burst in with their guns drawn. They both turned and looked at them, Hamed not making any move to turn his weapon towards them. He turned back to Bardari, a smile on his face, realizing he would be seeing Reza very shortly. He wanted to say something, opening his mouth, but no words came out as the sound of gunfire from the two security personnel filled the room. Hamed saw himself passing by Bardari's desk as he hit the floor with a thud, vaguely aware of the sensation of pain from various points on his body, including somewhere in his head. As he lay motionless, looking up at the ceiling with his eyes wide open, the two security guards slowly came into his field of vision, their guns drawn and pointed at him, then backed away, returning him his view of the ceiling.

"Is he dead?" he heard Bardari's voice.

"Yes, sir, he appears to be," one of the guards responded.

"Good work. Unfortunately, the colonel had gone mad. Something about losing his son. It happens to all of us with someone we know. Some of us can deal with it better than others. On your way out, send someone to remove his corpse from my office and clean up the mess on my carpet," he heard Bardari order them.

"Yes, sir." He heard them walk out.

"Ezter!" Bardari yelled for his secretary.

He heard the quick short footsteps of Bardari's secretary as she entered the office and the almost imperceptible gasp as she glimpsed of him on the floor.

"Yes, General," she stammered in a distressed voice.

"What's wrong, Ezter? Haven't you ever seen a dead body before?" he teased her sarcastically.

"Not like this, General." She was barely audible.

"Make sure those two idiots who made this mess get somebody up here to clean it up. But first, get me the commandant of Evin Prison on the line right away."

"Yes, General," he heard her footsteps tap away, then the door close.

Hamed's view of the ceiling was interrupted by the appearance of Bardari's face looking down at him. He stood there and stared at him with a contemptible expression on his face. He saw as Bardari jerk his head forward and spit on him, feeling it strike his face, then heard a phone ring. Bardari left his field of vision, then he heard Bardari pick up the phone and grunt, followed by a pause.

"Good morning, Colonel. I was informed Colonel Ahmadi had come there and removed the American prisoner from your custody," he heard Bardari say. There was a long pause, then Bardari again. "What time was that?" Another pause, then, "You are to tell no one about this. Do you understand? Good. *Salaam.*"

"Ezter!" He heard the footsteps of the rattled secretary.

"Yes, General," came her timid voice.

"Get me Brigadier General Hashdavi of the Border Guard right away."

"Yes, General." Then footsteps again and the door being shut.

He couldn't tell seconds from minutes as he waited, fixated on the ceiling. He finally heard the phone ring again, then Bardari's voice once again.

"Good morning, General. We have a situation with an escaped prisoner. At approximately twenty-three hundred last night, Ali Shiravi, an American of Iranian descent, escaped from IRGC custody here in Tehran. He had the assistance of some traitors. We believe he is on his way to the border, trying to make an escape over a land crossing. He could be heading in any direction, but I would guess he is heading northwest to Turkey, or possibly Azerbaijan or Armenia. But do not exclude any possibility. I want extra vigilance at every border crossing, and additional patrols and checkpoints at each border city and town. I will see about getting you a copy of his photo to distribute to all the border checkpoints. It is imperative he not get out of the country. Do what you have to do. Is that understood? Yes, yes." He heard Bardari listening to the more junior general on the other end.

Hamed suddenly detected a sensation of something in his right hand. At first, he didn't know if his mind was playing tricks on him, but as more time passed, he realized he was still grasping his gun. As feeling returned to his arm, it continued moving to his shoulder, then his torso and eventually past his waist down to his legs. His foot twitched as he felt his heel move along the floor. His view of the ceiling gradually shifted to the front of Bardari's desk as he let his head turn to the side. Slowly twisting his torso, he could feel sharp pain now in his upper chest and somewhere below his ribs. He methodically rolled his body along the floor, gradually bringing his knees around, bit by bit raising himself up onto his left elbow. Looking down on the floor beneath him, he didn't immediately recognize what he saw. He studied the small chunk of gray material with dark lines creating several bulging folds before finally recognizing what he was looking at. He had seen human brain before on several occasions. It was strange to be looking at it on the floor of Bardari's office, until he realized where it had come from. He wanted to reach up and feel his head but decided it didn't make any difference where it was missing from. He wouldn't need it for much longer. Beyond the view of Bardari in front of his desk, Hamed reached up and grabbed the edge of the large desk, slowly pulling himself up onto his knees, then up onto his left foot.

He heard Bardari bring the conversation to an end, then return the handset back to its cradle. Steadying himself while holding on to the edge of the desk, he slowly raised himself off the floor, standing up to face Bardari, whose eyes opened wide and mouth dropped open. Bardari tried to say something to the man missing part of his forehead pointing a gun at him, but no sound came out of the general's moving mouth.

"It is time for you to account for your sins. I hope you are ready to meet with Allah, General," Hamed said as he squeezed the trigger, discharging a round at point-blank range right between Bardari's eyes. Hamed saw the general's head fall back into his chair, his mouth and eyes still wide open from the shock of seeing him. He placed the gun down on the desk and turned his head, looking over to the side. He smiled, experiencing an overwhelming sense of joy when he saw Reza standing in the bright morning light shining in on him through the windows.

"Hello, my child. I missed you. We all have missed you, but I will keep you company until your mother and brother join us. It will not be long," Hamed said with happiness, realizing he was no longer in Bardari's office, but somewhere else, someplace where he could feel the lightness from having left the weight of his past behind him.

"Come, Baba, there is so much to see." His son waved for him to follow.

The Last Regret

Chapter 26

Defense Minister Rozen was sitting in the secure briefing room within Ministry of Defense Headquarters in the Matcal Tower in central Tel Aviv. Present was Prime Minister Akerman, who had come over to monitor the operation real-time as it was executed. Also, there was the deputy defense minister, the chief and deputy chief of the General Staff, and Major General Bachman. Rozen started with the briefing.

"Gentlemen, as we speak, all squadrons executing Operation Yem Sevp are having their final mission briefing. The mission will commence in approximately one and a half hours from now at eleven hundred hours. So that you all can understand and follow the progress of the mission, General Bachman will brief the technical aspects of the operation. General," Rozen said, turning it over to the head of the Air Force.

"Gentlemen, the target is the Fordow underground nuclear facility, near the city of Qom in central-northern Iran. The round-trip distance of the mission is two thousand and forty-six nautical miles. Mission aircraft are staged at Ramat David, Ramon, Tel Nof, and Nevatim, where the main strike team, our F-35 squadron, the Golden Eagles, are flying from. The operation will commence with six Re'em electronic warfare aircraft with the M'sanver Ma'or taking off first. They will be flying at forty-thousand feet, staggered fifty miles apart, opening a fifty-mile-wide-by-three-hundred-mile-long secure corridor from Israel through Syria and Iraq and into Iran, all the way to the target. Each of the Re'ems will be protected by six F-15C fighters. Two minutes later, two AEWCs, each escorted by six F-15s, will take off to assume tactical control and communications of mission aircraft. Five minutes later, four KC-135 aerial refuelers, escorted by eight F-15As with drop tanks, will follow and position themselves over eastern Iraq to top off the strike team prior to entering Iranian airspace. Twenty minutes later, the main strike team, composed of eight F-35s, each carrying two five thousand-pound GBU-28 bunker busters will take off. That is eighty thousand pounds of precision munitions that will be dropped on Fordow. Each GBU-28 will be released sequentially in two-second intervals, controlled by AEWCs via secure link with F-35s. An additional sixteen F-15E strike fighters, each carrying one GBU-28, will accompany the F-35s as backup, should anything unforeseen arise. Their bombing run can also be controlled remotely by the AEWCs. The strike team will be escorted by sixteen F-15D fighters, should they need to engage any aircraft attempting to interfere, which we believe is highly unlikely under the cover of the M'sanver Ma'or, but we are taking no chances. Fordow will be completely destroyed one way or another on this mission. The strike team should catch up with the refuelers just as they reach the rendezvous waypoint in northern Iraq at thirty-thousand feet and begin top off for the final leg to the target. Refuel time for each aircraft is two minutes with each tanker refueling eleven aircraft for a total of twenty-two minutes. Refuelers and their escorts will hold their positions within the secure corridor, while the strike team continues on the final three hundred miles, descending to twenty-five thousand feet and flying Mach 1.3 on afterburners into Iranian airspace to reach target in twenty minutes. The bombing run will take sixty seconds, with strike team returning at Mach 1.6 and out of Iranian airspace in sixteen minutes. The Re'em will begin the retrograde back to Israel, keeping all mission aircraft in the secure corridor, with all aircraft back in Israeli air space in four hours, seven minutes from start of mission. Any questions?"

"Do you anticipate any interference from Syrian, Russian or US assets operating in the area?" Akerman asked.

"We do not, Prime Minister. Any resistance from Syrian, Iraqi or Iranian air defense systems should be minimal. We will be staying clear of any Russian controlled airspace in Syria and avoiding US operating areas. Even if anyone should send any aircraft into the secure corridor, all their communications and sensor capability will be jammed. They will only have visual fighting ability. We do not anticipate any problems."

There was a moment of silence as Bachman waited for any other questions, until Rozen took back the briefing. "Thank you, General Bachman. Gentlemen, the damage estimate is ninety percent destruction of the facility and a one hundred percent casualty rate of all personnel in the facility. For as important it will be to destroy all their centrifuges, the loss of some of their top scientists and so many technicians will be far more valuable in crippling their nuclear program. We will be using approximately a quarter of our aircraft on this mission. The remaining tactical aircraft will be standing by on high alert for any possible, but highly unlikely, incursions by enemy aircraft into Israeli air space. The most likely form of retaliation from Iran will be significant missile attacks. We expect to be able to neutralize ninety percent of all incoming missiles with our Iron Dome Defense Shield."

"How many missiles do you believe they can launch at us?" asked Akerman.

"We believe they have approximately eighty Shahab 3s in the Bekaa Valley, each with a twelve-hundred-kilogram warhead, in addition to several hundred other smaller missiles," Rozen answered.

"That means at least eight of those monsters could possibly get through. If any hit civilian targets in Haifa, that would be tantamount to a declaration of war against us. I want a limited nuclear strike for Tehran ready to go, should their response be disproportionate," Akerman said, making it clear he wasn't going to stand for any aggression from Iran.

"Yes, Prime Minister, that is always on the table and available under warranted circumstances," Rozen replied, conditionally affirming that was an option. "If there is nothing else, I would suggest we all meet back in the tactical operations center by ten forty-five, fifteen minutes prior to when the mission commences."

***

Since departing Tabriz, Michael and Ali had spent the last three and a half hours talking nonstop as they closed in on Maku. Despite their physical and emotional exhaustion, there was an electricity amongst them, knowing they were quickly approaching their final destination and their way out of Iran. Michael had been thinking about how and where they would leave Karbashi's large Mercedes so that he could recover it afterwards. He figured he would drive into town and they would discreetly cruise through some secondary streets to search for a good location they could leave it where it could remain at least until tomorrow or the next day, until Karbashi could come and retrieve it. Then they would begin their walk back out of town to the extraction point.

Michael wasn't crazy about the two of them having to walk back down the shoulder of the main road heading out of town in the middle of the day, but the risk of getting spotted if they remained in town was too great. Maku wasn't Tehran. Hopefully there would be enough peasant and livestock traffic that they wouldn't stand out that much, despite Ali being dressed in Karbashi's dress shirt and slacks. There really was no other option, unless they drove the Mercedes as far up as the dirt road went, before they ditched it and begin their hike. The big blue luxury sedan would definitely not go unnoticed abandoned on the side of a dirt road, besides being an enormous inconvenience for Karbashi.

They would hike back up the ravine and bed down in the shade somewhere until nightfall, when Ercan would fly back in and pick them up. He would talk to Asya one more time to verify all the details. They had plenty of time to take things slow and make sure everyone was on the same page. Michael remembered from his Special Forces days long ago that going in was the easy part. Getting out was always tricky because of so many unforeseen variables that couldn't be planned for.

"How you feeling?" Michael asked Ali.

"Excited. A bit nervous, I suppose."

"Yeah, me too! Hard to believe we're both sitting here next to each other in this big blue Mercedes making our getaway out of Iran. Sometimes I think I'm going to wake up and say, wow, that was a wild dream."

"I wonder what I'm going to say to Roxanne about everything that has happened to me. I don't know how she will react. I don't know how to explain it to her so she can understand what it was like, especially what happened to me spiritually. What am I going to tell her?"

"I don't know, Ali. She seems like a very intelligent and squared-away young lady, but she's your daughter, so you know her better than anyone else. I know if it was my daughter, I would just tell it to her like it was. You don't have to tell her about any of the unpleasant details that would cause her nightmares, but I would tell her about how you felt, what you thought, how this has changed you and where you see life going from here. That's probably a talk I need to have with my daughter, Sam. I should have had it a long time ago, but I wasn't ready for it. Hopefully I'm ready for it now."

"So how are you going to answer the last two questions about how it has changed you and where your life goes from here? I'm not sure I have all that figured out yet," Ali said, asking him the hard questions.

"How am I going to answer? Well, just over a week ago, I tried to kill myself because I couldn't find a reason for living. Now all I can think about is being with the people I love; seeing if I can restore my relationship with my daughter, asking someone for forgiveness for the pain and sorrow I've caused them over the past twelve years, exploring the possibility of a future with a special person I've known for many years, but who until recently was never an option to be a part of my life. So, I guess I'm a completely different person one way or another. I know there's a whole lot of things I still have to figure out, especially this God thing. I didn't have the same firsthand, face-to-face with the Almighty that you had, but there are things that have happened to me that I still haven't come to terms with, things that defy rational explanation. Does that answer your question?"

"I suppose it tells me a lot about you I never realized. I always pictured you as having it so together with your life, sure of yourself, always knowing what needed to be done and how to do it. You never mentioned anything about God or talked about religion, but I just assumed from the self-assurance you always had that you had deep convictions, always sure about where you were spiritually."

"Hm. Yeah, I had deep convictions. But they were about myself. I was full of confidence, and maybe some cockiness too. I thought I could handle anything. That I was master of my domain; in control of my future. Turned out I was greatly mistaken about that. I think this whole experience has caused me to reevaluate everything and consider some other possibilities. I may have to accept the fact that someone else may have more say in the direction my life goes than I do. Still trying to sort all that out. Ask me again in a few months. How about you?"

"I have many things to consider also. It's somewhat overwhelming to have a real-life interaction with God, just as real as I'm sitting here talking with you. It's no longer an issue of whether I believe in Him. Now it's experiencing Him however I can, trying to get to know Him, learning who He is, figuring out what He wants from me, asking Him to guide me. I want to be able to share that experience with my daughter. If I can just get her to believe how real of an experience it was for me, make her understand that there is more to this world than what we can see with our eyes, that would be the greatest gift I could give to her as her father. Does that make sense?"

"Once you have God, you never go back?" Michael knew things would never be the same for Ali or him. They had experienced something that couldn't be explained away, something that had changed both of them forever. "Before I forget, let me give you my parents phone number in St. Augustine, Florida. There's a pen in the center console. Write it down on the inside of your forearm—just in case. You remember how, don't you? Add one digit, subtract a digit, and so on." Michael said the number slowly as Ali transposed it using the technique he had learned from Michael years ago in Athens.

Descending into the valley where Maku was located, they looked up ahead in the distance and saw that a line of traffic had formed before approaching the outskirts of town. They were still too far away to see what was causing the backup. Michael pulled over to the side of the highway while they were still a couple miles away to try to determine what was holding up traffic.

"What do you think's happened?" Ali asked.

"I don't know. I can't see, but I don't want to drive right up there and get stuck in traffic with no way out," Michael answered, putting it into neutral and pulling the parking brake.

Getting out of the car, Michael placed his hands over his eyes, shielding them from the sun as he tried to make out what was going on up ahead. Ali got out on the passenger side and did the same.

"Can you see what's going on?" Michael asked.

"I'm not sure. Maybe an accident?" Ali took a guess.

"I don't know, it's not stopping traffic coming this way," Michael observed as a large truck blew past them in the other direction, along with other traffic.

"Do you want to get a little closer for a better look?" asked Ali.

"Yeah, we can. The border inspection station isn't until a few miles past town. How about you take the driver's seat just to be safe?" Michael told him.

Ali got behind the wheel and pulled back onto the road. As they approached the line of stopped traffic, Ali pulled back over to the side of the road. They could see that the stopped traffic originated about half a mile ahead, just before the split in the highway—one way leading into Maku; the other passing behind a small mountain range, bypassing town, and leading directly to the border crossing at Bazargan. The curvature of the road and the large trucks up ahead, however, prevented them from seeing what the holdup was.

"What do you think?" Ali asked.

"I don't like not being able to see what's causing the backup, is what I think."

"What are we going to do?"

"It's not like we have many options. We can't just turn around and go back. We have to make our way into town and leave the car somewhere. It looks like traffic is slowly creeping up. We have plenty of time," Michael said, trying not to sound too concerned.

"Okay, you're the boss," Ali deferred.

Pulling back onto the highway, Ali drove slowly as he came up on the stopped traffic. He pulled in behind a large white coach bus with red Turkish writing that was most likely transporting a tour group back over the border to Turkey.

"I wonder where they're coming back from?" Michael commented.

"Maybe Tabriz. I know many groups go there to shop for Persian carpets. Tabriz is known for some of the best carpets in all of Iran."

"No kidding. You should have told me when we were back there earlier today. We could have stopped and done some shopping so I could spend some of my rial. I don't know when I'm going to have a chance to use them again."

Not sure if Michael was being serious, Ali asked, "Do you want to go back?"

"I was kidding," Michael responded, giving Ali a sideways glance.

They slowly inched their way up, moving a few feet at a time every few minutes. As the highway straightened and they drew near to the head of the line, they finally could look past the large bus in front of them and see what was causing the delay. What they saw severely alarmed them. Eight or nine vehicles ahead, they could see a police car parked on the side of the road and two officers stopping vehicles, inspecting their occupants.

"That's not good," Michael uttered.

"Uh-oh. What are we going to do now?" Ali asked, trying not to panic.

"Okay, let's keep calm. Do you think you can talk your way through this?" Michael asked.

"What am I going to say?"

"Mm, how about you say that you're having a meeting in town with some businessmen who have driven in from Turkey?"

"What kind of business?"

"Ah, tell them you're a pistachio exporter. Think you can swing that?"

"I don't know anything about pistachios, other than they grow on trees, don't they?"

"Yeah, I walked through orchards of them a few days ago. They're just cops. How much would they know about pistachios?" Michael tried to reassure him.

"What about when they ask for our documents or identification?"

"Can you bluff? Act like you're reaching for your wallet but can't find it? Say you must have forgotten it this morning when you left from home in Tabriz?"

"What about you?"

"I'll act like I'm sleeping. If they want to talk to me, I'll start in with my deaf-mute routine. It's what I've been using when I've been confronted. You can say I'm your disabled brother you brought along to make our mother happy, getting me out of the house, that sort of thing."

"I don't know if I can do this, Michael. Suppose they want us to get out of the car. Then what?"

"Whatever happens, we're not getting out of the car. If it comes to an impasse, I want you to floor it out of there as fast as you can and take the off-ramp to the right that crosses over the highway and goes into Maku. Before we get into town, we're going to turn off onto a dirt road to the left and drive as far it will take us up into the mountains. We'll ditch the car and hike as fast as we can and hopefully get a ride out by helo. I know it's not ideal, but right now, that's how we're going to have to play it," Michael told Ali as he reached into his bag and pulled out the Model 1911 Karbashi had given him.

Checking that a round was chambered, he cocked the hammer back and, folding his arms and turning slightly to the left, placed it under his armpit against the back of his seat. He hoped he didn't have to use it, but it would be ready just in case. Ali shot him a nervous look as he kept his eye on the bus in front of them, moving forward slowly as they drew closer to the police checkpoint.

"What do you think this is all about? Could they be looking for us?" Ali wondered.

"I have no idea. The colonel said he would give us as much time as possible. I don't know how the authorities would have any idea which way we were heading even if they have found out you escaped. Maybe it's something completely unrelated. I think now would be a good idea to use the phone Karbashi gave us while we still have a few minutes left," Michael said, pulling it from his pocket and turning it on.

He waited for a signal, then hit redial. Hearing the first ring, then the second, Michael was relieved when he heard the familiar voice from several hours ago. "Hello."

"It's me."

"Yes?"

"We have a situation. We're just outside of our final destination and there is a checkpoint on the road. Is there anything we should know?"

"My friend, there is very much you should know. Our other friend from last night went into work this morning and shot and killed his superior. He was killed himself. I do not have any details about what was said or exactly what happened. But you should know, his superior was the head of the organization, if you understand me. Everything here is in chaos this morning."

"Holy shit!"

"Yes, my sentiments exactly. There is a nationwide alert for our friend who is with you. I would assume the checkpoint is directly connected with that," Karbashi advised.

"We may not be able to leave your vehicle in a convenient location for you to recover. It will raise questions and create problems for you."

"Do what you must to do. Our friend paid the ultimate price with his life. Make it worth his sacrifice. Do not be concerned about me. I will handle things on my end."

"Okay my friend. Thank you again for everything."

"May Allah help you and protect you."

"You also. Goodbye."

"Goodbye." Karbashi ended the call.

Powering off the mobile phone, Michael looked at Ali. "You're not going to believe this. The colonel went into work this morning and shot and killed his boss, who I think is the general in command of the IRGC. The colonel was killed."

Stunned at the news, Ali sat behind the wheel in silence, trying to recover from the bomb Michael had just dropped on him. He inched up slowly as the next vehicle cleared the checkpoint, leaving only three, including the large bus, in front of them.

"You okay?" Michael asked.

"Yes, I'm fine. I'm just trying to process it."

"I know. It's like getting hit by a twenty-foot wave. But we both knew it couldn't have ended well for the colonel. The fact that he released us, broke us out, whatever you want to call it, was going to reach his superiors. He was going to have to suffer the consequences. Losing his child along with knowing what awaited so many of his own people was more than he could handle. Maybe he wanted to dictate the terms of how he left this life and do something to help, rather than end up in a prison cell or have his loved ones witness him being hung. Better to go out in a blaze of glory than rot away in a prison cell, knowing your family's out there. It's going to be tough on any other of his kids losing their dad like that, but at some point, they'll learn their father gave his life for a noble cause instead of being misled that he betrayed his country. That's how I would have wanted it, if I were in his place."

"If you look at it that way, I guess we should be happy for him that he could make that decision for himself. Not many people, especially in Iran, have that choice. I know he's done some terrible things to other men, but who knows? He could have asked God for forgiveness. He was a different man in the end. Maybe he's finally found peace with himself. Maybe he's with his son right now. You've spared my daughter from having to face that in her life. Thank you again, Michael, whatever happens to us from here."

"Hey, we'll get through this. We didn't come this far to have it all end here like this," Michael encouraged him as the bus in front of them pulled up to the checkpoint and the two officers stepped inside it.

"Please, God, I know You hear me. You told me so yourself. We need Your help right now. Get us through this somehow. Not just for our sake, but also for the millions of others who are depending on us to reveal the truth," Ali uttered.

"Amen to that, God, if hearing it from the both of us makes a difference to you," Michael seconded Ali's supplication. "Okay, we're up next. Get ready. Put your get your game face on."

The two officers stepped down from the bus and waited for it to pull on ahead, then waved the blue Mercedes up to the checkpoint. Ali let the car roll up slowly as Michael closed his eyes and adjusted his grip on his pistol. Coming to a stop and rolling his window down, Ali greeted the police officer who walked up to him as the other stood on the shoulder, looking through the window at the sleeping passenger.

"*Salaam,*" Ali initiated.

"*Salaam.* Where are you coming from?" the officer asked.

"Tabriz."

"Where are you going?"

"To Maku."

"For what purpose?"

"I have a business meeting."

"What kind of business?"

"I am a pistachio merchant. I export to Turkey and the rest of Europe. I am meeting some Turkish business associates who have come in."

"You must do a lot of business to afford a car like this."

"Praise Allah, business has been good for me."

"Who is your passenger?"

"It is my younger brother. I take him with me sometimes to get him out."

"What do you mean to get him out? Out of where?"

"My brother is disabled. He has been that way for most of his life. He fell out of a tree when we were young and hit his head. He lost his hearing and has never been quite right since then. He has lived at home with our parents all his life, with my mother now only, but she is elderly, eighty-two. She is still healthy, but a fully grown man is too much for her handle at her age, cooking, laundry. It makes our mother happy when I bring him along with me so he can get out of the house for a bit."

"And why do you place such a burden on your elderly mother, since you do so well in business? You should pay to have someone care for your brother. Why do you not take him into your house?" the officer asked judgmentally.

"Unfortunately, I have a cold-hearted, unsympathetic wife. She wouldn't stand for it. You know how some women can be," Ali said, trying to garner the officer's sympathy.

"I know what you mean, brother. My mother-in-law is Satan herself. I have never encountered a more mean-spirited woman in all my life."

"Sometimes even worse when it is a mother-in-law, always wanting to give her opinion and turn your household upside down."

"Yes, especially when they live with you," the officer said miserably.

"Sorry to hear that, brother. May we go now?"

"Yes, as soon as I see your license."

"Certainly," Ali responded as he reached inside his jacket, feigning searching for his wallet. "Hm, where is it?" He switched to his other side, then started looking around on his seat. "What? I don't understand. Did I forget it at home this morning? Oh, it must be in the jacket I wore yesterday. I returned home very late last night and hung up my clothes. I was in a rush this morning and must have forgotten to grab it. I'm sorry, Officer, I don't have it on me."

"Your name, sir?" the officer asked with a hint of annoyance.

"Hamed Ahmadi," Ali replied with the first name he could think of.

"Mr. Ahmadi, may I see your vehicle's documents."

"Oh, why yes, one moment," Ali reached for the glove box, not certain what he would find. Depressing the release, he opened the door and saw the owner's manual, a Quran, and some maps, but no registration or other documents. "Oh, I am so embarrassed, Officer, it is probably at my office. I do not like to leave important things in my auto. A car like this attracts thieves. I had already had it broken into once right in downtown Tabriz one night, if you can believe that. What is our country coming to?"

"What about your brother? Where is his identification?"

"Officer, my brother cannot function on his own. He would not know what to do with a wallet or money."

"Wake him up." The officer's tone was becoming increasingly unsympathetic.

"Yes, of course." Ali began nudging Michael's shoulder.

Not understanding their conversation, Michael could nonetheless tell Ali had played all his cards and the officer was becoming suspicious. Jumping into his previously played role, he pretended to stir from his sleep and started mouthing undistinguishable blather, releasing a bit of drool from his mouth. Ali turned back up to the officer and shrugged his shoulders, gesturing pitifully towards Michael.

Visibly annoyed by now, the officer snapped, "Wait here!" then walked around to the rear of the car and read off the license plate into his hand-held radio.

Realizing they had come to the end of their rope, Michael said to Ali under his breath, "Go, go, get out of here!"

Putting it into first, Ali stomped on the gas pedal and let out the clutch, squealing the tires as he launched forward, causing the officer on the side to jump back in surprise. Turning to look behind him, Michael was caught off guard as Ali shouted, "Hold on!" then swerved to the right, the next second making hard contact with the side of the police car parked on the shoulder of the road. The collision sent the patrol car sliding sideways down the seven-foot dirt embankment, then flipping over onto its side as it came to a sudden stop. Michael heard a gunshot, then another as he turned back around to see the two officers firing at them. Ali kept his foot on the gas as the big Mercedes sped away, increasing the distance from them. One of the bullets found its mark, shattering the safety glass of the rear windshield into hundreds of tiny chunks of glass, giving Michael and unimpeded view of the rear. He drew the .45 and aimed out the back but held his fire, knowing it would be a waste of his ammunition.

Turning back around when they had pulled a couple hundred meters away, Michael yelled excitedly, "Good move!"

"I thought it would buy us some time."

"It will, but they'll be on our tail within minutes, depending on how close another unit is. The turnoff is coming up here soon on the left. It's a dirt road," Michael warned as he reached inside his pocket and pulled out the mobile phone that was their lifeline to Asya. Powering it on and waiting for a signal, he kept his eyes on the road ahead, looking for their turn. "Here it is, coming up ahead, see it?"

"I see it, I see it!" Ali shouted as he let off the gas to slow down for the turn.

Almost certain they were on the right road, Michael turned his attention back to the cell phone and saw that he had a signal. He hurriedly dialed Asya's number as they were consumed by dust billowing in through the opening where the rear window used to be. Michael heard the other end ring once, twice, then a voice he was very happy to hear.

"Hello?"

"It's me. We have an urgent situation. We just had to run a police checkpoint not far from the extraction point. We're heading there now. I think we can make it in forty-five minutes. We'll have company on our tail very shortly. Can we get a ride out that quickly?" Michael tried to keep as calm and succinct as possible.

"I will call right now and call you back. Okay?" Asya fought to maintain her composure after the sudden shock of Michael's message.

"Okay," Michael ended the call.

Dialing Ercan's number while trying to stay calm, she could feel her heart start racing as she considered the situation. Expecting Ercan to be able to go in on such short notice in broad daylight was unrealistic. Even if he could make it there in time, flying in daylight would be highly risky, even dangerous. They would be highly visible and easy targets for any of the Iranian Air Force's Russian MIG 29s or Iranian-built HESA Saeqeh fighters, their own reverse-engineered version of the American Northrop F-5s still in their inventory from the days of the Shah. Asya heard Ercan's mobile phone ring, then ring again, and again. By the sixth ring, she was beginning to get a sick feeling in her stomach.

Finally, after the seventh ring, "*Evet.*"

"Thank Allah you answered. There has been an emergency. They had to run a police checkpoint and will shortly be under pursuit. They cannot wait until nightfall. I know what it is I am asking, but is it possible to get them out immediately? They can be at the extraction point in forty-five minutes."

There was quiet on the other end as Ercan contemplated the situation and weighed his options. The ten or so seconds of silence seemed like an eternity to Asya before she finally heard, "We are out in the middle of an exercise. We can be back at the camp in twenty minutes, ten minutes to refuel and another thirty minutes to get to them. Tell them if they can hold on for sixty minutes, we will be there to pull them out. If you still pray, we will need all the help we can get. I will call you as soon as we have them."

"Thank you, Ercan. Allah protect you." Asya ended the call and immediately dialed Michael back.

After the second ring, she heard a "Yeah!"

"They can be there in sixty minutes. Can you hold out until then?"

"Not like we have any other choice," Michael shouted over the rear wheels spinning and sliding as Ali floored it up the dirt road, kicking up a trail of dust.

"They will be there soon. Hold on just a little while longer. I will be praying for you," Asya encouraged him.

"Okay, we'll do what we can. Hey, you know, once this thing is all over, I was thinking about spending some time in Istanbul to recuperate, check out the old sights. Maybe you and I spend some time together, see what possibilities lie in the future, something like that, if you want?"

"Yes, I would like that very much. It would make me very happy."

"It would make me very happy also. So much has changed. There's a whole other side of you I want to get to know better. You've always been a very special person to me. I always felt a connection with you. I just want you to know that, just in case," he told her.

"I liked everything you said up until the just-in-case part. You can tell me all your innermost feelings about me in a few hours after I get there. I'll be taking the next flight out. I will see you then, my sweet."

"See you then." Michael ended the call and put the cell phone back in his pocket.

"Sorry, just had a few things I needed to say to her. Feels like it's taking a good beating. How's it handling?" Michael asked as they bounced around on the pothole-filled dirt road.

"It's a Mercedes. I think Farzan is going to need an alignment after this however," Ali answered, keeping his death grip on the steering wheel.

"And some body work. Watch out for cows or herds of goats. I saw some out here a few days ago," Michael shouted over the noise and dust.

"You mean flock of goats?"

"I thought it was flock of sheep and herd of goats. Or is it herd of cattle? Pull over the next shepherd you see and ask," Michael commented, reverting to his old habit when facing life-and-death situations.

"How far will this take us?" Ali asked, the dirt road beginning to climb as they passed by the pistachio orchards in the narrow agricultural valley.

"As far as it takes us. We'll have to hike up to the LZ. It's a pretty steep climb. How's your heart?"

"I do spin classes at the Y when I'm home. I only cook with olive oil."

"Hopefully the cops that come after us are overweight chain smokers." Michael continued with his sarcasm, if for no other reason than to keep Ali's mind off the desperate situation they were facing.

Having gained some elevation, Michael told Ali to stop the car after they had gone around a switchback that gave them partial cover from the road below. Waiting for the dust to settle, Michael looked back down to the main road for any pursuers. There was no one following behind them, but off in the distance, Michael could see a number of police vehicles flying past, heading towards the checkpoint with their lights flashing.

"Looks like they haven't caught on to us yet. Let's just wait here a moment to observe what's going on down below, so we can reassess our situation. We've got just under an hour until our ride shows up. I'm guessing it will take us thirty to forty-five minutes to get to the extraction point, depending on how far up we can drive. We're pretty well concealed here. I don't want to give us away. If we start moving up this road any further, they'll be able to see us from down below."

"Maybe we should just leave the car here and go on foot the rest of the way. Less chance anyone will see us," Ali suggested.

"That's what I was thinking. By the time they decide to check this road, we might already be out of here," Michael had just finished saying when they saw a police pickup truck speed by the dirt road turnoff, but then slam on the brakes, back up and turn up the dirt road. "Forget that idea. We're going to have company soon. Let's get moving."

Ali put it back into first and, with some quick footwork, popped the clutch to keep from rolling backwards as he gassed it back up the dirt road as fast as his nerves allowed him, keeping as far as possible from the steep embankment without guardrails.

"Slow down a bit. We don't want to go over the edge and make their job easy for them," Michael warned as the back end of the powerful Mercedes swung out towards the edge.

"Yeah, okay, calm down," Ali told himself.

The dust behind them blocked Michael's view of the police pickup truck. He was certain from down below they could see the trail of dust being left by them and were hot on their tail by now. The further they headed up the road, the narrower and more harrowing it became. By now the large Mercedes was bouncing up and down, bottoming out in the deep ruts and potholes, and it was becoming impossible to avoid the growing number of large rocks that had rolled down from above, littering the road. When it had finally gotten to the point that they were risking plunging off the side of what had essentially turned into a wide goat trail, Ali stopped the car, turned off the engine, pulled the parking brake and put it into first.

"I can't go any further. Otherwise, we're going to go over the edge," Ali declared, looking at his shaking hands.

"I'm impressed you managed to get us this far. Even if they have a four-wheel drive, there's not enough room for them to get by. They're going to have to huff it on foot from here also."

Grabbing his bag with the GPS satellite phone and the .45 pistol, Michael got out of the car. "Come on. We'll make quicker time huffing it up this road to the top. I came down through the ravine below, but it looks like this will get us there also from the way it comes around. It's not as direct, but a whole lot less steep. Give me the keys first."

Ali handed Michael the Mercedes key fob. Bringing his arm back, Michael heaved the key as far as he could down the ravine. "I hope Farzan has a spare set of keys, but that's going be the least of his concerns. We're putting him in a tough spot having to explain how his car was used by us to escape."

"He understood the risk, Michael. He wouldn't have given us his car otherwise."

"I know. I was just hoping we could leave his car somewhere he could discreetly retrieve it. Well, you ready to do this?"

"Ready as I'll ever be." Ali looked at Michael with trepidation.

"Okay, let's go, then."

Breaking into a trot with Ali falling in behind him, Michael started up the road. Shedding Karbashi's sport jacket, Ali kept up with Michael, who had twenty-five pounds on him and was carrying the bag full of pistachios with their equipment. They needed to get as much of a lead on the police as they could. Besides the unit pursuing them, Michael was certain several more wouldn't be far behind once they confirmed it was the blue Mercedes. Trying to maintain a pace they could both sustain, Michael could feel the fatigue in his body. His legs were heavy and he had to work on slowing down his breathing to keep from panting. This felt nothing like his last run ten days ago through the streets of Queen Anne at night. Of course, it didn't help that they were out in the warm sunshine and at an elevation of over four thousand feet. It wasn't long before they were both dripping in sweat.

"How you doing?" Michael glanced back, checking on Ali.

"I'm managing. Getting a workout in," Ali struggled, trying to suck as much air as possible into his lungs.

"No kidding. I'm too old to be doing this kind of stuff anymore."

"I have five years on you…How do you think I feel?"

"Yeah, but I got twenty-five or thirty pounds on you…Going uphill, it's a slight disadvantage."

"Weren't you ex-Special Forces, or something like that?" Ali teased him.

"That was over twenty years ago...when I foolishly thought I was indestructible. I'm starting to get AARP flyers in the mail already." Michael kept the banter going to distract them from their discomfort.

"I know what you mean. I have millennials holding doors open for me, addressing me as sir...treating me like I'm some kind of grandfather...At least you still have all your hair," Ali managed to get out in between breaths.

"Anybody ever tell you you could pass for a Hamid Karzai double if you grew a beard?"

"That's the reason, I don't. Thank you very much...coming from the man who doesn't look like he's aged a bit since the last time I saw you."

"Don't be fooled. I'm an old car with a cheap paint job...When I look in the mirror and notice the wrinkles under my eyes...it's a reminder that any misconception I still had of being relatively young...is long gone. I always ask myself the same question...'When did this happen?'"

"Well, it looks like you still keep yourself in good shape."

"We'll see how long that lasts. Seems like it's harder and harder to stay motivated...when you wake up every morning and everything hurts...and it takes a couple of minutes to straighten out completely." Michael let out in between gasps of air.

"Hard to believe twelve years have passed...since we were in Athens."

"I know. Life goes by so fast. Seems like the last twelve years somehow passed by...without me even realizing it. Sometimes it feels like everything before that was some kind of dream...like it wasn't me who did all that. It's like you know you did, but somehow it seems like...you saw it in a movie, instead of having really lived it. Sometimes I wish it was."

"Sounds like you have regrets."

"No regrets about life, just about some things that I did to those close to me."

"That's not unique just to you, Michael," Ali replied empathetically.

"My priorities were so screwed up."

"Welcome to the club. Isn't that what life is all about? Gaining wisdom... learning from our mistakes? Didn't you just tell me what...you want in your future? Haven't your priorities changed?"

"Yeah, they have. It just took a lot to get that to happen. Feels sometimes like…I didn't deserve a second chance to make up for the mistakes I made."

"Thank God, He thinks otherwise…We have to slow down…I can't keep up this pace for much longer." Ali gasped.

Michael broke from their jog to a fast walk as they both took in lungfuls of air. They had put about a half mile between them and the car. Looking back down the road, they saw the police pickup come around the corner and slam on its brakes, skidding to a dusty stop to keep from running into the back of the Mercedes. Two officers got out and inspected the Mercedes. Looking around, they spotted Ali and Michael up the trail in front of them. With their four-wheel drive, they could easily make it up the trail, which was exactly what they must have been thinking as they got back into their vehicle. Moving it forward until their front bumper made contact with the Mercedes, they attempted to push the Mercedes out of the way, down the cliffside. Despite both the front and back wheels of the Toyota pickup spinning up dirt, they weren't able to budge the large Mercedes. Giving up, they got back out of the pickup in frustration and looked up at Ali and Michael. Michael saw one of them reach into their vehicle and pull out a radio mic, holding it in front of his mouth and speaking.

"Looks like they're calling for backup," Ali commented.

"They most certainly are. We better get moving. Pretty soon there's going to be a few more than just the two of them," Michael said as he started jogging again at a slower pace.

He glanced at his watch. It was another thirty-five minutes before their ride out would show up. He didn't know if they would be able to hold out that long. Looking back down at the valley off in the distance, he saw a line of police cars with their lights flashing racing down the main road and turning onto theirs. There were going to be a lot more police, and much sooner than thirty-five minutes.

***

Bill Jackson and Sam Peters were sitting on the outdoor patio next to the chow hall with their bags packed and their equipment cases next to them. Since Captain Engil had dropped them off at their rooms last night, they hadn't seen a trace of him this morning. They had woken up after an uncomfortable night's sleep on two army cots in the barracks room they had been given. Having walked over to the chow hall to have a late breakfast, they were surprised at the flurry of activity throughout the base as ground crews buzzed around the eight F-35s and a dozen or so F-15s. Having finished breakfast and exiting the chow hall, they looked down the flight line and saw the F-35s and F-15s pull away from their aprons and taxi to the end of the runway in succession. With the F-35s taking off first from parallel runways, the roar from their engines engulfed the entire base.

"Something's definitely going on here besides a training exercise. Those GBU-28s they were putting on them Strike Eagles when we arrived weren't for no exercise," Jackson declared.

"Yep. The captain was wound way too uptight about getting the update done as fast as possible. I thought he was going to have a meltdown if we took any longer," Peters added.

"Well, so much for us getting out of here anytime soon, looks like. I haven't seen hide nor hair of him this morning. Must have forgotten about us with all this activity going on."

"You think we should give Barso another call and let him know what's going on?" Peters asked.

"Guess he'd be interested in knowing about this. Got the sat phone in your bag?"

Peters reached into his black backpack and pulled out the Iridium satellite phone, handing it to Jackson. "Here you go."

Jackson powered it on and waited for it to lock onto one of the satellites above them. Getting a signal, he dialed Harry Barso's number and waited for it to ring.

"You know it's just past four in the morning back in D.C.," Peters commented.

"Ah shit, you're right, I didn't think of that." Jackson was just about to hang up when he heard a brusque voice on the other end.

"Hello?"

"Oh, Mr. Barso, howdy, it's Bill Jackson. Sorry to call you at this hour. Forgot about the time difference."

"No worries. What's up?"

"Well, we finished our work last night, but we're still stuck here. I know you're interested in what's going on, and since we spoke last, this place here has been a beehive of activity this morning. Their F-35s and Strike Eagles, armed with GBU-28s, are taking off as we speak. That's what you're hearing in the background. I spent twenty-five years in the Air Force with F-15 and B-2 squadrons, and I know the difference between a training exercise and the real thing. All's I can tell you is that this ain't no training exercise, if you know what

I mean."

"Okay, Bill, thanks for the update. You guys getting out of there anytime soon?"

"Well, it don't appear to be the case right now. I'm guessing whenever this shindig here is over and done with, they might get back to remembering about us."

"All right. Call me if you can when the aircraft return, if you're still there."

"Roger that. Sorry again to start your morning out so early," Jackson apologized again.

"Not at all, I'm very appreciative you did. I owe you and your partner steak dinners and some good beers when you're back in town."

"We'll take you up on that. Out here."

"Out." Jackson heard the connection on the other side go silent.

"Hey, what are you doing?" Jackson and Peters heard an Israeli officer yell as he approached them.

"Waiting for our ride out of here," Jackson answered him.

"I mean who are you calling? That is forbidden while operations are taking place. Who are you?" the young lieutenant demanded.

"Hey, buddy, take it easy. We're the reason your Lightning IIs are flying this morning. We're from Lockheed Martin. Captain Engil was supposed to be setting up a ride out of here for us this morning, but he's disappeared."

"You are not permitted to be on the phone. Did he not tell you? Who were you calling?"

"Listen here, sonny, you guys ask us to come out here on a drop of a dime to get you up and running, then abandon us. I'm going to miss my wife's birthday because of this. I was just calling her to wish her a happy birthday, all right?"

"Well, that is understandable, but it is still not permitted. I am sure Captain Engil will attend to you as soon as possible. He is a bit preoccupied this morning." The lieutenant altered his tone somewhat.

"I'm sure he is," Jackson agreed, as the young lieutenant turned and marched off as if he was someone important.

"I didn't know you were married?" Peters commented.

"Been three times, just not right now," Jackson clarified.

***

Harry sat up in bed as Rose continued to sleep soundly next to him despite his conversation. She had learned to filter out his bellowing voice, much like city dwellers tune out the loud noises of garbage trucks making their rounds in the early-morning hours as the city sleeps. He thought about the implications of what he had just learned. The Israelis had launched what was obviously going to be a major attack against Iran. With that many strike aircraft carrying so many bunker-busting munitions, there weren't many targets they could be going after. It was most likely one of Iran's heavily fortified nuclear or ballistic missile facilities. There was only a handful that would require such a strike. If he had to take an educated guess, he would say Arak or Fordow, maybe Bushehr. This was it. It was the beginning of an escalation between Israel and Iran that would eventually lead to one inevitable outcome. Whether it would be a limited nuclear strike or a massive retaliation, depending on Iran's response, he knew Israel wouldn't hesitate to use their nuclear arsenal if the security of their nation felt threatened.

So, what now? What could he do with this information? Who was he going to call, and what would he even say? He hadn't heard anything from Michael, so he didn't even hold any cards over those individuals involved in setting these catastrophic events into motion. He looked at the clock. It was 4:20 a.m. A feeling of helplessness overcame him as he sat there in the darkness of his bedroom. Standing up and stepping into his slippers, he shuffled out of the bedroom and headed for the kitchen. He would make himself a pot of coffee and try to think of what to do, other than tune in to BBC to hear reporting about some massive attack in Iran, followed a few hours later by a barrage of missiles into Israel.

***

Michael and Ali kept a steady pace despite their hearts pounding and lungs burning, trying to supply oxygen to their drained legs. Glancing back, they could see that several other police units had arrived at the Mercedes, with what looked like twelve or so officers congregating around it and looking up in their direction. By now, they had added another mile between them and their pursuers, but that didn't mitigate the urgency of their situation. It wouldn't take long for them to catch up with Ali and Michael. Even if Ercan did arrive in time, it would be a precarious situation for the Blackhawks to come in if the police had rifles. Continuing to look behind them as they ran, what they saw next greatly alarmed them. With all the officers standing along one side of the Mercedes, Michael and Ali saw them begin to slowly push the large vehicle inch by inch across the dirt road toward the edge. It was a slow process, but the dozen officers finally managed to move it enough where first the rear tire, then the front tire were pushed off the edge, followed shortly afterwards with the remainder of the car, sending it flipping and bouncing down the steep cliffside until it came to crashing halt at the bottom of the ravine, bursting into flames and sending a fireball into the sky.

"Ah shit!" Michael exclaimed, realizing they would be shortly be catching up to them now that they could pursue them with their four-wheel drives.

"What are we going to do now?" Ali asked, trying not to panic.

Michael stopped a moment and searched their surroundings, looking for a way down into the ravine and above them on the mountainside. Neither was an option from where they stood. He tried to see what was further up the road, but his view was blocked by several curves around outcroppings. They had no choice other than to stay on the road for now.

"Come on, let's move. They'll be on us in five minutes or so," Michael said urgently as he started running again at a faster pace.

Ali followed closely behind him, both of them ignoring their pain as a surge of adrenaline allowed them to push their fifty-four and fifty-nine-year-old bodies beyond what would normally seem possible. Michael looked back down the road and saw the column of police pickup trucks was now slowly making their way up the road, not at a quick pace, but faster than the two of them were moving, despite the boost of the adrenaline. Michael looked at his watch. They still had twenty minutes left until their ride would arrive. It didn't look good. Michael began thinking about surrendering. It was either that or both of them getting killed. The seven rounds he had in the .45 were no match for the overwhelming firepower the officers had with them. Maybe there was a slight chance they would be listened to once they were back in Tehran. After all, they had Karbashi on their side. He might be able to support them somehow, that was, if he wasn't in Evin Prison himself. Michael just kept running, hoping for some miracle against all odds.

God, I know I've doubted you despite everything to the contrary, but if you're listening, we could use your help right now. I've got nothing more I can do on my own, nothing more I have to offer. This can't be the end after everything both of us have been through. Please, I'm asking for anything, Michael prayed as he kept moving up the road.

As they rounded the next bend, the road leveled off and their attention was immediately drawn to what they saw about a quarter mile ahead. In an open area along the side of the mountain was what appeared to be a quarry of some sort, littered with old rusted equipment and a variety of abandoned broken-down vehicles and trailers at its base. There were several shelves that had been notched out of the side of the mountainside above them.

"Looks like an abandoned granite quarry," Michael exclaimed in disbelief, pausing a moment to catch their breath.

"Yeah. Think we can make it, before they catch up?" Ali asked amidst his panting.

"We better, because we've run out of options," Michael answered, giving them another fifteen seconds to catch their breath before breaking into a run again. The level road was a welcome relief to their aching legs, which, despite their pounding hearts and burning lungs, had a newfound energy that drove them to almost a full-out sprint. Covering the distance in less than two minutes, they arrived at the base level of the quarry. Surveying the area quickly, Michael realized their only chance was to get the high ground and hopefully be able to hold them off with the few rounds Michael had in the .45 until their rescuers showed up. It was within the realm of possibility, but they weren't in the right location for their evac. The location where Michael had been dropped off four days ago was across the other side of the ravine on the next ridgeline, not visible from where they were currently located. Ercan wouldn't be able to see them from the direction they would be flying in from one hundred feet above the terrain. Michael's worst fears made their way into his head. While they were holding off the police, they would hear the sound of the Blackhawks come, then leave after not spotting them at the predetermined exfil point. There was nothing he could do about it now. They were here, and that's what they had to deal with.

"We need to get as far up to the top as we can if we have any chance of holding them off for a little bit," Michael told Ali in between gasps of air.

Ali nodded in acknowledgment, not able to say anything as he struggled with his breath.

"Looks like there's four other levels above us. The access road looks too rough even for their four-wheel drives. We'll go up that way," Michael pointed at the boulder-strewn utility road connecting each level.

Breaking out into a run again, they quickly made their way to the end of the quarry and started up the steep access road, where at one time large earth movers had transported rock down from where it was being mined out of the face of the mountain. Making their way up the first level, Michael paused for a few seconds for them to catch their breath, then started again up to the next level. Having finally reached the fourth and highest level, they stopped and looked back down the road from behind the cover of an old rusting giant excavator that looked like it had been abandoned decades before. They saw the first police vehicle come around the corner, followed by the rest of them, as they headed into the quarry. Reaching the main level, the convoy of pickup trucks came to a stop and several officers dismounted from the beds along with those in the cab. Altogether, Michael counted twelve officers, four of them with AK-47 rifles.

"Oh crap, they have AKs," Michael whispered as they spied on them from behind the excavator.

"Doesn't look like they have any idea where we are yet," Ali whispered back.

"Don't worry, they will soon enough."

"What are we going to do?"

Michael looked at his watch again. They still had another ten minutes until the Blackhawks were expected to arrive. That seemed like an eternity when it came to their current situation. Even with their advantage of having the high ground and the cover of the mining equipment, Michael knew he wouldn't be able to hold them off with the seven rounds in his handgun against their Russian assault rifles. The four AKs could keep them pinned down behind the equipment with a continuous barrage of 7.62-millimeter rounds as they made their way up the access road to their level. He might be able to buy them some time if he surprised them with a few well-placed rounds from his 1911, but they'd eventually figure out where they were hiding and overwhelm them with their superior firepower. If he went ahead with the fateful decision to fire first, any hope of surrender and being taken alive as prisoners would be greatly diminished. Things didn't look good.

"We're going to stay behind cover and hope for a miracle," Michael answered him.

"That's all you have? No other options, no other plan?"

"Plan? When did you start believing I had any kind of plan? I've been flying from the seat of my pants ever since I got here. It's out of my hands now," Michael whispered as he watched groups of two officers spread out in different directions with their weapons drawn.

They saw two of them start walking in the direction of the access road leading up to them. One of the officers carried an AK. Michael's mind raced, trying to decide on whether to fire at them once they started hiking up towards them. At approximately a hundred yards below them, it was pushing the limits of the 1911's accuracy. Once he opened fire, the rest of the officers would quickly run to their two comrades' assistance, and the assault to reach Michael and Ali would be on. The two officers turned up the access and began their ascent to the first level. Having run out of time, Michael made his decision. He had to keep them pinned down at the bottom, otherwise any hope of the Blackhawk making it in even if they were spotted, was gone. Steadying himself against the side of the excavator, he fired two rounds at the ground right in front of the two officers, shooting up a shower of dirt and dust by their feet as they dove for cover behind a mound of earth at the base of the road. Michael's fire had its intended effect in turning them back from their advance, along with announcing their presence to the remaining officers who were searching to identify the origin of gunfire echoing throughout the quarry. Michael and Ali heard the two officers shouting to the others, warning them where the shots had come from. Training their weapons above them, the officers ran to the aide of their two pinned down comrades. Michael had hedged his bets, deciding against killing or injuring the two innocent men who were just performing their duty as police officers, and hopefully leaving the possibility of surrender open for them, instead of almost certain death if he had hit either of them.

As the remaining officers spread out and took cover along the bottom of the access road, Michael could see them searching for where he and Ali were hiding. After a brief pause as the police officers regrouped, Michael and Ali heard who they assumed was the senior officer giving a command, then four others, two of them with AKs, come out from behind cover and start up the road crouched in single file behind each other, while the rest covered their advance. Taking aim, Michael unleashed three more rapidly fired rounds in succession towards the advancing officers hoping to have a similar effect as his last effort. He was successful once again in causing them to dive for cover, but it also unleashed a barrage of return fire that ricocheted off the old rusting machine they were taking cover behind. Peeking around the corner of the excavator, hoping not to get hit by the incoming fire, Michael saw the four officers return to their crouched advance up the dirt road. With only two rounds left in his .45, firing again at them wouldn't have accomplished much in stopping their progress. This was the end of the line for him and Ali. It was either surrender or be killed.

Just as he was about to tell Ali to shout out they were surrendering, Michael heard the "whop, whop, whop" of rotor blades off in the distance on the other side of the ridge. There was no way they would be able to spot them from where they were at. Turning and looking back at Ali crouched behind him, he said, "I'm sorry, Ali. They won't be able to see us on this side of the ridge. I gave it my best. I think we're finally at the point where we have to face reality and give ourselves up."

Not being able to come up with words to describe what he felt, Ali returned him a look of numbed acceptance. Words were not necessary for Michael to understand the letdown and devastation Ali felt after they had come so close. He felt the same. Peeking around the corner once more amidst the steady fire that was coming at them, he saw the four officers had advanced past the first level and were almost to the second level, not fifty yards from them.

Michael turned back to Ali and told him, "Shout out to them we're surrendering. Tell them not to—"

He hadn't finished his sentence when over the ridgeline appeared a Blackhawk swooping down towards them, followed by another behind it, off to its right side. Initially thinking they were Iranian helicopters, the police were caught off guard, creating momentary confusion amongst them as they paused their fire at Michael and Ali. Michael immediately stood up behind the cover of the excavator and began waving his arms, attempting to attract the Blackhawks' attention. Michael saw the lead Blackhawk come down and hover a few feet above the ground on the far side of the top level they were on, approximately two hundred yards away from them, where it was open and clear of any obstructions that the larger rotors might hit.

Realizing this was their chance, Michael yelled at Ali over the noise of the Blackhawks' loud turbines reverberating off the rock wall. "That's our ride out of here! Start running towards them. Keep along the face of the wall, so you're out of the line of fire from down below! I'll stay back and give you cover!"

"What about you?" Ali shouted.

"I'll be right behind you! Go! Go!" Michael urged him, giving him a nudge.

Ali stood up and hurried over to the rock wall as he began his sprint towards the waiting Blackhawk. Finally realizing the helicopters weren't Iranian, the police officers down below began firing at the Blackhawk. Seeing the lead helo taking fire, the door gunner of the second Blackhawk, hovering above and off to the side, opened fire with his M134 mini-gun, unleashing four thousand rounds per minute of 7.62-millimeter from the six-barrel rotary machine gun at the officers below, forcing them to dive for cover as a wall of flying dirt and rock was unleashed from the ground in front of them. Watching Ali make almost half the distance to the waiting Blackhawk, Michael turned his attention back to the four officers just below him. He saw them come out from behind their cover and begin their advance back up towards him as the other Blackhawk was preoccupied with keeping the heads of the officers below down. Knowing now was his only chance, he threw the 1911 in his bag and turned to sprint towards the Blackhawk, just as Ali reached it and was pulled inside by a crewmember. Running as fast as his fifty-four-year-old legs would carry him, Michael quickly closed the distance to the helo. With just about fifty yards to go, he didn't hear it above the thundering noise of the Blackhawk's turbines and rotor as he was suddenly struck hard in the back by something that knocked him face-first to the ground, followed by a sharp burning pain in his right chest. At first, he thought he had been struck by flying debris from the down-wash of the rotor and had the wind knocked out of him, but as he attempted to get back up, he fell straight back to the ground, not being able to take a breath.

From the open door of the hovering Blackhawk, Ercan saw what had happened and motioned the door gunner to open fire towards the four officers who were firing at Michael and them. Repeating the action of the door gunner in the other Blackhawk, he unleashed a burst from his M134 in front of the officers, causing them to dive to the ground for cover. Leaping out of the helo, Ercan ran towards Michael under the cover of his door gunner's fire. He reached Michael, who lay face-down in the dirt, motionless, the red bloodstain on his shirt telling Ercan he had been hit in the chest. Rolling him over, he saw a similar bloodstain in the front, and Michael's eyes open as he struggled to breathe. Grabbing Michael under one arm and by his belt, he heaved him up into a fireman's carry, turning back and running as fast as he could to the Blackhawk, Michael draped over his shoulder. With the help of Ali and another crewmember, they pulled Michael inside and laid him down on the deck as Ercan jumped in and signaled the pilot to take off. Opening up the throttle, the turbines roared to life as the Blackhawk lifted away from the cut-out ledge at the top of the quarry, while the door gunners continued with bursts from the mini-guns, keeping the Iranian officers down until they had cleared the ridgeline.

As they made a beeline back towards the border, hugging the mountainous terrain below them, Ercan grabbed the medic bag. From the bright red blood, Ercan realized Michael had taken a round in his lung, which was making it difficult and painful to breathe. With a pair of penny-cutter scissors, he cut open Michael's shirt from top to bottom, exposing the wound to his chest. Michael looked up at him from the deck of the helo, aware that he had been hit, and tried to say something, moving his lips. Ercan motioned him not to talk as he assessed his injury. The round had obviously gone through, indicated by the exit wound in front of his chest. Ercan could hear the classic sucking sound of a collapsed lung. He knew he had a few minutes to get dressings on both open wounds to prevent the air from escaping the lung and stop the bleeding. Otherwise, Michael wouldn't make it. Ercan would have the pilot fly directly to the hospital in Agri, where there was an operating room and surgery could be performed to try to save Michael. That was thirty minutes away. From the looks of the wound, Ercan wasn't sure Michael could hold out that long.

After placing a dressing on the exit wound, Ercan motioned Ali to help him roll Michael onto his side, where he cut open the back of his shirt, exposing the smaller entry wound. Placing a thick dressing on it, he gently rolled Michael back onto his back and grabbed a small bottle of oxygen, placing a mask over his mouth and turning on the flow. Bending down next to Michael's ear, Ercan shouted above the noise, "Hang on. We'll have you in a hospital in thirty minutes."

Reaching with his left arm, Michael pulled the oxygen mask away from his mouth and attempted to say something to Ercan.

"Don't talk," Ercan told him, placing the oxygen mask back over Michael's mouth.

Not giving up, Michael motioned with his hand as if writing something. Realizing what he wanted, Ercan pulled out a small field pad and pen from one of the pockets of his BDU shirt, handing Michael the pen and holding the writing pad for him. With his left hand, Michael managed to scribble, "Call Asya—tell Ali is out." Looking at what Michael wrote, Ercan nodded in acknowledgment. Putting on a flight helmet, Ercan plugged the audio jack into his cell phone and dialed, as Michael looked up at Ali. Ali looked down at him, trying to force a reassuring smile. Their eyes locked onto each other, Michael giving him a slight smile behind the clear plastic oxygen mask, signifying they had made it out.

As he lay there staring at Ali, Michael was surprised at how clearly he could hear his voice above the noise of the rotors. "You see, Michael, you did it. You served a purpose greater than you could have imagined in helping me. Why did you ever doubt that?"

Michael answered him from behind the mask. "I don't know. I suppose I didn't have faith that I could make a difference. I failed so badly before."

"Do you believe that now?"

"No, I don't. Once everyone finds out about you, everything will change. It will make a difference. I guess I played my part in that."

"It makes me happy you finally see things for how they really are. Safeguard that truth and you will always have the peace that comes along with knowing that."

"I will," he mouthed to Ali, who had grabbed his hand and was squeezing it comfortingly. As Michael lay there looking up at him, the whop, whop of the large rotor slowly faded away into the distance as Michael shut his eyes, letting a warm peace settle over him.

Chapter 27

Technical Sergeant Maria Vasquez was casually monitoring the NSA feed at her terminal inside the Combined Air and Space Operations Center, more commonly referred to as the CAOC, at Al Udeid Air Base in Qatar. What she saw focused her attention. The feed being streamed in was a combined depiction of all communications being swept up by NSA's satellites and ground stations monitoring CENTCOM's area of responsibility which included Israel, Syria, Iraq, and Iran, combined with US Air Force assets focused on intercepting military communications. Today's feed included all the radio waves being sucked up by one of the RC-135 Rivet Joint aircraft of the 21st Expeditionary Reconnaissance Squadron out of Naval Support Activity Souda Bay, on the island of Crete, Greece. The RC-135 was lingering about at forty-seven thousand feet above the Kurdistan region of northern Iraq, flying a routine mission monitoring military traffic coming out of Syria, Iraq and Iran, feeding it back to NSA where it was processed by the banks of petabyte-speed computers, which then streamed a graphic analysis back to the CAOC with a thirty second delay. What caught Vasquez's attention late that morning was something she hadn't previously seen during the regular course of her duties since starting in the COAC several months ago. Moving in a northeast direction within Syria along its border with Jordan was a three-hundred-mile-long-by-fifty-mile-wide radio-free traffic zone. Bringing it to the attention of Major Collins, her supervisor, she told him what she was seeing.

"Major, there's some very unusual activity along the Syrian-Jordan border on the Syrian side."

"What kind of activity?"

"I'm getting a blacked-out zone of nothing about three hundred miles long by fifty miles wide moving in a northeasterly direction, at around 500 knots." Vasquez explained.

"What?" the major asked as he walked over to where Vasquez was sitting.

"Right here, Major. See? It's like a black hole, other than some fragmentary comms being filtered through the mainframes at NSA," Vasquez explained, pointing to momentary blips that would appear for a few seconds then disappear again.

"That's really strange. Click on one of them when they pop up and bring up the audio so we can hear what it is," he instructed her.

Waiting for a fresh blip, Vasquez clicked on it, and they listened to see what it would tell them. What they heard at first only added to their confusion. They could only make out every fourth or fifth word of what sounded like radio traffic.

"What does that sound like to you?" Vasquez asked the major.

"Can't tell. I can't hear enough to make it out."

"It sounds like it could be Arabic, maybe," she guessed.

"Well, it's not Russian, that's for sure. Besides, there's no intel about Russian activity in that sector."

"Do you think it's the Syrians?"

"I don't think so. That's not Arabic. I think it's Hebrew we're hearing," he guessed just as that blip disappeared from the screen and the audio went silent.

"Israelis?"

"That's my guess. They're the only ones who would have the electronic warfare capability to do something like this. I'm guessing it's some kind of jamming system on a rolling frequency, which is why we're only picking up fragments of the communications. With it moving at five hundred knots on the track it's on, I'd be willing to bet my next paycheck they're flying some kind of mission. Maybe going after some Iranian targets in northern Syria."

"We haven't seen them use anything like this before when they've gone after targets in Syria."

"Maybe they're rolling out some new hardware," Collins suggested.

"Look, sir, the zone is shifting eastward into Iraq." Vasquez pointed to her monitor.

"What the heck?" Turning to Technical Sergeant Davis on the other side of the COAC, the major inquired, "Davis, do we have any real-time imagery from NRO over eastern Syria and western Iraq available?"

"Hold on sir, let me check what we got." Davis looked at his screen. "There's an older Keyhole 11 bird on station up above western Iran, but it's moving eastward. Going to have coverage for the sector you're asking about for maybe ten more minutes."

"Vasquez, send Davis your feed so he can see it on his screen. Davis, I want you to put in a flash request to NRO and have them redirect that bird's coverage straight down the middle of that fifty-mile-wide zone Vasquez is sending you. We're looking for any aircraft flying within its three-hundred-mile length. Make it fast."

"Yes, sir." Davis immediately started typing furiously on his terminal as he studied the image he was getting from Vasquez. Pausing after he had finished submitting his request to NRO back in Chantilly, Virginia, he stared at his terminal, waiting for a response. The seconds rolled by, turning into minutes as the three waited in suspenseful anticipation to receive something back.

"Got something, Major."

What came up on the large overhead wall monitor surprised them more than they had expected. Looking at a three-hundred-mile-long sector of real-time imagery, they saw what appeared to be multiple squadrons of fighter aircraft, some flying alongside larger aircraft.

"Davis, I want you to zoom in on that forward group of aircraft with that larger one," Major Collins directed him.

Moving his mouse and tapping his keyboard, Davis zoomed in and filled the large screen with a group of six smaller aircraft flying around a larger one.

"What does that look like to you, Davis?" Collins asked.

"Looks like six F-15s around what looks like a C-135 of some type," he said, referring to the airframe of the military version of a Boeing 707.

"That's what it looks like to me too. Okay, zoom back out. Now zoom in on that larger group of aircraft bringing up the rear. Yeah, that's it right there. What in the world...?" Collins stopped in mid-sentence.

"Holy crap, Major. Those look like F-35s with a bunch of F-15s keeping them company," Davis exclaimed.

"That's exactly what they are." Turning and heading to his desk behind the fourteen personnel he was supervising, he picked up his phone and dialed the direct number for Colonel Bazinsky, the COAC commander.

"Colonel, this is Major Collins. There's something you need to see right away," he said into his phone as he turned and looked at his commanding officer across the other side of the large operations center.

Asya was sitting at her desk back at her office, staring at the clock after relaying the info back to Michael about how quickly Ercan could get to them. Each minute seemed like an eternity. After an hour had passed, she hadn't heard anything yet. They should have been out by now. Something was wrong. Could they have been shot down? Her mind began to think the worst. As she watched the second hand make its way around the clock one more time, she almost jumped out of her chair when her phone rang.

Snatching it up with her good hand, she answered instantly. "Yes!"

"It's me," she heard Ercan say amidst the noise of the helicopter. "They are both out."

"Oh, thank you, Allah. How are they?"

"There is something I need to tell you." He paused. "Your friend has been shot. We are flying him right to the hospital. We should be there in twenty-five minutes. He wanted me to call right away and let you know his friend was out."

"He can talk?" Asya asked hopefully.

"No. He managed to scribble it on paper. He is in serious condition. He has lost a significant amount of blood," Ercan told her truthfully.

Asya sat there holding the phone to her ear in silence, listening to the sound of the whop, whop, whop in the background, not able to say anything as Ercan's news hit home.

"Are you there?" she heard him say.

"Yes, yes, I'm here."

"What do you want me to do with the other individual?"

"Keep him safe. I will be out there on the next flight," she said, recovering from her shock.

"I will do that. Call me once you have your flight information. I will come get you from the airport," he told her.

"Yes, yes, thank you." She ended the call.

Sitting behind her desk, she looked across her office, her gaze focusing on nothing in particular as she thought about what Ercan had said about Michael's condition. She knew Ercan didn't mince words when it came to describing the situation. Letting her know Michael had lost a lot of blood and was in serious condition was his way of telling her there was a good possibility he might not make it. She had prayed to Allah, asking him to help Michael and keep him safe. Part of her prayer had been answered, but the rest was yet to be determined on how Allah would respond. Looking down at her desk, she grasped her head with both hands and started to weep as she considered the possibility she would never see Michael again.

"Please, most merciful Allah. Do not let him die. You saved him once already to serve Your purpose. Save him once again. I know I am asking this for my own selfish reasons, but I humbly beg You to spare his life. Give him a chance for a new beginning. Give me that chance also," she prayed.

***

"I know it's still pretty early, Mr. President, but General Bob Marland over at CENTCOM just called me and told me he was just briefed by our forward operating headquarters in Doha that the Israeli Air Force has launched an extensive air attack against Iran. There's some four dozen aircraft involved. Right now, they're somewhere over central Iraq. Based upon our imagery, they also have refuelers in the air, so if they're going to top off their aircraft, depending on the target or targets, the attack should be commencing in somewhere between thirty and forty minutes." Secretary of Defense John Tapper broke the news to President Steele.

"Well, that's one hell of a way to start off my morning John," Martin Steele answered while peddling his Peloton exercise bicycle and watching how the markets in Europe were doing this morning on Bloomberg Television.

"I know how that feels, Mr. President. I've ordered General Marland to ensure there aren't any inadvertent air conflicts with any of our assets operating in eastern Syria and Iraq. That's all fine and dandy if they want to bloody Iran's nose some, but the damn Israelis never seem to think it's necessary to de-conflict with our folks over there when they decide to unilaterally go after somebody in their neighborhood. They're our only allies who do that kind of shit to us. One of these days we're going to have some kind of mishap, and both you and Ackerman are going to be standing behind the podium holding on to your balls while trying to explain how something so damn stupid could happen between two allies."

John Tapper was the only one who could speak to the President that way. On the boards of many of the same corporations as Martin Steele before he had become President, including Lockheed Martin, John Tapper had been asked by Steele to become his Secretary of Defense and oversee one of the largest military buildups since the days of Reagan. Both men had agreed the best way to put America back on the undisputed top internationally was to build up the military, and of course increase the profitability of those defense corporations. Steele, however, didn't find it necessary or wise to let Tapper in on his other little plan to put a choke hold on the world's petroleum supply with Russia. Steele needed Russia on his side as a junior partner to counter China's tremendous growth that was on track to unseat the US as the world's largest economy. Although Tapper was just as concerned about China, Steele knew he wouldn't go along with his plot to collude with Russia.

"John, I told you I already mentioned it once to Ackerman. I'll bring it up again next time we talk and make sure he understands we're serious about that." Steele tried to appease his annoyed Secretary of Defense.

"What do you want to do about this strike of theirs? Do you want me to call

Rozen and find out what the hell they're up to?"

"I'm sure they're pretty busy at this moment with everything that's going on. Just keep monitoring the situation and let me know what happens afterwards. I've got a meeting with Tom Barnum this morning to talk about loosening up some of those sanctions on Russia. Markov has been crying to me about how all his cronies over there are complaining their kids can't go to schools in Europe or the US because of the Magnitsky Act. We're going to see if there's some workaround we can do for their kids. You know, a gesture of goodwill without causing a lot of political fallout at home," he said, referring to the Secretary of Treasury.

"Yeah, well, Tom has a vested interest in going easy on the Russians. Since they have one-third of their currency and gold deposited over here, Tom's going to want to keep it unfrozen so his old pals over at Citigroup can count it towards part of their reserves."

"Now why do you always assume the worse about people?"

"Because I know people, especially the greedy ones."

"Takes one, to know one, John," Steele needled his Secretary of Defense and former business associate.

"That's why you know I'm speaking the truth, Martin."

"I'll pass on the warm regards from you to Tom this morning."

"You do that, Mr. President. Tell that greedy bastard, you sleep with dogs, you catch fleas," Tapper said, disclosing his disdain for Markov.

"All right, talk to you later, John," Steele hung up the phone.

Getting off the exercise bike, Steele walked out of the west bedroom across the hallway into the master bedroom, where the First Lady was sitting up in bed, drinking freshly squeezed orange juice and eating a piece of toast with cream cheese and smoked salmon, watching the morning news on CNN International. The President walked over to the large silver breakfast tray and grabbed the stainless-steel pitcher and a glass, pouring himself some orange juice.

"Well, it's finally happening. The Israelis have launched some major strike against Iran. The Iranians are going to get their nose bloodied pretty damn good and are going to have to respond with an attack of their own. I'll make it clear to him that we stand behind Israel's right to defend itself. As long as he gets the message we're behind him, he'll feel free to hit them as hard as possible if they suffer significant casualties from an Iranian response. It won't be long before Akerman feels he's boxed in and has no choice but to hit them with a nuke."

"I've never seen you so chipper this early in the morning, Martin. Nice to see how the death of a few million people can brighten the start of your day," Alexandra Kinkaid-Steele replied sarcastically.

"You are about as inspiring as a colonoscopy sometimes, Alexandra."

"Thank you, I love you too."

"Nonetheless, the cost is going to be worth the results. America is going to have its second heyday like we did in the 1950s, and the Middle East will be back in the same place it was in the 1950s. You see, everything comes around full circle."

"Whatever lets you sleep at night, Martin," The First Lady got up from the bed, taking her glass of orange juice with her into the master bath.

With her hands still grasping her head, Asya stayed like that in silence, not knowing what else she could pray for at the moment. Having lived the kind of life she had, seen the kind of things she had, she wasn't one to cry easily, but it had had a cathartic effect on her, at least for the moment. Her thoughts and her hopes since Michael had unexpectedly popped back into her life, had found their way past the protective layers she had built up around her heart in order to be able to function in her world of deception, betrayal and violence. That, and her unshakable faith that Allah ultimately had final say in all matters, both in this life and afterwards, was the only way she'd managed to survive all these years while still maintaining her humanity. The possibility of letting someone into her life once more, allowing herself to be vulnerable again, had cracked open the door to her heart. The pain from having that dangled in front of her and then abruptly snatched away felt like an arrow straight to the heart. She knew she had to collect herself. The pain she was feeling wouldn't compare to the pain thousands, even millions, would be experiencing if something wasn't done to bring an end to this monstrous plot.

Whatever she had already seen in her career was dwarfed by the evil that was trying to be unleashed now. It seemed that history always repeated itself, each generation forgetting the lessons from the past, allowing wicked men to gain power with false promises to make things better for them. Separating the internal politics and power struggles of her country while trying to faithfully carry out her duty was one of the most challenging struggles with her job. She guessed that was the case with many intelligence officers in every country. It was one thing how the general public formed its opinions from the modified facts and custom-tailored propaganda those in power fed to them, but she had been in the position to see things for how they truly were, had the benefit to know the oftentimes inconvenient truth. This was one of those times, and she knew she had to do more than just be a purveyor of that truth. She needed to act on it, even if it risked her own safety and well-being. Michael had done so and had paid the price for his decision. She was willing to do the same now. It was one thing to use a foreign asset to collect information, even to recover a person kidnapped from their country by a foreign adversary, but the unauthorized release of classified information to a foreign entity would not be something she could defend herself from. It could end up costing her dearly.

She picked up her mobile phone and dialed the number Michael had given her for his friend Harry. At this point, she wasn't concerned about there being any phone records of her making a call to him. She waited during the momentary silence while her call made its way through the international mobile network, finally ringing.

"Hello," she heard the gruff voice on the other end.

"Hello. This is Michael's friend. He told me the two of you like to visit the Hilton Galaxy Bar and that I should give you a call if he located your other old friend," Asya said, giving him the verification code Michael had told her to use.

"Yep, it was one of our favorite spots. He told me about you also and how you were a trusted friend. So, he's located our old pal?"

"Yes, and they are both back across the border. I will be traveling to that location shortly to meet your mutual friend and safeguard him until it is decided what is the best way to make use of his information."

"Okay. Knowing that helps me in doing what I need to on my end. How are they both doing?" Harry asked.

Asya paused a moment as she thought about how to answer his question. "From what I know, your missing friend is well. Michael..." She had to pause to collect herself. "Michael has been hit. He's in serious condition. They are flying him directly to the hospital. I do not know more than that. I will be there sometime later today."

Harry remained silent on his end as came to terms with what Asya had told him about Michael. He had prepared himself for that possibility, but actually hearing it, especially in light of the fact that Michael had actually succeeded with the mission, hit him hard.

"I see" was all he managed to reply as they shared each other's silence, considering the possibility of losing their friend.

"I need to make travel arrangements to get to their location. I just want you to know, I will do whatever is necessary to make sure the truth comes out, regardless of the cost. I will call you once I arrive and have more information about his condition," Asya said, breaking the silence, letting Harry know she was completely in.

"Yeah, okay, thanks, I appreciate that. I'll take it from here on my end. Talk to you again in a few hours," Harry told her, ending the call.

She had done all she could for now. She needed to get to the airport and grab the next flight to Agri. She would have plenty of time to contemplate the direction her life would take from here, with or without Michael. Either way, it would never be the same.

***

Harry sat at his desk in his office at home. The news about Michael had stung. In all his years with the CIA, he had never lost a close colleague or subordinate, let alone a friend. He had indirectly known some of the five CIA officers killed in 2009 at Forward Operating Base Chapman in Afghanistan, when the compromised CIA asset Al-Balawi, a Jordanian doctor recruited by the CIA to spy on Al-Qaeda, detonated a suicide vest after sidestepping security and making it inside the base. Michael had been more than just a subordinate and colleague. Although Harry hadn't seen him for years, Michael was one of the few people he had crossed paths with in life whom he considered a genuine individual and a true friend—something rare in the intelligence world where truth and loyalty were relative concepts. He knew Michael had struggled with what had unjustly happened to him as a result of Athens. Yet he was still willing to risk his life to save someone to whom he no longer owed any sense of responsibility or obligation.

Now Harry faced a similar decision about what he was willing to do in the face of a different type of danger, one that nonetheless could potentially bring significant risk to him. He would be inserting himself into a hornet's nest, throwing a wrench in the middle of a power play by the leaders of the two of the world's superpowers. Despite his experience and prowess from years of involvement in the highest levels of international intrigue, he knew he was just a tiny ant that could be crushed by those holding the reins of power, both in the United States and Moscow. At a minimum, his cushy life with his hefty salary could come to a crashing halt. What would he and Rose do then? Move to the Philippines and live off his government retirement? They wouldn't be able to touch that—at least he was fairly certain. It wasn't like he would be doing anything illegal, but he knew his actions would have repercussions. Yet he realized there were no other options at this point. How would he be able to live with himself if he remained quiet for fear of what might happen to him, knowing full well what was about to happen to millions of others. If nothing else, he owed it to his friend Michael, who had risked everything, to show the same courage right now.

He turned to his computer and typed in "White House switchboard" in his browser's search bar and came back with the telephone number he would dial that would set things in motion in a direction that would forever change his life. He took a deep breath and dialed the number on his mobile phone.

He heard it ring once, twice, then, "White House, how may I help you?"

"Hello. My name is Harry Barso. I'm a retired officer from the Central Intelligence Agency. I have some critical time-sensitive information concerning the national security of our country. Please connect me through to the duty officer in the Situation Room," he said, referring to the intelligence management center of the White House manned 24/7.

"May I ask what it is concerning?" the operator inquired.

"Lady, I just told you it is critical time-sensitive information about national security. If you have a top-secret clearance, I'd be happy to let you pass it on. Otherwise, if you don't connect me through in the next few seconds, you'll be answering to the chief of staff when the shit hits the fan in the next hour. Do you understand the urgency?"

"One moment, please."

Harry let out a sigh of exasperation, then waited as the seconds ticked by. Finally, after about thirty seconds that felt more like three minutes, the silence was broken.

"White House Situation Room. Lieutenant Colonel Huffman speaking. Can I help you?"

"Colonel, my name is Harry Barso. I'm a retired CIA officer. I currently work in the security department at Lockheed Martin. I have come into possession of critical time-sensitive information about our national security that needs to get to the President immediately. I know this is an unusual request, but I need you to put me through to him right now."

"Who is this?"

"Harry Barso. Listen, Colonel, you have a decision to make in the next thirty seconds. You can either hang up the phone and witness the consequences of your actions over all the international news networks in a couple of hours, or you can do as I say and break your protocols and put me through to the President just as if SECDEF or the DNI was calling with critical information for him, because apart from the fact I'm not SECDEF or the DNI, the information is no less critical. Do you understand what I am saying to you?"

There was a moment of silence as Harry waited. He thought he could hear the lieutenant colonel's breathing on the other end as he contemplated what to do. He finally came back on the line.

"How did you say you came by this information?"

"I didn't and that's not important right now. Listen, son, tens of thousands, if not significantly more, are going to die, not counting the devastation that will be caused all around the world if the President loses the chance to act within the next few minutes. Put me through now."

There was another moment of silence, then, "Stand by."

***

President Steele grabbed his glass of orange juice and brought it into the master bath, where he stood in front of the mirror shaving, frowning through the shave cream at the sight of First Lady behind him in the glass shower stall. He wished he had a better image to start off his day each morning instead of the aging body of his wife. Gone were the days where he could discreetly have arrangements made for him during business trips, at least for the next two years, hopefully six. Even then, afterwards, he guessed his membership in a very exclusive club would make such arrangements challenging, to say the least. He would be pushing seventy by then. Maybe his libido would have run its course, but then again, maybe not. It was annoying having to act so politically correct around all those young and attractive female interns working at the White House. Clinton had forever screwed that up for all his successors.

He wondered if he would learn about the events that were about to take place in Iran from his national security team or from the media first. He would have to make it clear when he spoke to Akerman that he didn't appreciate being blindsided with something like this, even though it was what he was so eagerly awaiting to hear. Assuming things moved along as anticipated, Iran would be reeling from the effects of an Israeli nuclear attack within the next few weeks. Then his ultimate plan would finally be set in motion, with Israel taking care of the dirty work and bearing the brunt of all the international blame. Akerman was such a bombastic fool for all his tough rhetoric. He never could think of what was in the long-term best interests of his country. It wasn't that difficult to send Akerman mixed signals about where the United States stood in support of his newfound aggressive posture towards Iran since his administration had taken office. Israel would survive, even if it meant the end of Akerman as a political force. Someone else would take his place, hopefully with more sense and less irritating.

Steele was surprised by the ring of the stand-alone phone line that was located throughout the private residence with a connection to only one place, the Situation Room in the basement of the West Wing. That was a bit earlier than he expected. Maybe Tapper had gotten the estimate wrong. The rinsed off the shaving cream and dried off with a towel, then picked up the receiver hanging from the wall.

"Yes?"

"Good morning, Mr. President. Lieutenant Colonel Huffman here."

"Good morning, Colonel. Whatcha got?"

"Sir, I am very sorry to disturb you like this, but I have an unusual call from an individual claiming to be a retired CIA officer with critical national security information, stating he needs to speak to you directly. He claims thousands of lives are at stake if the information isn't passed to you immediately. I know this highly irregular, Mr. President, but something makes me believe this isn't some kind of prank, or a crazy calling. I can hang up on him if you wish. I understand if this unacceptable to you, sir. I'm willing to submit my resignation if necessary for this complete breach of protocol," the lieutenant colonel offered apologetically.

Martin Steele stood holding the phone to his ear, temporarily speechless at what he had just heard. Who was calling him, claiming to have information about thousands of lives being at stake? Was it somebody from the media that had somehow been tipped off about something and was trying to get some kind of scoop or entrap him? That didn't make sense. No reporter would attempt something so outrageous and foolish, regardless of how much disdain some of the press had for him. Every bone in his body told him not to take the call, but another voice told him he couldn't afford to ignore this development and not find out who this person was and what they knew with so much at stake.

"Sir, are you still there?"

"Yes, Colonel, I'm here."

"Would you like me to hang up on him, sir?"

"Ah, no, no. I trust your judgment on this. Put him through."

"Very well, sir, stand by."

As the next few seconds ticked by, Martin Steele's mind raced trying to anticipate what he might hear. Could somebody actually have information implicating him in this plot? Had they told anyone else? He was getting ahead of himself. He needed to find out what this was about first.

"Mr. President?"

"Yes, this is President Steele. Who am I speaking to?"

"This is Harry Barso, Mr. President. I'm a retired CIA chief of station. I currently work for Lockheed Martin's security department. I have obtained information from two of our employees who have just witnessed the Israeli Air Force launch what appears to be a large-scale attack with dozens of aircraft carrying large bunker buster bombs. Also, the Secretary of State's interpreter that has been missing in Istanbul has been located and has information implicating Secretary Payton, a deputy director at CIA named Jonathan Canton, and the Russians, which I assume means President Markov, in a plot that was responsible for the assassination of the Iranian foreign minister with the intent of starting a war between Israel and Iran. I know Jonathan Canton. He had previously worked for me. I do not put it past him to be involved in something like this. I do not know if you were aware of any of this, but considering how things currently stand internationally, I'm sure you realize the direction things will go if Israel follows through with an attack like this. I don't believe there's much time left before the attack takes place, perhaps within minutes. I felt it was my duty to inform you about this immediately," Harry said, communicating everything as concisely as possible, making sure Steele understood the plot had been exposed.

"That is quite a story, Harry. Those are some pretty serious allegations against Secretary Payton, let alone the President of Russia. What makes you believe this Shiravi fella knows what he's talking about?"

"I didn't say his name, Mr. President."

"Oh yeah, I probably remembered it from the intelligence briefing. Anyhow, why should I believe any of these wild allegations about the foreign minister's assassination? Our intelligence folks think otherwise. Pretty brazen of you to call up demanding to speak to me and tell me a bunch of nonsense like this."

"Mr. President, it's your decision what you want to believe, but if asked afterwards about it, I am going to tell the truth about exactly what information I provided to you and when. It will be up to you to explain how you acted upon it," Harry said, calling the President on his attempt to intimidate him.

"And where is the Secretary's interpreter right now?"

"He's being kept in a safe place for the time being. He will be turned over to the FBI as soon as his safety can be assured."

"I see. Being that you have prior experience in these matters and are aware of the national security implications, I'm sure you understand the importance of keeping Mr. Shiravi's information from leaking to the press or our adversaries. Can you assure me you will keep this information from falling into the wrong hands?"

"It depends what you decide to do with it, Mr. President," Harry responded, applying as much pressure as he could, realizing he had to push Steele into saving his own skin if there was any chance he would take the necessary step and tell the Israelis to call off the attack in the next few minutes.

"Thank you for the call, Harry. I expect our national security establishment will get to the bottom of all this once we have Mr. Shiravi back in our custody. Now I apparently have to take care of some urgent matters as commander in chief to safeguard our country. I thank you for your patriotism. I'm sure we will be talking again soon." President Steele brought the conversation to an end, knowing he had no cards left to play.

"I'll be looking forward to seeing how you respond as our commander in chief. Goodbye, Mr. President." Harry ended the call, then let out a deep sigh of relief. That son of a bitch Steele knew all about it. President or not, Harry had experienced enough misdirection and deception throughout his career to know when he had confronted someone who was guilty and lying. Steele was in it as deep as Payton, Canton and Markov. The question now was, how was he going to react?

***

The last four of the F-15s that were accompanying the F-35s disconnected from the KC-135 refuelers and fell back into formation with the rest of the strike team. Waiting for the controller in the AEWC flying above them at forty-five thousand feet to give them the final execution order, Lieutenant Colonel Janner went over the last leg of the flight plan along with the vectors for the bomb run over Fordow. Topped off with full tanks of gas, his eight F-35s, followed by the accompanying sixteen F-15s twenty miles behind them, would drop down to twenty-five thousand feet and go to afterburners crossing over into Iranian airspace at Mach 1.3, getting them for Fordow in twenty minutes. At ten miles out, they would begin decelerating to six hundred knots and follow their vectors down to fifteen thousand feet to set up for their bomb run. At four miles out, the controller in the AEWC would begin the sequential release of each GBU-28 every two seconds, until all sixteen bombs were lined up and on their way, reaching the target thirty-one seconds later. Ten thousand pounds lighter, the F-35s would reengage afterburners, climbing to 30,000 feet and be out of Iranian airspace in sixteen minutes, without the Iranian air defenses even realizing what had happened.

"Gold Leader, Mission Command. You are clear to commence when ready," the AEWC controller released the strike team for their final stage.

"Mission Command, Gold Leader, roger," Janner acknowledged. "Gold Squadron, Gold Leader, on my three-count going to eleven hundred knots and descending to twenty-five thousand. Keep it tight."

"Gold 2."

"Gold 3."

"Gold 4."

"Gold 5."

"Gold 6."

"Gold 7."

"Gold 8."

"On my mark, three, two, one." Janner engaged his afterburners and felt the rush as he was pushed back into his seat and his flight suit tightened around his legs, keeping the blood from running out from his head as his F-35 began its acceleration from five hundred to eleven hundred knots in just under a minute.

***

Martin Steele slammed the receiver down on the cradle, causing the First Lady to look at him through the glass shower wall. He looked up at her through the mirror, giving her a look that made her recognize something had gone wrong. Turning off the shower, she opened the door and grabbed her towel off the bath mat, wrapping it around her.

"What happened?" she inquired.

He looked at her, but she could tell his attention was elsewhere else. Stepping out of the shower, she grabbed another towel and wrapped it around her head, then stepped into her slippers and walked to the counter, where he was standing in deep thought.

"What happened?" she asked again.

"What happened? I'll tell you what happened. I just got a call from some retired CIA guy who happened to tell me the Israelis had just launched an attack against Iran, and that Payton and your boy Canton were in cahoots with Markov in the assassination of Mohammedi. How is that for what happened?" he answered furiously.

"How did he know all that?"

"Apparently Payton's missing interpreter has been located and has that information."

"Where is he?"

"I don't know, he wouldn't say. Said Shiravi was being kept somewhere safe until he could be turned over to the FBI."

"Who is this person and why did he call you? If he's CIA, why didn't the DCI call?"

"I said he was retired CIA, and he called me to let me know the plot had been compromised and see how I was going to react. He works for Lockheed Martin now, and apparently a couple of their people are in Israel and somehow found out about the Israelis launching the attack."

"So where does that leave us?" she asked with concern.

"Us? You mean me. It's not you they'll impeach if this comes apart and I'm somehow implicated."

"My future is tied to yours. You need to do something and minimize the damage before it's too late."

"Don't you think I know that?"

"So what are you going to do?"

"Just shut up a minute so I can think, Alexandra!" he replied testily.

He stood there, running through various options in his head, while the First Lady stared at him. He had to distance himself from Payton as quickly as possible and make it appear he had been completely unaware of any Russian involvement. It would have to look like it was some kind of rogue effort on the part of the Secretary of State. Then there was the issue of the Israelis. How was he going to justify the fact that he had known about the attack yet did nothing to stop it? It would make him look complicit in whatever Payton had conspired to do with Markov. That bastard Barso had boxed him in. He couldn't risk letting the attack go through. For now, it was about minimizing the fallout. The less controversy surrounding him, the easier it would be to make it appear it had been some sort of effort to undermine him. He picked up the same phone he had just spoken on. It began to ring without him having to dial.

"Yes, Mr. President." He heard Lieutenant Colonel Huffman's voice again.

"Colonel, I need you to get Prime Minister Akerman on the line right now. I don't care where he is or what he's doing, just let him know the President of the United States wants to speak to him immediately. Is that understood?"

"Yes, sir! I'll connect him as soon as I have him on the line."

Steele hung the phone back up on the wall then grabbed his glass of orange juice and took a swig as he waited for it to ring again.

"What are you going to tell Akerman?" Alexandra Steele asked her husband.

"I'm going to tell him to stop the attack. What do you think I'm calling him for at this moment, to wish him a happy Passover?"

"Do you think you need to go that far?"

"How do you think it's going to look if it comes out that I either didn't know what the Israelis were up to, or that I actually did but denied it? I'll look either incompetent or complicit. Not a position I need to be in when the shit hits the fan about Mohammedi," he replied incredulously.

"I just meant if the attack doesn't go through, it brings everything to a grinding halt, for all practical purposes."

"That's exactly right, Alexandra. That's what needs to be done for now if we're going to survive this."

"I suppose, but daddy isn't going to be happy about this."

"F…," He was interrupted by the phone, snatching it off the cradle before it finished its first ring. "Yes."

"Mr. President, Prime Minister Akerman on the line for you."

"Mr. Prime Minister, this is President Steele. What the hell are you up to with your Air Force at this moment as we speak?" Steele put aside all pleasantries, going straight to the point.

"Hello, Mr. President. How nice to hear from you. I'm not sure exactly what you are referring to," Akerman replied, feigning ignorance.

"Don't bullshit me, Ehud. I know you have some four dozen planes up in the air right now somewhere over Iraq or Iran. I want you to give the order to turn them around and forget about any attack on Iran you decided on unilaterally without bothering to coordinate with me first."

"Whether or not we have planes in the air right now should not be of any concern to the United States, Mr. President. We are just exercising our sovereign right to defend ourselves from the terrorist state of Iran, which just recently launched an unprovoked missile attack against our country. I would think you would support our right to defend ourselves."

"Cut the shit, Ehud. With everything that's happened recently with the assassination of their foreign minister, and most of the international community wondering if Israel was behind it, do you think now is the best time to launch a major attack against them from Israeli soil?"

"When is a good time, Mr. President? After they develop a nuclear arsenal?"

"Listen here, you patronizing arrogant fool. Unless you call off the attack right now, I promise you the United States will completely withdraw any support for your actions. We will not block any vote by the Security Council against Israel. We will disavow any justification you try to use. You will lose my support completely on the Palestinian issue. I will pull back half our military aid to you. You will be completely on your own. Do you understand me?" Steele fumed with anger at him.

"I did not realize you would be so opposed to us striking them. I would have thought weakening their nuclear program and bringing instability to the regime is what you would have wanted."

"Not this way, Ehud. We will work together to figure out a permanent solution. I need you to call off the attack right now. Will you do that?"

"I am still not sure I understand your reasoning, but I will honor your wishes, Mr. President. The United States is our closest ally. I am sure you would never call on us to do something that would endanger our security."

"Just shut up and do what I asked, Ehud. I'll be standing by to get confirmation from CENTCOM that your planes are turned around. Goodbye." Steele hung up the phone.

Martin Steele looked at the First Lady. "That Yid better do as I told him," he declared, then picked up the phone again, speaking into it after a short pause. "Colonel, get me Secretary Payton on the line."

***

The fifteen minutes had passed quickly as the Golden Eagles raced across western Iran towards their final destination. Lieutenant Colonel Janner monitored the flight plan on his HUD as he prepared to give the command for the squadron to come off afterburners and begin the final stage for their bomb run. So far, everything had gone flawlessly. Communications with the AEWC had been crystal-clear, and there had been no indication of air defense systems attempting to lock onto them. He surmised the Iranian air defenses were in disarray trying to determine what was happening as a result of the M'sanver Ma'or jamming system blinding them to the presence of aircraft in their airspace.

"Gold Squadron, Gold Leader. On my three-count, to six hundred knots and follow me down to fifteen thousand."

"Gold 2."

"Gold 3."

"Gold 4."

"Gold 5."

"Gold 6."

"Gold 7."

"Gold 8."

"On my mark, three, two, one." Janner pulled back on the throttle and pushed forward on the stick as he led his squadron down to their final vectors, lining them up in bombing formation, before turning over their targeting computers to the controller in the AEWC who would release their bombs.

"Mission Command, Gold Leader. In position, ten miles from target. You have weapons control."

"Gold Leader, Mission Control. I have weapons." The AEWC controller began his thirty-second countdown as Colonel Eisler, the overall mission commander, stood behind him monitoring the countdown, until he was interrupted over his radio.

"Colonel, I have Prime Minister Akerman on the line for you," the communications officer told him.

"Put him through."

"Colonel, this is the prime minister. I need you to abort the mission immediately."

"Did you say abort, Prime Minister?" Eisler asked, not sure if he understood him correctly.

"That is what I said, Colonel. Abort, right now!"

"Yes, sir! Abort, abort, abort!" Colonel Eisler yelled at the controller who was lifting up the red security cover, preparing to flip the number one switch that would release the first GBU-28. "Gold Leader, Mission Control. Abort, abort, abort. I repeat, abort, abort, abort. Continue with flight plan exiting Iranian airspace. All aircraft. Mission Control. Mission is aborted, repeat, mission is aborted. Continue with egress flight plan." Switching back to the Akerman, the mission commander said, "Mr. Prime Minister, Colonel Eisler here. All aircraft have been recalled. No bombs have been dropped, but it came very close."

"Thank you, Colonel. We'll get them next time." Akerman sounded resolute.

"Yes, sir."

***

Bill Payton had just come out of the shower after getting up and running the five miles before that sun had come up, which he did three times a week. He had continued to do so religiously since getting his first star at the age of forty-seven, thirteen years ago. His security team always tagged along behind him, their Sig Sauer 9mms Velcro'd around them underneath their t-shirts as they kept up with the wiry retired four-star general. He had nothing in particular planned today, other than going into his office at Foggy Bottom.

It was unusual for him to have such a free and unscheduled day, but he needed it so he could regroup and try to come up with a solution to the dilemma Canton had put them in. His usefulness to them had greatly diminished, if not completely evaporated, with the position Canton found himself in. He knew this had the potential to become a major diplomatic headache for him. How did you explain the capture and interrogation of a foreign intelligence officer in their own country by the CIA and Russians? It had been an idiotic idea from the start, regardless of the circumstances. His immediate concern was finding a way to get Canton out of the country before he was picked up the Turkish authorities. That was the worst-case scenario. Then he would have even less room to maneuver diplomatically. He was trying to think of who he could call that still owed him favors in that part of the world, to arrange Canton's surreptitious departure out of Turkey. The last he wanted was to have to ask the Russians for assistance in making that happen.

As he was toweling off, he heard the ring of his STE encrypted phone on the nightstand next to his bed. Why was his office calling him at 6:05 a.m.? Didn't they know he was going to be there in just a short while? He walked out of the master bath into the bedroom and looked at the display on the STE. The White House? He rarely if ever received a call from there at home, unless it was some kind of emergency. What was going on? Had the Israelis gone ahead and dropped a nuke on Iran prematurely, or was it some other international crisis? He would have heard from the State Department's Operation Center before receiving a call from the White House. Maybe something had come up and President Steele wanted to meet with him this morning.

He grabbed the handset off the cradle and answered, "Payton."

"Sir, this is the Situation Room. Can you go secure?"

"Yep, go ahead."

"Going secure." There was a moment of silence, then the Situation Room watch officer came back on the line. "Mr. Secretary, I have President Steele standing by. I'm putting you through." Another short pause, then, "Mr. President, Secretary Payton. I'm dropping off."

President Steele waited for the symbol on his phone, telling him the call was direct with Payton. "Bill, where are you?"

"Good morning, Mr. President. I'm at home, getting ready to head into the office."

"Forget about going into the office. I need you on a plane right now on your way to Moscow."

"What's going on?"

"I'll tell you what's going on. I just got a call from some Harry Barso guy, claiming to be ex-CIA, telling me the Israelis just launched an attack against Iran and that your missing interpreter Shiravi has reappeared with information implicating you, Canton and Markov in Mohammedi's assassination."

"Who called you?" Payton asked, completely confused.

"I told you, some ex-CIA guy that works for Lockheed Martin. I don't know what his connection is to all this, but he made it clear he was letting me know about Mohammedi, wanting to see how I would react."

"I don't understand, how would he know any of this?"

"I don't know how he knows, but he knows. He said Shiravi is being kept somewhere safe until he can be turned over to the FBI. Can you believe that? The FBI?" Steele was livid.

"What about the Israelis? You said they launched an attack against Iran. I didn't hear anything about that."

"You didn't hear anything because I called Akerman and told him to turn his damn planes around while they were in the air. Otherwise, I was going to leave him completely on his own, with zero support from us."

"I thought that was what we wanted."

"That was before I got a call at five in the morning from some guy out of nowhere, insinuating I might somehow be connected to Mohammedi," Steele yelled into the phone, no longer able to contain himself.

"I understand, but there's nothing connecting you to any of this."

"I don't think you do, Bill. This has the potential to become a disaster. Whoever this Barso guy is, he knew more than what he was saying. Somehow, somewhere, there's been a compromise. We need to shut everything down and erase all our tracks. There can be no connections leading back to us. That includes Canton. Can you take care of that?"

"I'm not sure what you're asking, Mr. President."

"I'm telling you Canton has to disappear permanently. Do I need to make myself any clearer?"

"No, Mr. President, I understand perfectly. I'll take care of it. What do you want me to tell Markov?"

"Tell him to come up with some alternative facts, something that causes doubt and deflects the focus away from any official involvement on their part. He'll think of something, he's got experience in that area."

"What about Shiravi? Even with Canton out of the picture and the Russians denying everything, he's still going to claim I was involved."

"We'll think of something. Don't worry about that now. You and I have the same vision about what's necessary to put the United States back on top. It's hard to find men of your stature. You are a true patriot, Bill. I'm not going to leave you hanging out in the cold all on your own. Remember, the President has the power to pardon, so I wouldn't lose any sleep about any of this, regardless of which direction things go. You on board with what needs to be done? You with me?"

"Yes, sir! I'm with you all the way."

"Good. Now get yourself moving. I'll give Markov a call and tell him you're heading his way. I'm not going to discuss details on the phone with him. Not taking a chance someone on his end wouldn't use this as some sort of power play against him. Still need him around if we're going bring our vision to fruition. Call me as soon as the situation with Canton is resolved. I want it taken care of ASAP."

"I will do that, Mr. President," Payton assured him, realizing he had already hung up the phone.

Shit! Looks like I'm going to have to ask Markov for help after all. Payton cringed at the thought of having to rely on Markov.

Chapter 28

It was dark when Canton woke. He was disoriented at first, thinking he was back in his suite at the Ritz-Carlton. That idea quickly dissolved when he realized the mattress he was lying on felt like a hammock, along with the overwhelming foul stench the permeated the room. His memory quickly returned. He was in the dump of a hotel by the train station he had checked himself into the night before. He had gone through all of the bottles of the high-priced scotch he had brought with him from the mini-bar at the Ritz-Carlton, keeping himself steadily numbed while he remained holed up in his room waiting to hear back from Payton on how he was going to get him out of Turkey. Now he remembered. He had gone out after it had gotten dark and walked the streets around the train station until he had come across the area where the hookers congregated, making themselves available for travelers who had come in by train. The quality located around the train station was a far cry from what he was used to picking up in the more exclusive high-end areas, where he could find Russian or other Eastern European beauties. Tonight, he'd had to settle for some gypsy who was past her prime, but considering his situation, he didn't have many options. He had brought her back to his hotel room, catching the attention of the proprietor from the night before, who gave him a nod and a smile as they walked through the lobby to the stairs.

He couldn't remember if he had gotten her name. He couldn't remember much of anything, actually. He had finished off what he had brought with him from the mini-bar by early afternoon, then had walked around the corner to a small shop and bought a bottle of Johnnie Walker Red. It was like drinking paint thinner compared to the Blue Label, but he hadn't wanted to venture too far away from the anonymity and safety of his seedy hotel during daylight hours. His gypsy companion didn't speak any English, but that didn't bother him. He hadn't brought her back to his room for conversation. The last thing he remembered was her being on top of him while his head spun in circles, as he tried to concentrate on what he was doing. He felt like crap. He had a splitting headache, and his mouth tasted like a camel had defecated in it. Was she even still here? he wondered, groping the bed, but finding it empty. He turned and searched for a light next to the bed until he came across a lamp on a nightstand and turned the switch, bringing the room out of darkness. He gasped at what he saw when he looked down at his naked body. His groin was covered with blood. His next reaction was one of revulsion. *That disgusting bitch! She was on the rag and working?* He bristled with disgust. Had he even paid her? He couldn't remember. He looked around and saw his pants on the floor next to the bed, grabbing them and looking for his wallet. It wasn't where he normally kept it, in his back pocket. He immediately got a sick feeling in his stomach, dreading the possibility that was going through his head. Had she stolen his wallet?

He shot up out of bed and began looking around the room, catching sight of his wallet on the small table by the television. He grabbed it with a sigh of relief but immediately noticed it felt thin and light. He flipped it open to find it completely empty of all his bills. "That f.... whore stole all my money!" he shouted, enraged. He had over two thousand dollars in hundreds and another four thousand Turkish lira, the equivalent of roughly nine hundred dollars. He looked through the rest of his wallet and found that his credit cards were still there. That was a relief, he thought. He could at least pull some money out of an ATM. He didn't think MIT would be able to monitor his banking activity. His next thought brought alarm to him as he looked around for his black nylon briefcase bag, spotting it on the floor along the wall by his carry-on. Snatching it up, he unzipped the main compartment, hoping his worry was unfounded, the reality quickly hitting him that his worst fear had happened. His Glock 9mm was missing. He went to unzip another compartment within the main one and discovered it already unzipped. Reaching inside and grasping around frantically, he couldn't find his black diplomatic passport. He felt a sudden sharp pain in his right temple. Both his hands started shaking uncontrollably as his right eye began to twitch. His first impulse was to run back down to where he had picked her up and look for her. He wanted to choke her right on the spot, crush her throat until she couldn't breathe. He was hyperventilating and starting to feel dizzy. He had to calm down and pull himself together. Otherwise, he would make an already bad situation even worse.

He sat back down on the bed. He grabbed his pants again, checking the front pockets, and breathed a sigh of relief. He still had both his mobile phones, his official CIA phone and the clean phone he used to communicate with Rostov. At this point, those were the most important things he needed to make his escape. The money was lost, but it could be replaced. The gun was good to have, but realistically, if he needed to use it at this point, it meant his situation had gotten beyond bad. The loss of his passport wasn't good, but he wouldn't be needing it to get out of country. He would deal with the headache of explaining its loss when he got back to Langley. Those things did happen occasionally. He wouldn't be the first CIA officer to lose a passport. He looked at his watch. It was 2:00 a.m. Tuesday morning, about twenty-four hours since he had spoken to Payton. Why hadn't he called him yet? He would call him and find out what the holdup was. First, however, he needed to clean himself off. He headed to the bathroom, grabbing the bottle of Red Label. He needed to calm his nerves. What he needed was to drink a bunch of water, but this wasn't the type of hotel that provided bottled water, and he wasn't willing to take a chance with the tap water. It was one thing to have a hangover, another to get food poisoning from whatever parasites lived in the city's water supply.

**

Secretary Payton was ushered into an office within the Senate Building at 2:00 a.m. in the morning, where Victor Petrovich was waiting for him. He had gotten into Moscow at 12:30 a.m. local time. Catching a strong tailwind, his Gulfstream G550 made the flight from Andrews Air Force Base in eight and a half hours. Rather than meeting at Petrovich's office at SVR headquarters just outside the Ring Road southwest of Moscow, the Kremlin drew much less attention for Payton. As it was, it was highly unusual for his security detail, as well as the Regional Security Officer, the State Department official responsible for the overall security of the embassy, the ambassador and embassy personnel, to be secretly transporting the Secretary at this hour of the morning for a meeting. Then again, it had been unusual times with everything that was rapidly spiraling out of control in the Middle East since the assassination of the Iranian foreign minister. After escorting Payton in and doing a visual inspection of the room, his personal security officer exited, leaving the Secretary alone with Petrovich.

"Victor, thank you for meeting with me at this ungodly hour." Payton extended his hand to Petrovich.

"Mr. Secretary, please sit down," Petrovich gestured to the eighteenth-century sofa across the coffee table from him, declining Payton's hand.

"Sure, Victor. We're both pretty tired, so the faster we can deal with the situation at hand, the quicker we can get some rest."

"What is it, Mr. Secretary, that you need to discuss at this hour?"

"Well, I'll get straight to the point. I'm sure you've heard from your man in Istanbul what happened with the MIT chief of counterterrorism over there." Payton paused to gauge Petrovich's reaction.

"If you mean the tremendous debacle of your Mr. Canton's, I have."

"I'm not going to sit here and insult your intelligence, Victor, and try to defend him or disperse any of the blame. What he did was one hell of a colossal screw-up. He has caused everything to come undone and put all of us at risk. That's the reason President Steele has sent me here on such short notice. Canton has to be eliminated immediately. Is it possible for your man Rostov to take care of this for us?"

"Take care of it for us? I do not understand. He is your problem, not ours," Petrovich replied bluntly.

"Listen, Victor, he is all of our problem. If you want me to sit here and tell you we brought this on ourselves for relying on an idiot like Canton, I'll say it. Unlike you, we don't have our entire military and intelligence community at our disposal to carry out assassinations of foreign ministers, so we were limited to using the most unscrupulous individual we could find within the CIA. Never did I anticipate he would attempt such a foolish act as kidnapping a senior Turkish intelligence officer. If I could do it myself, I would personally put an end to that loathsome coward. I heard about how he abandoned one of your men and fled."

"It is interesting how you attribute this disaster to Canton. Was it not you along with Canton that your interpreter overheard discussing the details of our plan?"

"You know, Victor, it's a pretty sad testament to your Spetsnaz if they couldn't take care of such a simple task as putting a bullet in an unexpectant and unarmed fifty-some-year-old interpreter. There's plenty of blame to go around on how we got to this point. I didn't come here to hash out who's at fault. We have a vulnerability that threatens us all, and we need to deal with it. You are obviously in a better position to take care of it than we are. Can you do it, or will I have to tell President Steele in the morning that you won't because you're all bent out of shape?" Payton gambled with his ultimatum.

"Do you know where he is?" Petrovich relented for the time being.

"I can find out. He's been hiding out somewhere in Istanbul. Do you have any assets that can get to him?"

"Rostov and his men are standing by on a Russian cargo ship, waiting for it to depart from Istanbul in the morning. I will call him and see what he can do," Petrovich told Payton, then pulled out some type of encrypted mobile phone from the inside of his sports coat and dialed.

Petrovich broke into a conversation in Russian. Payton heard Canton's name mentioned and picked up *"ubey yevo,"* recognizing the phrase for "kill him" from what he still remembered of his limited Russian from his days as a young Army captain stationed in West Germany.

"Da, da, kanyeshna. Spaseeba, Dimitri Vladimirovich." Petrovich ended the conversation, agreeing with and thanking Rostov, calling him by his real name.

"Rostov will contact Canton and tell him to meet him by the water at some ferry terminal in an hour. Rostov will be there with a Zodiac and pick him up. He will take care of the matter," Petrovich informed Payton.

"Excellent. I'd like to wait here, if you wouldn't mind, until we have confirmation. I want to be able to report definitively to President Steele in the morning that it has been taken care of."

"When one of my men tells me something will be done, I can go to sleep, knowing in the morning when I wake that it has been done. It is unfortunate you do not have the same confidence with the men you have under your command." The subtlety of Petrovich's insult wasn't lost on Payton.

"Well, I suppose when you have men under you who fear they might take a fall out of a five-story window or swallow a radioactive cocktail if they screw up, it tends to grab their attention," Payton returned the slight with a smile as he settled in and waited to hear of Canton's demise.

***

Canton had just finished showering and was drying himself off with a dingy hand towel that at one time might have been white but was now a light shade of gray. Despite the risk, he had let the tap water run the entire time he was in the shower, then cupped his hands under the bathroom faucet, lapping up water as he tried to rehydrate himself and rinse the foul taste from his mouth. He didn't even have any money to buy a bottle of drinking water from one of the kiosks open all night around the train station. He would have to find an ATM a decent distance from his hotel, just in case his card activity was somehow being monitored, giving away his hideout location. He walked over to his carry-on and began foraging through it for a fresh change of clothes, when the silence in his room was broken by the sudden ring of one of his mobile phones.

He grabbed the phone. "I wasn't expecting to hear back from you."

"Apparently your boss contacted mine requesting assistance in getting you out. I was told to arrange that," Rostov said, attempting to sound displeased.

"Well, apparently your boss realizes who's running the show. You seemed to have a problem with that," Canton gloated over the phone.

"You need to be at the end of the breakwater at the Bostanci Ferry Terminal in one hour. If you are not there, then you will be left behind. A boat will meet you there and take you. Do not bring anything other than a small bag with your documents and any other important items. Leave your car in the parking lot. It is two twenty now. One hour. Do you understand?"

"Yes, but where is the Bostanci Ferry Terminal?"

"Across the bridge approximately half the distance from where you caused all this trouble. One hour." Rostov hung up his phone, a look of joyful anticipation on his face as he left his cabin and headed above deck, where his men were getting ready to lower the inflatable into the water.

Canton couldn't believe his good fortune. After the way Rostov had last spoken to him the last time, Canton took satisfaction in knowing he had been put back in his place. Payton had come through better than he had even expected, allowing him the opportunity to rub it in Rostov's face. He couldn't wait to see his expression. Grabbing clean underwear and socks, a black pair of pants and navy-blue pullover from his carry-on, he dressed quickly and gathered all his belongings as he prepared to leave. He wouldn't have to worry about finding an ATM to pull some cash out, after all. Vacating his room, he quickly made his way down the hallway and down the stairs to the empty lobby and out the front door. He located the BMW where he had parked it around the corner and down the street, throwing his carry-on in the trunk and taking his nylon briefcase bag with him in the passenger compartment. It didn't have anything valuable in it any longer, other than his CIA ID and a few of his official business cards. Starting the car, he pulled out into the quiet street and made his way to Kennedy Boulevard along the water, across the Galata Bridge, then up the Bosphorus Bridge, back across to the Asian side of Istanbul and back down Paşa Limanı Boulevard along the water, heading towards his escape from Turkey.

He needed to start thinking about a good cover story for what had happened. Maybe he would claim that he had confronted Tarhan about helping Blackstone, and she had threatened to blackmail him, claiming he had tried to rape her. Her allegation would seem so ludicrous without any evidence. It would be his word against hers. Once Langley found out about Blackstone's role in all this, she would lose all credibility. Things were starting to look up, he thought. For a short while, he had been beginning to fear the worst, that he would be rolled up by the Turkish authorities, starting a long and drawn-out diplomatic process to get him released. He knew the CIA would never allow one of its officers to be held by a foreign government, but the unwanted attention would end any hopes he had of being appointed DCI, regardless of how hard President Steele pushed for it. Now, everything would be contained internally and kept classified, away from the press and the public, and most importantly Congress. Maybe there was still some hope he would be DCI.

Making good time at that hour of the morning, he arrived at the ferry terminal in just under thirty minutes. Grabbing his briefcase, he left the BMW in the parking lot with his carry-on in the trunk and began walking down along the breakwater, which had pleasure craft and water taxis moored along the inside of the small harbor. Reaching the end, he scampered down over the huge boulders to the water's edge and sat down, waiting for his ride to show up. He guessed he would be accompanying Rostov's team back to Russia up through the Black Sea to either Sevastopol in Crimea or the commercial port in Novorossiysk. Either way, in a few days he would be washing down Beluga caviar with Russian vodka in the company of some beautiful young Russian whore. That would be a much-needed respite for a night or two after everything he had just been through, before having to go back to Langley and face the tricky process of navigating his way out of his current predicament. He was starting to feel better and better about himself. Despite his miscalculation with Tarhan, he had managed to evade capture and would shortly be on his way to freedom to fight another day.

He looked at his watch. It was 3:15 a.m. They should be here any minute. Looking out over the black waters of the Sea of Marmara, he picked up the faint sound of an outboard motor approaching, then the outline of a small boat came into view out of the darkness. As it drew nearer, Canton made out the outline of three individuals on the small inflatable. Pulling up next to the large boulders, Canton finally recognized Rostov sitting in the middle of the boat. Canton carefully made his way down to the inflatable, almost slipping on wet rocks and falling into the water, before one of Rostov's men in the front grabbed him and pulled him into the boat.

Finally coming face-to-face with Rostov, Canton declared sarcastically, "What's wrong? You don't look too happy to see me."

"It may surprise you, but I am overjoyed to see you," Rostov replied, the sincerity of his reply taking Canton by surprise.

"Yeah, well, I'm glad it was finally explained to you what needed to be done. No hard feelings." Canton stuck out his hand, not wanting to completely alienate himself since he had to spend the next few days with Canton and his men.

"Sit down." Rostov motioned him to the middle bench seat as his man on the outboard put it into reverse, slowly moving them away from the breakwater.

As they made their way slowly northward back up towards the Bosphorus Straits, Canton noticed Rostov staring at him with a strange look that made him feel uneasy. He wished he still had his Glock for reassurance. Why was he looking at him like that? When they got a little further away from shore, Rostov's man who was piloting the boat cut the throttle and let the boat come to a stop.

Confused, Canton asked uneasily, "Why are we stopping?"

Drawing his P-96 9mm from underneath his jacket, Rostov brought it up and pointed it at Canton. "We have some business that needs to be taken care of, as you Americans say."

"What's going on? You're supposed to be getting me out of here." Canton sounded bewildered and frightened for the first time.

"Is that the impression you were under? I believe you have greatly misjudged your circumstances. Put your hands behind your back," Rostov ordered him with a mocking smile.

"I don't understand. What's this all about? Why are you doing this?" He was surprised as he felt the powerful grip of the man behind him grab both his hands and wrench them behind his back, then the bite of a zip tie being cinched around his wrists.

"This is about your foolish and reckless actions that have brought disaster to the plans of your country and mine. What you have done has also jeopardized the safety of all of us. Dimitri almost died as a result of you abandoning him like the contemptible coward you are. You must now pay the price for your stupidity."

"Wait, wait, hold on a minute, I was just doing what needed to be done. Your man was the one who let some Turkish bitch get the better of him. I had it all worked out. She's the one who should be in this boat right now, not me." Canton began to panic.

"There is an old Russian saying: 'Do not dig a hole for somebody else; you yourself will fall into it.' Do you understand what that means?" Rostov asked him, a smile of satisfaction growing on his face as he pulled out his mobile phone and held it up in front of him.

Canton felt a hand reach from behind and grab his forehead in an iron grip. Twisting his head, he saw a black balaclava-covered face. "No, no, wait! We can make a deal! I can get you as much money as you want! Name your price! Don't do this! You're making a big mistake!" he pleaded.

Rostov's smile continued to grow as he videoed Canton's pathetic pleas. What Canton heard next made his eyes bulge wide open in terror. "*Allah a Akbar*" was the last thing he heard before he felt the sharp edge of a blade come across his from the left side of his throat to the right. He tried to scream but just heard a gurgle come from somewhere below his chin. His last image was the smile on Rostov's face as he was flung over the side into the water. Everything went black, then there was nothing.

***

Payton sat patiently in silence across from Petrovich, not bothering to try to make conversation. There was nothing more that needed to be said between them as they waited to hear that one of their liabilities had been eliminated. Payton didn't particularly care for him. He considered Petrovich just another one of Markov's thugs, like a mob boss's lieutenant responsible for taking care of dirty work. It irked Payton, having to stoop to the level of groveling for help from a hack like Petrovich, when he was the United States Secretary of State and a retired four-star general. Who was Petrovich to have a condescending attitude towards him? The minutes ticked by as the back-and-forth swing of the pendulum in the eighteenth-century French grandfather clock in the corner could be heard in the silence. Payton looked around at the opulent meeting room they sat in. The excess of the gold-leaf-covered crown molding, picture frames, doorknobs and chandeliers stood out to Payton as another indication of the Russians' insecurity about themselves. It was as if they were constantly trying to impress everyone with their superfluous grandiosity in everything they did and said in order to disguise their true weakness. Not like the United States, where a measure of true strength wasn't dependent on grandiose displays of military hardware in parades down Pennsylvania Avenue. Understatement was always a better strategy to keep your enemies off balance and prevent them from guessing what your true capabilities were.

Payton glanced at his Casio G-Shock watch. It was 3:30 a.m. He wondered how Petrovich's men would eliminate Canton. A bullet to the head would be the most humane thing they could do for that poor schmuck. He had known from the very beginning Canton had considerable character flaws, but with the First Lady vouching for him and the President's recommendation to check him out and consider using him in the plot, it had all but sealed his fate. Canton had been a fool if he'd truly believed Steele would appoint him as the DCI. One way or another, it wasn't going to end well for Canton. They could never have allowed such a liability to exist, having Canton hold that power over them, being able to implicate them in the plot. Any blame for how everything had unraveled, however, lay just as much at the feet of Steele as it did anyone else. That was what happened when a businessman tried to poke his nose into matters he had no expertise in. The President should have let him handle everything from the beginning. Then they wouldn't be in the mess they found themselves in currently. Payton's thoughts were interrupted by the ring of Petrovich's mobile phone.

"*Da*," Petrovich answered, then listened to the caller on the other end.

"*Harasho, Dimitri Vladimirovich. Paka*," Petrovich said, telling Rostov all was good, then hung up.

"There is something I want you to see," Petrovich told Payton, as he waited to receive an encrypted download. Getting up and coming over to him, Petrovich sat down next to him and held his mobile phone out for Payton to see, then pressed play.

"No, no, wait! We can make a deal! I can get you as much money as you want! Name your price! Don't do this! You're making a big mistake!"

"Allah ah Akbar!"

Payton grimaced at what he saw on Petrovich's phone. Watching a man undergo that type of death always troubled him. It wasn't that taking a man's life made him squeamish. He had dealt with death repeatedly over the course of his military career, especially during his stint as brigadier general commanding an infantry brigade of the 101st Airborne during the invasion of Iraq. It was the barbarity with which these jihadi terrorists took their victims lives, like they were butchering some kind of animal for slaughter. It always had the same effect on him, wanting to wipe the whole lot of them and where they came from off the face of the earth. They would have had a good start towards that effort if Canton hadn't messed it all up, but no one deserved to die like that.

"That's pretty damn barbaric, Victor. Was it necessary to do it that way? And what's with that jihadi Allah ah Akbar bullshit?" Payton asked in disgust.

"Mr. Secretary, you asked for our assistance in cleaning up your mess. Now you have video proof that one of your CIA officers was involved with the Chechnyan terrorist group responsible for the assassination of the Iranian foreign minister and the kidnapping of a Turkish government official. You, and we, now have, as you call it, plausible deniability of any official involvement with this travesty, shifting the responsibility to a rogue intelligence officer who was betrayed by the terrorists he was working with. The video looks quite convincing, wouldn't you agree?"

Payton thought about what he had just been told. As much as he hated to admit it, Petrovich was right. With the right spin, the administration could sell this narrative to Congress and the American public. There would be no way to dispute it, and it would cast significant doubt on Shiravi's claim of what had been overheard in his conversation with Canton. Payton would just have to feign complete shock that his CIA advisor was actually a traitor, working with international terrorists in order to subvert attempts in bringing peace and stability to the Middle East. It played perfectly with what every other rag head jihadi group was also striving for. Petrovich had done them a huge favor.

"Well, Victor, I'll be a monkey's uncle. I have to give credit where it's due. Did you think of this, or was it your man Rostov?" Payton commented, turning towards Petrovich pleasantly surprised.

"You are surprised? Why is it you Americans always take action without having a clear idea of what your goals are and considering all the possible outcomes? I warned President Markov about the risks of being involved in such a complex and sensitive undertaking with you Americans."

"Now that's something, Victor, hearing it from a regime that pushes people out of their five-story bathroom windows and tries to claim it was an accident, or uses a highly unique chemical weapon straight from their military stockpile to exact revenge on one of their own people. Do you think the rest of the world really buys any of the unbelievable bullshit coming from you?"

"Coming from a nation that continuously exerts itself in every corner of the world and invades other countries on fictitious intelligence of weapons of mass destruction, I do not believe it is Russia who had the problem of trust with the rest of the world."

"Well, all right, Victor, I'm not going to sit here and play tit for tat with you. I'm tired, as I'm sure you are. Thanks for your help. Maybe I'll see you around again, but then again, maybe I won't. I'm guessing Markov is not too happy with how all this turned out. He's going to have to blame someone for it. Maybe he'll reward you by demoting you to head up the local SVR office in Yakutsk. I've heard Siberia is a wonderful place to visit." Payton stood up and walked towards the door, not bothering to extend his hand again.

"Goodbye, Mr. Secretary. Enjoy your stay in Moscow, however long that may be," Payton heard as he exited the room, shutting the door behind him.

***

Harry sat in a wicker armchair inside his glassed-in patio. It was a clear night with a full moon shining in through the partial glass ceiling, illuminating the otherwise dark room. He was smoking a Cohiba while sipping a three-quarters-full tumbler of Macallan eighteen-year-old single malt scotch from a bottle he had just opened. Someone had given it to him for his retirement from the Agency. He couldn't remember who. Too many years had passed. He had been saving the expensive bottle for a special occasion. He figured bringing a stop to what had the potential to become a humanitarian catastrophe was as special as any occasion he was likely to experience in the years he had remaining. He wished he were celebrating the occasion with Michael rather than by himself. Rose had sensed something out of the ordinary in his demeanor when he had gotten home from work, but he had just told her he'd learned about an old friend who had fallen into bad health, declining to mention it was Michael. The less she knew, the better.

At sixty-five, he knew his best days were behind him. Regardless of how much time he still had left, the years would soon start catching up to him. It wouldn't be too long before age would start having its effect on his memory, and his mental acuity would begin to gradually decline. He had had an accomplished career at the CIA and had been fortunate to land his high paying job at Lockheed Martin. It had given him a comfortable lifestyle and still kept him in the intelligence arena, at least on the periphery, working for the world's largest defense contractor. Despite all his prior accomplishments, nothing had come close to having the impact of the phone call he had made earlier that day, which had potentially changed the course of history. It was a good way to go out after a forty-some-year career. Maybe it was a good time to consider calling it quits. Maybe he and Rose would move to the Philippines and build themselves a luxurious villa at a fraction of what he would make from selling his home in Bethesda. Between his government retirement, what he had in investments and what he would be getting from Lockheed Martin, they would be able to live very comfortably in the PI—like aristocrats.

Harry realized the position he had put himself in. Calling and confronting the President of the United States wasn't something that came with no repercussions, especially since he had made it clear in no uncertain terms that he was giving Steele an ultimatum. The plot with Markov had fortunately been foiled, at least for the time being. Bill Jackson had called him several hours later that morning and hurriedly told him all the aircraft had returned to base still armed with their GBU-28s. There had also been no reports on any of the international news outlets about an attack on Iran. The question now was, what, if anything, would Steele do about it. Would he just leave things be, or would there be consequences to pay? What could Steele actually do, try to have him killed? Who would attempt something like that? Canton was most likely toast from here on out, whether or not he was prosecuted. His days with the Agency would certainly be over. Considering the circumstances, Steele would have to be cautious with his future actions and appearances they would bring. He assumed the FBI and Justice Department, as well as the CIA, would be doing some extensive debriefing of Ali. He wondered what Ali would have to say about his trip to Iran and how he had escaped? Everything was far from being clear.

Then there was Michael. He hadn't heard back yet about his condition. He didn't want to read too much into that. He knew Michael's friend had her hands full handling the situation with Ali's sudden reappearance. But he knew the longer it took to hear something, the more likely the news wouldn't be good. *Mikey, old pal, I hope you realize just how significant it is what you pulled off.* Harry wished Michael could hear his thoughts. He knew what the odds were for Michael just to be able to make it back out himself. The fact that he had been able to get Ali out was incredible. In all his years at the Agency, he had never seen anything come close to the scope of what Michael had accomplished on his own with virtually no support. He knew Michael's reasons for undertaking what he did had never been about recognition or fame, but it was a shame such a selfless and heroic deed would never be publicly acknowledged, even if Ali disclosed everything that had happened. He knew the government would do everything possible to keep it highly classified.

Harry's thoughts wandered through all his options. Maybe he should hop on a plane and head to Turkey in order to help Ali navigate through the situation he currently found himself in. He still faced considerable risk and uncertainty in how things would turn out for him. Someone also needed to be there for Michael. One way or another, whether it was him or his remains, someone would need to take care of getting him back to the US. He felt compelled to do something more than his call to confront the President. He needed to do something. Things were far from being completely resolved. *Stop it, Harry. You need to stay put for the time being until you find out more. You're not with the Agency anymore. You've got no official clout to do anything,* he reminded himself. The ambassador and chief of station would certainly not appreciate him meddling in something that wasn't any of his business. His call to the President might or might not bring any consequences, especially if Steele was involved, but sticking his nose into something that was official classified government business wouldn't go unnoticed. He had to just sit tight until he heard back from Michael's MIT friend.

I'm getting too old for this kind of stuff anymore, he told himself. When all this was over, he thought about taking Rose on a nice long vacation to Thailand. On their way back, they could stop in the Philippines so she could visit her family. While there, they could look for some property to build their retirement villa. Maybe it was time for him to start enjoying his life. Better now, while he still had some life in him to enjoy, than later, sitting in a rocking chair, sipping prune juice through a straw. Harry took another puff from his Cohiba, then sipped his Macallan's. It tasted much better than prune juice.

***

Secretary Payton had finally checked into his hotel at 4:00 a.m. and managed to get six hours of sleep before being awakened by his aide in preparation for his 1:00 p.m. meeting with President Markov back at the Kremlin. It was to be a private one-on-one meeting without the presence of US Ambassador Richard Lakewood, to discuss sensitive issues regarding the tumultuous situation in the Middle East. It was to be a brief meeting with none of the usual formalities normally associated with high-profile diplomatic meetings between foreign ministers and heads of state. Payton was ushered into President Markov's office, leaving the two men alone.

Extending his hand towards Markov, who was sitting behind his desk, Payton was about to begin speaking when Markov raised his hand, signaling him to hold what he was about to say. Not bothering to offer him a seat, Markov waived all diplomatic formalities before addressing Payton, who remained standing in front of his desk.

"Mr. Secretary, I spoke to President Steele yesterday when you were on your way here. He attempted to reassure me that despite the colossal blunder you have caused as a result of your carelessness, our original goals for the Middle East have not changed. They will be achieved by other means at a later time, after things settle down and the situation becomes clearer. I have spoken to Victor Petrovich this morning, and he has advised me the liability with Mr. Canton has been eliminated. It appears you are the only remaining liability. That is President Steele's concern as to how he wishes to address that issue. The manner in which future diplomatic relations between our two countries continues will depend on how President Steele decides to proceed from here. Whatever course they may take, rest assured, this will be the last time you will have an audience with me."

Surprised at how Markov had addressed him, Payton was momentarily at a loss for words. What had he discussed with President Steele, and what did he mean by him being the only remaining liability? He hadn't had a chance to confer with the President before his meeting with Markov because of the seven-hour time difference, but he would find out what Markov was talking about as soon as he returned to the US embassy after his meeting, where he could have a secure telephone conversation with President Steele.

"President Markov, I understand your frustration at the unfortunate turn of events, but I can assure you, I continue to have the full confidence of President Steele," was all Payton could come up with under the circumstances.

"You may have his confidence, but not mine. Now, if there is nothing else, you may go." He gestured him to the door, not bothering to stand.

Payton stood there, stunned at what had just happened. Who did Markov think he was speaking to? He was the Secretary of State of the United States, representing the President. He wanted to say something, but what else could he say that would be appropriate in a situation like this? Markov, who continued holding his hand towards the door, maintained eye contact with him, waiting for him to leave.

Not being able to contain himself any longer, Payton expressed his true feelings to Markov before turning for the door. "You know, Dimitri, you're nothing but a pathetic two-bit dictator of a third-world country with oil and nukes. There's a reason the Soviet Union, and now Russia, has never been able to integrate with the rest of the industrialized world—because of small-minded insecure little men like you. I don't know what it is about the Russian people.

It seems like they just want to be fed a steady stream of bullshit excuses by their leaders as to why their country can never progress beyond a victim-hood mentality of always blaming others for their failures. Nothing ever changes with your sorry-assed country. *Dosvedania*, asshole." Payton turned and headed out the door to the hallway, where his personal security officer and aide were waiting for him. Not saying a thing, he strode down the hallway as the Russian protocol officer hurried after him to escort him to the front door, where his motorcade was waiting to take him back to the US embassy.

During the fifteen-minute drive to the embassy, Payton sat in the back of the ambassador's armored limo, stewing in silence. His aide knew not to question him when he had that look on his face. He looked out the window at the Muscovites going about their daily routines, just like in any other large city. What was it, he wondered, about these people that they could never get beyond the victim-hood mentality of believing others were the cause of all their problems? No wonder vodka was the national beverage. It was the only way to deal with the reality that everything in their society was rigged, no matter who was in charge. The rich and powerful would always hoard all the wealth and leave the crumbs for the average citizen wanting to believe the line of bullshit they were constantly being fed. Well, they got what they deserved with their leaders if they could be so easily misled.

He arrived back at the embassy to find Ambassador Lakewood and his entourage waiting for him at the front door as the motorcade pulled up. Stepping out of the limo when his security officer opened the door, Payton was greeted by Lakewood.

"Welcome, Mr. Secretary. How nice to see you again."

"Hello, Richard. Nice to see you too."

"This was quite an unexpected visit by you," Ambassador Lakewood said hesitantly.

"The President felt it was important for me to have a face-to-face with Markov on some sensitive matters concerning what's going on with the Iranians."

"I hope you had a productive meeting."

"Let's just say it was very candid."

"Always good to very clearly let him know where we stand."

"Yep." Payton's answer was short and to the point.

"Well, I suppose you would like to brief me on the issues at hand," Lakewood said as they walked down the main hallway towards the elevators, with embassy employees greeting Payton, who acknowledged with short nods.

"Not really, Richard. Nothing that directly pertains to US-Russian relations. I need to call the President and speak to him. What time is it back there now?" he asked, glancing at his watch. "Six thirty. He's up already."

"We'll go up to the SCIF, where you'll be away from the prying ears of our hosts. I can't even have a private moment with my wife in the residence without the FSB listening in on everything."

"Yeah, they're real sons of bitches, aren't they?" Payton replied, his thoughts still on how Markov had treated him.

He at least felt a sense of satisfaction at finally being able to tell Markov what he really thought of him. The question now was, exactly what he was going to say to President Steele about the way things had degenerated? He wondered if it was because Markov's conversation with Steele had also gone south. Maybe that was why Markov had been so hostile to him. They rode the elevator up to the top floor, where the ambassador's office was located, along with the sensitive compartmented information facility next door. Leading him there, Lakewood pulled open the heavy vault-like door, allowing Payton to step into the soundproof room that was specifically designed to thwart any type of electronic eavesdropping by the FSB, Russia's internal security service.

"I'll be next door in my office, Mr. Secretary." The ambassador left Payton to have his private conversation with the President as he shut the heavy door.

Payton sat down at the table and picked up the handset of the STE unit, dialing the number for Situation Room at the White House. After a brief pause while the secure satellite link was being established, the phone started ringing. It was answered on the second ring.

"Situation Room, Colonel Davidson."

"Good morning, Colonel. This is Secretary Payton. Put me through to the President, please."

"Yes, sir, right away. Please stand by."

As Payton waited, he thought about what he first wanted to say to Steele. Should he start off with his meeting with Markov, or on how the situation with Canton had been handled? He anticipated the President would share that same outrage at Markov's conduct as he felt. He wondered if he should tell him about how he had responded to Markov, letting him know exactly where he stood in relation to his position with the United States of America. He would play it by ear and see what the President had to say before deciding on that.

"Bill, how are you?" President Steele asked when he came on the line.

"I'm doing well, Mr. President. Hope I didn't call too early."

"No, not at all, Bill. I'm glad you did. So how did everything go taking care of our problem?"

"It's taken care of, Mr. President. They actually came through better than I had even hoped for. I saw it on video. It was pretty gruesome, but they staged it to look like he was being executed by some Chechnyan jihadis. Took a knife to his throat while he was pleading with them, then dumped his body into the Bosphorus. Gives them an out with what Shiravi thought he heard about Russian involvement, making it look like Canton was in cahoots with terrorists for money or whatever. Muddies the waters, and throws enough doubt into the picture that whatever Shiravi may claim he heard will be looked at very skeptically."

"That's really good, Bill. I knew I could count on you taking care of things."

"Thank you, Mr. President. I appreciate your confidence in me. I had a meeting with Markov just a short while ago."

"How did it go?"

"Well, he said some things that were of concern. He mentioned he had spoken to you yesterday while I was in the air on the way over here."

"We did talk. He obviously had some serious concerns about the direction things have gone as a result of Shiravi."

"Markov indicated you told him the overall goals concerning the Middle East have not changed, that we're just taking an operational pause to see how things shake out before deciding on a new approach?" Payton remarked probingly.

"That's right, Bill, that's what we agreed upon."

"He had some pretty harsh things to say about me."

"Yeah, he was pretty upset at how everything was handled. I can't really blame him. Can you?"

"Well, Mr. President, he seems to think that he's the one running the show and was going on about how—"

"Bill, Bill, just stop a minute," President Steele interrupted him. "Listen, you've served your country like a true patriot all these years. Your military service was exemplary, and your insights about geopolitics are second to none, which is why I selected you as my Secretary of State. But you really messed up big-time with how this completely unraveled because of your carelessness. You put our country in jeopardy, in addition to how far back you set us. We may never have such a good shot at this again. After all, we can't go around assassinating foreign ministers every other day. Now I'm sure despite what Shiravi says to the FBI about what he thought he heard you say, it will come down to your word against his, so I don't think they'll ever be able to prove anything against you, especially with Canton out of the picture. I hope you know, if somehow the unexpected did happen and you were convicted, I'd certainly pardon you at the end of my term, whether in two years or six. But either way, Bill, I can't afford to keep you on as my Secretary of State with all the negative publicity that's going to be swirling around. You know it's going to eventually make it to the press. Those bastards will try to destroy you. They could give a rat's ass about your service to our country."

Payton was taken aback by what the President had just said to him. He couldn't believe his ears. How could he just let him go like that? After all, he had risked everything agreeing with the President's vision and being his right-hand man in implementing it. Now he was just going to leave him out in the cold?

"Mr. President, I, I don't understand. I thought you said we were going to think of something. You said you weren't going to leave me out in the cold," Payton said, repeating Steele's assurances to him.

"Of course, Bill, I'm not going to let you hang, but we have to consider what's best for the country. You're a military man. You of all people should realize that. And besides, do you really want your reputation to be dragged through the mud the way it's going to be? I'd hate to see that happen after how valiantly you've served your country. I know you live by a certain code, which is why I'm going to suggest something that may be a hard decision, but it will give you an honorable way out of this. I promise you that I will vouch for your unwavering patriotism and how distraught you became when you found out Canton, your trusted advisor, was betraying his country to Islamic terrorists right under your nose. I'll tell the nation you did the only honorable thing a military officer of your stature would find acceptable when he believed he had let his country down. No one will think any less of you. On the contrary, they'll see you as a courageous man of principle and love for his country. Think of it, Bill, you'll be remembered as a patriot rather than being loathed and shunned."

Payton was silent as he let the President's words sink in. He realized what Steele was suggesting and the underhanded way he was packaging it. He was giving him the option of taking care of the final liability on his own terms, or else he would let him take the fall all on his own. He could just tell the world the truth about Steele's involvement with Markov in the plot, but what would that accomplish, other than bringing great harm to the country? The

President knew he would never let that happen to the country, even it meant his own demise. The only decision left to him now was how he was going to be remembered, his legacy. Even if he managed to escape prosecution, what kind of life would it leave him? He would be a pariah, shunned by all his former colleagues in the military and the establishment running the country. Even the corporate world would be a closed door for him. He wouldn't even be able to get a job as a guest commentator on CNN. That bastard Steele had him between a rock and a hard place.

"Bill, you still there?" he heard Steele ask.

"Yes, Mr. President, I am."

"Well, Bill, I know how hard of a decision you're facing, but I'd advise you to give some serious thought to what I suggested. I'm going to have to announce your resignation as soon as you get back if you choose to see this through and hope for the best."

"I understand, Mr. President. You know everything I've always done has been for the good of our country."

"I know that, Bill, and so will the country if you decide to take the honorable way out. Well, that's all I have to say. It's your call from here. Thank you for your service to your country, Bill. Goodbye." Payton heard the other end hang up.

He sat there thinking about what had just happened. He recalled his years in the military. Things were black and white back then, with well-defined lines regarding the values of honor, loyalty, integrity and personal courage, unlike the world of politicians. He should have just retired from the Army and taken a teaching position at West Point or some other university, where he could have instilled into young minds those values and how they related to the way history shaped the world we live in. At least there would have been some honor in a noble pursuit such as that. He stood up and opened the SCIF door, calling for his aide, who was standing outside in the hallway, to bring his briefcase.

The young aide brought Payton the brown leather case given to him by his father when he had graduated from West Point decades ago. It was well worn with marks from his many postings as he'd progressed from a second lieutenant up through four-star general.

"Thanks, Sam. Why don't you take a break and go grab a bite to eat down in the cafeteria? No rush to get back here, I'm going to be a while," he told his aide.

"Would you like me to bring you something back, sir?"

"No, thanks, Sam. I'm good." He took his briefcase and went back into the SCIF.

Sitting back down, he placed his briefcase on the table and opened it. Unsnapping a separate compartment, he pulled out another one of the items he had kept with him from when he'd gotten his first star as a young brigadier general. His father, still alive well into his eighties, had gotten him a Springfield Armory match grade stainless-steel Model 1911 .45ACP. He had carried it with him even after he had become Secretary of State. He would always be a general first. He studied the quality of the machining and the crossed cannons emblazoned walnut grips. It was an example of some of the best America had produced during its history of being at the forefront in leading the world during the past hundred years. He had been a part of that in some small way. He hoped his contribution would be remembered rather than his end.

He cocked the hammer, raised the pistol to his temple and pulled the trigger. Nothing was heard outside the thick sound-insulated walls of the SCIF.

Chapter 29

He looked at the television screen on the wall, the image of President Martin Steele standing behind the podium catching his attention, but the volume was too low to make out what was being said. A photograph of Secretary of State William Payton flashed on the screen next, followed by a video clip showing a ten-story beige concrete, glass and steel building with the American flag fluttering in the courtyard behind a twelve-foot tall heavy steel security fence, stainless-steel letters affixed to the wall with the words "Embassy of the United States of America" and the seal of the United States below it. It looked vaguely familiar, but he couldn't recall what country it was in. The screen then changed to a video clip of Secretary Payton shaking hands with Iranian Foreign Minister Farid Mohammedi from their recent meeting in Istanbul, prior to the foreign minister's assassination, before turning back to a male news anchor with his attractive female co-anchor. Next came video of a Turkish police patrol boat, followed by an image of a large beige stone building on top of a green hillside with a commanding view of the Bosphorus below. He couldn't tell if they were still on the same news story or had moved onto another, making it all the more confusing when the screen changed to Russian President Dimitri Markov speaking, then the gruesome image of several dead men in camouflage fatigues with black-clad Russian Spetsnaz soldiers standing by them, brandishing their 9mm AS Val assault rifles.

He wished he could hear what was being said, but he had no way of adjusting the volume of the television. Something significant had obviously taken place, but trying to connect the dots was beyond his ability at the moment. He was tired, and his eyes felt heavy. The last thing he remembered before nodding off was Iranian President Nouri Rostami on the screen, then the photo of some Iranian general in his trademark green uniform. His eyes gradually fell shut as he drifted off to sleep.

***

He had no idea how long he had been asleep or what time it was as he slowly opened his eyes to find a familiar-looking face sitting next to him, welcoming him with a loving smile and caring eyes.

"Hi," she said softly.

"Hi," Michael replied groggily.

"Welcome back."

"Thanks. Didn't think I was going to see you again."

"I wasn't certain I would see you either," Asya replied tenderly.

"I guess I got shot."

"You did."

"Feels like I got hit by a bus," Michael said in a raspy voice.

"Don't talk too much. You are still weak," she cautioned him.

"What day is it?"

"Friday."

"Friday? You mean I've been out for four days?"

"Yes, and considering how much blood you lost, it's amazing you are still alive."

"Guess you must have been praying for me."

"All the time."

"Thanks."

"You're welcome."

"How's Ali?"

"He is fine."

"Where is he?"

"He is at your consulate in Istanbul."

"Consulate? What about Canton?" Michael asked concerned.

"Don't worry. Canton is no longer a threat," Asya reassured him.

"What do you mean?"

"He is dead. His body washed up on the eastern shore of the Bosphorus Wednesday morning. His throat was slit."

"What happened?"

"Much has happened, and not just with Canton."

"So, tell me all that I've missed out on."

"Where to even begin? I suppose I need to tell you about my encounter with Canton and the Russians. After I returned from Agri, Canton contacted me and told me he had a source with information concerning the foreign minister's assassination. He said we had to meet the source at the shipyards down south of the city on the eastern shore. I should have known better but, never believing he would attempt something so brazen, I followed him to an abandoned warehouse. It was a trap. I was shot with some sort of tranquilizer. When I came to, Canton was there with two Russians. One of them looked familiar to me. Afterwards I realized why. I had seen his photo in our system of SVR officers suspected of having been in Turkey. His name is Dimitri Vladimirovich Kapalov. He goes by Rostov. Without going into all the details right now, I managed to escape after twenty-four hours. In the process, Canton shot one of the Russians. That was the last anyone had seen of him until his body was discovered." Asya paused, giving Michael a chance to take it all in.

After a moment of processing what he had just been told, he finally responded with, "Wow. And I thought I had a surprising story to tell you. That's how that happened?" He nodded towards her bandaged wrist.

"Yes. It's nothing. How do you say, just a scratch?"

"Did they hurt you in any other way?" Michael asked as sensitively as possible while still making it clear what he meant.

"No, thank Allah, I was unharmed. Canton had other intentions, but I managed to escape before he could go through with them."

"That's a pretty gruesome way for anybody to die. I don't like to judge anyone, because we all fall short in one way or another, but in his case, it's hard not to believe he got what he deserved in the end for all he's done and was planning on doing."

"I think the judgment he is facing now is much worse than what he faced in this life," Asya added to Michael's sentiments.

"What do you think happened?"

"Let me continue, and you tell me what you think. Yesterday, some Chechnyan jihadi group that has never been heard of before posted a video on the Internet of Canton being executed by a masked individual who shouted 'Allah ah Akbar' just as he cut Canton's throat. The group, calling themselves the Chechnyan Islamic Brigade, claimed they had executed the American spy on behalf of ISIS. They also claimed responsibility for the assassination of Mohammedi with the assistance of Canton, stating they had no more use for the infidel, which is why they killed him."

"Sounds like this Rostov guy was covering his tracks getting rid of Canton like that," Michael concluded.

"That's not all. Your Secretary of State committed suicide inside your embassy in Moscow on Wednesday. He shot himself in the head shortly after having a conversation with your President." Asya paused once again, letting Michael absorb what she had just dropped on him.

"The other person Ali heard implicated in the plot. They completely sanitized everything. I thought I was dreaming or something, but I realize now it's what I must have seen on the TV." He looked up at the old picture-tube television set mounted in the corner of his room. "I saw Payton's photo, then President Steele saying something, then President Markov, but I couldn't hear anything."

"Your President came on to tell the country about the tragic death of Secretary Payton. Steele said he had spoken to Payton when he was in Moscow, and that Payton had informed him the Russians had provided proof Canton was implicated with Chechnyan terrorists, who had paid him to provide them with security information on how to get to the Iranian foreign minister's room in order to assassinate him. President Steele said that Secretary Payton was distraught upon learning that the CIA officer who had been advising him during the summit, had plotted right under his nose with the terrorists that led to the foreign minister's assassination. Steele guessed Payton felt responsible in some way and could not live with that, tragically deciding to take his life. Steele went on to say what a patriot he had been serving his country all those years in the military and then as the Secretary of State. He also thanked the Russian government for uncovering the plot."

"Hm, a real convenient tragic explanation for public consumption. No real way to prove what involvement Steele may have had in any of this when the only two people who can implicate him are dead."

"Yes, but why would the Secretary of State kill himself, if President Steele himself was involved?" Asya asked.

"William Payton was a four-star general. He had an exemplary record while he was in the military—an Army Ranger, several high-profile commands, including Supreme Allied Commander of NATO, and of course Secretary of State. I'm guessing Steele gave him a choice, telling him what he would be facing, even if nothing was ever proven. Even if Steele was involved, it wouldn't be in Payton's nature to rat out his commander in chief. I'm guessing that from his perspective, it was the only honorable alternative he had."

"There's more," Asya continued. "Markov came on television, saying that the Russian intelligence services had uncovered the Chechnyan terrorist cell claiming they had been working under the direction of ISIS. Russian special forces killed their leader and six others during a raid, but one of them confessed their involvement in the assassination right before he died, saying they had assistance from the CIA spy Canton, whom they had paid to help them get to Mohammedi. The police in Istanbul found Canton's rental car parked at Bostanci Ferry Terminal with a bag containing fifty thousand euros in the trunk."

"Talk about covering every angle. They've created an airtight story with no one to contradict them, even with Ali's claims. No way to prove what Ali heard with both Canton and Payton dead. The way I see it, it's so convenient that it's almost proof that Steele and Markov were behind this."

"Yes, I agree with your conclusion."

"What about Ali? How did he end up at the consulate?" Michael asked.

"After I arrived in Agri on Monday, I debriefed Ali on everything that had happened. He told me about having overheard Secretary Payton and Canton talking about the plot with Russian to kill Mohammedi. He said that he heard Canton mention the name Rostov as the Russian who was in charge of the operation to kill the foreign minister. He said that he received a call from the Secretary telling him to meet him outside the Four Seasons by the water just before Mohammedi's assassination, how they attempted to kill him also but had missed, and how he had been able to escape by going into the water. He explained what happened afterwards, with him going to the Iranian consulate, being flown to Tehran, his interrogation at Evin Prison by the IRGC, then you showing up with Karbashi to break him out. I was not certain what to do, since the situation was unclear and nothing was known about Canton or Payton yet. After discussing everything with Ali and considering all the options, I decided it would make things unnecessarily complicated trying to explain how Ali got into Iran and how he got out. We decided he would stick close to his original story about Canton telling him to meet the Secretary of State outside just prior to the attack. He would say that he'd gone outside and felt a sharp sting on his neck, then the next thing he remembered was waking up as a captive in the warehouse I was held at, that he had been kept there as a prisoner, never seeing his captor's faces because they were always covered. He was there until I came and found him on Tuesday after receiving a call from Canton to meet him there. When I arrived, I found him tied there with no one else present. I took Ali there when we returned to Istanbul to actually see where he was imprisoned. That is what I told the chief of station when I brought him to the consulate. It was the only way I could think of ensuring what he knew was made available to the right people in your government while trying to protect him, you, Ercan and myself and leaving the Iranians out of it."

"Good thinking. I don't see how Ali telling about Iranian involvement contributes to anything other than casting doubt on his truthfulness and credibility, because it would be spun into an alternative narrative and used to discredit him by those with a vested interest in protecting themselves. They would probably claim that he was somehow acting on behalf of Iran, trying to frame him as being a traitor. I would never want to put him through a situation like that after what he's just been through, and I'm also not that keen on the thought of spending the next ten years in a Turkish prison with Ercan as my cell mate, writing letters to you over at the women's prison. Do they even let you write letters in prisons over here?" Michael let out a small chuckle that turned into a painful cough, reminding him of the fact that he had just been shot a few days ago. "Ow, that hurt." He winced in pain.

"See what happens? I told you not to talk, but you are going on like you just returned from holiday," Asya scolded him.

"I missed you," Michael said, trying to appease her.

"I missed you also."

There was a moment of awkward silence at the open display of one another's feelings towards each other. "Ah, I haven't even asked you the most obvious question. How did I get here, and where is here?"

"You're at the hospital in Agri. Ercan flew you directly here after you were shot."

"That's right. I remember now. I was lying down in the helo. Ali was saying something to me, or at least I thought he was. I remember hearing his voice, but I don't remember him talking to me, or how I could have even heard him above all the noise. That's strange." Michael paused as he pondered what had happened. "What did Ercan tell the hospital staff, flying some shot peasant into the hospital in a Blackhawk?"

"He spoke to the hospital administrator and told him it was a national security matter and someone would be coming to speak with him shortly. That someone was I."

"So, what did you tell him?"

"I told him what Ercan had told him. Your presence at his hospital was a national security matter, and he and his staff were not to discuss it or ask any questions. Otherwise, they could face serious consequences. Unlike in the United States, when someone here is told by a government official they may face serious consequences, the unknown of what their imagination comes up with is usually enough to ensure they will not say anything, especially coming from a special operations colonel and someone from MIT."

"You would sure intimidate me."

"Why do you say that?"

"Considering what you just went through and got out of, I wouldn't want to cross a gal like you." Michael smiled at her.

"I am not sure how to take that."

"Take it as a compliment. Canton's fatal mistake was thinking he could tangle with you. The bind they put themselves in with you escaping, could have had just as much to do with their plot coming apart as Ali did."

"Do you think their plan has been stopped?"

"Have the Iranians and Israelis been going tit for tat with each other while I've been getting my beauty sleep these past few days?"

"No, they have not. I had called your friend Harry and told him we had gotten you and Ali out, but I have not spoken to him since. I do not know if he had anything to do with any of that. What is even more astounding is one of our intelligence assets in Tehran has reported that General Mohammad Bardari, the commander of the IRGC, had been killed by someone within the IRGC, despite what Iranian television had been reporting about him having died from a heart attack. He was considered the main hardliner in their government who was pushing for a more confrontational stance towards Israel. It was he who would have ordered the missile strike against Israel last week, the day that you arrived in Istanbul."

"That's interesting; the same day Ali and I got out. Well, that's good, I suppose. Sounds like a strange thing to say about someone who was just killed, but I'm sure him not being around anymore will probably save a lot more lives."

"I hope that's the case. I am just so thankful to Allah you made it back and alive."

"Just barely, but here I am, staring at your pretty face. Can you lower this thing for me?" He motioned towards the bed rail. Reaching over after Asya had lowered it, he took hold of her hand and continued, "Awsh, I want to thank you for everything you've done for me. You put yourself at great risk and almost got killed for it. I just want you to know how grateful I am, and how much what you did, means to me. What I really mean is that you mean a lot to me. I just wanted you to know that," Michael fumbled as he tried to express his feeling towards her.

"You mean very much to me also, Michael. I am so happy to see you again after all these years. I never could have imagined it." She squeezed his hand.

"So where does that leave us?" he asked, peering into her eyes as he gently caressed her hand.

"I'm not sure. I have been, how do you say, off my balance since you have suddenly appeared back into my life. I have not felt this way before. I have no expectations."

"I don't have any expectations either. And if you think you're off balance, that's nothing compared to how things are spinning around in my head. I'm not sure what to think about everything that's happened. Two weeks ago, I couldn't think of anything I wanted to live for anymore. It's hard for me to understand how I got to that point. It's as if everything has changed now, like I'm a different person, or maybe the person I used to be. I don't know. The one thing I do know is that I like how it feels when I'm around you. I was thinking maybe I could spend some time recuperating in Istanbul, if you wouldn't mind the company for a little while?"

"I would like that very much."

"You sure? I'm not going to make things difficult for you with your work? I'm guessing people above you are going to be expecting some answers about Chechnyan terrorists conducting assassinations of foreign dignitaries in the heart of Istanbul. Me being around may just complicate your life at a time when you need it to be as uncluttered as possible."

"Don't worry about my work. Better that I know the truth, that way I will be able to navigate the situation despite what Steele and Markov are trying to have the world believe. Having you here, will only help. Who else could I tell any of this to? As far as clutter in my life, it has been uncluttered for too long. I would like some of your clutter in my life," she answered, letting him know just how sure she was about wanting him to stay.

"Since you put it that way, I guess I'll stick around for a little while."

Planting himself up on his elbow, Michael lifted himself, wincing slightly, and slowly moved towards Asya's. She met him halfway, their lips joining as they finally shared a moment of intimacy that both of them had been yearning for. Until now, they had both had their doubts about that ever becoming a reality. But somehow, against all odds, it had finally happened. It had become their reality.

***

Michael lay back slightly elevated in his hospital bed. His attending physician, who spoke English, had told him that he would need to remain in the hospital another week to check for infection and give his body a chance to heal more before he could be released and cleared to fly. Asya had needed to fly to Ankara in order to address some immediate concerns of her boss, the director of MIT. Steele and Markov's manufactured story about Chechnyan terrorists had thrown the Turkish government into turmoil, and President Ocsilan wanted some answers quickly. Michael had been given a private room and was receiving what seemed like exclusive treatment by the hospital staff; he wondered what Asya had said to the hospital administrator. She told Michael she planned on returning to Agri on Sunday and spending the day with him. Until then, he would have plenty of time to reflect on everything that had taken place. He thought about giving Harry a call, just to tell him he was still alive and kicking. He would keep it short, just a general conversation among friends, knowing it would be unwise to discuss anything over the phone. He would wait to fill him in on everything in person when he returned back home.

Michael's thoughts wandered back to the Friday two weeks ago. It was difficult for him to face the fact that he had attempted to end his life. It seemed like such an alien thing to him now, like he had seen it in a movie—never something he could imagine himself capable of doing. He searched inside himself for the person that had attempted such a drastic act but came up empty. Cognitively, he knew it was him. He was there, had pulled the trigger, had come to the next morning on his couch to discover the unexplainable had happened. Yet, he could no longer recognize that person. Something had changed inside him. He wanted to know what that was.

He reflected on everything that had taken place since then. His entire life had been upended, in a good way, a way he could never have imagined. Whereas two weeks ago, there'd seemed no reason why he should want to continue going on with life, now all he could think about was what possibilities lay before him. He thought about all that had occurred, his gun miraculously misfiring, the call from Ali's daughter, his decision to help Ali and the journey that followed with all the unexplainable things that had happened getting him through it all. And finally, there was Asya being thrust back into his life. He searched for an explanation, some meaning behind it all. He knew himself and what he was capable of. Everything that he had managed to accomplish was beyond his ability, defying any rational explanation. He knew what the odds were of everything that had occurred, one thing leading to the next and so on, bringing him to where he currently found himself at. They were astronomical.

He suddenly felt an overwhelming wave of emotion come over him and began to sob. He didn't know what had brought it about. Perhaps it was a delayed emotional release from all the stress from the past two weeks. They were not feelings of despair, but rather of thankfulness. Thankfulness that he had been pulled out of the abyss he had fallen into and had been given another chance at life. It was beyond anything he could have imagined. He knew that he had been living on borrowed time. He remembered hearing what he thought was Ali's voice when he was being flown out in Blackhawk, but thinking about it, he realized it would have been impossible to hear him over the deafening noise of the turbines and rotor. Maybe he had just been hallucinating from the trauma of hovering close to death. *Don't lie to yourself, Mike, you know you weren't hallucinating. You heard it.*

He thought about his discussion with Asya back at her apartment. She was so convinced about the existence of God, about his presence in the world, his active involvement in each of their lives. She had prayed for him. Had it helped? He was here, alive, wasn't he? Why was it so difficult for him to make that leap after everything he had just been through? There was so much circumstantial evidence, but no proof. But what proof did he need? Wasn't defying all the laws of probability and hearing God speak to him enough? It was an uncomfortable feeling for him to take that final step and put his faith into something larger than the physical world around him, something beyond what his senses and mind could comprehend. Yet all the evidence was there before him.

He shut his eyes, searching his innermost recesses, down to the core of his being. Not certain if he was speaking audibly or hearing himself inside his head, he began, "God, I don't know if you're there and can hear me, or I'm just going nuts thinking I'm talking to you. I know there's no rational explanation for everything that's happened to me. I could try to convince myself otherwise, that everything was just one coincidence after another, but I'd be lying to myself. I still don't understand why you chose me to stop this evil thing from taking place, but whatever the reason, you must have seen something in me. It's been one heck of a wild ride. I don't know how everything is going to play out from here, but I want to believe that you've got everything under control. What else am I going to believe in? Myself, the government, this crazy world? I know you obviously have a lot of more important things to take care of in the world than my issues, but I just want to thank you for being there for me. I'd really made a mess of things. I thought I was in control of everything in my life, but that illusion came to an abrupt end. I'm just asking if You would keep being there in my life. I want to have some kind of connection with you, but I'm not even sure how that's supposed to work. Do I pray to you, talk to you? I suppose you could call this praying, but it's kind of a one-sided conversation. It might even be considered delusional talking to myself like this, but unless I'm doing some kind of self-psychotherapy, I'll just assume you're listening. You showed yourself pretty dramatically over the past couple of weeks. I don't expect that I'll be hearing from you directly too often, like back in the helo, but maybe if you could just keep pointing me in the right direction, that would be a start. I guess I'll just have to look for signs of You working in my life somehow. I just ask You to keep bringing out the best of me. I don't ever want to go back to that dark place again. Thanks again, God, for everything."

Michael opened his eyes. He was in his hospital room. It still hurt each time he took a deep breath, but there was something different. He felt a lightness. Everything seemed brighter. There was a transformation taking place. There was hope. There was life.

CPSIA information can be obtained
at www.ICGtesting.com
Printed in the USA
FFHW020759110719
53548570-59220FF